NATION AND REGION
1860-1900

THE VIKING PORTABLE LIBRARY

AMERICAN
LITERATURE
SURVEY

EDITED BY

Milton R. Stern
The University of Connecticut

AND

Seymour L. Gross
The University of Detroit

☆

COLONIAL AND FEDERAL TO 1800
*General Introduction and Preface by
the Editors*

☆ ☆

THE AMERICAN ROMANTICS · 1800–1860
Prefatory Essay by Van Wyck Brooks

☆ ☆ ☆

NATION AND REGION · 1860–1900
Prefatory Essay by Howard Mumford Jones

☆ ☆ ☆ ☆

THE TWENTIETH CENTURY
Prefatory Essay by Malcolm Cowley

NATION
AND
REGION

1860-1900

REVISED AND EXPANDED

☆ ☆ ☆

*WITH A GENERAL INTRODUCTION BY THE EDITORS
AND A PREFATORY ESSAY BY*

Howard Mumford Jones

THE VIKING PRESS · NEW YORK

ACKNOWLEDGMENTS

Adams, Henry. "The Dynamo and the Virgin" from *The Education of Henry Adams*. By permission of Houghton Mifflin Company.

Dickinson, Emily. "After great pain a formal feeling comes," "Savior! I've no one else to tell," "A wife at daybreak I shall be," "The robin's criterion for time," " 'Twas warm at first like us," copyright 1929, © 1957 by Martha Dickinson Bianchi; "The first day's night had come," copyright 1935 by Martha Dickinson Bianchi; "Papa above," copyright 1914, 1952 by Martha Dickinson Bianchi; from *The Complete Poems of Emily Dickinson*. By permission of Little, Brown & Company. Some others from *The Poems of Emily Dickinson* edited by Thomas H. Johnson, copyright 1951, 1955 by the President and Fellows of Harvard College and the Trustees of Amherst College. By permission of the Belknap Press of Harvard University Press.

Howells, William Dean. "Editha." By permission of William White Howells.

James, Henry. "Daisy Miller" and "The Jolly Corner" from Volumes XVII and XVIII of *The Novels and Tales of Henry James* (New York Edition). Charles Scribner's Sons.

James, William. "What Pragmatism Means" from *Pragmatism*. Copyright 1907 by William James, 1934 by Henry James. By permission of Paul R. Reynolds & Son, agent.

Jewett, Sara Orne. "Miss Tempy's Watchers." Reprinted by permission of the publishers, Houghton Mifflin Company.

Wharton, Edith. "The Other Two" from *The Descent of Man*. By permission of Charles Scribner's Sons.

GENERAL
INTRODUCTION

In the spirit of his own time, Emerson insisted that every age must have its original relation to the universe. He reflected an older American belief that no age can hold a mortgage on any future time and that the world is for the living. Our Republic and our national literature share a democratic sense of time in which every age, besides shaping the world that exists, also remakes the past. Given the fact that history is never finally dead, all literary productions of the past can become meaningful in the human mind of the present. What, then, in our living moment, can we see of our identity in the total span of our literature?

One thing stands out clearly: American literature is a rebellious and iconoclastic body of art. The Puritan rebelled against the Anglican, the deist against the Puritan, the romantic against aspects of deism, the naturalist against aspects of romanticism, the symbolist against aspects of naturalism. In each case the rebellion was greeted with cries of outrage and prophecies of doom. It is true that almost any nation's literary history tells the same story: but besides this there is a deeper nay-saying that characterizes American literature and remains constant beneath the shifting faces of rebellion. On the surface it may seem strange that a nation in some ways tending toward a mass identity should produce a literature of which the underlying theme is revolutionary. But when one considers that the artist, with his keener sensibility and articulation, is most aware of tendencies in his society, including those he feels duty-bound to combat, and that the richest heritage of the Republic is its foundation in defense of freedom of the mind, then his rebelliousness becomes natural and inevitable. The American writer's "nay" is but a prelude to his resounding "yea!" uttered in behalf of new experience rather than hoarded conventions.

v

That constant and subterranean rebellion is a product of many forces which, to this day, make America a puzzle to observers. Our nation was founded in middle-class aspirations that were noble in many ways but still were capable of creating a business culture in which, as Edwin Arlington Robinson has it, "Your Dollar, Dove and Eagle make a Trinity that even you rate higher than you rate yourselves; it pays, it flatters, and it's new." On the other hand, those some aspirations demanded ideologies in which nothing is held to be greater than the integrity and freedom of the individual.

And still more contradictions. An extreme form of individualism, especially to be noted in the late nineteenth century, was a primitive, often savage, social and economic anarchy: each man for himself, but all with a common goal, which was the sack of a continent blessed with incredible resources that beckoned them ever westward. That same predatory impulse, however, was only one sequel to an image of America as the organic Great New West where the ultimate hungers of men's hearts could be satisfied, where the infinitude of human identity could be realized and personality could be fulfilled. Because the Republic faced away from the Old World, it was founded on a faith in experiment, newness, and youth. So founded, it could threaten to create a society in which age is a sin, human value is measured by personal appearance, and the teen-ager becomes the arbiter of popular taste. But this same naïve faith and innocence became something more than a mindless subject for the satire of a Sinclair Lewis: it also suggested an image of the American as a man free from stifling precedent who could break through old barriers in science, belief, and social institutions.

In short, the American writer began to see that there are really two Americas. One is the actual country that shares all the limitations of any human community in the Old World or the New; the other is the ideal America that, as Scott Fitzgerald told us, existed pure only as a wonderful and pathetically adolescent dream. One is a geographic location in the evolution of all human history; the other is a state of being that answers all human hopes. Whenever the ideal was put forward by mistaken patriotism as the real country, American writers protested—sometimes in full and bitter measure, as Mark

Twain, for one, has shown. And whenever the actual America threatened to destroy the ideal, American writers have again protested, with profound, poetic vigor, as Thoreau and Whitman have shown. It is because American culture is precariously and magnificently balanced in a bewildering variety of contradictions that the American writer has remained in a state of protest.

This is not to say that the present editors would return to the critical attitude of the 1930s, which regarded literature as a collection of social documents and interpreted every effort of artistic creation as an economic act. Rather, we think that there is a unifying identity in our cultural and intellectual production that is a deliberate dramatization of our total history. It is from this necessary and sensible orientation, as it seems to us, that we see the iconoclasm of the American writer as a major feature in our literature. What he expresses is a whole-voiced rejection of trammeling orthodoxies, conformities, hypocrisies, and delusions, wherever and whenever they are seen on the national landscape. Keeping that spirit in mind, we offer the following selections from American literature as a record of the continuing exploration that develops into and still speaks to our moment of time.

No student of American literature will feel that he has made a reasonably full perusal of the materials unless he has read complete Hawthorne's *The Scarlet Letter,* Thoreau's *Walden,* Melville's *Moby-Dick,* representative poems from Whitman's *Leaves of Grass,* and a novel or two each of James, Hemingway, and Faulkner. Those authors are most profitably read in full-length works, but before the reading revolution brought about by inexpensive paperback reprints, anthologists were forced to present them in more or less fragmented form. That is no longer necessary. The teacher today can include in his course, in addition to anthologized material, such representative works as those mentioned without feeling that his students are being asked to make an unreasonable expenditure for books.

In view of this change in the practical realities of courses in American literature, we have felt that it was both wise and necessary to omit from our anthology some of the authors who would, in any case, be read under separate cover. By deleting such material, we have been able to provide a wider selection than is usual from other authors, including Edward Taylor, Emily Dickinson, and Stephen Crane, who in many cases would not be read in separate editions. In this revised edition of *American Literature Survey,* we have added some representative works of Melville because it is impossible for students to buy an inexpensive reprint of *Moby-Dick* that also includes some of Melville's shorter fiction. We have added some basic poems by Whitman because in the majority of courses it is not feasible to read the entire *Leaves of Grass* in separate cover. And we have included some work by Henry James for the same reason we included Melville: none of the two or three James novels most commonly assigned is available in a volume that includes his shorter fiction and essays. Given the needs of courses in American literature, we feel that the present volumes maintain a proper balance of materials and meet the widest demands of common practice, flexibility, and usefulness.

As in the first edition of *American Literature Survey,* we have avoided excess editorial apparatus, in the belief that long historical interchapters, copious footnotes, and coercive critical judgments either duplicate or conflict with the teacher's work. The nature of interpretation and emphasis will vary from class to class, from teacher to teacher, and therefore we have been content to provide the student with a basic minimum of biographical, bibliographical, and textual information.

In general the selections are presented chronologically, though not where the logical placement of materials would make strict chronology a meaningless arrangement. In every case we have chosen texts that yield the highest combination of accuracy and readability, a principle which has led us to modernize the spelling and regularize the punctuation of the most reliable texts of some of the early writers. The dates placed after the works indicate publication; a second or third date indicates extensive revisions. In those instances where there has been a significant lapse of time between composition and publication, a "w." stands for date of writing, a "p." for date of publication.

Milton R. Stern
Seymour L. Gross

CONTENTS

PREFACE

By Howard Mumford Jones

From the point of view of contemporary American writing the interest in material produced in the United States in the period after the Civil War and until the "modernity" of the twentieth century is that it contains the roots and beginnings of many current interests, and this anthology is, on the whole, put together from this point of view. The point of view is consistent with itself. There is, however, another angle of vision from which the literary activity of the same period can be interpreted, a point of view more closely related to the slow process of literary history than is the one just sketched, and it is from this second and equally important standpoint that the following interpretation of the period is written.

From this second, but, I think, equally valid angle of vision the great achievement of American writing in the post-bellum period—that is, the years that stretch from Appomattox to the outbreak of World War I—was not that it saw published the poems of Emily Dickinson, the rise of naturalism, and various other notable elements with which we moderns find ourselves in immediate sympathy. The great achievement of the period was, on the contrary, craftsmanship, a craftsmanship desperately needed in the sixties but a craftsmanship we moderns, obsessed with nonrational psychology, existentialism, the cult of loneliness, the cult of myth, and the cult of symbolism, are not prepared to value at its true worth. We hold that stories should be unfinished or indirect, that poems should be collections of images for the reader to assemble or, if not that, lines that are deliberately made difficult. This is the more surprising since everybody admires Ernest Hemingway (or did), and Hemingway with his lean style and competent structure, both differing radically from the fuzziness of Sherwood Anderson's fiction or the Brahmsian rhetoric of Tom Wolfe or William Faulkner—Hemingway is the heir of the craftsmanship in question. The "note" of his prose at its best is (like the note of Bertrand Russell's inimitable excellence) a note of clarity, order, and economy. But clarity, order, and economy were precisely the ideals that both literary theory and literary practice were aiming for in the post-bellum years.

A radical reform was necessary. Romanticism had run its course. Although in painting romanticism had produced the ordered canvases of the Hudson River School, romanticism in literature, with the exception of Poe, was more notable as a producer of formlessness than as a creator of shape. The greatness of Emerson is aphoristic, not architectural. In *The Scarlet Letter* Hawthorne for one marvelous moment produced a novel as firmly molded as *Madame Bovary,* but except for a few short stories he could never do anything like it again, and nothing is more poignant than the collection of unfinished books with which his career reached its end. Thoreau has unity of tone, but not even *Walden* has real unity of structure. *Moby Dick* is stuffed with chapters that most readers, despite contemporary critical theory, wish away. Amos Bronson Alcott was orphic, Whittier never (or seldom) knew when he had finished a poem, Lowell is subject to whimsicality, and among the romantics Longfellow is almost alone in his mastery of poetical structure. Cooper sprawls. As for the minor figures one has to devote a good many hours of penitential reading in sentimental novels, melodramatic fiction, mawkish poetry, and bad plays to discover how invertebrate most of them are.

But in the post-bellum decades the movement was towards form and pattern. The American novel came firmly into its own as the vast sprawl of the Cooper or Simms prose epic was succeeded by the structured fiction of Howells and the cadenced novel of James. Not only is this great advance true of the major writers, it is true, increasingly, of many of the minor ones as well—Francis Marion Crawford, S. Weir Mitchell, Mary Johnston, and their kind, most of whom treat the novel respectfully as if it were a sonata, not an improvisation supposed to be divinely inspired by "genius." The change can be beautifully followed in Mark Twain, who begins with such books as *Roughing It,* virtually an endless succession of "funny" lectures, and ends with such works as *The Man That Corrupted Hadleyburg* and *The Mysterious Stranger,* tales like the tales of Voltaire, lucid, ironical, beautifully formed, and tragic or sardonic. Not only did Twain mature his sense of plot, shape, and character, but he and Howells extended their sense of craftsmanship into style, as the letters they exchanged amply testify. And of course in Henry James the Americans in this epoch produced the first great theorist of modern fiction. Let it not be forgotten that *French Poets and Novelists,* in which James maturely theorizes on his craft, was published as early as 1878.

Meanwhile the short story was going on from triumph to triumph. The tales of Washington Irving, charming though some of them are, are, after all, a mere succession of incidents. Poe, of course, anticipated the age of craftsmanship, and he saw that Hawthorne did also, but most American short stories before the Civil War were as shapeless as the worst of Irving's. In the post-bellum decades the insistence upon craftsmanship steadily heightens and matures the form. This was in part because the short story and the serialized novel were the life-blood of the great literary magazines of the Gilded Age and the 1890s. The firmness and clarity (one has perpetually to come back to these terms) of Sarah Orne Jewett, Mary Wilkins Freeman, Ambrose Bierce, Thomas Bailey Aldrich at his best, and a score of others has not been equaled in our time. Perhaps the triumph of craftsmanship was Frank R. Stockton's "The Lady or The Tiger," probably the most discussed short story in American literary history.

In poetry the movement toward craftsmanship produced less important work. Whitman, of course, stood steadily outside this movement (he it was who called Swinburne a "damned little simulacrum!"), and Longfellow, whose significance in the period few moderns realize, scarcely needed to go to school again. He is nowadays dismissed as insignificant, but the author of the finest sonnets in nineteenth-century American poetry cannot be made to disappear by a conjuring trick. Doubtless, as the preface to Stedman's

American Anthology (1900) more than hints, too much emphasis was placed upon the craft of rhyme. Certainly talent in the main had replaced genius, and talent, it has been remarked, does what it can, whereas genius does what it must. But the influence of the English romantics, notably that of Byron, was waning (except for Keats), the influence of Arnold, of the seventeenth-century poets, metaphysical and Cavalier, and by and by of the contemporary French masters steadily widened. So far as perfection of form according to the canon of craftsmanship is concerned, it would be hard to better certain lyrics by Thomas Bailey Aldrich, E. R. Sill, Lizette Woodworth Reese, and Louise Imogene Guiney. William Vaughn Moody, Trumbull Stickney, George Santayana, and George Cabot Lodge strove to re-create philosophic poetry—to fuse into a single whole a Darwinian philosophy, their studies in myth, and a modern outlook. They frequently chose to write a modernized variant of Greek drama, and sometimes they succeeded. Santayana's *Lucifer* is a failure as his sonnets and odes are not, but Stickney has the dry accuracy, mingled with the lyric cry, of Arnold and the Greeks. Moody, a superb technician, uneven and strong, left behind him an unfinished, yet Miltonic trilogy, and such remarkable interpretations of modernity as "The Menagerie" and "Ode on a Soldier Fallen in the Philippines," which time has made more relevant than ever.

Perhaps, however, aside from Whitman and the fictional trio, Twain, Howells, and James, the great creation of the era was its magnificent body of expository prose, in which one is almost tempted to place the naïve naturalism of writers like Frank Norris. For virtually the first time since Poe, criticism became an independent branch of thought. Beginning with Whipple and Stedman, critics insisted that literature is an autonomous art for which they sought "laws." It was not something that merely taught or merely uplifted. These critics were intensely aware of contemporary Europe, notably of French theorists like Taine, Brunetière and Scherer; and criticism was shortly to produce not merely Brownell's admirable books on French culture, but disquisitions on painting, sculpture, the decorative arts, music, and art history—Charles Eliot Norton is a case in point—more professional than anything we had to show in earlier decades if we except a few writers like Jarves and

Andrew Jackson Downing. Perhaps the most characteristic figure in criticism was Brander Matthews, who insisted that the art of writing, be it fiction, drama, verse, or criticism, is a craftsman's art. He brought to his books and essays, undoubtedly too numerous but widely read, the French passion for lucidity and order.

Moreover, the period nurtured and matured other types of expository or narrative writing. Romantic historians like Parkman had written well and were more skilled in narrative than their successors, but their task was simpler and so they could write pictorially. The task of Henry Adams and his generation was complex. He and his contemporaries —Schouler, McMaster, Rhodes, and others—brought weight and emphasis into history without losing order and structure. Theology likewise altered. It ceased to be an exercise in inhuman dialectics and concerned itself (like the moderns) with the human predicament, whatever that popular phrase may mean. It produced such a book as Rauschenbusch's *Christianity and the Social Crisis* (1907), which is several light-years distant from Jonathan Edwards. Nor should one forget the powerful anti-gospel taught by William Graham Sumner. His essays were not collected until 1934, but he began to be influential in the 1880s through articles written in a style that may be dull but that never lacks weight and onset.

Above all, however, these decades culminated in the most lucid philosophical prose the country has ever produced—the writing of Santayana, Royce, and William James. These men, with the possible exception of Royce, who strove for lightness but did not achieve it (except in *The Spirit of Modern Philosophy*), eschewed the crabbed style of German metaphysics and let light and air into philosophical discussion. We admire James and Santayana today; we forget that even minds as large and generous as theirs had to be shaped by the teaching of craftsmanship. If American literature has passed from a state more characterized by the amateur spirit than by professional competence, the long discipline of the postwar years (a discipline, by the by, for which we must be grateful to magazine editors and editors in publishing houses as influential as Maxwell Perkins ever was in our time) taught genius to write and talent to write better. It taught not merely that any lasting work of art demands fundamental brain work, it taught also the need for technical skill so unconscious that, like the technical skill of a pianist, it gets out of the way so that we may hear the music and understand the thought.

Much of the criticism and much of both the verse and the prose of the period have to go unrepresented in this anthology. There is only so much room in a box. The editors have given space to the naturalists and, naturally, do not have space for criticism, the importance of which is principally historical, and for lyrics, however exquisite, that do not now move us, though of course fashions may change. But the naturalists represent a real and fascinating problem of a transition of and in literary values. Hamlin Garland, in so far as he was a naturalist, perhaps never sufficiently escaped from the doctrine of craftsmanship to shape a major work—*Rose of Dutcher's Coolly,* for example, by which he at one time set great store, being vitiated from our point of view by too great subservience to what seems to us a pernicious doctrine of form. Yet Ambrose Bierce (if he be a naturalist), commonly held to be as self-conscious a shaper of short stories as was ever Edgar Allan Poe, managed to subdue workmanship to his ironic vision of a cruel and enigmatic universe, and the case of Frank Norris is endlessly debatable. *McTeague,* with its echoes of Zola, is certainly naturalistic, but is also shaped like a melodrama; and *The Octopus* is helped or hindered (it all depends on one's sympathies, one's point of view) by an overriding conception of some sort of prose epic that involves gigantism in landscape, mysticism in motivation, and brutality in conflict. Possibly Dreiser (see Volume IV) is our only thorough naturalist, at least for part of his career; the inevitability of Carrie Meeber's story in *Sister Carrie* still strikes us as superb. But the curious fascination of "epic" form that betrayed Zola and did not betray Flaubert came to fascinate Dreiser, as in the "Trilogy of Desire." Dreiser was no craftsman in the Brander Matthews sense, and endless fault has been found with his style and with his structure. He wrote as he must. The central question in his case is not so much the dull idiom and the clumsy "reflections" that too often mar his gigantic novels; the central question is to disentangle his "chemical" determinism from his general sense of structure and from a smothered idealism which held persistently to the belief that in America life means intensely and means well. Intelligent readers prefer the strength and drive of Dreiser, however clumsy its expression may be, to the negligible productions of the American aesthetic movement into which the doctrine of craftsmanship deliquesced as new forces and new interests took over at the end of a great, a misunderstood, and a crucial period in the development of American literary art.

NATION AND REGION
1860-1900

WALT WHITMAN

(1819–1892)

Editions of the works of Walt Whitman are *Complete Poems and Prose of Walt Whitman, 1855–1888* (1888–1889); *The Complete Prose Works of Walt Whitman* (1892); H. L. Traubel, R. M. Bucke, and T. B. Harned, eds., *The Complete Writings of Walt Whitman,* 10 vols. (1902); and E. Holloway, ed., *Leaves of Grass* (1924, 1954), the standard edition, taken from the edition of 1902. There is no complete collected edition of the works of Whitman, although one is under way: *The Collected Writings of Walt Whitman,* New York University Press. Whitman's published works include *Franklin Evans* (1842); *Leaves of Grass* (1855): hitherto unavailable, this was reissued in 1959, edited by M. Cowley, as *Walt Whitman's Leaves of Grass: The First (1855) Edition; Leaves of Grass* (1856): omits the 1855 Preface, adds poems 14 to 33; *Leaves of Grass* (1860–1861): adds 122 poems to second edition plus "Calamus" and "Children of Adam"; *Leaves of Grass* (1867): adds the following Annexes: *Drum Taps* (1865), *Sequel to Drum Taps* (1865–1866), and *Songs Before Parting; Democratic Vistas* (1871); *Passage to India* (1871); *After All, Not to Create Only* (1871); *Leaves of Grass* (1871): reissued in 1872, this edition adds *Passage to India* and 13 new poems; *As a Strong Bird on Pinions Free* (1872); *Memoranda During the War* (1875–1876); *Leaves of Grass* (1876), the "Author's Edition": the 1871 edition plus *Two Rivulets* (1876), including *Democratic Vistas, Centennial Songs,* and *Passage to India; Leaves of 1881*): the final arrangement of the poems exclusive of those that were later added, this (seventh) edition was reprinted in 1882 and 1888; *Specimen Days and Collect* (1882–1883); *November Boughs* (1888); *Leaves of Grass* (1889), with *Sands at Seventy* (incorporating *November Boughs*) and *A Backward Glance O'er Travel'd Roads; Good-bye My Fancy* (1891); *Autobiographia* (1892); *Leaves of Grass* (1891–1892), the "deathbed" (ninth) edition, adding pp. 381–411 to the edition of 1881, and including *Good-bye My Fancy;* R. M. Bucke, ed., *Calamus: Letters Written during the Years*

1868–1880 (1897); R. M. Bucke, ed., *The Wound Dresser* (1898, 1949); R. M. Bucke, ed., *Notes and Fragments* (1899); T. B. Harned, ed., *Letters Written by Walt Whitman to His Mother from 1866 to 1872* (1902); W. S. Kennedy, ed., *Walt Whitman's Diary in Canada* (1904); H. L. Traubel, ed., *An American Primer* (1904); *Lafayette in Brooklyn* (1905); *Criticism: An Essay* (1913); T. B. Harned, ed., *The Letters of Anne Gilchrist and Walt Whitman* (1918); C. Rodgers and J. Black, eds., *The Gathering of the Forces*, 2 vols. (1920); E. Holloway, ed., *The Uncollected Poetry and Prose of Walt Whitman*, 2 vols. (1921); E. Holloway, ed., *Pictures* (1927); T. O. Mabbott, ed., *The Half-Breed and Other Stories* (1927); C. J. Furness, ed., *Walt Whitman's Workshop* (1928); J. Catel, ed., *The Eighteenth Presidency!* (1928); T. O. Mabbott and R. G. Silver, eds., *A Child's Reminiscence* (1930); E. Holloway and V. Schwartz, eds., *I Sit and Look Out* (1932); C. I. Glicksberg, ed., *Walt Whitman and the Civil War* (1933); E. Holloway and R. Adimari, eds., *New York Dissected* (1936); K. Molinoff, ed., *An Unpublished Whitman Manuscript* (1941); C. Gohdes and R. G. Silver, eds., *Faint Clews and Indirections* (1949); F. B. Freedman, ed., *Walt Whitman Looks at the Schools* (1950); J. Rubin and C. Brown, eds., *Walt Whitman of the New York Aurora: Editor at Twenty-two* (1950); H. Frenz, ed., *Whitman and Rolleston, A Correspondence* (1951); E. F. Grier, ed., *The Eighteenth Presidency!* (1956); T. L. Brasher, ed., *The Early Poems and the Fiction* (1963); H. M. Christman, ed., *Walt Whitman's New York* (1963); F. Stovall, ed., *Prose Works 1892*, Vol. I (1963), Vol. II (1964); E. H. Miller, ed., *The Correspondence*, Vol. III (1964); H. W. Blodgett and S. Bradley, eds., *Leaves of Grass* (1965).

The Viking Portable Whitman, edited by Mark Van Doren, contains full selections from *Leaves of Grass*, including the Preface to the 1855 edition, selections from *Specimen Days*, and *A Backward Glance O'er Travel'd Roads*, and *Democratic Vistas* complete.

Studies of the man and his work are to be found in R. L. Stevenson, "The Gospel According to Walt Whitman," *New Quarterly*, X (1879); R. M. Bucke, *Walt Whitman* (1883); E. C. Stedman, *Poets of America* (1883); J. A. Symonds, *Walt Whitman: A Study* (1893); J. Burroughs, *Whitman: A Study* (1896); H. B. Binns, *A Life of Walt Whitman* (1905); B. Perry, *Walt Whitman: His Life and Works* (1906); S. Bradley, ed., H. L. Traubel, *With Walt Whitman in Camden*, I (1906), II and III (1908–1914), IV (1953), V (1964); F. B. Gummere, *Democracy and Poetry* (1911); B. De Selincourt, *Walt Whitman, A Critical Study* (1914); S. P. Sherman, *Americans* (1922); N. Foerster, *Nature in American Literature* (1923); E. Holloway, *Whitman: An Interpretation in Narrative* (1926); A. Lowell, "Walt Whitman and the New Poetry," *Yale Review*, XVI (1927); N. Foerster, *American Criticism* (1928); H. S. Canby, *Classic Americans* (1931); F. Schyberg, *Walt Whitman* (1933), trans. E. A. Allen (1951); H. Blodgett, *Walt Whitman in England* (1934); G. W. Allen, *American Prosody* (1935);

N. Arvin, *Whitman* (1938); S. Bradley, "The Fundamental Metrical Principle in Whitman's Poetry," *American Literature,* X (1938); E. Shephard, *Walt Whitman's Pose* (1938); F. O. Matthiessen, *American Renaissance* (1941); *Index to Early American Periodical Literature, 1728–1870: Part 3,* Walt Whitman (1941); G. W. Allen, *Twenty-five Years of Walt Whitman Bibliography, 1918–1942* (1943); H. S. Canby, *Walt Whitman, An American* (1943); G. W. Allen, *Walt Whitman Handbook* (1946); N. Resnick, *Walt Whitman and the Authorship of The Good Gray Poet* (1948); E. H. Eby, *Concordance of Walt Whitman's Leaves of Grass and Selected Prose Writings* (1949–1954); R. W. B. Lewis, "The Danger of Innocence: Adam as Hero in American Literature," *Yale Review,* XXXIX (1950); C. B. Willard, *Whitman's American Fame* (1950); J. Beaver, *Walt Whitman, Poet of Science* (1951); R. D. Faner, *Walt Whitman and Opera* (1951); A. Marks, "Whitman's Triadic Imagery," *American Literature,* XXIII (1951); F. Schyberg, *Walt Whitman* (1951); R. Jarrell, *Poetry and the Age* (1953); E. Shephard, "An Inquiry into Whitman's Method of Turning Prose into Poetry," *Modern Language Quarterly,* XIV (1953); R. Asselineau, *L'Evolution de Walt Whitman* (1954); R. P. Adams, "Whitman: A Brief Revaluation," *Tulane Studies in English,* V (1955); E. Allen and G. W. Allen, "Walt Whitman Bibliography 1944–1954," *Walt Whitman Foundation Bulletin,* April (1955); G. W. Allen, *The Solitary Singer* (1955); G. W. Allen, ed., *Walt Whitman Abroad* (1955); G. W. Allen, M. Van Doren, D. Daiches, *Walt Whitman: Man, Poet, Philosopher* (1955); R. Chase, *Walt Whitman Reconsidered* (1955); P. Miller, "The Shaping of the American Character," *New England Quarterly,* XXVIII (1955); M. Hindus, ed., *Leaves of Grass One Hundred Years After* (1955); W. Thorpe, "Walt Whitman," in F. Stovall, ed., *Eight American Authors: A Review of Research and Criticism* (1956); E. H. and R. S. Miller, *Walt Whitman's Correspondence: A Checklist* (1957); J. E. Miller, Jr., *A Critical Guide to Leaves of Grass* (1957); E. Sandeen, "Ego in Eden," in H. C. Gardiner, ed., *American Classics Reconsidered* (1958); K. Shapiro, "The First White Aboriginal," *Walt Whitman Review,* V (1959); R. Asselineau, *The Evolution of Walt Whitman: The Creation of a Personality* (1960); "Special Symposium Issue—Whitman: 1960," *Walt Whitman Review,* VI (1960); E. Holloway, *Free and Lonesome Heart: The Secret of Walt Whitman* (1960); L. Marx, ed., *The Americanness of Walt Whitman* (1960); W. Randal, "Walt Whitman and American Myths," *South Atlantic Quarterly,* LIX (1960); J. E. Miller, Jr., *Walt Whitman* (1962); R. H. Pearce, ed., *Whitman: A Collection of Critical Essays* (1962); C. F. Strauch, ed., "Symposium on Walt Whitman," *Emerson Society Quarterly,* No. 22 (1962); R. W. B. Lewis, ed., *The Presence of Walt Whitman* (1964); C. N. Stavrov, *Whitman and Nietzsche* (1964); V. K. Chari, *Whitman in the Light of Vedantic Philosophy* (1965); and H. J. Waskow, *Whitman: Explorations in Form* (1966). For continuing bibliography, consult issues of *The Walt Whitman Review.*

HENRY TIMROD

(1828–1867)

Timrod, who was born in Charleston, South Carolina, was the son of a poor man, a bookbinder. Nonetheless, he attended the Coates School, one of the finest in Charleston, where he met Paul Hamilton Hayne. Their friendship continued on into their literary association in the Charleston group. Encouraged by Hayne, Timrod began to send pseudonymous poems to the *Southern Literary Messenger* as early as 1848. These poems, however, like those collected in his volume of *Poems* (1860), were thin productions of a conventionally romantic nature.

Intending to become a professor, Timrod enrolled in the University of Georgia, but poor health and inadequate finances forced his withdrawal after only a year and a half. He read law, wrote poems, and tutored the children of plantation owners until 1861, when he enlisted in the Confederate Army. Again illness changed his plans and he withdrew from the army—only to become a war correspondent who encountered a succession of dismal experiences. His stint as a journalist led to his brief editorshop of the Columbia *South Carolinian* in 1864; but he was barely under way in this enterprise when Sherman's invading army burned the city. A few months later, his infant and only son died; depleted in health, spirit, and pocket, Timrod himself died of tuberculosis two years later.

It was the Civil War that gave Timrod his central theme and poetic identity; it changed his work from traditional prettiness to the synthesis of genuine fervor and cool, classical hardness that has led some critics to think of him as one of the most undervalued minor writers in American literature. The most lyrical poet of his time and place, he was acknowledged in his own day as the Laureate of the Confederacy.

Editions and accounts of the man and his work are to be found in P. H. Hayne, ed., *The Poems of Henry Timrod* (1873); *The Poems of Henry Timrod*, The Memorial Edition (1899); H. E. Shepherd, "Henry Timrod: Literary Estimate and Bibliography [bibliography by A. S. Salley, Jr.]," *Publications of the Southern Historical Association*, III (1899); G. A. Wauchope, *Henry Timrod, Man and Poet* (1915); H. T. Thompson, *Henry Timrod: Laureate of the Confederacy* (1928); A. C. Gordon, "Henry Timrod," *Dictionary of American Biography* (1936); E. W. Parks, ed., *Southern Poets* (1936); W. Fidler, "Unpublished Letters of Henry Timrod," *Southern Literary Messenger*, II (1940); J. B. Hubbell, *The Last Years of Henry Timrod* (1941); G. Cardwell, *The Uncollected Poems of Henry Timrod* (1942); E. W. Parks, ed., *The Essays of Henry Timrod* (1942); J. B. Hubbell, *The South in American Literature* (1954); L. D. Rubin, "Henry Timrod and the Dying of the Light," *Mississippi Quarterly*, XI (1958); E. W. Parks, *Henry Timrod* (1964); and E. W. Parks and A. Wells, eds., *Collected Poems* (1965).

Ethnogenesis

["Birth of a Nation"]

I

Hath not the morning dawned with added light?
And shall not evening call another star
Out of the infinite regions of the night,
To mark this day in Heaven? At last, we are
A nation among nations; and the world
Shall soon behold in many a distant port
    Another flag unfurled!
Now, come what may, whose favor need we court?
And, under God, whose thunder need we fear?
    Thank him who placed us here   10
Beneath so kind a sky—the very sun
Takes part with us; and on our errands run
All breezes of the ocean; dew and rain
Do noiseless battle for us; and the Year,
And all the gentle daughters in her train,
March in our ranks, and in our service wield
Long spears of golden grain!
A yellow blossom as her fairy shield,
June flings her azure banner to the wind,

While in the order of their birth   20
Her sisters pass, and many an ample field
Grows white beneath their steps, till now, behold,
  Its endless sheets unfold
THE SNOW OF SOUTHERN SUMMERS! Let the earth
Rejoice! beneath those fleeces soft and warm
  Our happy land shall sleep
  In repose as deep
As if we lay intrenched behind
Whole leagues of Russian ice and Arctic storm!

II

And what if, mad with wrongs themselves have wrought, 30
  In their own treachery caught,
  By their own fears made bold,
  And leagued with him of old,
Who long since in the limits of the North
Set up his evil throne, and warred with God—
What if, both mad and blinded in their rage,
Our foes should fling us down their mortal gage,
And with a hostile step profane our sod!
We shall not shrink, my brothers, but go forth
To meet them, marshaled by the Lord of Hosts,   40
And overshadowed by the mighty ghosts
Of Moultrie and Eutaw—who shall foil
Auxiliars such as these? Not these alone,
  But every stock and stone
  Shall help us; but the very soil,
And all the generous wealth it gives to toil,
And all for which we love our noble land,
Shall fight beside, and through us; sea and strand,
  The heart of woman, and her hand,
Tree, fruit, and flower, and every influence,   50
  Gentle, or grave, or grand;
  The winds in our defence
Shall seem to blow; to us the hills shall lend
  Their firmness and their calm;
And in our stiffened sinews we shall blend
The strength of pine and palm!

III

Nor would we shun the battleground,
  Though weak as we are strong;

Call up the clashing elements around,
    And test the right and wrong!   60
On one side, creeds that dare to teach
What Christ and Paul refrained to preach;
Codes built upon a broken pledge,
And Charity that whets a poniard's edge;
Fair schemes that leave the neighboring poor
To starve and shiver at the schemer's door
While in the world's most liberal ranks enrolled,
He turns some vast philanthropy to gold;
Religion, taking every mortal form
But that a pure and Christian faith makes warm,   70
Where not to vile fanatic passion urged,
Or not in vague philosophies submerged,
Repulsive with all Pharisaic leaven,
And making laws to stay the laws of Heaven!
And on the other, scorn of sordid gain,
Unblemished honor, truth without a stain,
Faith, justice, reverence, charitable wealth,
And, for the poor and humble, laws which give,
Not the mean right to buy the right to live,
    But life, and home, and health!   80
To doubt the end were want of trust in God,
    Who, if he has decreed
    That we must pass a redder sea
Than that which rang to Miriam's holy glee,
    Will surely raise at need
    A Moses with his rod!

IV

But let our fears—if fears we have—be still,
And turn us to the future! Could we climb
Some mighty Alp, and view the coming time,
The rapturous sight would fill   90
    Our eyes with happy tears!
Not only for the glories which the years
Shall bring us; not for lands from sea to sea,
And wealth, and power, and peace, though these shall be;
But for the distant peoples we shall bless,
And the hushed murmurs of a world's distress:
For, to give labor to the poor,
    The whole sad planet o'er,
And save from want and crime the humblest door,

Is one among the many ends for which   100
    God makes us great and rich!
The hour perchance is not yet wholly ripe
When all shall own it, but the type
Whereby we shall be known in every land
Is that vast gulf which lips our Southern strand,
And through the cold, untempered ocean pours
Its genial streams, that far off Arctic shores
May sometimes catch upon the softened breeze
Strange tropic warmth and hints of summer seas.

1861

Charleston

Calm as that second summer which precedes
    The first fall of the snow,
In the broad sunlight of heroic deeds
    The City bides the foe.

As yet, behind their ramparts stern and proud,
    Her bolted thunders sleep—
Dark Sumter like a battlemented cloud
    Looms o'er the solemn deep.

No Calpe frowns from lofty cliff or scar [Calpe: Gibraltar]
    To guard the holy strand;   10
But Moultrie holds in leash her dogs of war
    Above the level sand.

And down the dunes a thousand guns lie couched
    Unseen beside the flood,
Like tigers in some Orient jungle crouched,
    That wait and watch for blood.

Meanwhile, through streets still echoing with trade,
    Walk grave and thoughtful men
Whose hands may one day wield the patriot's blade
    As lightly as the pen.   20

And maidens with such eyes as would grow dim
   Over a bleeding hound
Seem each one to have caught the strength of him
   Whose sword she sadly bound.

Thus girt without and garrisoned at home,
   Day patient following day,
Old Charleston looks from roof and spire and dome
   Across her tranquil bay.

Ships, through a hundred foes, from Saxon lands
   And spicy Indian ports   30
Bring Saxon steel and iron to her hands
   And Summer to her courts.

But still, along yon dim Atlantic line
   The only hostile smoke
Creeps like a harmless mist above the brine
   From some frail, floating oak.

Shall the Spring dawn, and she, still clad in smiles
   And with an unscathed brow,
Rest in the strong arms of her palm-crowned isles
   As fair and free as now?   40

We know not: in the temple of the Fates
   God has inscribed her doom;
And, all untroubled in her faith, she waits
   The triumph or the tomb.

                     1862

Ode

Sung at the Occasion of Decorating the Graves of the
Confederate Dead, at Magnolia Cemetery, Charleston,
S.C., June 16, 1866

Sleep sweetly in your humble graves,
   Sleep, martyrs of a fallen cause;
Though yet no marble column craves
   The pilgrim here to pause.

In seeds of laurel in the earth
   The blossom of your fame is blown,
And somewhere, waiting for its birth,
   The shaft is in the stone!

Meanwhile, behalf the tardy years
   Which keep in trust your storied tombs,
Behold! your sisters bring their tears.   10
   And these memorial blooms.

Small tributes! but your shades will smile
   More proudly on these wreaths today,
Than when some cannon-molded pile
   Shall overlook this bay.

Stoop, angels, hither from the skies!
   There is no holier spot of ground
Than where defeated valor lies,
   By mourning beauty crowned!   20

                 1866

SIDNEY LANIER

(1842–1881)

Although Lanier's work is often uncontrolled and his imagery too soft or inaccurate to secure him a major niche in American poetry, Lanier's time and place as well as his relation to modern American writing mark him as an important minor figure. A lawyer's son, he was born in Macon, Georgia. His family background—urban and professional—kept him from sharing the aristocratic attitudes of the feudal great-planter class; nevertheless he served with the Macon volunteers for four years. Toward the end of the war he was a signal officer on a Southern blockade runner. Captured by Union blockade forces, he spent five months as a prisoner at Point Lookout, Maryland, and emerged with the tuberculosis that troubled his life until it finally killed him at the age of thirty-nine.

Lanier came out of the Civil War with a horror of warfare (illustrated in his only novel, *Tiger-Lilies*, 1867) that, together with his own sympathies, kept him from any lost-cause attitudes and made him a forward- rather than a backward-looking member of the Republic that emerged from the conflict. He married Mary Day of Macon, turned to law in his father's office, tried teaching and hotel clerking to earn his bread, and finally went north to Baltimore to find the kind of life he wanted.

A flutist and talented general musician since childhood, he played first flute with the Peabody Symphony Orchestra in Baltimore, interrupting his residence in that city for trips south and southwest in an attempt to find climatic respite from consumption. Long attracted to poetry, he dedicated himself to the articulation of the formal relationships between poetry and music. His poetical-musical researches led him to studies of Elizabethan literature and Old and Middle English. By 1875 he began to attract notice with his poems in *Lippincott's Magazine*, collected in *Poems* (1877). His poetry and his lectures on literature earned him an appointment to a lectureship at Johns Hopkins in 1879. He published a series of critical studies of the musical basis of poetry as *The Science of English Verse* (1880) and studies of fiction as *The English Novel* (1883). His career was interrupted by illness and he retired to Lynn, in the North Carolina mountains, to rebuild his health. He died there before the full development of his promise was realized.

After the war, with Hayne retired to the pine barrens and with Timrod dead, Lanier's emerged as the leading voice of Southern high seriousness in literature. Attempting, like Whitman, to adapt the rhythms of poetry to the natural bases of rhythm in music (which he held to be the greatest of the arts), he too found that no wide audience of his time would accept poetry that did not proceed according to fixed meters and rigid ideas of "poetic" cadence. He continued to write, however, exploring ideas of social and economic injustice that related him to what were to become the central materials of American literature. His dialect poems made him one of the pioneers of regional realism, and his view of poetry as music related him to the moderns in his Poelike view of his craft. While he agreed that the uses of poetry were social, he insisted that the impact and importance of poetry lay in its music.

Among Lanier's works, in addition to the titles mentioned above, are *The Centennial Meditation of Columbia, 1776–1876 . . . A Cantata . . .* [with music by Dudley Buck, written for the Centennial Exhibition in Philadelphia] (1876); *The Boy's Froissart* (1879); *The Boy's King Arthur* (1880); *Music and Poetry* (1898); and *Shakespeare and His Forerunners*, 2 vols. (1902).

Editions and accounts of the man and his work are to be found in M. Callaway, Jr., ed., *Select Poems of Sidney Lanier* (1895); H. Lanier, ed., *The Letters of Sidney Lanier, 1866–1881* (1899); E. Mims, *Sidney Lanier* (1905); H. W. Lanier, ed., *Selections from Sidney Lanier* (1916); S. T. Williams, "Lanier," in J. Macy, ed., *American Writers on American Literature* (1931); A. H. Starke, *Sidney Lanier* (1933); G. W. Allen, *American Prosody* (1935); L. Lorenz, *The Life of Sidney Lanier* (1935); E. W. Parks, ed., *Southern Poets* (1936); P. Graham and J. Jones, *A Concordance to the Poems of Sidney Lanier* (1939); R. Webb and E. R. Coulson, *Sidney Lanier, Poet and Prosodist* (1941); C. R. Anderson, ed., *The Centennial Edition of the Works of Sidney Lanier*, 10 vols. (1945);

S. Young, ed., *Selected Poems of Sidney Lanier* (1947); J. Beaver, "Lanier's Use of Science for Poetic Imagery," *American Literature*, XXIV (1953); P. Graham, "Sidney Lanier and the Pattern of Contrast," *American Quarterly*, XI (1959); J. A. De Bellis, "Sidney Lanier and the Morality of Feeling," *Dissertation Abstracts* (1964); and E. A. Havens, "Sidney Lanier's Concept and Use of Nature," *Dissertation Abstracts* (1965).

The Symphony

"O Trade! O Trade! would thou wert dead!
The Time needs heart—'tis tired of head:
We're all for love," the violins said.
"Of what avail the rigorous tale   [tale: count]
Of bill for coin and box for bale?
Grant thee, O Trade! thine uttermost hope:
Level red gold with blue sky-slope,
And base it deep as devils grope:
When all's done, what hast thou won
Of the only sweet that's under the sun?   10
Ay, canst thou buy a single sigh
Of true love's least, least ecstasy?"
Then, with a bridegroom's heart-beats trembling,
All the mightier strings assembling
Ranged them on the violin's side
As when the bridegroom leads the bride,
And, heart in voice, together cried:
"Yea, what avail the endless tale
Of gain by cunning and plus by sale?
Look up the land, look down the land,   20
The poor, the poor, the poor, they stand
Wedged by the pressing of Trade's hand
Against an inward-opening door
That pressure tightens evermore:
They sight a monstrous foul-air sigh
For the outside leagues of liberty,
Where Art, sweet lark, translates the sky
Into a heavenly melody.
'Each day, all day' (these poor folks say),
'In the same old year-long, drear-long way,   30
We weave in the mills and heave in the kilns,
We sieve mine-meshes under the hills,
And thieve much gold from the Devil's bank tills,

To relieve, O God, what manner of ills?—
The beasts, they hunger, and eat, and die;
And so do we, and the world's a sty;
Hush, fellow-swine: why nuzzle and cry?
Swinehood hath no remedy
Say many men, and hasten by,
Clamping the nose and blinking the eye.   40
But who said once, in the lordly tone,
Man shall not live by bread alone
But all that cometh from the Throne?
    Hath God said so?
    But Trade saith *No:*
And the kilns and the curt-tongued mills say *Go!*
There's plenty that can, if you can't: we know.
Move out, if you think you're underpaid.
The poor are prolific; we're not afraid;
Trade is trade.' "   50
Thereat this passionate protesting
Meekly changed, and softened till
It sank to sad requesting
And suggesting sadder still:
"And oh, if men might sometime see
How piteous-false the poor decree
That trade no more than trade must be!
Does business mean, *Die, you—live, I?*
Then 'Trade is trade' but sings a lie:
'Tis only war grown miserly.   60
If business is battle, name it so:
War-crimes less will shame it so,
And widows less will blame it so.
Alas, for the poor to have some part
In yon sweet living lands of Art,
Makes problem not for head, but heart.
Vainly might Plato's brain revolve it:
Plainly the heart of a child could solve it."

And then, as when from words that seem but rude
We pass to silent pain that sits abrood   70
Back in our heart's great dark and solitude,
So sank the strings to gentle throbbing
Of long chords change-marked with sobbing—
Motherly sobbing, not distinctlier heard
Than half wing-openings of the sleeping bird

Some dream of danger to her young hath stirred.
Then stirring and demurring ceased, and lo!
Every least ripple of the strings' song-flow
Died to a level with each level bow
And made a great chord tranquil-surface so,   80
As a brook beneath his curving bank doth go
To linger in the sacred dark and green
Where many boughs the still pool overlean
And many leaves make shadow with their sheen.
          But presently
A velvet flute-note fell down pleasantly
Upon the bosom of that harmony,
And sailed and sailed incessantly,
As if a petal from a wild-rose blown
Had fluttered down upon that pool of tone   90
And boatwise dropped o' the convex side
And floated down the glassy tide
And clarified and glorified
The solemn spaces where the shadows bide.
From the warm concave of that fluted note
Somewhat, half song, half odor, forth did float,
As if a rose might somehow be a throat:
"When Nature from her far-off glen
Flutes her soft messages to men,
          The flute can say them o'er again;   100
          Yea, Nature, singing sweet and lone,
Breathes through life's strident polyphone
The flute-voice in the world of tone.
          Sweet friends,
          Man's love ascends
To finer and diviner ends
Than man's mere thought e'er comprehends:
For I, e'en I,
As here I lie,
A petal on a harmony,   110
Demand of Science whence and why
Man's tender pain, man's inward cry,
When he doth gaze on earth and sky?
I am not overbold:
          I hold
Full powers from Nature manifold.
I speak for each no-tonguèd tree
That, spring by spring, doth nobler be,

And dumbly and most wistfully
His mighty prayerful arms outspreads   120
Above men's oft-unheeding heads,
And his big blessing downward sheds.
I speak for all-shaped blooms and leaves,
Lichens on stones and moss on eaves,
Grasses and grains in ranks and sheaves;
Broad-fronded ferns and keen-leaved canes,
And briery mazes bounding lanes,
And marsh-plants, thirsty-cupped for rains,
And milky stems and sugary veins;
For every long-armed woman-vine   130
That round a piteous tree doth twine;
For passionate odors, and divine
Pistils, and petals crystalline;
All purities of shady springs,
All shynesses of film-winged things
That fly from tree-trunks and bark-rings;
All modesties of mountain-fawns
That leap to covert from wild lawns,
And tremble if the day but dawns;
All sparklings of small beady eyes   140
Of birds, and sidelong glances wise
Wherewith the jay hints tragedies;
All piquancies of prickly burs,
And smoothnesses of downs and furs,
Of eiders and of minevers;
All limpid honeys that do lie
At stamen-bases, nor deny
The humming-birds' fine roguery,
Bee-thighs, nor any butterfly;
All gracious curves of slender wings,   150
Bark-mottlings, fibre-spiralings,
Fern-wavings and leaf-flickerings;
Each dial-marked leaf and flower-bell
Wherewith in every lonesome dell
Time to himself his hours doth tell;
All tree-sounds, rustlings of pine-cones,
Wind-sighings, doves' melodious moans,
And night's unearthly under-tones;
All placid lakes and waveless deeps,
All cool reposing mountain-steeps,   160
Vale-calms and tranquil lotos-sleeps;—

Yea, all fair forms, and sounds, and lights,
And warmths, and mysteries, and nights,
Of Nature's utmost depths and heights.
—These doth my timid tongue present,
Their mouthpiece and leal instrument   [leal: loyal]
And servant, all love-eloquent.
I heard, when '*All for love*' the violins cried:
So, Nature calls through all her system wide,
Give me thy love, O man, so long denied.   170
Much time is run, and man hath changed his ways,
Since Nature, in the antique fable-days,
Was hid from man's true love by proxy fays,
False fauns and rascal gods that stole her praise.
The nymphs, cold creatures of man's colder brain,
Chilled Nature's streams till man's warm heart was fain
Never to lave its love in them again.
Later, a sweet Voice *Love thy neighbor* said,
Then first the bounds of neighborhood outspread
Beyond all confines of old ethnic dread.   180
Vainly the Jew might wag his covenant head:
'*All men are neighbors,*' so the sweet Voice said.
So, when man's arms had circled all man's race,
The liberal compass of his warm embrace
Stretched bigger yet in the dark bounds of space;
With hands a-grope he felt smooth Nature's grace,
Drew her to breast and kissed her sweet-heart face:
Yea, man found neighbors in great hills and trees
And streams and clouds and suns and birds and bees,
And throbbed with neighbor-loves in loving these   190
But oh, the poor! the poor! the poor!
That stand by the inward-opening door
Trade's hand doth tighten ever more,
And sigh their monstrous foul-air sigh
For the outside hills of liberty,
Where Nature spreads her wild blue sky
For Art to make into melody!
Thou Trade! thou king of the modern days!
    Change thy ways,
    Change thy ways;   200
Let the sweaty laborers file
    A little while,
    A little while,
Where Art and Nature sing and smile.

Trade! is thy heart all dead, all dead?
And hast thou nothing but a head?
I'm all for heart," the flute-voice said.
And into sudden silence fled,
Like as a blush that while 'tis red
Dies to a still, still white instead.   210

Thereto a thrilling calm succeeds,
Till presently the silence breeds
A little breeze among the reeds
That seems to blow by sea-marsh weeds:
Then from the gentle stir and fret
Sings out the melting clarionet,
Like as a lady sings while yet
Her eyes with salty tears are wet.
"O Trade! O Trade!" the Lady said,
"I too will wish thee utterly dead   220
If all thy heart is in thy head.
For O my God! and O my God!
What shameful ways have women trod
At beckoning of Trade's golden rod!
Alas when sighs are traders' lies,
And heart's-ease eyes and violet eyes
    Are merchandise!
O purchased lips that kiss with pain!
O cheeks coin-spotted with smirch and stain!
O trafficked hearts that break in twain!   230
—And yet what wonder at my sisters' crime?
So hath Trade withered up Love's sinewy prime,
Men love not women as in olden time.
Ah, not in these cold merchantable days
Deem men their life an opal gray, where plays
The one red Sweet of gracious ladies' praise.
Now, comes a suitor with sharp prying eye—
Says, *Here, you Lady, if you'll sell, I'll buy:*
Come, heart for heart—a trade? What! weeping? why?
Shame on such wooers' dapper mercery!   240
I would my lover kneeling at my feet
In humble manliness should cry, *O sweet!*
I know not if thy heart my heart will greet;
I ask not if thy love my love can meet:
Whate'er thy worshipful soft tongue shall say,
I'll kiss thine answer, be it yea or nay:

I do but know I love thee, and I pray
To be thy knight until my dying day.
Woe him that cunning trades in hearts contrives!
Base love good women to base loving drives.   250
If men loved larger, larger were our lives;
And wooed they nobler, won they nobler wives."
There thrust the bold straightforward horn
To battle for that lady lorn,
With heartsome voice of mellow scorn,
Like any knight in knighthood's morn.
   "Now comfort thee," said he,
      "Fair Lady.
For God shall right thy grievous wrong,
And man shall sing thee a true-love song,   260
Voiced in act his whole life long,
   Yea, all thy sweet life long,
      Fair Lady.
Where's he that craftily hath said,
The day of chivalry is dead?
I'll prove that lie upon his head,
   Or I will die instead,
      Fair Lady.
Is Honor gone into his grave?
Hath Faith become a caitiff knave,   270
And Selfhood turned into a slave
   To work in Mammon's cave,
      Fair Lady?
Will Truth's long blade ne'er gleam again?
Hath Giant Trade in dungeons slain
All great contempts of mean-got gain
   And hates of inward stain,
      Fair Lady?
For aye shall name and fame be sold,
And place be hugged for the sake of gold,   280
And smirch-robed Justice feebly scold
   At Crime all money-bold,
      Fair Lady?
Shall self-wrapt husbands aye forget
Kiss-pardons for the daily fret
Wherewith sweet wifely eyes are wet—
   Blind to lips kiss-wise set—
      Fair Lady?
Shall lovers higgle, heart for heart,

Till wooing grows a trading mart   290
Where much for little, and all for part,
   Make love a cheapening art,
      Fair Lady?
Shall woman scorch for a single sin
That her betrayer may revel in,
And she be burnt, and he but grin
   When that the flames begin,
      Fair Lady?
Shall ne'er prevail the woman's plea,
We maids would far, far whiter be   300
If that our eyes might sometimes see
   Men maids in purity,
      Fair Lady?
Shall Trade aye salve his conscience-aches
With jibes at Chivalry's old mistakes—
The wars that o'erhot knighthood makes
   For Christ's and ladies' sakes,
      Fair Lady?
Now by each knight that e'er hath prayed
To fight like a man and love like a maid,   310
Since Pembroke's life, as Pembroke's blade,
   I' the scabbard, death, was laid,
      Fair Lady,
I dare avouch my faith is bright
That God doth right and God hath might.
Nor time hath changed His hair to white,
   Nor His dear love to spite,
      Fair Lady.
I doubt no doubts: I strive, and shrive my clay,
And fight my fight in the patient modern way   320
For true love and for thee—ah me! and pray
   To be thy knight until my dying day,
      Fair Lady."
Made end that knightly horn, and spurred away
Into the thick of the melodious fray.
And then the hautboy played and smiled,
And sang like any large-eyed child,
Cool-hearted and all undefiled.
   "Huge Trade!" he said,
"Would thou wouldst lift me on thy head   330
And run where'er my finger led!
Once said a Man—and wise was He—
Never shalt thou the heavens see,

Save as a little child thou be."
Then o'er sea-lashings of commingling tunes
The ancient wise bassoons,
 Like weird,
 Gray-beard
Old harpers sitting on the high sea-dunes,
 Chanted runes: 340
"Bright-waved gain, gray-waved loss,
The sea of all doth lash and toss,
One wave forward and one across:
But now 'twas trough, now 'tis crest,
And worst doth foam and flash to best,
 And curst to blest.

"Life! Life! thou sea-fugue, writ from east to west,
 Love, Love alone can pore
 On thy dissolving score
 Of harsh half-phrasings,   350
  Blotted ere writ,
 And double erasings
  Of chords most fit.
Yea, Love, sole music-master blest,
May read thy weltering palimpsest.
To follow Time's dying melodies through,
And never to lose the old in the new,
And ever to solve the discords true—
 Love alone can do.
And ever Love hears the poor-folks' crying,   360
And ever Love hears the women's sighing,
And ever sweet knighthood's death-defying,
And ever wise childhood's deep implying,
But never a trader's glozing and lying.

"And yet shall Love himself be heard,
Though long deferred, though long deferred:
O'er the modern waste a dove hath whirred:
Music is Love in search of a word."

          1875

The Mocking Bird

Superb and sole, upon a plumèd spray
That o'er the general leafage boldly grew,

He summ'd the woods in song; or typic drew
The watch of hungry hawks, the lone dismay
Of languid doves when long their lovers stray,
And all birds' passion-plays that sprinkle dew
At morn in brake or bosky avenue.
Whate'er birds did or dreamed, this bird could say.
Then down he shot, bounced airily along
The sward, twitched in a grasshopper, made song   10
Midflight, perched, prinked, and to his art again.
Sweet Science, this large riddle read me plain:
How may the death of that dull insect be
The life of yon trim Shakespeare on the tree?

1877

The Stirrup-Cup

Death, thou'rt a cordial old and rare:
Look how compounded, with what care!
Time got his wrinkles reaping thee
Sweet herbs from all antiquity.

David to thy distilling went,
Keats and Gotama excellent,
Omar Khayyám, and a Chaucer bright,
And Shakespeare for a king-delight.

Then, Time, let not a drop be spilt:
Hand me the cup whene'er thou wilt;   10
'Tis thy rich stirrup-cup to me;
I'll drink it down right smilingly.

1877

The Marshes of Glynn

Glooms of the live-oaks, beautiful-braided and woven
With intricate shades of the vines that myriad-cloven
    Clamber the forks of the multiform boughs,—
            Emerald twilights,—
            Virginal shy lights,
Wrought of the leaves to allure to the whisper of vows,
When lovers pace timidly down through the green colon-
                nades

Of the dim sweet woods, of the dear dark woods,
　Of the heavenly woods and glades,
That run to the radiant marginal sand-beach within　　10
　　　The wide sea-marshes of Glynn;—

Beautiful glooms, soft dusks in the noon-day fire,—
Wildwood privacies, closets of lone desire,
Chamber from chamber parted with wavering arras of
　　　　leaves,—
Cells for the passionate pleasure of prayer to the soul that
　　　　grieves,
Pure with a sense of the passing of saints through the wood,
Cool for the dutiful weighing of ill with good;—

O braided dusks of the oak and woven shades of the vine,
While the riotous noon-day sun of the June-day long did
　　　shine
Ye held me fast in your heart and I held you fast in
　　　mine;　　　　　　　　　　　　　　　　　　　　20
But now when the noon is no more, and riot is rest,
And the sun is a-wait at the ponderous gate of the West,
And the slant yellow beam down the wood-aisle doth seem
Like a lane into heaven that leads from a dream,—
Ay, now, when my soul all day hath drunken the soul of
　　　the oak,
And my heart is at ease from men, and the wearisome
　　　sound of the stroke
　Of the scythe of time and the trowel of trade is low,
　　And belief overmasters doubt, and I know that I know,
　　And my spirit is grown to a lordly great compass within,
That the length and the breadth and the sweep of the
　　　marshes of Glynn　　　　　　　　　　　　　30
Will work me no fear like the fear they have wrought me
　　　of yore
When length was fatigue, and when breadth was but
　　　bitterness sore,
And when terror and shrinking and dreary unnamable pain
Drew over me out of the merciless miles of the plain,—
Oh, now, unafraid, I am fain to face
　The vast sweet visage of space.
To the edge of the wood I am drawn, I am drawn,
Where the gray beach glimmering runs, as a belt of the
　　　dawn,

For a mete and a mark
    To the forest-dark:—   **40**
        So:
Affable live-oak, leaning low,—
Thus—with your favor—soft, with a reverent hand
(Not lightly touching your person, Lord of the land!),
Bending your beauty aside, with a step I stand
On the firm-packed sand,
        Free
By a world of marsh that borders a world of sea.
  Sinuous southward and sinuous northward the shimmer-
          ing band
  Of the sand-beach fastens the fringe of the marsh to the
          folds of the land.   **50**
Inward and outward to northward and southward the
          beach-lines linger and curl
As a silver-wrought garment that clings to and follows
          the firm sweet limbs of a girl.
Vanishing, swerving, evermore curving again into sight,
Softly the sand-beach wavers away to a dim gray looping
          of light.
And what if behind me to westward the wall of the woods
          stands high?
The world lies east: how ample, the marsh and the sea
          and the sky!
A league and a league of marsh-grass, waist-high, broad
          in the blade,
Green, and all of a height, and unflecked with a light or a
          shade,
Stretch leisurely off, in a pleasant plain,
To the terminal blue of the main.   **60**

Oh, what is abroad in the marsh and the terminal sea?
  Somehow my soul seems suddenly free
From the weighing of fate and the sad discussion of sin,
By the length and the breadth and the sweep of the marshes
         of Glynn.

Ye marshes, how candid and simple and nothing-withhold-
         ing and free
Ye publish yourselves to the sky and offer yourselves to the
         sea!

Tolerant plains, that suffer the sea and the rains and the
        sun,
Ye spread and span like the catholic man who hath mightily
        won
God out of knowledge and good out of infinite pain
And sight out of blindness and purity out of a stain.   70
As the marsh-hen secretly builds on the watery sod,
Behold I will build me a nest on the greatness of God:
I will fly in the greatness of God as the marsh-hen flies
In the freedom that fills all the space 'twixt the marsh and
        the skies:
By so many roots as the marsh-grass sends in the sod
I will heartily lay me a-hold on the greatness of God:
Oh, like to the greatness of God is the greatness within
The range of the marshes, the liberal marshes of Glynn.

And the sea lends large, as the marsh: lo, out of his plenty
        the sea
Pours fast: full soon the time of the flood-tide must be: 80
Look how the grace of the sea doth go
About and about through the intricate channels that flow
     Here and there,
     Everywhere,
Till his waters have flooded the uttermost creeks and the
        low-lying lanes,
And the marsh is meshed with a million veins,
That like as with rosy and silvery essences flow
  In the rose-and-silver evening glow.
      Farewell, my lord Sun!
The creeks overflow: a thousand rivulets run   90
'Twixt the roots of the sod; the blades of the marshgrass
       stir;
Passeth a hurrying sound of wings that westward whirr;
Passeth, and all is still; and the currents cease to run;
And the sea and the marsh are one.

How still the plains of the waters be!
The tide is in his ecstasy.
The tide is at his highest height:
      And it is night.

And now from the Vast of the Lord will the waters of sleep
Roll in on the souls of men,   100

But who will reveal to our waking ken
The forms that swim and the shapes that creep
   Under the waters of sleep?
And I would I could know what swimmeth below when
   the tide comes in
On the length and the breadth of the marvellous marshes
   of Glynn.

         1878

Marsh Song—At Sunset

Over the monstrous shambling sea,
 Over the Caliban sea,
Bright Ariel-cloud, thou lingerest:
Oh wait, oh wait, in the warm red West,—
 Thy Prospero I'll be.

Over the humped and fishy sea,
 Over the Caliban sea
O cloud in the West, like a thought in the heart
Of pardon, loose thy wind, and start,
 And do a grace for me.   10

Over the huge and huddling sea,
 Over the Caliban sea
Bring hither my brother Antonio,—Man,—
My injurer: night breaks the ban:
 Brother, I pardon thee.

       w. 1879–80
       p.1882

Opposition

Of fret, of dark, of thorn, of chill,
 Complain no more; for these, O heart,
Direct the random of the will
 As rhymes direct the rage of art.

The lute's fixed fret, that runs athwart
 The strain and purpose of the string,

For governance and nice consort
   Doth bar his wilful wavering.

The dark hath many dear avails;
   The dark distils divinest dews;   10
The dark is rich with nightingales,
   With dreams, and with the heavenly Muse.

Bleeding with thorns of petty strife,
   I'll ease (as lovers do) my smart
With sonnets to my lady Life
   Writ red in issues from the heart.

What grace may lie within the chill
   Of favor frozen fast in scorn!
When Good's a-freeze, we call it Ill!
   This rosy Time is glacier-born.   20

Of fret, of dark, of thorn, of chill,
   Complain thou not, O heart; for these
Bank-in the current of the will
   To uses, arts, and charities.

1880

FROM

The New South

It would seem that facts may now be arrayed which leave no doubt that upon the general cycle of American advance the South has described such an epicycle of individual growth that no profitable discussion of that region is possible at present which does not clearly define at the outset whether it is to be a discussion of the old South or the new South. Although the movement here called by the latter name is originally neither political, social, moral, nor aesthetic, yet the term in the present instance connotes all these with surprising completeness. The New South means small farming.

What Southern small farming really signifies, and how it has come to involve and determine the whole compass of civilization in that part of the republic, this paper proposes to show, (1) by briefly pointing out its true relation, in its last or (what one may call, its) poetic outcome, to the "large farming" now so imminent in the Northwest; (2) by presenting some statistics of the remarkable increase in the number of Southern small farms from 1860 to 1870, together with some details of the actual cultures and special conditions thereof; and (3) by contrasting with it a picture of large farming in England three hundred years ago. Indeed, one has only to recall how the connection between marriage and the price of corn is but a crude and partial statement of the intimate relation between politics, social life, morality, art, on the one hand, and the bread-giver earth on the other; one has only to remember that, particularly here in America, whatever crop we hope to reap in the future,—whether it be a crop of poems, of paintings, of symphonies, of constitutional safeguards, of virtuous behaviors, of religious exaltations,—we have got to bring it out of the ground with palpable ploughs and with plain farmers' forethought: in order to see that a vital revolution in the farming economy of the South, if it is actually occurring, is necessarily carrying with it all future Southern politics and Southern social relations and Southern art, and that, therefore, such an agricultural change is the one substantial fact upon which any really new South can be predicated.

Approached from this direction, the quiet rise of the small farmer in the Southern States during the last twenty years becomes the notable circumstance of the period, in comparison with which noisier events signify nothing.

As just now hinted, small farming in the South becomes clear in its remoter bearings when seen over against the precisely opposite tendency toward large farming in the West. Doubtless recent reports of this tendency have been sometimes exaggerated. In reading them, one has been obliged to remember that small minds love to bring large news, and, failing a load, will make one. But certainly enough appears, if only in the single apparently well-authenticated item of the tempting profits realized by some of the great northwestern planters, to authorize the inference that the tendency to cultivate wheat on enormous farms, where the economies possible only to corporation-management can secure the greatest yield with the least expense, is a growing one.

And, this being so, the most rapid glance along the peculiar details of the northwestern large farm opens before us a path of thought which quickly passes beyond wheat-raising, and leads among all those other means of life which appertain to this complex creature who cannot live by bread alone. For instance, classify, as a social and moral factor, a farm like the Grandin place, near Fargo, where 4,855 acres are sown in wheat; where five hands do all the work during the six winter months, while as many as two hundred and fifty must be employed in midsummer; where the day's work is nearly thirteen hours; where, out of the numerous structures for farm purposes, but two have any direct relation to man,—one a residence for the superintendent and foreman, the other a boarding-house for the hands; where no women, children, nor poultry are to be seen; where the economies are such as are wholly out of the power of the small wheat-raisers, insomuch that even the railways can give special rates for grain coming in such convenient large quantities; where the steam machine, the telephone, and the telegraph are brought to the last degree of skilful service; where, finally, the net profits for the current year are $52,239.

It appears plainly enough from these details that, looked upon from the midst of all those associations which cluster about the idea of the farm, large farming is not farming at all. It is mining for wheat.

Or a slight change in the point of view presents it as a manufacturing business, in which clods are fed to the mill, and grain appears in carloads at Chicago. And perhaps the most exact relations of this large farming to society in general are to be drawn by considering such farmers as corporations, their laborers as mill-operatives for six months in each year and tramps for the other six, their farms as mills where nature mainly turns the wheel, their investment as beyond the reach of strikes or fires, foreign distress their friend, and the world's hunger their steady customer.

It appears further that, while such agricultural communities are so merely in name and are manufacturing communities in fact, they are manufacturing communities only as to the sterner features of that guild,—the order, the machine, the minimum of expense, the maximum of product,—and not as to those pleasanter features, the school-house, the church, the little workingmen's library, the sewing-class, the cookery-class, the line of promotion, the rise of the bright boy and the steady workman,—all the gentler matters which will spring up, even out of the dust-heaps, about any spot where men have the rudest abiding-place. On the large farm is no abiding-place; the laborer must move on; life cannot stand still, to settle and clarify.

It would not seem necessary to disclaim any design to inveigh against the owners of these great factory-farms, if indignation had not been already expressed in such a way as to oblige one to declare that no obligations can be cited, as between them and their laborers, which would not equally apply to every manufacturer. If it is wrong to discharge all but ten laborers when only ten are needed, then the mill-owners of Massachusetts must be held bound to run day and night when the market is over-stocked because they ran so when it was booming; and if it is criminal to pay the large-farmhands no more than will hardly support them for thirteen hours' work, every mill-company in the world which pays market rates for work is *particeps* [a partner in crime]. But, with the coast thus cleared of personality; with the large farm thus classed as a manufacturing company in all its important incidents; and recognizing in the fullest manner that, if wheat can be made most cheaply in this way, it must be so made: a very brief train of thought brings us upon a situation, as between the small farmer on the one hand and the corporation on the other, which reveals them as embodying two tendencies in the republic at this moment whose relations it is the business of statesmanship and of citizenship to understand with the utmost clearness, since we are bound to foster both of them.

For, if we stop our ears to the noisy child's-play of current politics, and remember (1) that in all ages and countries two spirits, or motives, or tendencies exist which are essentially opposed to each other, but both of which are necessary to the state; (2) that the problem of any given period or society is to recognize the special forms in which these two tendencies are then and there embodying themselves, and to keep them in such relations that neither shall crush, while each shall healthily check, the other; (3) that these tendencies may be called the spirit of control and the spirit of independence, and that they are so intimately connected with the two undeniable facts which lie at the bottom of moral behavior—namely, the facts of influence from without, on the one hand, and free will on the other—that the questions of morals and of politics coalesce at their roots; (4) that these two tendencies are now most tangibly embodied among us in the corporation and the small farmer —the corporation representing the spirit of control, and the small farmer representing in many curious ways, the spirit of independence; (5) that our republic vitally needs the corporation for the mighty works which only the corporation can do, while it as vitally needs the small farmer for the pure substance of individual and self-reliant manhood which he digs out of the ground, and which, the experience of all peoples would seem to show, must primarily come that way and no other: we are bound to conclude that the practical affair in the United States at the present juncture is to discover how we may cherish at once the corporation and the small farmer into the highest state of competitive activity, less by constitution-straining laws which forbid the corporation to do this and that, or which coddle the small farmer with sop and privilege, than by affording free scope for both to adjust themselves, and by persistently holding sound moral principles to guide the adjustment. . . .

The phrase "small farming," used of the South, crops out in directions curious enough to one unacquainted with the special economies and relations of existence in that part of our country. While large farming in the South means exclusive cotton-growing,—as it means in the West exclusive wheat-growing or exclusive corn-growing,—small farming means *diversified farm-products;* and a special result of the Southern conditions of agriculture has brought about a still more special sense of the word, so that in Georgia, for example, the term "small farmer" brings up to every native mind the idea of a farmer who, besides his cotton crop, raises corn enough to "do" him. But again, the incidents hinging upon this apparently simple matter of making corn enough to do him are so numerous as, in turn, to render *them* the distinctive feature of small farming. Small farming means, in short, meat and bread for which there are no notes in bank; pigs fed with home-made corn, and growing of themselves while the corn and cotton were being tended; yarn spun, stockings knit, butter made and sold (instead of bought); eggs, chickens, peaches, watermelons, the four extra sheep and a little wool, two calves and a beef, —all to sell every year, besides a colt who is now suddenly become, all of himself, a good, serviceable horse; the four oxen, who are as good as gifts made by the grass; and a hundred other items, all representing income from a hundred sources to the small farmer, which equally represent outgo to the large farmer,—items, too, scarcely appearing at all on the expense side of the strictest account-book, because they are either products of odd moments which, if not so applied, would not have been at all applied, or products of natural animal growth, and grass at nothing a ton. All these ideas are inseparably connected with that of the small farmer in the South.

. . .

Nothing seems more sure than that an entirely new direction of cleavage in the structure of Southern polity must come with the wholly different aggregation of particles implied in this development of small farming.

In the identical aims of the small-farmer class, whatever now remains of the color-line must surely disappear out of the Southern political situation. This class, consisting as it already does of black small-farmers and white small-farmers, must necessarily be a body of persons whose privileges, needs, and relations are *not* those which exist as between the black man on the one hand and the white man on the other, but those which exist as between the small farmer on the one hand and whatever affects small farming on the other. For here—as cannot be too often said—the relation of politics to agriculture is that of the turnip-top to the turnip.

. . .

It does not seem possible to doubt . . . that there is, in Georgia at least, a strong class of small farmers which powerfully tends to obliterate color from politics, in virtue of its merger of all conflicting elements into the common interest of common agricultural pursuit. . . .

It is impossible to end without advertising to a New South which exists in a far more literal sense than that of small farming. How much of this gracious land is yet new to all real cultivation, how much of it lies groaning for the muscle of men, and how doubly mournful is this newness, in view of the fair and fruitful conditions which here hold perpetual session, and press perpetual invitation upon all men to come and have plenty! Surely, along that ample stretch of generous soil, where the Appalachian ruggednesses calm themselves into pleasant hills before dying quite away into the sea-board levels, a man can find such temperance of heaven and earth—enough of struggle with nature to draw out manhood, with enough of bounty to sanction the struggle—that a more exquisite co-adaptation of all blessed circumstances for man's life need not be sought. It is with a part of that region that this writer is most familiar, and one cannot but remember that, as one stands at a certain spot thereof and looks off up and across the Ocmulgee River, the whole prospect seems distinctly to yearn for men. Everywhere the huge and gentle slopes kneel and pray for vineyards, for cornfields, for cottages, for spires to rise up from beyond the oak-groves. It is a land where there is never a day of summer nor of winter when a man cannot do a full day's work in the open field; all the products meet there, as at nature's own agricultural fair; rice grows alongside of wheat, corn alongside of sugar-cane, cotton alongside of clover, apples alongside of peaches, so that a small farm may often miniature the whole United States in growth; the little valleys everywhere run with living waters, asking grasses and cattle and quiet grist-mills; all manner of timbers for economic uses and trees for finer arts cover the earth; in short, here is such a neighborly congregation of climates, soils, minerals, and vegetables, that within the compass of many a hundred-acre farm a man may find wherewithal to build his house of stone, of brick, of oak, or of pine, to furnish it in woods that would delight the most curious eye, and to supply his family with all the necessaries, most of the comforts, and many of the luxuries, of the whole world. It is the country of homes.

And, as said, it is because these blissful ranges are still clamorous for human friendship; it is because many of them are actually virgin to plough, pillar, axe, or mill-wheel, while others have known only the insulting and mean cultivation of the earlier immigrants who scratched the surface for cotton a year or two, then carelessly abandoned all to sedge and sassafras, and sauntered on toward Texas: it is thus that these lands are, with sadder significance than that of small farming, also a New South.

1880

EMILY DICKINSON

(1830–1886)

Born in the closed and rigid society of early nineteenth-century Puritan Amherst, Massachusetts, Emily Dickinson demonstrates, as almost no other American writer can, the vast discrepancy sometimes discernible between the art and the biography of a single human being. It has become fashionable to minimize the impression of Emily Dickinson as a "New England nun," as the white-clad genteel spinster isolated from society, devoting herself to her garden, her books, and her poetry. (Indeed, a new biography, Jay Leyda's *The Years and Hours of Emily Dickinson,* suggests the possibility of a promiscuous Emily in a mad household.) Yet when all is said and done, the impression of isolation remains constant and probably valid. Perhaps the most amazing aspect of Emily Dickinson's personality is the fact that such rebellious, strong-souled, hard-minded, iconoclastic, and excellent poetry came, not from a robust man, but from precisely the kind of old maid with whom one would associate the production of scatterbrained verses of prettiness, turgidity, and convention. The tough, fine-spun filaments of feeling that catch outward from each diamond-hard poem indicate a woman who can be measured only by her work, for her biography leaves little on which to build.

She was the daughter of Edward Dickinson, lawyer, Congressman, and trustee and treasurer of Amherst College. Immersed in the proper bosom of her Calvinist household, she was educated at home except for a year (1847) at Mount Holyoke Female Seminary, at South Hadley. An active girl with a pixyish bent of humor, at Mount Holyoke she met Helen

Fiske (later Helen Hunt Jackson, of *Ramona* fame), who would remain a friend and one of Miss Dickinson's few contemporaries to recognize the universal and lyrical power of her intense poetic genius. She probably had few male companions, although she enjoyed the company of Benjamin F. Newton, who worked in her father's law office and who tried to guide her in her poetry and reading. His death in 1853 left her shaken, but probably more by the loss of a decent and sensitive friend than by that of a potential mate. A year later, while her father was in Congress, she traveled to Washington; during the trip she visited Philadelphia, where she met and perhaps became infatuated with a married minister, Charles Wadsworth. As in the case of Ben Newton, it is not possible to be certain about her emotional involvement with the man; we only know that in her twenty-third year she began to exchange letters with him. In 1860 he visited her, probably quite properly; the next year he accepted a pastorate in San Francisco, to which he moved with his family. From that time on Miss Dickinson began to withdraw into her house and into herself; this, however, might merely have been a consequence of her life, her upbringing, and her personality. With the withdrawal into the heat of her emotional innerness came the beginning of her real poetic productivity.

By the time she was thirty-two, Amherst gossip had already begun to create the picture of the recluse lady in the substantial family that lived on Main Street. By 1870 she hardly "went out." When her father died in 1874 and her mother became paralyzed a year later, she was scarcely seen any more. In 1886 she died as uneventfully—outwardly—as she had lived.

Her public poetic career was even less eventful than her personal life. She asked the editor of the *Atlantic Monthly*, Colonel Thomas Wentworth Higginson, to judge a handful of poems, and he became a lifelong friend, trying to regularize her poetry: it was advice she hardly accepted. During her lifetime she published, as accurately as can be determined, only seven poems, and they were printed anonymously. After Emily's death, her sister Lavinia discovered a wealth of fragments and manuscript poems, and the publication that Emily scorned during her life began to catch up with her through death. Lavinia turned to a neighbor, Mrs. Mabel Loomis Todd, to set the manuscripts in order for publication. In 1890 Mrs. Todd and Colonel Higginson brought out *Poems by Emily Dickinson*.

In 1891 they brought out *Poems . . . Second Series.* In 1896 they published *Poems . . . Third Series.* Until 1914 the three volumes, together with *Letters of Emily Dickinson* (1894), which included an additional 102 poetic items, constituted all that the world had of Emily Dickinson's poems.

A falling out between Lavinia and Mrs. Todd, together with family jealousies, further complicated the fate of the manuscripts; but in 1914 Martha Dickinson Bianchi, Emily's niece, added to the Dickinson canon with still other poems collected in *The Single Hound.* The editions of the 1890's had influenced only Stephen Crane and a few fellow innovators, but in 1914 Miss Dickinson's work began to receive wider attention. The renaissance of modern American poetry, the time of literary manifestoes, the air of rebellion, all combined to allow readers to find in Emily Dickinson's work the gem-clear imagery and the modern attitudes that new voices in poetry were demanding. In her intense honesty and amazing figures the age caught an echo of its own revolt in perceptions and styles, a revolt that triumphed after World War I. From 1914 on, Emily Dickinson's reputation began to change from that of the queer, interesting, but unimportant minor poet to that of the major new voice (together with Whitman) of modern times. In 1924 Mrs. Bianchi published *The Complete Poems of Emily Dickinson,* which was anything but complete and which contained all the poems of the Higginson-Todd editions, *The Single Hound,* and five new pieces. In 1929 Mrs. Bianchi and Alfred Leete Hampson edited *Further Poems of Emily Dickinson Withheld from Publication by Her Sister Lavinia.* Mrs. Bianchi and Hampson compiled all the poems published to date in 1930 in *The Poems of Emily Dickinson,* adding *Unpublished Poems of Emily Dickinson* in 1936. Then in 1937 they combined all editions in another *Poems of Emily Dickinson.* But all was not yet done; for in 1945 Mrs. Todd and her daughter, Millicent Todd Bingham, brought out 668 hitherto unpublished poems in *Bolts of Melody.*

For a decade there was a serious need for a complete and definitive edition of Emily Dickinson's poems. This was finally supplied in 1955 by Thomas H. Johnson in *The Poems of Emily Dickinson* in three volumes. These volumes present all 1775 of Emily Dickinson's known poems, their chronology and all their variants, and there the matter rests. (The poems presented here are arranged in the sequence Johnson suggests. Those poems which were changed from first printing by the revisions published by Johnson are indicated by Johnson's numbering following the title.)

The influences on Emily Dickinson's poetry were, most largely, Puritanism, the verse meters of her English hymnal, the Bible, Shakespeare, and Emerson. From the Bible and Shakespeare she took precedents for her conceits and wild imagery. From Emerson (she had received a copy of his 1846 *Poems* on her twentieth birthday and probably met him when he visited Amherst in 1855) she took the condensed form, the gnomic, epigrammatic verse that was willing to violate grammar, agreement, mood, voice, tense, and expectation to achieve vigor of thought or of image; Emily Dickinson carried the device further than Emerson ever cared to. Influences, however, must be treated very specially in her case. So "untouched" was her life that all influences were fused in the crucible of her inner feelings, in which she was able to transfigure crumbs, bees, stars, broken dishes, or God into the special meanings and conjunctions that mark her verse as unmistakably her own. Puritan and recluse that she was, she found her meanings in the most common, everyday objects and experiences, which she transmuted with a power that left the commonplace vibrating with an energy it had not had before.

In addition to the books mentioned above, the following are some of the editions and accounts of Emily Dickinson and her work: G. Bradford, *Portraits of American Women* (1919); C. Aiken, ed., *Selected Poems of Emily Dickinson* (1924); R. W. Brown, *Lonely Americans* (1929); J. Pollitt, *Emily Dickinson: The Human Background of her Poetry* (1930); G. Taggard, *The Life and Mind of Emily Dickinson* (1930); G. F. Whicher, *Emily Dickinson: A Bibliography* (1931); M. D. Bianchi, *Emily Dickinson Face to Face* (1932); G. F. Whicher, *This Was a Poet* (1938); M. Jenkins, *Emily Dickinson, Friend and Neighbor* (1930, 1939); M. J. Power, *In the Name of the Bee* (1943); M. T. Bingham, *Ancestors' Brocades* (1945); H. W. Wells, *Introduction to Emily Dickinson* (1947); R. Chase, *Emily Dickinson* (1951); T. H. Johnson, *Emily Dickinson: An Interpretive Biography* (1955); T. H. Johnson, ed., *The Letters of Emily Dickinson*, 3 vols. (1958); C. R. Anderson, *Emily Dickinson's Poetry* (1960); J. Leyda, *The Years and Hours of Emily Dickinson*, 2 vols. (1960); T. H. Johnson, ed., *Final Harvest: Emily Dickinson's Poems* (1962); R. B. Sewall, ed., *Emily Dickinson: A Collection of Critical Essays* (1963); C. R. Blake and C. F. Wells, eds., *The Recognition of Emily Dickinson* (1964); C. Griffith, *The Long Shadow: Emily Dickinson's Tragic Poetry* (1964); S. P. Rosenbaum, ed., *A Concordance to the Poems of Emily Dickinson* (1964); D. Douglas, *Emily Dickinson* (1965); A. J. Gelpi, *Emily Dickinson, The Mind of the Poet* (1965); J. L.

Capps, *Emily Dickinson's Reading, 1836–1886* (1966); D. T. Porter, *The Art of Emily Dickinson's Early Poetry* (1966); and T. W. Ford, *Heaven Beguiles the Tired: Death in the Poetry of Emily Dickinson* (1966).

Sic Transit Gloria Mundi

Sic transit gloria mundi,
How doth the busy bee—
Dum vivimus vivamus,
I stay mine enemy.

Oh, *veni, vidi, vici,*
Oh, *caput, cap-a-pie,*
And oh, *memento mori*
When I am far from thee.

Hurrah for Peter Parley,
Hurrah for Daniel Boone,   10
Three cheers, sir, for the gentlemen
Who first observed the moon.

Peter put up the sunshine,
Pattie arrange the stars,
Tell Luna tea is waiting,
And call your brother Mars.

Put down the apple, Adam,
And come away with me;
So shall thou have a pippin
From off my father's tree.   20

I climb the hill of science
I "view the landscape o'er,"
Such transcendental prospect
I ne'er beheld before.

Unto the Legislature
My country bids me go.
I'll take my india-rubbers,
In case the wind should blow.

During my education,
It was announced to me   30
That gravitation, stumbling,
Fell from an apple-tree.

The earth upon its axis
Was once supposed to turn,
By way of a gymnastic
In honor to the sun.

It was the brave Columbus,
A-sailing on the tide,
Who notified the nations
Of where I would reside.   40

Mortality is fatal,
Gentility is fine,
Rascality heroic,
Insolvency sublime.

Our fathers being weary
Lay down on Bunker Hill,
And though full many a morning,
Yet they are sleeping still.

The trumpet, sir, shall wake them,
In dream I see them rise,   50
Each with a solemn musket
A-marching to the skies.

A coward will remain, sir,
Until the fight is done,
But an immortal hero
Will take his hat and run.

Good-by, sir, I am going—
My country calleth me.
Allow me, sir, at parting
To wipe my weeping e'e.   60

In token of our friendship
Accept this *Bonnie Doon,*
And when the hand that plucked it
Has passed beyond the moon,

The memory of my ashes
Will consolation be.
Then farewell, Tuscarora,
And farewell, sir, to thee.

p. 1852

The Morns Are Meeker Than They Were

The morns are meeker than they were,
The nuts are getting brown;
The berry's cheek is plumper,
The rose is out of town.

The maple wears a gayer scarf,
The field a scarlet gown.
Lest I should be old-fashioned,
I'll put a trinket on.

w. c1858
p. 1890

I Never Lost as Much but Twice

I never lost as much but twice,
And that was in the sod;
Twice have I stood a beggar
Before the door of God!

Angels, twice descending,
Reimbursed my store.
Burglar, banker, father,
I am poor once more!

w. c1858
p. 1890

If I Should Die, and You Should Live

If I should die, and you should live,
   And time should gurgle on,
And morn should beam, and noon should burn,
   As it has usual done;
If birds should build as early,

And bees as bustling go,—
One might depart at option
  From enterprise below!

'Tis sweet to know that stocks will stand
  When we with daisies lie,   10
That commerce will continue,
  And trades as briskly fly.
It makes the parting tranquil
  And keeps the soul serene,
That gentlemen so sprightly
  Conduct the pleasing scene!

w. c1858
p. 1891

Papa Above!

Papa above!
          Regard a Mouse
O'erpowered by the Cat;
Reserve within thy Kingdom
A "mansion" for the Rat!

Snug in seraphic cupboards
To nibble all the day,
While unsuspecting cycles
Wheel pompously away.

w. c1859
p. 1914

Success Is Counted Sweetest

Success is counted sweetest
By those who ne'er succeed.
To comprehend a nectar
Requires sorest need.

Not one of all the purple host
Who took the flag to-day
Can tell the definition,
So clear, of victory,

As he, defeated, dying,
On whose forbidden ear   10
The distant strains of triumph
Break, agonized and clear.

w. 1859
p. 1878

"Arcturus" Is His Other Name

[J70]

"Arcturus" is his other name—
I'd rather call him "star."
It's very mean of science
To go and interfere!

I slew a worm the other day—
A "savan" passing by
Murmured "resurgam"—"centipede!"
"Oh Lord how frail are we!"

I pull a flower from the woods—
A monster with a glass   10
Computes the stamens in a breath,
And has her in a "class!"

Whereas I took the butterfly
Aforetime in my hat,
He sits erect in "cabinets,"
The clover bells forgot.

What once was "heaven,"
Is *"zenith"* now;
Where I proposed to go
When time's brief masquerade was done,   20
Is mapped and charted too.

What if the poles should frisk about,
And stand upon their heads!
I hope I'm ready for "the worst,"
Whatever prank betides!

Perhaps the "Kingdom of Heaven's" changed.
I hope the "children" there
Won't be "new fashioned" when I come,
And laugh at me, and stare

I hope the Father in the skies   30
Will lift his little girl—
Old fashioned, naughty, everything,
Over the stile of "pearl."

w. c1859
p. 1891, 1947

Exultation Is the Going

Exultation is the going
Of an inland soul to sea,—
Past the houses, past the headlands,
Into deep eternity!

Bred as we, among the mountains,
Can the sailor understand
The divine intoxication
Of the first league out from land?

w. c1859
p. 1890

I Never Hear the Word "Escape"

I never hear the word "escape"
Without a quicker blood,
A sudden expectation,
A flying attitude.

I never hear of prisons broad
By soldiers battered down,
But I tug childish at my bars,—
Only to fail again!

w. c1859
p. 1891

Some Things That Fly There Be

Some things that fly there be,—
Birds, hours, the bumble-bee:
Of these no elegy.

Some things that stay there be,—
Grief, hills, eternity:
Nor this behooveth me.

There are, that resting, rise.
Can I expound the skies?
How still the riddle lies!

w. c1859
p. 1890

My Nosegays Are for Captives

My nosegays are for captives;
    Dim, long-expectant eyes,
Fingers denied the plucking,
    Patient till paradise.

To such, if they should whisper
    Of morning and the moor,
They bear no other errand,
    And I, no other prayer.

w. c1859
p. 1891

To Fight Aloud Is Very Brave

To fight aloud is very brave,
But gallanter, I know,
Who charge within the bosom,
The cavalry of woe.

Who win, and nations do not see,
Who fall, and none observe,
Whose dying eyes no country
Regards with patriot love.

We trust, in plumed procession,
For such the angels go,   10
Rank after rank, with even feet
And uniforms of snow.

w. c1859
p. 1890

These Are the Days When Birds Come Back

These are the days when birds come back,
A very few, a bird or two,
To take a backward look.

These are the days when skies put on
The old, old sophistries of June,—
A blue and gold mistake.

Oh, fraud that cannot cheat the bee,
Almost thy plausibility
Induces my belief,

Till ranks of seeds their witness bear,   10
And softly through the altered air
Hurries a timid leaf!

Oh, sacrament of summer days,
Oh, last communion in the haze,
Permit a child to join,

Thy sacred emblems to partake,
Thy consecrated bread to break,
Taste thine immortal wine!

w. c1859
p. 1890

Just Lost When I Was Saved!

Just lost when I was saved!
Just felt the world go by!
Just girt me for the onset with eternity,
When breath blew back,
And on the other side
I heard recede the disappointed tide!

Therefore, as one returned, I feel,
Odd secrets of the line to tell!
Some sailor, skirting foreign shores,
Some pale reporter from the awful doors   10
Before the seal!

Next time, to stay!
Next time, the things to see
By ear unheard,
Unscrutinized by eye.

Next time, to tarry,
While the ages steal,—
Slow tramp the centuries,
And the cycles wheel.

w. c1860
p. 1891

A Wounded Deer Leaps Highest

A wounded deer leaps highest,
I've heard the hunter tell;
'Tis but the ecstasy of death,
And then the brake is still.

The smitten rock that·gushes,
The trampled steel that springs:
A cheek is always redder
Just where the hectic stings!

Mirth is the mail of anguish,
In which it cautious arm,   10
Lest anybody spy the blood
And "You're hurt" exclaim!

w. c1860
p. 1890

If I Shouldn't Be Alive

If I shouldn't be alive
When the robins come,
Give the one in red cravat
A memorial crumb.

If I couldn't thank you,
Being just asleep,
You will know I'm trying
With my granite lip!

w. c1860
p. 1890

Faith Is a Fine Invention

Faith is a fine invention
For gentlemen who see;
But microscopes are prudent
In an emergency!

w. c1860
p.1891

It's Such a Little Thing to Weep

[J189]

It's such a little thing to weep,
So short a thing to sigh;
And yet by trades the size of these
We men and women die!

w. c1860
p. 1896

The Thought beneath So Slight a Film

The thought beneath so slight a film
Is more distinctly seen,—
As laces just reveal the surge,
Or mists the Apennine.

w. c1860
p. 1891

Come Slowly, Eden!

Come slowly, Eden!
Lips unused to thee,
Bashful, sip thy jasmines,
As the fainting bee,

Reaching late his flower,
Round her chamber hums,
Counts his nectars—enters,
And is lost in balms!

w. c1860
p. 1890

Did the Harebell Loose Her Girdle

Did the harebell loose her girdle
To the lover bee,
Would the bee the harebell hallow
Much as formerly?

Did the paradise, persuaded,
Yield her moat of pearl,
Would the Eden be an Eden,
Or the earl an earl?

w. c1860
p. 1891

I Taste a Liquor Never Brewed

I taste a liquor never brewed,
From tankards scooped in pearl;
Not all the vats upon the Rhine
Yield such an alcohol!

Inebriate of air am I,
And debauchée of dew,
Reeling, through endless summer days,
From inns of molten blue.

When landlords turn the drunken bee
Out of the foxglove's door,   10
When butterflies renounce their drams,
I shall but drink the more!

Till seraphs swing their snowy hats,
And saints to windows run,
To see the little tippler
Leaning against the sun!

w. c1860
p. 1861, 1890

Savior! I've No One Else to Tell

Savior! I've no one else to tell,
And so I trouble *thee*.
I am the one forgot thee so—
Dost thou remember me?
Nor for myself I came so far—
That were the little load;
I brought thee the imperial heart
I had not strength to hold,
The heart I carried in my own
Till mine too heavy grew—   10
Yet strangest, *heavier* since it went.
Is it too large for *you*?

w. 1861
p. 1896, 1929

God Permits Industrious Angels

God permits industrious angels
Afternoons to play.
I met one,—forgot my school-mates,
All, for him, straightway.

God calls home the angel promptly
At the setting sun;
I missed mine. How dreary marbles,
After playing Crown!

w. c1861
p. 1890

I Like a Look of Agony

I like a look of agony,
Because I know it's true;
Men do not sham convulsion,
Nor simulate a throe.

The eyes glaze once, and that is death.
Impossible to feign
The beads upon the forehead
By homely anguish strung.

w. c1861
p. 1890

Wild Nights! Wild Nights!

Wild nights! Wild nights!
Were I with thee,
Wild nights should be
Our luxury!

Futile the winds
To a heart in port,—
Done with the compass,
Done with the chart.

Rowing in Eden!
Ah! the sea!   10
Might I but moor
To-night in thee!

w. c1861
p. 1891

I Can Wade Grief

I can wade grief,
Whole pools of it,—
I'm used to that.
But the least push of joy
Breaks up my feet,
And I tip—drunken.
Let no pebble smile,
'Twas the new liquor,—
That was all!

Power is only pain,   10
Stranded, through discipline,
Till weights will hang.
Give balm to giants,
And they'll wilt, like men.
Give Himmaleh,— [Himmaleh: the Himalayas personified]
They'll carry him!

w. 1861
p. 1891

Hope Is the Thing with Feathers

Hope is the thing with feathers
That perches in the soul,
And sings the tune without the words,
And never stops at all,

And sweetest in the gale is heard;
And sore must be the storm
That could abash the little bird
That kept so many warm.

I've heard it in the chillest land,
And on the strangest sea;   10
Yet, never, in extremity,
It asked a crumb of me.

w. c1861
p. 1891

There's a Certain Slant of Light

There's a certain slant of light,
On winter afternoons,
That oppresses, like the weight
Of cathedral tunes.

Heavenly hurt it gives us;
We can find no scar,
But internal difference
Where the meanings are.

None may teach it anything,   10
'Tis the seal, despair,—
An imperial affliction
Sent us of the air.

When it comes, the landscape listens,
Shadows hold their breath;
When it goes, 'tis like the distance
On the look of death.

w. c1861
p. 1890

The Robin's My Criterion for Tune

[J 2 8 5]

The robin's my criterion for tune
Because I grow where robins do;
But were I Cuckoo born
I'd swear by him—
The ode familiar rules the noon.
The Buttercup's my whim for bloom

Because we're orchard-sprung—
But were I Britain-born
I'd daisies spurn—
None but the nut October fit   10
Because through dropping it
The seasons flit, I'm taught.
Without the snow's tableau
Winter were lie to me—
Because I see New Englandly.
The Queen discerns like me—
Provincially

w. c1861
p. 1929

I'm Nobody! Who Are You?

I'm nobody! Who are you?
Are you nobody, too?
Then there's a pair of us—don't tell!
They'd banish us, you know.

How dreary to be somebody!
How public, like a frog
To tell your name the livelong day
To an admiring bog!

w. c1861
p. 1891

I Reason, Earth Is Short

I reason, earth is short,
And anguish absolute,
And many hurt;
But what of that?

I reason, we could die:
The best vitality
Cannot excel decay;
But what of that?

I reason that in heaven
Somehow, it will be even,   10
Some new equation given;
But what of that?

w. c1862
p. 1890

The Soul Selects Her Own Society

The soul selects her own society,
Then shuts the door;
On her divine majority
Obtrude no more.

Unmoved, she notes the chariot's pausing
At her low gate;
Unmoved, an emperor is kneeling
Upon her mat.

I've known her from an ample nation
Choose one;   10
Then close the valves of her attention
Like stone.

w. c1862
p. 1890

The Day Came Slow, Till Five O'Clock

[J304]

The day came slow, till five o'clock,
Then sprang before the hills
Like hindered rubies, or the light
A sudden musket spills.

The purple could not keep the east,
The sunrise shook abroad,
Like breadths of topaz, packed a night,
The lady just unrolled.

The happy winds their timbrels took;
The birds, in docile rows,   10
Arranged themselves around their prince—
The wind is prince of those.

The orchard sparkled like a Jew—
How mighty 'twas to be
A guest in this stupendous place,
The parlor of the day!

w. c1862
p. 1891

I'll Tell You How the Sun Rose

I'll tell you how the sun rose,—
A ribbon at a time.
The steeples swam in amethyst,
The news like squirrels ran.

The hills untied their bonnets,
The bobolinks begun.
Then I said softly to myself,
"That must have been the sun!"

*   *   *

But how he set, I know not.
There seemed a purple stile   10
Which little yellow boys and girls
Were climbing all the while

Till when they reached the other side,
A dominie in gray
Put gently up the evening bars,
And led the flock away.

w. c1860
p. 1890

There Came a Day at Summer's Full

[J 3 2 2]

There came a day at summer's full
Entirely for me;
I thought that such were for the saints,
Where resurrections be.

The sun, as common, went abroad,
The flowers, accustomed, blew,
As if no soul the solstice passed
That maketh all things new.

The time was scarce profaned by speech;
The symbol of a word   10
Was needless, as at sacrament
The wardrobe of our Lord.

Each was to each the sealed church,
Permitted to commune this time,
Lest we too awkward show
At supper of the Lamb.

The hours slid fast, as hours will,
Clutched tight by greedy hands;
So faces on two decks look back,
Bound to opposing lands.   20

And so, when all the time had leaked
Without external sound,
Each bound the other's crucifix—
We gave no other bond.

Sufficient troth that we shall rise—
Deposed, at length, the grave—
To that new marriage, justified
Through Calvaries of Love!

w. 1861
p. 1890

Some Keep the Sabbath Going to Church

Some keep the Sabbath going to church;
I keep it staying at home,
With a bobolink for a chorister,
And an orchard for a dome.

Some keep the Sabbath in surplice;
I just wear my wings,
And instead of tolling the bell for church,
Our little sexton sings.

God preaches,—a noted clergyman,—
And the sermon is never long;   10
So instead of getting to heaven at last,
I'm going all along!

w. c1860
p. 1864

A Bird Came down the Walk

A bird came down the walk:
He did not know I saw;
He bit an angle-worm in halves
And ate the fellow, raw.

And then he drank a dew
From a convenient grass,
And then hopped sidewise to the wall
To let a beetle pass.

He glanced with rapid eyes
That hurried all abroad,—   10
They looked like frightened beads, I thought
He stirred his velvet head

Like one in danger; cautious,
I offered him a crumb,
And he unrolled his feathers
And rowed him softer home

Than oars divide the ocean,
Too silver for a seam,
Or butterflies, off banks of noon,
Leap, plashless, as they swim.   20

w. 1862
p. 1891

The Grass So Little Has to Do

[J333]

The grass so little has to do,—
A sphere of simple green,
With only butterflies to brood,
And bees to entertain;

And stir all day to pretty tunes
The breezes fetch along,
And hold the sunshine in its lap
And bow to everything;

And thread the dews all night, like pearls,
And make itself so fine,—   10
A duchess were too common
For such a noticing.

And even when it dies, to pass
In odors so divine,
Like lowly spices lain to sleep,
Or spikenards perishing.

And then in sovereign barns to dwell,
And dream the days away,—
The grass so little has to do,
I wish I were a hay.   20

w. 1862
p. 1890

'Tis Not That Dying Hurts Us So

[J335]

'Tis not that dying hurts us so—
'Tis living hurts us more;
But dying is a different way,
A kind behind the door—

The southern custom of the bird
That ere the frosts are due
Accepts a better latitude.
We are the birds that stay,

The shiverers round farmers' doors,
For whose reluctant crumb   10
We stipulate, till pitying snows
Persuade our feathers home.

w. 1862
p. 1894, 1945

I Know That He Exists

I know that he exists
Somewhere, in silence.
He has hid his rare life
From our gross eyes.

'Tis an instant's play,
'Tis a fond ambush,
Just to make bliss
Earn her own surprise!

But should the play
Prove piercing earnest,   10
Should the glee glaze
In death's stiff stare,

Would not the fun
Look too expensive?

Would not the jest
Have crawled too far?

w. 1862
p. 1891

After Great Pain a Formal Feeling Comes

[J 3 4 1]

After great pain a formal feeling comes—
The nerves sit ceremonious, like tombs;
The stiff Heart questions—was it He that bore?
And yesterday—or centuries before?

The feet, mechanical, go round
A wooden way
Of ground, or air, or ought,
Regardless grown,
A quartz contentment, like a stone.

This is the hour of lead   10
Remembered if outlived,
As freezing persons recollect the snow—
First chill, then stupor, then the letting go.

w. 1862
p. 1929

I Dreaded That First Robin So

I dreaded that first robin so,
But he is mastered now,
And I'm accustomed to him grown,—
He hurts a little, though.

I thought if I could only live
Till that first shout got by,
Not all pianos in the woods
Had power to mangle me.

I dared not meet the daffodils,
For fear their yellow gown   10

Would pierce me with a fashion
So foreign to my own.

I wished the grass would hurry,
So when 'twas time to see,
He'd be too tall, the tallest one
Could stretch to look at me.

I could not bear the bees should come,
I wished they'd stay away
In those dim countries where they go:
What word had they for me?   20

They're here, though; not a creature failed,
No blossom stayed away
In gentle deference to me,
The Queen of Calvary.

Each one salutes me as he goes,
And I my childish plumes
Lift, in bereaved acknowledgment
Of their unthinking drums.

w. 1862
p. 1891

What Soft Cherubic Creatures

What soft, cherubic creatures
    These gentlewomen are!
One would as soon assault a plush
    Or violate a star.

Such dimity convictions,
    A horror so refined
Of freckled human nature,
    Of Deity ashamed,—

It's such a common glory,
    A fisherman's degree!   10
Redemption, brittle lady,
    Be so ashamed of thee.

w. c1862
p. 1896

The First Day's Night Had Come

[J 4 1 0]

The first day's night had come,
And grateful that a thing
So terrible had been endured,
I told my soul to sing.

She said her strings were snapt,
Her bow to atoms blown,
And so to mend her gave me work
Until another morn.

And then a day as huge
As yesterdays in pairs   10
Unrolled its horror in my face,
Until it blocked my eyes;

My brain, begun to laugh,
I mumbled, like a fool;
And tho 'tis years ago—that day—
My brain keeps giggling still.

And something's odd within—
That person that I was,
And this one, do not feel the same.
Could it be madness—this?   20

w. c1862
p. 1935, 1947

'Twas Like a Maelstrom, with a Notch

[J 4 1 4]

'Twas like a maelstrom, with a notch,
That nearer every day
Kept narrowing its boiling wheel
Until the agony

Toyed cooly with the final inch
Of your delirious hem;
And you dropt, lost,
When something broke,
And let you from a dream,

As if a goblin with a gauge   10
Kept measuring the hours
Until you felt your second
Weigh helpless in his paws;

And not a sinew stirred, could help,
And sense was setting numb,
When God remembered, and the Fiend
Let go, overcome,

As if your sentence stood pronounced,
And you were frozen led
From dungeon's luxury of doubt   20
to gibbets and the dead;

And when the film had stitched your eyes,
A creature gasped "Reprieve!"
Which anguish was the utterest then,
To perish, or to live?

w. c1862
p. 1945

Much Madness Is Divinest Sense

Much madness is divinest sense
To a discerning eye;
Much sense the starkest madness.
'Tis the majority
In this, as all, prevails.
Assent, and you are sane;
Demur,—you're straightway dangerous,
And handled with a chain.

w. c1862
p. 1890

Prayer Is the Little Implement

Prayer is the little implement
Through which men reach
Where presence is denied them.
They fling their speech

By means of it in God's ear;
If then He hear,
This sums the apparatus
Comprised in prayer.

w. c1862
p. 1891

This Is My Letter to the World

This is my letter to the world,
  That never wrote to me,—
The simple news that Nature told,
  With tender majesty.

Her message is committed
  To hands I cannot see;
For love of her, sweet countrymen,
  Judge tenderly of me!

w. 1862
p. 1890

I Died for Beauty, but Was Scarce

I died for beauty, but was scarce
Adjusted in the tomb,
When one who died for truth was lain
In an adjoining room.

He questioned softly why I failed?
"For beauty," I replied.
"And I for truth—the two are one;
We brethren are," he said.

And so, as kinsmen met a night,
We talked between the rooms,   10
Until the moss had reached our lips,
And covered up our names.

w. c1862
p. 1890

A Wife at Daybreak I Shall Be

[J 461]

A wife at daybreak I shall be.
Sunrise, hast thou a flag for me?
At midnight I am but a maid—
How short it takes to make a bride!
Then, midnight, I have passed from thee
Unto the East, and victory.

Midnight, Good Night! I hear them call.
The angels bustle in the hall,
Softly my future climbs the stair,
I fumble at my childhood's prayer—   10
So soon to be a child no more.
Eternity, I'm coming, Sir—
Savior, I've seen the face before!

w. c1862
p. 1929

I Heard a Fly Buzz When I Died

[J 465]

I heard a fly buzz when I died;
The stillness in the room
Was like the stillness in the air
Between the heaves of storm.

The eyes around had wrung them dry
And breaths were gathering firm
For that last onset when the King
Be witnessed in the room.

I willed my keepsakes, signed away
What portion of me be   10
Assignable—and then it was
There interposed a fly,

With blue, uncertain, stumbling buzz,
Between the light and me.
And then the windows failed, and then
I could not see to see.

w. c1862
p. 1896

'Tis Little I Could Care for Pearls

'Tis little I could care for pearls
  Who own the ample sea;
Or brooches, when the Emperor
  With rubies pelteth me;

Or gold, who am the Prince of Mines;
  Or diamonds, when I see
A diadem to fit a dome
  Continual crowning me.

w. c1862
p. 1896

I Had No Time to Hate, Because

I had no time to hate, because
The grave would hinder me,
And life was not so ample I
Could finish enmity.

Nor had I time to love; but since
Some industry must be,
The little toil of love, I thought,
Was large enough for me.

w. c1862
p. 1890

At Least to Pray Is Left, Is Left

[J502]

At least to pray is left, is left.
Oh Jesus! in the air,
I know not which thy chamber is—
I'm knocking everywhere.

Thou settest earthquake in the South,
And maelstrom in the sea—
Say, Jesus Christ of Nazareth,
Hast thou no arm for me?

w. 1862
p. 1891

I'm Ceded, I've Stopped Being Theirs

I'm ceded, I've stopped being theirs;
The name they dropped upon my face
With water, in the country church,
Is finished using now,
And they can put it with my dolls,
My childhood, and the string of spools
I've finished threading too.

Baptized before without the choice,
But this time consciously, of grace
Unto supremest name,   10
Called to my full, the crescent dropped,
Existence's whole arc filled up
With one small diadem.

My second rank, too small the first,
Crowned, crowing on my father's breast,
A half unconscious queen;
But this time, adequate, erect,
With will to choose or to reject,
And I choose—just a throne.

w. 1862
p. 1890

If You Were Coming in the Fall

[J 5 1 1]

If you were coming in the fall,
I'd brush the summer by
With half a smile and half a spurn,
As housewives do a fly.

If I could see you in a year,
I'd wind the months in balls,
And put them each in separate drawers,
For fear the numbers fuse.

If only centuries delayed,
I'd count them on my hand,   10
Subtracting till my fingers dropped
Into Van Diemen's Land.

If certain, when this life was out,
That yours and mine should be,
I'd toss it yonder like a rind,
And taste eternity.

But now, uncertain of the length
Of this that is between,
It goads me, like the goblin bee,
That will not state its sting.   20

w. 1862
p. 1890

'Twas Warm at First Like Us

'Twas warm at first like us,
Until there crept thereon
A chill, like frost upon a glass,
Till all the scene be gone.

The forehead copied stone,
The fingers grew too cold

To ache, and like a skater's brook
The busy eyes congealed.

It straightened—that was all—
It crowded cold to cold—   10
It multiplied indifference
As Pride were all it could.

And even when with cords
'Twas lowered like a freight,
It made no signal, nor demurred,
But dropped like adamant.

w. c1862
p. 1929

To Hear an Oriole Sing

To hear an oriole sing
May be a common thing,
Or only a divine.

It is not of the bird
Who sings the same, unheard,
As unto crowd.

The fashion of the ear
Attireth that it hear
In dun or fair.

So whether it be rune,   10
Or whether it be none,
Is of within;

The "tune is in the tree,"
The sceptic showeth me;
"No, sir! In thee!"

w. c1862
p. 1891

I Took My Power in My Hand

I took my power in my hand
And went against the world;
'Twas not so much as David had,
But I was twice as bold.

I aimed my pebble, but myself
Was all the one that fell.
Was it Goliath was too large,
Or only I too small?

w. c1862
p. 1891

I've Seen a Dying Eye

I've seen a dying eye
Run round and round a room
In search of something, as it seemed,
Then cloudier become;
And then, obscure with fog,
And then be soldered down,
Without disclosing what it be,
'Twere blessed to have seen.

w. c1862
p. 1890

The Brain within Its Groove

The brain within its groove
Runs evenly and true;
But let a splinter swerve,
'Twere easier for you
To put the water back
When floods have slit the hills,
And scooped a turnpike for themselves,
And blotted out the mills!

w. c1862
p. 1890

I Had Been Hungry All the Years

[J579]

I had been hungry all the years;
My noon had come to dine;
I, trembling, drew the table near,
And touched the curious wine.

'Twas this on tables I had seen,
When turning, hungry, home
I looked in windows, for the wealth
I could not hope for mine.

I did not know the ample bread,
'Twas so unlike the crumb   10
The birds and I had often shared
In Nature's dining-room.

The plenty hurt me, 'twas so new—
Myself felt ill and odd,
As berry of a mountain bush
Transplanted to the road.

Nor was I hungry; so I found
That hunger was a way
Of persons outside windows,
The entering takes away.   20

w. c1862
p. 1891

I Found the Phrase to Every Thought

I found the phrase to every thought
I ever had, but one;
And that defies me,—as a hand
Did try to chalk the sun

To races nurtured in the dark;—
How would your own begin?

Can blaze be done in cochineal,
Or noon in mazarin?

w. c1862
p. 1891

I Like to See It Lap the Miles

I like to see it lap the miles,
And lick the valleys up,
And stop to feed itself at tanks;
And then, prodigious, step

Around a pile of mountains,
And, supercilious, peer
In shanties by the sides of roads;
And then a quarry pare

To fit its sides, and crawl between,
Complaining all the while   10
In horrid, hooting stanza;
Then chase itself down hill

And neigh like Boanerges; [Boanerges: "Sons of thunder"]
Then, punctual as a star,
Stop,—docile and omnipotent—
At its own stable door.

w. c1862
p. 1891

Like Mighty Footlights Burned the Red

Like mighty footlights burned the red
At bases of the trees,—
The far theatricals of day
Exhibiting to these.

'Twas universe that did applaud
While, chiefest of the crowd,
Enabled by his royal dress,
Myself distinguished God.

w. c1862
p. 1891

Afraid? Of Whom Am I Afraid?

Afraid? Of whom am I afraid?
Not death; for who is he?
The porter of my father's lodge
As much abasheth me.

Of life? 'Twere odd I fear a thing
That comprehendeth me
In one or more existences
At Deity's decree.

Of resurrection? Is the east
Afraid to trust the morn   10
With her fastidious forehead?
As soon impeach my crown!

w. c1862
p. 1890

The Brain Is Wider Than the Sky

[J 6 3 2]

The brain is wider than the sky,
For, put them side by side,
The one the other will contain
With ease—and you beside.

The brain is deeper than the sea,
For, hold them, blue to blue,
The one the other will absorb,
As sponges, buckets do.

The brain is just the weight of God,
For, heft them, pound for pound,   10
And they will differ—if they do—
As syllable from sound.

w. c1862
p. 1896

The Way I Read a Letter's This

[J636]

The way I read a letter's this—
'Tis first I lock the door,
And push it with my fingers next,
For transport it be sure.

And then I go the furthest off
To counteract a knock;
Then draw my little letter forth
And slowly pick the lock.

Then, glancing narrow at the wall,
And narrow at the floor,   10
For firm conviction of a mouse
Not exorcised before,

Peruse how infinite I am
To—no one that you know!
And sigh for lack of heaven,—but not
The heaven God bestow.

w. c1862
p. 1891

I Cannot Live with You

I cannot live with you,
It would be life,
And life is over there
Behind the shelf

The sexton keeps the key to,
Putting up
Our life, his porcelain,
Like a cup

Discarded of the housewife,
Quaint or broken;   10

A newer Sèvres pleases,
Old ones crack.

I could not die with you,
For one must wait
To shut the other's gaze down,—
You could not.

And I, could I stand by
And see you freeze,
Without my right of frost,
Death's privilege?   20

Nor could I rise with you,
Because your face
Would put out Jesus',
That new grace

Glow plain and foreign
On my homesick eye,
Except that you, than he
Shone closer by.

They'd judge us—how?
For you served Heaven, you know,   30
Or sought to;
I could not,

Because you saturated sight,
And I had no more eyes
For sordid excellence
As Paradise.

And were you lost, I would be,
Though my name
Rang loudest
On the heavenly fame.   40

And were you saved,
And I condemned to be
Where you were not,
That self were hell to me.

So we must keep apart,
You there, I here,
With just the door ajar
That oceans are,
And prayer,
And that pale sustenance,   50
Despair!

w. c1862
p. 1890

Pain Has an Element of Blank

Pain has an element of blank;
It cannot recollect
When it began, or if there were
A day when it was not.

It has no future but itself,
Its infinite realms contain
Its past, enlightened to perceive
New periods of pain.

w. c1862
p. 1890

Of All the Souls That Stand Create

Of all the souls that stand create
I have elected one.
When sense from spirit files away,
And subterfuge is done;

When that which is and that which was
Apart, intrinsic, stand,
And this brief tragedy of flesh
Is shifted like a sand;

When figures show their royal front
And mists are carved away,—   10
Behold the atom I preferred
To all the lists of clay!

w. c1862
p. 1891

One Need Not Be a Chamber to Be Haunted

[J*670*]

One need not be a chamber to be haunted,
One need not be a house;
The brain has corridors surpassing
Material place.

Far safer, of a midnight meeting
External ghost,
Than its interior confronting
That cooler host.

Far safer through an abbey gallop,
The stones achase,   10
Than, unarmed, one's a'self encounter
In lonesome place.

Ourself, behind ourself concealed,
Should startle most;
Assassin, hid in our apartment,
Be horror's least.

The body borrows a revolver,
He bolts the door,
O'erlooking a superior spectre,
Or more.   20

w. c1862
p. 1891

They Say That "Time Assuages"

They say that "time assuages,"—
    Time never did assuage;
An actual suffering strengthens,
    As sinews do, with age.

Time is a test of trouble,
    But not a remedy.

If such it prove, it prove too
   There was no malady.

w. 1863
p. 1896

A Thought Went up My Mind To-Day

A thought went up my mind to-day
That I have had before,
But did not finish,—some way back,
I could not fix the year,

Nor where it went, nor why it came
The second time to me,
Nor definitely what it was,
Have I the art to say.

But somewhere in my soul, I know
I've met the thing before;   **10**
It just reminded me—'twas all—
And came my way no more.

w. c1863
p. 1891

Because I Could Not Stop for Death

[J712]

Because I could not stop for Death,
He kindly stopped for me—
The carriage held but just ourselves
And Immortality.

We slowly drove, he knew no haste,
And I had put away
My labor, and my leisure too,
For his civility.

We passed the school, where children strove
At recess in the ring;   **10**

We passed the fields of gazing grain,
We passed the setting sun.

Or rather, he passed us.
The dews grew quivering and chill,
For only gossamer my gown,
My tippet only tulle.

We paused before a house that seemed
A swelling of the ground;
The roof was scarcely visible,
The cornice in the ground.   20

Since then 'tis centuries, and yet
Feels shorter than the day
I first surmised the horses' heads
Were toward eternity.

w. c1863
p. 1890

She Rose to His Requirement, Dropped

She rose to his requirement, dropped
The playthings of her life
To take the honorable work
Of woman and of wife.

If aught she missed in her new day
Of amplitude, or awe,
Or first prospective, or the gold
In using wore away,

It lay unmentioned, as the sea
Develops pearl and weed,   10
But only to himself is known
The fathoms they abide.

w. c1863
p. 1890

I Many Times Thought Peace Had Come

[J739]

I many times thought peace had come,
When peace was far away,
As wrecked men deem they sight the land
At centre of the sea;

And struggle slacker but to prove
As hopelessly as I,
How many the fictitious shores,
Or any harbor be.

w. c1863
p. 1891

It Dropped So Low in My Regard

It dropped so low in my regard
  I heard it hit the ground,
And go to pieces on the stones
  At bottom of my mind;

Yet blamed the fate that fractured, less
  Than I reviled myself
For entertaining plated wares
  Upon my silver shelf.

w. c1863
p. 1896

Presentiment Is That Long Shadow on the Lawn

Presentiment is that long shadow on the lawn
Indicative that suns go down;
The notice to the startled grass
That darkness is about to pass.

w. c1863
p. 1890

A Death-Blow Is a Life-Blow to Some

A death-blow is a life-blow to some
Who, till they died, did not alive become;
Who, had they lived, had died, but when
They died, vitality begun.

w. c1864
p. 1891

The Poets Light But Lamps

[J883]

The poets light but lamps,
Themselves go out;
The wicks they stimulate,
If vital light,

Inhere as do the suns—
Each age a lens
Disseminating their
Circumference.

w. c1864
p. 1945

A Narrow Fellow in the Grass

A narrow fellow in the grass
Occasionally rides;
You may have met him—did you not,
His notice instant is.
The grass divides as with a comb,
A spotted shaft is seen;
And then it closes at your feet,
And opens further on.

He likes a boggy acre,
A floor too cool for corn.   10
Yet when a boy, and barefoot,

I more than once, at noon,
Have passed, I thought, a whip-lash
Unbraiding in the sun,—
When, stooping to secure it,
It wrinkled, and was gone.

Several of nature's people
I know, and they know me;
I feel for them a transport
Of cordiality;   20
Yet never met this fellow,
Attended or alone,
Without a tighter breathing,
And zero at the bone.

w. 1865
p. 1866

Crumbling Is Not an Instant's Act

[J997]

Crumbling is not an instant's act,
A fundamental pause—
Delapidation's processes
Are organized decays.

'Tis first a cobweb on the soul,
A cuticle of dust,
A borer in the axis,
An elemental rust.

Ruin is formal—devil's work,
Consecutive and slow;   10
Fail in an instant no man did—
Slipping is crash's law.

w. c1865
p. 1945

That Such Have Died Enables

That such have died enables
  The tranquiller to die;
That such have lived, certificate
  For immortality.

                 w. c1865
                 p. 1896

I Never Saw a Moor

I never saw a moor,
I never saw the sea;
Yet know I how the heather looks,
And what a wave must be.

I never spoke with God,
Nor visited in heaven;
Yet certain am I of the spot
As if the chart were given.

                 w. c1865
                 p. 1890

The Sky Is Low, the Clouds Are Mean

The sky is low, the clouds are mean,
A travelling flake of snow
Across a barn or through a rut
Debates if it will go.

A narrow wind complains all day
How some one treated him;
Nature, like us, is sometimes caught
Without her diadem.

                 w. c1866
                 p. 1890

The Bustle in a House

The bustle in a house
The morning after death
Is solemnest of industries
Enacted upon earth,—

The sweeping up the heart,
And putting love away
We shall not want to use again
Until eternity.

w. c1866
p. 1890

The Last Night That She Lived

[J1100]

The last night that she lived,
It was a common night,
Except the dying; this to us
Made nature different.

We noticed smallest things,—
Things overlooked before,
By this great light upon our minds
Italicized, as 'twere.

As we went out and in
Between ᴜ˙ final room   10
And rooms where those to be alive
Tomorrow were, a blame

That others could exist
While she must finish quite,
A jealousy for her arose
So nearly infinite.

We waited while she passed;
It was a narrow time,

Too jostled were our souls to speak,
At length the notice came.   20

She mentioned, and forgot;
Then lightly as a reed
Bent to the water, shivered scarce,
Consented, and was dead.

And we, we placed the hair,
And drew the head erect;
And then an awful leisure was,
Our faith to regulate.

w. c1866
p. 1890

Tell All the Truth, but Tell It Slant

[*J 1129*]

Tell all the truth, but tell it slant—
Success in circuit lies.
Too bright for our infirm delight,
The truth's superb surprise,
As lightning to the children eased
With explanation kind.
The truth must dazzle gradually,
Or every man be blind.

w. c1868
p. 1945

After a Hundred Years

After a hundred years
Nobody knows the place,—
Agony, that enacted there,
Motionless as peace.

Weeds triumphant ranged,
Strangers strolled and spelled
At the lone orthography
Of the elder dead.

Winds of summer fields
Recollect the way,—
Instinct picking up the key
Dropped by memory.

10

w. c1869
p. 1891

The Clouds Their Backs Together Laid

The clouds their backs together laid,
The north begun to push,
The forests galloped till they fell,
The lightning skipped like mice;
The thunder crumbled like a stuff—
How good to be safe in tombs,
Where nature's temper cannot reach,
Nor vengeance ever comes!

w. c1870
p. 1890

We Never Know How High We Are

We never know how high we are
  Till we are called to rise;
And then, if we are true to plan,
  Our statures touch the skies.

The heroism we recite
  Would be a daily thing,
Did not ourselves the cubits warp
  For fear to be a king.

w. c1870
p. 1896

The Show Is Not the Show

The show is not the show,
But they that go.
Menagerie to me
My neighbor be.

Fair play—
Both went to see.

w. 1872
p. 1891

He Preached upon "Breadth"
Till It Argued Him Narrow

He preached upon "breadth" till it argued him narrow,—
The broad are too broad to define;
And of "truth" until it proclaimed him a liar,—
The truth never flaunted a sign.

Simplicity fled from his counterfeit presence
As gold the pyrites would shun.
What confusion would cover the innocent Jesus
To meet so enabled a man!

w. 1872
p. 1891

Who Goes to Dine Must Take His Feast

[J 1 2 2 3]

Who goes to dine must take his feast
Or find the banquet mean—
The table is not laid without
Till it is laid within.

For pattern is the mind bestowed,
That imitating her,
Our most ignoble services
Exhibit worthier.

w. c1872
p. 1945

The Butterfly's Assumption-Gown

The butterfly's assumption-gown,
In chrysoprase apartments hung,
    This afternoon put on.

How condescending to descend,
And be of buttercups the friend
  In a New England town!

w c1873
p. 1890

A Word Dropped Careless on a Page

[J 1 2 6 1]

A word dropped careless on a page
May stimulate an eye
When folded in perpetual seam
The wrinkled maker lie.

Infection in the sentence breeds—
We may inhale despair
At distances of centuries
From the malaria.

w. c1873
p. 1894, 1947

Pink, Small, and Punctual

Pink, small, and punctual,
Aromatic. low.
Covert in April,
Candid in May,

Dear to the moss,
Known to the knoll,

Next to the robin
In every human soul.

Bold little beauty,
Bedecked with thee,   10
Nature forswears
Antiquity.

w. c1875
p. 1890

Summer Has Two Beginnings

[J1422]

Summer has two beginnings—
Beginning once in June,
Beginning in October,
Affectingly again,

Without, perhaps, the riot,
But graphicer for grace,
As finer is a going
Than a remaining face;

Departing then forever,
Forever until May—   10
Forever is deciduous,
Except to those who die.

w. c1877
p. 1945

A Route of Evanescence

A route of evanescence
With a revolving wheel;
A resonance of emerald,
A rush of cochineal;
And every blossom on the bush
Adjusts its tumbled head,—
The mail from Tunis, probably,
An easy morning's ride.

w. c1879
p. 1891

Before You Thought of Spring

Before you thought of spring,
Except as a surmise,
You see, God bless his suddenness,

A fellow in the skies
Of independent hues,
A little weather-worn,
Inspiriting habiliments
Of indigo and brown.

With specimens of song,
As if for you to choose,   10
Discretion in the interval,
With gay delays he goes
To some superior tree
Without a single leaf,
And shouts for joy to nobody
But his seraphic self!

w. 1879
p. 1891

How Happy Is the Little Stone

How happy is the little stone
That rambles in the road alone,
And doesn't care about careers,
And exigencies never fears;
Whose coat of elemental brown
A passing universe put on;
And independent as the sun,
Associates or glows alone,
Fulfilling absolute decree
In casual simplicity.   10

w. c1881
p. 1891

As Imperceptibly as Grief

As imperceptibly as grief
The summer lapsed away,—
Too imperceptible, at last,
To seem like perfidy.

A quietness distilled,
As twilight long begun,

Or Nature, spending with herself
Sequestered afternoon.

The dusk drew earlier in,
The morning foreign shone,—   10
A courteous, yet harrowing grace,
As guest who would be gone.

And thus, without a wing,
Or service of a keel,
Our summer made her light escape
Into the beautiful.

w. 1865, 1882
p. 1891

Those Dying Then

[*J1551*]

Those dying then
Knew where they went—
They went to God's right hand;
That hand is amputated now,
And God cannot be found.

The abdication of belief
Makes the behavior small—
Better an ignis fatuus   [ignis fatuus: deceptive light]
Than no illume at all.

w. c1882
p. 1945

He Ate and Drank the Precious Words

He ate and drank the precious words,
His spirit grew robust;
He knew no more that he was poor,
Nor that his frame was dust.
He danced along the dingy days,
And this bequest of wings

Was but a book. What liberty
A loosened spirit brings!

w. c1883
p. 1890

The Going from a World We Know

The going from a world we know
    To one a wonder still
Is like the child's adversity
    Whose vista is a hill,
Behind the hill is sorcery
    And everything unknown,
But will the secret compensate
    For climbing it alone?

w. 1884
p. 1894

Apparently with No Surprise

Apparently with no surprise
To any happy flower,
The frost beheads it at its play
In accidental power.
The blond assassin passes on,
The sun proceeds unmoved
To measure off another day
For an approving God.

w. c1884
p. 1890

My Life Closed Twice before Its Close

My life closed twice before its close;
    It yet remains to see
If Immortality unveil
    A third event to me,

So huge, so hopeless to conceive,
    As these that twice befell.

Parting is all we know of heaven,
   And all we need of hell.

p. 1896

The Mob within the Heart

[J 1 7 4 5]

The mob within the heart,
Police cannot suppress;
The riot given at the first
Is authorized as peace,

Uncertified of scene,
Or signified of sound,
But growing like a hurricane
In a congenial ground.

p. 1945

To Make a Prairie It Takes a Clover and One Bee

To make a prairie it takes a clover and one bee,—
One clover, and a bee,
And revery.
The revery alone will do
If bees are few.

p. 1896

Elysium Is as Far as to

Elysium is as far as to
The very nearest room,
If in that room a friend await
Felicity or doom.

What fortitude the soul contains,
That it can so endure
The accent of a coming foot,
The opening of a door!

w. 1882
p. 1890

CHARLES FARRAR BROWNE
"Artemus Ward" (1834–1867)

The development of American humor is a fascinating and complex matter, for it is impossible to divorce regional literature, local color, and folk sources from American humor. Crude yet often surprisingly sophisticated, earthy yet often the product of fantastic imagination, American humor is one of the most important measures of our culture. It reflects our native and historical attitudes to the land and all its properties, to our politics and all its disillusionments, and to ourselves with all our expensive innocence, pragmatism, lustiness, and boastfulness. Except for Mark Twain and certain twentieth-century authors, the writers who fostered the growth of native humor have been consigned to minor positions in literary if not cultural history; yet no presentation of the national character in literature would be complete without at least one of them.

There are many studies and collections and bibliographies that discuss the development of humor and regionalism, including M. J. Moses, *The Literature of the Old South* (1910); C. Holliday, *The Wit and Humor of Colonial Days* (1912); R. L. Rusk, *The Literature of the Middle Western Frontier*, 2 vols. (1925); J. Tandy, *Crackerbox Philosophers in American Humor and Satire* (1925); N. Wilt, *Some American Humorists* (1929); C. McWilliams, *The New Regionalism in American Literature* (1930); F. J. Meine, ed., *Tall Tales of the Southwest* (1930); F. Shay, *Here's Audacity! American Legendary Heroes* (1930); T. L. Masson, *Our American Humorists* (1931); C. M. Rourke, *American Humor* (1931); R. A. Coleman, ed., *Western Prose and Poetry* (1932); W. Murrell, *A History of American Graphic Humor*, 2 vols. (1933–1938); A. P. Hudson, ed., *Humor of the Old Deep South* (1936); W. J. Snelling, *Tales of the Northwest* (1936); W. Blair, ed., *Native American Humor, 1800–1900* (1937); M. Major, *Southwest Heritage* (1938); H. W. Odum and H. E. Moore, *American Regionalism* (1938); T. D. Clark, *The Rampaging Frontier* (1939); L. J. Davidson and P. Bostwick, eds., *The Literature of the Rocky Mountain West, 1803–1903* (1939); H. W. Thompson, *Body, Boots and Britches* (1940); V. L. O. Chittick, *Ring-Tailed Roarers* (1941); W. Blair, *Horse Sense in American Humor from Benjamin*

Franklin to Ogden Nash (1942); J. R. Masterson, ed., *Tall Tales of Arkansaw* (1942); C. M. Rourke, *The Roots of American Culture and Other Essays* (1942); J. F. Dobie, *Guide to Life and Literature of the Southwest* (1943); W. C. Hendricks, ed., *Bundle of Troubles* (1943); W. Blair, *Tall Tale America* (1944); S. H. Holbrook, ed., *Promised Land* (1945); J. R. Aswell, ed., *Native American Humor* (1947); M. C. Boatright, ed., *Folk Laughter on the American Frontier* (1949); J. N. Tidwell, ed., *A Treasury of American Folk Humor* (1956); W. Thorp, *American Humorists* (1957); K. S. Lynn, ed., *The Comic Tradition in America* (1958); A. P. Dudden, ed., *The Assault of Laughter: A Treasury of American Political Humor* (1962); W. H. Hall, "A Study of Southern Humor, 1865–1913," *Dissertation Abstracts*, XXII (1962); B. Weber, ed., *An Anthology of American Humor* (1962); J. C. Austin, "The Cycle of American Humor," *Papers on English Language and Literature*, I (1965); J. C. Kitch, "Dark Laughter: A Study of the Pessimistic Tradition in American Humor," *Dissertation Abstracts*, XXV (1965); and W. Hall, *The Smiling Phoenix* (1966).

The best and the most influential humorist before Mark Twain was "Artemus Ward." Born in Waterford, Maine, Charles Farrar Browne early became a printer's apprentice in Lancaster, New Hampshire. Familiar with the trade by the time he was fourteen, Browne wandered about New England working for various newspapers. At one time he worked in Boston on B. P. Shillaber's *Carpet Bag*, a comic paper that had an early influence on Mark Twain. Browne drifted out of Boston into the South and the Midwest, and ended up as a local editor on the Cleveland *Plain Dealer*. In 1857 he began to contribute his letters from "Artemus Ward" to the *Plain Dealer*, introducing to a remarkably receptive American public the misspellings and misadventures of that puppeteer, menagerie keeper, and owner of publicly decent waxworks. Ward's success was immediate, and two years later Browne moved to New York, where he worked for *Vanity Fair*, came to know Whitman and the bohemians who frequented Pfaff's restaurant, and began public lecturing in 1861.

His extensive and popular lecture tours resulted in *Artemus Ward: His Book* in 1862, *Artemus Ward: His Travels* in 1865, and *Artemus Ward in London and Other Papers* posthumously in 1867. In the course of his travels, Ward met a struggling young journalist named Samuel Clemens in Virginia City, Nevada, and helped him publish a story, "The Celebrated Jumping Frog." Unlike the writer that Clemens would become, Browne, as a professional "phunny phellow," used the vernacular and the semiliteracy of the lowbrow for the sake of whatever jokes they could produce rather than for the specifics and subtleties of characterization. Nonetheless, he taught Clemens many tricks of the trade and helped bring the rough, earthy attributes of frontier experience into the house of "acceptable" literature through the entry of folk humor. Lincoln was even known to interrupt a Cabinet meeting to read Artemus Ward.

In 1866 Browne went to England. Again, in his lectures and in his work for *Punch*, he met with enormous success. Tuberculosis claimed him a year later, and he died in England at the height of his powers, not yet quite thirty-three years old. *Sandwiches* appeared posthumously in 1869.

See also, in addition to the bibliography above, E. P. Hingston, *The Genial Showman* (1870); F. Hudson, *Journalism in the United States* (1873); M. D. Landon, ed., *Artemus Ward: His Works, Complete* (1875); H. R. Haweis, *American Humorists* (1883); T. W. Robertson and E. D. Hingston, eds., *The Complete Works of Artemus Ward* (1903); D. C. Seitz, *Artemus Ward . . . A Biography and a Bibliography* (1919); A. J. Nock, *Selected Works of Artemus Ward* (1924); S. T. Williams, "Artemus the Delicious," *Virginia Quarterly Review*, XXVIII (1952); J. Blanck, *Bibliography of American Literature*, I (1955); J. Q. Reed, "Civil War Humor: Artemus Ward," *Civil War History*, II (1956); J. C. Austin, *Artemus Ward* (1964); and C. F. Browne, *Artemus Ward, His Book* (1964).

FROM

Artemus Ward: His Book

Interview with President Lincoln

I hav no politics. Nary a one. I'm not in the bizness. If I was I spose I should holler versiffrusly in the streets at nite and go home to Betsy Jane smellin of coal ile and gin in the mornin. I should go to the Poles arly. I should stay there all day. I should see to it that my nabers was thar. I should git carriges to take the kripples, the infirm, and the indignant thar. I should be on guard agin frauds and sich. I should be on the look out for the infamus lise of the enemy, got up jest be4 elecshun for perlitical effeck. When all was over, and my candydate was elected, I should move

heving & arth—so to speak—until I got orfice, which if I
didn't git a orfice I should turn round and abooze the Administration with all my mite and maine. But I'm not in the
bizniss. I'm in a far more respectful bizniss nor what pol-
lertics is. I wouldn't give two cents to be a Congresser. The
wus insult I ever received was when sertin citizens of Bal-
dinsville axed me to run fur the Legislater. Sez I, "My
frends, dostest think I'd stoop to that there?" They turned
as white as a sheet. I spoke in my most orfullest tones &
they knowed I wasn't to be trifled with. They slunked out
of site to onct.

There4, having no politics, I made bold to visit Old Abe
at his humstid in Springfield. I found the old feller in his
parler, surrounded by a perfeck swarm of orfice-seekers.
Knowin he had been capting of a flat boat on the roarin
Mississippy I thought I'd address him in sailor lingo, so sez
I, "Old Abe, ahoy! Let out yer main-suls, reef hum the
forecastle & throw yer jibpoop over-board! Shiver my timbers, my harty!" (N.B. This is ginuine mariner langwidge.
I know, becawz I've seen sailor plays acted out by them
New York theater fellers.) Old Abe lookt up quite cross &
sez, "Send in yer petition by & by. I can't possibly look at
it now. Indeed I can't. It's onpossible, sir!"

"Mr. Linkin, who do you spect I air?" sed I.

"A orfice-seeker, to be sure!" sed he.

"Wall, sir," sed I, "you's never more mistaken in your
life. You hain't gut a orfiss I'd take under no circumstances.
I'm A. Ward. Wax figgers is my perfeshun. I'm the father
of Twins, and they look like me—both of them. I cum to
pay a frendly visit to the President eleck of the United
States. If so be you wants to see me, say so—if not, say so,
& I'm orf like a jug handle."

"Mr. Ward, sit down. I am glad to see you, sir."

"Repose in Abraham's Buzzum!" sed one of the orfice-
seekers, his idee bein to git orf a goak at my expense.

"Wall," sez I, "ef all you fellers repose in that there
Buzzum thar'll be mity poor nussin for sum of you!"
Whereupon Old Abe buttoned his weskit clear up and
blusht like a maiden of sweet 16. Jest at this pint of the
conversation another swarm of orfice-seekers arrove & cum
pilin into the parler. Sum wanted post-orfices, sum wanted
collectorships, sum wantid furrin missions, and all wanted
sumthin. I thought Old Abe would go crazy. He hadn't

more than had time to shake hands with 'em, before another tremenjis crowd cum porein onto his premises. His house and dooryard was now perfeckly overflowed with orfice-seekers, all clameruss for a immejit interview with Old Abe. One man from Ohio, who had about seven inches of corn whiskey into him, mistook me for Old Abe, and addrest me as "The Prahayrie Flower of the West!" Thinks I, *you* want a orfiss putty bad. Another man with a gold heded cane and a red nose, told Old Abe he was "a seckind Washington & the Pride of the Boundliss West."

Sez I, "Square, you wouldn't take a small post-offiss if you could git it, would you?"

Sez he, "A patrit is abuv them things, sir!"

"There's a putty big crop of patrits this season, ain't there, Square?" sez I, when *another* crowd of offiss-seekers pored in. The house, dooryard, barn, & woodshed was now all full, and when *another* crowd cum I told 'em not to go away for want of room, as the hog-pen was still empty. One patrit from a small town in Michygan went up on top the house, got into the chimney and slid down into the parlor where Old Abe was endevrin to keep the hungry pack of orfice-seekers from chawin him up alive without benefit of clergy. The minit he reached the fireplace he jumpt up, brusht the soot out of his eyes, and yelled: "Don't make eny pintment at the Spunkville post-offiss till you've read my papers. All the respectful men in our town is signers to that there docyment!"

"Good God!" cried Old Abe, "they cum upon me from the skize—down the chimneys, and from the bowels of the yearth!" He hadn't more'n got them words out of his delikit mouth before two fat offiss-seekers from Wisconsin, in endeverin to crawl atween his legs for the purpuss of applyin for the tollgateship at Milwawky, upsot the President eleck, & he would hev gone sprawlin into the fire-place if I hadn't caught him in these arms. But I hadn't more'n stood him up strate, before another man cum crashing down the chimney, his head strikin me vilently agin the inards and prostratin my voluptoous form onto the floor. "Mr. Linkin," shoutid the infatooated being, "my papers is signed by every clergyman in our town, and likewise the skoolmaster!"

Sez I, "You egrejis ass," gittin up & brushin the dust from my eyes, "I'll sign your papers with this bunch of bones, if you don't be a little more keerful how you make my breadbasket a depot in the futur. How do you like that air perfumery?" sez I, shuving my fist under his nose. "Them's the kind of papers I'll giv you! Them's the papers *you* want!"

"But I workt hard for the ticket; I toiled night and day! The patrit should be rewarded!"

"Virtoo," sed I, holdin' the infatooated man by the coat-collar, "virtoo, sir, is its own reward. Look at me!" He did look at me, and qualed be4 my gase. "The fact is," I continued, lookin round on the hungry crowd, "there is scacely a offiss for every ile lamp carried round durin' this campane. I wish thare was. I wish thare was furrin missions to be filled on varis lonely Islands where eppydemics rage incesantly, and if I was in Old Abe's place I'd send every mother's son of you to them. What air you here for?" I continnered, warmin up considerable, "can't you give Abe a minit's peace? Don't you see he's worrid most to death? Go home, you miserable men, go home & till the sile! Go to peddlin tinware—go to choppin wood—go to bilin sope—stuff sassengers—black boots—git a clerkship on sum respectable manure cart—go round as original Swiss Bell Ringers—becum 'origenal and only' Campbell Minstrels—if to lecturin at 50 dollars a nite—imbark in the peanut bizniss—*write for the Ledger*—saw off your legs and go round givin concerts, with techin appeals to a charitable public, printed on your handbills—anything for a honest living, but don't come round here drivin Old Abe crazy by your outrajis cuttings up! Go home. 'Stand not upon the order of your goin' but go to onct! If in five minits from this time," sez I pullin' out my new sixteen dollar huntin cased watch, and brandishin' it before their eyes, "Ef in five minits from this time a single sole of you remains on these here premises, I'll go out to my cage near by, and let my Boy Constructor loose! & ef he gits amung you, you'll think old Solferino has cum again and no mistake!" You ought to hev seen them scamper, Mr. Fair. They run orf as tho Satun his self was arter them with a red hot ten pronged pitchfork. In five minits the premises was clear.

"How kin I ever repay you, Mr. Ward, for your kindness?" sed Old Abe, advancin and shakin me warmly by the hand. "How kin I ever repay you, sir?"

"By givin the whole country a good, sound administration. By poerin' ile upon the troubled waturs, North and South. By pursooin' a patriotic, firm, and just course, and then if any State wants to secede, let 'em Sesesh!"

"How 'bout my Cabinit, Mister Ward?" sed Abe.

"Fill it up with Showmen sir! Showmen is devoid of politics. They hain't got any principles! They know how to cater for the public. They know what the public wants, North & South Showmen, sir, is honest men. Ef you doubt their literary ability, look at their posters, and see small bills! Ef you want a Cabinit as is a Cabinit fill it up with showmen, but don't call on me. The moral wax figger perfeshun musn't be permitted to go down while there's a drop of blood in these vains! A. Linkin, I wish you well! Ef Powers or Walcutt wus to pick out a model for a beautiful man, I scarcely think they'd sculp you; but ef you do the fair thing by your country you'll make as putty a angel as any of us! A. Linkin, use the talents which Nature has put into you judishusly and firmly, and all will be well. A. Linkin, adoo!"

He shook me cordyully by the hand—we exchanged picters, so we could gaze upon each others' liniments when far away from one another—he at the hellum of the ship of State, and I at the hellum of the show bizniss—admittance only 15 cents.

1862

FROM

Artemus Ward: His Travels

California

We reach San Francisco one Sunday afternoon. I am driven to the Occidental Hotel by a kind-hearted hackman, who states that inasmuch as I have come out there to amuse people, he will only charge me five dollars. I pay it in gold, of course, because greenbacks are not current on the Pacific coast.

Many of the citizens of San Francisco remember the Sabbath-day to keep it jolly; and the theatres, the circus, the minstrels, and the music halls are all in full blast to-night.

I "compromise" and go to the Chinese theatre, thinking perhaps, there can be no great harm in listening to worldly sentiments when expressed in a language I don't understand.

The Chinaman at the door takes my ticket with the remark, "Ki hi-hi ki!" Shoolah!"

And I tell him that on the whole I think he is right.

The Chinese play is "continued," like a Ledger story, from night to night. It commences with the birth of the hero or heroine, which interesting event occurs publicly on the stage; and then follows him or her down to the grave, where it cheerfully ends.

Sometimes a Chinese play lasts six months. The play I am speaking of had been going on for about two months. The heroine had grown up into womanhood, and was on the point, as I inferred, of being married to a young Chinaman in spangled pantaloons and a long black tail. The bride's father comes in with his arms full of tea chests, and bestows them, with his blessing, upon the happy couple. As this play is to run four months longer, however, and as my time is limited, I go away at the close of the second act, while the orchestra is performing an overture on gongs and one-stringed fiddles.

The door-keeper again says, "Ki hi-hi ki! Shoolah!" adding this time, however, "Chow-wow." I agree with him in regard to the ki hi and hi ki, but tell him I don't feel altogether certain about the chow-wow. . . .

I go to the mountain towns. The sensational mining days are over, but I find the people jolly and hospitable nevertheless.

At Nevada I am called upon, shortly after my arrival, by an athletic scarlet-faced man, who politely says his name is Blaze.

"I have a little bill against you, sir," he observes.

"A bill—what for?"

"For drinks."

"Drinks?"

"Yes, sir—at my bar, I keep the well-known and highly-respected coffee-house down street."

"But, my dear sir, there is a mistake—I never drank at your bar in my life."

"I know it, sir. That isn't the point. The point is this: I pay out money for good liquors, and it is people's own fault if they don't drink them. There are the liquors—do as you please about drinking them, *but you must pay for them!* Isn't that fair?"

His enormous body (which Puck wouldn't put a girdle round for forty dollars) shook gleefully while I read this eminently original bill.

Years ago Mr. Blaze was an agent of the California Stage Company. There was a formidable and well-organized opposition to the California Stage Company at that time, and Mr. Blaze rendered them such signal service in his capacity of agent that they were very sorry when he tendered his resignation.

"You are some sixteen hundred dollars behind in your accounts, Mr. Blaze," said the President, "but in view of your faithful and efficient services, we shall throw off eight hundred dollars of that amount."

Mr. Blaze seemed touched by this generosity. A tear stood in his eye, and his bosom throbbed audibly.

"You will throw off eight hundred dollars—you *will?*" he at last cried, seizing the President's hand, and pressing it passionately to his lips.

"I will," returned the President.

"Well, sir," said Mr. Blaze, "I'm a gentleman, I *am,* you bet! And I won't allow no Stage Company to surpass me in politeness. *I'll throw off the other eight hundred dollars, and we'll call it square!* No gratitude, sir—no thanks; it is my duty." . . .

I get back to San Francisco in a few weeks, and am to start home Overland from here.

The distance from Sacramento to Atchison, Kansas, by the Overland stage route, is twenty-two hundred miles, but you can happily accomplish a part of the journey by railroad. The Pacific railroad is completed twelve miles to Folsom, leaving only two thousand and one hundred and eighty-eight miles to go by stage. This breaks the monotony; but as it is mid-winter, and as there are well substantiated reports of Overland passengers freezing to death, and of the Piute savages being in one of their sprightly moods when they scalp people, I do not—I may say that I do not leave the capital of California in a light-hearted and joyous manner. But "leaves have their time to fall," and I have my time to leave, which is now.

We ride all day and all night, and ascend and descend

some of the most frightful hills I ever saw. We make Johnson's Pass, which is 6,752 feet high, about two o'clock in the morning, and go down the great Kingsbury grade with locked wheels. The driver, with whom I sit outside, informs me, as we slowly roll down this fearful mountain road, which looks down on either side into an appalling ravine, that he has met accidents in his time, and cost the California Stage Company a great deal of money; "because," he says, "juries is agin us on principle, and every man who sues us is sure to recover. But it will never be so agin, not with *me,* you bet."

"How is that?" I said.

It was frightfully dark. It was snowing withal, and notwithstanding the brakes were kept hard down, the coach slewed wildly, often fairly touching the brink of the black precipice.

"How is that?" I said.

"Why, you see," he replied, "that corpses never sue for damages, but maimed people do. And the next time I have an overturn I shall go round and keerfully examine the passengers. Them as is dead, I shall let alone; but them as is mutilated I shall finish with the king-bolt! Dead folks don't sue. They ain't on it."

Thus with anecdote did this driver cheer me up.

1865

FROM

Artemus Ward in London and Other Papers

The Tower of London

MR. PUNCH, MY DEAR SIR,—

I skurcely need inform you that your excellent Tower is very pop'lar with peple from the agricultooral districks, and it was chiefly them class which I found waitin at the gates the other mornin.

I saw at once that the Tower was established on a firm basis. In the entire history of firm basisis I don't find a basis more firmer than this one.

"You have no Tower in America?" said a man in the crowd, who had somehow detected my denomination.

"Alars! no," I ansered; "we boste of our enterprise and improovements, and yit we are devoid of a Tower. America, oh my onhappy country! thou hast not got no Tower! It's a sweet Boon."

The gates was opened after awhile, and we all purchist tickets and went into a waitin-room.

"My frens," said a pale-faced little man, in black close, "this is a sad day."

"Inasmuch as to how?" I said.

"I mean it is sad to think that so many peple have been killed within these gloomy walls. My frens, let us drop a tear!"

"No," I said, "you must excuse me. Others may drop one if they feel like it; but as for me, I decline. The early managers of this institootion were a bad lot, and their crimes were trooly orful; but I can't sob for those who died four or five hundred years ago. If they was my own relations I couldn't. It's absurd to shed sobs over things which occurd durin the rain of Henry the Three. Let us be cheerful," I continnered. "Look at the festiv Warders, in their red flannil jackets. They are cheerful, and why should it not be thusly with us?"

A Warder now took us in charge, and showed us the Trater's Gate, the armers, and things. The Trater's Gate is wide enuff to admit about twenty traters abrest, I should jedge; but beyond this, I couldn't see that it was superior to gates in gen'ral.

Traters, I will here remark, are a onfortnit class of peple. If they wasn't they wouldn't be traters. They conspire to bust up a country—they fail, and they're traters. They bust her, and they become statesmen and heroes.

Take the case of Gloster, afterwards Old Dick the Three, who may be seen at the Tower, on horseback, in a heavy tin overcoat—take Mr. Gloster's case. Mr. G. was a conspirater of the basist dye, and if he'd failed, he would have been hung on a sour apple tree. But Mr. G. succeeded, and became great. He was slewd by Col. Richmond, but he lives in histry, and his equestrian figger may be seen daily for a sixpence, in conjunction with other em'nent persons, and no extra charge for the Warder's able and bootiful lectur.

There's one king in the room who is mounted onto a foamin steed, his right hand graspin a barber's pole. I didn't learn his name.

The room where the daggers and pistils and other weppins is kept is interestin. Among this collection of choice cutlery I notist the bow and arrer which those hot-heded old chaps used to conduct battles with. It is quite like the bow and arrer used at this day by certin tribes of American Injuns, and they shoot 'em off with such a excellent precision that I almost sigh'd to be a Injun, when I was in the Rocky Mountin regin. They are a pleasant lot them Injuns. Mr. Cooper and Dr. Catlin have told us of the red man's wonerful eloquence, and I found it so. Our party was stopt on the plains of Utah by a band of Shoshones, whose chief said, "Brothers! the pale-face is welcome. Brothers! the sun is sinkin in the West, and Warra-bucky-she will soon cease speakin. Brothers! the poor red man belongs to a race which is fast becomin extink." He then whooped in a shrill manner, stole all our blankets and whisky, and fled to the primeval forest to conceal his emotions.

I will remark here, while on the subjeck of Injuns, that they are in the main a very shaky set, with even less sense than the Fenians, and when I hear philanthropists bewailin the fack that every year "carries the noble red man nearer the settin sun," I simply have to say I'm glad of it, tho' it is rough on the settin sun. They call you by the sweet name of Brother one minit, and the next they scalp you with their Tomashawks. But I wander. Let us return to the Tower.

At one end of the room where the weppins is kept, is a wax figger of Queen Elizabeth, mounted on a fiery stuffed hoss, whose glass eye flashes with pride, and whose red morocker nostril dilates hawtily, as if conscious of the royal burden he bears. I have associated Elizabeth with the Spanish Armady. She's mixed up with it at the Surry Theater, where *Troo to the Core* is being acted, and in which a full bally core is introjooced on board the Spanish Admiral's ship, givin the audiens the idee that he intends openin a moosic-hall in Plymouth the moment he conkers that town. But a very interesting drammer is *Troo to the Core*, notwithstandin the eccentric conduck of the Spanish Admiral; and very nice it is in Queen Elizabeth to make Martin Truegold a baronet.

The Warder shows us some instrooments of tortur, such as thumbscrews, throat-collars, etc., statin that these was conkered from the Spanish Armady, and addin what a crooil peple the Spaniards was in them days—which elissited from a bright eyed little girl of about twelve summers the remark that she tho't it *was* rich to talk about the crooilty of the Spaniards usin thumbscrews, when we was in a Tower where so many poor peple's heads had been cut off. This made the Warder stammer and turn red.

I was so blessed with the little girl's brightness that I could have kissed the dear child, and I would if she'd been six years older.

I think my companions intended makin a day of it, for they all had sandwiches, sassiges, etc. The sad-lookin man, who had wanted us to drop a tear afore we started to go round, fling'd such quantities of sassige into his mouth, that I expected to see him choke hisself to death. He said to me, in the Beauchamp Tower, where the poor prisoners writ their onhappy names on the cold wall, "This is a sad sight."

"It is, indeed," I ansered. "You're black in the face. You shouldn't eat sassige in public without some rehearsals beforehand. You manage it orkwardly."

"No," he said, "I mean this sad room."

Indeed, he was quite right. Tho' so long ago all these drefful things happened, I was very glad to git away from this gloomy room, and go where the rich and sparklin Crown Jewils is kept. I was so pleased with the Queen's Crown, that it occurd to me what a agree-ble surprise it would be to send a sim'lar one home to my wife; and I asked the Warder what was the vally of a good, well-constructed Crown like that. He told me, but on cypherin up with a pencil the amount of funs I have in the Jint Stock Bank, I conclooded I'd send her a genteel silver watch instid.

And so I left the Tower. It is a solid and commandin edifis, but I deny that it is cheerful. I bid it adoo without a pang.

I was droven to my hotel by the most melancholy driver of a four-wheeler that I ever saw. He heaved a deep sigh as I gave him two shillings. "I'll give you six *d.'s* more," I said, "if it hurts you so."

"It isn't that," he said, with a hartrendin groan, "it's only a way I have. My mind's upset to-day. I at one time tho't I'd drive you into the Thames. I've been readin all the daily papers to try and understand about Governor

Ayre, and my mind is totterin. It's really wonderful I didn't drive you into the Thames."

I asked the onhappy man what his number was, so I could redily find him in case I should want him agin, and bad him good-bye. And then I tho't what a frollicksome day I'd made of it.

Respectably, &c.

ARTEMUS WARD

1867

GEORGE WASHINGTON CABLE

(1844–1925)

Cable was fitted by Louisiana and his own history for the local-color fiction he was to write, fiction that demanded both materials exciting in their very strangeness and stories that would serve a didactic function. He was born in New Orleans to a mother who was a daughter of New England Puritans and to a father who was a slave-holding Virginian. The father saw his business go to ruin in 1849 and died a decade later, leaving the fifteen-year-old George to support the penniless family with only the sporadic help of his sister. Escaping from New Orleans when it was captured by Union forces, Cable joined the Fourth Mississippi Cavalry and was seriously wounded, but served until the cessation of hostilities.

After the war, he was a bookkeeper and a surveyor and worked for a firm of cotton factors, rising to an official function in the New Orleans Cotton Exchange. During this time he became interested in the rich heritage of Creole culture in his native region and began to study that culture with avid antiquarian interest. He began his writing as an occasional reporter for the New Orleans *Picayune* and contributed fugitive pieces to *Scribner's Monthly* and the *Century Magazine*. Through the influence and interest of Edward King, he placed his first story, " 'Sieur George," in *Scribner's Monthly* for October, 1873. His early stories, representing his best writing, were collected in 1879 under the title of *Old Creole Days* and established him as a leading figure in the emerging literature of regionalist fiction. Cable's New Orleans had the same appeal of the strange, bizarre, and unknown that the Sierras of Bret Harte exercised over the general American public. In his own day Cable ranked high in contemporary estimates of national popularity.

He became a familiar figure in the lyceum circuits, sometimes appearing together with Mark Twain from 1884 to 1886, and occasionally singing the African folk songs that he and Lafcadio Hearn had collected in New Orleans more than a dozen years earlier. *Old Creole Days* was followed by his first novel, *The Grandissimes*, in 1880, and by *Madame Delphine* in 1881.

The refrain of a postwar folk song was, "I won't be reconstructed, and I do not give a damn," but Cable cared very much about national sociology and was very much a reconstructed rebel; in 1884 he moved with his family to the North. The cosmopolitanism of his life as a lecturer and a writer may have shriveled his roots somewhat and thereby sapped the vigor of his fiction, but it allowed him broader perspectives for his economic, social, and political thinking. Finally he turned against the ideals and traditions of a departed South and began to reflect his increasingly reformist energies in such contemplations of the Negro problem as *The Silent South* (1885) and *The Negro Question* (1890). The resentment and unpopularity that these books earned him in his homeland were compensated by the satisfactions of his life in Northampton, Massachusetts, his home for the last forty years of his long life.

In addition to the titles mentioned above, some of Cable's works are *The Creoles of Louisiana* (1884); *Dr. Sevier* (1885); *Bonaventure* (1888); *Strange True Stories of Louisiana* (1889); *The Busy Man's Bible* (1891); *John March: Southerner* (1894); *The Cavalier* (1901); *Bylow Hill* (1902); *"Posson Jone' "* and *Père Raphaël* (1909); and *Lovers of Louisiana* (1918).

Editions and accounts of the man and his work are to be found in W. M. Baskerville, *Southern Writers*, I (1897); H. A. Toulmin, *Social Historians* (1911); F. L. Pattee, *A History of American Literature since 1870* (1915); L. L. C. Biklé, *George Washington Cable: His Life and Letters* (1928); E. L. Tinker, "Cable and the Creoles," *American Literature*, V (1934); A. H. Quinn, *American Fiction* (1936); K. Ekstrom, *George Washington Cable* (1950); G. Cardwell, *Twins of Genius* (1953); J. B. Hubbell, *The South in American Literature* (1954); A. Turner, *George Washington Cable, A Biography* (1956); J. Blanck, *Bibliography of American Literature*, II (1957); A. Turner, ed., *The Negro Question. . . .* (1958); P. Butcher, *George Washington Cable: The Northampton Years* (1959); P. Butcher, *George W. Cable* (1962); and J. K. King, "George Washington Cable and Thomas Nelson Page," *Dissertation Abstracts*, XXV (1964).

Belles Demoiselles Plantation

The original grantee was Count ————, assume the name to be De Charleu; the old Creoles never forgive a public mention. He was the French king's commissary. One day, called to France to explain the lucky accident of the commissariat having burned down with his account-books inside, he left his wife, a Choctaw Comptesse, behind.

Arrived at court, his excuses were accepted, and that tract granted him where afterwards stood Belles Demoiselles Plantation. A man cannot remember every thing! In a fit of forgetfulness he married a French gentlewoman, rich and beautiful, and "brought her out." However, "All's well that ends well"; a famine had been in the colony, and the Choctaw Comptesse had starved, leaving nought but a half-caste orphan family lurking on the edge of the settlement, bearing our French gentlewoman's own new name, and being mentioned in Monsieur's will.

And the new Comptesse—she tarried but a twelve-month, left Monsieur a lovely son, and departed, led out of this vain world by the swamp-fever.

From this son sprang the proud Creole family of De Charleu. It rose straight up, up, up, generation after generation, tall, branchless, slender, palm-like; and finally, in the time of which I am to tell, flowered with all the rare beauty of a century-plant, in Artemise, Innocente, Felicité, the twins Marie and Martha, Leontine and little Septima; the seven beautiful daughters for whom their home had been fitly named Belles Demoiselles.

The Count's grant had once been a long Pointe, round which the Mississippi used to whirl, and seethe, and foam, that it was horrid to behold. Big whirlpools would open and wheel about in the savage eddies under the low bank, and close up again, and others open, and spin, and disappear. Great circles of muddy surface would boil up from hundreds of feet below, and gloss over, and seem to float away,—sink, come back again under water, and with only a soft hiss surge up again, and again drift off, and vanish.

Every few minutes the loamy bank would tip down a great load of earth upon its besieger, and fall back a foot,— sometimes a yard,—and the writhing river would press after, until at last the Pointe was quite swallowed up, and the great river glided by in a majestic curve, and asked no more; the bank stood fast, the 'caving' became a forgotten misfortune, and the diminished grant was a long, sweeping, willowy bend, rustling with miles of sugar-cane.

Coming up the Mississippi in the sailing craft of those early days, about the time one first could descry the white spires of the old St. Louis Cathedral, you would be pretty sure to spy, just over to your right under the levee, Belles Demoiselles Mansion, with its broad veranda and red painted cypress roof, peering over the embankment, like a bird in the nest, half hid by the avenue of willows which one of the departed De Charleus,—he that married a Marot,—had planted on the levee's crown.

The house stood unusually near the river, facing eastward, and standing four-square, with an immense veranda about its sides, and a flight of steps in front spreading broadly downward, as we open arms to a child. From the veranda nine miles of river were seen; and in their compass, near at hand, the shady garden full of rare and beautiful flowers; farther away broad fields of cane and rice, and the distant quarters of the slaves, and on the horizon everywhere a dark belt of cypress forest.

The master was old Colonel De Charleu,—Jean Albert Henri Joseph De Charleu-Marot, and "Colonel" by the grace of the first American governor. Monsieur,—he would not speak to any one who called him "Colonel,"—was a hoary-headed patriarch. His step was firm, his form erect, his intellect strong and clear, his countenance classic, serene, dignified, commanding, his manners courtly, his voice musical,—fascinating. He had had his vices,—all his life; but had borne them, as his race do, with a serenity of conscience and a cleanness of mouth that left no outward blemish on the surface of the gentleman. He had gambled in Royal Street, drunk hard in Orleans Street, run his adversary through in the duelling-ground at Slaughter-house Point, and danced and quarrelled at the St. Philippe-street-theatre quadroon balls. Even now, with all his courtesy and bounty, and a hospitality which seemed to be entertaining angels, he was bitter-proud and penurious, and deep down in his hard-finished heart loved nothing but himself, his name, and his motherless children. But these! —their ravishing beauty was all but excuse enough for the unbounded idolatry of their father. Against these seven goddesses he never rebelled. Had they even required him to defraud old De Carlos—

I can hardly say.

Old De Carlos was his extremely distant relative on the Choctaw side. With this single exception, the narrow thread-like line of descent from the Indian wife, diminished to a mere strand by injudicious alliances, and deaths in the gutters of old New Orleans, was extinct. The name, by Spanish contact, had become De Carlos; but this one surviving bearer of it was known to all, and known only, as Injin Charlie.

One thing I never knew a Creole to do. He will not utterly go back on the ties of blood, no matter what sort of knots those ties may be. For one reason, he is never ashamed of his or his father's sins; and for another,—he will tell you—he is "all heart!"

So the different heirs of the De Charleu estate had always strictly regarded the rights and interests of the De Carloses, especially their ownership of a block of dilapidated buildings in a part of the city, which had once been very poor property, but was beginning to be valuable. This block had much more than maintained the last De Carlos through a long and lazy lifetime, and, as his household consisted only of himself, and an aged and crippled negress, the inference was irresistible that he "had money." Old Charlie, though by *alias* an "Injin," was plainly a dark white man, about as old as Colonel De Charleu, sunk in the bliss of deep ignorance, shrewd, deaf, and, by repute at least, unmerciful.

The Colonel and he always conversed in English. This rare accomplishment, which the former had learned from his Scotch wife,—the latter from up-river traders,—they found an admirable medium of communication, answering better than French could, a similar purpose to that of the stick which we fasten to the bit of one horse and breast-gear of another, whereby each keeps his distance. Once in a while, too, by way of jest, English found its way among the ladies of Belles Demoiselles, always signifying that their sire was about to have business with old Charlie.

Now a long-standing wish to buy out Charlie troubled the Colonel. He had no desire to oust him unfairly; he was proud of being always fair; yet he did long to engross the whole estate under one title. Out of his luxurious idleness he had conceived this desire, and thought little of so slight an obstacle as being already somewhat in debt to old Charlie for money borrowed, and for which Belles Demoiselles was, of course, good, ten times over. Lots, buildings, rents, all, might as well be his, he thought, to give, keep, or destroy. "Had he but the old man's heritage. Ah! he might bring that into existence which his *belles demoiselles* had been begging for, 'since many year'; a home,—and such a home,—in the gay city. Here he should tear down this row of cottages, and make his garden wall; there that long rope-walk should give place to vine-covered arbors; the bakery yonder should make way for a costly conservatory; that wine warehouse should come down, and the mansion go up. It should be the finest in the state. Men should never pass it, but they should say—'the palace of the De Charleus; a family of grand descent, a people of elegance and bounty, a line as old as France, a fine old man, and seven daughters as beautiful as happy; whoever dare attempt to marry there must leave his own name behind him!'

"The house should be of stones fitly set, brought down in ships from the land of 'les Yankees,' and it should have an airy belvedere, with a gilded image tip-toeing and shining on its peak, and from it you should see, far across the gleaming folds of the river, the red roof of Belles Demoiselles, the country-seat. At the big stone gate there should be a porter's lodge, and it should be a privilege even to see the ground."

Truly they were a family fine enough, and fancy-free enough to have fine wishes, yet happy enough where they were, to have had no wish but to live there always.

To those, who, by whatever fortune, wandered into the garden of Belles Demoiselles some summer afternoon as the sky was reddening towards evening, it was lovely to see the family gathered out upon the tiled pavement at the foot of the broad front steps, gayly chatting and jesting, with that ripple of laughter that comes so pleasingly from a bevy of girls. The father would be found seated in their midst, the center of attention and compliment, witness, arbiter, umpire, critic, by his beautiful children's unanimous appointment, but the single vassal, too, of seven absolute sovereigns.

Now they would draw their chairs near together in eager discussion of some new step in the dance, or the adjustment of some rich adornment. Now they would start about him with excited comments to see the eldest fix a bunch of violets in his button-hole. Now the twins would move down a walk after some unusual flower, and be greeted on their return with the high pitched notes of delighted feminine surprise.

As evening came on they would draw more quietly about their paternal center. Often their chairs were forsaken, and they grouped themselves on the lower steps, one above another, and surrendered themselves to the tender influences of the approaching night. At such an hour the passer on the river, already attracted by the dark figures of the broad-roofed mansion, and its woody garden standing against the glowing sunset, would hear the voices of the hidden group rise from the spot in the soft harmonies of an evening song; swelling clearer and clearer as the thrill of music warmed them into feeling, and presently joined by the deeper tones of the father's voice; then, as the daylight passed quite away, all would be still, and he would know that the beautiful home had gathered its nestlings under its wings.

And yet, for mere vagary, it pleased them not to be pleased.

"Arti!" called one sister to another in the broad hall, one morning,—mock amazement in her distended eyes, —"something is goin' to took place!"

"Comm-e-n-t?"—long-drawn perplexity.

"Papa is goin' to town!"

The news passed up stairs.

"Inno!"—one to another meeting in a doorway,—"something is goin' to took place!"

"Qu'est-ce-que c'est!"—vain attempt at gruffness.

"Papa is goin' to town!"

The unusual tidings were true. It was afternoon of the same day that the Colonel tossed his horse's bridle to his groom, and stepped up to old Charlie, who was sitting on his bench under a China-tree, his head, as was his fashion, bound in a Madras handkerchief. The "old man" was plainly under the effect of spirits, and smiled a deferential salutation without trusting himself to his feet.

"Eh, well Charlie!"—the Colonel raised his voice to suit his kinsman's deafness,—"how is those times with my friend Charlie?"

"Eh?" said Charlie, distractedly.

"Is that goin' well with my friend Charlie?"

"In de house,—call her,"—making a pretence of rising.

"Non, non! I don't want," the speaker paused to breathe —" 'ow is collection?"

"Oh!" said Charlie, "every day he make me more poorer!"

"What do you hask for it?" asked the planter indifferently, designating the house by a wave of his whip.

"Ask for w'at?" said Injin Charlie.

"De *house*! What you ask for it?"

"I don't believe," said Charlie.

"What you would *take* for it!" cried the planter.

"Wait for w'at?"

"What you would *take* for the whole block?"

"I don't want to sell him!"

"I'll give you *ten thousand dollah* for it."

"Ten t'ousand dollah for dis house? Oh, no, dat is no price. He is blame good old house,—dat old house." (Old Charlie and the Colonel never swore in presence of each other.) "Forty years dat old house didn't had to be paint! I easy can get fifty t'ousand dollah for dat old house."

"Fifty thousand picayunes; yes," said the Colonel.

"She's a good house. Can make plenty money," pursued the deaf man.

"That's what make you so rich, eh, Charlie?"

"Non, I don't make nothing. Too blame clever, me dat's de troub'. She's a good house,—make money fast like a steamboat,—make a barrel full in a week! Me I lose money all de days. Too blame clever."

"Charlie!"

"Eh?"

"Tell me what you'll take."

"Make? I don't make *nothing*. Too blame clever."

"What will you *take?*"

"Oh! I got enough already,—half drunk now."

"What will you take for the 'ouse?"

"You want to buy her?"

"I don't know,"—(shrug),—"maybe,—if you sell it cheap."

"She's a bully old house."

There was a long silence. By and by old Charlie commenced—

"Old Injin Charlie is a low-down dog."

"C'est vrai, oui!" retorted the Colonel in an undertone.

"He's got Injin blood in him."

The Colonel nodded assent.

"But he's got some blame good blood, too, ain't it?"

The Colonel nodded impatiently.

"Bien! Old Charlie's Injin blood says, 'sell de house, Charlie, you blame old fool!' *Mais,* old Charlie's good blood says, 'Charlie! if you sell dat old house, Charlie, you low-down old dog, Charlie, what de Compte De Charleu make for you grace-granmuzzer, de dev' can eat you, Charlie, I don't care.' "

"But you'll sell it anyhow, won't you, old man?"

"No!" And the *no* rumbled off in muttered oaths like thunder out on the Gulf. The incensed old Colonel wheeled and started off.

"Curl!" (Colonel) said Charlie, standing up unsteadily.

The planter turned with an inquiring frown.

"I'll trade with you!" said Charlie.

The Colonel was tempted. " 'Ow'l you trade?" he asked.

"My house for yours!"

The old Colonel turned pale with anger. He walked very quickly back, and came close up to his kinsman.

"Charlie!" he said.

"Injin Charlie,"—with a tipsy nod.

But by this time self-control was returning. "Sell Belles Demoiselles to you?" he said in a high key, and then laughed "Ho, ho, ho!" and rode away.

A cloud, but not a dark one, overshadowed the spirits of Belles Demoiselles' plantation. The old master, whose beaming presence had always made him a shining Saturn, spinning and sparkling within the bright circle of his daughters, fell into musing fits, started out of frowning reveries, walked often by himself, and heard business from his overseer fretfully.

No wonder. The daughters knew his closeness in trade, and attributed to it his failure to negotiate for the Old

Charlie buildings,—so to call them. They began to depre-
ciate Belles Demoiselles. If a north wind blew, it was too
cold to ride. If a shower had fallen, it was too muddy to
drive. In the morning the garden was wet. In the evening
the grasshopper was a burden. *Ennui* was turned into
capital; every headache was interpreted a premonition of
ague; and when the native exuberance of a flock of ladies
without a want or a care burst out in laughter in the father's
face, they spread their French eyes, rolled up their little
hands, and with rigid wrists and mock vehemence vowed
and vowed again that they only laughed at their misery, and
should pine to death unless they could move to the sweet
city. "Oh! the theatre! Oh! Orleans Street! Oh! the masquerade! the Place d'Armes! the ball!" and they would
call upon Heaven with French irreverence, and fall into
each other's arms, and whirl down the hall singing a waltz,
end with a grand collision and fall, and, their eyes streaming merriment, lay the blame on the slippery floor, that
would some day be the death of the whole seven.

Three times more the fond father, thus goaded, managed, by accident,—business accident,—to see old Charlie
and increase his offer; but in vain. He finally went to him
formally.

"Eh?" said the deaf and distant relative. "For what
you want him, eh? Why you don't stay where you halways
be 'appy? Dis is a blame old rat-hole,—good for old Injin
Charlie,—da's all. Why you don't stay where you be halways 'appy? Why you don't buy somewheres else?"

"That's none of your business," snapped the planter.
Truth was, his reasons were unsatisfactory even to himself.

A sullen silence followed. Then Charlie spoke:

"Well, now, look here; I sell you old Charlie's house."

"*Bien!* and the whole block," said the Colonel.

"Hold on," said Charlie. "I sell you de 'ouse and de
block. Den I go and git drunk, and go to sleep; de dev'
comes along and says, 'Charlie! old Charlie, you blame
low-down old dog, wake up! What you doin' here? Where's
de 'ouse what Monsieur le Compte give your grace-granmuzzer? Don't you see dat fine gentyman, De Charleu,
done gone and tore him down and make him over new,
you blame old fool, Charlie, you low-down old Injin dog!'"

"I'll give you forty thousand dollars," said the Colonel.
"For de 'ouse?"

"For all."

The deaf man shook his head.

"Forty-five!" said the Colonel.

"What a lie? For what you tell me 'What a lie?' I don't tell you no lie."

"Non, non! I give you *forty-five!"* shouted the Colonel.

Charlie shook his head again.

"Fifty!"

He shook it again.

The figures rose and rose to—

"Seventy-five!"

The answer was an invitation to go away and let the owner alone, as he was, in certain specified respects, the vilest of living creatures, and no company for a fine gentyman.

The "fine gentyman" longed to blaspheme,—but before old Charlie!—in the name of pride, how could he? He mounted and started away.

"Tell you what I'll make wid you," said Charlie.

The other, guessing aright, turned back without dismounting, smiling.

"How much Belles Demoiselles hoes me now?" asked the deaf one.

"One hundred and eighty thousand dollars," said the Colonel, firmly.

"Yass," said Charlie. "I don't want Belles Demoiselles."

The old Colonel's quiet laugh intimated it made no difference either way.

"But me," continued Charlie, "me,—I'm got le Compte De Charleu's blood in me, any'ow,—a litt' bit, any'ow, ain't it?"

The Colonel nodded that it was.

"Bien! If I go out of dis place and don't go to Belles Demoiselles, de peoples will say,—dey will say, 'Old Charlie he been all doze time tell a blame *lie!* He ain't no kin to his old grace-granmuzzer, not a blame bit! He don't got nary drop of De Charleu blood to save his blame low-down old Injin soul!' No, sare! What I want wid money, den? No, sare! My place for yours!"

He turned to go into the house, just too soon to see the Colonel make an ugly whisk at him with his riding-whip. Then the Colonel, too, moved off.

Two or three times over, as he ambled homeward,

laughter broke through his annoyance, as he recalled old Charlie's family pride and the presumption of his offer. Yet each time he could but think better of—not the offer to swap, but the preposterous ancestral loyalty. It was so much better than he could have expected from his "low-down" relative, and not unlike his own whim withal—the proposition which went with it was forgiven.

This last defeat bore so harshly on the master of Belles Demoiselles, that the daughters, reading chagrin in his face, began to repent. They loved their father as daughters can, and when they saw their pretended dejection harassing him seriously they restrained their complaints, displayed more than ordinary tenderness, and heroically and ostentatiously concluded there was no place like Belles Demoiselles. But the new mood touched him more than the old, and only refined his discontent. Here was a man, rich without the care of riches, free from any real trouble, happiness as native to his house as perfume to his garden, deliberately, as it were with premeditated malice, taking joy by the shoulder and bidding her be gone to town, whither he might easily have followed, only that the very same ancestral nonsense that kept Injin Charlie from selling the old place for twice its value prevented him from choosing any other spot for a city home.

But by and by the charm of nature and the merry hearts around him prevailed; the fit of exalted sulks passed off, and after a while the year flared up at Christmas, flickered, and went out.

New Year came and passed; the beautiful garden of Belles Demoiselles put on its spring attire; the seven fair sisters moved from rose to rose; the cloud of discontent had warmed into invisible vapor in the rich sunlight of family affection, and on the common memory the only scar of last year's wound was old Charlie's sheer impertinence in crossing the caprice of the De Charleus. The cup of gladness seemed to fill with the fil'ing of the river.

How high that river was! Its tremendous current rolled and tumbled and spun along, hustling the long funeral flotillas of drift,—and how near shore it came! Men were out day and night, watching the levee. On windy nights even the old Colonel took part, and grew light-hearted with occupation and excitement, as every minute the river threw a white arm over the levee's top, as though it would vault over. But all held fast, and, as the summer drifted in, the water sunk down into its banks and looked quite incapable of harm.

On a summer afternoon of uncommon mildness, old Colonel Jean Albert Henri Joseph de Charleu-Marot, being in a mood for revery, slipped the custody of his feminine rulers and sought the crown of the levee, where it was his wont to promenade. Presently he sat upon a stone bench,—a favorite seat. Before him lay his broad-spread fields; near by, his lordly mansion; and being still,—perhaps by female contact,—somewhat sentimental, he fell to musing on his past. It was hardly worthy to be proud of. All its morning was reddened with mad frolic, and far toward the meridian it was marred with elegant rioting. Pride had kept him well-nigh useless, and despised the honors won by valor; gaming had dimmed prosperity; death had taken his heavenly wife; voluptuous ease had mortgaged his lands; and yet his house still stood, his sweet-smelling fields were still fruitful, his name was fame enough; and yonder and yonder, among the trees and flowers, like angels walking in Eden, were the seven goddesses of his only worship.

Just then a slight sound behind him brought him to his feet. He cast his eyes anxiously to the outer edge of the little strip of bank between the levee's base and the river. There was nothing visible. He paused, with his ear toward the water, his face full of frightened expectation. Ha! There came a single plashing sound, like some great beast slipping into the river, and little waves in a wide semi-circle came out from under the bank and spread over the water!

"My God!"

He plunged down the levee and bounded through the low weeds to the edge of the bank. It was sheer, and the water about four feet below. He did not stand quite on the edge, but fell upon his knees a couple of yards away, wringing his hands, moaning and weeping, and staring through his watery eyes at a fine, long crevice just discernible under the matted grass, and curving outward on either hand toward the river.

"My God!" he sobbed aloud; "my God!" and even while he called, his God answered: the tough Bermuda grass stretched and snapped, the crevice slowly became a gape, and softly, gradually, with no sound but the closing of the water at last, a ton or more of earth settled into the boiling eddy and disappeared.

At the same instant a pulse of the breeze brought from the garden behind, the joyous, thoughtless laughter of the fair mistresses of Belles Demoiselles.

The old Colonel sprang up and clambered over the levee. Then forcing himself to a more composed movement, he hastened into the house and ordered his horse.

"Tell my children to make merry while I am gone," he left word. "I shall be back to-night," and the horse's hoofs clattered down a by-road leading to the city.

"Charlie," said the planter, riding up to a window, from which the old man's nightcap was thrust out, "what you say, Charlie,—my house for yours, eh, Charlie—what you say?"

"Ello!" said Charlie; "from where you come from dis time of to-night?"

"I come from the Exchange in St. Louis Street." (A small fraction of the truth.)

"What you want?" said matter-of-fact Charlie.

"I come to trade."

The low-down relative drew the worsted off his ears. "Oh! yass," he said with an uncertain air.

"Well, old man Charlie, what you say: my house for yours,—like you said,—eh, Charlie?"

"I dunno," said Charlie; "it's nearly mine now. Why you don't stay dare youse'f?"

"Because I don't want!" said the Colonel savagely. "Is dat reason enough for you? You better take me in de notion, old man, I tell you,—yes!"

Charlie never winced; but how his answer delighted the Colonel! Quoth Charlie:

"I don't care—I take him!—*mais,* possession give right off."

"Not the whole plantation, Charlie; only"—

"I don't care," said Charlie; "we easy can fix dat. *Mais,* what for you don't want to keep him? I don't want him. You better keep him."

"Don't you try to make no fool of me, old man," cried the planter.

"Oh, no!" said the other. "Oh, no! but you make a fool of yourself, ain't it?"

The dumbfounded Colonel stared; Charlie went on:

"Yass! Belles Demoiselles is more wort' dan tree block like dis one. I pass by dare since two weeks. Oh, pritty Belles Demoiselles! De cane was wave in de wind, de garden smell like a bouquet, de white-cap was jump up and down on de river; seven *belles demoiselles* was ridin' on horses. 'Pritty, pritty, pritty!' says old Charlie. Ah! *Monsieur le père,* 'ow 'appy, 'appy, 'appy!

"Yass!" he continued—the Colonel still staring—"le Compte De Charleu have two familie. One was low-down Choctaw, one was high up *noblesse*. He gave the low-down Choctaw dis old rat-hole; he give Belles Demoiselles to you gran-fozzer; and now you don't be *satisfait*. What I'll do wid Belles Demoiselles? She'll break me in two years, yass. And what you'll do wid old Charlie's house, eh? You'll tear her down and make you'se'f a blame old fool. I rather wouldn't trade!"

The planter caught a big breathful of anger, but Charlie went straight on:

"I rather wouldn't, *mais* I will do it for you;—just the same, like Monsieur le Compte would say, 'Charlie, you old fool, I want to shange houses wid you.'"

So long as the Colonel suspected irony he was angry, but as Charlie seemed, after all, to be certainly in earnest, he began to feel conscience-stricken. He was by no means a tender man, but his lately-discovered misfortune had unhinged him, and this strange, undeserved, disinterested family fealty on the part of Charlie touched his heart. And should he still try to lead him into the pitfall he had dug? He hesitated;—no, he would show him the place by broad daylight, and if he chose to overlook the "caving bank," it would be his own fault;—a trade's a trade.

"Come," said the planter, "come at my house to-night; to-morrow we look at the place before breakfast, and finish the trade."

"For what?" said Charlie.

"Oh, because I got to come in town in the morning."

"I don't want," said Charlie. "How I'm goin' to come dere?"

"I git you a horse at the liberty stable."

"Well—anyhow—I don't care—I'll go." And they went.

When they had ridden a long time, and were on the road darkened by hedges of Cherokee rose, the Colonel called behind him to the "low-down" scion:

"Keep the road, old man."

"Eh?"

"Keep the road."

"Oh, yes; all right; I keep my word; we don't goin' to play no tricks, eh?"

But the Colonel seemed not to hear. His ungenerous design was beginning to be hateful to him. Not only old Charlie's unprovoked goodness was prevailing; the eulogy on Belles Demoiselles had stirred the depths of an intense love for his beautiful home. True, if he held to it, the caving of the bank, at its present fearful speed, would let the house into the river within three months; but were it not better to lose it so, than sell his birthright? Again,—coming back to the first thought,—to betray his own blood! It was only Injin Charlie; but had not the De Charleu blood just spoken out in him? Unconsciously he groaned.

After a time they struck a path approaching the plantation in the rear, and a little after, passing from behind a clump of live-oaks, they came in sight of the villa. It looked so like a gem, shining through its dark grove, so like a great glow-worm in the dense foliage, so significant of luxury and gayety, that the poor master, from an overflowing heart, groaned again.

"What?" asked Charlie.

The Colonel only drew his rein, and, dismounting mechanically, contemplated the sight before him. The high, arched doors and windows were thrown wide to the summer air; from every opening the bright light of numerous candelabra darted out upon the sparkling foliage of magnolia and bay, and here and there in the spacious verandas a colored lantern swayed in the gentle breeze. A sound of revel fell on the ear, the music of harps; and across one window, brighter than the rest, flitted, once or twice, the shadows of dancers. But oh! the shadows flitting across the heart of the fair mansion's master!

"Old Charlie," said he, gazing fondly at his house, "You and me is both old, eh?"

"Yaas," said the stolid Charlie.

"And we has both been bad enough in our time, eh, Charlie?"

Charlie, surprised at the tender tone, repeated "Yaas."

"And you and me is mighty close?"

"Blame close, yaas."

"But you never know me to cheat, old man!"

"No,"—impassively.

"And do you think I would cheat you now?"

"I dunno," said Charlie. "I don't believe."

"Well, old man, old man,"—his voice began to quiver, —"I sha'n't cheat you now. My God!—old man, I tell you —you better not make the trade!"

"Because for what?" asked Charlie in plain anger; but both looked quickly toward the house! The Colonel tossed his hands wildly in the air, rushed forward a step or two, and giving one fearful scream of agony and fright, fell forward on his face in the path. Old Charlie stood transfixed with horror. Belles Demoiselles, the realm of maiden beauty, the home of merriment, the house of dancing, all in the tremor and glow of pleasure, suddenly sunk, with one short, wild wail of terror—sunk, sunk, down, down, down, into the merciless, unfathomable flood of the Mississippi.

Twelve long months were midnight to the mind of the childless father; when they were only half gone, he took his bed; and every day, and every night, old Charlie, the "low-down," the "fool," watched him tenderly, tended him lovingly, for the sake of his name, his misfortunes, and his broken heart. No woman's step crossed the floor of the sick-chamber, whose western dormer-windows overpeered the dingy architecture of old Charlie's block; Charlie and a skilled physician, the one all interest, the other all gentleness, hope, and patience—these only entered by the door; but by the window came in a sweet-scented evergreen vine, transplanted from the caving bank of Belles Demoiselles. It caught the rays of sunset in its flowery net and let them softly in upon the sick man's bed; gathered the glancing beams of the moon at midnight, and often wakened the sleeper to look, with his mindless eyes, upon their pretty silver fragments strewn upon the floor.

By and by there seemed—there was—a twinkling dawn of returning reason. Slowly, peacefully, with an increase unseen from day to day, the light of reason came into the eyes, and speech became coherent; but withal there came a failing of the wrecked body, and the doctor said that monsieur was both better and worse.

One evening, as Charlie sat by the vineclad window with

his fireless pipe in his hand, the old Colonel's eyes fell full upon his own, and rested there.

"Charl—," he said with an effort, and his delighted nurse hastened to the bedside and bowed his best ear. There was an unsuccessful effort or two, and then he whispered, smiling with sweet sadness,—

"We didn't trade."

The truth, in this case, was a secondary matter to Charlie; the main point was to give a pleasing answer. So he nodded his head decidedly, as who should say—"Oh yes, we did, it was a bona-fide swap!" but when he saw the smile vanish, he tried the other expedient and shook his head with still more vigor, to signify that they had not so much as approached a bargain; and the smile returned.

Charlie wanted to see the vine recognized. He stepped backward to the window with a broad smile, shook the foliage, nodded and looked smart.

"I know," said the Colonel, with beaming eyes, "—many weeks."

The next day—

"Charl—"

The best ear went down.

"Send for a priest."

The priest came, and was alone with him a whole afternoon. When he left, the patient was very haggard and exhausted, but smiled and would not suffer the crucifix to be removed from his breast.

One more morning came. Just before dawn Charlie, lying on a pallet in the room, thought he was called, and came to the bedside.

"Old man," whispered the failing invalid, "is it caving yet?"

Charlie nodded.

"It won't pay you out."

"Oh, dat makes not'ing," said Charlie. Two big tears rolled down his brown face. "Dat makes not'in'."

The Colonel whispered once more:

"*Mes belles demoiselles!* in paradise;—in the garden—I shall be with them at sunrise," and so it was.

1874

JOEL CHANDLER HARRIS

(1848–1908)

Before Harris was born, in Eatonton, Georgia, his father deserted the family, leaving the mother to support the boy by dressmaking. Between the ages of thirteen and seventeen, Harris lived on the "Turnwold" plantation, working for and influenced by the plantation's master, Joseph Addison Turner. There he set type, learned the rudiments of journalism, and completed his first writing as he worked on Turner's weekly paper, the *Countryman*. Harris learned from Turner the necessity for conciseness and the urbane swift stroke of telling wit— Joseph Addison Turner modeled the *Countryman* after the *Spectator*, and his style was indicated by his name. Yet Harris took from "Turnwold" a greater gift than eighteenth-century elegance and control. He learned and mastered the Negro dialect and the inflections and materials of the stories told by firelight in the slave quarters. From the folk bestiaries of American slaves—stories in which, as he pointed out, helplessness wins out against the fox, the bear, and the wolf—he took a record of a humor and of attitudes that provided him with regional materials offering a greater communication with his times than he could find in the English literature of an earlier century.

In November, 1864, Sherman's March ended the "Turnwold" part of Harris's development. After the war he worked for various newspapers, continuing to learn his trade from men such as William Tappan Thompson, a famous Southern humorist of the times and editor of the Savannah *Morning News*. In 1876 Harris began his fruitful twenty-four-year association with the Atlanta *Constitution*, where he strengthened his reputation as a humorist and journalist. A friend of the Atlanta orator of the New South, Henry W. Grady, Harris began to write his "Uncle Remus" stories for political purposes. Painstakingly and with many revisions, he artfully perfected his faithful record of the deceptively artless Negro storyteller, and he remains to this day unsurpassed in his chosen materials. Mark Twain called him the only master of the Negro dialect, and the success of his stories helped make the *Constitution* the most influential newspaper of the South. "Uncle Remus," innocently exposing the foibles of mankind in his animal tales, aimed toward reconciliation in every way and laughed—sometimes painfully—at the idiocy and destructiveness of sectional antagonism. Harris extended his attempt at reconciliation from politics to literature: local color, he insisted, is not sectionalism, as the "Free Joe" and "Daddy Jake" stories indicate. Sectionalism, Harris said, aims at separateness; local color is a regional instrument for talking to the entire nation and, indeed, to every man.

The "Uncle Remus" stories were first collected in 1880 in *Uncle Remus, His Songs and Sayings;* the immediate and wide national reception of the book prompted the production of *Nights with Uncle Remus* in 1883, *Uncle Remus and his Friends* in 1892, *The Tar Baby and Other Rhymes of Uncle Remus* in 1904, *Told by Uncle Remus* in 1905, *Uncle Remus and Brer Rabbit* in 1907, and the posthumous *Uncle Remus and the Little Boy* (1910) and *Uncle Remus Returns* (1918). Although his poems and novels neither received nor merited wide attention, some of Harris's stories of Georgia cracker life, such as *Gabriel Tolliver: A Story of Reconstruction* (1902), pointed accurately toward the kind of realism into which Southern local color was to develop. Although Southern literature of high and universal seriousness has shaded Harris into a second rank, he remains important, not only for historical purposes, but also for his own real achievement in his given genre.

In addition to the works mentioned above, Harris wrote many books, including *Mingo and Other Sketches in Black and White* (1884); *Free Joe* (1887); *Daddy Jake the Runaway* (1889); *Balsam and His Friends* (1892); *On the Plantation* (1892); *Stories of Georgia* (1896); *Tales of the Home Folks in Peace and War* (1898); *Plantation Pageants* (1899); *On the Wing of Occasions* (1900); and *The Making of a Statesman* (1902).

Editions and accounts of the man and his work are to be found in W. M. Baskerville, *Southern Writers* (1902); H. A. Toulmin, *Social Historians* (1911); J. C. Harris, *The Life and*

Letters of Joel Chandler Harris (1918); R. L. Wiggins, *The Life of Joel Chandler Harris* (1918); F. L. Pattee, *The Development of the American Short Story* (1923); F. P. Gaines, *The Southern Plantation* (1924); J. C. Harris, ed., *Joel Chandler Harris, Editor and Essayist* (1931); A. H. Quinn, *American Fiction* (1936); P. H. Buck, *The Road to Reunion* (1937); T. H. English, "In Memory of Uncle Remus," *Southern Literary Messenger*, II (1940); A. F. Harlow, *Joel Chandler Harris* (1941); J. Stafford, "Patterns of Meaning in *Nights with Uncle Remus*," *American Literature*, XVIII (1946); L. Dauner, "Myth and Humor in the Uncle Remus Fables," *American Literature*, XX (1948); B. Wolfe, "Uncle Remus and the Malevolent Rabbit," *Commentary*, VIII (1949); S. B. Brookes, *Joel Chandler Harris, Folklorist* (1950); J. B. Hubbell, *The South in American Literature* (1954); H. F. Smith, "Joel Chandler Harris's Contributions to Scribner's *Monthly* and *Century Magazine*," *Georgia Historical Quarterly*, XLVII (1963); and D. A. Walton, "Joel Chandler Harris as Folklorist," *Keystone Folklore Quarterly*, XI (1966).

FROM

Nights with Uncle Remus

The Moon in the Mill-Pond

One night when the little boy made his usual visit to Uncle Remus, he found the old man sitting up in his chair fast asleep. The child said nothing. He was prepared to exercise a good deal of patience upon occasion, and the occasion was when he wanted to hear a story. But, in making himself comfortable, he aroused Uncle Remus from his nap.

"I let you know, honey," said the old man, adjusting his spectacles, and laughing rather sheepishly—"I let you know, honey, w'en I git's my head r'ar'd back dat away, en my eyeleds shot, en my mouf open, en my chin p'intin' at de rafters, den dey's some mighty quare gwines on in my min'. Dey is dat, des ez sho ez youer settin' dar. W'en I fus year you comin' down de paf," Uncle Remus continued, rubbing his beard thoughtfully, "I 'uz sorter fear'd you mought 'spicion dat I done gone off on my journeys fer ter see ole man Nod."

This was accompanied by a glance of inquiry, to which the little boy thought it best to respond.

"Well, Uncle Remus," he said, "I did think I heard you snoring when I came in."

"Now you see dat!" exclaimed Uncle Remus, in a tone of grieved astonishment; "you see dat! Man can't lean hisse'f 'pun his 'membunce, 'ceppin' dey's some un fer ter come high-primin' roun' en 'lowin' dat he done gone ter sleep. *Shoo!* W'en you stept in dat do' dar I 'uz right in 'mungs some mighty quare notions—mighty quare notions. Dey aint no two ways; ef I 'uz ter up en let on 'bout all de notions w'at I gits in 'mungs, folks 'ud hatter come en kyar me off ter de place whar dey puts 'stracted people.

"Atter I sop up my supper," Uncle Remus went on, "I tuck'n year some flutterments up dar 'mungs de rafters, en I look up, en dar wuz a Bat sailin' 'roun'. 'Roun'· en 'roun' en 'roun' she go—und' de rafters, 'bove de rafters —en ez she sail she make noise lak she grittin' 'er toofies. Now, w'at dat Bat atter, I be bless ef I kin tell you, but dar she wuz; 'roun' en 'roun', over en under. I ax 'er w'at do she want up dar, but she aint got no time fer ter tell; 'roun' en 'roun', en over en under. En bimeby, out she flip, en I boun' she grittin' 'er toofies en gwine 'roun' en 'roun' out dar, en dodgin' en flippin' des lak de elements wuz full er rafters en cobwebs.

"W'en she flip out I le'nt my head back, I did, en 'twa'nt no time 'fo' I git mix up wid my notions. Dat Bat wings so limber en 'er will so good dat she done done 'er day's work dar 'fo' you could 'er run ter de big house en back. De Bat put me in min' er folks," continued Uncle Remus, settling himself back in his chair, "en folks put me in min' er de creeturs."

Immediately the little boy was all attention.

"Dey wuz times," said the old man, with something like a sigh, "w'en de creeturs 'ud segashuate tergedder des like dey aint had no fallin' out. Dem wuz de times w'en ole Brer Rabbit 'ud 'ten' lak he gwine quit he 'havishness, en dey'd all go 'roun' des lak dey b'long ter de same fambly connexion.

"One time after dey bin gwine in cohoots dis away, Brer Rabbit 'gun ter feel his fat, he did, en dis make 'im git projecky terreckly. De mo' peace w'at dey had, de mo' wuss Brer Rabbit feel, twel bimeby he git restless in de min'. W'en de sun shine he'd go en lay off in de grass en kick at de gnats, en nibble at de mullen stalk en waller in de san'. One night atter supper, w'iles he 'uz romancin' 'roun', he run up wid ole Brer Tarrypin, en atter dey shuck han's dey sot down on de side er de road en run on 'bout ole times. Dey talk en dey talk, dey did, en bimeby Brer Rabbit say it done come ter dat pass whar he bleedz ter have some fun, en Brer Tarrypin 'low dat Brer Rabbit des de ve'y man he bin lookin fer.

" 'Well den,' sez Brer Rabbit, sezee, 'we'll des put Brer Fox, en Brer Wolf, en Brer B'ar on notice, en termorrer night we'll meet down by de mill-pon' en have a little fishin' frolic. I'll do de talkin',' sez Brer Rabbit, sezee, 'en you kin set back en say *yea*,' sezee.

"Brer Tarrypin laugh.

" 'Ef I aint dar,' sezee, 'den you may know de grasshopper done fly 'way wid me,' sezee.

" 'En you neenter bring no fiddle, n'er,' sez Brer Rabbit, sezee, 'kaze dey aint gwineter be no dancin' dar,' sezee.

"Wid dat," continued Uncle Remus, "Brer Rabbit put out fer home, en went ter bed, en Brer Tarrypin bruise 'roun' en make his way todes de place so he kin be dar 'gin de 'p'inted time.

"Nex' day Brer Rabbit sont wud ter de yuther creeturs, en dey all make great 'miration, kaze dey aint think 'bout dis deyse'f. Brer Fox, he 'low, he did, dat he gwine atter Miss Meadows en Miss Motts, en de yuther gals.

"Sho nuff, w'en de time come dey wuz all dar. Brer B'ar, he fotch a hook en line; Brer Wolf, he fotch a hook en line; Brer Fox, he fotch a dip-net, en Brer Tarrypin, not ter be outdone, he fotch de bait."

"What did Miss Meadows and Miss Motts bring?" the little boy asked.

Uncle Remus dropped his head slightly to one side, and looked over his spectacles at the little boy.

"Miss Meadows en Miss Motts," he continued, "dey tuck'n stan' way back fum de aidge er de pon' en squeal eve'y time Brer Tarrypin shuck de box er bait at um. Brer B'ar 'low he gwine ter fish fer mud-cats; Brer Wolf 'low he gwine ter fish fer horneyheads; Brer Fox 'low he gwine ter fish fer peerch fer de ladies; Brer Tarrypin 'low he gwine ter fish fer minners, en Brer Rabbit wink at Brer Tarrypin en 'low he gwine ter fish fer suckers.

"Dey all git ready, dey did, en Brer Rabbit march up ter de pon' en make fer ter th'ow he hook in de water, but des 'bout dat time hit seem lak he see sump'n. De t'er creeturs, dey stop en watch his motions. Brer Rabbit, he drap he pole, he did, en he stan' dar scratchin' he head en lookin' down in de water.

"De gals dey 'gun ter git oneasy w'en dey see dis, en Miss Meadows, she up en holler out, she did:

" 'Law, Brer Rabbit, w'at de name er goodness de marter in dar?'

"Brer Rabbit scratch he head en look in de water. Miss Motts, she hilt up 'er petticoats, she did, en 'low she monstus fear'd er snakes. Brer Rabbit keep on scratchin' en lookin'.

"Bimeby he fetch a long bref, he did, en he 'low:

" 'Ladies en gentermuns all, we des might ez well make tracks fum dish yer place, kaze dey aint no fishin' in dat pon' fer none er dish yer crowd.'

"Wid dat, Brer Tarrypin, he scramble up ter de aidge en look over, en he shake he head, en 'low:

" 'Tooby sho'—tooby sho'! Tut-tut-tut!' en den he crawl back, he did, en do lak he wukkin' he min'.

" 'Don't be skeert, ladies, kaze we er boun' ter take keer un you, let come w'at will, let go w'at mus',' sez Brer Rabbit, sezee. 'Accidents got ter happen unter we all, des same ez dey is unter yuther folks; en dey aint nuthin' much de marter, 'ceppin' dat de Moon done drap in de water. Ef you don't b'leeve me you kin look fer yo'se'f,' sezee.

"Wid dat dey all went ter de bank en lookt in; en, sho nuff, dar lay de Moon, a-swingin' an' a-swayin' at de bottom er de pon'."

The little boy laughed. He had often seen the reflection of the sky in shallow pools of water, and the startling depths that seemed to lie at his feet had caused him to draw back with a shudder.

"Brer Fox, he look in, he did, en he 'low, 'Well, well, well!' Brer Wolf, he look in, en he 'low, 'Mighty bad, mighty bad!' Brer B'ar, he look in, en he 'low, 'Tum, tum, tum!' De ladies dey look in, en Miss Meadows she squall out, 'Aint dat too much?' Brer Rabbit, he look in ag'in, en he up en 'low, he did:

" 'Ladies en gentermuns, you all kin hum en haw, but less'n we gits dat Moon out er de pon', dey aint no fish kin be ketch 'roun' yer dis night; en ef you'll ax Brer Tarrypin, he'll tell you de same.'

"Den dey ax how kin dey git de Moon out er dar, en Brer Tarrypin 'low dey better lef' dat wid Brer Rabbit.

Brer Rabbit he shot he eyes, he did, en make lak he wukkin he min'. Bimeby, he up'n 'low:

" 'De nighes' way out'n dish yer diffikil is fer ter sen' roun' yer too ole Mr. Mud-Turkle en borry his sane, en drag dar Moon up fum dar,' sezee.

" 'I 'clar' ter gracious I mighty glad you mention dat,' says Brer Tarrypin, sezee. 'Mr. Mud-Turkle is setch clos't kin ter me dat I calls 'im Unk Muck, en I lay ef you sen' dar atter dat sane you won't fine Unk Muck so mighty disaccomerdatin'.'

"Well," continued Uncle Remus, after one of his tantalizing pauses, "dey sont atter de sane, en wiles Brer Rabbit wuz gone, Brer Tarrypin, he 'low dat he done year tell time en time ag'in dat dem w'at fine de Moon in de water en fetch 'im out, lakwise dey ull fetch out a pot er money. Dis make Brer Fox, en Brer Wolf, en Brer B'ar feel mighty good, en day 'low, dey did, dat long ez Brer Rabbit been so good ez ter run atter de sane, dey ull do de sanein'.

"Time Brer Rabbit git back, he see how de lan' lay, en he make lak he wanter go in atter de Moon. He pull off he coat, en he 'uz fixin' fer ter shuck he wescut, but de yuther creeturs dey 'low dey wa'nt gwine ter let dryfoot man lak Brer Rabbit go in de water. So Brer Fox, he tuck holt er one staff er de sane, Brer Wolf he tuck holt er de yuther staff, en Brer B'ar he wade' long behime fer ter lif' de sane 'cross logs en snags.

"Dey make one haul—no Moon; n'er haul—no Moon; n'er haul—no Moon. Den bimeby dey git out furder fum de bank. Water run in Brer Fox year, he shake he head; water run in Brer Wolf year, he shake he head; water run in Brer B'ar year, he shake he head. En de fus news you know, w'iles dey wuz a-shakin', dey come to whar de bottom shelfed off. Brer Fox he step off en duck hisse'f; den Brer Wolf duck hisse'f; en Brer B'ar he make a splunge en duck hisse'f; en, bless gracious, dey kick en splatter twel it look lak dey 'uz gwine ter slosh all de water outer de mill pon'.

"W'en dey come out, de gals 'uz all a-snickerin' en agigglin', en dey well mought, 'kase go whar you would, dey wa'nt no wuss lookin' creeturs dan dem; en Brer Rabbit, he holler, sezee:

" 'I speck you all, gents, better go home en git some

dry duds, en n'er time we'll be in better luck, sezee. 'I hear talk dat de Moon'll bite at a hook ef you take fools fer baits, en I lay dat's de onliest way fer ter ketch 'er,' sezee.

"Brer Fox en Brer Wolf en Brer B'ar went drippin' off, en Brer Rabbit en Brer Tarrypin, dey went home wid de gals."

1881, 1883

Free Joe and the Rest of the World

The name of Free Joe strikes humorously upon the ear of memory. It is impossible to say why, for he was the humblest, the simplest, and the most serious of all God's living creatures, sadly lacking in all those elements that suggest the humorous. It is certain, moreover, that in 1850 the sober-minded citizens of the little Georgian village of Hillsborough were not inclined to take a humorous view of Free Joe, and neither his name nor his presence provoked a smile. He was a black atom, drifting hither and thither without an owner, blown about by all the winds of circumstance, and given over to shiftlessness.

The problems of one generation are the paradoxes of a succeeding one, particularly if war, or some such incident, intervenes to clarify the atmosphere and strengthen the understanding. Thus, in 1850, Free Joe represented not only a problem of large concern, but, in the watchful eyes of Hillsborough, he was the embodiment of that vague and mysterious danger that seemed to be forever lurking on the outskirts of slavery, ready to sound a shrill and ghostly signal in the impenetrable swamps, and steal forth under the midnight stars to murder, rapine, and pillage— a danger always threatening, and yet never assuming shape; intangible, and yet real; impossible, and yet not improbable. Across the serene and smiling front of safety, the pale outlines of the awful shadow of insurrection sometimes fell. With this invisible panorama as a background, it was natural that the figure of Free Joe, simple and humble as it was, should assume undue proportions. Go where he would, do what he might, he could not escape the finger of observation and the kindling eye of suspicion. His lightest words were noted, his slightest actions marked.

Under all the circumstances it was natural that his peculiar condition should reflect itself in his habits and manners. The slaves laughed loudly day by day, but Free Joe rarely laughed. The slaves sang at their work and danced at their frolics, but no one ever heard Free Joe sing or saw him dance. There was something painfully plaintive and appealing in his attitude, something touching in his anxiety to please. He was of the friendliest nature, and seemed to be delighted when he could amuse the little children who had made a playground of the public square. At times he would please them by making his little dog Dan perform all sorts of curious tricks, or he would tell them quaint stories of the beasts of the field and birds of the air; and frequently he was coaxed into relating the story of his own freedom. That story was brief, but tragical.

In the year of our Lord 1840, when a negro speculator of a sportive turn of mind reached the little village of Hillsborough on his way to the Mississippi region, with a caravan of likely negroes of both sexes, he found much to interest him. In that day and at that time there were a number of young men in the village who had not bound themselves over to repentance for the various misdeeds of the flesh. To these young men the negro speculator (Major Frampton was his name) proceeded to address himself. He was a Virginian, he declared; and, to prove the statement, he referred all the festively inclined young men of Hillsborough to a barrel of peach-brandy in one of his covered wagons. In the minds of these young men there was less doubt in regard to the age and quality of the brandy than there was in regard to the negro trader's birthplace. Major Frampton might or might not have been born in the Old Dominion—that was a matter for consideration and inquiry—but there could be no question as to the mellow pungency of the peach-brandy.

In his own estimation, Major Frampton was one of the most accomplished of men. He had summered at the Virginia Springs; he had been to Philadelphia, to Washington, to Richmond, to Lynchburg, and to Charleston, and had accumulated a great deal of experience which he found useful. Hillsborough was hid in the woods of Middle Georgia, and its general aspect of innocence impressed him. He looked on the young men who had shown their readiness to test his peach-brandy as overgrown country boys who needed to be introduced to some of the arts and sciences he had at his command. Thereupon the major pitched his tents, figuratively speaking, and became, for the time being, a part and parcel of the innocence that characterized Hillsborough. A wiser man would doubtless have made the same mistake.

The little village possessed advantages that seemed to be providentially arranged to fit the various enterprises that Major Frampton had in view. There was the auction block in front of the stuccoed court-house, if he desired to dispose of a few of his negroes; there was a quarter-track, laid out to his hand and in excellent order, if he chose to enjoy the pleasures of horse-racing; there were secluded pine thickets within easy reach, if he desired to indulge in the exciting pastime of cock-fighting; and variously lonely and unoccupied rooms in the second story of the tavern, if he cared to challenge the chances of dice or cards.

Major Frampton tried them all with varying luck, until he began his famous game of poker with Judge Alfred Wellington, a stately gentleman with a flowing white beard and mild blue eyes that gave him the appearance of a benevolent patriarch. The history of the game in which Major Frampton and Judge Alfred Wellington took part is something more than a tradition in Hillsborough, for there are still living three or four men who sat around the table and watched its progress. It is said that at various stages of the game Major Frampton would destroy the cards with which they were playing, and send for a new pack, but the result was always the same. The mild blue eyes of Judge Wellington, with few exceptions, continued to overlook "hands" that were invincible—a habit they had acquired during a long and arduous course of training from Sarotoga to New Orleans. Major Frampton lost his money, his horses, his wagons, and all his negroes but one, his body-servant. When his misfortune had reached this limit, the major adjourned the game. The sun was shining brightly, and all nature was cheerful. It is said that the major also seemed to be cheerful. However this may be, he visited the court-house, and executed the papers that gave his body-servant his freedom. This being done, Major Frampton sauntered into a convenient pine thicket, and blew out his brains.

The negro thus freed came to be known as Free Joe. Compelled, under the law, to choose a guardian, he chose Judge Wellington, chiefly because his wife Lucinda was among the negroes won from Major Frampton. For several years Free Joe had what may be called a jovial time. His wife Lucinda was well provided for, and he found it a comparatively easy matter to provide for himself; so that, taking all the circumstances into consideration, it is not matter for astonishment that he became somewhat shiftless.

When Judge Wellington died, Free Joe's troubles began. The judge's negroes, including Lucinda, went to his half-brother, a man named Calderwood, who was a hard master and a rough customer generally —a man of many eccentricities of mind and character. His neighbors had a habit of alluding to him as "Old Spite"; and the name seemed to fit him so completely that he was known far and near as "Spite" Calderwood. He probably enjoyed the distinction the name gave him, at any rate he never resented it, and it was not often that he missed an opportunity to show that he deserved it. Calderwood's place was two or three miles from the village of Hillsborough, and Free Joe visited his wife twice a week, Wednesday and Saturday nights.

One Sunday he was sitting in front of Lucinda's cabin, when Calderwood happened to pass that way.

"Howdy, marster?" said Free Joe, taking off his hat.

"Who are you?" exclaimed Calderwood abruptly, halting and staring at the negro.

"I'm name' Joe, marster. I'm Lucindy's ole man."

"Who do you belong to?"

"Marse John Evans is my gyardeen, marster."

"Big name—gyardeen. Show your pass."

Free Joe produced that document, and Calderwood read it aloud slowly, as if he found it difficult to get at the meaning:

"To whom it may concern: This is to certify that the boy Joe Frampton has my permission to visit his wife Lucinda."

This was dated at Hillsborough, and signed *"John W. Evans."*

Calderwood read it twice, and then looked at Free Joe, elevating his eyebrows, and showing his discolored teeth.

"Some mighty big words in that there. Evans owns this place, I reckon. When's he comin' down to take hold?"

Free Joe fumbled with his hat. He was badly frightened.

"Lucindy say she speck you wouldn't min' my comin', long ez I behave, marster."

Calderwood tore the pass in pieces and flung it away.

"Don't want no free niggers 'round here," he exclaimed. "There's the big road. It'll carry you to town. Don't let me catch you here no more. Now, mind what I tell you."

Free Joe presented a shabby spectacle as he moved off with his little dog Dan slinking at his heels. It should be said in behalf of Dan, however, that his bristles were up, and that he looked back and growled. It may be that the dog had the advantage of insignificance, but it is difficult to conceive how a dog bold enough to raise his bristles under Calderwood's very eyes could be as insignificant as Free Joe. But both the negro and his little dog seemed to give a new and more dismal aspect to forlornness as they turned into the road and went toward Hillsborough.

After this incident Free Joe appeared to have clearer ideas concerning his peculiar condition. He realized the fact that though he was free he was more helpless than any slave. Having no owner, every man was his master. He knew that he was the object of suspicion, and therefore all his slender resources (ah! how pitifully slender they were!) were devoted to winning, not kindness and appreciation, but toleration; all his efforts were in the direction of mitigating the circumstances that tended to make his condition so much worse than that of the negroes around him—negroes who had friends because they had masters.

So far as his own race was concerned, Free Joe was an exile. If the slaves secretly envied him his freedom (which is to be doubted, considering his miserable condition), they openly despised him, and lost no opportunity to treat him with contumely. Perhaps this was in some measure the result of the attitude which Free Joe chose to maintain toward them. No doubt his instinct taught him that to hold himself aloof from the slaves would be to invite from the whites the toleration which he coveted, and without which even his miserable condition would be rendered more miserable still.

His greatest trouble was the fact that he was not allowed to visit his wife; but he soon found a way out of his difficulty. After he had been ordered away from the Calderwood place, he was in the habit of wandering as far in that direction as prudence would permit. Near the Calderwood place, but not on Calderwood's land, lived an old man named Micajah Staley and his sister Becky Staley. These people were old and very poor. Old Micajah had a palsied arm and hand; but, in spite of this, he managed to earn a precarious living with his turning-lathe.

When he was a slave Free Joe would have scorned these representatives of a class known as poor white trash, but now he found them sympathetic and helpful in various ways. From the back door of their cabin he could hear the Calderwood negroes singing at night, and he sometimes fancied he could distinguish Lucinda's shrill treble rising above the other voices. A large poplar grew in the woods some distance from the Staley cabin, and at the foot of this tree Free Joe would sit for hours with his face turned toward Calderwood's. His little dog Dan would curl up in the leaves near by, and the two seemed to be as comfortable as possible.

One Saturday afternoon Free Joe, sitting at the foot of this friendly poplar, fell asleep. How long he slept, he could not tell; but when he awoke little Dan was licking his face, the moon was shining brightly, and Lucinda his wife stood before him laughing. The dog, seeing that Free Joe was asleep, had grown somewhat impatient, and he concluded to make an excursion to the Calderwood place on his own account. Lucinda was inclined to give the incident a twist in the direction of superstition.

"I 'uz settn' down front er de fireplace," she said, "cookin' me some meat, w'en all of a sudden I year sumpin at de do'—scratch, scratch. I tuck'n tu'n de meat over, en make out I ain't year it. Bimeby it come dar 'gin—scratch, scratch. I up en open de do', I did, en, bless de Lord! dar wuz little Dan, en it look like ter me dat his ribs done grow terge'er. I gin 'im some bread, en den, w'en he start out, I tuck'n foller 'im, kaze, I say ter myse'f, maybe my nigger man mought be some'rs 'roun'. Dat ar little dog got sense, mon."

Free Joe laughed and dropped his hand lightly on Dan's head. For a long time after that he had no difficulty in seeing his wife. He had only to sit by the poplar tree until little Dan could run and fetch her. But after a while the other negroes discovered that Lucinda was meeting Free Joe in the woods, and information of the fact soon reached Calderwood's ears. Calderwood was what is called a man of action. He said nothing; but one day he put Lucinda in his buggy, and carried her to Macon, sixty miles away. He carried her to Macon, and came back without her; and

nobody in or around Hillsborough, or in that section, ever
saw her again.

For many a night after that Free Joe sat in the woods
and waited. Little Dan would run merrily off and be gone
a long time, but he always came back without Lucinda.
This happened over and over again. The "willis-whistlers"
would call and call, like fantom huntsmen wandering on a
far-off shore; the screech-owl would shake and shiver in the
depths of the woods; the night-hawks, sweeping by on
noiseless wings, would snap their beaks as though they
enjoyed the huge joke of which Free Joe and little Dan
were the victims; and the whip-poor-wills would cry to
each other through the gloom. Each night seemed to be
lonelier than the preceding, but Free Joe's patience was
proof against loneliness. There came a time, however, when
little Dan refused to go after Lucinda. When Free Joe
motioned him in the direction of the Calderwood place, he
would simply move about uneasily and whine; then he
would curl up in the leaves and make himself comfortable.

One night, instead of going to the poplar tree to wait
for Lucinda, Free Joe went to the Staley cabin, and, in
order to make his welcome good, as he expressed it, he
carried with him an armful of fat-pine splinters. Miss
Becky Staley had a great reputation in those parts as a
fortune-teller, and the schoolgirls, as well as older people,
often tested her powers in this direction, some in jest and
some in earnest. Free Joe placed his humble offering of
light-wood in the chimney corner, and then seated himself
on the steps, dropping his hat on the ground outside.

"Miss Becky," he said presently, "whar in de name er
gracious you reckon Lucindy is?"

"Well, the Lord he'p the nigger!" exclaimed Miss Becky,
in a tone that seemed to reproduce, by some curious agreement of sight with sound, her general aspect of peakedness.
"Well, the Lord he'p the nigger! hain't you been a-seein'
her all this blessed time? She's over at old Spite Calderwood's, if she's anywheres, I reckon."

"No'm, dat I ain't, Miss Becky. I ain't seen Lucindy in
now gwine on mighty nigh a mont'."

"Well, it hain't a-gwine to hurt you," said Miss Becky,
somewhat sharply. "In my day an' time it wuz allers took
to be a bad sign when niggers got to honeyin' 'roun' an'
gwine on."

"Yessum," said Free Joe, cheerfully assenting to the proposition—"yessum, dat's so, but me an' my ole 'oman, we 'uz raise terge'er, en dey ain't bin many days w'en we 'uz' 'way fum one 'n'er like we is now."

"Maybe she's up an' took up wi' some un else," said Micajah Staley from the corner. "You know what the sayin' is: 'New master, new nigger.' "

"Dat's so, dat's de sayin', but tain't wid my ole 'oman like 'tis wid yuther niggers. Me en her wuz des natally raise up terge'er. Dey's lots likelier niggers dan w'at I is," said Free Joe, viewing his shabbiness with a critical eye, "but I knows Lucindy mos' good ez I does little Dan dar—dat I does."

There was no reply to this, and Free Joe continued:

"Miss Becky, I wish you please, ma'am, take en run yo' kyards en see sump'n n'er 'bout Lucindy; kaze ef she sick, I'm gwine dar. Dey ken take en take me up en gimme a stroppin', but I'm gwine dar."

Miss Becky got her cards, but first she picked up a cup, in the bottom of which were some coffee-grounds. These she whirled slowly round and round, ending finally by turning the cup upside down on the hearth and allowing it to remain in that position.

"I'll turn the cup first," said Miss Becky, "and then I'll run the cards and see what they say."

As she shuffled the cards the fire on the hearth burned low, and in its fitful light the gray-haired, thin-featured woman seemed to deserve the weird reputation which rumor and gossip had given her. She shuffled the cards for some moments, gazing intently in the dying fire; then, throwing a piece of pine on the coals, she made three divisions of the pack, disposing them about in her lap. Then she took the first pile, ran the cards slowly through her fingers, and studied them carefully. To the first she added the second pile. The study of these was evidently not satisfactory. She said nothing, but frowned heavily; and the frown deepened as she added the rest of the cards until the entire fifty-two had passed in review before her. Though she frowned, she seemed to be deeply interested. Without changing the relative position of the cards, she ran them all over again. Then she threw a larger piece of pine on the fire, shuffled the cards afresh, divided them into three piles, and subjected them to the same careful and critical examination.

"I can't tell the day when I've seed the cards run this a-way," she said after a while. "What is an' what ain't, I'll never tell you; but I know what the cards sez."

"W'at does dey say, Miss Becky?" the negro inquired, in a tone the solemnity of which was heightened by its eagerness.

"They er runnin' quare. These here that I'm a-lookin' at," said Miss Becky, "they stan' for the past. Them there, they er the present; and the t'others, they er the future. Here's a bundle"—tapping the ace of clubs with her thumb— "an' here's a journey as plain as the nose on a man's face. Here's Lucinda—"

"Whar she, Miss Becky?"

"Here she is—the queen of spades."

Free Joe grinned. The idea seemed to please him immensely.

"Well, well, well!" he exclaimed. "Ef dat don't beat my time! De queen er spades! W'en Lucindy year dat hit'll tickle 'er, sho'!"

Miss Becky continued to run the cards back and forth through her fingers.

"Here's a bundle an' a journey, and here's Lucinda. An' here's ole Spite Calderwood."

She held the cards toward the negro and touched the king of clubs.

"De Lord he'p my soul!" exclaimed Free Joe with a chuckle. "De faver's dar. Yesser, dat's him! W'at de matter 'long wid all un um, Miss Becky?"

The old woman added the second pile of cards to the first, and then the third, still running them through her fingers slowly and critically. By this time the piece of pine in the fireplace had wrapped itself in a mantle of flame, illuminating the cabin and throwing into strange relief the figure of Miss Becky as she sat studying the cards. She frowned ominously at the cards and mumbled a few words to herself. Then she dropped her hands in her lap and gazed once more into the fire. Her shadow danced and capered on the wall and floor behind her, as if, looking over her shoulder into the future, it could behold a rare spectacle. After a while she picked up the cup that had been turned on the hearth. The coffee grounds, shaken around, presented what seemed to be a most intricate map.

"Here's the journey," said Miss Becky, presently; "here's the big road, here's rivers to cross, here's the bundle to tote." She paused and sighed. "They hain't no names writ here, an' what it all means I'll never tell you. Cajy, I wish you'd be so good as to han' me my pipe."

"I hain't no hand wi' the kyards," said Cajy, as he handed the pipe, "but I reckon I can patch out your misinformation, Becky, bekaze the other day, whiles I was a-finishin' up Mizzers Perdue's rollin'-pin, I hearn a rattlin' in the road. I looked out, an' Spite Calderwood was a-drivin' by in his buggy, an' thar sot Lucinda by him. It'd in-about drapt out er my min'."

Free Joe sat on the door-sill and fumbled at his hat, flinging it from one hand to the other.

"You ain't see um gwine back, is you, Mars Cajy?" he asked after a while.

"Ef they went back by this road," said Mr. Staley, with the air of one who is accustomed to weigh well his words, "it must 'a' bin endurin' of the time whiles I was asleep, bekaze I hain't bin no furder from my shop than to yon bed."

"Well, sir!" exclaimed Free Joe in an awed tone, which Mr. Staley seemed to regard as a tribute to his extraordinary powers of statement.

"Ef it's my beliefs you want," continued the old man, "I'll pitch 'em at you fair and free. My beliefs is that Spite Calderwood is gone an' took Lucindy outen the county. Bless your heart and soul! when Spite Calderwood meets the Old Boy in the road they'll be a turrible scuffle. You mark what I tell you."

Free Joe, still fumbling with his hat, rose and leaned against the door-facing. He seemed to be embarrassed. Presently he said:

"I speck I better be gittin' 'long. Nex' time I see Lucindy, I'm gwine tell 'er w'at Miss Becky say 'bout de queen er spades—dat I is. Ef dat don't tickle 'er, dey ain't no nigger 'oman never bin tickle'."

He paused a moment, as though waiting for some remark or comment, some confirmation of misfortune, or, at the very least, some endorsement of his suggestion that Lucinda would be greatly pleased to know that she had figured as the queen of spades; but neither Miss Becky nor her brother said anything.

"One minnit ridin' in the buggy 'longside er Mars Spite, en de nex' highfalutin' 'roun' playin' de queen er spades.

Mon, deze yer nigger gals gittin' up in de pictur's; dey sholy
is."

With a brief "Good night, Miss Becky, Mars Cajy," Free
Joe went out into the darkness, followed by little Dan. He
made his way to the poplar, where Lucinda had been in
the habit of meeting him, and sat down. He sat there a
long time; he sat there until little Dan, growing restless,
trotted off in the direction of the Calderwood place. Dozing
against the poplar, in the gray dawn of the morning, Free
Joe heard Spite Calderwood's fox-hounds in full cry a mile
away.

"Shoo!" he exclaimed, scratching his head, and laughing to himself, "dem ar dogs is des a-warmin' dat old fox
up."

But it was Dan the hounds were after, and the little dog
came back no more. Free Joe waited and waited, until he
grew tired of waiting. He went back the next night and
waited, and for many nights thereafter. His waiting was in
vain, and yet he never regarded it as in vain. Careless and
shabby as he was, Free Joe was thoughtful enough to have
his theory. He was convinced that little Dan had found
Lucinda, and that some night when the moon was shining
brightly through the trees, the dog would rouse him from
his dreams as he sat sleeping at the foot of the poplar tree,
and he would open his eyes and behold Lucinda standing
over him, laughing merrily as of old; and then he thought
what fun they would have about the queen of spades.

How many long nights Free Joe waited at the foot of
the poplar tree for Lucinda and little Dan no one can ever
know. He kept no account of them, and they were not
recorded by Micajah Staley nor by Miss Becky. The season
ran into summer and then into fall. One night he went to
the Staley cabin, cut the two old people an armful of wood,
and seated himself on the doorsteps, where he rested. He
was always thankful—and proud, as it seemed—when
Miss Becky gave him a cup of coffee, which she was sometimes thoughtful enough to do. He was especially thankful
on this particular night.

"You er still layin' off for to strike up wi' Lucindy out
thar in the woods, I reckon," said Micajah Staley, smiling
grimly. The situation was not without its humorous aspects.

"Oh, dey er comin', Mars Cajy, dey er comin', sho," Free
Joe replied. "I boun' you dey'll come; en w'en dey does

come, I'll des take en fetch um yer, whar you kin see um wid you own eyes, you en Miss Becky."

"No," said Mr. Staley, with a quick and emphatic gesture of disapproval. "Don't! don't fetch 'em anywheres. Stay right wi' 'em as long as may be."

Free Joe chuckled, and slipped away into the night, while the two old people sat gazing in the fire. Finally Micajah spoke.

"Look at that nigger; look at 'im. He's pine-blank as happy now as a killdee by a mill-race. You can't faze 'em. I'd in-about give up my t'other hand ef I could stan' flat-footed, an' grin at trouble like that there nigger."

"Niggers is niggers," said Miss Becky, smiling grimly, "an' you can't rub it out; yit I lay I've seed a heap of white people lots meaner'n Free Joe. He grins—an' that's nigger —but I've ketched his under jaw a-tremblin' when Lucindy's name uz brung up. An' I tell you," she went on, bridling up a little, and speaking with almost fierce emphasis, "the Old Boy's done sharpened his claws for Spite Calderwood. You'll see it."

"Me, Rebecca?" said Mr. Staley, hugging his palsied arm; "me? I hope not."

"Well, you'll know it then," said Miss Becky, laughing heartily at her brother's look of alarm.

The next morning Micajah Staley had occasion to go into the woods after a piece of timber. He saw Free Joe sitting at the foot of the poplar, and the sight vexed him somewhat.

"Git up from there," he cried, "an' go an' arn your livin'. A mighty purty pass it's come to, when great big buck niggers can lie a-snorin' in the woods all day, when t'other folks is got to be up an' a-gwine. Git up from there!"

Receiving no response, Mr. Staley went to Free Joe, and shook him by the shoulder; but the negro made no response. He was dead. His hat was off, his head was bent, and a smile was on his face. It was as if he had bowed and smiled when death stood before him, humble to the last. His clothes were ragged; his hands were rough and callous; his shoes were literally tied together with strings; he was shabby in the extreme. A passer-by, glancing at him, could have no idea that such a humble creature had been summoned as a witness before the Lord God of Hosts.

1887

BRET HARTE

(1836–1902)

Albany-born Bret Harte came from a family in which nothing seemed certain, one whose instability and social pretensions led to a constant search for identity, foreshadowing careers of writers such as F. Scott Fitzgerald. The paternal grandfather, Bernard Hart, was a man of substantial position. He married Catherine Brett, and the couple separated after the birth of Henry, Bret's father. Nine years after Bret Harte's birth, Henry died, leaving a family with a haunting sense of social belonging that family relationships and financial circumstances did not warrant. The young Harte lived with his mother in Brooklyn and Manhattan and then, with his sister, followed his mother and older brother out to California in 1854.

As a Wells Fargo messenger, a drugstore clerk, and possibly a miner, the semiaristocratic Harte was roundly exposed to the frontier life of California and the mining-camp territory, where he made his luckiest strike in the lode of literary materials that was to brighten his life into a brief nova of American fame and fortune. Driven out of Union, California, where, as a newspaperman on the *Northern Californian* he aroused the vigilantes' wrath by his denunciation of a massacre of Indians, he wandered on to San Francisco in 1860. Working for the *Golden Era*, he began to exploit the romantic stories of Spanish California. This early work in its own way was indicative of the causes of both fame and failure in Harte's writings. He tended to sentimentalize in a theatrical way the romantic aspects of the legends he dealt with; though his handling led to quick popularity with a novelty-seeking public, it failed to grapple with the deep roots of American identity in the national vision of the West.

While editing the *Californian* he had begun to build a local reputation and to sharpen his literary skills; he was even able to obtain regular contributions from Mark Twain. In 1868, as editor of the new and influential *Overland Monthly*, he tried to establish what he saw as "a peculiarly characteristic Western American literature." Failing to discover appropriate contributions, he wrote, by way of illustration of what he sought, "The Luck of Roaring Camp" and included it in the August issue. When it made its way East, the story became an immediate sensation. It gave to the beginnings of local-color writing a drive and intensification that led some critics erroneously to see Harte as the father of American regional writing. But it did establish the West as a theme that is still popular today, as current television programs indicate. Moreover, "The Luck's" new "realism," which reversed the formula characterization of the "good guys" and the "bad guys," and which dared to picture motherhood in terms other than those demanded by the fetishes of gentility, had a tremendous impact on the American short story and its conventions. Although Harte never did become the authentic voice of the West that he thought he was, his influence on American writing is considerable.

In 1869 the *Overland* published "The Outcasts of Poker Flat" (another immediate sensation in the East); with its sentimentalized picture (now a cliché) of noble gamblers and warmhearted prostitutes, the story completed the materials begun in "The Luck." When in 1870 Harte published "Plain Language from Truthful James" (in the *Overland*) and *The Luck of Roaring Camp and Other Sketches,* he was catapulted into a frenzy of national fame, being hailed on all sides as a foremost literary genius. He turned down a professorship at the new University of California, turned down Chicago's bid for his literary residence, and made a triumphal cross-country tour to Boston, where he consented to become the most gleefully publicized property of the *Atlantic Monthly*. However, like many "Westerners" who exploited their region only as a passport to acceptance by the East, he could merely repeat himself in his stories. The *Atlantic* paid him an advance of $10,000 for any twelve items he would write in 1871, and was disappointed in all of them. Once he had combined the sketch-by-Irving with the characterization-by-Dickens in order to create a West he had never understood, he had nothing new to offer. Not even collaboration with Mark Twain in playwrighting (*Ah Sin,* in

1877) could rejuvenate him, and as suddenly as they had come, fame, fortune, and invention deserted him.

He was saved by an appointment, in 1878, as United States Commercial Agent in Prussia. In 1880 he was appointed United States Consul in Glasgow; five years later he lost his position, but stayed abroad, where he still had some of the fame and marketplace that his stories had once enjoyed at home. He remained in England, rewriting his once successful stories under new titles, in order to support his family, which had stayed in the United States to enjoy the earnings he regularly sent them. After twenty-four years abroad, during which he had never once returned home, he died in England of throat cancer.

Some of Harte's many books are *The Lost Galleon and other Tales* (1867); *Condensed Novels* (1867); *East and West Poems* (1871); *Stories of the Sierras* (1872); *The Little Drummer* (1872); *Mrs. Skaggs's Husbands* (1873); *Tales of the Argonauts* (1875); *Echoes of the Foot-Hills* (1875); *Gabriel Conroy* (1876); *Maruja* (1885); *A Millionaire of Rough-and-Ready* (1887); *A Sappho of Green Springs* (1891); *Colonel Stabottle's Client* (1892); *Susy: A Story of the Plains* (1893); *A Protégée of Jack Hamlin's* (1894); *The Bell-Ringer of Angel's* (1894); *Three Partners* (1897); *Mr. Jack Hamlin's Meditation* (1899); *Condensed Novels: Second Series* (1902); and *The Story of Enriquez* (1924).

Editions and accounts of the man and his works are to be found in B. Harte, ed., *The Complete Works of Bret Harte,* 10 vols. (1880—1912); *The Writings of Bret Harte,* Standard Library Edition, 19 vols. (1896—1914); *The Writings of Bret Harte,* The Overland Edition and the Riverside Edition, adding a supplement to the Standard Library, 20 vols. (1896—1914); H. W. Boynton, *Bret Harte* (1903); T. E. Pemberton, *Life of Bret Harte* (1903); H. C. Merwin, *Life of Bret Harte* (1911); C. M. Kozlay, ed., *The Lectures of Bret Harte* (1909); J. Erskine, *Leading American Novelists* (1910); T. D. Beasley, *A Tramp through the Bret Harte Country* (1914); C. M. Kozlay, ed., *Stories and Poems and Other Uncollected Writings by Bret Harte* (1914); *The Works of Bret Harte, the Argonaut Edition,* 25 vols. (1914); F. L. Pattee, *A History of American Literature Since 1870* (1915); G. B. Harte, ed., *The Letters of Bret Harte* (1926); G. R. Stewart, Jr., *Bret Harte, Argonaut and Exile* (1931); G. R. Stewart, Jr., ed., "A Bibliography of the Writings of Bret Harte in the Magazines of California, 1857—1871," *University of California Publications in English,* III (1933); J. Gaer, ed., *Bret Harte: Bibliographical and Biographical Data* (1935); A. H. Quinn, *American Fiction* (1936); F. Walker, *San Francisco's Literary Frontier* (1939); J. B. Harrison, ed., *Bret Harte* (1941); O. Lewis, ed., *Tales of the Gold Rush* (1944); M. Duckett, "Bret Harte's Portrayal of Half-Breeds," *American Literature,* XXV (1953); M. Duckett,

"Plain Language from Bret Harte," *Nineteenth-Century Fiction,* XI (1957); D. S. Brady, "A New Look at Bret Harte and *The Overland Monthly,*" *Dissertation Abstracts,* XXII (1962); M. Duckett, *Mark Twain and Bret Harte* (1964); and R. O'Connor, *Bret Harte, A Biography* (1966).

The Luck of Roaring Camp

There was commotion in Roaring Camp. It could not have been a fight, for in 1850 that was not novel enough to have called together the entire settlement. The ditches and claims were not only deserted, but "Tuttle's grocery" had contributed its gamblers, who, it will be remembered, calmly continued their game the day that French Pete and Kanaka Joe shot each other to death over the bar in the front room. The whole camp was collected before a rude cabin on the outer edge of the clearing. Conversation was carried on in a low tone, but the name of a woman was frequently repeated. It was a name familiar enough in the camp,—"Cherokee Sal."

Perhaps the less said of her the better. She was a coarse, and it is to be feared, a very sinful woman. But at that time she was the only woman in Roaring Camp, and was just then lying in sore extremity, when she most needed the ministration of her own sex. Dissolute, abandoned, and irreclaimable, she was yet suffering a martyrdom hard enough to bear even when veiled by sympathizing womanhood, but now terrible in her loneliness. The primal curse had come to her in that original isolation which must have made the punishment of the first transgression so dreadful. It was, perhaps, part of the expiation of her sin, that, at a moment when she most lacked her sex's intuitive tenderness and care, she met only the half-contemptuous faces of her masculine associates. Yet a few of the spectators were, I think, touched by her sufferings. Sandy Tipton thought it was "rough on Sal," and, in the contemplation of her condition, for a moment rose superior to the fact that he had an ace and two bowers in his sleeve.

It will be seen, also, that the situation was novel. Deaths were by no means uncommon in Roaring Camp, but a birth was a new thing. People had been dismissed from the camp effectively, finally, and with no possibility of return; but this was the first time that anybody had been introduced *ab initio*. Hence the excitement.

"You go in there, Stumpy," said a prominent citizen known as "Kentuck," addressing one of the loungers. "Go in there, and see what you kin do. You've had experience in them things."

Perhaps there was a fitness in the selection. Stumpy, in other climes, had been the putative head of two families; in fact, it was owing to some legal informality in these proceedings that Roaring Camp—a city of refuge—was indebted to his company. The crowd approved the choice, and Stumpy was wise enough to bow to the majority. The door closed upon the extemporc surgeon and midwife, and Roaring Camp sat down outside, smoked its pipe, and awaited the issue.

The assemblage numbered about a hundred men. One or two of these were actual fugitives from justice, some were criminal, and all were reckless. Physically, they exhibited no indication of their past lives and character. The greatest scamp had a Raphael face, with a profusion of blond hair; Oakhurst, a gambler, had the melancholy air and intellectual abstraction of a Hamlet; the coolest and most courageous man was scarcely over five feet in height, with a soft voice and an embarrassed, timid manner. The term "roughs" applied to them was a distinction rather than a definition. Perhaps in the minor details of fingers, toes, ears, etc., the camp may have been deficient, but these slight omissions did not detract from their aggregate force. The strongest man had but three fingers on his right hand; the best shot had but one eye.

Such was the physical aspect of the men that were dispersed around the cabin. The camp lay in a triangular valley, between two hills and a river. The only outlet was a steep trail over the summit of a hill that faced the cabin, now illuminated by the rising moon. The suffering woman might have seen it from the rude bunk whereon she lay,—seen it winding like a silver thread until it was lost in the stars above.

A fire of withered pine boughs added sociability to the gathering. By degrees the natural levity of Roaring Camp returned. Bets were freely offered and taken regarding the result. Three to five that "Sal would get through with it"; even, that the child would survive; side bets as to the sex and complexion of the coming stranger. In the midst of an excited discussion an exclamation came from those nearest the door, and the camp stopped to listen. Above the swaying and moaning of the pines, the swift rush of the river, and the crackling of the fire rose a sharp, querulous cry—a cry unlike anything heard before in the camp. The pines stopped moaning, the river ceased to rush, and the fire to crackle. It seemed as if Nature had stopped to listen too.

The camp rose to its feet as one man! It was proposed to explode a barrel of gun-powder, but, in consideration of the situation of the mother, better counsels prevailed, and only a few revolvers were discharged; for, whether owing to the rude surgery of the camp, or some other reason, Cherokee Sal was sinking fast. Within an hour she had climbed, as it were, that rugged road that led to the stars, and so passed out of Roaring Camp, its sin and shame forever. I do not think that the announcement disturbed them much, except in speculation as to the fate of the child. "Can he live now?" was asked of Stumpy. The answer was doubtful. The only other being of Cherokee Sal's sex and maternal condition in the settlement was an ass. There was some conjecture as to fitness, but the experiment was tried. It was less problematical than the ancient treatment of Romulus and Remus, and apparently as successful.

When these details were completed, which exhausted another hour, the door was opened, and the anxious crowd, who had already formed themselves into a queue, entered in single file. Beside the low bunk or shelf, on which the figure of the mother was starkly outlined below the blankets, stood a pine table. On this a candle-box was placed, and within it, swathed in staring red flannel, lay the last arrival at Roaring Camp. Beside the candle-box was placed a hat. Its use was soon indicated. "Gentlemen," said Stumpy, with a singular mixture of authority and *ex officio* complacency —"Gentlemen will please pass in at the front door, round the table, and out at the back door. Them as wishes to contribute anything toward the orphan will find a hat handy." The first man entered with his hat on; he uncovered, however, as he looked about him, and so, unconsciously, set an example to the next. In such communities good and bad actions are catching. As the procession filed in, comments were audible,—criticisms addressed, perhaps, rather to Stumpy, in the character of showman,—"Is that him?" "Mighty small specimen"; "Hasn't more'n got the color"; "Ain't bigger nor a derringer." The contributions were as characteristic: A silver tobacco box; a doubloon; a navy revolver, silver mounted; a gold specimen; a very beautifully embroidered lady's handkerchief (from Oakhurst the gambler); a diamond breastpin, a diamond ring (suggested by the pin, with the remark from the giver that he "saw that pin and went two diamonds better"); a slung shot; a Bible (contributor not detected); a golden spur; a silver teaspoon (the initials, I regret to say, were not the giver's); a pair of surgeon's shears; a lancet; a Bank of England note for £5; and about $200 in loose gold and silver coin. During these proceedings Stumpy maintained a silence as impassive as the dead on his left—a gravity as inscrutable as that of the newly-born on his right. Only one incident occurred to break the monotony of the curious procession. As Kentuck bent over the candle-box half curiously, the child turned, and, in a spasm of pain. caught at his groping finger, and held it fast for a moment. Kentuck looked foolish and embarrassed. Something like a blush tried to assert itself in his weather-bcaten cheek. "The d—d little cuss!" he said, as he extricated his finger, with, perhaps, more tenderness and care than he might have been deemed capable of showing. He held that finger a little apart from its fellows as he went out, and examined it curiously. The examination provoked the same original remark in regard to the child. In fact, he seemed to enjoy repeating it. "He rastled with my finger," he remarked to Tipton, holding up the member, "the d—d little cuss!"

It was four o'clock before the camp sought repose. A light burnt in the cabin where the watchers sat, for Stumpy did not go to bed that night. Nor did Kentuck. He drank quite freely and related with great gusto his experience, invariably ending with his characteristic condemnation of the newcomer. It seemed to relieve him of any unjust implication of sentiment, and Kentuck had the weaknesses of the nobler sex. When everybody else had gone to bed, he walked down to the river, and whistled reflectingly. Then he walked up the gulch, past the cabin, still whistling with demonstrative unconcern. At a large redwood tree he paused and retraced his steps, and again passed the cabin. Halfway down to the river's bank he again paused, and then returned and knocked at the door. It was opened by

Stumpy. "How goes it?" said Kentuck, looking past Stumpy toward the candle-box. "All serene," replied Stumpy. "Anything up?" "Nothing." There was a pause—an embarrassing one—Stumpy still holding the door. Then Kentuck had recourse to his finger, which he held up to Stumpy. "Rastled with it,—the d—d little cuss," he said, and retired.

The next day Cherokee Sal had such rude sepulture as Roaring Camp afforded. After her body had been committed to the hillside, there was a formal meeting of the camp to discuss what should be done with her infant. A resolution to adopt it was unanimous and enthusiastic. But an animated discussion in regard to the manner and feasibility of providing for its wants at once sprung up. It was remarkable that the argument partook of none of those fierce personalities with which discussions were usually conducted at Roaring Camp. Tipton proposed that they should send the child to Red Dog—a distance of forty miles —where female attention could be procured. But the unlucky suggestion met with fierce and unanimous opposition. It was evident that no plan which entailed parting from their new acquisition would for a moment be entertained. "Besides," said Tom Ryder, "them fellows at Red Dog would swap it, and ring in somebody else on us." A disbelief in the honesty of other camps prevailed at Roaring Camp as in other places.

The introduction of a female nurse in the camp also met with objection. It was argued that no decent woman could be prevailed to accept Roaring Camp as her home, and the speaker urged that "they didn't want any more of the other kind." This unkind allusion to the defunct mother, harsh as it may seem, was the first spasm of propriety—the first symptom of the camp's regeneration. Stumpy advanced nothing. Perhaps he felt a certain delicacy in interfering with the selection of a possible successor in office. But when questioned, he averred stoutly that he and "Jinny"—the mammal before alluded to—could manage to rear the child. There was something original, independent, and heroic about the plan that pleased the camp. Stumpy was retained. Certain articles were sent for to Sacramento. "Mind," said the treasurer, as he pressed a bag of gold-dust into the expressman's hand, "the best that can be got— lace, you know, and filigree-work and frills,—d—n the cost!"

Strange to say, the child thrived. Perhaps the invigorating climate of the mountain camp was compensation for material deficiencies. Nature took the foundling to her broader breast. In that rare atmosphere of the Sierra foothills—that air pungent with balsamic odor, that ethereal cordial, at once bracing and exhilarating, he may have found food and nourishment, or a subtle chemistry that transmuted asses' milk to lime and phosphorus. Stumpy inclined to the belief that it was the latter and good nursing. "Me and that ass," he would say, "has been father and mother to him! Don't you," he would add, apostrophizing the helpless bundle before him, "never go back on us."

By the time he was a month old, the necessity of giving him a name became apparent. He had generally been known as "the Kid," "Stumpy's boy," "the Cayote" (an allusion to his vocal powers) and even by Kentuck's endearing diminutive of "the d—d little cuss." But these were felt to be vague and unsatisfactory, and were at last dismissed under another influence. Gamblers and adventurers are generally superstitious, and Oakhurst one day declared that the baby had brought "the luck" to Roaring Camp. It was certain that of late they had been successful. "Luck" was the name agreed upon, with the prefix of Tommy for greater convenience. No allusion was made to the mother, and the father was unknown. "It's better," said the philosophical Oakhurst, "to take a fresh deal all round. Call him Luck, and start him fair." A day was accordingly set apart for the christening. What was meant by this ceremony the reader may imagine, who has already gathered some idea of the reckless irreverence of Roaring Camp. The master of ceremonies was one "Boston," a noted wag, and the occasion seemed to promise the greatest facetiousness. This ingenious satirist had spent two days in preparing a burlesque of the church service, with pointed local allusions. The choir was properly trained, and Sandy Tipton was to stand godfather. But after the procession had marched to the grove with music and banners, and the child had been deposited before a mock altar, Stumpy stepped before the expectant crowd. "It ain't my style to spoil fun, boys," said the little man, stoutly, eyeing the faces around him, "but it strikes me that this thing ain't exactly on the squar. It's playing it pretty low down on this yer baby to ring in fun on him that he ain't goin' to understand. And ef there's going to be any god-fathers round, I'd like to see who's got any better rights than me." A silence followed Stumpy's speech. To the credit of all humorists be it said that the first man to acknowledge its justice was the satirist, thus stopped of his fun. "But," said Stumpy, quickly, following up his advantage, "we're here for a christening, and we'll have it. I proclaim you Thomas Luck, according to the laws of the United States and the State of California, so help me God." It was the first time that the name of the Deity had been uttered otherwise but profanely in the camp. The form of christening was perhaps even more ludicrous than the satirist had conceived; but strangely enough, nobody saw it and nobody laughed. "Tommy" was christened as seriously as he would have been under a Christian roof, and cried and was comforted in as orthodox fashion.

And so the work of regeneration began in Roaring Camp. Almost imperceptibly a change came over the settlement. The cabin assigned to "Tommy Luck"—or "The Luck," as he was more frequently called—first showed signs of improvement. It was kept scrupulously clean and whitewashed. Then it was boarded, clothed and papered. The rosewood cradle—packed eighty miles by mule—had, in Stumpy's way of putting it, "sorter killed the rest of the furniture." So the rehabilitation of the cabin became a necessity. The men who were in the habit of lounging in at Stumpy's to see "how The Luck got on" seemed to appreciate the change, and, in self-defense, the rival establishment of "Tuttle's grocery" bestirred itself, and imported a carpet and mirrors. The reflections of the latter on the appearance of Roaring Camp tended to produce stricter habits of personal cleanliness. Again Stumpy imposed a kind of quarantine upon those who aspired to the honor and privilege of holding "The Luck." It was a cruel mortification to Kentuck—who, in the carelessness of a large nature and the habits of frontier life, had begun to regard all garments as a second cuticle, which, like a snake's, only sloughed off through decay—to be debarred this privilege from certain prudential reasons. Yet such was the subtle influence of innovation that he thereafter appeared regularly every afternoon in a clean shirt, and face still shining from his ablutions. Nor were moral and social sanitary laws neglected. "Tommy," who was supposed to spend his whole existence in a persistent attempt to repose, must not be disturbed by noise. The shouting and yelling which had gained the camp its infelicitous title were not permitted within hearing distance of Stumpy's. The men conversed in whispers, or smoked with Indian gravity. Profanity was tacitly given up in these sacred precincts, and throughout the camp a popular form of expletive, known as "D—n the luck!" and "Curse the luck!" was abandoned, as having a new personal bearing. Vocal music was not interdicted, being supposed to have a soothing, tranquilizing quality, and one song, sung by "Man-o'-War Jack," an English sailor from Her Majesty's Australian colonies, was quite popular as a lullaby. It was a lugubrious recital of the exploits of "the *Arethusa*, Seventy-four," in a muffled minor, ending with a prolonged dying fall at the burden of each verse, "On b-o-o-o-ard of the *Arethusa*." It was a fine sight to see Jack holding The Luck, rocking from side to side as if with the motion of a ship, and crooning forth this naval ditty. Either through the peculiar rocking of Jack or the length of his song—it contained ninety stanzas, and was continued with conscientious deliberation to the bitter end —the lullaby generally had the desired effect. At such times the men would lie at full length under the trees, in the soft summer twilight, smoking their pipes and drinking in the melodious utterances. An indistinct idea that this was pastoral happiness pervaded the camp. "This 'ere kind o' think," said the Cockney Simmons, meditatively reclining on his elbow, "is 'evingly." It reminded him of Greenwich.

On the long summer days The Luck was usually carried to the gulch, from whence the golden store of Roaring Camp was taken. There, on a blanket spread over pine boughs, he would lie while the men were working in the ditches below. Latterly, there was a rude attempt to decorate this bower with flowers and sweet-smelling shrubs, and generally some one would bring him a cluster of wild honey-suckles, azaleas, or the painted blossoms of Las Mariposas. The men had suddenly awakened to the fact that there were beauty and significance in these trifles, which they had so long trodden carelessly beneath their feet. A flake of glittering mica, a fragment of variegated quartz, a bright pebble from the bed of the creek, became beautiful to eyes thus cleared and strengthened, and were invariably put aside for "The Luck." It was wonderful how many treasures the woods and hillsides yielded that "would do for Tommy." Surrounded by playthings such as never child out of fairyland had before, it is to be hoped that Tommy was content. He appeared to be serenely happy, albeit there was an infantine gravity about him, a contemplative light in his round gray eyes, that sometimes worried Stumpy. He was always tractable and quiet, and it is recorded that once, having crept beyond his "corral"—a hedge of tessellated pine boughs, which surrounded his bed —he dropped over the bank on his head in the soft earth, and remained with his mottled legs in the air in that position for at least five minutes with unflinching gravity. He was extricated without a murmur. I hesitate to record the many other instances of his sagacity, which rest, unfortunately, upon the statements of prejudiced friends. Some of them were not without a tinge of superstition. "I crep' up the bank just now," said Kentuck one day, in a breathless state of excitement, "and dern my skin if he wasn't a talking to a jaybird as was a-sittin on his lap. There they was, just as free and sociable as anything you please, a-jawin at each other just like two cherrybums." Howbeit, whether creeping over the pine boughs or lying lazily on his back, blinking at the leaves above him, to him the birds sang, the squirrels chattered, and the flowers bloomed. Nature was his nurse and playfellow. For him she would let slip between the leaves golden shafts of sunlight that fell just within his grasp; she would send wandering breezes to visit him with the balm of bay and resinous gums; to him the tall redwoods nodded familiarly and sleepily, the bumblebees buzzed, and the rooks cawed a slumbrous accompaniment.

Such was the golden summer of Roaring Camp. They were "flush times"—and the Luck was with them. The claims had yielded enormously. The camp was jealous of its privileges and looked suspiciously on strangers. No encouragement was given to immigration, and, to make their seclusion more perfect, the land on either side of the mountain wall that surrounded the camp they duly pre-empted. This, and a reputation for singular proficiency with the revolver, kept the reserve of Roaring Camp inviolate. The expressman—their only connecting link with the surrounding world—sometimes told wonderful stories of the camp. He would say, "They've a street up there in 'Roaring,' that would lay over any street up there in Red Dog. They've got vines and flowers round their houses, and they wash themselves twice a day. But they're mighty rough on strangers, and they worship an Ingin baby."

With the prosperity of the camp came a desire for further improvement. It was proposed to build a hotel in the following spring, and to invite one or two decent families to reside there for the sake of "The Luck," who might perhaps profit by female companionship. The sacrifice that this concession to the sex cost these men, who were fiercely skeptical in regard to its general virtue and usefulness, can only be accounted for by their affection for Tommy. A few still held out. But the resolve could not be carried into effect for three months, and the minority meekly yielded in the hope that something might turn up to prevent it. And it did.

The winter of '51 will long be remembered in the foothills. The snow lay deep on the sierras, and every mountain creek became a river, and every river a lake. Each gorge and gulch was transformed into a tumultuous watercourse that descended the hillsides, tearing down giant trees and scattering its drift and debris along the plain. Red Dog had been twice under water, and Roaring Camp had been forewarned. "Water put the gold into them gulches," said Stumpy; "it's been here once and will be here again!" And that night the North Fork suddenly leaped over its banks, and swept up the triangular valley of Roaring Camp.

In the confusion of rushing water, crashing trees, and crackling timber, and the darkness which seemed to flow with the water and blot out the fair valley, but little could be done to collect the scattered camp. When the morning broke, the cabin of Stumpy nearest the river-bank was gone. Higher up the gulch they found the body of its unlucky owner; but the pride—the hope—the joy—the Luck —of Roaring Camp had disappeared. They were returning with sad hearts, when a shout from the bank recalled them.

It was a relief-boat from down the river. They had picked up, they said, a man and an infant, nearly exhausted, about two miles below. Did anybody know them, and did they belong here?

It needed but a glance to show them Kentuck lying there, cruelly crushed and bruised, but still holding The Luck of Roaring Camp in his arms. As they bent over the strangely assorted pair, they saw that the child was cold and pulseless. "He is dead," said one. Kentuck opened his eyes. "Dead?" he repeated feebly. "Yes, my man, and you are dying too." A smile lit the eyes of the expiring Kentuck. "Dying!" he repeated, "he's a-taking me with him—tell the boys I've got the Luck with me now"; and the strong man, clinging to the frail babe as a drowning man is said to cling to a straw, drifted away into the shadowy river that flows forever to the unknown sea.

1868

FROM

Condensed Novels

Muck-a-Muck

A MODERN INDIAN NOVEL

After Cooper

Chapter I

It was toward the close of a bright October day. The last rays of the setting sun were reflected from one of those sylvan lakes peculiar to the Sierras of California. On the right the curling smoke of an Indian village rose between the columns of the lofty pines, while to the left the log cottage of Judge Tompkins, embowered in buckeyes, completed the enchanting picture.

Although the exterior of the cottage was humble and unpretentious, and in keeping with the wildness of the landscape, its interior gave evidence of the cultivation and refinement of its inmates. An aquarium, containing goldfishes, stood on a marble center-table at one end of the apartment, while a magnificent grand piano occupied the other. The floor was covered with a yielding tapestry carpet, and the walls were adorned with paintings from the pencils of Van Dyck, Rubens, Tintoretto, Michelangelo, and the productions of the more modern Turner, Kensett, Church, and Bierstadt. Although Judge Tompkins had chosen the frontiers of civilization as his home, it was impossible for him to entirely forego the habits and tastes of his former life. He was seated in a luxurious armchair, writing at a mahogany *écritoire,* while his daughter, a lovely young girl of seventeen summers, plied her crochet-needle on an ottoman beside him. A bright fire of pine logs flickered and flamed on the ample hearth.

Genevra Octavia Tompkins was Judge Tompkins's only child. Her mother had long since died on the Plains. Reared in affluence, no pains had been spared with the daughter's education. She was a graduate of one of the principal seminaries, and spoke French with a perfect Benicia accent. Peerlessly beautiful, she was dressed in a white *moiré antique* robe trimmed with *tulle.* That simple rosebud, with which most heroines exclusively decorate their hair, was all she wore in her raven locks.

The Judge was the first to break the silence.

"Genevra, the logs which compose yonder fire seem to have been incautiously chosen. The sibilation produced by the sap, which exudes copiously therefrom, is not conducive to composition."

"True, father, but I thought it would be preferable to the constant crepitation which is apt to attend the combustion of more seasoned ligneous fragments."

The Judge looked admiringly at the intellectual features of the graceful girl, and half forgot the slight annoyances of the green wood in the musical accents of his daughter. He was smoothing her hair tenderly, when the shadow of a tall figure, which suddenly darkened the doorway, caused him to look up.

Chapter II

It needed but a glance at the newcomer to detect at once the form and features of the haughty aborigine—the untaught and untrammeled son of the forest. Over one shoulder a blanket, negligently but gracefully thrown, disclosed a bare and powerful breast, decorated with a quantity of three-cent postage-stamps which he had despoiled from an Overland Mail stage a few weeks previous. A cast-off beaver of Judge Tompkins's, adorned by a simple feather, covered his erect head, from beneath which his straight locks descended. His right hand hung lightly by his side, while his left was engaged in holding on a pair of pantaloons, which the lawless grace and freedom of his lower limbs evidently could not brook.

"Why," said the Indian, in a low sweet tone—"why does the Pale Face still follow the track of the Red Man? Why does he pursue him, even as *O-kee-chow,* the wildcat, chases *Ka-ka,* the skunk? Why are the feet of *Sorrel-top,* the white chief, among the acorns of *Muck-a-Muck,* the mountain forest? Why," he repeated, quietly but firmly abstracting a silver spoon from the table—"why do you seek to drive him from the wigwams of his fathers? His brothers are already gone to the happy hunting-grounds. Will the Pale Face seek him there?" And, averting his face from the Judge, he hastily slipped a silver cake-basket beneath his blanket, to conceal his emotion.

"Muck-a-Muck has spoken," said Genevra, softly. "Let him now listen. Are the acorns of the mountain sweeter than the esculent and nutritious bean of the Pale Face miner? Does my brother prize the edible qualities of the snail above that of the crisp and oleaginous bacon? Delicious are the grasshoppers that sport on the hillside —are they better than the dried apples of the Pale Faces? Pleasant is the gurgle of the torrent, *Kish-Kish,* but is it better than the cluck-cluck of old Bourbon from the öld stone bottle?"

"Ugh!" said the Indian—"ugh! good. The White Rabbit is wise. Her words fall as the snow on Tootoonolo, and the rocky heart of Muck-a-Muck is hidden. What says my brother the Gray Gopher of Dutch Flat?"

"She has spoken, Muck-a-Muck," said the Judge, gazing fondly on his daughter. "It is well. Our treaty is concluded. No, thank you—you need *not* dance the Dance of Snow Shoes, or the Moccasin Dance, the Dance of Green Corn, or the Treaty Dance. I would be alone. A strange sadness overpowers me."

"I go," said the Indian. "Tell your great chief in Washington, the Sachem Andy, that the Red Man is retiring before the footsteps of the adventurous Pioneer. Inform him, if you please, that westward the star of empire takes its way, that the chiefs of the Pi-Ute nation are for Reconstruction to a man, and that Klamath will poll a heavy Republican vote in the fall."

And folding his blanket more tightly around him, Muck-a-Muck withdrew.

Chapter III

Genevra Tompkins stood at the door of the log cabin, looking after the retreating Overland Mail stage which conveyed her father to Virginia City. "He may never return again," sighed the young girl as she glanced at the frightfully rolling vehicle and wildly careering horses—"at least, with unbroken bones. Should he meet with an accident! I mind me now a fearful legend, familiar to my childhood. Can it be that the drivers on this line are privately instructed to despatch all passengers maimed by accident, to prevent tedious litigation? No, no. But why this weight upon my heart?"

She seated herself at the piano and lightly passed her hand over the keys. Then, in a clear mezzo-soprano voice, she sang the first verse of one of the most popular Irish ballads:

"O *Arrah, ma dheelish,* the distant *dudheen*
Lies soft in the moonlight, *ma bouchal vourneen:*
The springing *gossoons* on the heather are still,
And the *caubeens* and *colleens* are heard on the hills."

But as the ravishing notes of her sweet voice died upon the air, her hands sank listlessly to her side. Music could not chase away the mysterious shadow from her heart. Again she rose. Putting on a white crape bonnet, and carefully drawing a pair of lemon-colored gloves over her taper fingers, she seized her parasol and plunged into the depths of the pine forest.

Chapter IV

Genevra had not proceeded many miles before a weariness seized upon her fragile limbs, and she would fain seat herself upon the trunk of a prostrate pine, which she previously dusted with her handkerchief. The sun was just sinking below the horizon, and the scene was one of gorgeous and sylvan beauty. "How beautiful is Nature!" murmured the innocent girl, as, reclining gracefully against the root of the tree, she gathered up her skirts and tied a handkerchief around her throat. But a low growl interrupted her meditation. Starting to her feet, her eyes met a sight which froze her blood with terror.

The only outlet to the forest was the narrow path, barely wide enough for a single person, hemmed in by trees and rocks, which she had just traversed. Down this path, in Indian file, came a monstrous grizzly, closely followed by a California lion, a wildcat, and a buffalo, the rear being brought up by a wild Spanish bull. The mouths of the three first animals were distended with frightful significance; the horns of the last were lowered as ominously. As Genevra was preparing to faint, she heard a low voice behind her.

"Eternally dog-gone my skin ef this ain't the puttiest chance yet."

At the same moment, a long, shining barrel dropped lightly from behind her, and rested over her shoulder.

Genevra shuddered.

"Dern ye—don't move!"

Genevra became motionless.

The crack of a rifle rang through the woods. Three frightful yells were heard, and two sullen roars. Five animals bounded into the air and five lifeless bodies lay upon the plain. The well-aimed bullet had done its work. Entering the open throat of the grizzly, it had traversed his body only to enter the throat of the California lion, and in like manner the catamount, until it passed through into the respective foreheads of the bull and the buffalo, and finally fell flattened from the rocky hillside.

Genevra turned quickly. "My preserver!" she shrieked, and fell into the arms of Natty Bumpo, the celebrated Pike Ranger of Donner Lake.

Chapter V

The moon rose cheerfully above Donner Lake. On its placid bosom a dugout canoe glided rapidly, containing Natty Bumpo and Genevra Tompkins.

Both were silent. The same thought possessed each, and perhaps there was sweet companionship even in the unbroken quiet. Genevra bit the handle of her parasol and blushed. Natty Bumpo took a fresh chew of tobacco. At length Genevra said, as if in half-spoken revery:

"The soft shining of the moon and the peaceful ripple of the waves seem to say to us various things of an instructive and moral tendency."

"You may bet yer pile on that, Miss," said her companion, gravely. "It's all the preachin' and psalm-singin' I've heern since I was a boy."

"Noble being!" said Miss Tompkins to herself, glancing at the stately Pike as he bent over his paddle to conceal his emotion. "Reared in this wild seclusion, yet he has become penetrated with visible consciousness of a Great First Cause." Then, collecting herself, she said aloud: "Me-thinks 't were pleasant to glide ever thus down the stream of life, hand in hand with the one being whom the soul claims as its affinity. But what am I saying?"—and the delicate-minded girl hid her face in her hands.

A long silence ensued, which was at length broken by her companion.

"Ef you mean you're on the marry," he said, thoughtfully, "I ain't in no wise partikler!"

"My husband," faltered the blushing girl; and she fell into his arms.

In ten minutes more the loving couple had landed at Judge Tompkins's.

Chapter VI

A year has passed away. Natty Bumpo was returning from Gold Hill, where he had been to purchase provisions. On his way to Donner Lake, rumors of an Indian uprising met his ears. "Dern their pesky skins, ef they dare to touch my Jenny," he muttered between his clenched teeth.

It was dark when he reached the borders of the lake. Around a glittering fire he dimly discerned dusky figures dancing. They were in war paint. Conspicuous among them was the renowned Muck-a-Muck. But why did the fingers of Natty Bumpo tighten convulsively around his rifle?

The chief held in his hand long tufts of raven hair. The heart of the pioneer sickened as he recognized the clustering curls of Genevra. In a moment his rifle was at his shoulder, and with a sharp "ping," Muck-a-Muck leaped into the air a corpse. To knock out the brains of the remaining savages, tear the tresses from the stiffening hand of Muck-a-Muck, and dash rapidly forward to the cottage of Judge Tompkins, was the work of a moment.

He burst open the door. Why did he stand transfixed with open mouth and distended eyeballs? Was the sight too horrible to be borne? On the contrary, before him, in her peerless beauty, stood Genevra Tompkins, leaning on her father's arm.

"Ye'r not scalped, then!" gasped her lover.

"No. I have no hesitation in saying that I am not; but why this abruptness?" responded Genevra.

Bumpo could not speak, but frantically produced the silken tresses. Genevra turned her face aside.

"Why, that's her waterfall!" said the Judge.

Bumpo sank fainting to the floor.

The famous Pike chieftain never recovered from the deceit, and refused to marry Genevra, who died, twenty years afterwards, of a broken heart. Judge Tompkins lost his fortune in Wild Cat. The stage passes twice a week the deserted cottage at Donner Lake. Thus was the death of Muck-a-Muck avenged.

1871

The Society upon the Stanislaus

I reside at Table Mountain, and my name is Truthful
    James;
I am not up to small deceit or any sinful games;
And I'll tell in simple language what I know about the row
That broke up our Society upon the Stanislow.

But first I would remark, that it is not a proper plan
For any scientific gent to whale his fellow-man,
And, if a member don't agree with his peculiar whim,
To lay for that same member for to "put a head" on him.

Now nothing could be finer or more beautiful to see
Than the first six months' proceedings of that same So-
    ciety,   10
Till Brown of Calaveras brought a lot of fossil bones
That he found within a tunnel near the tenement of Jones.

Then Brown he read a paper, and he reconstructed there,
From those same bones, an animal that was extremely rare;
And Jones then asked the Chair for a suspension of the
    rules,
Till he could prove that those same bones was one of his
    lost mules.

Then Brown he smiled a bitter smile, and said he was at
    fault.
It seemed he had been trespassing on Jones's family vault;
He was a most sarcastic man, this quiet Mr. Brown,
And on several occasions he had cleaned out the town.   20

Now I hold it is not decent for a scientific gent
To say another is an ass,—at least, to all intent;
Nor should the individual who happens to be meant
Reply by heaving rocks at him, to any great extent.

Then Abner Dean of Angel's raised a point of order, when
A chunk of old red sandstone took him in the abdomen,
And he smiled a kind of sickly smile, and curled up on the
    floor,
And the subsequent proceedings interested him no more.

For, in less time than I write it, every member did engage
In a warfare with the remnants of a palæozoic age;   30
And the way they heaved those fossils in their anger was
    a sin,
Till the skull of an old mammoth caved the head of Thomp-
    son in.

And this is all I have to say of these improper games,
For I live at Table Mountain, and my name is Truthful
    James;
And I've told in simple language what I know about the
    row
That broke up our Society upon the Stanislow.

                                1868

SARAH ORNE JEWETT

(1849–1909)

Sarah Orne Jewett was born in South Berwick, Maine, which remained her life-long home. During her youth, the Civil War,
Western emigration, changes in shipping conditions, and industrial mechanization were in the process of emptying the once
prosperous rural and coastal towns of New England of significance and self-respect. It is her pained but poised confrontation of the economic and social deterioration resulting from a
history in which the national direction swerved past her native
region that lies at the heart of Miss Jewett's fiction. The pain,
naturally enough, stemmed from having to witness the decay
of the once splendid past of "one's own kind," aggravated, as
she herself said, by the arrogant condescension of city boarders
who "misconstrued the country people and made game of their
peculiarities." The poise—that quality in her writing which
makes Miss Jewett the most accomplished regional writer of her
time—stemmed from her refusal to expend her creative energies either in the nostalgic romanticizing of a glorious past or
in the sentimentalizing of a pathetic present. "I determined to
teach the world that country people were not the awkward,
ignorant set those people [the city boarders] seemed to think. I
wanted the world to know their grand simple lives." And in this
she was eminently successful, catching the moral durability of
people whose rude exteriors mask a stubborn refusal to become
as spiritually abandoned as the weathered farmhouses that
scarred the New England landscape.

Sarah Jewett was fortunate in her father, Dr. Theodore Her-
man Jewett, to whom she paid loving tribute in *A Country Doc-*

tor (1884). Not only did he allow his daughter to accompany him on countless medical rounds, thereby enabling her to gain first-hand knowledge of the Maine villagers she was to write about, but he was also her first intellectual and literary stimulus. "Great writers don't try to write *about* people and things," Dr. Jewett once told his daughter; "they tell them just as they are" —a principle of realistic method which Miss Jewett tried to follow throughout her literary career. Her formal education was irregular, and, by modern standards, incomplete; but in her father's excellent library she began learning her craft through reading the great masters of the English and Continental novel, especially Jane Austen and Flaubert. Harriet Beecher Stowe's *The Pearl of Orr's Island*, which Miss Jewett read as a young lady, opened her eyes to the possibilities of local-color fiction, and the work of William Dean Howells helped to solidify her conviction that the quiet and commonplace, in the hands of "a master writer [who] makes you feel the distinction and importance of it," could furnish the occasion for highly significant fiction. How right she was can be seen in a reading of *The Country of the Pointed Firs* (1896), her finest achievement, which demonstrates that the faithful portrayal of human nature, no matter how restricted in time and place, tends to become universal almost in spite of itself.

In addition to the books mentioned above, Miss Jewett's work includes *Deephaven* (1877), *Old Friends and New* (1879), *Country By-Ways* (1881), *The Mate of the Daylight and Friends Ashore* (1883), *A Marsh Island* (1885), *A White Heron, and Other Stories* (1886), *The King of Folly Island, and Other People* (1888), *Strangers and Wayfarers* (1890), *A Native of Winby, and Other Tales* (1893), *The Life of Nancy* (1895), *The Queen's Twin and Other Stories* (1899), *The Tory Lover*, 1901.

Editions and accounts of the woman and her work are to be found in C. M. Thompson, "The Art of Miss Jewett," *Atlantic Monthly*, XCIV (1904); *Stories and Tales*, 7 vols. (1910); A. Fields, ed., *The Letters of Sarah Orne Jewett* (1911); E. M. Chapman, "The New England of Sarah Orne Jewett," *Yale Review*, n.s. III (1913); M. H. Shackford, "Sarah Orne Jewett," *Sewanee Review*, XXX (1922); W. Cather, ed., *The Best Stories of Sarah Orne Jewett*, 2 vols. (1925); F. O. Matthiessen, *Sarah Orne Jewett* (1929), the best study; W. Cather, "Miss Jewett," *Not Under Forty* (1936); C. J. Weber, "Whittier and Sarah Orne Jewett," *New England Quarterly*, XVIII (1945); C. J. Weber, ed., *Letters of Sarah Orne Jewett Now in the Colby College Library* (1947); C. C. Weber and C. J. Weber, eds., *A Bibliography of the Published Writings of Sarah Orne Jewett* (1949); A. M. Buchan, "*Our Dear Sarah*": *An Essay on Sarah Orne Jewett* (1953); R. Carey, ed., *Sarah Orne Jewett*

Letters (1956); W. Berthoff, "The Art of Jewett's *Pointed Firs*," *New England Quarterly*, XXXII (1959); H. H. Waggoner, "The Unity of *The Country of the Pointed Firs*," *Twentieth Century Literature*, V (1959); R. Cary, *Sarah Orne Jewett* (1962); D. B. Green, ed., *The World of Dunnett Landing* (1962); the Jewett issue of *Colby Library Quarterly*, Ser. VI, X (1964); M. A. McGuire, "Sarah Orne Jewett," *Dissertation Abstracts*, XXV (1965); and M. F. Thorp, *Sarah Orne Jewett* (1966).

Miss Tempy's Watchers

The time of year was April; the place was a small farming town in New Hampshire, remote from any railroad. One by one the lights had been blown out in the scattered houses near Miss Tempy Dent's; but as her neighbors took a last look out-of-doors, their eyes turned with instinctive curiosity toward the old house, where a lamp burned steadily. They gave a little sigh. "Poor Miss Tempy!" said more than one bereft acquaintance; for the good woman lay dead in her north chamber, and the light was a watcher's light. The funeral was set for the next day, at one o'clock.

The watchers were two of the oldest friends, Mrs. Crowe and Sarah Ann Binson. They were sitting in the kitchen, because it seemed less awesome than the unused best room, and they beguiled the long hours by steady conversation. One would think that neither topics nor opinions would hold out, at that rate, all through the long spring night; but there was a certain degree of excitement just then, and the two women had risen to an unusual level of expressiveness and confidence. Each had already told the other more than one fact that she had determined to keep secret; they were again and again tempted into statements that either would have found impossible by daylight. Mrs. Crowe was knitting a blue yarn stocking for her husband; the foot was already so long that it seemed as if she must have forgotten to narrow it at the proper time. Mrs. Crowe knew exactly what she was about, however; she was of a much cooler disposition than Sister Binson, who made futile attempts at some sewing, only to drop her work into her lap whenever the talk was most engaging.

Their faces were interesting—of the dry, shrewd, quick-witted New England type, with thin hair twisted neatly back out of the way. Mrs. Crowe could look vague and benignant, and Miss Binson was, to quote her neighbors, a little too sharp-set; but the world knew that she had need to be, with the load she must carry of supporting an inefficient widowed sister and six unpromising and unwilling nieces and nephews. The eldest boy was at last placed with a good man to learn the mason's trade. Sarah Ann Binson, for all her sharp, anxious aspect, never defended herself when her sister whined and fretted. She was told every week of her life that the poor children never would have had to lift a finger if their father had lived, and yet she had kept her steadfast way with the little farm, and patiently taught the young people many useful things, for which, as everybody said, they would live to thank her. However pleasureless her life appeared to outward view, it was brimful of pleasure to herself.

Mrs. Crowe, on the contrary, was well-to-do, her husband being a rich farmer and an easy-going man. She was a stingy woman, but for all that she looked kindly; and when she gave away anything, or lifted a finger to help anybody, it was thought a great piece of beneficence, and a compliment, indeed, which the recipient accepted with twice as much gratitude as double the gift that came from a poorer and more generous acquaintance. Everybody liked to be on good terms with Mrs. Crowe. Socially she stood much higher than Sarah Ann Binson. They were both old schoolmates and friends of Temperance Dent, who had asked them, one day, not long before she died, if they would not come together and look after the house, and manage everything, when she was gone. She may have had some hope that they might become closer friends in this period of intimate partnership, and that the richer woman might better understand the burdens of the poorer. They had not kept the house the night before; they were too weary with the care of their old friend, whom they had not left until all was over.

There was a brook which ran down the hillside very near the house, and the sound of it was much louder than usual. When there was silence in the kitchen, the busy stream had a strange insistence in its wild voice, as if it tried to make the watchers understand something that related to the past.

"I declare, I can't begin to sorrow for Tempy yet. I am

so glad to have her at rest," whispered Mrs. Crowe. "It is strange to set here without her, but I can't make it clear that she has gone. I feel as if she had got easy and dropped off to sleep, and I'm more scared about waking her up than knowing any other feeling."

"Yes," said Sarah Ann, "it 's just like that, ain't it? But I tell you we are goin' to miss her worse than we expect. She's helped me through with many a trial, has Temperance. I ain't the only one who says the same, neither."

These words were spoken as if there were a third person listening; somebody besides Mrs. Crowe. The watchers could not rid their minds of the feeling that they were being watched themselves. The spring wind whistled in the window crack, now and then, and buffeted the little house in a gusty way that had a sort of companionable effect. Yet, on the whole, it was a very still night, and the watchers spoke in a half-whisper.

"She was the freest-handed woman that ever I knew," said Mrs. Crowe, decidedly. "According to her means, she gave away more than anybody. I used to tell her 't wa'n't right. I used really to be afraid that she went without too much, for we have a duty to ourselves."

Sister Binson looked up in a half-amused, unconscious way, and then recollected herself.

Mrs. Crowe met her look with a serious face. "It ain't so easy for me to give as it is for some," she said simply, but with an effort which was made possible only by the occasion. "I should like to say, while Tempy is laying here yet in her own house, that she has been a constant lesson to me. Folks are too kind, and shame me with thanks for what I do. I ain't such a generous woman as poor Tempy was, for all she had nothin' to do with, as one may say."

Sarah Binson was much moved at this confession, and was even pained and touched by the unexpected humility. "You have a good many calls on you"—she began, and then left her kind little compliment half finished.

"Yes, yes, but I've got means enough. My disposition's more of a cross to me as I grow older, and I made up my mind this morning that Tempy's example should be my pattern henceforth." She began to knit faster than ever.

" 'T ain't no use to get morbid: that's what Tempy used to say herself," said Sarah Ann, after a minute's silence. "Ain't it strange to say 'used to say?' " and her own voice choked a little. "She never did like to hear folks git goin' about themselves."

" 'T was only because they're apt to do it so as other folks will say 't was n't so, an' praise 'em up," humbly replied Mrs. Crowe, "and that ain't my object. There wa'n't a child but what Tempy set herself to work to see what she could do to please it. One time my brother's folks had been stopping here in the summer, from Massachusetts. The children was all little, and they broke up a sight of toys, and left 'em when they were going away. Tempy come right up after they rode by, to see if she could n't help me set the house to rights, and she caught me just as I was going to fling some of the clutter into the stove. I was kind of tired out, starting 'em off in season. 'Oh, give me them!' says she, real pleading; and she wropped 'em up and took 'em home with her when she went, and she mended 'em up and stuck 'em together, and made some young one or other happy with every blessed one. You 'd thought I 'd done her the biggest favor. 'No thanks to me. I should ha' burnt 'em, Tempy,' says I."

"Some of 'em came to our house, I know," said Miss Binson. "She 'd take a lot o' trouble to please a child, 'stead o' shoving of it out o' the way, like the rest of us when we're drove."

"I can tell you the biggest thing she ever done, and I don't know 's there's anybody left but me to tell it. I don't want it forgot," Sarah Binson went on, looking up at the clock to see how the night was going. "It was that pretty-looking Trevor girl, who taught the Corners school, and married so well afterwards, out in New York State. You remember her, I dare say?"

"Certain," said Mrs. Crowe, with an air of interest.

"She was a splendid scholar, folks said, and give the school a great start; but she 'd overdone herself getting her education, and working to pay for it, and she all broke down one spring, and Tempy made her come and stop with her a while—you remember that? Well, she had an uncle, her mother's brother, out in Chicago, who was well off and friendly, and used to write to Lizzie Trevor, and I dare say make her some presents; but he was a lively, driving man, and did n't take time to stop and think about his folks. He hadn't seen her since she was a little girl. Poor Lizzie was so pale and weakly that she just got through the term o' school. She looked as if she was just going straight off in a decline. Tempy, she cosseted her up a while, and then, next thing folks knew, she was tellin' round how Miss Trevor had gone to see her uncle, and meant to visit Niagary Falls on the way, and stop over night. Now I happened to know, in ways I won't dwell on to explain, that the poor girl was in debt for her schoolin' when she come here, and her last quarter's pay had just squared it off at last, and left her without a cent ahead, hardly; but it had fretted her thinking of it, so she paid it all; those might have dunned her that she owed it to. An' I taxed Tempy about the girl's goin' off on such a journey till she owned up, rather 'n have Lizzie blamed, that she'd given her sixty dollars, same 's if she was rolling in riches, and sent her off to have a good rest and vacation."

"Sixty dollars!" exclaimed Mrs. Crowe. "Tempy only had ninety dollars a year that came in to her; rest of her livin' she got by helpin' about, with what she raised off this little piece o' ground, sand one side an' clay the other. An' how often I 've heard her tell, years ago, that she 'd rather see Niagary than any other sight in the world!"

The women looked at each other in silence; the magnitude of the generous sacrifice was almost too great for their comprehension.

"She was just poor enough to do that!" declared Mrs. Crowe at last, in an abandonment of feeling. "Say what you may, I feel humbled to the dust," and her companion ventured to say nothing. She never had given away sixty dollars at once, but it was simply because she never had it to give. It came to her very lips to say in explanation, "Tempy was so situated"; but she checked herself in time, for she would not betray her own loyal guarding of a dependent household.

"Folks say a great deal of generosity, and this one's being public-sperited, and that one free-handed about giving," said Mrs. Crowe, who was a little nervous in the silence. "I suppose we can't tell the sorrow it would be to some folks not to give, same 's 't would be to me not to save. I seem kind of made for that, as if 't was what I 'd got to do. I should feel sights better about it if I could make it evident what I was savin' for. If I had a child, now, Sarah Ann," and her voice was a little husky—"if I had a child, I should think I was heapin' of it up because he was the one trained by the Lord to scatter it again for good. But here 's Mr. Crowe and me, we can't do anything with money, and both of as like to keep things same 's they 've always been. Now Priscilla Dance was talking away like a mill-clapper, week before last. She 'd think I would go right off and get one o' them new-fashioned gilt-and-white papers for the best room, and some new furniture, an' a marble-top table. And I looked at her, all struck up. 'Why,' says I, 'Priscilla, that nice old velvet paper ain't hurt a mite. I should n't feel 't was my best room without it. Dan'el says 't is the first thing he can remember rubbin' his little baby fingers on to it, and how splendid he thought them red roses was.' I maintain," continued Mrs. Crowe stoutly, "that folks wastes sights o' good money doin' just such foolish things. Tearin' out the insides o' meetin'-houses, and fixin' the pews different; 't was good enough as 't was with mendin'; then times come, an' they want to put it all back same 's 't was before."

This touched upon an exciting subject to active members of that parish. Miss Binson and Mrs. Crowe belonged to opposite parties, and had at one time come as near hard feelings as they could, and yet escape them. Each hastened to speak of other things and to show her untouched friendliness.

"I do agree with you," said Sister Binson, "that few of us know what use to make of money, beyond every-day necessities. You 've seen more o' the world than I have, and know what 's expected. When it comes to taste and judgment about such things, I ought to defer to others"; and with this modest avowal the critical moment passed when there might have been an improper discussion.

In the silence that followed, the fact of their presence in a house of death grew more clear than before. There was something disturbing in the noise of a mouse gnawing at the dry boards of a closet wall near by. Both the watchers looked up anxiously at the clock; it was almost the middle of the night, and the whole world seemed to have left them alone with their solemn duty. Only the brook was awake.

"Perhaps we might give a look upstairs now," whispered Mrs. Crowe, as if she hoped to hear some reason against their going just then to the chamber of death; but Sister Binson rose, with a serious and yet satisfied countenance, and lifted the small lamp from the table. She was much more used to watching than Mrs. Crowe, and much less affected by it. They opened the door into a small entry with a steep stairway; they climbed the creaking stairs, and entered the cold upper room on tiptoe. Mrs. Crowe's heart began to beat very fast as the lamp was put on a high bureau and made long, fixed shadows about the walls. She went hesitatingly toward the solemn shape under its white drapery, and felt a sense of remonstrance as Sarah Ann gently, but in a business-like way, turned back the thin sheet.

"Seems to me she looks pleasanter and pleasanter," whispered Sarah Ann Binson impulsively, as they gazed at the white face with its wonderful smile. "To-morrow 't will all have faded out. I do believe they kind of wake up a day or two after they die, and it 's then they go." She replaced the light covering, and they both turned quickly away; there was a chill in this upper room.

" 'T is a great thing for anybody to have got through, ain't it?" said Mrs. Crowe softly, as she began to go down the stairs on tiptoe. The warm air from the kitchen beneath met them with a sense of welcome and shelter.

"I don' know why it is, but I feel as near again to Tempy down here as I do up there," replied Sister Binson. "I feel as if the air was full of her, kind of. I can sense things, now and then, that she seems to say. Now I never was one to take up with no nonsense of sperits and such, but I declare I felt as if she told me just now to put some more wood into the stove."

Mrs. Crowe preserved a gloomy silence. She had suspected before this that her companion was of a weaker and more credulous disposition than herself. " 'T is a great thing to have got through," she repeated, ignoring definitely all that had last been said. "I suppose you know as well as I that Tempy was one that always feared death. Well, it 's all put behind her now; she knows what 't is." Mrs. Crowe gave a little sigh, and Sister Binson's quick sympathies were stirred toward this other old friend, who also dreaded the great change.

"I 'd never like to forget almost those last words Tempy spoke plain to me," she said gently, like the comforter she truly was. "She looked up at me once or twice, that last afternoon after I come to set by her, and let Mis' Owen go home; and I says, 'Can I do anything to ease you, Tempy?' and the tears come into my eyes so I could n't see what kind of a nod she give me. 'No, Sarah Ann, you can't, dear,' says she; and then she got her breath again, and says she, looking at me real meanin', 'I 'm only a-gettin' sleepier and sleepier; that 's all there is,' says she, and smiled up at me kind of wishful, and shut her eyes. I knew well enough all she meant. She 'd been lookin' out for a chance to tell me, and I don' know's she ever said much afterwards."

Mrs. Crowe was not knitting; she had been listening too eagerly. "Yes, 't will be a comfort to think of that sometimes," she said, in acknowledgment.

"I know that old Dr. Prince said once, in evenin' meetin', that he 'd watched by many a dyin' bed, as we well knew, and enough o' his sick folks had been scared o' dyin' their whole lives through; but when they come to the last, he 'd never seen one but was willin', and most were glad, to go. ' 'T is as natural as bein' born or livin' on,' he said. I don't know what had moved him to speak that night. You know he wa'n't in the habit of it, and 't was the monthly concert of prayer for foreign missions anyways," said Sarah Ann; "but 't was a great stay to the mind to listen to his words of experience."

"There never was a better man," responded Mrs. Crowe, in a really cheerful tone. She had recovered from her feeling of nervous dread, the kitchen was so comfortable with lamplight and firelight; and just then the old clock began to tell the hour of twelve with leisurely whirring strokes.

Sister Binson laid aside her work, and rose quickly and went to the cupboard. "We 'd better take a little to eat," she explained. "The night will go fast after this. I want to know if you went and made some o' your nice cupcake, while you was home to-day?" she asked, in a pleased tone; and Mrs. Crowe acknowledged such a gratifying piece of thoughtfulness for this humble friend who denied herself all luxuries. Sarah Ann brewed a generous cup of tea, and the watchers drew their chairs up to the table presently, and quelled their hunger with good country appetites. Sister Binson put a spoon into a small, old-fashioned glass of preserved quince, and passed it to her friend. She was most familiar with the house, and played the part of hostess. "Spread some o' this on your bread and butter," she said to Mrs. Crowe. "Tempy wanted me to use some three or four times, but I never felt to. I know she 'd like to have us comfortable now, and would urge us to make a good supper, poor dear."

"What excellent preserves she did make!" mourned Mrs. Crowe. "None of us has got her light hand at doin' things tasty. She made the most o' everything, too. Now, she only had that one old quince-tree down in the far corner of the piece, but she 'd go out in the spring and tend to it, and look at it so pleasant, and kind of expect the old thorny thing into bloomin'."

"She was just the same with folks," said Sarah Ann. "And she'd never git more 'n a little apernful o' quinces, but she'd have every mite o' goodness out o' those, and set the glasses up onto her best-room closet shelf, *so* pleased. 'T wa'n't but a week ago to-morrow mornin' I fetched her a little taste o' jelly in a teaspoon; and she says 'Thank ye,' and took it, an' the minute she tasted it she looked up at me as worried as could be. 'Oh, I don't want to eat that,' says she. 'I always keep that in case o' sickness.' 'You 're goin' to have the good o' one tumbler yourself,' says I. 'I 'd just like to know who 's sick now, if you ain't!' An' she could n't help laughin', I spoke up so smart. Oh, dear me, how I shall miss talkin' over things with her! She always sensed things, and got just the p'int you meant."

"She did n't begin to age until two or three years ago, did she?" asked Mrs. Crowe. "I never saw anybody keep her looks as Tempy did. She looked young long after I begun to feel like an old woman. The doctor used to say 't was her young heart, and I don't know but what he was right. How she did do for other folks! There was one spell she was n't at home a day to a fortnight. She got most of her livin' so, and that made her own potatoes and things last her through. None o' the young folks could get married without her, and all the old ones was disappointed if she wa'n't round when they was down with sickness and had to go. An' cleanin', or tailorin' for boys, or rug-hookin'—there was nothin' but what she could do as handy as most. 'I do love to work'—ain't you heard her say that twenty times a week?"

Sarah Ann Binson nodded, and began to clear away the

empty plates. "We may want a taste o' somethin' more towards mornin'," she said. "There 's plenty in the closet here; and in case some comes from a distance to the funeral, we 'll have a little table spread after we get back to the house."

"Yes, I was busy all the mornin'. I 've cooked up a sight o' things to bring over," said Mrs. Crowe. "I felt 't was the last I could do for her."

They drew their chairs near the stove again, and took up their work. Sister Binson's rocking-chair creaked as she rocked; the brook sounded louder than ever. It was more lonely when nobody spoke, and presently Mrs. Crowe returned to her thoughts of growing old.

"Yes, Tempy aged all of a sudden. I remember I asked her if she felt as well as common, one day, and she laughed at me good. There, when Mr. Crowe begun to look old, I could n't help feeling as if somethin' ailed him, and like as not 't was somethin' he was goin' to git right over, and I dosed him for it stiddy, half of one summer."

"How many things we shall be wanting to ask Tempy!" exclaimed Sarah Ann Binson, after a long pause. "I can't make up my mind to doin' without her. I wish folks could come back just once, and tell us how 'tis where they 've gone. Seems then we could do without 'em better."

The brook hurried on, the wind blew about the house now and then; the house itself was a silent place, and the supper, the warm fire, and an absence of any new topics for conversation made the watchers drowsy. Sister Binson closed her eyes first, to rest them for a minute; and Mrs. Crowe glanced at her compassionately, with a new sympathy for the hard-worked little woman. She made up her mind to let Sarah Ann have a good rest, while she kept watch alone; but in a few minutes her own knitting was dropped, and she, too, fell asleep. Overhead, the pale shape of Tempy Dent, the outworn body of that generous, loving-hearted, simple soul, slept on also in its white raiment. Perhaps Tempy herself stood near, and saw her own life and its surroundings with new understanding. Perhaps she herself was the only watcher.

Later, by some hours, Sarah Ann Binson woke with a start. There was a pale light of dawn outside the small windows. Inside the kitchen, the lamp burned dim. Mrs. Crowe awoke, too.

"I think Tempy 'd be the first to say 'twas just as well we both had some rest," she said, not without a guilty feeling.

Her companion went to the outer door, and opened it wide. The fresh air was none too cold, and the brook's voice was not nearly so loud as it had been in the midnight darkness. She could see the shapes of the hills, and the great shadows that lay across the lower country. The east was fast growing bright.

" 'T will be a beautiful day for the funeral," she said, and turned again, with a sigh, to follow Mrs. Crowe up the stairs.

1879, 1914

MARY E. WILKINS FREEMAN

(1852–1930)

Although there are some significant differences between them, the customary association of Mary Wilkins Freeman with Sarah Orne Jewett (whose stories Mrs. Freeman insisted she never read) has ample justification. Both wrote of decaying New England village life and of its inhabitants, whose only defense against the imminent collapse of their way of life is a ruggedly Yankee will to survive——on their own terms. But there is an edge of austerity in much of Mrs. Freeman's work which is absent from Miss Jewett's, ascribable, perhaps, to a life that was not without its own grim aspects.

She was born in Randolph, Massachusetts, to an old New England family (among whom, it is said, a Salem witchcraft judge is numbered). Her education was hampered by ill health. After the rest of her family died, she nursed her invalid father in the isolated, lonely life of Brattleboro, Vermont, to which they had moved. By 1883 Mary Wilkins was left alone in the world with an aged aunt to support. She returned to her birthplace to try to write for a living, choosing the short story as the medium most likely to give immediate financial returns. Her first two collections of short stories (fifty-two tales), *A Humble Romance* (1887) and *A New England Nun and Other Stories* (1891) comprise about a fourth of her short-fiction output and include her finest work. Her novels, such as *Jane Field* (1893), *Pembroke* (1894), and *Jerome, A Poor Man* (1897) are structurally diffuse, revealing that her real talent lay in the short story, where her imagination was controlled by the focused nature of the form. Her one venture into drama, *Giles Corey, Yeoman* (1893), a play about the Salem witchcraft trials, was a failure. Her last collection of short stories, *Edgewater People* .

179

(1918), returns to the type and nearly the excellence of her early work. In 1902, at the age of fifty, she married Dr. Charles M. Freeman and moved to Metuchen, New Jersey, where she lived until her death. The marriage was not happy.

Like Miss Jewett, Mrs. Freeman centers her attention on the proud, stoical, eccentric people of her native region, utilizing social and dialectal notation as means, not ends. But there is in her work a greater toughmindedness, if one may so call it, reflected in her willingness to confront the ugly and in her spare, objective, restrained prose style. Although she is capable of finding the comic in the stark, her work does not exhibit the tender sense of humor that softly pervades much of Miss Jewett's writing; and her portraits of nearly hysterical repression (in the psychiatric sense) tend to strike today's Freudian-oriented reader as decidedly modern.

In addition to the books mentioned above, Mrs. Freeman's work includes *The Pot of Gold and Other Stories* (1892), *Young Lucretia and Other Stories* (1892), *Comfort Pease and Her Gold Ring* (1895), *Madelon* (1896), *Silence and Other Stories* (1898), *The People of Our Neighborhood* (1898), *In Colonial Times* (1899), *The Jamesons* (1899), *The Heart's Highway* (1900), *The Love of Parson Lord and Other Stories* (1900), *Understudies* (1901), *The Portion of Labor* (1901), *Six Trees* (1903), *The Wind in the Rose-Bush* (1903), *The Givers* (1904), *The Debtor* (1905), *"Doc" Gordon* (1906), *By the Light of the Soul* (1906), *The Fair Lavinia* (1907), *The Shoulders of Atlas* (1908), *The Winning Lady* (1909), *The Green Door* (1910), *The Butterfly House* (1912), *The Yates Pride* (1912), *The Copy-Cat and Other Stories* (1914).

Editions and accounts of Mrs. Freeman's work are to be found in C. M. Thompson, "Miss Wilkins: An Idealist in Masquerade," *Atlantic Monthly, LXXXIII* (1899); F. L. Pattee, *A History of American Literature Since 1870* (1915); B. C. Williams, *Our Short Story Writers* (1920); H. W. Lanier, ed., *The Best Stories of Mary E. Wilkins* (1927); A. H. Quinn, *American Fiction* (1936); B. M. Levy, "Mutations in New England Local Color," *New England Quarterly, XIX* (1946); E. treatment; and A. A. Hamblen, *The New England Art of Mary E. Wilkins Freeman* (1966).

The Revolt of "Mother"

"Father!"

"What is it?"

"What are them men diggin' over there in the field for?"
There was a sudden dropping and enlarging of the lower

part of the old man's face, as if some heavy weight had
settled therein; he shut his mouth tight, and went on har-
nessing the great bay mare. He hustled the collar on to
her neck with a jerk.

"Father!"

The old man slapped the saddle upon the mare's back.

"Look here, father, I want to know what them men are
diggin' over in the field for, an' I'm goin' to know."

"I wish you'd go into the house, mother, an' 'tend to
your own affairs," the old man said then. He ran his words
together, and his speech was almost as inarticulate as a
growl.

But the woman understood; it was her most native
tongue. "I ain't goin' into the house till you tell me what
them men are doin' over there in the field," said she.

Then she stood waiting. She was a small woman, short
and straight-waisted like a child in her brown cotton gown.
Her forehead was mild and benevolent between the smooth
curves of gray hair; there were meek downward lines
about her nose and mouth; but her eyes, fixed upon the
old man, looked as if the meekness had been the result of
her own will, never of the will of another.

They were in the barn, standing before the wide open
doors. The spring air, full of the smell of growing grass
and unseen blossoms, came in their faces. The deep yard
in front was littered with farm wagons and piles of wood;
on the edges, close to the fence and the house, the grass
was a vivid green, and there were some dandelions.

The old man glanced doggedly at his wife as he tight-
ened the last buckles on the harness. She looked as immovable to him as one of the rocks in his pasture-land,
bound to the earth with generations of blackberry vines.
He slapped the reins over the horse, and started forth
from the barn.

"Father!" said she.

The old man pulled up. "What is it?"

"I want to know what them men are diggin' over there
in that field for."

"They're diggin' a cellar, I s'pose, if you've got to know."

"A cellar for what?"

"A barn."

"A barn? You ain't goin' to build a barn over there
where we was goin' to have a house, father?"

The old man said not another word. He hurried the horse into the farm wagon, and clattered out of the yard, jouncing as sturdily on his seat as a boy.

The woman stood a moment looking after him, then she went out of the barn across a corner of the yard to the house. The house, standing at right angles with the great barn and a long reach of sheds and out-buildings, was infinitesimal compared with them. It was scarcely as commodious for people as the little boxes under the barn eaves were for doves.

A pretty girl's face, pink and delicate as a flower, was looking out of one of the house windows. She was watching three men who were digging over in the field which bounded the yard near the road line. She turned quietly when the woman entered.

"What are they digging for, mother?" said she. "Did he tell you?"

"They're diggin' for—a cellar for a new barn."

"Oh, mother, he ain't going to build another barn?"

"That's what he says."

A boy stood before the kitchen glass combing his hair. He combed slowly and painstakingly, arranging his brown hair in a smooth hillock over his forehead. He did not seem to pay any attention to the conversation.

"Sammy, did you know father was going to build a new barn?" asked the girl.

The boy combed assiduously.

"Sammy!"

He turned, and showed a face like his father's under his smooth crest of hair. "Yes, I s'pose I did," he said, reluctantly.

"How long have you known it?" asked his mother.

" 'Bout three months, I guess."

"Why didn't you tell of it?"

"Didn't think 'twould do no good."

"I don't see what father wants another barn for," said the girl, in her sweet, slow voice. She turned again to the window, and stared out at the digging men in the field. Her tender, sweet face was full of a gentle distress. Her forehead was as bald and innocent as a baby's with the light hair strained back from it in a row of curl-papers. She was quite large, but her soft curves did not look as if they covered muscles.

Her mother looked sternly at the boy. "Is he goin' to buy more cows?"

The boy did not reply; he was tying his shoes.

"Sammy, I want you to tell me if he's goin' to buy more cows."

"I s'pose he is."

"How many?"

"Four, I guess."

His mother said nothing more. She went into the pantry, and there was a clatter of dishes. The boy got his cap from a nail behind the door, took an old arithmetic from the shelf, and started for school. He was lightly built, but clumsy. He went out of the yard with a curious spring in the hips, that made his loose home-made jacket tilt up in the rear.

The girl went to the sink, and began to wash the dishes that were piled up there. Her mother came promptly out of the pantry, and shoved her aside. "You wipe 'em," said she, "I'll wash. There's a good many this mornin'."

The mother plunged her hands vigorously into the water, the girl wiped the plates slowly and dreamily. "Mother," said she, "don't you think it's too bad father's going to build that new barn, much as we need a decent house to live in?"

Her mother scrubbed a dish fiercely. "You ain't found out yet we're women-folks, Nanny Penn," said she. "You ain't seen enough of men-folks yet to. One of these days you'll find it out, an' then you'll know that we know only what men-folks think we do, so far as any use of it goes, an' how we'd ought to reckon men-folks in with Providence, an' not complain of what they do any more than we do of the weather."

"I don't care; I don't believe George is anything like that, anyhow," said Nanny. Her delicate face flushed pink, her lips pouted softly, as if she were going to cry.

"You wait an' see. I guess George Eastman ain't no better than other men. You hadn't ought to judge father, though. He can't help it, 'cause he don't look at things jest the way we do. An' we've been pretty comfortable here, after all. The roof don't leak—ain't never but once —that's one thing. Father's kept it shingled right up."

"I do wish we had a parlor."

"I guess it won't hurt George Eastman any to come to

see you in a nice clean kitchen. I guess a good many girls don't have as good a place as this. Nobody's ever heard me complain."

"I ain't complained either, mother."

"Well, I don't think you'd better, a good father an' a good home as you've got. S'pose your father made you go out an' work for your livin'? Lots of girls have to that ain't no stronger an' better able to than you be."

Sarah Penn washed the frying-pan with a conclusive air. She scrubbed the outside of it as faithfully as the inside. She was a masterly keeper of her box of a house. Her one living-room never seemed to have in it any of the dust which the friction of life with inanimate matter produces. She swept, and there seemed to be no dirt to go before the broom; she cleaned, and one could see no difference. She was like an artist so perfect that he has apparently no art. To-day she got out a mixing bowl and a board, and rolled some pies, and there was no more flour upon her than upon her daughter who was doing finer work. Nanny was to be married in the fall, and she was sewing on some white cambric and embroidery. She sewed industriously while her mother cooked; her soft milk-white hands and wrists showed whiter than her delicate work.

"We must have the stove moved out in the shed before long," said Mrs. Penn. "Talk about not havin' things, it's been a real blessin' to be able to put a stove up in that shed in hot weather. Father did one good thing when he fixed that stove-pipe out there."

Sarah Penn's face as she rolled her pies had that expression of meek vigor which might have characterized one of the New Testament saints. She was making mince-pies. Her husband, Adoniram Penn, liked them better than any other kind. She baked twice a week. Adoniram often liked a piece of pie between meals. She hurried this morning. It had been later than usual when she began, and she wanted to have a pie baked for dinner. However deep a resentment she might be forced to hold against her husband, she would never fail in sedulous attention to his wants.

Nobility of character manifests itself at loop-holes when it is not provided with large doors. Sarah Penn's showed itself to-day in flaky dishes of pastry. So she made the pies faithfully, while across the table she could see, when she glanced up from her work, the sight that rankled in her patient and steadfast soul—the digging of the cellar of the new barn in the place where Adoniram forty years ago had promised her their new house should stand.

The pies were done for dinner. Adoniram and Sammy were home a few minutes after twelve o'clock. The dinner was eaten with serious haste. There was never much conversation at the table in the Penn family. Adoniram asked a blessing, and they ate promptly, then rose up and went about their work.

Sammy went back to school, taking soft sly lopes out of the yard like a rabbit. He wanted a game of marbles before school, and feared his father would give him some chores to do. Adoniram hastened to the door and called after him, but he was out of sight.

"I don't see what you let him go for, mother," said he. "I wanted him to help me unload that wood."

Adoniram went to work out in the yard unloading wood from the wagon. Sarah put away the dinner dishes, while Nanny took down her curl papers and changed her dress. She was going down to the store to buy some more embroidery and thread.

When Nanny was gone, Mrs. Penn went to the door. "Father!" she called.

"Well, what is it!"

"I want to see you jest a minute, father."

"I can't leave this wood nohow. I've got to git it unloaded an' go for a load of gravel afore two o'clock. Sammy had ought to helped me. You hadn't ought to let him go to school so early."

"I want to see you jest a minute."

"I tell ye I can't, nohow, mother."

"Father, you come here." Sarah Penn stood in the door like a queen; she held her head as if it bore a crown; there was that patience which makes authority royal in her voice. Adoniram went.

Mrs. Penn led the way into the kitchen, and pointed to a chair. "Sit down, father," said she; "I've got somethin' I want to say to you."

He sat down heavily; his face was quite stolid, but he looked at her with restive eyes. "Well, what is it, mother?"

"I want to know what you're buildin' that new barn for, father?"

"I ain't got nothin' to say about it."

"It can't be you think you need another barn?"

"I tell ye I ain't got nothin' to say about it, mother; an' I ain't goin' to say nothin'."

"Be you goin' to buy more cows?"

Adoniram did not reply; he shut his mouth tight.

"I know you be, as well as I want to. Now, father, look here"—Sarah Penn had not sat down; she stood before her husband in the humble fashion of a Scripture woman—"I'm goin' to talk real plain to you; I never have sence I married you, but I'm goin' to now. I ain't never complained, an' I ain't goin' to complain now, but I'm goin' to talk plain. You see this room here, father; you look at it well. You see there ain't no carpet on the floor, an' you see the paper is all dirty, an' droppin' off the wall. We ain't had no new paper on it for ten year, an' then I put it on myself, an' it didn't cost but ninepence a roll. You see this room, father; it's all the one I've had to work in an' eat in an' sit in sence we was married. There ain't another woman in the whole town whose husband ain't got half the means you have but what's got better. It's all the room Nanny's got to have her company in; an' there ain't one of her mates but what's got better, an' their fathers not so able as hers is. It's all the room she'll have to be married in. What would you have thought, father, if we had had our weddin' in a room no better than this? I was married in my mother's parlor, with a carpet on the floor, an' stuffed furniture, an' a mahogany card-table. An' this is all the room my daughter will have to be married in. Look here, father!"

Sarah Penn went across the room as though it were a tragic stage. She flung open a door and disclosed a tiny bedroom, only large enough for a bed and bureau, with a path between. "There, father," said she—"there's all the room I've had to sleep in forty year. All my children were born there—the two that died, an' the two that's livin'. I was sick with a fever there."

She stepped to another door and opened it. It led into the small, ill-lighted pantry. "Here," said she, "is all the buttery I've got—every place I've got for my dishes, to set away my victuals in, an' to keep my milk-pans in.

Father, I've been takin' care of the milk of six cows in this place, an' now you're goin' to build a new barn, an' keep more cows, an' give me more to do in it."

She threw open another door. A narrow crooked flight of stairs wound upward from it. "There, father," said she, "I want you to look at the stairs that go up to them two un-finished chambers that are all the places our son an' daugh-ter have had to sleep in all their lives. There ain't a prettier girl in town nor a more ladylike one than Nanny, an' that's the place she has to sleep in. It ain't so good as your horse's stall; it ain't so warm an' tight."

Sarah Penn went back and stood before her husband. "Now, father," said she, "I want to know if you think you're doin' right an' accordin' to what you profess. Here, when we was married, forty year ago, you promised me faithful that we should have a new house built in that lot over in the field before the year was out. You said you had money enough, an' you wouldn't ask me to live in no such place as this. It is forty year now, an' you've been makin' more money, an' I've been savin' of it for you ever since, an' you ain't built no house yet. You've built sheds an' cow-houses an' one new barn, an' now you're goin' to build another. Father, I want to know if you think it's right. You're lodgin' your dumb beasts better than you are your own flesh an' blood. I want to know if you think it's right."

"I ain't got nothin' to say."

"You can't say nothin' without ownin' it ain't right, father. An' there's another thing—I ain't complained; I've got along forty year, an' I s'pose I should forty more, if it wasn't for that—if we don't have another house. Nanny she can't live with us after she's married. She'll have to go somewhere else to live away from us, an' it don't seem as if I could have it so, noways, father. She wasn't ever strong. She's got considerable color, but there wasn't never any backbone to her. I've always took the heft of everything off her, an' she ain't fit to keep house an' do everything herself. She'll be all worn out inside of a year. Think of her doin' all the washin' an' ironin' an' bakin' with them soft white hands an' arms, an' sweepin'! I can't have it so, noways, father."

Mrs. Penn's face was burning; her mild eyes gleamed. She had pleaded her little cause like a Webster; she had ranged from severity to pathos; but her opponent employed that obstinate silence which makes eloquence futile with mocking echoes. Adoniram arose clumsily.

"Father, ain't you got nothin' to say?" said Mrs. Penn.

"I've got to go off after that load of gravel. I can't stan' here talkin' all day."

"Father, won't you think it over, an' have a house built there instead of a barn?"

"I ain't got nothin' to say."

Adoniram shuffled out. Mrs. Penn went into her bedroom. When she came out, her eyes were red. She had a roll of unbleached cotton cloth. She spread it out on the kitchen table, and began cutting out some shirts for her husband. The men over in the field had a team to help them this afternoon; she could hear their halloos. She had a scanty pattern for the shirts; she had to plan and piece the sleeves.

Nanny came home with her embroidery, and sat down with her needlework. She had taken down her curl-papers, and there was a soft roll of fair hair like an aureole over her forehead; her face was as delicately fine and clear as porcelain. Suddenly she looked up, and the tender red flamed all over her face and neck. "Mother," said she.

"What say?"

"I've been thinking—I don't see how we're goin' to have any—wedding in this room. I'd be ashamed to have his folks come if we didn't have anybody else."

"Mebbe we can have some new paper before then; I can put it on. I guess you won't have no call to be ashamed of your belongin's."

"We might have the wedding in the new barn," said Nanny, with gentle pettishness. "Why, mother, what makes you look so?"

Mrs. Penn had started, and was staring at her with a curious expression. She turned again to her work, and spread out a pattern carefully on the cloth. "Nothin'," said she.

Presently Adoniram clattered out of the yard in his two-wheeled dump cart, standing as proudly upright as a Roman charioteer. Mrs. Penn opened the door and stood there a minute looking out; the halloos of the men sounded louder.

It seemed to her all through the spring months that she

heard nothing but the halloos and the noises of saws and hammers. The new barn grew fast. It was a fine edifice for this little village. Men came on pleasant Sundays, in their meeting suits and clean shirt bosoms, and stood around it admiringly. Mrs. Penn did not speak of it, and Adoniram did not mention it to her, although sometimes, upon a return from inspecting it, he bore himself with injured dignity.

"It's a strange thing how your mother feels about the new barn," he said, confidentially, to Sammy one day.

Sammy only grunted after an odd fashion for a boy; he had learned it from his father.

The barn was all completed ready for use by the third week in July. Adoniram had planned to move his stock in on Wednesday; on Tuesday he received a letter which changed his plans. He came in with it early in the morning. "Sammy's been to the post-office," said he, "an' I've got a letter from Hiram." Hiram was Mrs. Penn's brother, who lived in Vermont.

"Well," said Mrs. Penn, "what does he say about the folks?"

"I guess they're all right. He says he thinks if I .come up country right off there's a chance to buy jest the kind of a horse I want." He stared reflectively out of the window at the new barn.

Mrs. Penn was making pies. She went on clapping the rolling-pin into the crust, although she was very pale, and her heart beat loudly.

"I dun' know but what I'd better go," said Adoniram. "I hate to go off jest now, right in the midst of hayin', but the ten-acre lot's cut, an' I guess Rufus an' the others can git along without me three or four days. I can't get a horse around here to suit me, nohow, an' I've got to have another for all that wood-haulin' in the fall. I told Hiram to watch out, an' if he got wind of a good horse to let me know. I guess I'd better go."

"I'll get out your clean shirt an' collar," said Mrs. Penn calmly.

She laid out Adoniram's Sunday suit and his clean clothes on the bed in the little bedroom. She got his shaving-water and razor ready. At last she buttoned on his collar and fastened his black cravat.

Adoniram never wore his collar and cravat except on

extra occasions. He held his head high, with a rasped dignity. When he was all ready, with his coat and hat brushed, and a lunch of pie and cheese in a paper bag, he hesitated on the threshold of the door. He looked at his wife, and his manner was definitely apologetic. "*If* them cows come to-day, Sammy can drive 'em into the new barn," said he; "an' when they bring the hay up, they can pitch it in there."

"Well," replied Mrs. Penn.

Adoniram set his shaven face ahead and started. When he had cleared the door-step, he turned and looked back with a kind of nervous solemnity. "I shall be back by Saturday if nothin' happens," said he.

"Do be careful, father," returned his wife.

She stood in the door with Nanny at her elbow and watched him out of sight. Her eyes had a strange, doubtful expression in them; her peaceful forehead was contracted. She went in, and about her baking again. Nanny sat sewing. Her wedding-day was drawing nearer, and she was getting pale and thin with her steady sewing. Her mother kept glancing at her.

"Have you got that pain in your side this mornin'?" she asked.

"A little."

Mrs. Penn's face, as she worked, changed, her perplexed forehead smoothed, her eyes were steady, her lips firmly set. She formed a maxim for herself, although incoherently with her unlettered thoughts. "Unsolicited opportunities are the guide-posts of the Lord to the new roads of life," she repeated in effect, and she made up her mind to her course of action.

"S'posin' I *had* wrote to Hiram," she muttered once, when she was in the pantry—"s'posin' I had wrote, an' asked him if he knew of any horse? But I didn't, an' father's goin' wa'n't none of my doin'. It looks like a providence." Her voice rang out quite loud at the last.

"What you talkin' about, mother?" called Nanny.

"Nothin'."

Mrs. Penn hurried her baking; at eleven o'clock it was all done. The load of hay from the west field came slowly down the cart track, and drew up at the new barn. Mrs. Penn ran out. "Stop!" she screamed, "stop!"

The men stopped and looked; Sammy upreared from the top of the load, and stared at his mother.

"Stop!" she cried out again. "Don't you put the hay in that barn; put it in the old one."

"Why, he said to put it in here," returned one of the haymakers, wonderingly. He was a young man, a neighbor's son, whom Adoniram hired by the year to help on the farm.

"Don't you put the hay in the new barn; there's room enough in the old one, ain't there?" said Mrs. Penn.

"Room enough," returned the hired man, in his thick, rustic tones. "Didn't need the new barn, nohow, far as room's concerned. Well, I s'pose he changed his mind." He took hold of the horses' bridles.

Mrs. Penn went back to the house. Soon the kitchen windows were darkened, and a fragrance like warm honey came into the room.

Nanny laid down her work. "I thought father wanted them to put the hay into the new barn?" she said, wonderingly.

"It's all right," replied her mother.

Sammy slid down from the load of hay, and came in to see if dinner was ready.

"I ain't goin' to get a regular dinner to-day, as long as father's gone," said his mother. "I've let the fire go out. You can have some bread an' milk an' pie. I thought we could get along." She set out some bowls of milk, some bread, and a pie on the kitchen table. "You'd better eat your dinner now," said she. "You might jest as well get through with it. I want you to help me afterwards."

Nanny and Sammy stared at each other. There was something strange in their mother's manner. Mrs. Penn did not eat anything herself. She went into the pantry, and they heard her moving dishes while they ate. Presently she came out with a pile of plates. She got the clothes-basket out of the shed, and packed them in it. Nanny and Sammy watched. She brought out cups and saucers, and put them in with the plates.

"What you goin' to do, mother?" inquired Nanny, in a timid voice. A sense of something unusual made her tremble, as if it were a ghost. Sammy rolled his eyes over his pie.

"You'll see what I'm goin' to do," replied Mrs. Penn.
"If you're through, Nanny, I want you to go up-stairs an'
pack up your things; an' I want you, Sammy, to help me
take down the bed in the bedroom."

"Oh, mother, what for?" gasped Nanny.

"You'll see."

During the next few hours a feat was performed by this
simple, pious New England mother which was equal in its
way to Wolfe's storming of the Heights of Abraham. It
took no more genius and audacity of bravery for Wolfe to
cheer his wondering soldiers up those steep precipices,
under the sleeping eyes of the enemy, than for Sarah Penn,
at the head of her children, to move all their little household goods into the new barn while her husband was away.

Nanny and Sammy followed their mother's instructions
without a murmur; indeed, they were overawed. There is
a certain uncanny and superhuman quality about all such
purely original undertakings as their mother's was to them.
Nanny went back and forth with her light load, and Sammy
tugged with sober energy.

At five o'clock in the afternoon the little house in which
the Penns had lived for forty years had emptied itself into
the new barn.

Every builder builds somewhat for unknown purposes,
and is in a measure a prophet. The architect of Adoniram
Penn's barn, while he designed it for the comfort of four-
footed animals, had planned better than he knew for the
comfort of humans. Sarah Penn saw at a glance its possibilities. Those great box-stalls, with quilts hung before
them, would make better bedrooms than the one she had
occupied for forty years, and there was a tight carriage-
room. The harness-room, with its chimney and shelves,
would make a kitchen of her dreams. The great middle
space would make a parlor, by-and-by, fit for a palace.
Up-stairs there was as much room as down. With partitions
and windows, what a house would there be! Sarah looked
at the row of stanchions before the allotted space for cows,
and reflected that she would have her front entry there.

At six o'clock the stove was up in the harness room, the
kettle was boiling, and the table set for tea. It looked almost
as home-like as the abandoned house across the yard had
ever done. The young hired man milked, and Sarah directed
him calmly to bring the milk to the new barn. He came

gaping, dropping little blots of foam from the brimming pails on the grass. Before the next morning he had spread the story of Adoniram Penn's wife moving into the new barn all over the little village. Men assembled in the store and talked it over, women with shawls over their heads scuttled into each other's houses before their work was done. Any deviation from the ordinary course of life in this quiet town was enough to stop all progress in it. Everybody paused to look at the staid, independent figure on the side track. There was a difference of opinion with regard to her. Some held her to be insane; some, of a lawless and rebellious spirit.

Friday the minister went to see her. It was in the forenoon, and she was at the barn door shelling peas for dinner. She looked up and returned his salutation with dignity, then she went on with her work. She did not invite him in. The saintly expression of her face remained fixed, but there was an angry flush over it.

The minister stood awkwardly before her, and talked. She handled the peas as if they were bullets. At last she looked up, and her eyes showed the spirit that her meek front had covered for a lifetime.

"There ain't no use talkin', Mr. Hersey," said she. "I've thought it all over an' over, an' I believe I'm doin' what's right. I've made it the subject of prayer, an' it's betwixt me an' the Lord an' Adoniram. There ain't no call for nobody else to worry about it."

"Well, of course, if you have brought it to the Lord in prayer, and feel satisfied that you are doing right, Mrs. Penn," said the minister, helplessly. His thin gray-bearded face was pathetic. He was a sickly man; his youthful confidence had cooled; he had to scourge himself up to some of his pastoral duties as relentlessly as a Catholic ascetic, and then he was prostrated by the smart.

"I think it's right jest as much as I think it was right for our forefathers to come over here from the old country 'cause they didn't have what belonged to 'em," said Mrs. Penn. She arose. The barn threshold might have been Plymouth Rock from her bearing. "I don't doubt you mean well, Mr. Hersey," said she, "but there are things people hadn't ought to interfere with. I've been a member of the church for over forty years. I've got my own mind an' my own feet, an' I'm goin' to think my own thoughts an' go my own way, an' nobody but the Lord is goin' to dictate to me unless I've a mind to have him. Won't you come in an' set down? How is Mis' Hersey?"

"She is well, I thank you," replied the minister. He added some more perplexed apologetic remarks; then he retreated.

He could expound the intricacies of every character study in the Scriptures, he was competent to grasp the Pilgrim Fathers and all historical innovators, but Sarah Penn was beyond him. He could deal with primal cases, but parallel ones worsted him. But, after all, although it was aside from his province, he wondered more how Adoniram Penn would deal with his wife than how the Lord would. Everybody shared the wonder. When Adoniram's four new cows arrived, Sarah ordered three to be put in the old barn, the other in the house shed where the cooking-stove had stood. That added to the excitement. It was whispered that all four cows were domiciled in the house.

Towards sunset on Saturday, when Adoniram was expected home, there was a knot of men in the road near the new barn. The hired man had milked, but he still hung around the premises. Sarah Penn had supper all ready. There were brown-bread and baked beans and a custard pie; it was the supper that Adoniram loved on a Saturday night. She had on a clean calico, and she bore herself imperturbably. Nanny and Sammy kept close at her heels. Their eyes were large, and Nanny was full of nervous tremors. Still there was to them more pleasant excitement than anything else. An inborn confidence in their mother over their father asserted itself.

Sammy looked out of the harness-room window. "There he is," he announced, in an awed whisper. He and Nanny peeped around the casing. Mrs. Penn kept on about her work. The children watched Adoniram leave the new horse standing in the drive while he went to the house door. It was fastened. Then he went around to the shed. That door was seldom locked, even when the family was away. The thought how her father would be confronted by the cow flashed upon Nanny. There was a hysterical sob in her throat. Adoniram emerged from the shed and stood looking about in a dazed fashion. His lips moved; he was saying something, but they could not hear what it was. The hired man was peeping around a corner of the old barn, but nobody saw him.

Adoniram took the new horse by the bridle and led him across the yard to the new barn. Nanny and Sammy slunk close to their mother. The barn doors rolled back, and there stood Adoniram, with the long mild face of the great Canadian farm horse looking over his shoulder.

Nanny kept behind her mother, but Sammy stepped suddenly forward, and stood in front of her.

Adoniram stared at the group. "What on airth you all down here for?" said he. "What's the matter over to the house?"

"We've come here to live, father," said Sammy. His shrill voice quavered out bravely.

"What"—Adoniram sniffed—"what is it smells like cookin'?" said he. He stepped forward and looked in the open door of the harness-room. Then he turned to his wife. His old bristling face was pale and frightened. "What on airth does this mean, mother?" he gasped.

"You come in here, father," said Sarah. She led the way into the harness-room and shut the door. "Now, father," said she, "you needn't be scared. I ain't crazy. There ain't nothin' to be upset over. But we've come here to live, an' we're goin' to live here. We've got jest as good a right here as new horses an' cows. The house wasn't fit for us to live in any longer, an' I made up my mind I wa'n't goin' to stay there. I've done my duty by you forty year, an' I'm goin' to do it now; but I'm goin' to live here. You've got to put in some windows and partitions; an' you'll have to buy some furniture."

"Why, mother!" the old man gasped.

"You'd better take your coat off an' get washed—there's the wash basin—an' then we'll have supper."

"Why, mother!"

Sammy went past the window, leading the new horse to the old barn. The old man saw him, and shook his head speechlessly. He tried to take off his coat, but his arms seemed to lack the power. His wife helped him. She poured some water into the tin basin, and put in a piece of soap. She got the comb and brush, and smoothed his thin gray hair after he had washed. Then she put the beans, hot bread, and tea on the table. Sammy came in, and the family drew up. Adoniram sat looking dazedly at his plate, and they waited.

"Ain't you goin' to ask a blessin', father?" said Sarah.

And the old man bent his head and mumbled.

All through the meal he stopped eating at intervals, and stared furtively at his wife; but he ate well. The home food tasted good to him, and his old frame was too sturdily healthy to be affected by his mind. But after supper he went out, and sat down on the step of the smaller door at the right of the barn, through which he had meant his Jerseys to pass in stately file, but which Sarah designed for her front house door, and he leaned his head on his hands.

After the supper dishes were cleared away and the milk-pans washed, Sarah went out to him. The twilight was deepening. There was a clear green glow in the sky. Before them stretched the smooth level of field; in the distance was a cluster of hay-stacks like the huts of a village; the air was very cool and calm and sweet. The landscape might have been an ideal one of peace.

Sarah bent over and touched her husband on one of his thin, sinewy shoulders. "Father!"

The old man's shoulders heaved: he was weeping.

"Why, don't do so, father," said Sarah.

"I'll—put up the—partitions, an'—everything you—want, mother."

Sarah put her apron up to her face; she was overcome by her own triumph.

Adoniram was like a fortress whose walls had no active resistance, and went down the instant the right besieging tools were used. "Why, mother," he said, hoarsely, "I hadn't no idee you was so set on't as all this comes to."

1890

MARK TWAIN
(Samuel Langhorne Clemens)
(1835–1910)

Editions of the work of Mark Twain are *The Writings of Mark Twain*, 22 vols. (1899–1900), the Autograph edition; *The Writings of Mark Twain*, 25 vols. (1901–1907), the Underwood edition; *The Writings of Mark Twain*, 25 vols. (1907–1918), the Author's National edition; *The Writings of Mark Twain*, 37 vols. (1922–1925), the standard (Albert B. Paine) edition; and *Mark Twain's Works*, 23 vols. (1933).

Twain's published works include *The Celebrated Jumping Frog of Calaveras County* (1867); *The Innocents Abroad* (1869); *Mark Twain's (Burlesque) Autobiography* (1871); *Roughing It* (1872); *The Gilded Age* (1873) with Charles Dudley Warner; *Mark Twain's Sketches* (1875); *The Adventures of Tom Sawyer* (1876); *A True Story* (1877); *Punch, Brothers, Punch!* (1878); *A Tramp Abroad* (1880); *The Prince and the Pauper* (1882); *The Stolen White Elephant* (1882); *Life on the Mississippi* (1883); *Adventures of Huckleberry Finn* (1884); *A Connecticut Yankee in King Arthur's Court* (1889); *The American Claimant* (1892); *Merry Tales* (1892); *The £1,-000,000 Bank-Note* (1893); *Tom Sawyer Abroad* (1894); *Pudd'nhead Wilson* (1894); *Personal Recollections of Joan of Arc* (1896); *Tom Sawyer, Detective* (1896); *Following the Equator* (1897); *How to Tell a Story and Other Essays* (1897); *The Man that Corrupted Hadleyburg* (1900); *A Double Barrelled Detective Story* (1902); *My Debut as a Literary Person* (1903); *A Dog's Tale* (1904); *Extracts from Adam's Diary* (1904); *King Leopold's Soliloquy* (1905); *What Is Man?* (1906); *The $30,000 Bequest* (1906); *Eve's Diary* (1906); *Christian Science* (1907); *A Horse's Tale* (1907); *Is Shakespeare Dead?* (1909); *Captain Stormfield's Visit to Heaven* (1909); *Mark Twain's Speeches* (1910); *The Mysterious Stranger* (1916); *What Is Man? and Other Essays* (1917); *Mark Twain's Letters*, 2 vols. (1917); *The Curious Republic of Gondour* (1919); *The*

Mysterious Stranger and Other Stories (1922); *Europe and Elsewhere* (1923); *Mark Twain's Autobiography*, 2 vols. (1924), re-edited by C. Neider as *The Autobiography of Mark Twain, Including Chapters Now Published for the First Time* (1959); *Mark Twain's Notebook* (1935); G. E. Dane, ed., *Letters from the Sandwich Islands* (1937); F. Walker, ed., *The Washoe Giant in San Francisco* (1938); F. J. Meine, ed., *1601* (1939) though there were various surreptitious printings during Twain's lifetime; T. Nickerson, ed., *Letters from Honolulu* (1939); B. DeVoto, ed., *Mark Twain in Eruption* (1940); F. Walker and G. E. Dane, eds., *Mark Twain's Travels with Mr. Brown* (1940); C. Clemens, ed., *Republican Letters* (1941); T. Hornberger, ed., *Mark Twain's Letters to Will Bowen* (1941); E. M. Branch, ed., *Mark `Twain's Letters in the Muscatine Journal* (1942); D. Wecter, ed., *Mark Twain in Three Moods* (1948); D. Wecter, ed., *The Love Letters of Mark Twain* (1949); D. Wecter, ed., *Mark Twain to Mrs. Fairbanks* (1949); D. Wecter, ed., *Report from Paradise* (1952); H. N. Smith and F. Anderson, eds., *Mark Twain of the Enterprise* (1957); H. N. Smith and W. Gibson, eds., *Mark Twain—Howells Letters*, 2 vols. (1960); W. Blair, ed., *Selected Shorter Writings of Mark Twain* (1962); B. DeVoto, ed., *Letters from the Earth* (1962); and C. Neider, ed., *The Complete Essays of Mark Twain* (1963).

The Viking Portable Mark Twain, edited by Bernard DeVoto, contains *Huckleberry Finn* and *The Mysterious Stranger* complete. Twain's fiction is further represented by "The Notorious Jumping Frog of Calaveras County" and selections from *A Tramp Abroad* and from *A Connecticut Yankee in King Arthur's Court*. Autobiography, opinion, essay, and épigram are represented by "The Private History of a Campaign that Failed," "Fenimore Cooper's Literary Offenses," and selections from *Old Times on the Mississippi, Pudd'nhead Wilson, Following the Equator, Mark Twain in Eruption, Europe and Elsewhere,* and Mark Twain's *Autobiography*. The volume also includes twenty-eight Mark Twain letters.

Studies of the man and his work are to be found in, W. D. Howells, *My Mark Twain* (1910); A. B. Paine, *Mark Twain, A Biography,* 3 vols. (1912); V. W. Brooks, *The Ordeal of Mark Twain* (1920, 1933); C. Clemens, *My Father: Mark Twain* (1931); B. DeVoto, *Mark Twain's America* (1932); S. Leacock, *Mark Twain* (1933); M. Brashear, *Mark Twain: Son of Missouri* (1934); T. Dreiser, "Mark the Double Twain," *English Journal*, XXIV (1935); F. L. Pattee, ed., *Mark Twain: Representative Selections* (1935); E. Wagenknecht, *Mark Twain: The Man and His Work* (1935, 1961); E. L. Masters, *Mark Twain: A Portrait* (1938); E. H. Hemminghaus, *Mark Twain in Germany* (1939); O. Read, *Mark Twain and I* (1940); B. DeVoto, *Mark Twain at Work* (1942); W. F. Taylor, *The Economic Novel in America* (1942); C. Clemens, *Young Sam Clemens* (1943); J. D. Ferguson, *Mark Twain: Man and Legend* (1943); S. C. Webster, *Mark Twain: Businessman* (1946); W. F. Freer, *Mark Twain and Hawaii* (1947); A. Cowie, *The Rise of the American Novel* (1948); R. W. West, Jr., "Mark

Twain's Idyl of Frontier America," *University of Kansas City Review,* XV (1948); A. Byrnes, "Boy-Men and Man-Boys," *Yale Review,* XXXVIII (1949); K. Andrews, *Nook Farm: Twain's Hartford Circle* (1950); G. C. Bellamy, *Mark Twain as Literary Artist* (1950); E. M. Branch, *The Literary Apprenticeship of Mark Twain* (1950); J. Jones, "Utopia as Dirge," *American Quarterly,* II (1950); H. S. Canby, *Turn West, Turn East: Mark Twain and Henry James* (1951); D. Wecter, *Sam Clemens of Hannibal* (1952); G. A. Cardwell, *Twins of Genius* (1953); L. Marx, "Mr. Eliot, Mr. Trilling, and *Huckleberry Finn,*" *American Scholar,* XXII (1953); R. Asselineau, *The Literary Reputation of Mark Twain from 1910 to 1950* (1954); A. L. Scott, ed., *Mark Twain, Selected Criticism* (1955); H. H. Clark, "Mark Twain," *Eight American Authors: A Review of Research and Criticism* (1956); A. E. Jones, "Mark Twain and Sexuality," *PMLA,* LXXI (1956); J. Blanck, *Bibliography of American Literature,* II (1957); R. Chase, *The American Novel and Its Tradition* (1957); G. P. Elliott, "Wonder for *Huckleberry Finn,*" in C. Shapiro, ed., *Twelve Original Essays on Great American Novels* (1958); P. S. Foner, *Mark Twain: Social Critic* (1958); H. E. Long, *Mark Twain Handbook* (1958); D. M. McKeithan, *Court Trials in Mark Twain and Other Essays* (1958); B. Marks, ed., *Mark Twain's Huckleberry Finn* (1959); W. Blair, *Mark Twain & Huck Finn* (1960); P. Fatout, *Mark Twain on the Lecture Circuit* (1960); C. T. Harnsberger, *Mark Twain: Family Man* (1960); K. S. Lynn, *Mark Twain and Southwestern Humor* (1960); *Mark Twain Anniversary Number, Journal of the Central Mississippi Valley American Studies Association,* I (1960); F. R. Rogers, *Mark Twain's Burlesque Patterns as Seen in the Novels and Narratives, 1855–1885* (1960); A. Turner, *Mark Twain and George W. Cable* (1960); L. J. Budd, *Mark Twain: Social Philosopher* (1962); S. Bradley et al., eds., *Adventures of Huckleberry Finn, an Annotated Text* (1962); P. Covici, Jr., *Mark Twain's Humor* (1962); H. Hill and W. Blair, *The Art of Huckleberry Finn* (1962); L. Leary, ed., *A Casebook on Mark Twain's Wound* (1962); H. N. Smith, *Mark Twain: The Development of a Writer* (1962); D. Grant, *Mark Twain* (1963); H. N. Smith, ed., *Mark Twain: Collection of Critical Essays* (1963); J. S. Tuckey, *Mark Twain and Little Satan* (1963); the Clemens issue of *American Quarterly,* XVI (1964); P. Fatout, *Mark Twain in Virginia City* (1964); H. Hill, *Mark Twain and Elisha Bliss* (1964); H. N. Smith, *Mark Twain's Fable of Progress* (1964); R. A. Wiggins, *Mark Twain: Jackleg Novelist* (1964); M. Duckett, *Mark Twain and Bret Harte* (1965); B. M. French, *Mark Twain and the Gilded Age* (1965); E. C. Salisbury, ed., *Susy and Mark Twain* (1965); I. M. Cox, *Mark Twain* (1966); J. Kaplan, *Mr. Clemens and Mark Twain* (1966); R. Regan, *Unpromising Heroes: Mark Twain and His Characters* (1966); and W. Spengemann, *Mark Twain and the Backwoods Angel* (1967).

WILLIAM DEAN HOWELLS

(1837–1920)

In the world of literature, the middle way is not always the safest—one tends to get hit from both sides. Although at the height of his fame Howells was the unofficial Dean of American Letters, having put on a one-man literary show of extraordinary energy and much merit (in his publishing life he produced over one hundred books), his brand of "homely average" realism was periodically attacked on the one hand by the champions of the romance (such as Robert Louis Stevenson) as being emotionally stultifying, and on the other by the naturalists as being morally timid. Toward the opponents of the right—the sentimentalizing idealists—Howells was unequivocally severe: having turned away from "the fruitful fields of our common life," they tended toward "silly slop" that was "false and impossible." Toward the opponents of the left—the naturalistic realists who began to emerge around the turn of the century—his attitude was more complex: he recognized the vitality in such robust writers as Stephen Crane and Frank Norris and enthusiastically encouraged them, but his own work tended to stop decorously this side of the presentation of crime and sexual passion. To be sure, in his critical essays he attempted to formulate a theoretical basis for such novelistic inhibitions (bizarre crime was eccentric and sexual passion inappropriate for the Young Girl audience), but one suspects that his personal attraction to the "cleanly respectabilities" lies very much at the heart of both his theory and practice. That he was aware, no less than the naturalists, of the darker dimensions of the American experience, of the undemocratic aspects of the Democracy ("grotesquely illogical," he once called it), is undeniable. His strong Socialist sympathies were the result of his reading of such theorists as Tolstoy, Morris, Bellamy, and Laurence Gronlund (*The Co-operative Commonwealth*). These sympathies, his increasing interest during the 1880's in the problems of our industrial society, and his novels of social injustice—such as *A Hazard of New Fortunes* (1890) and *The Quality of Mercy* (1892)—bear ample testimony that Howells was not an ostrich-optimist. Rather, he was very much afraid (as he confessed to Henry James) that the American Experiment was going to "come out all wrong in the end, unless it bases itself anew on a real equality." But the harshly angry response to America's undeniable defects struck Howells as potentially distortive, for in its outrage the pessimism tended to lose sight of "the more smiling aspects of life," which, in the final analysis, Howells felt to be "the more American."

Howells's life was long, productive, and, for the most part, smiling. Born in Martin's Ferry, Ohio, Howells was the son of a printer-publisher of a mystical (specifically Swedenborgian) turn of mind. His formal schooling was almost nil, but so thoroughly did he educate himself in languages and literature that he had occasion in his later life to decline professorships at Harvard, Yale, and Johns Hopkins. The Howells family hopped from Ohio town to Ohio town, including in its jaunts a year in a log cabin. In Hamilton, at the age of nine, William Dean set type in his father's newspaper office; in Dayton, at the age of twelve, he was a compositor in a printing shop; in Ashtabula and Jefferson and Columbus and Cincinnati he did newspaper work, becoming, before he was twenty, political editorialist of the Columbus *Ohio State Journal*. In 1860, he published (with J. J. Piatt) *Poems of Two Friends* and wrote a Lincoln campaign biography for which, in the following year, he was rewarded with a consulship in Venice. To his four years in Venice he owed not only such travel books as *Venetian Life* (1866) and *Italian Journeys* (1867) but also the locale for such "international" novels of Americans in Europe as *A Foregone Conclusion* (1875), *The Lady of the Aroostook* (1879), and *A Fearful Responsibility* (1881). Back in America, he worked for *The Nation* for a brief time before going to Boston to join the staff of the *Atlantic Monthly;* in five years he became its chief editor. Howells's great range of critical appreciation can be seen in his publishing in the pages of the *Atlantic* such opposite literary talents as "redskin" Mark Twain and "paleface" Henry James, both of whom became his friends. In 1881 he resigned his editorship and spent four years abroad. From 1886 until 1892 he conducted "The Editor's Study" for *Harper's Magazine*, in which he fought the good fight for realism in fiction. *Criticism and Fiction* (1891) is a collection of some of his *Harper's* essays. In 1900 he returned as the "Easy Chair" essayist for *Harper's*, continuing in that capacity until his death in 1920. For the last twelve years of his life he was the president of the American Academy of Arts and Letters.

In 1912, on the occasion of his seventy-fifth birthday, Howells was given a dinner attended by many notables, including President Taft. But despite the fact that his last years were filled with honors, he had, as he himself knew, outlived his time. The realism that he had championed and helped to establish had gone so far beyond him that it could turn around to sneer without a sense of ingratitude. Only eleven years after Howells's death, Sinclair Lewis could speak of him as "a pious old maid" who had established for American literature "a very bad standard." Fortunately we have repudiated such facile deprecations and have come to assess more accurately Howells's contribution to the literature of our national life. His enormous understanding of the commonplace and the trivial and his quiet sense of life's limitations remind us (as his beloved Jane Austen reminds us) of how much moral reality is couched in the "foolish and insipid face" of "poor Real Life."

In addition to the titles mentioned above, Howells's fiction includes *Their Wedding Journey* (1872); *The Undiscovered Country* (1880); *Doctor Breen's Practice* (1881); *A Modern Instance* (1882); *The Rise of Silas Lapham* (1885); *Indian Summer* (1886); *April Hopes* (1888); *The Shadow of a Dream* (1890); *An Imperative Duty* (1892); *A Traveler from Altruria* (1894); *The Landlord at Lion's Head* (1897); *The Kentons* (1902); *The Son of Royal Langbrith* (1904); *Through the Eye of the Needle* (1907); *New Leaf Mills* (1913); and *The Leatherwood God* (1916). His books of criticism and biography include, in addition to the titles mentioned above, *Three Villages* (1884); *Modern Italian Poets* (1887); *A Boy's Town* (1890); *My Year in a Log Cabin* (1893); *My Literary Passions* (1895); *Impressions and Experiences* (1896); *Literary Friends and Acquaintance* (1900); *Heroines of Fiction* (1901); *Literature and Life* (1902); *My Mark Twain* (1910); and *Years of My Youth* (1916). Howells also wrote thirty-one plays and four books of poetry in addition to the joint effort with Piatt.

There is no collected edition of Howells' works. Accounts of the man and his work can be found in H. Garland, "Sanity in Fiction," *North American Review*, CLXXVI (1903); Mark Twain, "William Dean Howells," *Harper's Magazine*, CXIII (1906); H. L. Mencken, *Prejudices: First Series* (1919); D. Cooke, *William Dean Howells: A Critical Study* (1922); O. Firkins, *William Dean Howells: A Study* (1924); A. Howells, ed.,

Life in Letters of William Dean Howells, 2 vols. (1928); V. Parrington, *Main Currents in American Thought,* III (1930); J. Getzels, "William Dean Howells and Socialism," *Science and Society,* II (1938); B. Smith, *Forces in American Criticism* (1939); V. W. Brooks, *New England: Indian Summer* (1940); W. Taylor, *The Economic Novel in America* (1942); W. Gibson and G. Arms, *A Bibliography of William Dean Howells* (1948); H. Commager, ed., *Selected Writings of William Dean Howells* (1950); C. Kirk and R. Kirk, eds., *William Dean Howells: Representative Selections* (1950); L. Trilling, "W. D. Howells and the Roots of Modern Taste," *Partisan Review,* XVIII (1951); J. Woodress, *Howells and Italy* (1952); E. Carter, *Howells and the Age of Realism* (1954); E. Cady, *The Road to Realism: The Early Years, 1837–1885, of William Dean Howells* (1956); E. Cady, *The Realist at War: The Mature Years, 1885–1920, of William Dean Howells* (1958); O. Fryckstedt, *In Quest of America: A Study of Howells's Early Development as a Novelist* (1958); G. Bennett, *William Dean Howells: The Development of a Novelist* (1959); V. W. Brooks, *Howells: His Life and World* (1959); R. Hough, *The Quiet Rebel: William Dean Howells as Social Commentator* (1959); C. Kirk and R. Kirk, eds., *Criticism and Fiction and Other Essays* (1959); W. Wasserstrom, *The Heiress of All the Ages: Sex and Sentiment in the Genteel Tradition* (1959); W. Meserve, ed., *The Complete Plays of William Dean Howells* (1960); H. N. Smith and W. Gibson, eds., *Mark Twain–Howells Letters,* 2 vols. (1960); E. H. Cady and D. L. Frazier, eds., *The War of the Critics over William Dean Howells* (1962); K. E. Eble, ed., *Howells: A Century of Criticism* (1962); C. M. Kirk, W. D. Howells: Traveler from Altruria* (1962); C. M. Kirk and R. Kirk, *William Dean Howells* (1962); M. Millgate, *American Social Fiction: James to Cozzens* (1964); C. M. Kirk, *W. D. Howells and Art in His Time* (1965); N. Wright, *American Novelists in Italy* (1965); R. W. Schneider, *Five Novelists of the Progressive Era* (1965); and G. C. Carrington, Jr., *The Immense Complex Drama: The World and Art of the Howells Novel* (1966).

A Romance of Real Life

It was long past the twilight hour, which has been elsewhere mentioned as so oppressive in suburban places, and it was even too late for visitors, when a resident, whom I shall briefly describe as the Contributor, was startled by a ring at his door, in the vicinity of one of our great maritime cities,—say Plymouth or Manchester. As any thoughtful person would have done upon the like occasion, he ran over his acquaintance in his mind, speculating whether it were such or such a one, and dismissing the whole list of improbabilities, before laying down the book he was reading, and answering the bell. When at last he did this, he was rewarded by the apparition of an utter stranger on his threshold,—a gaunt figure of forlorn and curious smartness towering far above him, that jerked him a nod of the head, and asked if Mr. Hapford lived there. The face which the lamplight revealed was remarkable for a harsh two days' growth of beard, and a single bloodshot eye; yet it was not otherwise a sinister countenance, and there was something in the strange presence that appealed and touched. The contributor, revolving the facts vaguely in his mind, was not sure, after all, that it was not the man's clothes rather than his expression that softened him towards the rugged visage: they were so tragically cheap, and the misery of helpless needlewomen and the poverty and ignorance of the purchaser were so apparent in their shabby newness, of which they appeared still conscious enough to have led the way to the very window, in the Semitic quarter of the city, where they had lain ticketed, "This nobby suit for $15."

But the stranger's manner put both his face and his clothes out of mind, and claimed a deeper interest when, being answered that the person for whom he asked did not live there, he set his bristling lips hard together, and sighed heavily.

"They told me," he said, in a hopeless way, "that he lived on this street, and I've been to every other house. I'm very anxious to find him, Cap'n,"—the contributor, of course, had no claim to the title with which he was thus decorated,—"for I've a daughter living with him, and I want to see her; I've just got home from a two years' voyage, and"—there was a struggle of the Adam's-apple in the man's gaunt throat—"I find she's about all there is left of my family."

How complex is every human motive! This contributor had been lately thinking, whenever he turned the pages of some foolish traveller,—some empty prattler of Southern or Eastern lands, where all sensation was long ago exhausted, and the oxygen has perished from every sentiment, so has it been breathed and breathed again,—that nowadays the wise adventurer sat down beside his own register and waited for incidents to seek him out. It seemed to him that the cultivation of a patient and receptive spirit was the sole condition needed to insure the occurrence of all manner of surprising facts within the range of one's own personal knowledge; that not only the Greeks were at our doors, but the fairies and the genii, and all the people of romance, who had but to be hospitably treated in order to develop the deepest interest of fiction, and to become the characters of plots so ingenious that the most cunning invention were poor beside them. I myself am not so confident of this, and would rather trust Mr. Charles Reade, say, for my amusement than any chance combination of events. But I should be afraid to say how much his pride in the character of the stranger's sorrows, as proof of the correctness of his theory, prevailed with the contributor to ask him to come in and sit down; though I hope that some abstract impulse of humanity, some compassionate and unselfish care for the man's misfortunes as misfortunes, was not wholly wanting. Indeed, the helpless simplicity with which he had confided his case might have touched a harder heart. "Thank you," said the poor fellow, after a moment's hesitation. "I believe I will come in. I've been on foot all day, and after such a long voyage it makes a man dreadfully sore to walk about so much. Perhaps you can think of a Mr. Hapford living somewhere in the neighborhood."

He sat down, and, after a pondering silence, in which he had remained with his head fallen upon his breast, "My name is Jonathan Tinker," he said, with the unaffected air which had already impressed the contributor, and as if he felt that some form of introduction was necessary, "and the girl that I want to find is Julia Tinker." Then he said, resuming the eventful personal history which the listener exulted while he regretted to hear: "You see, I shipped first to Liverpool, and there I heard from my family; and then I shipped again for Hong-Kong, and after that I never heard a word: I seemed to miss the letters everywhere. This morning, at four o'clock, I left my ship as soon as she had hauled into the dock, and hurried up home. The house was shut, and not a soul in it; and I didn't know what to do, and I sat down on the doorstep to wait till the neighbors woke up, to ask them what had become of my family. And the first one come out he told me my wife had been dead a year and a half, and the baby I'd never seen, with her; and one of my boys was dead; and he didn't know where the rest of the children was, but he'd heard two of the little ones was with a family in the city."

The man mentioned these things with the half-apologetic air observable in a certain kind of Americans when some accident obliges them to confess the infirmity of the natural feelings. They do not ask your sympathy, and you offer it quite at your own risk, with a chance of having it thrown back upon your hands. The contributor assumed the risk so far as to say, "Pretty rough!" when the stranger paused; and perhaps these homely words were best suited to reach the homely heart. The man's quivering lips closed hard again, a kind of spasm passed over his dark face, and then two very small drops of brine shone upon his weather-worn cheeks. This demonstration, into which he had been surprised, seemed to stand for the passion of tears into which the emotional races fall at such times. He opened his lips with a kind of dry click, and went on:—

"I hunted about the whole forenoon in the city, and at last I found the children. I'd been gone so long they didn't know me, and somehow I thought the people they were with weren't overglad I'd turned up. Finally the oldest child told me that Julia was living with a Mr. Hapford on this street, and I started out here to-night to look her up. If I can find her, I'm all right. I can get the family together, then, and start new."

"It seems rather odd," mused the listener aloud, "that the neighbors let them break up so, and that they should all scatter as they did."

"Well, it ain't so curious as it seems, Cap'n. There was money for them at the owners', all the time; I'd left part of my wages when I sailed; but they didn't know how to get at it, and what could a parcel of children do? Julia's a good girl, and when I find her I'm all right."

The writer could only repeat that there was no Mr. Hapford living on that street, and never had been, so far as he knew. Yet there might be such a person in the neighborhood; and they would go out together, and ask at some of the houses about. But the stranger must first take a glass of wine; for he looked used up.

The sailor awkwardly but civilly enough protested that he did not want to give so much trouble, but took the glass, and, as he put it to his lips, said formally, as if it were a toast or a kind of grace, "I hope I may have the opportunity of returning the compliment." The contributor thanked him; though, as he thought of all the circumstances of the case, and considered the cost at which the stranger had come to enjoy his politeness, he felt little eagerness to secure the return of the compliment at the same price, and added, with the consequence of another set phrase, "Not at all." But the thought had made him the more anxious to befriend the luckless soul fortune had cast in his way; and so the two sallied out together, and rang doorbells wherever lights were still seen burning in the windows, and asked the astonished people who answered their summons whether any Mr. Hapford were known to live in the neighborhood.

And although the search for this gentleman proved vain, the contributor could not feel that an expedition which set familiar objects in such novel lights was altogether a failure. He entered so intimately into the cares and anxieties of his "protégé," that at times he felt himself in some inexplicable sort a shipmate of Jonathan Tinker, and almost personally a partner of his calamities. The estrangement of all things which takes place, within doors and without, about midnight, may have helped to cast this doubt upon his identity;—he seemed to be visiting now for the first time the streets and neighborhoods nearest his own, and his feet stumbled over the accustomed walks. In his quality of houseless wanderer, and,—so far as appeared to others, —possibly, worthless vagabond, he also got a new and instructive effect upon the faces which, in his real character, he knew so well by their looks of neighborly greeting, and it is his belief that the first hospitable prompting of the human heart is to shut the door in the eyes of homeless strangers who present themselves after eleven o'clock. By that time the servants are all abed, and the gentleman of the house answers the bell, and looks out with a loath and bewildered face, which gradually changes to one of suspicion, and of wonder as to what those fellows can possibly want of *him,* till at last the prevailing expression is one of contrite desire to atone for the first reluctance by any sort of service. The contributor professes to have observed these changing phases in the visages of those whom he that night called from their dreams, or arrested in the act of going to bed; and he drew the conclusion—very proper for his imaginable connection with the garroting and other adventurous brotherhoods—that the most flattering moment for knocking on the head people who answer a late ring at night is either in their first selfish bewilderment, or their final self-abandonment to their better impulses. It does not seem to have occurred to him that he would himself have been a much more favorable subject for the predatory arts than any of his neighbors, if his shipmate, the unknown companion of his researches for Mr. Hapford, had been at all so minded. But the faith of the gaunt giant upon which he reposed was good, and the contributor continued to wander about with him in perfect safety. Not a soul among those they asked had ever heard of a Mr. Hapford,—far less of a Julia Tinker living with him. But they all listened to the contributor's explanation with interest and eventual sympathy; and in truth,—briefly told, with a word now and then thrown in by Jonathan Tinker, who kept at the bottom of the steps, showing like a gloomy spectre in the night, or, in his grotesque length and gauntness, like the other's shadow cast there by the lamplight,—it was a story which could hardly fail to awaken pity.

At last, after ringing several bells where there were no lights, in the mere wantonness of good-will, and going away before they could be answered (it would be entertaining to know what dreams they caused the sleepers within), there seemed to be nothing for it but to give up the search till morning, and go to the main street and wait for the last horse-car to the city.

There, seated upon the curbstone, Jonathan Tinker, being plied with a few leading questions, told in hints and scraps the story of his hard life, which was at present that of a second mate, and had been that of a cabin-boy and of a seaman before the mast. The second mate's place he held to be the hardest aboard ship. You got only a few dollars more than the men, and you did not rank with the officers; you took your meals alone, and in everything you belonged by yourself. The men did not respect you, and sometimes the captain abused you awfully before the passengers. The hardest captain that Jonathan Tinker ever sailed with was Captain Gooding; and Jonathan Tinker was with him only one voyage. When he had been home awhile, he saw an advertisement for a second mate, and he went round to the owners'. They had kept it secret who the captain was;

but there was Captain Gooding in the owners' office. "Why, here's the man, now, that I want for a second mate," said he, when Jonathan Tinker entered; "he knows me." "Captain Gooding, I know you 'most too well to want to sail under you," answered Jonathan. "I might go if I hadn't been with you one voyage too many already."

"And then the men!" said Jonathan, "the men coming aboard drunk, and having to be pounded sober! And the hardest of the fight falls on the second mate! Why, there isn't an inch of me that hasn't been cut over or smashed into a jell. I've had three ribs broken; I've got a scar from a knife on my cheek; and I've been stabbed bad enough, half a dozen times, to lay me up."

Here he gave a sort of desperate laugh, as if the notion of so much misery and such various mutilation were too grotesque not to be amusing. "Well, what can you do?" he went on. "If you don't strike, the men think you're afraid of them; and so you have to begin hard and go on hard. I always tell a man, 'Now, my man, I always begin with a man the way I mean to keep on. You do your duty and you're all right. But if you don't—' Well, the men ain't Americans any more,—Dutch, Spaniards, Chinese, Portugee,—and it ain't like abusing a white man."

Jonathan Tinker was plainly part of the horrible tyranny which we all know exists on shipboard; and his listener respected him the more that, though he had heart enough to be ashamed of it, he was too honest not to own it.

Why did he still follow the sea? Because he did not know what else to do. When he was younger, he used to love it, but now he hated it. Yet there was not a prettier life in the world if you got to be captain. He used to hope for that once, but not now; though he *thought* he could navigate a ship. Only let him get his family together again, and he would—yes, he would—try to do something ashore.

No car had yet come in sight, and so the contributor suggested that they should walk to the car-office, and look in the Directory which is kept there for the name of Hapford, in search of whom it had already been arranged that they should renew their acquaintance on the morrow. Jonathan Tinker, when they had reached the office, heard with constitutional phlegm that the name of the Hapford for whom he inquired was not in the Directory. "Never mind," said the other, "come round to my house in the morning. We'll find him yet." So they parted with a shake of the hand, the second mate saying that he believed he should go down to the vessel and sleep aboard,—if he could sleep,—and murmuring at the last moment the hope of returning the compliment, while the other walked homeward, weary as to the flesh, but, in spite of his sympathy for Jonathan Tinker, very elate in spirit. The truth is,—and however disgraceful to human nature, let the truth still be told,—he had recurred to his primal satisfaction in the man as calamity capable of being used for such and such literary ends, and, while he pitied him, rejoiced in him as an episode of real life quite as striking and complete as anything in fiction. It was literature made to his hand. Nothing could be better, he mused; and once more he passed the details of the story in review, and beheld all those pictures which the poor fellow's artless words had so vividly conjured up: he saw him leaping ashore in the gray summer dawn as soon as the ship hauled into the dock, and making his way, with his vague sea-legs unaccustomed to the pavements, up through the silent and empty city streets; he imagined the tumult of fear and hope which the sight of the man's home must have caused in him, and the benumbing shock of finding it blind and deaf to all his appeals; he saw him sitting down upon what had been his own threshold, and waiting in a sort of bewildered patience till the neighbors should be awake, while the noises of the streets gradually arose, and the wheels began to rattle over the stones, and the milkman and the iceman came and went, and the waiting figure began to be stared at, and to challenge the curiosity of the passing policeman; he fancied the opening of the neighbor's door, and the slow, cold understanding of the case; the manner, whatever it was, in which the sailor was told that one year before his wife had died, with her babe, and that his children were scattered, none knew where. As the contributor dwelt pityingly upon these things, but at the same time estimated their aesthetic value one by one, he drew near the head of his street, and found himself a few paces behind a boy slouching onward through the night, to whom he called out, adventurously, and with no real hope of information,—

"Do you happen to know anybody on this street by the name of Hapford?"

"Why no, not in this town," said the boy; but he added

that there was a street by the same name in a neighboring suburb, and a Hapford living on it.

"By Jove!" thought the contributor, "this is more like literature than ever"; and he hardly knew whether to be more provoked at his own stupidity in not thinking of a street of the same name in the next village, or delighted at the element of fatality which the fact introduced into the story; for Tinker, according to his own account, must have landed from the cars a few rods from the very door he was seeking, and so walked farther and farther from it every moment. He thought the case so curious, that he laid it briefly before the boy, who, however he might have been inwardly affected, was sufficiently true to the national traditions not to make the smallest conceivable outward sign of concern in it.

At home, however, the contributor related his adventures and the story of Tinker's life, adding the fact that he had just found out where Mr. Hapford lived. "It was the only touch wanting," said he; "the whole thing is now perfect."

"It's *too* perfect," was answered from a sad enthusiasm. "Don't speak of it! I can't take it in."

"But the question is," said the contributor, penitently taking himself to task for forgetting the hero of these excellent misfortunes in his delight over their perfection, "how am I to sleep to-night, thinking of that poor soul's suspense and uncertainty? Never mind,—I'll be up early, and run over and make sure that it is Tinker's Hapford, before he gets out here, and have a pleasant surprise for him. Would it not be a justifiable *coup de theatre* to fetch his daughter here, and let her answer his ring at the door when he comes in the morning?"

This plan was discouraged. "No, no; let them meet in their own way. Just take him to Hapford's house and leave him."

"Very well. But he's too good a character to lose sight of. He's got to come back here and tell us what he intends to do."

The birds, next morning, not having had the second mate on their minds either as an unhappy man or a most fortunate episode, but having slept long and soundly, were singing in a very sprightly way in the wayside trees; and the sweetness of their notes made the contributor's heart light as he climbed the hill and rang at Mr. Hapford's door.

The door was opened by a young girl of fifteen or sixteen, whom he knew at a glance for the second mate's daughter, but of whom, for form's sake, he asked if there were a girl named Julia Tinker living there.

"My name's Julia Tinker," answered the maid, who had rather a disappointing face.

"Well," said the contributor, "your father's got back from his Hong-Kong voyage."

"Hong-Kong voyage?" echoed the girl, with a stare of helpless inquiry, but no other visible emotion.

"Yes. He had never heard of your mother's death. He came home yesterday morning, and was looking for you all day."

Julia Tinker remained open-mouthed but mute; and the other was puzzled at the want of feeling shown, which he could not account for even as a national trait. "Perhaps there's some mistake," he said.

"There must be," answered Julia: "my father hasn't been to sea for a good many years. *My* father," she added, with a diffidence indescribably mingled with a sense of distinction,—"*my* father's in State's Prison. What kind of looking man was this?"

The contributor mechanically described him.

Julia Tinker broke into a loud, hoarse laugh. "Yes, it's him, sure enough." And then, as if the joke were too good to keep: "Miss Hapford, Miss Hapford, father's got out. Do come here!" she called into a back room.

When Mrs. Hapford appeared, Julia fell back, and, having deftly caught a fly on the door-post, occupied herself in plucking it to pieces, while she listened to the conversation of the others.

"It's all true enough," said Mrs. Hapford, when the writer had recounted the moving story of Jonathan Tinker, "so far as the death of his wife and baby goes. But he hasn't been to sea for a good many years, and he must have just come out of State's Prison, where he was put for bigamy. There's always two sides to a story, you know; but they say it broke his first wife's heart, and she died. His friends don't want him to find his children, and this girl especially."

"He's found his children in the city," said the contributor, gloomily, being at a loss what to do or say, in view of the wreck of his romance.

"O, he's found 'em, has he?" cried Julia, with heightened amusement. "Then he'll have me next, if I don't pack and go."

"I'm very, very sorry," said the contributor, secretly resolved never to do another good deed, no matter how temptingly the opportunity presented itself. "But you may depend he won't find out from *me* where you are. Of course I had no earthly reason for supposing his story was not true."

"Of course," said kind-hearted Mrs. Hapford, mingling a drop of honey with the gall in the contributor's soul, "you only did your duty."

And indeed, as he turned away, he did not feel altogether without compensation. However Jonathan Tinker had fallen in his esteem as a man, he had even risen as literature. The episode which had appeared so perfect in its pathetic phases did not seem less finished as a farce; and this person, to whom all things of everyday life presented themselves in periods more or less rounded, and capable of use as facts or illustrations, could not but rejoice in these new incidents, as dramatically fashioned as the rest. It occurred to him that, wrought into a story, even better use might be made of the facts now than before, for they had developed questions of character and of human nature which could not fail to interest. The more he pondered upon his acquaintance with Jonathan Tinker, the more fascinating the erring mariner became, in his complex truth and falsehood, his delicately blending shades of artifice and *naïveté*. He must, it was felt, have believed to a certain point in his own inventions: nay, starting with that groundwork of truth,—the fact that his wife was really dead, and that he had not seen his family for two years,—why should he not place implicit faith in all the fictions reared upon it? It was probable that he felt a real sorrow for her loss, and that he found a fantastic consolation in depicting the circumstances of her death so that they should look like his inevitable misfortunes rather than his faults. He might well have repented his offence during those two years of prison; and why should he not now cast their dreariness and shame out of his memory, and replace them with the freedom and adventure of a two years' voyage to China,—so probable, in all respects, that the fact should appear an impossible nightmare? In the experiences of his life he had abundant mate-

rial to furnish forth the facts of such a voyage, and in the
weariness and lassitude that should follow a day's walking
equally after a two years' voyage and two years' imprison-
ment, he had as much physical proof in favor of one hypothesis as the other. It was doubtless true, also, as he said,
that he had gone to his house at dawn, and sat down on
the threshold of his ruined home; and perhaps he felt the
desire he had expressed to see his daughter, with a purpose
of beginning life anew; and it may have cost him a veritable
pang when he found that his little ones did not know him.
All the sentiments of the situation were such as might
persuade a lively fancy of the truth of its own inventions;
and as he heard these continually repeated by the contributor in their search for Mr. Hapford, they must have acquired an objective force and repute scarcely to be resisted.
At the same time, there were touches of nature throughout
Jonathan Tinker's narrative which could not fail to take
the faith of another. The contributor, in reviewing it,
thought it particularly charming that his mariner had not
overdrawn himself or attempted to paint his character
otherwise than as it probably was; that he had shown his
ideas and practices of life to be those of a second mate,
nor more nor less, without the gloss of regret or the
pretences of refinement that might be pleasing to the supposed philanthropist with whom he had fallen in. Captain
Gooding was of course a true portrait, and there was nothing in Jonathan Tinker's statement of the relations of a
second mate to his superiors and his inferiors which did not
agree perfectly with what the writer had just read in *Two
Years before the Mast,*—a book which had possibly cast its
glamour upon the adventure. He admired also the just and
perfectly characteristic air of grief in the bereaved husband
and father,—those occasional escapes from the sense of
loss into a brief hilarity and forgetfulness, and those re-
lapses into the hovering gloom, which every one has observed in this poor, crazy human nature when oppressed by
sorrow, and which it would have been hard to simulate.
But, above all, he exulted in that supreme stroke of the
imagination given by the second mate when, at parting, he
said he believed he would go down and sleep on board the
vessel. In view of this, the State's Prison theory almost appeared a malign and foolish scandal.

Yet even if this theory were correct, was the second

mate wholly answerable for beginning his life again with the imposture he had practised? The contributor had either so fallen in love with the literary advantages of his forlorn deceiver that he would see no moral obliquity in him, or he had touched a subtler verity at last in pondering the affair. It seemed now no longer a farce, but had a pathos which, though very different from that of its first aspect, was hardly less tragical. Knowing with what coldness, or, at the best, uncandor, he (representing Society in its attitude toward convicted Error) would have met the fact had it been owned to him at first, he had not virtue enough to condemn the illusory stranger, who must have been helpless to make at once evident any repentance he felt or good purpose he cherished. Was it not one of the saddest consequences of the man's past,—a dark necessity of misdoing, —that, even with the best will in the world to retrieve himself, his first endeavor must involve a wrong? Might he not, indeed, be considered a martyr, in some sort, to his own admirable impulses? I can see clearly enough where the contributor was astray in this reasoning, but I can also understand how one accustomed to value realities only as they resembled fables should be won with such pensive sophistry; and I can certainly sympathize with his feeling that the mariner's failure to reappear according to appointment added its final and most agreeable charm to the whole affair, and completed the mystery from which the man emerged and which swallowed him up again.

1871

Editha

The air was thick with the war feeling, like the electricity of a storm which has not yet burst. Editha sat looking out into the hot spring afternoon, with her lips parted, and panting with the intensity of the question whether she could let him go. She had decided that she could not let him stay, when she saw him at the end of the still leafless avenue, making slowly up toward the house, with his head down, and his figure relaxed. She ran impatiently out on the veranda, to the edge of the steps, and imperatively demanded greater haste of him with her will before she called aloud to him, "George!"

He had quickened his pace in mystical response to her

mystical urgence, before he could have heard her; now he looked up and answered "Well?"

"Oh, how united we are!" she exulted, and then she swooped down the steps to him. "What is it?" she cried.

"It's war," he said, and he pulled her up to him, and kissed her.

She kissed him back intensely, but irrelevantly, as to their passion, and uttered from deep in her throat, "How glorious!"

"It's war," he repeated, without consenting to her sense of it; and she did not know just what to think at first. She never knew what to think of him; that made his mystery, his charm. All through their courtship, which was contemporaneous with the growth of the war feeling, she had been puzzled by his want of seriousness about it. He seemed to despise it even more than he abhorred it. She could have understood his abhorring any sort of bloodshed; that would have been a survival of his old life when he thought he would be a minister, and before he changed and took up the law. But making light of a cause so high and noble seemed to show a want of earnestness at the core of his being. Not but that she felt herself able to cope with a congenital defect of that sort, and make his love for her save him from himself. Now perhaps the miracle was already wrought in him. In the presence of the tremendous fact that he announced, all triviality seemed to have gone out of him; she began to feel that. He sank down on the top step, and wiped his forehead with his handkerchief, while she poured out upon him her question of the origin and authenticity of his news.

All the while, in her duplex emotioning, she was aware that now at the very beginning she must put a guard upon herself against urging him, by any word or act, to take the part that her whole soul willed him to take, for the completion of her ideal of him. He was very nearly perfect as he was, and he must be allowed to perfect himself. But he was peculiar, and he might very well be reasoned out of his peculiarity. Before her reasoning went her emotioning: her nature pulling upon his nature, her womanhood upon his manhood, without her knowing the means she was using to the end she was willing. She had always supposed that the man who won her would have done something to win her; she did not know what, but something. George Gearson had simply asked her for her love, on the way home from a concert, and she gave her love to him, without, as it were, thinking. But now, it flashed upon her, if he could do something worthy to *have* won her—be a hero, *her* hero—it would be even better than if he had done it before asking her; it would be grander. Besides, she had believed in the war from the beginning.

"But don't you see, dearest," she said, "that it wouldn't have come to this, if it hadn't been in the order of Providence? And I call any war glorious that is for the liberation of people who have been struggling for years against the cruelest oppression. Don't you think so too?"

"I suppose so," he returned, languidly. "But war! Is it glorious to break the peace of the world?"

"That ignoble peace! It was no peace at all, with that crime and shame at our very gates." She was conscious of parroting the current phrases of the newspapers, but it was no time to pick and choose her words. She must sacrifice anything to the high ideal she had for him, and after a good deal of rapid argument she ended with the climax: "But now it doesn't matter about the how or why. Since the war has come, all that is gone. There are no two sides, any more. There is nothing now but our country."

He sat with his eyes closed and his head leant back against the veranda, and he said with a vague smile, as if musing aloud, "Our country—right or wrong."

"Yes, right or wrong!" she returned fervidly. "I'll go and get you some lemonade." She rose rustling, and whisked away; when she came back with two tall glasses of clouded liquid, on a tray, and the ice clucking in them, he still sat as she had left him, and she said as if there had been no interruption: "But there is no question of wrong in this case. I call it a sacred war. A war for liberty, and humanity, if ever there was one. And I know you will see it just as I do, yet."

He took half the lemonade at a gulp, and he answered as he set the glass down: "I know you always have the highest ideal. When I differ from you, I ought to doubt myself."

A generous sob rose in Editha's throat for the humility of a man, so very nearly perfect, who was willing to put himself below her.

Besides, she felt, more subliminally, that he was never so

near slipping through her fingers as when he took that meek way.

"You shall not say that! Only, for once I happen to be right." She seized his hand in her two hands, and poured her soul from her eyes into his. "Don't you think so?" she entreated him.

He released his hand and drank the rest of his lemonade, and she added, "Have mine, too," but he shook his head in answering, "I've no business to think so, unless I act so, too."

Her heart stopped a beat before it pulsed on with leaps that she felt in her neck. She had noticed that strange thing in men; they seemed to feel bound to do what they believed, and not think a thing was finished when they said it, as girls did. She knew what was in his mind, but she pretended not, and she said, "Oh, I am not sure," and then faltered.

He went on as if to himself without apparently heeding her, "There's only one way of proving one's faith in a thing like this."

She could not say that she understood, but she did understand.

He went on again. "If I believed—if I felt as you do about this war—Do you wish me to feel as you do?"

Now she was really not sure; so she said, "George, I don't know what you mean."

He seemed to muse away from her as before. "There is a sort of fascination in it. I suppose that at the bottom of his heart every man would like at times to have his courage tested; to see how he would act."

"How can you talk in that ghastly way?"

"It *is* rather morbid. Still, that's what it comes to, unless you're swept away by ambition, or driven by conviction. I haven't the conviction or the ambition, and the other thing is what it comes to with me. I ought to have been a preacher, after all; then I couldn't have asked it of myself, as I must, now I'm a lawyer. And you believe it's a holy war, Editha?" he suddenly addressed her. "Or, I know you do! But you wish me to believe so, too?"

She hardly knew whether he was mocking or not, in the ironical way he always had with her plainer mind. But the only thing was to be outspoken with him.

"George, I wish you to believe whatever you think is true, at any and every cost. If I've tried to talk you into anything, I take it all back."

"Oh, I know that, Editha. I know how sincere you are, and how—I wish I had your undoubting spirit! I'll think it over; I'd like to believe as you do. But I don't, now; I don't, indeed. It isn't this war alone; though this seems peculiarly wanton and needless; but it's every war—so stupid; it makes me sick. Why shouldn't this thing have been settled reasonably?"

"Because," she said, very throatily again, "God meant it to be war."

"You think it was God? Yes, I suppose that is what people will say."

"Do you suppose it would have been war if God hadn't meant it?"

"I don't know. Sometimes it seems as if God had put this world into men's keeping to work it as they pleased."

"Now, George, that is blasphemy."

"Well, I won't blaspheme. I'll try to believe in your pocket Providence," he said, and then he rose to go.

"Why don't you stay to dinner?" Dinner at Balcom's Works was at one o'clock.

"I'll come back to supper, if you'll let me. Perhaps I shall bring you a convert."

"Well, you may come back, on that condition."

"All right. If I don't come, you'll understand."

He went away without kissing her, and she felt it a suspension of their engagement. It all interested her intensely; she was undergoing a tremendous experience, and she was being equal to it. While she stood looking after him, her mother came out through one of the long windows, on to the veranda, with a catlike softness and vagueness.

"Why didn't he stay to dinner?"

"Because—because—war has been declared," Editha pronounced, without turning.

Her mother said, "Oh, my!" and then said nothing more until she had sat down in one of the large Shaker chairs, and rocked herself for some time. Then she closed whatever tacit passage of thought there had been in her mind with the spoken words, "Well, I hope *he* won't go."

"And I hope he *will*," the girl said, and confronted her

mother with a stormy exultation that would have frightened any creature less unimpressionable than a cat.

Her mother rocked herself again for an interval of cogitation. What she arrived at in speech was, "Well, I guess you've done a wicked thing, Editha Balcom."

The girl said, as she passed indoors through the same window her mother had come out by, "I haven't done anything—yet."

In her room, she put together all her letters and gifts from Gearson, down to the withered petals of the first flower he had offered, with that timidity of his veiled in that irony of his. In the heart of the packet she enshrined her engagement ring which she had restored to the pretty box he had brought it her in. Then she sat down, if not calmly yet strongly, and wrote:

"George: I understood—when you left me. But I think we had better emphasize your meaning that if we cannot be one in everything we had better be one in nothing. So I am sending these things for your keeping till you have made up your mind.

"I shall always love you, and therefore I shall never marry any one else. But the man I marry must love his country first of all, and be able to say to me,

> 'I could not love thee, dear, so much,
> Loved I not honor more.'

"There is no honor above America with me. In this great hour there is no other honor.

"Your heart will make my words clear to you. I have never expected to say so much, but it has come upon me that I must say the utmost.

Editha."

She thought she had worded her letter well, worded it in a way that could not be bettered; all had been implied and nothing expressed.

She had it ready to send with the packet she had tied with red, white, and blue ribbon, when it occurred to her that she was not just to him, that she was not giving him a fair chance. He had said he would go and think it over, and she was not waiting. She was pushing, threatening, compelling. That was not a woman's part. She must leave him free, free, free. She could not accept for her country or herself a forced sacrifice.

In writing her letter she had satisfied the impulse from

which it sprang; she could well afford to wait till he had thought it over. She put the packet and the letter by, and rested serene in the consciousness of having done what was laid upon her by her love itself to do, and yet used patience, mercy, justice.

She had her reward. Gearson did not come to tea, but she had given him till morning, when, late at night there came up from the village the sound of a fife and drum with a tumult of voices, in shouting, singing, and laughing. The noise drew nearer and nearer; it reached the street end of the avenue; there it silenced itself, and one voice, the voice she knew best, rose over the silence. It fell; the air was filled with cheers; the fife and drum struck up, with the shouting, singing, and laughing again, but now retreating; and a single figure came hurrying up the avenue.

She ran down to meet her lover and clung to him. He was very gay, and he put his arm around her with a bois-terous laugh. "Well, you must call me Captain, now; or Cap, if you prefer; that's what the boys call me. Yes, we've had a meeting at the town hall, and everybody has volun-teered; and they selected me for captain, and I'm going to the war, the big war, the glorious war, the holy war or-dained by the pocket Providence that blesses butchery. Come along; let's tell the whole family about it. Call them from their downy beds, father, mother, Aunt Hitty, and all the folks!"

But when they mounted the veranda steps he did not wait for a larger audience; he poured the story out upon Editha alone.

"There was a lot of speaking, and then some of the fools set up a shout for me. It was all going one way, and I thought it would be a good joke to sprinkle a little cold water on them. But you can't do that with a crowd that adores you. The first thing I knew I was sprinkling hell-fire on them. 'Cry havoc, and let slip the dogs of war.' That was the style. Now that it had come to the fight, there were no two parties; there was one country, and the thing was to fight the fight to a finish as quick as possible. I suggested volunteering then and there, and I wrote my name first of all on the roster. Then they elected me—that's all. I wish I had some ice-water!"

She left him walking up and down the veranda, while she ran for the ice-pitcher and a goblet, and when she came back he was still walking up and down, shouting the story he had told her to her father and mother, who had come out more sketchily dressed than they commonly were by day. He drank goblet after goblet of the ice-water without noticing who was giving it, and kept on talking, and laughing through his talk wildly. "It's astonishing," he said, "how well the worse reason looks when you try to make it appear the better. Why, I believe I was the first convert to the war in that crowd to-night! I never thought I should like to kill a man; but now, I shouldn't care; and the smokeless powder lets you see the man drop that you kill. It's all for the country! What a thing it is to have a country that *can't* be wrong, but if it is, is right anyway!"

Editha had a great, vital thought, an inspiration. She set down the ice-pitcher on the veranda floor, and ran up-stairs and got the letter she had written him. When at last he noisily bade her father and mother, "Well, good night. I forgot I woke you up; I sha'n't want any sleep myself," she followed him down the avenue to the gate. There, after the whirling words that seemed to fly away from her thoughts and refuse to serve them, she made a last effort to solemnize the moment that seemed so crazy, and pressed the letter she had written upon him.

"What's this?" he said. "Want me to mail it?"

"No, no. It's for you. I wrote it after you went this morning. Keep it—keep it—and read it sometime—" She thought, and then her inspiration came: "Read it if ever you doubt what you've done, or fear that I regret your having done it. Read it after you've started."

They strained each other in embraces that seemed as ineffective as their words, and he kissed her face with quick, hot breaths that were so unlike him, that made her feel as if she had lost her old lover and found a stranger in his place. The stranger said, "What a gorgeous flower you are, with your red hair, and your blue eyes that look black now, and your face with the color painted out by the white moonshine! Let me hold you under my chin, to see whether I love blood, you tiger-lily!" Then he laughed Gearson's laugh, and released her, scared and giddy. Within her wilfulness she had been frightened by a sense of subtler force in him, and mystically mastered as she had never been before.

She ran all the way back to the house, and mounted

the steps panting. Her mother and father were talking of the great affair. Her mother said: "Wa'n't Mr. Gearson in rather of an excited state of mind? Didn't you think he acted curious?"

"Well, not for a man who'd just been elected captain and had to set 'em up for the whole of Company A," her father chuckled back.

"What in the world do you mean, Mr. Balcom? Oh! There's Editha!" She offered to follow the girl indoors.

"Don't come, mother!" Editha called, vanishing.

Mrs. Balcom remained to reproach her husband. "I don't see much of anything to laugh at."

"Well, it's catching. Caught it from Gearson. I guess it won't be much of a war, and I guess Gearson don't think so, either. The other fellows will back down as soon as they see we mean it. I wouldn't lose any sleep over it. I'm going back to bed, myself."

Gearson came again next afternoon, looking pale, and rather sick, but quite himself, even to his languid irony. "I guess I'd better tell you, Editha, that I consecrated myself to your god of battles last night by pouring too many libations to him down my own throat. But I'm all right, now. One has to carry off the excitement, somehow."

"Promise me," she commanded, "that you'll never touch it again!"

"What! Not let the canniken clink? Not let the soldier drink? Well, I promise."

"You don't belong to yourself now; you don't even belong to *me*. You belong to your country, and you have a sacred charge to keep yourself strong and well for your country's sake. I have been thinking, thinking all night and all day long."

"You look as if you had been crying a little, too," he said with his queer smile.

"That's all past. I've been thinking, and worshipping *you*. Don't you suppose I know all that you've been through, to come to this? I've followed you every step from your old theories and opinions."

"Well, you've had a long row to hoe."

"And I know you've done this from the highest motives—"

"Oh, there won't be much pettifogging to do till this cruel war is—"

"And you haven't simply done it for my sake. I couldn't respect you if you had."

"Well, then we'll say I haven't. A man that hasn't got his own respect intact wants the respect of all the other people he can corner. But we won't go into that. I'm in for the thing now, and we've got to face our future. My idea is that this isn't going to be a very protracted struggle; we shall just scare the enemy to death before it comes to a fight at all. But we must provide for contingencies, Editha. If anything happens to me—"

"Oh, George!" She clung to him sobbing.

"I don't want you to feel foolishly bound to my memory. I should hate that, wherever I happened to be."

"I am yours, for time and eternity—time and eternity." She liked the words; they satisfied her famine for phrases.

"Well, say eternity; that's all right; but time's another thing; and I'm talking about time. But there is something! My mother! If anything happens—"

She winced, and he laughed. "You're not the bold soldier-girl of yesterday!" Then he sobered. "If anything happens, I want you to help my mother out. She won't like my doing this thing. She brought me up to think war a fool thing as well as a bad thing. My father was in the civil war; all through it; lost his arm in it." She thrilled with the sense of the arm round her; what if that should be lost? He laughed as if divining her: "Oh, it doesn't run in the family, as far as I know!" Then he added, gravely, "He came home with misgivings about war, and they grew on him. I guess he and mother agreed between them that I was to be brought up in his final mind about it; but that was before my time. I only knew him from my mother's report of him and his opinions; I don't know whether they were hers first; but they were hers last. This will be a blow to her. I shall have to write and tell her—"

He stopped, and she asked, "Would you like me to write too, George?"

"I don't believe that would do. No, I'll do the writing. She'll understand a little if I say that I thought the way to minimize it was make war on the largest possible scale at once—that I felt I must have been helping on the war somehow if I hadn't helped keep it from coming, and I knew I hadn't; when it came, I had no right to stay out of it."

Whether his sophistries satisfied him or not, they satisfied her. She clung to his breast, and whispered, with closed eyes and quivering lips, "Yes, yes, yes!"

"But if anything should happen, you might go to her, and see what you could do for her. You know? It's rather far off; she can't leave her chair—"

"Oh, I'll go, if it's the ends of the earth! But nothing will happen! Nothing *can!* I—"

She felt herself lifted with his rising, and Gearson was saying, with his arm still around her, to her father: "Well, we're off at once, Mr. Balcom. We're to be formally accepted at the capital, and then bunched up with the rest somehow, and sent into camp somewhere, and got to the front as soon as possible. We all want to be in the van, of course; we're the first company to report to the Governor. I came to tell Editha, but I hadn't got round to it."

She saw him again for a moment at the capital, in the station, just before the train started southward with his regiment. He looked well, in his uniform, and very soldierly, but somehow girlish, too, with his clean-shaven face and slim figure. The manly eyes and the strong voice satisfied her, and his preoccupation with some unexpected details of duty flattered her. Other girls were weeping and bemoaning themselves, but she felt a sort of noble distinction in the abstraction, the almost unconsciousness, with which they parted. Only at the last moment he said, "Don't forget my mother. It mayn't be such a walkover as I supposed," and he laughed at the notion.

He waved his hand to her, as the train moved off—she knew it among a score of hands that were waved to other girls from the platform of the car, for it held a letter which she knew was hers. Then he went inside the car to read it, doubtless, and she did not see him again. But she felt safe for him through the strength of what she called her love. What she called her God, always speaking the name in a deep voice and with the implication of a mutual understanding, would watch over him and keep him and bring him back to her. If with an empty sleeve, then he should have three arms instead of two, for both of hers should be his for life. She did not see, though, why she should always be thinking of the arm his father had lost.

There were not many letters from him, but they were

such as she could have wished, and she put her whole strength into making hers such as she imagined he could have wished, glorifying and supporting him. She wrote to his mother glorifying him as their hero, but the brief answer she got was merely to the effect that Mrs. Gearson was not well enough to write herself, and thanking her for her letter by the hand of some one who called herself "Yrs truly, Mrs. W. J. Andrews."

Editha determined not to be hurt, but to write again quite as if the answer had been all she expected. But before it seemed as if she could have written, there came news of the first skirmish, and in the list of the killed which was telegraphed as a trifling loss on our side, was Gearson's name. There was a frantic time of trying to make out that it might be, must be, some other Gearson; but the name, and the company and the regiment, and the State were too definitely given.

Then there was a lapse into depths out of which it seemed as if she never could rise again; then a lift into clouds far above all grief, black clouds, that blotted out the sun, but where she soared with him, with George, George! She had the fever that she expected of herself, but she did not die in it; she was not even delirious, and it did not last long. When she was well enough to leave her bed, her one thought was of George's mother, of his strangely worded wish that she should go to her and see what she could do for her. In the exultation of the duty laid upon her—it buoyed her up instead of burdening her—she rapidly recovered.

Her father went with her on the long railroad journey from northern New York to western Iowa; he had business out at Davenport, and he said he could just as well go then as any other time; and he went with her to the little country town where George's mother lived in a little house on the edge of illimitable corn-fields, under trees pushed to a top of the rolling prairie. George's father had settled there after the civil war, as so many other old soldiers had done; but they were Eastern people, and Editha fancied touches of the East in the June rose overhanging the front door, and the garden with early summer flowers stretching from the gate of the paling fence.

It was very low inside the house, and so dim, with the closed blinds, that they could scarcely see one another:

Editha tall and black in her crapes which filled the air
with the smell of their dyes; her father standing decorously
apart with his hat on his forearm, as at funerals; a woman
rested in a deep armchair, and the woman who had let the
strangers in stood behind the chair.

The seated woman turned her head round and up, and
asked the woman behind her chair, "*Who* did you say?"

Editha, if she had done what she expected of herself,
would have gone down on her knees at the feet of the
seated figure and said, "I am George's Editha," for answer.

But instead of her own voice she heard that other
woman's voice, saying, "Well, I don't know as I *did* get
the name just right. I guess I'll have to make a little more
light in here," and she went and pushed two of the shutters
ajar.

Then Editha's father said in his public will-now-address-
a-few-remarks tone, "My name is Balcom, ma'am; Junius
H. Balcom, of Balcom's Works, New York; my daughter—"

"Oh!" The seated woman broke in, with a powerful
voice, the voice that always surprised Editha from Gearson's slender frame. "Let me see you! Stand round where
the light can strike on your face," and Editha dumbly
obeyed. "So, you're Editha Balcom," she sighed.

"Yes," Editha said, more like a culprit than a comforter.

"What did you come for?" Mrs. Gearson asked.

Editha's face quivered, and her knees shook. "I came—
because—because George—" She could go no farther.

"Yes," the mother said, "he told me he had asked you
to come if he got killed. You didn't expect that, I suppose,
when you sent him."

"I would rather have died myself than done it!" Editha
said with more truth in her deep voice than she ordinarily
found in it. "I tried to leave him free—"

"Yes, that letter of yours, that came back with his other
things, left him free."

Editha saw now where George's irony came from.

"It was not to be read before—unless—until—I told
him so," she faltered.

"Of course, he wouldn't read a letter of yours, under
the circumstances, till he thought you wanted him to. Been
sick?" the woman abruptly demanded.

"Very sick," Editha said, with self-pity.

"Daughter's life," her father interposed, "was almost despaired of, at one time."

Mrs. Gearson gave him no heed. "I suppose you would have been glad to die, such a brave person as you! I don't believe *he* was glad to die. He was always a timid boy, that way; he was afraid of a good many things; but if he was afraid he did what he made up his mind to. I suppose he made up his mind to go, but I knew what it cost him, by what it cost me when I heard of it. I had been through *one* war before. When you sent him you didn't expect he would get killed."

The voice seemed to compassionate Editha, and it was time. "No," she huskily murmured.

"No, girls don't; women don't, when they give their men up to their country. They think they'll come marching back, somehow, just as gay as they went, or if it's an empty sleeve, or even an empty pantaloon, it's all the more glory, and they're so much the prouder of them, poor things."

The tears began to run down Editha's face; she had not wept till then; but it was now such a relief to be understood that the tears came.

"No, you didn't expect him to get killed," Mrs. Gearson repeated in a voice which was startlingly like George's again. "You just expected him to kill some one else, some of those foreigners, that weren't there because they had any say about it, but because they had to be there, poor wretches—conscripts, or whatever they call 'em. You thought it would be all right for my George, *your* George, to kill the sons of those miserable mothers and the husbands of those girls that you would never see the faces of." The woman lifted her powerful voice in a psalmlike note. "I thank my God he didn't live to do it! I thank my God they killed him first, and that he ain't livin' with their blood on his hands!" She dropped her eyes which she had raised with her voice, and glared at Editha. "What you got that black on for?" She lifted herself by her powerful arms so high that her helpless body seemed to hang limp its full length. "Take it off, take it off, before I tear it from your back!"

The lady who was passing the summer near Balcom's Works was sketching Editha's beauty, which lent itself wonderfully to the effects of a colorist. It had come to that confidence which is rather apt to grow between artist and sitter, and Editha had told her everything.

"To think of your having such a tragedy in your life!" the lady said. She added: "I suppose there are people who feel that way about war. But when you consider the good this war has done—how much it has done for the country! I can't understand such people, for my part. And when you had come all the way out there to console her—got up out of a sick bed! Well!"

"I think," Editha said, magnanimously, "she wasn't quite in her right mind; and so did papa."

"Yes," the lady said, looking at Editha's lips in nature and then at her lips in art, and giving an empirical touch to them in the picture. "But how dreadful of her! How perfectly—excuse me—how *vulgar!*"

A light broke upon Editha in the darkness which she felt had been without a gleam of brightness for weeks and months. The mystery that had bewildered her was solved by the word; and from that moment she rose from grovelling in shame and self-pity, and began to live again in the ideal.

1905

FROM

Criticism and Fiction

From Chapter II

· · ·

"As for those called critics," the author [Burke] says, "they have generally sought the rule of the arts in the wrong place; they have sought among poems, pictures, engravings, statues, and buildings; but art can never give the rules that make an art. This is, I believe, the reason why artists in general, and poets principally, have been confined in so narrow a circle; they have been rather imitators of one another than of nature. Critics follow them, and therefore can do little as guides. I can judge but poorly of anything while I measure it by no other standard than itself. The true standard of the arts is in every man's power; and an easy observation of the most common, sometimes of the meanest things, in nature will give the truest lights, where the greatest sagacity and industry that slights such observation must leave us in the dark, or, what is worse, amuse and mislead us by false lights."

If this should happen to be true—and it certainly commends itself to acceptance—it might portend an immediate danger to the vested interests of criticism, only that it was written a hundred years ago; and we shall probably have the "sagacity and industry that slights the observation" of nature long enough yet to allow most critics the time to learn some more useful trade than criticism as they pursue it. Nevertheless, I am in hopes that the communistic era in taste foreshadowed by Burke is approaching, and that it will occur within the lives of men now over-awed by the foolish old superstition that literature and art are anything but the expression of life, and are to be judged by any other test than that of their fidelity to it. The time is coming, I hope, when each new author, each new artist, will be considered, not in his proportion to any other author or artist, but in his relation to the human nature, known to us all, which it is his privilege, his high duty, to interpret. "The true standard of the artist is in every man's power" already, as Burke says; Michelangelo's "light of the piazza," the glance of the common eye, is and always was the best light on a statue; Goethe's "boys and blackbirds" have in all ages been the real connoisseurs of berries; but hitherto the mass of common men have been afraid to apply their own simplicity, naturalness, and honesty to the appreciation of the beautiful. They have always cast about for the instruction of some one who professed to know better, and who browbeat wholesome common-sense into the self-distrust that ends in sophistication. They have fallen generally to the worst of this bad species, and have been "amused and misled" (how pretty that quaint old use of amuse is!) "by the false lights" of critical vanity and self-righteousness. They have been taught to compare what they see and what they read, not with the things that they have observed and known, but with the things that some other artist or writer has done. Especially if they have themselves the artistic impulse in any direction they are taught to form themselves, not upon life, but upon the masters who became masters only by forming themselves upon life. The seeds of death are planted in them, and they can produce only the stillborn, the academic. They are not told to take their work into the public square and see if it seems true to the chance passer, but to test it by the work of the very men who refused and decried any other test of their own work. The young writer who attempts to report the phrase and carriage of every-day life, who tries to tell just how he has heard men talk and seen them look, is made to feel guilty of something low and unworthy by the stupid people who would like to have him show how Shakespeare's men talked and looked, or Scott's, or Thackeray's, or Balzac's, or Hawthorne's, or Dickens's; he is instructed to idealize his personages, that is, to take the life-likeness out of them, and put the book-likeness into them. He is approached in the spirit of the wretched pedantry into which learning, much or little, always decays when it withdraws itself and stands apart from experience in an attitude of imagined superiority, and which would say with the same confidence to the scientist: "I see that you are looking at a grass-hopper there which you have found in the grass, and I suppose you intend to describe it. Now don't waste your time and sin against culture in that way. I've got a grasshopper here, which has been evolved at considerable pains and expense out of the grasshopper in general; in fact, it's a type. It's made up of wire and card-board, very prettily painted in a conventional tint, and it's perfectly inde-structible. It isn't very much like a real grasshopper, but it's a great deal nicer, and it's served to represent the notion of a grasshopper ever since man emerged from barbarism. You may say that it's artificial. Well, it is artificial; but then it's ideal too; and what you want to do is to cultivate the ideal. You'll find the books full of my kind of grass-hopper, and scarcely a trace of yours in any of them. The thing that you are proposing to do is commonplace; but if you say that it isn't commonplace, for the very reason that it hasn't been done before, you'll have to admit that it's photographic."

As I said, I hope the time is coming when not only the artist, but the common, average man, who always "has the standard of the arts in his power," will have also the courage to apply it, and will reject the ideal grasshopper wherever he finds it, in science, in literature, in art, be-cause it is not "simple, natural, and honest," because it is not like a real grasshopper. But I will own that I think the time is yet far off, and that the people who have been brought up on the ideal grasshopper, the heroic grasshopper, the impassioned grasshopper, the self-devoted, adventureful, good old romantic card-board grasshopper, must die out before the simple, honest, and natural grasshopper can have a fair field. I am in no haste to compass the end of these good people, whom I find in the mean time very amusing. It is delightful to meet one of them, either in print or out of it—some sweet elderly lady or excellent gentleman whose youth was pastured on the literature of thirty or forty years ago—and to witness the confidence with which they preach their favorite authors as all the law and the prophets. They have commonly read little or nothing since, or, if they have, they have judged it by a standard taken from these authors, and never dreamed of judging it by nature; they are destitute of the documents in the case of the later writers; they suppose that Balzac was the beginning of realism, and that Zola is its wicked end; they are quite ignorant, but they are ready to talk you down, if you differ from them, with an assumption of knowledge sufficient for any occasion. The horror, the resentment, with which they receive any question of their literary saints is genuine; you descend at once very far in the moral and social scale, and anything short of offensive personality is too good for you; it is expressed to you that you are one to be avoided, and put down even a little lower than you have naturally fallen.

These worthy persons are not to blame; it is part of their intellectual mission to represent the petrifaction of taste, and to preserve an image of a smaller and cruder and emptier world than we now live in, a world which was feeling its way towards the simple, the natural, the honest, but was a good deal "amused and misled" by lights now no longer mistakable for heavenly luminaries. They belong to a time, just passing away, when certain authors were considered authorities in certain kinds, when they must be accepted entire and not questioned in any particular. Now we are beginning to see and to say that no author is an authority except in those moments when he held his ear close to Nature's lips and caught her very accent. These moments are not continuous with any authors in the past, and they are rare with all. Therefore I am not afraid to say now that the greatest classics are sometimes not at all great, and that we can profit by them only when we hold them, like our meanest contemporaries, to a strict accounting, and verify their work by the standard of the arts which we all have in our power, the simple, the natural, and the honest.

Those good people, these curious and interesting if somewhat musty back-numbers, must always have a hero, an idol of some sort, and it is droll to find Balzac, who suffered from their sort such bitter scorn and hate for his realism while he was alive, now become a fetich in his turn, to be shaken in the faces of those who will not blindly worship him. But it is no new thing in the history of literature: whatever is established is sacred with those who do not think. At the beginning of the century, when romance was making the same fight against effete classicism which realism is making to-day against effete romanticism, the Italian poet Monti declared that "the romantic was the cold grave of the Beautiful," just as the realistic is now supposed to be. The romantic of that day and the real of this are in certain degree the same. Romanticism then sought, as realism seeks now, to widen the bounds of sympathy, to level every barrier against æsthetic freedom, to escape from the paralysis of tradition. It exhausted itself in this impulse; and it remained for realism to assert that fidelity to experience and probability of motive are essential conditions of a great imaginative literature. It is not a new theory, but it has never before universally characterized literary endeavor. When realism becomes false to itself, when it heaps up facts merely, and maps life instead of picturing it, realism will perish too. Every true realist instinctively knows this, and it is perhaps the reason why he is careful of every fact, and feels himself bound to express or to indicate its meaning at the risk of over-moralizing. In life he finds nothing insignificant; all tells for destiny and character; nothing that God has made is contemptible. He cannot look upon human life and declare this thing or that thing unworthy of notice, any more than the scientist can declare a fact of the material world beneath the dignity of his inquiry. He feels in every nerve the equality of things and the unity of men; his soul is exalted, not by vain shows and shadows and ideals, but by realities, in which alone the truth lives. In criticism it is his business to break the images of false gods and misshapen heroes, to take away the poor silly toys that many grown people still like to play with. He cannot keep terms with Jack the Giant-killer or Puss in Boots, under any name or in any place, even when they reappear as the convict Vautrec, or the Marquis de Montrivaut, or the Sworn Thirteen Noblemen. He must say to himself that Balzac, when he imagined these monsters, was not Balzac, he was Dumas; he was not realistic, he was romantic.

From Chapter XXI

. . .

It is the difference of the American novelist's ideals from those of the English novelist that gives him his advantage, and seems to promise him the future. The love of the passionate and the heroic, as the Englishman has it, is such a crude and unwholesome thing, so deaf and blind to all the most delicate and important facts of art and life, so insensible to the subtle values in either that its presence or absence makes the whole difference, and enables one who is not obsessed by it to thank Heaven that he is not as that other man is.

There can be little question that many refinements of thought and spirit which every American is sensible of in the fiction of this continent, are necessarily lost upon our good kin beyond seas, whose thumb-fingered apprehension requires something gross and palpable for its assurance of reality. This is not their fault, and I am not sure that it is wholly their misfortune: they are made so as not to miss what they do not find, and they are simply content without those subtleties of life and character which it gives us so keen a pleasure to have noted in literature. If they perceive them at all it is as something vague and diaphanous, something that filmily wavers before their sense and teases them, much as the beings of an invisible world might mock one of our material frame by intimations of their presence. It is with reason, therefore, on the part of an Englishman, that Mr. Henley complains of our fiction as a shadow-land, though we find more and more in it the faithful report of our life, its motives and emotions, and all the comparatively etherealized passions and ideals that influence it.

In fact, the American who chooses to enjoy his birthright to the full, lives in a world wholly different from the Englishman's, and speaks (too often through his nose) another language: he breathes a rarefied and nimble air full of shining possibilities and radiant promises which the fog-and-soot-clogged lungs of those less-favored islanders struggle in vain to fill themselves with. But he ought to be modest in his advantage, and patient with the coughing and sputtering of his cousin who complains of finding himself in an exhausted receiver on plunging into one of our novels. To be quite just to the poor fellow, I have had some such experience as that myself in the atmosphere of some of our more attenuated romances.

Yet every now and then I read a book with perfect comfort and much exhilaration, whose scenes the average Englishman would gasp in. Nothing happens; that is, nobody murders or debauches anybody else; there is no arson or pillage of any sort; there is not a ghost, or a ravening beast, or a hair-breadth escape, or a shipwreck, or a monster of self-sacrifice, or a lady five thousand years old in the whole course of the story; "no promenade, no band of music, nossing!" as Mr. Du Maurier's Frenchman said of the meet for a fox-hunt. Yet it is all alive with the keenest interest for those who enjoy the study of individual traits and general conditions as they make themselves known to American experience.

These conditions have been so favorable hitherto (though they are becoming always less so) that they easily account for the optimistic faith of our novel which Mr. Hughes notices. It used to be one of the disadvantages of the practice of romance in America, which Hawthorne more or less whimsically lamented, that there were so few shadows and inequalities in our broad level of prosperity; and it is one of the reflections suggested by Dostoïevsky's novel, *The Crime and the Punishment,* [sic] that whoever struck a note so profoundly tragic in American fiction would do a false and mistaken thing—as false and as mistaken in its way as dealing in American fiction with certain nudities which the Latin peoples seem to find edifying. Whatever their deserts, very few American novelists have been led out to be shot, or finally exiled to the rigors of a winter at Duluth; and in a land where journeymen carpenters and plumbers strike for four dollars a day the sum of hunger and cold is comparatively small, and the wrong from class to class has been almost inappreciable, though all this is changing for the worse. Our novelists, therefore, concern themselves with the more smiling aspects of life, which are the more American, and seek the universal in the individual rather than the social interests. It is worth while, even at the risk of being called commonplace, to be true to our well-to-do actualities; the very passions themselves seem to be softened and modified by conditions which formerly at least could not be said to wrong any one, to cramp endeavor, or to cross lawful desire. Sin and suffering and shame there must always be in the world, I suppose, but I believe that in this new world of ours it is still mainly from one to another one, and oftener still from one to one's self. We have death too in America, and a great deal of disagreeable and painful disease, which the multiplicity of our patent medicines does not seem to cure; but this is tragedy that comes in the very nature of things, and is not peculiarly American, as the large, cheerful average of health and success and happy life is. It will not do to boast, but it is well to be true to the facts, and to see that, apart from these purely mortal troubles, the race here has enjoyed conditions in which most of the ills that have darkened its annals might be averted by honest work and unselfish behavior.

Fine artists we have among us, and right-minded as far as they go; and we must not forget this at evil moments when it seems as if all the women had taken to writing hysterical improprieties, and some of the men were trying to be at least as hysterical in despair of being as improper. If we kept to the complexion of a certain school—which sadly needs a school-master—we might very well be despondent; but after all, that school is not representative of our conditions or our intentions. Other traits are much more characteristic of our life and our fiction. In most American novels, vivid and graphic as the best of them are, the people are segregated if not sequestered, and the scene is sparsely populated. The effect may be in instinctive response to the vacancy of our social life, and I shall not make haste to blame it. There are few places, few occasions among us, in which a novelist can get a large number of polite people together, or at least keep them together. Unless he carries a snap-camera his picture of them has no probability; they affect one like the figures perfunctorily associated in such deadly old engravings as that of "Washington Irving and his Friends." Perhaps it is for this reason that we excel in small pieces with three or four figures, or in studies of rustic communities, where there is propinquity if not society. Our grasp of more urbane life is feeble; most attempts to assemble it in our pictures are failures, possibly because it is too transitory, too intangible in its nature with us, to be truthfully represented as really existent.

I am not sure that the Americans have not brought the short story nearer perfection in the all-round sense than almost any other people, and for reasons very simple and near at hand. It might be argued from the national hurry and impatience that it was a literary form peculiarly adapted to the American temperament, but I suspect that its extraordinary development among us is owing much more to more tangible facts. The success of American magazines, which is nothing less than prodigious, is only commensurate with their excellence. Their sort of success is not only from the courage to decide which ought to please, but from the knowledge of what does please; and it is probable that, aside from the pictures, it is the short stories which please the readers of our best magazines. The serial novels they must have, of course; but rather more of course they must have short stories, and by operation of the law of supply and demand, the short stories, abundant in quantity and excellent in quality, are forthcoming because they are wanted. By another operation of the same law, which political economists have more recently taken account of, the demand follows the supply, and short stories are sought for because there is a proven ability to furnish them, and people read them willingly because they are usually very good. The art of writing them is now so disciplined and diffused with us that there is no lack either for the magazines or for the newspaper "syndicates" which deal in them almost to the exclusion of the serials. In other countries the feuilleton of the journals is a novel continued from day to day, but with us the papers, whether daily or weekly, now more rarely print novels, whether they get them at first hand from the writers, as a great many do, or through the syndicates, which purvey a vast variety of literary wares, chiefly for the Sunday editions of the city journals. In the country papers the short story takes the place of the chapters of a serial which used to be given.

From Chapter XXII

An interesting fact in regard to the different varieties of the short story among us is that the sketches and studies by the women seem faithfuller and more realistic than those of the men, in proportion to their number. Their tendency is more distinctly in that direction, and there is a solidity, an honest observation, in the work of such women as Mrs. Cooke, Miss Murfree, Miss Wilkins and Miss Jewett, which often leaves little to be desired. I should, upon the whole, be disposed to rank American short stories only below those of such Russian writers as I have read, and I should praise rather than blame their free use of our different local parlances, or "dialects," as people call them. I like this because I hope that our inherited English may be constantly freshened and revived from the native sources which our literary decentralization will help to keep open, and I will own that as I turn over novels coming from Philadelphia, from New Mexico, from Boston, from Tennessee, from rural New England, from New York, every local flavor of diction gives me courage and pleasure. M. Alphonse Daudet, in a conversation which Mr. H. H. Boyesen has set down in a recently recorded interview with him, said, in speaking of Tourguéneff: "What a luxury it must be to have a great big untrodden barbaric language to wade into! We poor fellows who work in the language of an old civilization, we may sit and chisel our little verbal felicities, only to find in the end that it is a borrowed jewel we are polishing. The crown jewels of our French tongue have passed through the hands of so many generations of monarchs that is seems like presumption on the part of any late-born pretender to attempt to wear them."

This grief is, of course, a little whimsical, yet it has a certain measure of reason in it, and the same regret has been more seriously expressed by the Italian poet Aleardi:

"Muse of an aged people, in the eve
Of fading civilization, I was born.
       . . . Oh, fortunate,*

My sisters, who in the heroic dawn
Of races sung! To them did destiny give
The virgin fire and chaste ingenuousness
Of their land's speech; and, reverenced, their hands
Ran over potent strings."

It will never do to allow that we are at such a desperate pass in English, but something of this divine despair we may feel too in thinking of "the spacious times of great Elizabeth," when the poets were trying the stops of the young language, and thrilling with the surprises of their own music. We may comfort ourselves, however, unless we prefer a luxury of grief, by remembering that no language is ever old on the lips of those who speak it, no matter how decrepit it drops from the pen. We have only to leave our studies, editorial and other, and go into the shops and fields to find the "spacious times" again; and from the beginning Realism, before she had put on her capital letter, had divined this near-at-hand truth along with the rest. Mr. Lowell, almost the greatest and finest realist who ever wrought in verse, showed us that Elizabeth was still Queen where he heard Yankee farmers talk. One need not invite slang into the company of its betters, though perhaps slang has been dropping its "s" and becoming language ever since the world began, and is certainly sometimes delightful and forcible beyond the reach of the dictionary. I would not have any one go about for new words, but if one of them came aptly, not to reject its help. For our novelists to try to write Americanly, from any motive, would be a dismal error, but being born Americans, I would have them use "Americanisms" whenever these serve their turn; and when their characters speak, I should like to hear them speak true American, with all the varying Tennesseean, Philadelphian, Bostonian, and New York accents. If we bother ourselves to write what the critics imagine to be "English," we shall be priggish and artificial, and still more so if we make our Americans talk "English." There is also this serious disadvantage about "English," that if we wrote the best "English" in the world, probably the English themselves would not know it, or, if they did, certainly would not own it. It has always been supposed by grammarians and purists that a language can be kept as they find it; but languages, while they live, are perpetually changing. God apparently meant them for the common people—whom Lincoln believed God liked because he had made so many of them; and the common people will use them freely as they use other gifts of God. On their lips our continental English will differ more and more from the insular English, and I believe that this is not deplorable, but desirable.

In fine, I would have our American novelists be as American as they unconsciously can. Matthew Arnold complained that he found no "distinction" in our life, and I would gladly persuade all artists intending greatness in any kind among us that the recognition of the fact pointed out by Mr. Arnold ought to be a source of inspiration to them, and not discouragement. We have been now some hundred years building up a state on the affirmation of the essential equality of men in their rights and duties, and whether we have been right or been wrong the gods have taken us at our word, and have responded to us with a civilization in which there is no "distinction" perceptible to the eye that loves and values it. Such beauty and such grandeur as we have is common beauty, common grandeur, or the beauty and grandeur in which the quality of solidarity so prevails that neither distinguishes itself to the disadvantage of anything else. It seems to me that these conditions invite the artists to the study and the appreciation of the common, and to the portrayal in every art of those finer and higher aspects which unite rather than sever humanity, if he would thrive in our new order of things. The talent that is robust enough to front the every-day world and catch the charm of its work-worn, care-worn, brave, kindly face, need not fear the encounter, though it seems terrible to the sort nurtured in the superstition of the romantic, the bizarre, the heroic, the distinguished, as the things alone worthy of painting or carving or writing. The arts must become democratic, and then we shall have the expression of America in art; and the reproach which Mr. Arnold was half right in making us shall have no justice in it any longer; we shall be "distinguished."

From Chapter XXIV

One of the great newspapers the other day invited the prominent American authors to speak their minds upon a point in the theory and practice of fiction which had already vexed some of them. It was the question of how much or how little the American novel ought to deal with certain facts of life which are not usually talked of before young people, and especially young ladies. Of course the question was not decided, and I forget just how far the balance inclined in favor of a larger freedom in the matter. But it certainly inclined that way; one or two writers of the sex which is somehow supposed to have purity in its keeping (as if purity were a thing that did not practically concern the other sex, preoccupied with serious affairs) gave it a rather vigorous tilt to that side. In view of this fact it would not be the part of prudence to make an effort to dress the balance; and indeed I do not know that I was going to make any such effort. But there are some things to say, around and about the subject, which I should like to have some one else say, and which I may myself possibly be safe in suggesting.

One of the first of these is the fact, generally lost sight of by those who censure the Anglo-Saxon novel for its prudishness, that it is really not such a prude after all; and that if it is sometimes apparently anxious to avoid those experiences of life not spoken of before young people, this may be an appearance only. Sometimes a novel which has this shuffling air, this effect of truckling to propriety, might defend itself, if it could speak for itself, by saying that such experiences happened not to come within its scheme, and that, so far from maiming or mutilating itself in ignoring them, it was all the more faithfully representative of the tone of modern life in dealing with love that was chaste, and with passion so honest that it could be openly spoken of before the tenderest society bud at dinner. It might say that the guilty intrigue, the betrayal, the extreme flirtation even, was the exceptional thing in life, and unless the scheme of the story necessarily involved it, that it would be bad art to lug it in, and as bad taste as to introduce such topics in a mixed company. It could say very justly that the novel in our civilization now always addresses a mixed company, and that the vast majority of the company are ladies, and that very many, if not most, of these ladies are young girls. If the novel were written for men and for married women alone, as in continental Europe, it might be altogether different. But the simple fact is that it is not written for them alone among us, and it is a question of writing, under cover of our universal acceptance, things for young girls to read which you would be put out-of-doors for saying to them, or of frankly giving notice of your intention, and so cutting yourself off from the pleasure—and it is a very high and sweet one—of appealing to these vivid, responsive intelligences, which are none the less brilliant and admirable because they are innocent.

One day a novelist who liked, after the manner of other men, to repine at his hard fate, complained to his friend, a critic, that he was tired of the restriction he had put upon himself in this regard; for it is a mistake, as can be readily shown, to suppose that others impose it. "See how free those French fellows are!" he rebelled. "Shall we always be shut up to our tradition of decency?"

"Do you think it's much worse than being shut up to their tradition of indecency?" said his friend.

Then that novelist began to reflect, and he remembered how sick the invariable motive of the French novel made him. He perceived finally that, convention for convention, ours was not only more tolerable, but on the whole was truer to life, not only to its complexion, but also to its texture. No one will pretend that there is not vicious love beneath the surface of our society; if he did, the fetid explosions of the divorce trials would refute him; but if he pretended that it was in any just sense characteristic of our society, he could be still more easily refuted. Yet it exists, and it is unquestionably the material of tragedy, the stuff from which intense effects are wrought. The question, after owning this fact, is whether these intense effects are not rather cheap effects. I incline to think they are, and I will try to say why I think so, if I may do so without offence. The material itself, the mere mention of it, has an instant fascination; it arrests, it detains, till the last word is said, and while there is anything to be hinted. This is what makes a love intrigue of some sort all but essential to the popularity of any fiction. Without such an intrigue the intellectual equipment of the author must be of the highest, and then he will succeed only with the highest class of readers. But any author who will deal with a guilty love intrigue holds all readers in his hand, the highest with the lowest, as long as he hints the slightest hope of the smallest potential naughtiness. He need not at all be a great author; he may be a very shabby wretch, if he has but the courage or the trick of that sort of thing. The critics will call him "virile" and "passionate"; decent people will be ashamed to have been limned by him; but the low average will only ask another chance of flocking into his net. If he happens to be an able writer, his really fine and costly work will be unheeded, and the lure to the appetite will be chiefly remembered. There may be other qualities which make reputations for other men, but in his case they will count for nothing. He pays this penalty for his success in that kind; and every one pays some such penalty who deals with some such material. It attaches in like manner to the triumphs of the writers who now almost form a school among us, and who may be said to have established themselves in an easy popularity simply by the study of erotic shivers and fervors. They may find their account in the popularity, or they may not; there is no question of the popularity.

But I do not mean to imply that their case covers the whole ground. So far as it goes, though, it ought to stop the mouths of those who complain that fiction is enslaved to propriety among us. It appears that of a certain kind of impropriety it is free to give us all it will, and more. But this is not what serious men and women writing fiction mean when they rebel against the limitations of their art in our civilization. They have no desire to deal with nakedness, as painters and sculptors freely do in the worship of beauty; or with certain facts of life, as the stage does, in the service of sensation. But they ask why, when the conventions of the plastic and histrionic arts liberate their followers to the portrayal of almost any phase of the physical or of the emotional nature, an American novelist may not write a story on the lines of *Anna Karénina* or *Madame Bovary*. Sappho they put aside, and from Zola's work they avert their eyes. They do not condemn him or Daudet, necessarily, or accuse their motives; they leave them out of the question; they do not want to do that kind of thing. But they do sometimes wish to do another kind, to touch one of the most serious and sorrowful problems of life in the spirit of Tolstoi and Flaubert, and they ask why they may not. At one time, they remind us, the Anglo-Saxon novelist did deal with such problems—De Foe in his spirit, Richardson in his, Goldsmith in his. At what moment did our fiction lose this privilege? In what fatal hour did the Young Girl arise and seal the lips of Fiction, with a touch of her finger, to some of the most vital interests of life?

Whether I wished to oppose them in their aspiration for greater freedom, or whether I wished to encourage them, I should begin to answer them by saying that the Young Girl had never done anything of the kind. The manners of the novel have been improving with those of its readers; that is all. Gentlemen no longer swear or fall drunk under the table, or abduct young ladies and shut them up in lonely country-houses, or so habitually set about the ruin of their neighbors' wives, as they once did. Generally, people now call a spade an agricultural implement; they have not grown decent without having also grown a little squeamish, but they have grown comparatively decent; there is no doubt about that. They require of a novelist whom they respect unquestionable proof of his seriousness, if he proposes to deal with certain phases of life; they require a sort of scientific decorum. He can no longer expect to be received on the ground of entertainment only; he assumes a higher function, something like that of a physician or a priest, and they expect him to be bound by laws as sacred as those of such professions; they hold him solemnly pledged not to betray them or abuse their confidence. If he will accept the conditions, they give him their confidence, and he may then treat to his greater honor, and not at all to his disadvantage, of such experiences, such relations of men and women as George Eliot treats in *Adam Bede,* in *Daniel Deronda,* in *Romola,* in almost all her books; such as Hawthorne treats in the *Scarlet Letter;* such as Dickens treats in *David Copperfield;* such as Thackeray treats in *Pendennis,* and glances at in every one of his fictions; such as most of the masters of English fiction have at some time treated more or less openly. It is quite false or quite mistaken to suppose that our novels have left untouched these most important realities of life. They have only not made them their stock in trade; they have kept a true perspective in regard to them; they have relegated them in their pictures of life to the space and place they occupy in life itself, as we know it in England and America. They have kept a correct proportion, knowing perfectly well that unless the novel is to be a map, with everything scrupulously laid down in it, a faithful record of life in far the greater extent could be made to the exclusion of guilty love and all its circumstances and consequences.

I justify them in this view not only because I hate what is cheap and meretricious, and hold in peculiar loathing the cant of the critics who require "passion" as something in itself admirable and desirable in a novel, but because I prize fidelity in the historian of feeling and character. Most of these critics who demand "passion" would seem to have no conception of any passion but one. Yet there are several other passions; the passion of grief, the passion of avarice, the passion of pity, the passion of ambition, the passion of hate, the passion of envy, the passion of devotion, the passion of friendship; and all these have a greater part in the drama of life than the passion of love, and infinitely greater than the passion of guilty love. Wittingly or unwittingly, English fiction and American fiction have recognized this truth, not fully, not in the measure it merits, but in greater degree than most other fiction.

1891

HENRY JAMES

(1843–1916)

If Henry James could in any sense be accused of provincialism, it could only be the kind with which Howells charged him when he blamed James for emphasizing Hawthorne's shortcomings and overlooking the unregenerate provincialism of the English upper classes. Indeed, it was difficult for James to find American cosmopolitan virtues ascendant over those of Europeans; what American charm and superiority existed at all for him existed in the frank good nature and honestly materialistic cheerfulness which bespoke a good heart innocent of sophistication and subtlety. Yet, as with every question raised by James's fictions, no simple statement is satisfactory. James's attitudes toward America and Europe were complex and shifting. If in his early fiction there was a tendency to see the American as the possible, though uncouth, moral redeemer of people who had had their ethical vigor Europeanized out of them by conventions and an ultra-refined sense of the social self ("Daisy Miller," *The American*), his later work reversed the order and made Europe the liberator of Americans who had been too narrowed by philistine, petit-bourgeois conformity (*The Ambassadors*). Though a statement of a shift away from America toward Europe is a justifiable generalization, the fuller truth lies in the complexities created by the fact that the American remains the bringer of exquisite moral sensibilities both in early works such as *The Portrait of a Lady* and in late works such as *The Wings of the Dove*. In short, it is not possible to talk about James's famous "international theme" without an understanding of his concern with "form as morality," with the artist as the culture hero, and with his double perspective of both Americans and Europeans as "artists" and spoilers.

James was uniquely suited by his education for the double perspective which allowed him in his novels to use Europe and America as reciprocating energies whose contrasts provided moral measures of each other. His father, Henry, Sr., led his sons through an intensely liberal and liberating set of experiences. Study and travel abroad, he felt, would provide his children with a wider and deeper education than the usual, formal course of American study. New York became not so much the family's home, though it was that too, as a home-base for constant excursions into and experiments within international culture and society. After private tutoring in their New York childhood, Henry and his brother William (see page 581) were exposed to various kinds of schooling. Henry studied painting for a while but decided to attend Harvard Law School, while his older brother attended Harvard Medical School. In their later careers William went from medicine to psychology to philosophy and Henry from law to literature. The brilliant pair exemplified the intellectual possibilities of American versatility and openness of expectation.

Henry James influenced American literature both as a critic and as an artist. He was a bachelor who replaced marriage with a productive, exhausting, and excruciating search for form. From European novelists such as Turgenev and Flaubert, James learned that fiction must be approached, like any art, through a long and disciplined attempt to fashion the particular idiom of the art into the just and perfect instrument of the point of view to be expressed. His "early period," in which he wrote such superb works as *The American* (1877) and *The Portrait of a Lady* (1881), his only novel which approached popularity in America in his lifetime, set for him the "international theme" which was to engage his imagination to the end of his life. This subject afforded him a means of exploring the problems of evil, both personal and social, and of moral identity, both private and public, as well as that of point of view as an important means by which a writer can control both meaning and value. By contrasting sweet and sometimes foolish, gauche innocence with worldly sophistication, he was able to dramatize his ideas that culture is a highly organized expression of noble impulses which humanize experience and people— especially people. Many of James's "people," and not only in the ghost stories, are chilling portraits of what for James is the ultimate and most monstrous dehumanization: the loss of ability to treat human beings with honor, altruism, and decency.

His experimental "middle period," during which he "retired" to refine the instruments of language with which he treated his interwoven themes of humanity and society, is characterized by such books as *The Spoils of Poynton* (1897), which has as its literal subject matter the possession of furniture. Such precious plot material, together with his exquisite search for the exact word and the exact syntax and the exact nuance, led to a kind of prose that encouraged many critics to accuse James of a dissociation from real life and of a bloodless preoccupation with finesse for its own sake. James, however, replied that an artist can work only with what he has, and that every artist's "given" is different. The fruitful critical question, he insisted, is raised not by sympathy with or hostility toward a writer's *donnée* but by an examination of what he does with it.

What makes plots "interesting" will differ with differing

temperaments, but if fiction is to achieve anything, James suggested, it must be morally, psychologically, and stylistically interesting. Its interest is generated by the extent to which action is dictated by characterization, following its own inevitability, in the context of the "scene"—relationships of characters to each other in their sensibility, morality, and accepted society, for all of which the physical setting is often a symbol in James's work. Consequently, James concluded, a writer must concentrate on the internal life within the thematic landscape rather than saturate his fiction with external details of verisimilitude in an attempt to make his writing look like "real life." (Among examples of the "novel of saturation" to which he pointed in his critical writings were the works of H. G. Wells.)

The critical questions that James opened into a dialogue with his age have not been resolved: who, after all, is to say for certain what is the one ultimate definition of art? But in his "final phase," emerging from the experimental prose of the "middle period," he had so brilliantly mastered his complicated syntax in the creation of the late, great novels (*The Wings of the Dove, The Ambassadors, The Golden Bowl*) and his critical writings became so compelling that his theories established the beginning of a whole new body of criticism in America and Europe. The European and American writers who are recognized as the great, classic moderns were all influenced by James. Because of him the writer's sense of vocation in America, as well as the very concept of literary craft, has been irrevocably changed. Editions of the work of Henry James are *The Novels and Tales of Henry James*, 26 vols. (1907–1917), the New York edition; and *The Novels and Tales of Henry James*, 35 vols. (1921–1923).

The published writings of Henry James include *A Passionate Pilgrim* (1875); *Transatlantic Sketches* (1875); *Roderick Hudson* (1876); *The American* (1877); *Watch and Ward* (1878); *French Poets and Novelists* (1878); *The Europeans* (1878); *Daisy Miller* (1879); *An International Episode* (1879); *The Madonna of the Future* (1879); *Hawthorne* (1879); *The Diary of a Man of Fifty*, and *A Bundle of Letters* (1880); *Confidence* (1880); *Washington Square* (1881); *The Portrait of a Lady* (1881); *The Siege of London, The Pension Beaurepas*, and *The Point of View* (1883); *Portraits of Places* (1883); *Tales of Three Cities* (1884); *A Little Tour in France* (1885); *Stories Revived* (1885); *The Bostonians* (1886); *The Princess Cassamassima* (1886); *Partial Portraits* (1888); *The Aspern Papers and Other Stories* (1888); *The Reverberator* (1888); *A London Life, The Patagonia*, and *The Liar and Mrs. Temperley* (1889); *The Tragic Muse* (1890); *The Lesson of the Master, and Other Stories* (1892); *The Private Life* (1893); *The Wheel of Time* (1893); *The Real Thing and Other Tales* (1893); *Picture and*

Text (1893); *Essays in London and Elsewhere* (1893); *Theatricals: Two Comedies* (1894); *Theatricals, Second Series* (1895); *Terminations, The Death of the Lion, and Others* (1895); *Embarrassments* (1896); *The Other House* (1896); *The Spoils of Poynton* (1897); *What Maisie Knew* (1897); *The Two Magics, The Turn of the Screw,* and *Covering End* (1898); *In the Cage* (1898); *The Awkward Age* (1899); *The Soft Side* (1900); *The Sacred Fount* (1901); *The Wings of the Dove* (1902); *William Wetmore Story and His Friends* (1903); *The Better Sort* (1903); *The Ambassadors* (1903); *The Golden Bowl* (1904); *The Question of Our Speech,* and *The Lesson of Balzac* (1905); *English Hours* (1905); *The American Scene* (1907); *Views and Reviews* (1908); *Julia Bride* (1909); *Italian Hours* (1909); *The Finer Grain* (1910); *The Outcry* (1911); *A Small Boy and Others* (1913); *Notes on Novelists* (1914); *Notes of a Son and Brother* (1914); *The Ivory Tower* (1917); *The Middle Years* (1917); *The Sense of the Past* (1917); *Within the Rim and Other Essays 1914–1915* (1918); *Gabrielle de Bergerac* (1918); *Travelling Companions* (1919); P. Lubbock, ed., *The Letters of Henry James,* 2 vols. (1920); P. de Chaignon la Rose, ed., *Notes and Reviews by Henry James* (1921); *The Letters of Henry James to Walter Berry* (1928); E. F. Benson, ed., *Henry James: Letters to A. C. Benson and Auguste Monod* (1930); E. Robins, ed., *Theater and Friendship: Some Henry James Letters* (1932); F. O. Matthiessen and K. B. Murdock, eds., *The Notebooks of Henry James* (1947); A. Wade, ed., *The Scenic Art, Notes on Acting and the Drama* (1948); L. Edel, ed., *The Complete Plays of Henry James* (1949); J. A. Smith, ed., *Henry James and Robert Louis Stevenson: A Record of Friendship and Criticism* (1949); E. Kenton, ed., *Eight Uncollected Tales of Henry James* (1950); L. Edel, ed., *The Selected Letters of Henry James* (1955); J. L. Sweeney, ed., *The Painter's Eye: Notes and Essays on the Pictorial Arts* (1956); L. Edel and I. D. Lind, eds., *Parisian Sketches: Letters to the New York Tribune, 1875–1876* (1957); A. Mordell, ed., *Literary Reviews and Essays: American, English, and French Literature* (1957); L. Edel and G. Ray, eds., *Henry James and H. G. Wells: A Record of Their Friendship, Their Debate on the Art of Fiction, and Their Quarrel* (1958); and L. Edel, ed., *The Complete Tales of Henry James,* 12 vols. (1962–1965).

THE VIKING PORTABLE HENRY JAMES, edited by Morton Dauwen Zabel, contains three nouvelles, *The Pupil, The Turn of the Screw,* and *The Beast in the Jungle.* There are three tales, "Four Meetings," "Grenville Fane," and

"The Real Thing." The essay is represented by ten of James' most famous pieces of criticism and by four "portraits of places." The volume further contains five selections of autobiography and journal, twenty-two letters, a James chronology, biography, and bibliography.

Studies of the man and his work are to be found in W. D. Howells, "Henry James, Jr.," *Century Magazine*, n.s. III (1882); W. D. Howells, "Mr. Henry James's Later Work," *North American Review*, CLXXVI (1903); J. Conrad, "Henry James: An Appreciation," *North American Review*, CLXXX (1905); W. C. Brownell, *American Prose Masters* (1909); F. M. Ford, *Henry James: A Critical Study* (1913); R. West, *Henry James* (1916); J. W. Beach, *The Method of Henry James* (1918, 1954); Henry James Number, *Little Review*, V (August, 1918); S. B. Liljegren, *American and European in the Works of Henry James* (1920); D. Bethurum, "Morality and Henry James," *Sewanee Review*, XXXI (1923); V. W. Brooks, *The Pilgrimage of Henry James* (1925); P. Edgar, *Henry James: Man and Author* (1927); M. Roberts, *Henry James's Criticism* (1929); M. Josephson, *Portrait of the Artist as American* (1930); C. P. Kelley, *The Early Development of Henry James* (1930, revised 1965); L. Edel, *The Prefaces of Henry James* (1931); J. W. Beach, *The Twentieth-Century Novel* (1932); H. Grattan, *The Three Jameses* (1932); R. P. Blackmur, ed., *The Art of the Novel* (1934); H. Hartwick, *The Foreground of American Fiction* (1934); W. Lewis, *Men Without Art* (1934); S. Spender, "The School of Experience in the Early Novels," *Hound and Horn*, VII (1934); E. M. Snell, *The Modern Fables of Henry James* (1935); F. M. Ford, *Portraits from Life* (1937); A. J. A. Waldock, *James, Joyce, and Others* (1937); Y. Winters, *Maule's Curse* (1938); V. W. Brooks, *New England: Indian Summer* (1940); C. Van Doren, *The American Novel* (1940); L. N. Richardson, ed., *Henry James: Representative Selections* (1941); Henry James Number, *Kenyon Review*, V (1943); R. N. Foley, *Criticism in American Periodicals of the Works of Henry James from 1866 to 1916* (1944); F. O. Matthiessen, *Henry James: The Major Phase* (1944); F. W. Dupee, ed., *The Question of Henry James* (1945); Q. Anderson, "Henry James and the New Jerusalem," *Kenyon Review*, VIII (1946); E. K. Brown, "James and Conrad," *Yale Review*, XXXV (1946); K. Hoskins, "Henry James and the Future of the Novel," *Sewanee Review*, LIV (1946); W. H. Auden, "Henry James's 'The American Scene,'" *Horizon*, XV (1947); F. O. Matthiessen, *The James Family* (1947); S. H. Nowell-Smith, *The Legend of the Master* (1947); O. Andreas, *Henry James and the Expanding Horizon* (1948); F. R. Leavis, *The Great Tradition* (1948); A. Warren, *Rage for Order* (1948); G. Hemphill, "Hemingway and James," *Kenyon Review*, XI (1949); E. Stevenson, *The Crooked Corridor: A*

Study of Henry James (1949); G. Greene, "Henry James," Table Ronde, XXIX (1950); H. S. Canby, Turn West, Turn East: Twain and James (1951); F. W. Dupee, Henry James (1951); M. Bewley, The Complex Fate (1952); M. Swan, Henry James (1952); L. Edel, Henry James: The Untried Years 1843–1870 (1953); R. C. LeClair, Young Henry James, 1843–1870 (1955); E. T. Bowdon, The Themes of Henry James: A System of Observation through the Visual Arts (1956); Q. Anderson, The American Henry James (1957); F. C. Crews, The Tragedy of Manners: Moral Drama in the Later Novels of Henry James (1957); C. G. Hoffman, The Short Novels of Henry James (1957); Henry James Number, Modern Fiction Studies, III (Spring 1957); Henry James Number, Nineteenth-Century Fiction, XII (June 1957); L. Edel and D. H. Laurence, A Bibliography of Henry James (1958, revised 1961); R. Marks, James's Later Novels (1960); R. Poirier, The Comic Sense of Henry James: A Study of the Early Novels (1960); G. Willen, ed., A Casebook on Henry James's The Turn of the Screw (1960); R. W. Stallman, The Houses that James Built (1961), L. Edel, Henry James: The Conquest of London (1962); L. Edel, Henry James: The Middle Years (1962); D. Krook, The Ordeal of Consciousness in Henry James (1962); N. Lebowitz, ed., Discussions of Henry James (1962); W. F. Wright, The Madness of Art: A Study of Henry James (1962); M. Geismar, Henry James and the Jacobites (1963); Sister M. C. Sharp, The Confidante in Henry James (1963); J. Weisenfarth, Henry James and the Dramatic Analogy (1963); L. Edel, ed., Henry James: A Collection of Critical Essays (1964); R. L. Gale, The Caught Image (1964); L. B. Holland, The Expense of Vision (1964); D. W. Jefferson, Henry James and the Modern Reader (1964); K. B. Vaid, Technique in the Tales of Henry James (1964); R. F. Sayre, The Examined Self (1964); M. Millgate, American Social Fiction: James to Cozzens (1964); B. Lowery, Marcel Proust et Henry James (1964); J. A. Clair, The Ironic Dimension in the Work of Henry James (1965); R. L. Gale, Plots and Characters in the Fiction of Henry James (1965); B. R. McElderry, Henry James (1965); G. Monteiro, Henry James and John Hay (1965); E. Stone, The Battle and the Books: Some Aspects of Henry James (1965); R. W. B. Lewis, Trials of the Word (1965); N. Wright, American Novelists in Italy (1965); M. Bell, Edith Wharton and Henry James (1965); L. B. Holland, The Expense of Greatness: Essays on the Craft of Henry James (1966); N. Lebowitz, The Imagination of Loving: Henry James's Legacy to the Novel (1966); A. Mizener, ed., A Reader's Guide to Henry James; and the Henry James issue of Modern Fiction Studies, XII (1966).

Daisy Miller

I

At the little town of Vevey, in Switzerland, there is a particularly comfortable hotel; there are indeed many hotels, since the entertainment of tourists is the business of the place, which, as many travellers will remember, is seated upon the edge of a remarkably blue lake—a lake that it behooves every tourist to visit. The shore of the lake presents an unbroken array of establishments of this order, of every category, from the "grand hotel" of the newest fashion, with a chalk-white front, a hundred balconies, and a dozen flags flying from its roof, to a small Swiss pension of an elder day, with its name inscribed in German-looking lettering upon a pink or yellow wall and an awkward summer-house in the angle of the garden. One of the hotels at Vevey, however, is famous, even classical, being distinguished from many of its upstart neighbours by an air both of luxury and of maturity. In this region, through the month of June, American travellers are extremely numerous; it may be said indeed that Vevey assumes at that time some of the characteristics of an American watering-place. There are sights and sounds that evoke a vision, an echo, of Newport and Saratoga. There is a flitting hither and thither of "stylish" young girls, a rustling of muslin flounces, a rattle of dance-music in the morning hours, a sound of high-pitched voices at all times. You receive an impression of these things at the excellent inn of the "Trois Couronnes," and are transported in fancy to the Ocean House or to Congress Hall. But at the "Trois Couronnes," it must be added, there are other features much at variance with these suggestions: neat German waiters who look like secretaries of legation; Russian princesses sitting in the garden; little Polish boys walking about, held by the hand, with their governors; a view of the snowy crest of the Dent du Midi and the picturesque towers of the Castle of Chillon.

I hardly know whether it was the analogies or the differences that were uppermost in the mind of a young American, who, two or three years ago, sat in the garden of the "Trois Couronnes," looking about him rather idly at some of the graceful objects I have mentioned. It was a beautiful summer morning, and in whatever fashion the young American looked at things they must have seemed to him charming. He had come from Geneva the day before, by the little steamer, to see his aunt, who was staying at the hotel—Geneva having been for a long time his place of residence. But his aunt had a headache—his aunt had almost always a headache—and she was now shut up in her room smelling camphor, so that he was at liberty to wander about. He was some seven-and-twenty years of age; when his friends spoke of him they usually said that he was at Geneva "studying." When his enemies spoke of him they said—but after all he had no enemies: he was extremely amiable and generally liked. What I should say is simply that when certain persons spoke of him they conveyed that the reason of his spending so much time at Geneva was that he was extremely devoted to a lady who lived there—a foreign lady, a person older than himself. Very few Americans—truly I think none—had ever seen this lady, about whom there were some singular stories. But Winterbourne had an old attachment for the little capital of Calvinism; he had been put to school there as a boy and had afterwards even gone, on trial—trial of the grey old "Academy" on the steep and stony hillside—to college there; circumstances which had led to his forming a great many youthful friendships. Many of these he had kept, and they were a source of great satisfaction to him.

After knocking at his aunt's door and learning that she was indisposed he had taken a walk about the town and then he had come in to his breakfast. He had now finished that repast, but was enjoying a small cup of coffee which had been served him on a little table in the garden by one of the waiters who looked like *attachés*. At last he finished his coffee and lit a cigarette. Presently a small boy came walking along the path—an urchin of nine or ten. The child, who was diminutive for his years, had an aged expression of countenance, a pale complexion, and sharp little features. He was dressed in knickerbockers and had red stockings that displayed his poor little spindle-shanks; he also wore a brilliant red cravat. He carried in his hand a long alpenstock, the sharp point of which he thrust into everything he approached—the flower-beds, the garden-benches, the trains of the ladies' dresses. In front of Winterbourne he paused, looking at him with a pair of bright and penetrating little eyes.

"Will you give me a lump of sugar?" he asked in a small sharp hard voice—a voice immature and yet somehow not young.

Winterbourne glanced at the light table near him, on which his coffee-service rested, and saw that several morsels of sugar remained. "Yes, you may take one," he answered; "but I don't think too much sugar good for little boys."

This little boy stepped forward and carefully selected three of the coveted fragments, two of which he buried in the pocket of his knickerbockers, depositing the other as promptly in another place. He poked his alpenstock, lance-fashion, into Winterbourne's bench and tried to crack the lump of sugar with his teeth.

"Oh blazes; it's har-r-d!" he exclaimed, divesting vowel and consonants, pertinently enough, of any taint of softness.

Winterbourne had immediately gathered that he might have the honour of claiming him as a countryman. "Take care you don't hurt your teeth," he said paternally.

"I haven't got any teeth to hurt. They've all come out. I've only got seven teeth. Mother counted them last night, and one came out right afterwards. She said she'd slap me if any more came out. I can't help it. It's this old Europe. It's the climate that makes them come out. In America they didn't come out. It's these hotels."

Winterbourne was much amused. "If you eat three lumps of sugar your mother will certainly slap you," he ventured.

"She's got to give me some candy then," rejoined his young interlocutor. "I can't get any candy here—any American candy. American candy's the best candy."

"And are American little boys the best little boys?" Winerbourne asked.

"I don't know. *I'm* an American boy," said the child.

"I see you're one of the best!" the young man laughed.

"Are you an American man?" pursued this vivacious infant. And then on his friend's affirmative reply, "American men are the best," he declared with assurance.

His companion thanked him for the compliment, and

the child, who had now got astride of his alpenstock, stood
looking about him while he attacked another lump of
sugar. Winterbourne wondered if he himself had been like
this in his infancy, for he had been brought to Europe at
about the same age.

"Here comes my sister!" cried his young compatriot.
"She's an American girl, you bet!"

Winterbourne looked along the path and saw a beautiful young lady advancing. "American girls are the best
girls," he thereupon cheerfully remarked to his visitor.

"My sister ain't the best!" the child promptly returned.
"She's always blowing at me."

"I imagine that's your fault, not hers," said Winterbourne. The young lady meanwhile had drawn near. She
was dressed in white muslin, with a hundred frills and
flounces and knots of pale-coloured ribbon. Bareheaded,
she balanced in her hand a large parasol with a deep
border of embroidery; and she was strikingly, admirably
pretty. "How pretty they are!" thought our friend, who
straightened himself in his seat as if he were ready to rise.

The young lady paused in front of his bench, near the
parapet of the garden, which overlooked the lake. The
small boy had now converted his alpenstock into a vault-
ing-pole, by the aid of which he was springing about in
the gravel and kicking it up not a little. "Why, Randolph,"
she freely began, "what *are* you doing?"

"I'm going up the Alps!" cried Randolph. "This is the
way!" And he gave another extravagant jump, scattering
the pebbles about Winterbourne's ears.

"That's the way they come down," said Winterbourne.

"He's an American man!" proclaimed Randolph in his
harsh little voice.

The young lady gave no heed to this circumstance, but
looked straight at her brother. "Well, I guess you'd better
be quiet," she simply observed.

It seemed to Winterbourne that he had been in a manner presented. He got up and stepped slowly toward the
charming creature, throwing away his cigarette. "This little
boy and I have made acquaintance," he said with great
civility. In Geneva, as he had been perfectly aware, a
young man wasn't at liberty to speak to a young unmarried lady save under certain rarely-occurring conditions;
but here at Vevey what conditions could be better than

these?—a pretty American girl coming to stand in front of you in a garden with all the confidence in life. This pretty American girl, whatever that might prove, on hearing Winterbourne's observation simply glanced at him; she then turned her head and looked over the parapet, at the lake and the opposite mountains. He wondered whether he had gone too far, but decided that he must gallantly advance rather than retreat. While he was thinking of something else to say the young lady turned again to the little boy, whom she addressed quite as if they were alone together. "I should like to know where you got that pole."

"I bought it!" Randolph shouted.

"You don't mean to say you're going to take it to Italy!"

"Yes, I'm going to take it t' Italy!" the child rang out.

She glanced over the front of her dress and smoothed out a knot or two of ribbon. Then she gave her sweet eyes to the prospect again. "Well, I guess you'd better leave it somewhere," she dropped after a moment.

"Are you going to Italy?" Winterbourne now decided very respectfully to enquire.

She glanced at him with lovely remoteness. "Yes, sir," she then replied. And she said nothing more.

"And are you—a—thinking of the Simplon?" he pursued with a slight drop of assurance.

"I don't know," she said. "I suppose it's some mountain. Randolph, what mountain are we thinking of?"

"Thinking of?"—the boy stared.

"Why going right over."

"Going to where?" he demanded.

"Why right down to Italy"—Winterbourne felt vague emulations.

"I don't know," said Randolph. "I don't want to go t' Italy. I want to go to America."

"Oh Italy's a beautiful place!" the young man laughed.

"Can you get candy there?" Randolph asked of all the echoes.

"I hope not," said his sister. "I guess you've had enough candy, and mother thinks so too."

"I haven't had any for ever so long—for a hundred weeks!" cried the boy, still jumping about.

The young lady inspected her flounces and smoothed her ribbons again; and Winterbourne presently risked an observation on the beauty of the view. He was ceasing to be in doubt, for he had begun to perceive that she was really not in the least embarrassed. She might be cold, she might be austere, she might even be prim; for that was apparently—he had already so generalised—what the most "distant" American girls did: they came and planted themselves straight in front of you to show how rigidly unapproachable they were. There hadn't been the slightest flush in her fresh fairness however; so that she was clearly neither offended nor fluttered. Only she was composed— he had seen that before too—of charming little parts that didn't match and that made no *ensemble;* and if she looked another way when he spoke to her, and seemed not particularly to hear him, this was simply her habit, her manner, the result of her having no idea whatever of "form" (with such a tell-tale appendage as Randolph where in the world would she have got it?) in any such connexion. As he talked a little more and pointed out some of the objects of interest in the view, with which she appeared wholly unacquainted, she gradually, none the less, gave him more of the benefit of her attention; and then he saw that act unqualified by the faintest shadow of reserve. It wasn't however what would have been called a "bold" front that she presented, for her expression was as decently limpid as the very cleanest water. Her eyes were the very prettiest conceivable, and indeed Winterbourne hadn't for a long time seen anything prettier than his fair countrywoman's various features—her complexion, her nose, her ears, her teeth. He took a great interest generally in that range of effects and was addicted to noting and, as it were, recording them; so that in regard to this young lady's face he made several observations. It wasn't at all insipid, yet at the same time wasn't pointedly—what point, on earth, could she ever make?—expressive; and though it offered such a collection of small finenesses and neatnesses he mentally accused it—very forgivingly—of a want of finish. He thought nothing more likely than that its wearer would have had her own experience of the action of her charms, as she would certainly have acquired a resulting confidence; but even should she depend on this for her main amusement her bright sweet superficial little visage gave out neither mockery nor irony. Before long it became clear that, however these things might be, she was much disposed to conversation. She remarked to Winterbourne that they were going to Rome for the winter—she and her mother and Randolph. She asked him if he was a "real American"; she wouldn't have taken him for one; he seemed more like a German—this flower was gathered as from a large field of comparison—especially when he spoke. Winterbourne, laughing, answered that he had met Germans who spoke like Americans, but not, so far as he remembered, any American with the resemblance she noted. Then he asked her if she mightn't be more at ease should she occupy the bench he had just quitted. She answered that she liked hanging round, but she none the less resignedly, after a little, dropped to the bench. She told him she was from New York State—"if you know where that is"; but our friend really quickened this current by catching hold of her small slippery brother and making him stand a few minutes by his side.

"Tell me your honest name, my boy." So he artfully proceeded.

In response to which the child was indeed unvarnished truth. "Randolph C. Miller. And I'll tell you hers." With which he levelled his alpenstock at his sister.

"You had better wait till you're asked!" said this young lady quite at her leisure.

"I should like very much to know *your* name," Winterbourne made free to reply.

"Her name's Daisy Miller!" cried the urchin. "But that ain't her real name; that ain't her name on her cards."

"It's a pity you haven't got one of my cards!" Miss Miller quite as naturally remarked.

"Her real name's Annie P. Miller," the boy went on.

It seemed, all amazingly, to do her good. "Ask him *his* now"—and she indicated their friend.

But to this point Randolph seemed perfectly indifferent; he continued to supply information with regard to his own family. "My father's name is Ezra B. Miller. My father ain't in Europe—he's in a better place than Europe." Winterbourne for a moment supposed this the manner in which the child had been taught to intimate that Mr. Miller had been removed to the sphere of celestial rewards. But Randolph immediately added: "My father's in Schenectady. He's got a big business. My father's rich, you bet."

"Well!" ejaculated Miss Miller, lowering her parasol and looking at the embroidered border. Winterbourne presently released the child, who departed, dragging his alpenstock along the path. "He don't like Europe," said the girl as with an artless instinct for historic truth. "He wants to go back."

"To Schenectady, you mean?"

"Yes, he wants to go right home. He hasn't got any boys here. There's one boy here, but he always goes round with a teacher. They won't let him play."

"And your brother hasn't any teacher?" Winterbourne enquired.

It tapped, at a touch, the spring of confidence. "Mother thought of getting him one—to travel round with us. There was a lady told her of a very good teacher; an American lady—perhaps you know her—Mrs. Sanders. I think she came from Boston. She told her of this teacher, and we thought of getting him to travel round with us. But Randolph said he didn't want a teacher travelling round with us. He said he wouldn't have lessons when he was in the cars. And we *are* in the cars about half the time. There was an English lady we met in the cars—I think her name was Miss Featherstone; perhaps you know her. She wanted to know why I didn't give Randolph lessons—give him 'instruction,' she called it. I guess he could give me more instruction than I could give him. He's very smart."

"Yes," said Winterbourne; "he seems very smart."

"Mother's going to get a teacher for him as soon as we get t' Italy. Can you get good teachers in Italy?"

"Very good, I should think," Winterbourne hastened to reply.

"Or else she's going to find some school. He ought to learn some more. He's only nine. He's going to college." And in this way Miss Miller continued to converse upon the affairs of her family and upon other topics. She sat there with her extremely pretty hands, ornamented with very brilliant rings, folded in her lap, and with her pretty eyes now resting upon those of Winterbourne, now wandering over the garden, the people who passed before her and the beautiful view. She addressed her new acquaintance as if she had known him a long time. He found it very pleasant. It was many years since he had heard a young girl talk so much. It might have been said of this wandering maiden who had come and sat down beside him upon a bench that she chattered. She was very quiet, she sat in a charming tranquil attitude; but her lips and her eyes were constantly moving. She had a soft slender agreeable voice, and her tone was distinctly sociable. She gave Winterbourne a report of her movements and intentions, and those of her mother and brother, in Europe, and enumerated in particular the various hotels at which they had stopped. "That English lady in the cars," she said —"Miss Featherstone—asked me if we didn't all live in hotels in America. I told her I had never been in so many hotels in my life as since I came to Europe. I've never seen so many—it's nothing but hotels." But Miss Miller made this remark with no querulous accent; she appeared to be in the best humour with everything. She declared that the hotels were very good when once you got used to their ways and that Europe was perfectly entrancing. She wasn't disappointed—not a bit. Perhaps it was because she had heard so much about it before. She had ever so many intimate friends who had been there ever so many times, and that way she had got thoroughly posted. And then she had had ever so many dresses and things from Paris. Whenever she put on a Paris dress she felt as if she were in Europe.

"It was a kind of a wishing-cap," Winterbourne smiled.

"Yes," said Miss Miller at once and without examining this analogy; "it always made me wish I was here. But I needn't have done that for dresses. I'm sure they send all the pretty ones to America; you see the most frightful things here. The only thing I don't like," she proceeded, "is the society. There ain't any society—or if there is I don't know where it keeps itself. Do you? I suppose there's some society somewhere, but I haven't seen anything of it. I'm very fond of society and I've always had plenty of it. I don't mean only in Schenectady, but in New York. I used to go to New York every winter. In New York I had lots of society. Last winter I had seventeen dinners given me, and three of them were by gentlemen," added Daisy Miller. "I've more friends in New York than in Schenectady—more gentlemen friends; and more young lady friends too," she resumed in a moment. She paused again for an instant; she was looking at Winterbourne with all her prettiness in her frank gay eyes and in her clear rather uniform smile. "I've always had," she said, "a great deal of gentlemen's society."

Poor Winterbourne was amused and perplexed—above

all he was charmed. He had never yet heard a young girl express herself in just this fashion; never at least save in cases where to say such things was to have at the same time·some rather complicated consciousness about them. And yet was he to accuse Miss Daisy Miller of an actual or a potential *arrière-pensée,* as they said at Geneva? He felt he had lived at Geneva so long as to have got morally muddled; he had lost the right sense for the young American tone. Never indeed since he had grown old enough to appreciate things had he encountered a young compatriot of so "strong" a type as this. Certainly she was very charming, but how extraordinarily communicative and how tremendously easy! Was she simply a pretty girl from New York State—were they all like that, the pretty girls who had had a good deal of gentlemen's society? Or was she also a designing, an audacious, in short an expert young person? Yes, his instinct for such a question had ceased to serve him, and his reason could but mislead. Miss Daisy Miller looked extremely innocent. Some people had told him that after all American girls *were* exceedingly innocent, and others had told him that after all they weren't. He must on the whole take Miss Daisy Miller for a flirt— a pretty American flirt. He had never as yet had relations with representatives of that class. He had known here in Europe two or three women—persons older than Miss Daisy Miller and provided, for respectability's sake, with husbands—who were great coquettes; dangerous terrible women with whom one's light commerce might indeed take a serious turn. But this charming apparition wasn't a coquette in that sense; she was very unsophisticated; she was only a pretty American flirt. Winterbourne was almost grateful for having found the formula that applied to Miss Daisy Miller. He leaned back in his seat; he remarked to himself that she had the finest little nose he had ever seen; he wondered what were the regular conditions and limitations of one's intercourse with a pretty American flirt. It presently became apparent that he was on the way to learn.

"Have you been to that old castle?" the girl soon asked, pointing with her parasol to the far-shining walls of the Château de Chillon.

"Yes, formerly, more than once," said Winterbourne. "You too, I suppose, have seen it?"

"No, we haven't been there. I want to go there dreadfully. Of course I mean to go there. I wouldn't go away from here without having seen that old castle."

"It's a very pretty excursion," the young man returned, "and very easy to make. You can drive, you know, or you can go by the little steamer."

"You can go in the cars," said Miss Miller.

"Yes, you can go in the cars," Winterbourne assented.

"Our courier says they take you right up to the castle," she continued. "We were going last week, but mother gave out. She suffers dreadfully from dyspepsia. She said she couldn't any more go—!" But this sketch of Mrs. Miller's plea remained unfinished. "Randolph wouldn't go either; he says he don't think much of old castles. But I guess we'll go this week if we can get Randolph."

"Your brother isn't interested in ancient monuments?" Winterbourne indulgently asked.

He now drew her, as he guessed she would herself have said, every time. "Why no, he says he don't care much about old castles. He's only nine. He wants to stay at the hotel. Mother's afraid to leave him alone, and the courier won't stay with him; so we haven't been to many places. But it will be too bad if we don't go up there." And Miss Miller pointed again at the Château de Chillon.

"I should think it might be arranged," Winterbourne was thus emboldened to reply. "Couldn't you get some one to stay—for the afternoon—with Randolph?"

Miss Miller looked at him a moment, and then with all serenity, "I wish *you'd* stay with him!" she said.

He pretended to consider it. "I'd much rather go to Chillon with you."

"With me?" she asked without a shadow of emotion.

She didn't rise blushing, as a young person at Geneva would have done; and yet, conscious that he had gone very far, he thought it possible she had drawn back. "And with your mother," he answered very respectfully.

But it seemed that both his audacity and his respect were lost on Miss Daisy Miller. "I guess mother wouldn't go—for *you,*" she smiled. "And she ain't much *bent* on going, anyway. She don't like to ride round in the afternoon." After which she familiarly proceeded: "But did you really mean what you said just now—that you'd like to go up there?"

"Most earnestly I meant it," Winterbourne declared.

"Then we may arrange it. If mother will stay with Randolph I guess Eugenio will."

"Eugenio?" the young man echoed.

"Eugenio's our courier. He doesn't like to stay with Randolph—he's the most fastidious man I ever saw. But he's a splendid courier. I guess he'll stay at home with Randolph if mother does, and then we can go to the castle."

Winterbourne reflected for an instant as lucidly as possible: "we" could only mean Miss Miller and himself. This prospect seemed almost too good to believe; he felt as if he ought to kiss the young lady's hand. Possibly he would have done so—and quite spoiled his chance; but at this moment another person—presumably Eugenio—appeared. A tall handsome man, with superb whiskers and wearing a velvet morning-coat and a voluminous watch-guard, approached the young lady, looking sharply at her companion. "Oh Eugenio!" she said with the friendliest accent.

Eugenio had eyed Winterbourne from head to foot; he now bowed gravely to Miss Miller. "I have the honour to inform Mademoiselle that luncheon's on table."

Mademoiselle slowly rose. "See here, Eugenio, I'm going to that old castle anyway."

"To the Château de Chillon, Mademoiselle?" the courier enquired. "Mademoiselle has made arrangements?" he added in a tone that struck Winterbourne as impertinent.

Eugenio's tone apparently threw, even to Miss Miller's own apprehension, a slightly ironical light on her position. She turned to Winterbourne with the slightest blush. "You won't back out?"

"I shall not be happy till we go!" he protested.

"And you're staying in this hotel?" she went on. "And you're really American?"

The courier still stood there with an effect of offence for the young man so far as the latter saw in it a tacit reflexion on Miss Miller's behaviour and an insinuation that she "picked up" acquaintances. "I shall have the honour of presenting to you a person who'll tell you all about me," he said, smiling, and referring to his aunt.

"Oh well, we'll go some day," she beautifully answered; with which she gave him a smile and turned away. She put up her parasol and walked back to the inn beside

Eugenio. Winterbourne stood watching her, and as she moved away, drawing her muslin furbelows over the walk, he spoke to himself of her natural elegance.

II

He had, however, engaged to do more than proved feasible in promising to present his aunt, Mrs. Costello, to Miss Daisy Miller. As soon as that lady had got better of her headache he waited on her in her apartment and, after a show of the proper solicitude about her health, asked if she had noticed in the hotel an American family—a mamma, a daughter and an obstreperous little boy.

"An obstreperous little boy and a preposterous big courier?" said Mrs. Costello. "Oh yes, I've noticed them. Seen them, heard them, and kept out of their way." Mrs. Costello was a widow of fortune, a person of much distinction and who frequently intimated that if she hadn't been so dreadfully liable to sick-headaches she would probably have left a deeper impress on her time. She had a long pale face, a high nose, and a great deal of very striking white hair, which she wore in large puffs and over the top of her head. She had two sons married in New York and another who was now in Europe. This young man was amusing himself at Hamburg and, though guided by his taste, was rarely observed to visit any particular city at the moment selected by his mother for her appearance there. Her nephew, who had come to Vevey expressly to see her, was therefore more attentive than, as she said, her very own. He had imbibed at Geneva the idea that one must be irreproachable in all such forms. Mrs. Costello hadn't seen him for many years and was now greatly pleased with him, manifesting her approbation by initiating him into many of the secrets of that social sway which, as he could see she would like him to think, she exerted from her stronghold in Forty-Second Street. She admitted that she was very exclusive, but if he had been better acquainted with New York he would see that one had to be. And her picture of the minutely hierarchical constitution of the society of that city, which she presented to him in many different lights, was, to Winterbourne's imagination, almost oppressively striking.

He at once recognised from her tone that Miss Daisy Miller's place in the social scale was low. "I'm afraid you don't approve of them," he pursued in reference to his new friends.

"They're horribly common"—it was perfectly simple. "They're the sort of Americans that one does one's duty by just ignoring."

"Ah you just ignore them?"—the young man took it in.

"I can't *not,* my dear Frederick. I wouldn't if I hadn't to, but I have to."

"The little girl's very pretty," he went on in a moment.

"Of course she's very pretty But she's of the last crudity."

"I see what you mean of course," he allowed after another pause.

"She has that charming look they all have," his aunt resumed. "I can't think where they pick it up; and she dresses in perfection—no, you don't know how well she dresses. I can't think where they get their taste."

"But, my dear aunt, she's not, after all, a Comanche savage."

"She is a young lady," said Mrs. Costello, "who has an intimacy with her mamma's courier!"

"An 'intimacy' with him?" Ah there it was!

"There's no other name for such a relation. But the skinny little mother's just as bad! They treat the courier as a familiar friend—as a gentleman and a scholar. I shouldn't wonder if he dines with them. Very likely they've never seen a man with such good manners, such fine clothes, so *like* a gentleman—or a scholar. He probably corresponds to the young lady's idea of a count. He sits with them in the garden of an evening. I think he smokes in their faces."

Winterbourne listened with interest to these disclosures; they helped him to make up his mind about Miss Daisy. Evidently she was rather wild. "Well," he said, "I'm not a courier and I didn't smoke in her face, and yet she was very charming to me."

"You had better have mentioned at first," Mrs. Costello returned with dignity, "that you had made her valuable acquaintance."

"We simply met in the garden and talked a bit."

"By appointment—no? Ah that's still to come! Pray what did you say?"

"I said I should take the liberty of introducing her to my admirable aunt."

"Your admirable aunt's a thousand times obliged to you."

"It was to guarantee my respectability."

"And pray who's to guarantee hers?"

"Ah you're cruel!" said the young man. "She's a very innocent girl."

"You don't say that as if you believed it," Mrs. Costello returned.

"She's completely uneducated," Winterbourne acknowledged, "but she's wonderfully pretty, and in short she's very nice. To prove I believe it I'm going to take her to the Château de Chillon."

Mrs. Costello made a wondrous face. "You two are going off there together? I should say it proved just the contrary. How long had you known her, may I ask, when this interesting project was formed? You haven't been twenty-four hours in the house."

"I had known her half an hour!" Winterbourne smiled.

"Then she's just what I supposed."

"And what do you suppose?"

"Why that she's a horror."

Our youth was silent for some moments. "You really think then," he presently began, and with a desire for trustworthy information, "you really think that—" But he paused again while his aunt waited.

"Think what, sir?"

"That she's the sort of young lady who expected a man sooner or later to—well, we'll call it carry her off?"

"I haven't the least idea what such young ladies expect a man to do. But I really consider you had better not meddle with little American girls who are uneducated, as you mildly put it. You've lived too long out of the country. You'll be sure to make some great mistake. You're too innocent."

"My dear aunt, not so much as that comes to!" he protested with a laugh and a curl of his moustache.

"You're too guilty then!"

He continued all thoughtfully to finger the ornament in question. "You won't let the poor girl know you then?" he asked at last.

"Is it literally true that she's going to the Château de Chillon with you?"

"I've no doubt she fully intends it."

"Then, my dear Frederick," said Mrs. Costello, "I must decline the honour of her acquaintance. I'm an old woman, but I'm not too old—thank heaven—to be honestly shocked!"

"But don't they all do these things—the little American girls at home?" Winterbourne enquired.

Mrs. Costello stared a moment. "I should like to see my granddaughters do them!" she then grimly returned.

This seemed to throw some light on the matter, for Winterbourne remembered to have heard his pretty cousins in New York, the daughters of this lady's two daughters, called "tremendous flirts." If therefore Miss Daisy Miller exceeded the liberal licence allowed to these young women it was probable she did go even by the American allowance rather far. Winterbourne was impatient to see her again, and it vexed, it even a little humiliated him, that he shouldn't by instinct appreciate her justly.

Though so impatient to see her again, he hardly knew what ground he should give for his aunt's refusal to become acquainted with her; but he discovered promptly enough that with Miss Daisy Miller there was no great need of walking on tiptoe. He found her that evening in the garden, wandering about in the warm starlight after the manner of an indolent sylph and swinging to and fro the largest fan he had ever beheld. It was ten o'clock. He had dined with his aunt, had been sitting with her since dinner, and had just taken leave of her till the morrow. His young friend frankly rejoiced to renew their intercourse; she pronounced it the stupidest evening she had ever passed.

"Have you been all alone?" he asked with no intention of an epigram and no effect of her perceiving one.

"I've been walking round with mother. But mother gets tired walking round," Miss Miller explained.

"Has she gone to bed?"

"No, she doesn't like to go to bed. She doesn't sleep scarcely any—not three hours. She says she doesn't know how she lives. She's dreadfully nervous. I guess she sleeps more than she thinks. She's gone somewhere after Randolph; she wants to try to get him to go to bed. He doesn't like to go to bed."

The soft impartiality of her *constatations,* as Winterbourne would have termed them, was a thing by itself—exquisite little fatalist as they seemed to make her. "Let us hope she'll persuade him," he encouragingly said.

"Well, she'll talk to him all she can—but he doesn't like her to talk to him": with which Miss Daisy opened and closed her fan. "She's going to try to get Eugenio to talk to him. But Randolph ain't afraid of Eugenio. Eugenio's a splendid courier, but he can't make much impression on Randolph! I don't believe he'll go to bed before eleven." Her detachment from any invidious judgement of this was, to her companion's sense, inimitable; and it appeared that Randolph's vigil was in fact triumphantly prolonged, for Winterbourne attended her in her stroll for some time without meeting her mother. "I've been looking round for that lady you want to introduce me to," she resumed—"I guess she's your aunt." Then on his admitting the fact and expressing some curiosity as to how she had learned it, she said she had heard all about Mrs. Costello from the chambermaid. She was very quiet and very *comme il faut;* she wore white puffs; she spoke to no one and she never dined at the common table. Every two days she had a headache. "I think that's a lovely description, headache and all!" said Miss Daisy, chattering along in her thin gay voice. "I want to know her ever so much. I know just what *your* aunt would be; I know I'd like her. She'd be very exclusive. I like a lady to be exclusive; I'm dying to be exclusive myself. Well, I guess we *are* exclusive, mother and I. We don't speak to anyone—or they don't speak to us. I suppose it's about the same thing. Anyway, I shall be ever so glad to meet your aunt."

Winterbourne was embarrassed—he could but trump up some evasion. "She'd be most happy, but I'm afraid those tiresome headaches are always to be reckoned with."

The girl looked at him through the fine dusk.

"Well, I suppose she doesn't have a headache every day."

He had to make the best of it. "She tells me she wonderfully does." He didn't know what else to say.

Miss Miller stopped and stood looking at him. Her prettiness was still visible in the darkness; she kept flapping to and fro her enormous fan. "She doesn't want to know me!" she then lightly broke out. "Why don't you say so? You needn't be afraid. *I'm* not afraid!" And she quite crowed for the fun of it.

Winterbourne distinguished however a wee false note in this: he was touched, shocked, mortified by it. "My dear young lady, she knows no one. She goes through life immured. It's her wretched health."

The young girl walked on a few steps in the glee of the thing. "You needn't be afraid," she repeated. "Why should she want to know me?" Then she paused again; she was close to the parapet of the garden, and in front of her was the starlit lake. There was a vague sheen on its surface, and in the distance were dimly-seen mountain forms. Daisy Miller looked out at these great lights and shades and again proclaimed a gay indifference—"Gracious! she *is* exclusive!" Winterbourne wondered if she were seriously wounded and for a moment almost wished her sense of injury might be such as to make it becoming in him to reassure and comfort her. He had a pleasant sense that she would be all accessible to a respectful tenderness at that moment. He felt quite ready to sacrifice his aunt—conversationally; to acknowledge she was a proud rude woman and to make the point that they needn't mind her. But before he had time to commit himself to this questionable mixture of gallantry and impiety, the young lady, resuming her walk, gave an exclamation in quite another tone. "Well, here's mother! I guess she *hasn't* got Randolph to go to bed." The figure of a lady appeared, at a distance, very indistinct in the darkness; it advanced with a slow and wavering step and then suddenly seemed to pause.

"Are you sure it's your mother? Can you make her out in this thick dusk?" Winterbourne asked.

"Well," the girl laughed, "I guess I know my own mother! And when she has got on my shawl too. She's always wearing my things."

The lady in question, ceasing now to approach, hovered vaguely about the spot at which she had checked her steps.

"I'm afraid your mother doesn't see you," said Winterbourne. "Or perhaps," he added—thinking, with Miss Miller, the joke permissible—"perhaps she feels guilty about your shawl."

"Oh it's a fearful old thing!" his companion placidly answered. "I told her she could wear it if she didn't mind looking like a fright. She won't come here because she sees you."

"Ah then," said Winterbourne, "I had better leave you."

"Oh no—come on!" the girl insisted.

"I'm afraid your mother doesn't approve of my walking with you."

She gave him, he thought, the oddest glance. "It isn't for me; it's for you—that is, it's for *her*. Well, I don't know who it's for! But mother doesn't like any of my gentlemen friends. She's right down timid. She always makes a fuss if I introduce a gentleman. But I *do* introduce them—almost always. If I didn't introduce my gentlemen friends to mother," Miss Miller added, in her small flat monotone, "I shouldn't think I was natural."

"Well, to introduce me," Winterbourne remarked, "you must know my name." And he proceeded to pronounce it.

"Oh my—I can't say all that!" cried his companion, much amused. But by this time they had come up to Mrs. Miller, who, as they drew near, walked to the parapet of the garden and leaned on it, looking intently at the lake and presenting her back to them. "Mother!" said the girl in a tone of decision—upon which the elder lady turned round. "Mr. Frederick Forsyth Winterbourne," said the latter's young friend, repeating his lesson of a moment before and introducing him very frankly and prettily. "Common" she might be, as Mrs. Costello had pronounced her; yet what provision was made by that epithet for her queer little native grace?

Her mother was a small spare light person, with a wandering eye, a scarce perceptible nose, and, as to make up for it, an unmistakeable forehead, decorated—but too far back, as Winterbourne mentally described it—with thin much-frizzled hair. Like her daughter Mrs. Miller was dressed with extreme elegance; she had enormous diamonds in her ears. So far as the young man could observe she gave him no greeting—she certainly wasn't looking at him. Daisy was near her, pulling her shawl straight. "What are you doing, poking round here?" this young lady enquired—yet by no means with the harshness of accent her choice of words might have implied.

"Well, I don't know"—and the newcomer turned to the lake again.

"I shouldn't think you'd want that shawl!" Daisy familiarly proceeded.

"Well—I do!" her mother answered with a sound that partook for Winterbourne of an odd strain between mirth and woe.

"Did you get Randolph to go to bed?" Daisy asked.

"No, I couldn't induce him"—and Mrs. Miller seemed to confess to the same mild fatalism as her daughter. "He wants to talk to the waiter. He *likes* to talk to that waiter."

"I was just telling Mr. Winterbourne," the girl went on; and to the young man's ear her tone might have indicated that she had been uttering his name all her life.

"Oh yes!" he concurred—"I've the pleasure of knowing your son."

Randolph's mamma was silent; she kept her attention on the lake. But at last a sigh broke from her. "Well, I don't see how he lives!"

"Anyhow, it isn't so bad as it was at Dover," Daisy at least opined.

"And what occurred at Dover?" Winterbourne desired to know.

"He wouldn't go to bed at all. I guess he sat up all night —in the public parlour. He wasn't in bed at twelve o'clock: it seemed as if he couldn't budge."

"It was half-past twelve when I gave up," Mrs. Miller recorded with passionless accuracy.

It was of great interest to Winterbourne. "Does he sleep much during the day?"

"I guess he doesn't sleep *very* much," Daisy rejoined.

"I wish he just *would!*" said her mother. "It seems as if he *must* make it up somehow."

"Well, I guess it's we that make it up. I think he's real tiresome," Daisy pursued.

After which, for some moments, there was silence. "Well, Daisy Miller," the elder lady then unexpectedly broke out, "I shouldn't think you'd want to talk against your own brother!"

"Well, he *is* tiresome, mother," said the girl, but with no sharpness of insistence.

"Well, he's only nine," Mrs. Miller lucidly urged.

"Well, he wouldn't go up to that castle, anyway," her daughter replied as for accommodation. "I'm going up there with Mr. Winterbourne."

To this announcement, very placidly made, Daisy's parent offered no response. Winterbourne took for granted on this that she opposed such a course; but he said to himself at the same time that she was a simple easily-managed person and that a few deferential protestations would modify her attitude. "Yes," he therefore interposed, "your daughter has kindly allowed me the honour of being her guide."

Mrs. Miller's wandering eyes attached themselves with an appealing air to her other companion, who, however, strolled a few steps further, gently humming to herself. "I presume you'll go in the cars," she then quite colourlessly remarked.

"Yes, or in the boat," said Winterbourne.

"Well, of course I don't know," Mrs. Miller returned. "I've never been up to that castle."

"It is a pity you shouldn't go," he observed, beginning to feel reassured as to her opposition. And yet he was quite prepared to find that as a matter of course she meant to accompany her daughter.

It was on this view accordingly that light was projected for him. "We've been thinking ever so much about going, but it seems as if we couldn't. Of course Daisy—she wants to go round everywhere. But there's a lady here—I don't know her name—she says she shouldn't think we'd want to go to see castles *here;* she should think we'd want to wait till we got t' Italy. It seems as if there would be so many there," continued Mrs. Miller with an air of increasing confidence. "Of course we only want to see the principal ones. We visited several in England," she presently added.

"Ah yes, in England there are beautiful castles," said Winterbourne. "But Chillon here is very well worth seeing."

"Well, if Daisy feels up to it—" said Mrs. Miller in a tone that seemed to break under the burden of such conceptions. "It seems as if there's nothing she won't undertake."

"Oh I'm pretty sure she'll enjoy it!" Winterbourne declared. And he desired more and more to make it a certainty that he was to have the privilege of a *tête-à-tête* with the young lady who was still strolling along in front of them and softly vocalising. "You're not disposed, madam," he enquired, "to make the so interesting excursion yourself?"

So addressed, Daisy's mother looked at him an instant with a certain scared obliquity and then walked forward in silence. Then, "I guess she had better go alone," she said simply.

It gave him occasion to note that this was a very different type of maternity from that of the vigilant matrons who massed themselves in the forefront of social intercourse in the dark old city at the other end of the lake. But his meditations were interrupted by hearing his name very distinctly pronounced by Mrs. Miller's unprotected daughter. "Mr. Winterbourne!" she piped from a considerable distance.

"Mademoiselle!" said the young man.

"Don't you want to take me out in a boat?"

"At present?" he asked.

"Why of course!" she gaily returned.

"Well, Annie Miller!" exclaimed her mother.

"I beg you, madam, to let her go," he hereupon eagerly pleaded; so instantly had he been struck with the romantic side of this chance to guide through the summer starlight a skiff freighted with a fresh and beautiful young girl.

"I shouldn't think she'd want to," said her mother. "I should think she'd rather go indoors."

"I'm sure Mr. Winterbourne wants to *take* me," Daisy declared. "He's so awfully devoted!"

"I'll row you over to Chillon under the stars."

"I don't believe it!" Daisy laughed.

"Well!" the elder lady again gasped, as in rebuke of this freedom.

"You haven't spoken to me for half an hour," her daughter went on.

"I've been having some very pleasant conversation with your mother," Winterbourne replied.

"Oh pshaw! I want you to take me out in a boat!" Daisy went on as if nothing else had been said. They had all stopped and she had turned round and was looking at her friend. Her face wore a charming smile, her pretty eyes gleamed in the darkness, she swung her great fan about. No, he felt, it was impossible to be prettier than that.

"There are half a dozen boats moored at that landing-place," and he pointed to a range of steps that descended from the garden to the lake. "If you'll do me the honour to accept my arm we'll go and select one of them."

She stood there smiling; she threw back her head; she laughed as for the drollery of this. "I like a gentleman to be formal!"

"I assure you it's a formal offer."

"I was bound I'd make you say something," Daisy agreeably mocked.

"You see it's not very difficult," said Winterbourne. "But I'm afraid you're chaffing me."

"I think not, sir," Mrs. Miller shyly pleaded.

"Do then let me give you a row," he persisted to Daisy.

"It's quite lovely, the way you say that!" she cried in reward.

"It will be still more lovely to do it."

"Yes, it would be lovely!" But she made no movement to accompany him; she only remained an elegant image of free light irony.

"I guess you'd better find out what time it is," her mother impartially contributed.

"It's eleven o'clock, madam," said a voice with a foreign accent out of the neighbouring darkness; and Winterbourne, turning, recognised the florid personage he had already seen in attendance. He had apparently just approached.

"Oh Eugenio," said Daisy, "I'm going out with Mr. Winterbourne in a boat!"

Eugenio bowed. "At this hour of the night, Mademoiselle?"

"I'm going with Mr. Winterbourne," she repeated with her shining smile. "I'm going this very minute."

"Do tell her she can't, Eugenio," Mrs. Miller said to the courier.

"I think you had better not go out in a boat, Mademoiselle," the man declared.

Winterbourne wished to goodness this pretty girl were not on such familiar terms with her courier; but he said nothing, and she meanwhile added to his ground. "I suppose you don't think it's proper! My!" she wailed; "Eugenio doesn't think anything's proper."

"I'm nevertheless quite at your service," Winterbourne hastened to remark.

"Does Mademoiselle propose to go alone?" Eugenio asked of Mrs. Miller.

"Oh no, with this gentleman!" cried Daisy's mamma for reassurance.

"I *meant* alone with the gentleman." The courier looked for a moment at Winterbourne—the latter seemed to make out in his face a vague presumptuous intelligence as at the expense of their companions—and then solemnly and with a bow, "As Mademoiselle pleases!" he said.

But Daisy broke off at this. "Oh I hoped you'd make a fuss! I don't care to go now."

"Ah but I myself shall make a fuss if you don't go," Winterbourne declared with spirit.

"That's all I want—a little fuss!" With which she began to laugh again.

"Mr. Randolph has retired for the night!" the courier hereupon importantly announced.

"Oh Daisy, now we can go then!" cried Mrs. Miller.

Her daughter turned away from their friend, all lighted with her odd perversity. "Good-night—I hope you're disappointed or disgusted or something!"

He looked at her gravely, taking her by the hand she offered. "I'm puzzled, if you want to know!" he answered.

"Well, I hope it won't keep you awake!" she said very smartly; and, under the escort of the privileged Eugenio, the two ladies passed toward the house.

Winterbourne's eyes followed them; he was indeed quite mystified. He lingered beside the lake a quarter of an hour, baffled by the question of the girl's sudden familiarities and caprices. But the only very definite conclusion he came to was that he should enjoy deucedly "going off" with her somewhere.

Two days later he went off with her to the Castle of Chillon. He waited for her in the large hall of the hotel, where the couriers, the servants, the foreign tourists were lounging about and staring. It wasn't the place he would have chosen for a tryst, but she had placidly appointed it. She came tripping downstairs, buttoning her long gloves, squeezing her folded parasol against her pretty figure, dressed exactly in the way that consorted best, to his fancy, with their adventure. He was a man of imagination and, as our ancestors used to say, of sensibility; as he took in her charming air and caught from the great staircase her impatient confiding step the note of some small sweet strain of romance, not intense but clear and sweet, seemed to sound for their start. He could have believed he was *really* going "off" with her. He led her out through all the idle people assembled—they all looked at her straight and hard: she had begun to chatter as soon as she joined him. His preference had been that they should be conveyed to Chillon in a carriage, but she expressed a lively wish to go in the little steamer—there would be such a lovely breeze upon the water and they should see such lots of people. The sail wasn't long, but Winterbourne's companion found time for many characteristic remarks and other demonstrations, not a few of which were, from the extremity of their candour, slightly disconcerting. To the young man himself their small excursion showed so for delightfully irregular and incongruously intimate that, even allowing for her habitual sense of freedom, he had some expectation of seeing her appear to find in it the same savour. But it must be confessed that he was in this particular rather disappointed. Miss Miller was highly animated, she was in the brightest spirits; but she was clearly not at all in a nervous flutter—as she should have been to match *his* tension; she avoided neither his eyes nor those of any one else; she neither coloured from an awkward consciousness when she looked at him nor when she saw that people were looking at herself. People continued to look at her a great deal, and Winterbourne could at least take pleasure in his pretty companion's distinguished air. He had been privately afraid she would talk loud, laugh overmuch, and even perhaps desire to move extravagantly about the boat. But he quite forgot his fears; he sat smiling with his eyes on her face while, without stirring from her place, she delivered herself of a great number of original reflexions. It was the most charming innocent prattle he had ever heard, for, by his own experience hitherto, when young persons were so ingenuous they were less articulate and when they were so confident were more sophisticated. If he had assented to the idea that she was "common," at any rate, *was* she proving so, after all, or was he simply getting used to her commonness? Her discourse was for the most part of what immediately and superficially surrounded them, but there were moments when it threw out a longer look or took a sudden straight plunge.

"What on *earth* are you so solemn about?" she suddenly demanded, fixing her agreeable eyes on her friend's.

"*Am* I solemn?" he asked. "I had an idea I was grinning from ear to ear."

"You look as if you were taking me to a prayer-meeting or a funeral. If that's a grin your ears are very near together."

"Should you like me to dance a hornpipe on the deck?"

"Pray do, and I'll carry round your hat. It will pay the expenses of our journey."

"I never was better pleased in my life," Winterbourne returned.

She looked at him a moment, then let it renew her amusement. "I like to make you say those things. You're a queer mixture!"

In the castle, after they had landed, nothing could exceed the light independence of her humour. She tripped about the vaulted chambers, rustled her skirts in the corkscrew staircases, flirted back with a pretty little cry and a shudder from the edge of the oubliettes and turned a singularly well-shaped ear to everything Winterbourne told her about the place. But he saw she cared little for mediæval history and that the grim ghosts of Chillon loomed but faintly before her. They had the good fortune to have been able to wander without other society than that of their guide; and Winterbourne arranged with this companion that they shouldn't be hurried—that they should linger and pause wherever they chose. He interpreted the bargain generously—Winterbourne on his side had been generous—and ended by leaving them quite to themselves. Miss Miller's observations were marked by no logical consistency; for anything she wanted to say she was sure to find a pretext. She found a great many, in the tortuous passages and rugged embrasures of the place, for asking her young man sudden questions about himself, his family, his previous history, his tastes, his habits, his designs, and for supplying information on corresponding points in her own situation. Of her own tastes, habits, and designs the charming creature was prepared to give the most definite and indeed the most favourable account.

"Well, I hope you know enough!" she exclaimed after Winterbourne had sketched for her something of the story of the unhappy Bonnivard. "I never saw a man that knew so much!" The history of Bonnivard had evidently, as they say, gone into one ear and out of the other. But this easy erudition struck her none the less as wonderful, and she was soon quite sure she wished Winterbourne would travel with them and "go round" with them: they too in that case might learn something about something. "Don't you want to come and teach Randolph?" she asked; "I guess he'd improve with a gentleman teacher." Winterbourne was certain that nothing could possibly please him so much, but that he had unfortunately other occupations. "Other occupations? I don't believe a speck of it!" she protested. "What do you mean now? You're not in business." The young man allowed that he was not in business, but he had engagements which even within a day or two would necessitate his return to Geneva. "Oh bother!" she panted, "I don't believe it!" and she began to talk about something else. But a few moments later, when he was pointing out to her the interesting design of an antique fireplace, she broke out irrelevantly: "You don't mean to say you're going back to Geneva?"

"It is a melancholy fact that I shall have to report myself there to-morrow."

She met it with a vivacity that could only flatter him. "Well, Mr. Winterbourne, I think you're horrid!"

"Oh don't say such dreadful things!" he quite sincerely pleaded—"just at the last."

"The last?" the girl cried; "I call it the very first! I've half a mind to leave you here and go straight back to the hotel alone." And for the next ten minutes she did nothing but call him horrid. Poor Winterbourne was fairly bewildered; no young lady had as yet done him the honour to be so agitated by the mention of his personal plans. His companion, after this, ceased to pay any attention to the curiosities of Chillon or the beauties of the lake; she opened fire on the special charmer in Geneva whom she appeared to have instantly taken it for granted that he was hurrying back to see. How did Miss Daisy Miller know of that agent of his fate in Geneva? Winterbourne, who denied the existence of such a person, was quite unable to discover; and he was divided between amazement at the rapidity of her induction and amusement at the directness of her criticism. She struck him afresh, in all this, as an extraordinary mixture of innocence and crudity. "Does she never allow you more than three days at a time?" Miss Miller wished ironically to know. "Doesn't she give you a vacation in summer? there's no one so hard-worked but they can get leave to go off somewhere at this season. I suppose if you stay another day she'll come right after you in the boat. Do wait over till Friday and I'll go down to the landing to see her arrive!" He began at last even to feel he had been wrong to be disappointed in the temper in which his young lady had embarked. If he had missed the personal accent, the personal accent was now making its appearance. It sounded very distinctly, toward the end, in her telling him she'd stop "teasing" him if he'd promise her solemnly to come down to Rome that winter.

"That's not a difficult promise to make," he hastened to acknowledge. "My aunt has taken an apartment in Rome from January and has already asked me to come and see her."

"I don't want you to come for your aunt," said Daisy; "I want you just to come for me." And this was the only allusion he was ever to hear her make again to his invidious kinswoman. He promised her that at any rate he would certainly come, and after this she forbore from teasing. Winterbourne took a carriage and they drove back to Vevey in the dusk; the girl at his side, her animation a little spent, was now quite distractingly passive.

In the evening he mentioned to Mrs. Costello that he had spent the afternoon at Chillon with Miss Daisy Miller.

"The Americans—of the courier?" asked this lady.

"Ah happily the courier stayed at home."

"She went with you all alone?"

"All alone."

Mrs. Costello sniffed a little at her smelling-bottle. "And that," she exclaimed, "is the little abomination you wanted me to know!"

III

Winterbourne, who had returned to Geneva the day after his excursion to Chillon, went to Rome toward the end of January. His aunt had been established there a considerable time, and he had received from her a couple of characteristic letters. "Those people you were so devoted to last summer at Vevey have turned up here, courier and all," she wrote. "They seem to have made several acquaintances, but the courier continues to be the most *intime*. The young lady, however, is also very intimate with various third-rate Italians, with whom she rackets about in a way that makes much talk. Bring me that pretty novel of Cherbuliez's— 'Paule Méré'—and don't come later than the 23d."

Our friend would in the natural course of events, on arriving in Rome, have presently ascertained Mrs. Miller's address at the American banker's and gone to pay his compliments to Miss Daisy. "After what happened at Vevey I certainly think I may call upon them," he said to Mrs. Costello.

"If after what happens—at Vevey and everywhere—you desire to keep up the acquaintance, you're very welcome. Of course you're not squeamish—a man may know every one. Men are welcome to the privilege!"

"Pray what is it then that 'happens'—here for instance?" Winterbourne asked.

"Well, the girl tears about alone with her unmistakeably low foreigners. As to what happens further you must apply elsewhere for information. She has picked up half a dozen of the regular Roman fortune-hunters of the inferior sort and she takes them about to such houses as she may put *her* nose into. When she comes to a party—such a party as she can come to—she brings with her a gentleman with a good deal of manner and a wonderful moustache."

"And where's the mother?"

"I haven't the least idea. They're very dreadful people."

Winterbourne thought them over in these new lights. "They're very ignorant—very innocent only, and utterly uncivilised. Depend on it they're not 'bad.' "

"They're hopelessly vulgar," said Mrs. Costello. "Whether or no being hopelessly vulgar is being 'bad' is a question for the metaphysicians. They're bad enough to blush for, at any rate; and for this short life that's quite enough."

The news that his little friend the child of nature of the Swiss lakeside was now surrounded by half a dozen wonderful moustaches checked Winterbourne's impulse to go straightway to see her. He had perhaps not definitely flattered himself that he had made an ineffaceable impression upon her heart, but he was annoyed at hearing of a state of affairs so little in harmony with an image that had lately flitted in and out of his own meditations; the image of a very pretty girl looking out of an old Roman window and asking herself urgently when Mr. Winterbourne would arrive. If, however, he determined to wait a little before reminding this young lady of his claim to her faithful remembrance, he called with more promptitude on two or three other friends. One of these friends was an American lady who had spent several winters at Geneva, where she had placed her children at school. She was a very accomplished woman and she lived in Via Gregoriana. Winterbourne found her in a little crimson drawing-room on a third floor; the room was filled with southern sunshine. He hadn't been there ten minutes when the servant, appearing in the doorway, announced complacently "Madame Mila!" This announcement was presently followed by the entrance of little Randolph Miller, who stopped in the middle of the room and stood staring at Winterbourne. An instant later his pretty sister crossed the threshold; and then, after a considerable interval, the parent of the pair slowly advanced.

"I guess I know you!" Randolph broke ground without delay.

"I'm sure you know a great many things"—and his old friend clutched him all, interestedly by the arm. "How's your education coming on?"

Daisy was engaged in some pretty babble with her hostess, but when she heard Winterbourne's voice she quickly turned her head with a "Well, I declare!" which he met smiling. "I told you I should come, you know."

"Well, I didn't believe it," she answered.

"I'm much obliged to you for that," laughed the young man.

"You might have come to see me then," Daisy went on as if they had parted the week before.

"I arrived only yesterday."

"I don't believe any such thing!" the girl declared afresh.

Winterbourne turned with a protesting smile to her mother, but this lady evaded his glance and, seating herself, fixed her eyes on her son. "We've got a bigger place than this," Randolph hereupon broke out. "It's all gold on the walls."

Mrs. Miller, more of a fatalist apparently than ever,

turned uneasily in her chair. "I told you if I was to bring you you'd say something!" she stated as for the benefit of such of the company as might hear it.

"I told *you!*" Randolph retorted. "I tell *you,* sir!" he added jocosely, giving Winterbourne a thump on the knee. "It *is* bigger too!"

As Daisy's conversation with her hostess still occupied her, Winterbourne judged it becoming to address a few words to her mother—such as "I hope you've been well since we parted at Vevey."

Mrs Miller now certainly looked at him—at his chin. "Not very well, sir," she answered.

"She's got the dyspepsia," said Randolph. "I've got it too. Father's got it bad. But I've got it worst!"

This proclamation, instead of embarrassing Mrs. Miller, seemed to soothe her by reconstituting the environment to which she was most accustomed. "I suffer from the liver," she amiably whined to Winterbourne. "I think it's this climate; it's less bracing than Schenectady, especially in the winter season. I don't know whether you know we reside at Schenectady. I was saying to Daisy that I certainly hadn't found any one like Dr. Davis and I didn't believe I *would.* Oh up in Schenectady, he stands first; they think everything of Dr. Davis. He has so much to do, and yet there was nothing he wouldn't do for *me.* He said he never saw anything like my dyspepsia, but he was bound to get at it. I'm sure there was nothing he wouldn't try, and I didn't care what he did to me if he only brought me relief. He was just going to try something new, and I just longed for it, when we came right off. Mr. Miller felt as if he wanted Daisy to see Europe for herself. But I couldn't help writing the other day that I supposed it was all right for Daisy, but that I didn't know as I *could* get on much longer without Dr. Davis. At Schenectady he stands at the very top; and there's a great deal of sickness there too. It affects my sleep."

Winterbourne had a good deal of pathological gossip with Dr. Davis's patient, during which Daisy chattered unremittingly to her own companion. The young man asked Mrs. Miller how she was pleased with Rome. "Well, I must say I'm disappointed," she confessed. "We had heard so much about it—I suppose we had heard too much. But we couldn't help that. We had been led to expect something different."

Winterbourne, however, abounded in reassurance. "Ah wait a little, and you'll grow very fond of it."

"I hate it worse and worse every day!" cried Randolph.

"You're like the infant Hannibal," his friend laughed.

"No I ain't—like any infant!" Randolph declared at a venture.

"Well, that's so—and you never *were!*" his mother concurred. "But we've seen places," she resumed, "that I'd put a long way ahead of Rome." And in reply to Winterbourne's interrogation, "There's Zürich—up there in the mountains," she instanced; "I think Zürich's real lovely, and we hadn't heard half so much about it."

"The best place we've seen's the *City of Richmond!*" said Randolph.

"He means the ship," Mrs. Miller explained. "We crossed in that ship. Randolph had a good time on the *City of Richmond.*"

"It's the best place *I've* struck," the child repeated. "Only it was turned the wrong way."

"Well, we've got to turn the right way sometime," said Mrs. Miller with strained but weak optimism. Winterbourne expressed the hope that her daughter at least appreciated the so various interest of Rome, and she declared with some spirit that Daisy was quite carried away. "It's on account of the society—the society's splendid. She goes round everywhere; she has made a great number of acquaintances. Of course she goes round more than I do. I must say they've all been very sweet—they've taken her right in. And then she knows a great many gentlemen. Oh she thinks there's nothing like Rome. Of course it's a great deal pleasanter for a young lady if she knows plenty of gentlemen."

By this time Daisy had turned her attention again to Winterbourne, but in quite the same free form. "I've been telling Mrs. Walker how mean you were!"

"And what's the evidence you've offered?" he asked, a trifle disconcerted, for all his superior gallantry, by her inadequate measure of the zeal of an admirer who on his way down to Rome had stopped neither at Bologna nor at Florence, simply because of a certain sweet appeal to his fond fancy, not to say to his finest curiosity. He remembered how a cynical compatriot had once told him that American women—the pretty ones, and this gave a largeness to the axiom—were at once the most exacting in the world and the least endowed with a sense of indebtedness.

"Why you were awfully mean up at Vevey," Daisy said. "You wouldn't do most anything. You wouldn't stay there when I asked you."

"Dearest young lady," cried Winterbourne, with generous passion, "have I come all the way to Rome only to be riddled by your silver shafts?"

"Just hear him say that!"—and she gave an affectionate twist to a bow on her hostess's dress. "Did you ever hear anything so quaint?"

"So 'quaint,' my dear?" echoed Mrs. Walker more critically—quite in the tone of a partisan of Winterbourne.

"Well, I don't know"—and the girl continued to finger her ribbons. "Mrs. Walker, I want to tell you something."

"Say, mother-r," broke in Randolph with his rough ends to his words, "I tell you you've got to go. Eugenio'll raise something!"

"I'm not afraid of Eugenio," said Daisy with a toss of her head. "Look here, Mrs. Walker," she went on, "you know I'm coming to your party."

"I'm delighted to hear it."

"I've got a lovely dress."

"I'm very sure of that."

"But I want to ask a favour—permission to bring a friend."

"I shall be happy to see any of your friends," said Mrs. Walker, who turned with a smile to Mrs. Miller.

"Oh they're not my friends," cried that lady, squirming in shy repudiation. "It seems as if they didn't take to me —I never spoke to one of them!"

"It's an intimate friend of mine, Mr. Giovanelli," Daisy pursued without a tremor in her young clearness or shadow on her shining bloom.

Mrs. Walker had a pause and gave a rapid glance at Winterbourne. "I shall be glad to see Mr. Giovanelli," she then returned.

"He's just the finest kind of Italian," Daisy pursued with the prettiest serenity. "He's a great friend of mine and the handsomest man in the world—except Mr. Win-

terbourne! He knows plenty of Italians, but he wants to
know some Americans. It seems as if he was crazy
about Americans. He's tremendously bright. He's perfectly lovely!"

It was settled that this paragon should be brought to
Mrs. Walker's party, and then Mrs. Miller prepared to
take her leave. "I guess we'll go right back to the hotel,"
she remarked with a confessed failure of the larger imagination.

"You may go back to the hotel, mother," Daisy replied,
"but I'm just going to walk round."

"She's going to go it with Mr. Giovanelli," Randolph
unscrupulously commented.

"I'm going to go it on the Pincio," Daisy peaceably
smiled, while the way that she "condoned" these things almost melted Winterbourne's heart.

"Alone, my dear—at this hour?" Mrs. Walker asked.
The afternoon was drawing to a close—it was the hour
for the throng of carriages and of contemplative pedestrians. "I don't consider it's safe, Daisy," her hostess firmly
asserted.

"Neither do I then," Mrs. Miller thus borrowed confidence to add. "You'll catch the fever as sure as you live.
Remember what Dr. Davis told you!"

"Give her some of that medicine before she starts in,"
Randolph suggested.

The company had risen to its feet; Daisy, still showing
her pretty teeth, bent over and kissed her hostess. "Mrs.
Walker, you're too perfect," she simply said. "I'm not going alone; I'm going to meet a friend."

"Your friend won't keep you from catching the fever
even if it *is* his own second nature," Mrs. Miller observed.

"Is it Mr. Giovanelli that's the dangerous attraction?"
Mrs. Walker asked without mercy.

Winterbourne was watching the challenged girl; at this
question his attention quickened. She stood there smiling
and smoothing her bonnet-ribbons; she glanced at Winterbourne. Then, while she glanced and smiled, she brought
out all affirmatively and without a shade of hesitation:
"Mr. Giovanelli—the beautiful Giovanelli."

"My dear young friend"—and, taking her hand, Mrs.
Walker turned to pleading—"don't prowl off to the Pincio
at this hour to meet a beautiful Italian."

"Well, he speaks first-rate English," Mrs. Miller incoherently mentioned.

"Gracious me," Daisy piped up, "I don't want to do anything that's going to affect my health—or my character either! There's an easy way to settle it." Her eyes continued to play over Winterbourne. "The Pincio's only a hundred yards off, and if Mr. Winterbourne were as polite as he pretends he'd offer to walk right in with me!"

Winterbourne's politeness hastened to proclaim itself, and the girl gave him gracious leave to accompany her. They passed downstairs before her mother, and at the door he saw Mrs. Miller's carriage drawn up, with the ornamental courier whose acquaintance he had made at Vevey seated within. "Good-bye, Eugenio," cried Daisy; "I'm going to take a walk!" The distance from Via Gregoriana to the beautiful garden at the other end of the Pincian Hill is in fact rapidly traversed. As the day was splendid, however, and the concourse of vehicles, walkers and loungers numerous, the young Americans found their progress much delayed. This fact was highly agreeable to Winterbourne, in spite of his consciousness of his singular situation. The slow-moving, idly-gazing Roman crowd bestowed much attention on the extremely pretty young woman of English race who passed through it, with some difficulty, on his arm; and he wondered what on earth had been in Daisy's mind when she proposed to exhibit herself unattended to its appreciation. His own mission, to her sense, was apparently to consign her to the hands of Mr. Giovanelli; but, at once annoyed and gratified, he resolved that he would do no such thing.

"Why haven't you been to see me?" she meanwhile asked. "You can't get out of that."

"I've had the honour of telling you that I've only just stepped out of the train."

"You must have stayed in the train a good while after it stopped!" she derisively cried. "I suppose you were asleep. You've had time to go to see Mrs. Walker."

"I knew Mrs. Walker—" Winterbourne began to explain.

"I know where you knew her. You knew her at Geneva. She told me so. Well, you knew me at Vevey. That's just as good. So you ought to have come." She asked him no other question than this; she began to prattle about her own affairs. "We've got splendid rooms at the hotel; Eugenio says they're the best rooms in Rome. We're going to stay all winter—if we don't die of the fever; and I guess we'll stay then! It's a great deal nicer than I thought; I thought it would be fearfully quiet—in fact I was sure it would be deadly pokey. I foresaw we should be going round all the time with one of those dreadful old men who explain about the pictures and things. But we only had about a week of that, and now I'm enjoying myself. I know ever so many people, and they're all so charming. The society's extremely select. There are all kinds—English and Germans and Italians. I think I like the English best. I like their style of conversation. But there are some lovely Americans. I never saw anything so hospitable. There's something or other every day. There's not much dancing—but I must say I never thought dancing was everything. I was always fond of conversation. I guess I'll have plenty at Mrs. Walker's—her rooms are so small." When they had passed the gate of the Pincian Gardens Miss Miller began to wonder where Mr. Giovanelli might be. "We had better go straight to that place in front, where you look at the view."

Winterbourne at this took a stand. "I certainly shan't help you to find him."

"Then I shall find him without you," Daisy said with spirit.

"You certainly won't leave me!" he protested.

She burst into her familiar little laugh. "Are you afraid you'll get lost—or run over? But there's Giovanelli leaning against that tree. He's staring at the women in the carriages: did you ever see anything so cool?"

Winterbourne descried hereupon at some distance a little figure that stood with folded arms and nursing its cane. It had a handsome face, a hat artfully poised, a glass in one eye and a nosegay in its buttonhole. Daisy's friend looked at it a moment and then said: "Do you mean to speak to that thing?"

"Do I mean to speak to him? Why you don't suppose I mean to communicate by signs!"

"Pray understand then," the young man returned, "that I intend to remain with you."

Daisy stopped and looked at him without a sign of troubled consciousness, with nothing in her face but her charming eyes, her charming teeth, and her happy dimples. "Well, she's a cool one!" he thought.

"I don't like the way you say that," she declared. "It's too imperious."

"I beg your pardon if I say it wrong. The main point's to give you an idea of my meaning."

The girl looked at him more gravely, but with eyes that were prettier than ever. "I've never allowed a gentleman to dictate to me or to interfere with anything I do."

"I think that's just where your mistake has come in," he retorted. "You should sometimes listen to a gentleman— the right one."

At this she began to laugh again. "I do nothing but listen to gentlemen! Tell me if Mr. Giovanelli is the right one."

The gentleman with the nosegay in his bosom had now made out our two friends and was approaching Miss Miller with obsequious rapidity. He bowed to Winterbourne as well as to the latter's compatriot; he seemed to shine, in his coxcombical way, with the desire to please and the fact of his own intelligent joy, though Winterbourne thought him not a bad-looking fellow. But he nevertheless said to Daisy: "No, he's not the right one."

She had clearly a natural turn for free introductions; she mentioned with the easiest grace the name of each of her companions to the other. She strolled forward with one of them on either hand; Mr. Giovanelli, who spoke English very cleverly—Winterbourne afterwards learned that he had practised the idiom upon a great many American heiresses—addressed her a great deal of very polite nonsense. He had the best possible manners, and the young American, who said nothing, reflected on that depth of Italian subtlety, so strangely opposed to Anglo-Saxon simplicity, which enables people to show a smoother surface in proportion as they're more acutely displeased. Giovanelli of course had counted upon something more intimate—he had not bargained for a party of three; but he kept his temper in a manner that suggested far-stretching intentions. Winterbourne flattered himself he had taken his measure. "He's anything but a gentleman," said the young American; "he isn't even a very plausible imitation of one. He's a music-master or a penny-a-liner or a third-rate artist. He's awfully on his good behaviour, but damn his fine eyes!" Mr. Giovanelli had indeed great advantages; but it was deeply disgusting to Daisy's other friend that something in her shouldn't have instinctively discriminated against such a type. Giovanelli chattered and jested and made himself agreeable according to his honest Roman lights. It was true that if he was an imitation the imitation was studied. "Nevertheless," Winterbourne said to himself, "a nice girl ought to know!" And then he came back to the dreadful question of whether this *was* in fact a nice girl. Would a nice girl—even allowing for her being a little American flirt—make a rendezvous with a presumably low-lived foreigner? The rendezvous in this case indeed had been in broad daylight and in the most crowded corner of Rome; but wasn't it possible to regard the choice of these very circumstances as a proof more of vulgarity than of anything else? Singular though it may seem, Winterbourne was vexed that the girl, in joining her *amoroso,* shouldn't appear more impatient of his own company, and he was vexed precisely because of his inclination. It was impossible to regard her as a wholly unspotted flower— she lacked a certain indispensable fineness; and it would therefore much simplify the situation to be able to treat her as the subject of one of the visitations known to romancers as "lawless passions." That she should seem to wish to get rid of him would have helped him to think more lightly of her, just as to be able to think more lightly of her would have made her less perplexing. Daisy at any rate continued on this occasion to present herself as an inscrutable combination of audacity and innocence.

She had been walking some quarter of an hour, attended by her two cavaliers and responding in a tone of very childish gaiety, as it after all struck one of them, to the pretty speeches of the other, when a carriage that had detached itself from the revolving train drew up beside the path. At the same moment Winterbourne noticed that his friend Mrs. Walker—the lady whose house he had lately left—was seated in the vehicle and was beckoning to him. Leaving Miss Miller's side, he hastened to obey her summons—and all to find her flushed, excited, scandalised. "It's really too dreadful"—she earnestly appealed to him. "That crazy girl mustn't do this sort of thing. She mustn't walk here with you two men. Fifty people have remarked her."

Winterbourne—suddenly and rather oddly rubbed the wrong way by this—raised his grave eyebrows. "I think it's a pity to make too much fuss about it."

"It's a pity to let the girl ruin herself!"

"She's very innocent," he reasoned in his own troubled interest.

"She's very reckless," cried Mrs. Walker, "and goodness knows how far—left to itself—it may go. Did you ever," she proceeded to enquire, "see anything so blatantly imbecile as the mother? After you had all left me just now I couldn't sit still for thinking of it. It seemed too pitiful not even to attempt to save them. I ordered the carriage and put on my bonnet and came here as quickly as possible. Thank heaven I've found you!"

"What do you propose to do with us?" Winterbourne uncomfortably smiled.

"To ask her to get in, to drive her about here for half an hour—so that the world may see she's not running absolutely wild—and then take her safely home."

"I don't think it's a very happy thought," he said after reflexion, "but you're at liberty to try."

Mrs. Walker accordingly tried. The young man went in pursuit of their young lady who had simply nodded and smiled, from her distance, at her recent patroness in the carriage and then had gone her way with her own companion. On learning, in the event, that Mrs. Walker had followed her, she retraced her steps, however, with a perfect good grace and with Mr. Giovanelli at her side. She professed herself "enchanted" to have a chance to present this gentleman to her good friend, and immediately achieved the introduction; declaring with it, and as if it were of as little importance, that she had never in her life seen anything so lovely as that lady's carriage-rug.

"I'm glad you admire it," said her poor pursuer, smiling sweetly. "Will you get in and let me put it over you?"

"Oh no, thank you!"—Daisy knew her mind. "I'll admire it ever so much more as I see you driving round with it."

"Do get in and drive round *with* me," Mrs. Walker pleaded.

"That would be charming, but it's so fascinating just as I am!"—with which the girl radiantly took in the gentlemen on either side of her.

"It may be fascinating, dear child, but it's not the custom here," urged the lady of the victoria, leaning forward in this vehicle with her hands devoutly clasped.

"Well, it ought to be then!" Daisy imperturbably laughed. "If I didn't walk I'd expire."

"You should walk with your mother, dear," cried Mrs. Walker with a loss of patience.

"With my mother dear?" the girl amusedly echoed. Winterbourne saw she scented interference. "My mother never walked ten steps in her life. And then, you know," she blandly added, "I'm more than five years old."

"You're old enough to be more reasonable. You're old enough, dear Miss Miller, to be talked about."

Daisy wondered to extravagance. "Talked about? What do you mean?"

"Come into my carriage and I'll tell you."

Daisy turned shining eyes again from one of the gentlemen beside her to the other. Mr. Giovanelli was bowing to and fro, rubbing down his gloves and laughing irresponsibly; Winterbourne thought the scene the most unpleasant possible. "I don't think I want to know what you mean," the girl presently said. "I don't think I should like it."

Winterbourne only wished Mrs. Walker would tuck up her carriage-rug and drive away; but this lady, as she afterwards told him, didn't feel she could "rest there." "Should you prefer being thought a very reckless girl?" she accordingly asked.

"Gracious me!" exclaimed Daisy. She looked again at Mr. Giovanelli, then she turned to her other companion. There was a small pink flush in her cheek; she was tremendously pretty. "Does Mr. Winterbourne think," she put to him with a wonderful bright intensity of appeal, "that—to save my reputation—I ought to get into the carriage?"

It really embarrassed him; for an instant he cast about—so strange was it to hear her speak that way of her "reputation." But he himself in fact had to speak in accordance with gallantry. The finest gallantry here was surely just to tell her the truth; and the truth, for our young man, as the few indications I have been able to give have made him known to the reader, was that his charming friend should listen to the voice of civilised society. He took in again her exquisite prettiness and then said the more distinctly: "I think you should get into the carriage."

Daisy gave the rein to her amusement. "I never heard anything so stiff! If this is improper, Mrs. Walker," she pursued, "then I'm *all* improper, and you had better give me right up. Good-bye; I hope you'll have a lovely ride!" —and with Mr. Giovanelli, who made a triumphantly obsequious salute, she turned away.

Mrs. Walker sat looking after her, and there were tears in Mrs. Walker's eye. "Get in here, sir," she said to Winterbourne, indicating the place beside her. The young man answered that he felt bound to accompany Miss Miller; whereupon the lady of the victoria declared that if he refused her this favour she would never speak to him again. She was evidently wound up. He accordingly hastened to overtake Daisy and her more faithful ally, and, offering her his hand, told her that Mrs. Walker had made a stringent claim on his presence. He had expected her to answer with something rather free, something still more significant of the perversity from which the voice of society, through the lips of their distressed friend, had so earnestly endeavoured to dissuade her. But she only let her hand slip, as she scarce looked at him, through his slightly awkward grasp; while Mr. Giovanelli, to make it worse, bade him farewell with too emphatic a flourish of the hat.

Winterbourne was not in the best possible humour as he took his seat beside the author of his sacrifice. "That was not clever of you," he said candidly, as the vehicle mingled again with the throng of carriages.

"In such a case," his companion answered, "I don't want to be clever—I only want to be *true!*"

"Well, your truth has only offended the strange little creature—it has only put her off."

"It has happened very well"—Mrs. Walker accepted her work. "If she's so perfectly determined to compromise herself the sooner one knows it the better—one can act accordingly."

"I suspect she meant no great harm, you know," Winterbourne maturely opined.

"So I thought a month ago. But she has been going too far."

"What has she been doing?"

"Everything that's not done here. Flirting with any man

she can pick up; sitting in corners with mysterious Italians; dancing all the evening with the same partners; receiving visits at eleven o'clock at night. Her mother melts away when the visitors come."

"But her brother," laughed Winterbourne, "sits up till two in the morning."

"He must be edified by what he sees. I'm told that at their hotel everyone's talking about her and that a smile goes round among the servants when a gentleman comes and asks for Miss Miller."

"Ah we needn't mind the servants!" Winterbourne compassionately signified. "The poor girl's only fault," he presently added, "is her complete lack of education."

"She's naturally indelicate," Mrs. Walker, on her side, reasoned. "Take that example this morning. How long had you known her at Vevey?"

"A couple of days."

"Imagine then the taste of her making it a personal matter that you should have left the place!"

He agreed that taste wasn't the strong point of the Millers—after which he was silent for some moments; but only at last to add: "I suspect, Mrs. Walker, that you and I have lived too long at Geneva!" And he further noted that he should be glad to learn with what particular design she had made him enter her carriage.

"I wanted to enjoin on you the importance of your ceasing your relations with Miss Miller; that of your not appearing to flirt with her; that of your giving her no further opportunity to expose herself; that of your in short letting her alone."

"I'm afraid I can't do anything quite so enlightened as *that*," he returned. "I like her awfully, you know."

"All the more reason you shouldn't help her to make a scandal."

"Well, there shall be nothing scandalous in, my attentions to her," he was willing to promise.

"There certainly will be in the way she takes them. But I've said what I had on my conscience," Mrs. Walker pursued. "If you wish to rejoin the young lady I'll put you down. Here, by the way, you have a chance."

The carriage was engaged in that part of the Pincian drive which overhangs the wall of Rome and overlooks the beautiful Villa Borghese. It is bordered by a large parapet, near which are several seats. One of these, at a distance, was occupied by a gentleman and a lady, toward whom Mrs. Walker gave a toss of her head. At the same moment these persons rose and walked to the parapet. Winterbourne had asked the coachman to stop; he now descended from the carriage. His companion looked at him a moment in silence and then, while he raised his hat, drove majestically away. He stood where he had alighted; he had turned his eyes toward Daisy and her cavalier. They evidently saw no one; they were too deeply occupied with each other. When they reached the low garden-wall they remained a little looking off at the great flat-topped pine-clusters of Villa Borghese; then the girl's attendant admirer seated himself familiarly on the broad ledge of the wall. The western sun in the opposite sky sent out a brilliant shaft through a couple of cloud-bars; whereupon the gallant Giovanelli took her parasol out of her hands and opened it. She came a little nearer and he held the parasol over her; then, still holding it, he let it so rest on her shoulder that both of their heads were hidden from Winterbourne. This young man stayed but a moment longer; then he began to walk. But he walked—not toward the couple united beneath the parasol, rather toward the residence of his aunt Mrs. Costello.

IV

He flattered himself on the following day that there was no smiling among the servants when he at least asked for Mrs. Miller at her hotel. This lady and her daughter, however, were not at home; and on the next day after, repeating his visit, Winterbourne again was met by a denial. Mrs. Walker's party took place on the evening of the third day, and in spite of the final reserves that had marked his last interview with that social critic our young man was among the guests. Mrs. Walker was one of those pilgrims from the younger world who, while in contact with the elder, make a point, in their own phrase, of studying European society; and she had on this occasion collected several specimens of diversely-born humanity to serve, as might be, for textbooks. When Winterbourne arrived the little person he desired most to find wasn't there; but in a few moments he saw Mrs. Miller come in alone, very shyly and ruefully. This lady's hair, above the dead waste of her temples, was more frizzled than ever. As she approached their hostess Winterbourne also drew near.

"You see I've come all alone," said Daisy's unsupported parent. "I'm so frightened I don't know what to do; it's the first time I've ever been to a party alone—especially in this country. I wanted to bring Randolph or Eugenio or some one, but Daisy just pushed me off by myself. I ain't used to going round alone."

"And doesn't your daughter intend to favour us with her society?" Mrs. Walker impressively enquired.

"Well, Daisy's all dressed," Mrs. Miller testified with that accent of the dispassionate, if not of the philosophic, historian with which she always recorded the current incidents of her daughter's career. "She got dressed on purpose before dinner. But she has a friend of hers there; that gentleman—the handsomest of the Italians—that she wanted to bring. They've got going at the piano—it seems as if they couldn't leave off. Mr. Giovanelli does sing splendidly. But I guess they'll come before very long," Mrs. Miller hopefully concluded.

"I'm sorry she should come—in that particular way," Mrs. Walker permitted herself to observe.

"Well, I told her there was no use in her getting dressed before dinner if she was going to wait three hours," returned Daisy's mamma. "I didn't see the use of her putting on such a dress as that to sit around with Mr. Giovanelli."

"This is most horrible!" said Mrs. Walker, turning away and addressing herself to Winterbourne. "*Elle s'affiche, la malheureuse.* It's her revenge for my having ventured to remonstrate with her."

Daisy came after eleven o'clock, but she wasn't, on such an occasion, a young lady to wait to be spoken to. She rustled forward in radiant loveliness, smiling and chattering, carrying a large bouquet and attended by Mr. Giovanelli. Every one stopped talking and turned and looked at her while she floated up to Mrs. Walker. "I'm afraid you thought I never was coming, so I sent mother off to tell you. I wanted to make Mr. Giovanelli practise some things before he came; you know he sings beautifully, and I want you to ask him to sing. This is Mr. Giovanelli; you know I introduced him to you; he's got the most lovely voice and he knows the most charming set of songs. I made him go over them this evening on purpose; we had the greatest time at the hotel." Of all this Daisy delivered herself with the sweetest brightest loudest confidence, looking now at her hostess and now at all the room, while she gave a series of little pats, round her very white shoulders, to the edges of her dress. "Is there anyone I know?" she undiscourageably asked.

"I think everyone knows you!" said Mrs. Walker as with a grand intention; and she gave a very cursory greeting to Mr. Giovanelli. This gentleman bore himself gallantly; he smiled and bowed and showed his white teeth, he curled his moustaches and rolled his eyes and performed all the proper functions of a handsome Italian at an evening party. He sang, very prettily, half a dozen songs, though Mrs. Walker afterwards declared that she had been quite unable to find out who asked him. It was apparently not Daisy who had set him in motion—this young lady being seated a distance from the piano and, though she had publicly, as it were, professed herself his musical patroness or guarantor, giving herself to gay and audible discourse while he warbled.

"It's a pity these rooms are so small; we can't dance," she remarked to Winterbourne as if she had seen him five minutes before.

"I'm not sorry we can't dance," he candidly returned. "I'm incapable of a step."

"Of course you're incapable of a step," the girl assented. "I should think your legs *would* be stiff cooped in there so much of the time in that victoria."

"Well, they were very restless there three days ago," he amicably laughed; "all they really wanted was to dance attendance on you."

"Oh my other friend—my friend in need—stuck to me; he seems more at one with his limbs than you are—I'll say that for him. But did you ever hear anything so cool," Daisy demanded, "as Mrs. Walker's wanting me to get into her carriage and drop poor Mr. Giovanelli, and under the pretext that it was proper? People have different ideas! It would have been most unkind; he had been talking about that walk for ten days."

"He shouldn't have talked about it at all," Winterbourne decided to make answer on this: "he would never have proposed to a young lady of this country to walk about the streets of Rome with him."

"About the streets?" she cried with her pretty stare. "Where then would he have proposed to her to walk? The Pincio ain't the streets either, I guess; and I besides, thank goodness, am not a young lady of this country. The young ladies of this country have a dreadfully pokey time of it, by what I can discover; I don't see why I should change my habits for *such* stupids."

"I'm afraid your habits are those of a ruthless flirt," said Winterbourne with studied severity.

"Of course they are!"—and she hoped, evidently, by the manner of it, to take his breath away. "I'm a fearful frightful flirt! Did you ever hear of a nice girl that wasn't? But I suppose you'll tell me now I'm not a nice girl."

He remained grave indeed under the shock of her cynical profession. "You're a very nice girl, but I wish you'd flirt with me, and me only."

"Ah thank you, thank you very much: you're the last man I should think of flirting with. As I've had the pleasure of informing you, you're too stiff."

"You say that too often," he resentfully remarked.

Daisy gave a delighted laugh. "If I could have the sweet hope of making you angry I'd say it again."

"Don't do that—when I'm angry I'm stiffer than ever. But if you won't flirt with me do cease at least to flirt with your friend at the piano. They don't," he declared as in full sympathy with "them," "understand that sort of thing here."

"I thought they understood nothing else!" Daisy cried with startling world-knowledge.

"Not in young unmarried women."

"It seems to me much more proper in young unmarried than in old married ones," she retorted.

"Well," said Winterbourne, "when you deal with natives you must go by the custom of the country. American flirting is a purely American silliness; it has—in its ineptitude of innocence—no place in *this* system. So when you show yourself in public with Mr. Giovanelli and without your mother—"

"Gracious, poor mother!"—and she made it beautifully unspeakable.

Winterbourne had a touched sense for this, but it didn't alter his attitude. "Though *you* may be flirting, Mr. Giovanelli isn't—he means something else."

"He isn't preaching at any rate," she returned. "And if you want very much to know, we're neither of us flirting—not a little speck. We're too good friends for that. We're real intimate friends."

He was to continue to find her thus at moments inimitable. "Ah," he then judged, "if you're in love with each other it's another affair altogether!"

She had allowed him up to this point to speak so frankly that he had no thought of shocking her by the force of his logic; yet she now none the less immediately rose, blushing visibly and leaving him mentally to exclaim that the name of little American flirts was incoherence. "Mr. Giovanelli at least," she answered, sparing but a single small queer glance for it, a queerer small glance, he felt, than he had ever yet had from her—"Mr. Giovanelli never says to me such very disagreeable things."

It had an effect on him—he stood staring. The subject of their contention had finished singing; he left the piano, and his recognition of what—a little awkwardly—didn't take place in celebration of this might nevertheless have been an acclaimed operatic tenor's series of repeated ducks before the curtain. So he bowed himself over to Daisy. "Won't you come to the other room and have some tea?" he asked—offering Mrs. Walker's slightly thin refreshment as he might have done all the kingdoms of the earth.

Daisy at last turned on Winterbourne a more natural and calculable light. He was but the more muddled by it, however, since so inconsequent a smile made nothing clear —it seemed at the most to prove in her a sweetness and softness that reverted instinctively to the pardon of offenses. "It has never occurred to Mr. Winterbourne to offer me any tea," she said with her finest little intention of torment and triumph.

"I've offered you excellent advice," the young man permitted himself to growl.

"I prefer weak tea!" cried Daisy, and she went off with the brilliant Giovanelli. She sat with him in the adjoining room, in the embrasure of the window, for the rest of the evening. There was an interesting performance at the piano, but neither of these conversers gave heed to it. When

Daisy came to take leave of Mrs. Walker this lady consci-
entiously repaired the weakness of which she had been
guilty at the moment of the girl's arrival—she turned her
back straight on Miss Miller and left her to depart with
what grace she might. Winterbourne happened to be near
the door; he saw it all. Daisy turned very pale and looked
at her mother, but Mrs. Miller was humbly unconscious
of any rupture of any law or of any deviation from any
custom. She appeared indeed to have felt an incongruous
impulse to draw attention to her own striking conformity.
"Good-night, Mrs. Walker," she said; "we've had a beautiful evening. You see if I let Daisy come to parties without me; I don't want her to go away without me." Daisy
turned away, looking with a small white prettiness, a
blighted grace, at the circle near the door: Winterbourne
saw that for the first moment she was too much shocked
and puzzled even for indignation. He on his side was
greatly touched.

"That was very cruel," he promptly remarked to Mrs.
Walker.

But this lady's face was also as a stone. "She never enters my drawing-room again."

Since Winterbourne then, hereupon, was not to meet
her in Mrs. Walker's drawing-room he went as often as
possible to Mrs. Miller's hotel. The ladies were rarely at
home, but when he found them the devoted Giovanelli
was always present. Very often the glossy little Roman,
serene in success, but not unduly presumptuous, occupied
with Daisy alone the florid salon enjoyed by Eugenio's
care, Mrs. Miller being apparently ever of the opinion that
discretion is the better part of solicitude. Winterbourne
noted, at first with surprise, that Daisy on these occasions
was neither embarrassed nor annoyed by his own entrance;
but he presently began to feel that she had no more surprises for him and that he really liked, after all, not making out what she was "up to." She showed no displeasure
for the interruption of her *tête-à-tête* with Giovanelli; she
could chatter as freshly and freely with two gentlemen as
with one, and this easy flow had ever the same anomaly
for her earlier friend that it was so free without availing
itself of its freedom. Winterbourne reflected that if she was
seriously interested in the Italian it was odd she shouldn't
take more trouble to preserve the sanctity of their inter-

views, and he liked her the better for her innocent-looking indifference and her inexhaustible gaiety. He could hardly have said why, but she struck him as a young person not formed for a troublesome jealousy. Smile at such a betrayal though the reader may, it was a fact with regard to the women who had hitherto interested him that, given certain contingencies, Winterbourne could see himself afraid—literally afraid—of these ladies. It pleased him to believe that even were twenty other things different and Daisy should love him and he should know it and like it, he would still never be afraid of Daisy. It must be added that this conviction was not altogether flattering to her: it represented that she was nothing every way if not light.

But she was evidently very much interested in Giovanelli. She looked at him whenever he spoke; she was perpetually telling him to do this and to do that; she was constantly chaffing and abusing him. She appeared completely to have forgotten that her other friend had said anything to displease her at Mrs. Walker's entertainment. One Sunday afternoon, having gone to Saint Peter's with his aunt, Winterbourne became aware that the young woman held in horror by that lady was strolling about the great church under escort of her coxcomb of the Corso. It amused him, after a debate, to point out the exemplary pair—even at the cost, as it proved, of Mrs. Costello's saying when she had taken them in through her eye-glass: "That's what makes you so pensive in these days, eh?"

"I hadn't the least idea I was pensive," he pleaded.

"You're very much preoccupied; you're always thinking of something."

"And what is it," he asked, "that you accuse me of thinking of?"

"Of that young lady's, Miss Baker's, Miss Chandler's—what's her name?—Miss Miller's intrigue with that little barber's block."

"Do you call it an intrigue," he asked—"an affair that goes on with such peculiar publicity?"

"That's their folly," said Mrs. Costello, "it's not their merit."

"No," he insisted with a hint perhaps of the preoccupation to which his aunt had alluded—"I don't believe there's anything to be called an intrigue."

"Well"—and Mrs. Costello dropped her glass—"I've

heard a dozen people speak of it: they say she's quite carried away by him."

"They're certainly as thick as thieves," our embarrassed young man allowed.

Mrs. Costello came back to them, however, after a little; and Winterbourne recognised in this a further illustration —than that supplied by his own condition—of the spell projected by the case. "He's certainly very handsome. One easily sees how it is. She thinks him the most elegant man in the world, the finest gentleman possible. She has never seen anything like him—he's better even than the courier. It was the courier probably who introduced him, and if he succeeds in marrying the young lady the courier will come in for a magnificent commission."

"I don't believe she thinks of marrying him," Winterbourne reasoned, "and I don't believe he hopes to marry her."

"You may be very sure she thinks of nothing at all. She romps on from day to day, from hour to hour, as they did in the Golden Age. I can imagine nothing more vulgar," said Mrs. Costello, whose figure of speech scarcely went on all fours. "And at the same time," she added, "depend upon it she may tell you any moment that she is 'engaged.'"

"I think that's more than Giovanelli really expects," said Winterbourne.

"And who is Giovanelli?"

"The shiny—but, to do him justice, not greasy—little Roman. I've asked questions about him and learned something. He's apparently a perfectly respectable little man. I believe he's in a small way a *cavaliere avvocato*. But he doesn't move in what are called the first circles. I think it really not absolutely impossible the courier introduced him. He's evidently immensely charmed with Miss Miller. If she thinks him the finest gentleman in the world, he, on his side, has never found himself in personal contact with such splendour, such opulence, such personal daintiness, as this young lady's. And then she must seem to him wonderfully pretty and interesting. Yes, he can't really hope to pull it off. That must appear to him too impossible a piece of luck. He has nothing but his handsome face to offer, and there's a substantial, a possibly explosive Mr. Miller in that mysterious land of dollars and six-shooters.

Giovanelli's but too conscious that he hasn't a title to offer. If he were only a count or a *marchese!* What on earth can he make of the way they've taken him up?"

"He accounts for it by his handsome face and thinks Miss Miller a young lady *qui se passe ses fantaisies!*"

"It's very true," Winterbourne pursued, "that Daisy and her mamma haven't yet risen to that stage of—what shall I call it?—of culture, at which the idea of catching a count or a *marchese* begins. I believe them intellectually incapable of that conception."

"Ah but the *cavaliere avvocato* doesn't believe them!" cried Mrs. Costello.

Of the observation excited by Daisy's "intrigue" Winterbourne gathered that day at Saint Peter's sufficient evidence. A dozen of the American colonists in Rome came to talk with his relative, who sat on a small portable stool at the base of one of the great pilasters. The vesper-service was going forward in splendid chants and organ-tones in the adjacent choir, and meanwhile, between Mrs. Costello and her friends, much was said about poor little Miss Miller's going really "too far." Winterbourne was not pleased with what he heard; but when, coming out upon the great steps of the church, he saw Daisy, who had emerged before him, get into an open cab with her accomplice and roll away through the cynical streets of Rome, the measure of her course struck him as simply there to take. He felt very sorry for her—not exactly that he believed she had completely lost her wits, but because it was painful to see so much that was pretty and undefended and natural sink so low in human estimation. He made an attempt after this to give a hint to Mrs. Miller. He met one day in the Corso a friend—a tourist like himself—who had just come out of the Doria Palace, where he had been walking through the beautiful gallery. His friend "went on" for some moments about the great portrait of Innocent X, by Velasquez, suspended in one of the cabinets of the palace, and then said: "And in the same cabinet, by the way, I enjoyed sight of an image of a different kind; that little American who's so much more a work of nature than of art and whom you pointed out to me last week." In answer to Winterbourne's enquiries his friend narrated that the little American—prettier now than ever—was seated with a companion in the secluded nook in which the papal presence is enshrined.

"All alone?" the young man heard himself disingenuously ask.

"Alone with a little Italian who sports in his buttonhole a stack of flowers. The girl's a charming beauty, but I thought I understood from you the other day that she's a young lady *du meilleur monde*."

"So she is!" said Winterbourne; and having assured himself that his informant had seen the interesting pair but ten minutes before, he jumped into a cab and went to call on Mrs. Miller. She was at home, but she apologised for receiving him in Daisy's absence.

"She's gone out somewhere with Mr. Giovanelli. She's always going round with Mr. Giovanelli."

"I've noticed they're intimate indeed," Winterbourne concurred.

"Oh it seems as if they couldn't live without each other!" said Mrs. Miller. "Well, he's a real gentleman anyhow. I guess I have the joke on Daisy—that she *must* be engaged!"

"And how does your daughter *take* the joke?"

"Oh she just says she ain't. But she might as *well* be!" this philosophic parent resumed. "She goes on as if she was. But I've made Mr. Giovanelli promise to tell me if Daisy don't. I'd want to write to Mr. Miller about it—wouldn't you?"

Winterbourne replied that he certainly should; and the state of mind of Daisy's mamma struck him as so unprecedented in the annals of parental vigilance that he recoiled before the attempt to educate at a single interview either her conscience or her wit.

After this Daisy was never at home and he ceased to meet her at the houses of their common acquaintance, because, as he perceived, these shrewd people had quite made up their minds as to the length she must have gone. They ceased to invite her, intimating that they wished to make, and make strongly, for the benefit of observant Europeans, the point that though Miss Daisy Miller was a pretty American girl all right, her behaviour wasn't pretty at all—was in fact regarded by her compatriots as quite monstrous. Winterbourne wondered how she felt about all the cold shoulders that were turned upon her, and sometimes found himself suspecting with impatience that she simply didn't feel and didn't know. He set her down as hopelessly childish and shallow, as such mere giddiness and ignorance incarnate as was powerless either to heed or to suffer. Then at other moments he couldn't doubt that she carried about in her elegant and irresponsible little organism a defiant, passionate, perfectly observant consciousness of the impression she produced. He asked himself whether the defiance would come from the consciousness of innocence or from her being essentially a young person of the reckless class. Then it had to be admitted, he felt, that holding fast to a belief in her "innocence" was more and more but a matter of gallantry too fine-spun for use. As I have already had occasion to relate, he was reduced without pleasure to this chopping of logic and vexed at his poor fallibility, his want of instinctive certitude as to how far her extravagance was generic and national and how far it was crudely personal. Whatever it was he had helplessly missed her, and now it was too late. She was "carried away" by Mr. Giovanelli.

A few days after his brief interview with her mother he came across her at that supreme seat of flowering desolation known as the Palace of the Caesars. The early Roman spring had filled the air with bloom and perfume, and the rugged surface of the Palatine was muffled with tender verdure. Daisy moved at her ease over the great mounds of ruin that are embanked with mossy marble and paved with monumental inscriptions. It seemed to him he had never known Rome so lovely as just then. He looked off at the enchanting harmony of line and colour that remotely encircles the city—he inhaled the softly humid odours and felt the freshness of the year and the antiquity of the place reaffirm themselves in deep interfusion. It struck him also that Daisy had never showed to the eye for so utterly charming; but this had been his conviction on every occasion of their meeting. Giovanelli was of course at her side, and Giovanelli too glowed as never before with something of the glory of his race.

"Well," she broke out upon the friend it would have been such mockery to designate as the latter's rival, "I should think you'd be quite lonesome!"

"Lonesome?" Winterbourne resignedly echoed.

"You're always going round by yourself. Can't you get anyone to walk with you?"

"I'm not so fortunate," he answered, "as your gallant companion."

Giovanelli had from the first treated him with distinguished politeness; he listened with a deferential air to his remarks; he laughed punctiliously at his pleasantries; he attached such importance as he could find terms for to Miss Miller's cold compatriot. He carried himself in no degree like a jealous wooer; he had obviously a great deal of tact; he had no objection to anyone's expecting a little humility of him. It even struck Winterbourne that he almost yearned at times for some private communication in the interest of his character for common sense; a chance to remark to him as another intelligent man that, bless him, *he* knew how extraordinary was their young lady and didn't flatter himself with confident—at least *too* confident and too delusive—hopes of matrimony and dollars. On this occasion he strolled away from his charming charge to pluck a sprig of almond-blossom which he carefully arranged in his button-hole.

"I know why you say that," Daisy meanwhile observed. "Because you think I go round too much with *him!*" And she nodded at her discreet attendant.

"Everyone thinks so—if you care to know," was all Winterbourne found to reply.

"Of course I care to know!"—she made this point with much expression. "But I don't believe a word of it. They're only pretending to be shocked. They don't really care a straw what I do. I don't go round so much."

"I think you'll find they do care. They'll show it—disagreeably," he took on himself to state.

Daisy weighed the importance of that idea. "How—disagreeably?"

"Haven't you noticed anything?" he compassionately asked.

"I've noticed *you*. But I noticed you've no more 'give' than a ramrod the first time ever I saw you."

"You'll find at least that I've more 'give' than several others," he patiently smiled.

"How shall I find it?"

"By going to see the others."

"What will they do to me?"

"They'll show you the cold shoulder. Do you know what that means?"

Daisy was looking at him intently; she began to colour. "Do you mean as Mrs. Walker did the other night?"

"Exactly as Mrs. Walker did the other night."

She looked away at Giovanelli, still titivating with his almond-blossom. Then with her attention again on the important subject: "I shouldn't think you'd let people be so unkind!"

"How can I help it?"

"I should think you'd want to say something."

"I do want to say something"—and Winterbourne paused a moment. "I want to say that your mother tells me she believes you engaged."

"Well, I guess she does," said Daisy very simply.

The young man began to laugh. "And does Randolph believe it?"

"I guess Randolph doesn't believe anything." This testimony to Randolph's scepticism excited Winterbourne to further mirth, and he noticed that Giovanelli was coming back to them. Daisy, observing it as well, addressed herself again to her countryman. "Since you've mentioned it," she said, "I *am* engaged." He looked at her hard—he had stopped laughing. "You don't believe it!" she added.

He asked himself, and it was for a moment like testing a heart-beat; after which, "Yes, I believe it!" he said.

"Oh no, you don't," she answered. "But *if* you possibly do," she still more perversely pursued—"well, I ain't."

Miss Miller and her constant guide were on their way to the gate of the enclosure, so that Winterbourne, who had but lately entered, presently took leave of them. A week later on he went to dine at a beautiful villa on the Caelian Hill, and, on arriving, dismissed his hired vehicle. The evening was perfect and he promised himself the satisfaction of walking home beneath the Arch of Constantine and past the vaguely-lighted monuments of the Forum. Above was a moon half-developed, whose radiance was not brilliant but veiled in a thin cloud-curtain that seemed to diffuse and equalise it. When on his return from the villa at eleven o'clock he approached the dusky circle of the Colosseum the sense of the romantic in him easily suggested that the interior, in such an atmosphere, would well repay a glance. He turned aside and walked to one of the empty arches, near which, as he observed, an open carriage—one of the little Roman street-cabs—was stationed. Then he passed in among the cavernous shadows of the great structure and emerged upon the clear and silent arena. The place had never seemed to him more impressive. One half of the gigantic circus was in deep shade while the other slept in the luminous dusk. As he stood there he began to murmur Byron's famous lines out of "Manfred"; but before he had finished his quotation he remembered that if nocturnal meditation thereabouts was the fruit of a rich literary culture it was none the less deprecated by medical science. The air of other ages surrounded one; but the air of other ages, coldly analysed, was no better than a villainous miasma. Winterbourne sought, however, toward the middle of the arena, a further reach of vision, intending the next moment a hasty retreat. The great cross in the center was almost obscured; only as he drew near did he make it out distinctly. He thus also distinguished two persons stationed on the low steps that formed its base. One of these was a woman seated; her companion hovered before her.

Presently the sound of the woman's voice came to him distinctly in the warm night-air. "Well, he looks at us as one of the old lions or tigers may have looked at the Christian martyrs!" These words were winged with their accent, so that they fluttered and settled about him in the darkness like vague white doves. It was Miss Daisy Miller who had released them for flight.

"Let us hope he's not very hungry"—the bland Giovanelli fell in with her humour. "He'll have to take *me* first; you'll serve for dessert."

Winterbourne felt himself pulled up with final horror now—and, it must be added, with final relief. It was as if a sudden clearance had taken place in the ambiguity of the poor girl's appearances and the whole riddle of her contradictions had grown easy to read. She was a young lady about the *shades* of whose perversity a foolish puzzled gentleman need no longer trouble his head or his heart. That once questionable quantity *had* no shades—it was a mere black little blot. He stood there looking at her, looking at her companion too, and not reflecting that though he saw them vaguely he himself must have been more brightly presented. He felt angry at all his shiftings of view—he felt ashamed of all his tender little scruples and all his witless little mercies. He was about to advance again, and then again checked himself; not from the fear of doing her injustice, but from a sense of the danger of showing undue exhilaration for this disburdenment of cautious criticism. He turned away toward the entrance of the place; but as he did so he heard Daisy speak again.

"Why it was Mr. Winterbourne! He saw me and he cuts me dead!"

What a clever little reprobate she was, he was amply able to reflect at this, and how smartly she feigned, how promptly she sought to play off on him, a surprised and injured innocence! But nothing would induce him to cut her either "dead" or to within any measureable distance even of the famous "inch" of her life. He came forward again and went toward the great cross. Daisy had got up and Giovanelli lifted his hat. Winterbourne had now begun to think simply of the madness, on the ground of exposure and infection, of a frail young creature's lounging away such hours in a nest of malaria. What if she *were* the most plausible of little reprobates? That was no reason for her dying of the *perniciosa.* "How long have you been 'fooling round' here?" he asked with conscious roughness.

Daisy, lovely in the sinister silver radiance, appraised him a moment, roughness and all. "Well, I guess all the evening." She answered with spirit and, he could see even then, with exaggeration. "I never saw anything so quaint."

"I'm afraid," he returned, "you'll not think a bad attack of Roman fever very quaint. This is the way people catch it. I wonder," he added to Giovanelli, "that you, a native Roman, should countenance such extraordinary rashness."

"Ah," said this seasoned subject, "for myself I have no fear."

"Neither have I—for you!" Winterbourne retorted in French. "I'm speaking for this young lady."

Giovanelli raised his well-shaped eyebrows and showed his shining teeth, but took his critic's rebuke with docility, "I assured Mademoiselle it was a grave indiscretion, but when was Mademoiselle ever prudent?"

"I never was sick, and I don't mean to be!" Mademoiselle declared. "I don't look like much, but I'm healthy! I was bound to see the Colosseum by moonlight—I wouldn't have wanted to go home without *that;* and we've had the most beautiful time, haven't we, Mr. Giovanelli? If there has been any danger Eugenio can give me some pills. Eugenio has got some splendid pills."

"*I* should advise you then," said Winterbourne, "to drive home as fast as possible and take one!"

Giovanelli smiled as for the striking happy thought. "What you say is very wise. I'll go and make sure the carriage is at hand." And he went forward rapidly.

Daisy followed with Winterbourne. He tried to deny himself the small fine anguish of looking at her, but his eyes themselves refused to spare him, and she seemed moreover not in the least embarrassed. He spoke no word; Daisy chattered over the beauty of the place: "Well, I *have* seen the Colosseum by moonlight—that's one thing I can rave about!" Then noticing her companion's silence she asked him why he was so stiff—it had always been her great word. He made no answer, but he felt his laugh an immense negation of stiffness. They passed under one of the dark archways; Giovanelli was in front with the carriage. Here Daisy stopped a moment, looking at her compatriot. "*Did* you believe I was engaged the other day?"

"It doesn't matter now what I believed the other day!" he replied with infinite point.

It 'was a wonder how she didn't wince for it. "Well, what do you believe now?"

"I believe it makes very little difference whether you're engaged or not!"

He felt her lighted eyes fairly penetrate the thick gloom of the vaulted passage—as if to seek some access to him she hadn't yet compassed. But Giovanelli, with a graceful inconsequence, was at present all for retreat. "Quick, quick; if we get in by midnight we're quite safe!"

Daisy took her seat in the carriage and the fortunate Italian placed himself beside her. "Don't forget Eugenio's pills!" said Winterbourne as he lifted his hat.

"I don't care," she unexpectedly cried out for this, "whether I have Roman fever or not!" On which the cabdriver cracked his whip and they rolled across the desultory patches of antique pavement.

Winterbourne—to do him justice, as it were—mentioned to no one that he had encountered Miss Miller at midnight in the Colosseum with a gentleman; in spite of which deep discretion, however, the fact of the scandalous adventure was known a couple of days later, with a dozen vivid details, to every member of the little American circle, and was commented accordingly. Winterbourne judged thus that the people about the hotel had been thoroughly empowered to testify, and that after Daisy's return there would have been an exchange of jokes between the porter and the cab-driver. But the young man became aware at the same moment of how thoroughly it had ceased to ruffle him that the little American flirt should be "talked about" by low-minded menials. These sources of current criticism a day or two later abounded still further: the little American flirt was alarmingly ill and the doctors now in possession of the scene. Winterbourne, when the rumour came to him, immediately went to the hotel for more news. He found that two or three charitable friends had preceded him and that they were being entertained in Mrs. Miller's salon by the all-efficient Randolph.

"It's going round at night that way, you bet—that's what has made her so sick. She's always going round at night. I shouldn't think she'd want to—it's so plaguey dark over here. You can't see anything over here without the moon's right up. In America they don't go round by the moon!" Mrs. Miller meanwhile wholly surrendered to her genius for unapparent uses; her salon knew her less than ever, and she was presumably now at least giving her daughter the advantage of her society. It was clear that Daisy was dangerously ill.

Winterbourne constantly attended for news from the sick-room, which reached him, however, but with worrying indirectness, though he once had speech, for a moment, of the poor girl's physician and once saw Mrs. Miller, who, sharply alarmed, struck him as thereby more happily inspired than he could have conceived and indeed as the most noiseless and light-handed of nurses. She invoked a good deal the remote shade of Dr. Davis, but Winterbourne paid her the compliment of taking her after all for less monstrous a goose. To this indulgence indeed something she further said perhaps even more insidiously disposed him. "Daisy spoke of you the other day quite pleasantly. Half the time she doesn't know what she's saying, but that time I think she did. She gave me a message

—she told me to tell you. She wanted you to know she never was engaged to that handsome Italian who was always round. I'm sure I'm very glad; Mr. Giovanelli hasn't been near us since she was taken ill. I thought he was so much of a gentleman, but I don't call that very polite! A lady told me he was afraid I hadn't approved of his being round with her so much evenings. Of course it ain't as if their evenings were as pleasant as ours—since *we* don't seem to feel that way about the poison. I guess I *don't* see the point now; but I suppose he knows I'm a lady and I'd scorn to raise a fuss. Anyway, she wants you to realise she ain't engaged. I don't know why she makes so much of it, but she said to me three times 'Mind you tell Mr. Winterbourne.' And then she told me to ask if you remembered the time you went up to that castle in Switzerland. But I said I wouldn't give any such messages as *that*. Only if she ain't engaged I guess I'm glad to realise it too."

But, as Winterbourne had originally judged, the truth on this question had small actual relevance. A week after this the poor girl died; it had been indeed a terrible case of the *perniciosa*. A grave was found for her in the little Protestant cemetery, by an angle of the wall of imperial Rome, beneath the cypresses and the thick spring-flowers. Winterbourne stood there beside it with a number of other mourners; a number larger than the scandal excited by the young lady's career might have made probable. Near him stood Giovanelli, who came nearer still before Winterbourne turned away. Giovanelli, in decorous mourning, showed but a whiter face; his button-hole lacked its nosegay and he had visibly something urgent—and even to distress—to say, which he scarce knew how to "place." He decided at last to confide it with a pale convulsion to Winterbourne. "She was the most beautiful young lady I ever saw, and the most amiable." To which he added in a moment: "Also—naturally!—the most innocent."

Winterbourne sounded him with hard dry eyes, but presently repeated his words, "The most innocent?"

"The most innocent!"

It came somehow so much too late that our friend could only glare at its having come at all. "Why the devil," he asked, "did you take her to that fatal place?"

Giovanelli raised his neat shoulders and eyebrows to

within suspicion of a shrug. "For myself I had no fear; and *she*—she did what she liked."

Winterbourne's eyes attached themselves to the ground. "She did what she liked!"

It determined on the part of poor Giovanelli a further pious, a further candid, confidence. "If she had lived I should have got nothing. She never would have married me."

It had been spoken as if to attest, in all sincerity, his disinterestedness, but Winterbourne scarce knew what welcome to give it. He said, however, with a grace inferior to his friend's: "I dare say not."

The latter was even by this not discouraged. "For a moment I hoped so. But no. I'm convinced."

Winterbourne took it in; he stood staring at the raw protuberance among the April daisies. When he turned round again his fellow mourner had stepped back.

He almost immediately left Rome, but the following summer he again met his aunt Mrs. Costello at Vevey. Mrs. Costello extracted from the charming old hotel there a value that the Miller family hadn't mastered the secret of. In the interval Winterbourne had often thought of the most interesting member of the trio—of her mystifying manners and her queer adventure. One day he spoke of her to his aunt—said it was on his conscience he had done her injustice.

"I'm sure I don't know"—that lady showed caution. "How did your injustice affect her?"

"She sent me a message before her death which I didn't understand at the time. But I've understood it since. She would have appreciated one's esteem."

"She took an odd way to gain it! But do you mean by what you say," Mrs. Costello asked, "that she would have reciprocated one's affection?"

As he made no answer to this she after a little looked round at him—he hadn't been directly within sight; but the effect of that wasn't to make her repeat her question. He spoke, however, after a while. "You were right in that remark that you made last summer. I was booked to make a mistake. I've lived too long in foreign parts." And this time she herself said nothing.

Nevertheless he soon went back to live at Geneva, whence there continue to come the most contradictory accounts of his motives of sojourn: a report that he's "study-ing" hard—an intimation that he's much interested in a very clever foreign lady.

1879, 1909

The Art of Fiction

I should not have affixed so comprehensive a title to these few remarks, necessarily wanting in any complete-ness upon a subject the full consideration of which would carry us far, did I not seem to discover a pretext for my temerity in the interesting pamphlet lately published under this name by Mr. Walter Besant. Mr. Besant's lecture at the Royal Institution—the original form of his pamphlet —appears to indicate that many persons are interested in the art of fiction, and are not indifferent to such remarks as those who practise it may attempt to make about it. I am therefore anxious not to lose the benefit of this favour-able association, and to edge in a few words under cover of the attention which Mr. Besant is sure to have excited. There is something very encouraging in his having put into form certain of his ideas on the mystery of story-telling.

It is a proof of life and curiosity—curiosity on the part of the brotherhood of novelists as well as on the part of their readers. Only a short time ago it might have been supposed that the English novel was not what the French call *discutable*. It had no air of having a theory, a con-viction, a consciousness of itself behind it—of being the expression of an artistic faith, the result of choice and comparison. I do not say it was necessarily the worse for that: it would take much more courage than I possess to intimate that the form of the novel as Dickens and Thack-eray (for instance) saw it had any taint of incompleteness. It was, however, *naïf* (if I may help myself out with another French word); and evidently if it be destined to suffer in any way for having lost its *naïveté* it has now an idea of making sure of the corresponding advantages. During the period I have alluded to there was a comfort-able, good-humoured feeling abroad that a novel is a novel, as a pudding is a pudding, and that our only busi-ness with it could be to swallow it. But within a year or two, for some reason or other, there have been signs of returning animation—the era of discussion would appear to have been to a certain extent opened. Art lives upon discussion, upon experiment, upon curiosity, upon variety of attempt, upon the exchange of views and the comparison of standpoints; and there is a presumption that those times when no one has anything particular to say about it, and has no reason to give for practice or preference, though they may be times of honour, are not times of development—are times, possibly even, a little of dullness. The successful application of any art is a delightful spectacle, but the theory too is interesting; and though there is a great deal of the latter without the former I suspect there has never been a genuine success that has not had a latent core of conviction. Discussion, suggestion, formulation, these things are fertilizing when they are frank and sincere. Mr. Besant has set an excellent example in saying what he thinks, for his part, about the way in which fiction should be written, as well as about the way in which it should be published; for his view of the "art," carried on into an appendix, covers that too. Other labourers in the same field will doubtless take up the argument, they will give it the light of their experience, and the effect will surely be to make our interest in the novel a little more what it had for some time threatened to fail to be—a serious, active, inquiring interest, under protection of which this delightful study may, in moments of confidence, venture to say a little more what it thinks of itself.

It must take itself seriously for the public to take it so. The old superstition about fiction being "wicked" has doubtless died out in England; but the spirit of it lingers in a certain oblique regard directed toward any story which does not more or less admit that it is only a joke. Even the most jocular novel feels in some degree the weight of the proscription that was formerly directed against literary levity: the jocularity does not always succeed in passing for orthodoxy. It is still expected, though perhaps people are ashamed to say it, that a production which is after all only a "make-believe" (for what else is a "story"?) shall be in some degree apologetic—shall renounce the pretension of attempting really to represent life. This, of course, any sensible, wide-awake story declines to do, for it quickly perceives that the tolerance granted to it on such a condition is only an attempt to stifle it disguised in the form of generosity. The old evangelical hostility to the novel, which was as explicit as it was narrow, and which regarded it as little less favourable to our immortal part than a stage-play, was in reality far less insulting. The only reason for the existence of a novel is that it does attempt to represent life. When it relinquishes this attempt, the same attempt that we see on the canvas of the painter, it will have arrived at a very strange pass. It is not expected of the picture that it will make itself humble in order to be forgiven; and the analogy between the art of the painter and the art of the novelist is, so far as I am able to see, complete. Their inspiration is the same, their process (allowing for the different quality of the vehicle) is the same, their success is the same. They may learn from each other, they may explain and sustain each other. Their cause is the same, and the honour of one is the honour of another. The Mahometans think a picture an unholy thing, but it is a long time since any Christian did, and it is therefore the more odd that in the Christian mind the traces (dissimulated though they may be) of a suspicion of the sister art should linger to this day. The only effectual way to lay it to rest is to emphasize the analogy to which I just alluded—to insist on the fact that as the picture is reality, so the novel is history. That is the only general description (which does it justice) that we may give of the novel. But history also is allowed to represent life; it is not, any more than painting, expected to apologize. The subject-matter of fiction is stored up likewise in documents and records, and if it will not give itself away, as they say in California, it must speak with assurance, with the tone of the historian. Certain accomplished novelists have a habit of giving themselves away which must often bring tears to the eyes of people who take their fiction seriously. I was lately struck, in reading over many pages of Anthony Trollope, with his want of discretion in this particular. In a digression, a parenthesis, or an aside, he concedes to the reader that he and this trusting friend are only "making believe." He admits that the events he narrates have not really happened, and that he can give his narrative any turn the reader may like best. Such a betrayal of a sacred office seems to me, I confess, a terrible crime; it is what I mean by the attitude of apology, and it shocks me every whit as much in Trollope as it would have shocked me in Gibbon or Macaulay. It implies that the novelist is less occupied in looking for the truth (the truth, of course I mean, that he assumes, the premises that we must grant him, whatever they may be) than the historian, and in doing so it deprives him at a stroke of all his standing-room. To represent and illustrate the past, the actions of men, is the task of either writer, and the only difference that I can see is, in proportion as he succeeds, to the honour of the novelist, consisting as it does in his having more difficulty in collecting his evidence, which is so far from being purely literary. It seems to me to give him a great character, the fact that he has at once so much in common with the philosopher and the painter; this double analogy is a magnificent heritage.

It is of all this evidently that Mr. Besant is full when he insists upon the fact that fiction is one of the *fine* arts, deserving in its turn of all the honours and emoluments that have hitherto been reserved for the successful profession of music, poetry, painting, architecture. It is impossible to insist too much on so important a truth, and the place that Mr. Besant demands for the work of the novelist may be represented, a trifle less abstractly, by saying that he demands not only that it shall be reputed artistic, but that it shall be reputed very artistic indeed. It is excellent that he should have struck this note, for his doing so indicates that there was need of it, that his proposition may be to many people a novelty. One rubs one's eyes at the thought; but the rest of Mr. Besant's essay confirms the revelation. I suspect in truth that it would be possible to confirm it still further, and that one would not be far wrong in saying that in addition to the people to whom it has never occurred that a novel ought to be artistic, there are a great many others who, if this principle were urged upon them, would be filled with an indefinable mistrust. They would find it difficult to explain their repugnance, but it would operate strongly to put them on their guard. "Art" in our Protestant communities, where so many things have got so strangely twisted about, is supposed in certain circles to have some vaguely injurious effect upon those who make it an important consideration, who let it weigh in the balance. It is assumed to be opposed in some mysterious manner to morality, to amusement, to instruction. When it is embodied in the work of the painter (the sculptor is another affair!) you know what it is: it stands there before you, in the honesty of pink and green and a gilt frame; you can see the worst of it at a glance, and you can be on your guard. But when it is introduced into literature it becomes more insidious—there is danger of its hurting you before you know it. Literature should be either instructive or amusing, and there is in many minds an impression that these artistic preoccupations, the search for form, contribute to neither end, interfere indeed with both. They are too frivolous to be edifying, and too serious to be diverting; and they are moreover priggish and paradoxical and superfluous. That, I think, represents the manner in which the latent thought of many people who read novels as an exercise in skipping would explain itself if it were to become articulate. They would argue, of course, that a novel ought to be "good," but they would interpret this term in a fashion of their own, which indeed would vary considerably from one critic to another. One would say that being good means representing virtuous and aspiring characters, placed in prominent positions; another would say that it depends on a "happy ending," on a distribution at the last of prizes, pensions, husbands, wives, babies, millions, appended paragraphs, and cheerful remarks. Another still would say that it means being full of incident and movement, so that we shall wish to jump ahead, to see who was the mysterious stranger, and if the stolen will was ever found, and shall not be distracted from this pleasure by any tiresome analysis or "description." But they would all agree that the "artistic" idea would spoil some of their fun. One would hold it accountable for all the description, another would see it revealed in the absence of sympathy. Its hostility to a happy ending would be evident, and it might even in some cases render any ending at all impossible. The "ending" of a novel is, for many persons, like that of a good dinner, a course of dessert and ices, and the artist in fiction is regarded as a sort of meddlesome doctor who forbids agreeable aftertastes. It is therefore true that this conception of Mr. Besant's of the novel as a superior form encounters not only a negative but a positive indifference. It matters little that as a work of art it should really be as little or as much of its essence to supply happy endings, sympathetic characters, and an objective tone, as if it were a work of mechanics: the association of ideas, however incongruous, might easily be too much for it if an eloquent voice were not sometimes raised to call attention to the fact that it is at once as free and as serious a branch of literature as any other.

Certainly this might sometimes be doubted in presence of the enormous number of works of fiction that appeal to the credulity of our generation, for it might easily seem that there could be no great character in a commodity so quickly and easily produced. It must be admitted that good novels are much compromised by bad ones, and that the field at large suffers discredit from overcrowding. I think, however, that this injury is only superficial, and that the superabundance of written fiction proves nothing against the principle itself. It has been vulgarized, like all other kinds of literature, like everything else to-day, and it has proved more than some kinds accessible to vulgarization. But there is as much difference as there ever was between a good novel and a bad one: the bad is swept with all the daubed canvases and spoiled marble into some unvisited limbo, or infinite rubbish-yard beneath the back-windows of the world, and the good subsists and emits its light and stimulates our desire for perfection. As I shall take the liberty of making but a single criticism of Mr. Besant, whose tone is so full of the love of his art, I may as well have done with it at once. He seems to me to mistake in attempting to say so definitely beforehand what sort of an affair the good novel will be. To indicate the danger of such an error as that has been the purpose of these few pages; to suggest that certain traditions on the subject, applied *a priori,* have already had much to answer for, and that the good health of an art which undertakes so immediately to reproduce life must demand that it be perfectly free. It lives upon exercise, and the very meaning of exercise is freedom. The only obligation to which in advance we may hold a novel, without incurring the accusation of being arbitrary, is that it be interesting. That general responsibility rests upon it, but it is the only one I can think of. The ways in which it is at liberty to accomplish this result (of interesting us) strike me as innumerable, and such as can only suffer from being marked out or fenced in by prescription. They are as various as the temperament of man, and they are successful in proportion as they reveal a particular mind, different from others. A novel is in its broadest definition a personal, a direct impression of life: that, to begin with, constitutes its value, which is greater or less according to the intensity of the impression. But there will be no intensity at all, and therefore no value, unless there is freedom to feel and say. The tracing of a line to be followed, of a tone to be taken, of a form to be filled out, is a limitation of that freedom and a suppression of the very thing that we are most curious about. The form, it seems to me, is to be appreciated after the fact: then the author's choice has been made, his standard has been indicated; then we can follow lines and directions and compare tones and resemblances. Then in a word we can enjoy one of the most charming of pleasures, we can estimate quality, we can apply the test of execution. The execution belongs to the author alone; it is what is most personal to him, and we measure him by that. The advantage, the luxury, as well as the torment and responsibility of the novelist, is that there is no limit to what he may attempt as an executant—no limit to his possible experiments, efforts, discoveries, successes. Here it is especially that he works, step by step, like his brother of the brush, of whom we may always say that he has painted his picture in a manner best known to himself. His manner is his secret, not necessarily a jealous one. He cannot disclose it as a general thing if he would; he would be at a loss to teach it to others. I say this with a due recollection of having insisted on the community of method of the artist who paints a picture and the artist who writes a novel. The painter *is* able to teach the rudiments of his practice, and it is possible, from the study of good work (granted the aptitude), both to learn how to paint and to learn how to write. Yet it remains true, without injury to the *rapprochement,* that the literary artist would be obliged to say to his pupil much more than the other, "Ah, well, you must do it as you can!" It is a question of degree, a matter of delicacy. If there are exact sciences, there are also exact arts, and the grammar of painting is so much more definite that it makes the difference.

I ought to add, however, that if Mr. Besant says at the beginning of his essay that the "laws of fiction may be laid down and taught with as much precision and exactness as the laws of harmony, perspective, and proportion," he mitigates what might appear to be an extravagance by applying his remark to "general" laws, and by expressing most of these rules in a manner with which it would certainly be unaccommodating to disagree. That the novelist must write from his experience; that his "characters must be real and such as might be met with in actual life"; that "a young lady brought up in a quiet country village should avoid descriptions of garrison life," and "a writer whose friends and personal experiences belong to the lower middle-class should carefully avoid introducing his characters into society"; that one should enter one's notes in a commonplace book; that one's figures should be clear in outline; that making them clear by some trick of speech or of carriage is a bad method, and "describing them at length" is a worse one; that English Fiction should have a "conscious moral purpose"; that "it is almost impossible to estimate too highly the value of careful workmanship—that is, of style"; that "the most important point of all is the story," that "the story is everything": these are principles with most of which it is surely impossible not to sympathize. That remark about the lower-middle-class writer and his knowing his place is perhaps rather chilling; but for the rest I should find it difficult to dissent from any one of these recommendations. At the same time, I should find it difficult positively to assent to them, with the exception, perhaps, of the injunction as to entering one's notes in a commonplace book. They scarcely seem to me to have the quality that Mr. Besant attributes to the rules of the novelist—the "precision and exactness" of "the laws of harmony, perspective, and proportion." They are suggestive, they are even inspiring, but they are not exact, though they are doubtless as much so as the case admits of: which is a proof of that liberty of interpretation for which I just contended. For the value of these different injunctions—so beautiful and so vague—is wholly in the meaning one attaches to them. The characters, the situations, which strike one as real will be those that touch and interest one most, but the measure of reality is very difficult to fix. The reality of Don Quixote or of Mr. Micawber is a very delicate shade; it is a reality so coloured by the author's vision that, vivid as it may be, one would hesitate to propose it as a model: one would expose one's self to some very embarrassing questions on the part of a pupil. It goes without saying that you will not write a good novel unless you possess the sense of reality; but it will be difficult to give you a recipe for calling that sense into being. Humanity is immense, and reality has myriad forms; the most one can affirm is that some of the flowers of fiction have the odour of it, and others have not; as for telling you in advance how your nosegay should be composed, that is another affair. It is equally excellent and inconclusive to say that one must write from experience; to our suppositious aspirant such a declaration might savour of mockery. What kind of experience is intended, and where does it begin and end? Experience is never limited, and it is never complete; it is an immense sensibility, a kind of huge spider-web of the finest silken threads suspended in the chamber of consciousness, and catching every air-borne particle in its tissue. It is the very atmosphere of the mind; and when the mind is imaginative—much more when it happens to be that of a man of genius—it takes to itself the faintest hints of life, it converts the very pulses of the air into revelations. The young lady living in a village has only to be a damsel upon whom nothing is lost to make it quite unfair (as it seems to me) to declare to her that she shall have nothing to say about the military. Greater miracles have been seen than that, imagination assisting, she should speak the truth about some of these gentlemen. I remember an English novelist, a woman of genius, telling me that she was much commended for the impression she had managed to give in one of her tales of the nature and way of life of the French Protestant youth. She had been asked where she learned so much about this recondite being, she had been congratulated on her peculiar opportunities. These opportunities consisted in her having once, in Paris, as she ascended a staircase, passed an open door where, in the household of a *pasteur*, some of the young Protestants were seated at table round a finished meal. The glimpse made a picture; it lasted only a moment, but that moment was experience. She had got her direct personal impression, and she turned out her type. She knew what youth was, and what Protestantism; she also had the advantage of having seen what it was to be French, so that she converted these ideas into a concrete image and produced a reality. Above all, however, she was blessed with the faculty which when you give it an inch takes an ell, and which for the artist is a much greater source of strength than any accident of residence or of place in the social scale. The power to guess the unseen from the seen, to trace the implication of things, to judge the whole piece by the pattern, the condition of feeling life in general so completely that you are well on your way to knowing any particular corner of it—this cluster of gifts may almost be said to constitute experience, and they occur in country and in town, and in the most differing stages of education. If experience consists of impressions, it may be said that impressions *are* experience, just as (have we not seen it?) they are the very air we breathe. Therefore, if I should certainly say to a novice, "Write from experience and experience only," I should feel that this was rather a tantalizing monition if I were not careful immediately to add, "Try to be one of the people on whom nothing is lost!"

I am far from intending by this to minimize the importance of exactness—of truth of detail. One can speak best from one's own taste, and I may therefore venture to say that the air of reality (solidity of specification) seems to me to be the supreme virtue of a novel—the merit on which all its other merits (including that conscious moral purpose of which Mr. Besant speaks) helplessly and submissively depend. If it be not there they are all as nothing, and if these be there, they owe their effect to the success with which the author has produced the illusion of life. The cultivation of this success, the study of this exquisite process, form, to my taste, the beginning and the end of the art of the novelist. They are his inspiration, his despair, his reward, his torment, his delight. It is here in very truth that he competes with life; it is here that he competes with his brother the painter in *his* attempt to render the look of things, the look that conveys their meaning, to catch the colour, the relief, the expression, the surface, the substance of the human spectacle. It is in regard to this that Mr. Besant is well inspired when he bids him take notes. He cannot possibly take too many, he cannot possibly take enough. All life solicits him, and to "render" the simplest surface, to produce the most momentary illusion, is a very complicated business. His case would be easier, and the rule would be more exact, if Mr. Besant had been able to tell him what notes to take. But this, I fear, he can never learn in any manual; it is the business of his life. He has to take a great many in order to select a few, he has to work them up as he can, and even the guides and philosophers who might have most to say to him must leave him alone when it comes to the application of precepts, as we leave the painter in communion with his palette. That his characters "must be clear in outline," as Mr. Besant says—he feels that down to his boots; but how he shall make them so is a secret between his good angel and himself. It would be absurdly simple if he could be taught that a great deal of "description" would make them so, or that on the contrary the absence of description and the cultivation of dialogue, or the absence of dialogue and the multiplication of "incident," would rescue him from his difficulties. Nothing, for instance, is more possible than that he be of a turn of mind for which this odd, literal opposition of description and dialogue, incident and description, has little meaning and light. People often talk of these things as if they had a kind of internecine distinctness, instead of melting into each other at every breath, and being intimately associated parts of one general effort of expression. I cannot imagine composition existing in a series of blocks, nor conceive, in any novel worth discussing at all, of a passage of description that is not in its intention narrative, a passage of dialogue that is not in its intention descriptive, a touch of truth of any sort that does not partake of the nature of incident, or an incident that derives its interest from any other source than the general and only source of the success of a work of art— that of being illustrative. A novel is a living thing, all one and continuous, like any other organism, and in proportion as it lives will it be found, I think, that in each of the parts there is something of each of the other parts. The critic who over the close texture of a finished work shall pretend to trace a geography of items will mark some frontiers as artificial, I fear, as any that have been known to history. There is an old-fashioned distinction between the novel of character and the novel of incident which must have cost many a smile to the intending fabulist who was keen about his work. It appears to me as little to the point as the equally celebrated distinction between the novel and the romance—to answer as little to any reality.

There are bad novels and good novels, as there are bad pictures and good pictures; but that is the only distinction in which I see any meaning, and I can as little imagine speaking of a novel of character as I can imagine speaking of a picture of character. When one says picture one says of character, when one says novel one says of incident, and the terms may be transposed at will. What is character but the determination of incident? What is incident but the illustration of character? What is either a picture or a novel that is *not* of character? What else do we seek in it and find in it? It is an incident for a woman to stand up with her hand resting on a table and look out at you in a certain way; or if it be not an incident I think it will be hard to say what it is. At the same time it is an expression of character. If you say you don't see it (character in *that—allons donc!*), this is exactly what the artist who has reasons of his own for thinking he *does* see it undertakes to show you. When a young man makes up his mind that he has not faith enough after all to enter the church as he intended, that is an incident, though you may not hurry to the end of the chapter to see whether perhaps he doesn't change once more. I do not say that these are extraordinary or startling incidents. I do not pretend to estimate the degree of interest proceeding from them, for this will depend upon the skill of the painter. It sounds almost puerile to say that some incidents are intrinsically much more important than others, and I need not take this precaution after having professed my sympathy for the major ones in remarking that the only classification of the novel that I can understand is into that which has life and that which has it not.

The novel and the romance, the novel of incident and that of character—these clumsy separations appear to me to have been made by critics and readers for their own convenience, and to help them out of some of their occasional queer predicaments, but to have little reality or interest for the producer, from whose point of view it is of course that we are attempting to consider the art of fiction. The case is the same with another shadowy category which Mr. Besant apparently is disposed to set up—that of the "modern English novel"; unless indeed it be that in this matter he has fallen into an accidental confusion of standpoints. It is not quite clear whether he intends the remarks in which he alludes to it to be didactic or historical. It is as difficult to suppose a person intending to write a modern English as to suppose him writing an ancient English novel: that is a label which begs the question. One writes the novel, one paints the picture, of one's language and of one's time, and calling it modern English will not, alas! make the difficult task any easier. No more, unfortunately, will calling this or that work of one's fellow-artist a romance—unless it be, of course, simply for the pleasantness of the thing, as for instance when Hawthorne gave this heading to his story of *Blithedale*. The French, who have brought the theory of fiction to remarkable completeness, have but one name for the novel, and have not attempted smaller things in it, that I can see, for that. I can think of no obligation to which the "romancer" would not be held equally with the novelist; the standard of execution is equally high for each. Of course it is of execution that we are talking—that being the only point of a novel that is open to contention. This is perhaps too often lost sight of, only to produce interminable confusions and cross-purposes. We must grant the artist his subject, his idea, his *donnée:* our criticism is applied only to what he makes of it. Naturally I do not mean that we are bound to like it or find it interesting: in case we do not our course is perfectly simple—to let it alone. We may believe that of a certain idea even the most sincere novelist can make nothing at all, and the event may perfectly justify our belief; but the failure will have been a failure to execute, and it is in the execution that the fatal weakness is recorded. If we pretend to respect the artist at all, we must allow him his freedom of choice, in the face, in particular cases, of innumerable presumptions that the choice will not fructify. Art derives a considerable part of its beneficial exercise from flying in the face of presumptions, and some of the most interesting experiments of which it is capable are hidden in the bosom of common things. Gustave Flaubert has written a story about the devotion of a servant-girl to a parrot, and the production, highly-finished as it is, cannot on the whole be called a success. We are perfectly free to find it flat, but I think it might have been interesting; and I, for my part, am extremely glad he should have written it; it is a contribution to our knowledge of what can be done—or what cannot. Ivan Turgenev has written a tale about a deaf and dumb serf and a lap-dog, and the thing is touching, loving, a little masterpiece. He struck the note of life where Gustave Flaubert missed it—he flew in the face of a presumption and achieved a victory.

Nothing, of course, will ever take the place of the good old fashion of "liking" a work of art or not liking it: the most improved criticism will not abolish that primitive, that ultimate test. I mention this to guard myself from the accusation of intimating that the idea, the subject, of a novel or a picture, does not matter. It matters, to my sense, in the highest degree, and if I might put up a prayer it would be that artists should select none but the richest. Some, as I have already hastened to admit, are much more remunerative than others, and it would be a world happily arranged in which persons intending to treat them should be exempt from confusions and mistakes. This fortunate condition will arrive only, I fear, on the same day that critics become purged from error. Meanwhile, I repeat, we do not judge the artist with fairness unless we say to him,

"Oh, I grant you your starting-point, because if I did not I should seem to prescribe to you, and heaven forbid I should take that responsibility. If I pretend to tell you what you must not take, you will call upon me to tell you then what you must take; in which case I shall be prettily caught. Moreover, it isn't till I have accepted your data that I can begin to measure you. I have the standard, the pitch; I have no right to tamper with your flute and then criticize your music. Of course I may not care for your idea at all; I may think it silly, or stale, or unclean; in which case I wash my hands of you altogether. I may content myself with believing that you will not have succeeded in being interesting, but I shall, of course, not attempt to demonstrate it, and you will be as indifferent to me as I am to you. I needn't remind you that there are all sorts of tastes: who can know it better? Some people, for excellent reasons, don't like to read about carpenters; others, for reasons even better, don't like to read about courtesans. Many object to Americans. Others (I believe they are mainly editors and publishers) won't look at Italians. Some readers don't like quiet subjects; others don't like bustling ones. Some enjoy a complete illusion, others the consciousness of large concessions. They choose their novels accordingly, and if they don't care about your idea they won't, *a fortiori,* care about your treatment."

So that it comes back very quickly, as I have said, to the liking: in spite of M. Zola, who reasons less powerfully than he represents, and who will not reconcile himself to this absoluteness of taste, thinking that there are certain things that people ought to like, and that they can be made to like. I am quite at a loss to imagine anything (at any rate in this matter of fiction) that people *ought* to like or to dislike. Selection will be sure to take care of itself, for it has a constant motive behind it. That motive is simply experience. As people feel life, so they will feel the art that is most closely related to it. This closeness of relation is what we should never forget in talking of the effort of the novel. Many people speak of it as a factitious, artificial form, a product of ingenuity, the business of which is to alter and arrange the things that surround us, to translate them into conventional, traditional moulds. This, however, is a view of the matter which carries us but a very short way, condemns the art to an eternal repetition of a few familiar *clichés,* cuts short its development, and leads us straight up to a dead wall. Catching the very note and trick, the strange irregular rhythm of life, that is the attempt whose strenuous force keeps Fiction upon her feet. In proportion as in what she offers us we see life *without* rearrangement do we feel that we are touching the truth; in proportion as we see it *with* rearrangement do we feel that we are being put off with a substitute, a compromise and convention. It is not uncommon to hear an extraordinary assurance of remark in regard to this matter of rearranging, which is often spoken of as if it were the last word of art. Mr. Besant seems to me in danger of falling into the great error with his rather unguarded talk about "selection." Art is essentially selection, but it is a selection whose main care is to be typical, to be inclusive. For many people art means rose-coloured window-panes, and selection means picking a bouquet for Mrs. Grundy. They will tell you glibly that artistic considerations have nothing to do with the disagreeable, with the ugly; they will rattle off shallow commonplaces about the province of art and the limits of art till you are moved to some wonder in return as to the province and the limits of ignorance. It appears to

me that no one can ever have made a seriously artistic
attempt without becoming conscious of an immense increase—a kind of revelation—of freedom. One perceives
in that case—by the light of a heavenly ray—that the
province of art is all life, all feeling, all observation, all
vision. As Mr. Besant so justly intimates, it is all experience.
That is a sufficient answer to those who maintain that it
must not touch the sad things of life, who stick into its
divine unconscious bosom little prohibitory inscriptions on
the end of sticks, such as we see in public gardens—
"It is forbidden to walk on the grass; it is forbidden to
touch the flowers; it is not allowed to introduce dogs or to
remain after dark; it is requested to keep to the right." The
young aspirant in the line of fiction whom we continue to
imagine will do nothing without taste, for in that case his
freedom would be of little use to him; but the first advantage of his taste will be to reveal to him the absurdity of
the little sticks and tickets. If he have taste, I must add, of
course he will have ingenuity, and my disrespectful reference to that quality just now was not meant to imply that
it is useless in fiction. But it is only a secondary aid; the
first is a capacity for receiving straight impressions.

Mr. Besant has some remarks on the question of "the
story" which I shall not attempt to criticize, though they
seem to me to contain a singular ambiguity, because I do
not think I understand them. I cannot see what it meant
by talking as if there were a part of a novel which is the
story and part of it which for mystical reasons is not—
unless indeed the distinction be made in a sense in which
it is difficult to suppose that any one should attempt to
convey anything. "The story," if it represents anything,
represents the subject, the idea, the *donnée* of the novel;
and there is surely no "school"—Mr. Besant speaks of a
school—which urges that a novel should be all treatment
and no subject. There must assuredly be something to
treat; every school is intimately conscious of that. This
sense of the story being the idea, the starting-point, of the
novel, is the only one that I see in which it can be spoken
of as something different from its organic whole; and since
in proportion as the work is successful the idea permeates
and penetrates it, informs and animates it, so that every
word and every punctuation-point contribute directly to
the expression, in that proportion do we lose our sense of

the story being a blade which may be drawn more or less out of its sheath. The story and the novel, the idea and the form, are the needle and thread, and I never heard of a guild of tailors who recommended the use of the thread without the needle, or the needle without the thread. Mr. Besant is not the only critic who may be observed to have spoken as if there were certain things in life which constitute stories, and certain others which do not. I find the same odd implication in an entertaining article in the *Pall Mall Gazette*, devoted, as it happens, to Mr. Besant's lecture. "The story is the thing!" says this graceful writer, as if with a tone of opposition to some other idea. I should think it was, as every painter who, as the time for "sending in" his picture looms in the distance, finds himself still in quest of a subject—as every belated artist not fixed about his theme will heartily agree. There are some subjects which speak to us and others which do not, but he would be a clever man who should undertake to give a rule—an *index expurgatorius*—by which the story and the no-story should be known apart. It is impossible (to me at least) to imagine any such rule which shall not be altogether arbitrary. The writer in the *Pall Mall* opposes the delightful (as I suppose) novel of *Margot la Balafrée* to certain tales in which "Bostonian nymphs" appear to have "rejected English dukes for psychological reasons." I am not acquainted with the romance just designated, and can scarcely forgive the *Pall Mall* critic for not mentioning the name of the author, but the title appears to refer to a lady who may have received a scar in some heroic adventure. I am inconsolable at not being acquainted with this episode, but am utterly at a loss to see why it is a story when the rejection (or acceptance) of a duke is not, and why a reason, psychological or other, is not a subject when a cicatrix is. They are all particles of the multitudinous life with which the novel deals, and surely no dogma which pretends to make it lawful to touch the one and unlawful to touch the other will stand for a moment on its feet. It is the special picture that must stand or fall, according as it seem to possess truth or to lack it. Mr. Besant does not, to my sense, light up the subject by intimating that a story must, under penalty of not being a story, consist of "adventures." Why of adventures more than of green spectacles? He mentions a category of impossible things, and among them he places "fiction without adventure." Why without adventure, more than without matrimony, or celibacy, or parturition, or cholera, or hydropathy, or Jansenism? This seems to me to bring the novel back to the hapless little *rôle* of being an artificial, ingenious thing—bring it down from its large, free character of an immense and exquisite correspondence with life. And what *is* adventure, when it comes to that, and by what sign is the listening pupil to recognize it? It is an adventure—an immense one—for me to write this little article; and for a Bostonian nymph to reject an English duke is an adventure only less stirring, I should say, than for an English duke to be rejected by a Bostonian nymph. I see dramas within dramas in that, and innumerable points of view. A psychological reason is, to my imagination, an object adorably pictorial; to catch the tint of its complexion—I feel as if that idea might inspire one to Titianesque efforts. There are few things more exciting to me, in short, than a psychological reason, and yet, I protest, the novel seems to me the most magnificent form of art. I have just been reading, at the same time, the delightful story of *Treasure Island,* by Mr. Robert Louis Stevenson and, in a manner less consecutive, the last tale from M. Edmond de Goncourt, which is entitled *Chérie.* One of these works treats of murders, mysteries, islands of dreadful renown, hair-breadth escapes, miraculous coincidences, and buried doubloons. The other treats of a little French girl who lived in a fine house in Paris and died of wounded sensibility because no one would marry her. I call *Treasure Island* delightful, because it appears to me to have succeeded wonderfully in what it attempts; and I venture to bestow no epithet upon *Chérie,* which strikes me as having failed deplorably in what it attempts— that is, in tracing the development of the moral consciousness of a child. But one of these productions strikes me as exactly as much of a novel as the other, and as having a "story" quite as much. The moral consciousness of a child is as much a part of life as the islands of the Spanish Main, and the one sort of geography seems to me to have those "surprises" of which Mr. Besant speaks quite as much as the other. For myself (since it comes back in the last resort, as I say, to the preference of the individual), the picture of the child's experience has the advantage that I can at successive steps (an immense luxury, near to the "sensual pleasure" of which Mr. Besant's critic in the *Pall Mall* speaks) say Yes or No, as it may be, to what the artist puts before me. I have been a child in fact, but I have been on a quest for a buried treasure only in supposition, and it is a simple accident that with M. de Goncourt I should have for the most part to say No. With George Eliot, when she painted that country with a far other intelligence, I always said Yes.

The most interesting part of Mr. Besant's lecture is unfortunately the briefest passage—his very cursory allusion to the "conscious moral purpose" of the novel. Here again it is not very clear whether he be recording a fact or laying down a principle; it is a great pity that in the latter case he should not have developed his idea. This branch of the subject is of immense importance, and Mr. Besant's few words point to considerations of the wildest reach, not to be lightly disposed of. He will have treated the art of fiction but superficially who is not prepared to go every inch of the way that these considerations will carry him. It is for this reason that at the beginning of these remarks I was careful to notify the reader that my reflections on so large a theme have no pretension to be exhaustive. Like Mr. Besant, I have left the question of the morality of the novel till the last, and at the last I find I have used up my space. It is a question surrounded with difficulties, as witness the very first that meets us, in the form of a definite question, on the threshold. Vagueness, in such a discussion, is fatal, and what is the meaning of your morality and your conscious moral purpose? Will you not define your terms and explain how (a novel being a picture) a picture can be either moral or immoral? You wish to paint a moral picture or carve a moral statue: will you not tell us how you would set about it? We are discussing the Art of Fiction; questions of art are questions (in the widest sense) of execution; questions of morality are quite another affair, and will you not let us see how it is that you find it so easy to mix them up? These things are so clear to Mr. Besant that he has deduced from them a law which he sees embodied in English Fiction, and which is "a truly admirable thing and a great cause for congratulation." It is a great cause for congratulation indeed when such thorny problems become as smooth as silk. I may add that in so far as Mr. Besant perceives that in point of fact English Fiction has addressed itself preponderantly to these delicate questions he will appear to many people to have made a vain discovery. They will have been positively struck, on the contrary, with the moral timidity of the usual English novelist; with his (or with her) aversion to face the difficulties with which on every side the treatment of reality bristles. He is apt to be extremely shy (whereas the picture that Mr. Besant draws is a picture of boldness), and the sign of his work, for the most part, is a cautious silence on certain subjects. In the English novel (by which of course I mean the American as well), more than in any other, there is a traditional difference between that which people know and that which they agree to admit that they know, that which they see and that which they speak of, that which they feel to be a part of life and that which they allow to enter into literature. There is the great difference, in short, between what they talk of in conversation and what they talk of in print. The essence of moral energy is to survey the whole field, and I should directly reverse Mr. Besant's remark and say not that the English novel has a purpose, but that it has a diffidence. To what degree a purpose in a work of art is a source of corruption I shall not attempt to inquire; the one that seems to me least dangerous is the purpose of making a perfect work. As for our novel, I may say lastly on this score that as we find it in England to-day it strikes me as addressed in a large degree to "young people," and that this in itself constitutes a presumption that it will be rather shy. There are certain things which it is generally agreed not to discuss, not even to mention, before young people. That is very well, but the absence of discussion is not a symptom of the moral passion. The purpose of the English novel—"a truly admirable thing, and a great cause for congratulation"—strikes me therefore as rather negative.

There is one point at which the moral sense and the artistic sense lie very near together; that is in the light of the very obvious truth that the deepest quality of a work of art will always be the quality of the mind of the producer. In proportion as that intelligence is fine will the novel, the picture, the statue partake of the substance of beauty and truth. To be constituted of such elements is, to my vision, to have purpose enough. No good novel will ever proceed from a superficial mind; that seems to me an axiom which, for the artist in fiction, will cover all needful moral ground: if the youthful aspirant take it to heart it will illuminate for him many of the mysteries of "purpose." There are many other useful things that might be said to him, but I have come to the end of my article, and can only touch them as I pass. The critic in the *Pall Mall Gazette*, whom I have already quoted, draws attention to the danger, in speaking of the art of fiction, of generalizing. The danger that he has in mind is rather, I imagine, that of particularizing, for there are some comprehensive remarks which, in addition to those embodied in Mr. Besant's suggestive lecture, might without fear of misleading him be addressed to the ingenuous student. I should remind him first of the magnificence of the form that is open to him, which offers to sight so few restrictions and such innumerable opportunities. The other arts, in comparison, appear confined and hampered; the various conditions under which they are exercised are so rigid and definite. But the only condition that I can think of attaching to the composition of the novel is, as I have already said, that it be sincere. This freedom is a splendid privilege, and the first lesson of the young novelist is to learn to be worthy of it.

"Enjoy it as it deserves [I should say to him]; take possession of it, explore it to its utmost extent, publish it, rejoice in it. All life belongs to you, and do not listen either to those who would shut you up into corners of it and tell you that it is only here and there that art inhabits, or to those who would persuade you that this heavenly messenger wings her way outside of life altogether, breathing a superfine air, and turning away her head from the truth of things. There is no impression of life, no manner of seeing it and feeling it, to which the plan of the novelist may not offer a place; you have only to remember that talents so dissimilar as those of Alexandre Dumas and Jane Austen, Charles Dickens and Gustave Flaubert have worked in this field with equal glory. Do not think too much about optimism and pessimism; try and catch the colour of life itself. In France to-day we see a prodigious effort (that of Émile Zola, to whose solid and serious work no explorer of the capacity of the novel can allude without respect), we see an extraordinary effort vitiated by a spirit of pessimism on a narrow basis. M. Zola is magnificent, but he strikes an English reader as ignorant; he has an air of working in the dark; if he had as much light as energy, his results would be of the highest value. As for the aberrations of a shallow optimism, the ground (of English fiction especially) is strewn with their brittle particles as with broken glass. If you must indulge in conclusions, let them have the taste of a wide knowledge. Remember that your first duty is to be as complete as possible —to make as perfect a work. Be generous and delicate and pursue the prize."

1888

The Jolly Corner

I

"Everyone asks me what I 'think' of everything," said Spencer Brydon; "and I make answer as I can—begging or dodging the question, putting them off with any nonsense. It wouldn't matter to any of them really," he went on, "for, even were it possible to meet in that stand-and-deliver way so silly a demand on so big a subject, my 'thoughts' would still be almost altogether about something that concerns only myself." He was talking to Miss Staverton, with whom for a couple of months now he had availed himself of every possible occasion to talk; this disposition and this resource, this comfort and support, as the situation in fact presented itself, having promptly enough taken the first place in the considerable array of rather unattenuated surprises attending his so strangely belated return to America. Everything was somehow a surprise; and that might be natural when one had so long and so consistently neglected everything, taken pains to give surprises so much margin for play. He had given them more than thirty years —thirty-three, to be exact; and they now seemed to him to have organised their performance quite on the scale of that licence. He had been twenty-three on leaving New York—he was fifty-six today: unless indeed he were to reckon as he had sometimes, since his repatriation, found himself feeling; in which case he would have lived longer than is often allotted to man. It would have taken a century, he repeatedly said to himself, and said also to Alice Staverton, it would have taken a longer absence and a more averted mind than those even of which he had been guilty, to pile up the differences, the newnesses, the queernesses, above all the bignesses, for the better or the worse, that at present assaulted his vision wherever he looked.

The great fact all the while however had been the incalculability; since he *had* supposed himself, from decade to decade, to be allowing, and in the most liberal and intelligent manner, for brilliancy of change. He actually saw that he had allowed for nothing; he missed what he would have been sure of finding, he found what he would never have imagined. Proportions and values were upside-down; the ugly things he had expected, the ugly things of his faraway youth, when he had too promptly waked up to a sense of the ugly—these uncanny phenomena placed him rather, as it happened, under the charm; whereas the "swagger" things, the modern, the monstrous, the famous things, those he had more particularly, like thousands of ingenuous enquirers every year, come over to see, were exactly his sources of dismay. They were as so many set traps for displeasure, above all for reaction, of which his restless tread was constantly pressing the spring. It was interesting, doubtless, the whole show, but it would have been too disconcerting hadn't a certain finer truth saved the situation. He had distinctly not, in this steadier light, come over *all* for the monstrosities; he had come, not only in the last analysis but quite on the face of the act, under an impulse with which they had nothing to do. He had come—putting the thing pompously—to look at his "property," which he had thus for a third of a century not been within four thousand miles of; or, expressing it less sordidly, he had yielded to the humour of seeing again his house on the jolly corner, as he usually, and quite fondly, described it—the one in which he had first seen the light, in which various members of his family had lived and had died, in which the holidays of his over-schooled boyhood had been passed and the few social flowers of his chilled adolescence gathered, and which, alienated then for so long a period, had, through the successive deaths of his two brothers and the termination of old arrangements, come wholly into his hands. He was the owner of another, not quite so "good"—the jolly corner having been, from far back, superlatively extended and consecrated; and the value of the pair represented his main capital, with an income consisting, in these later years, of their respective rents which (thanks precisely to their original excellent type) had never been depressingly low. He could live in "Europe," as he had been in the habit of living, on the product of these flourishing New York leases, and all the better since, that of the second structure, the mere number in its long row, having within a twelvemonth fallen in, renovation at a high advance had proved beautifully possible.

These were items of property indeed, but he had found himself since his arrival distinguishing more than ever between them. The house within the street, two bristling blocks westward, was already in course of reconstruction as a tall mass of flats; he had acceded, some time before, to overtures for this conversion—in which, now that it was going forward, it had been not the least of his astonishments to find himself able, on the spot, and though without a previous ounce of such experience, to participate with a certain intelligence, almost with a certain authority. He had lived his life with his back so turned to such concerns and his face addressed to those of so different an order that he scarce knew what to make of this lively stir, in a compartment of his mind never yet penetrated, of a capacity for business and a sense for construction. These virtues, so common all round him now, had been dormant in his own organism—where it might be said of them perhaps that they had slept the sleep of the just. At present, in the splendid autumn weather—the autumn at least was a pure boon in the terrible place—he loafed about his "work" undeterred, secretly agitated; not in the least "minding" that the whole proposition, as they said, was vulgar and sordid, and ready to climb ladders, to walk the plank, to handle materials and look wise about them, to ask questions, in fine, and challenge explanations and really "go into" figures.

It amused, it verily quite charmed him; and, by the same stroke, it amused, and even more, Alice Staverton, though perhaps charming her perceptibly less. She wasn't however going to be better off for it, as *he* was—and so astonishingly much: nothing was now likely, he knew, ever to make her better off than she found herself, in the afternoon of life, as the delicately frugal possessor and tenant of the small house in Irving Place to which she had subtly managed to cling through her almost unbroken New York career. If he knew the way to it now better than to any other address among the dreadful multiplied numberings which seemed to him to reduce the whole place to some vast ledger-page, overgrown, fantastic, of ruled and crisscrossed lines and figures—if he had formed, for his consolation, that habit, it was really not a little because of the charm of his having encountered and recognised, in the vast wilderness of the wholesale, breaking through the mere gross generalisation of wealth and force and success, a small still scene where items and shades, all delicate things, kept the sharpness of the notes of a high voice perfectly trained, and where economy hung about like the scent of a garden. His old friend lived with one maid and herself dusted her relics and trimmed her lamps and polished her silver; she stood off, in the awful modern crush, when she could, but she sallied forth and did battle when the challenge was really to "spirit," the spirit she after all confessed to, proudly and a little shyly, as to that of the better time, that of *their* common, their quite faraway and antediluvian social period and order. She made use of the street-cars when need be, the terrible things that people scrambled for as the panic-stricken at sea scramble for the boats; she affronted, inscrutably, under stress, all the public concussions and ordeals; and yet, with that slim mystifying grace of her appearance, which defied you to say if she were a fair young woman who looked older through trouble, or a fine smooth older one who looked young through successful indifference; with her precious reference, above all, to memories and histories into which he could enter, she was as exquisite for him as some pale pressed flower (a rarity to begin with), and, failing other sweetnesses, she was a sufficient reward of his effort. They had communities of knowledge, "their" knowledge (this discriminating possessive was always on her lips) of presences of the other age, presences all overlaid, in his case, by the experience of a man and the freedom of a wanderer, overlaid by pleasure, by infidelity, by passages of life that were strange and dim to her, just by "Europe" in short, but still unobscured, still exposed and cherished, under that pious visitation of the spirit from which she had never been diverted.

She had come with him one day to see how his "apartment-house" was rising; he had helped her over gaps and explained to her plans, and while they were there had happened to have, before her, a brief but lively discussion with the man in charge, the representative of the building-firm that had undertaken his work. He had found himself quite "standing-up" to this personage over a failure on the latter's part to observe some detail of one of their noted conditions, and had so lucidly urged his case that, besides ever so prettily flushing, at the time, for sympathy in his triumph, she had afterwards said to him (though to a slightly greater effect of irony) that he had clearly for too many years neglected a real gift. If he had but stayed at home he would have anticipated the inventor of the sky-scraper. If he had but stayed at home he would have discovered his genius in time really to start some new variety of awful architectural hare and run it till it burrowed in a gold-mine. He was to remember these words, while the weeks elapsed, for the small silver ring they had sounded over the queerest and deepest of his own lately most disguised and most muffled vibrations.

It had begun to be present to him after the first fortnight, it had broken out with the oddest abruptness, this particular wanton wonderment: it met him there—and this was the image under which he himself judged the matter, or at least, not a little, thrilled and flushed with it —very much as he might have been met by some strange figure, some unexpected occupant, at a turn of one of the dim passages of an empty house. The quaint analogy quite hauntingly remained with him, when he didn't indeed rather improve it by a still intenser form: that of his opening a door behind which he would have made sure of finding nothing, a door into a room shuttered and void, and yet so coming, with a great suppressed start, on some quite erect confronting presence, something planted in the middle of the place and facing him through the dusk. After that visit to the house in construction he walked with his companion to see the other and always so much the better one, which in the eastward direction formed one of the corners, the "jolly" one precisely, of the street now so

generally dishonoured and disfigured in its westward
reaches, and of the comparatively conservative Avenue.
The Avenue still had pretensions, as Miss Staverton said,
to decency; the old people had mostly gone, the old names
were unknown, and here and there an old association
seemed to stray, all vaguely, like some very aged person,
out too late, whom you might meet and feel the impulse
to watch or follow, in kindness, for safe restoration to
shelter.

They went in together, our friends; he admitted himself
with his key, as he kept no one there, he explained, pre-
ferring, for his reasons, to leave the place empty, under
a simple arrangement with a good woman living in the
neighbourhood and who came for a daily hour to open
windows and dust and sweep. Spencer Brydon had his reasons and was growingly aware of them; they seemed to
him better each time he was there, though he didn't name
them all to his companion, any more than he told her as
yet how often, how quite absurdly often, he himself came.
He only let her see for the present, while they walked
through the great blank rooms, that absolute vacancy
reigned and that, from top to bottom, there was nothing
but Mrs. Muldoon's broomstick, in a corner, to tempt the
burglar. Mrs. Muldoon was then on the premises, and she
loquaciously attended the visitors, preceding them from
room to room and pushing back shutters and throwing
up sashes—all to show them, as she remarked, how little
there was to see. There was little indeed to see in the great
gaunt shell where the main dispositions and the general
apportionment of space, the style of an age of ampler
allowances, had nevertheless for its master their honest
pleading message, affecting him as some good old servant's,
some lifelong retainer's appeal for a character, or even for
a retiring-pension; yet it was also a remark of Mrs. Muldoon's that, glad as she was to oblige him by her noonday
round, there was a request she greatly hoped he would
never make of her. If he should wish her for any reason to
come in after dark she would just tell him, if he "plased,"
that he must ask it of somebody else.

The fact that there was nothing to see didn't militate for
the worthy woman against what one *might* see, and she put
it frankly to Miss Staverton that no lady could be expected to like, could she? "craping up to thim top storeys

in the ayvil hours." The gas and the electric light were off.
the house, and she fairly evoked a gruesome vision of her
march through the great grey rooms—so many of them as
there were too!—with her glimmering taper. Miss Staverton
met her honest glare with a smile and the profession that
she herself certainly would recoil from such an adventure.
Spencer Brydon meanwhile held his peace—for the moment; the question of the "evil" hours in his old home
had already become too grave for him. He had begun
some time since to "crape," and he knew just why a
packet of candles addressed to that pursuit had been stowed
by his own hand, three weeks before, at the back of a
drawer of the fine old sideboard that occupied, as a
"fixture," the deep recess in the dining-room. Just now he
laughed at his companions—quickly however changing
the subject; for the reason that, in the first place, his laugh
struck him even at that moment as starting the odd echo,
the conscious human resonance (he scarce knew how
to qualify it) that sounds made while he was there alone
sent back to his ear or his fancy; and that, in the second,
he imagined Alice Staverton for the instant on the point
of asking him, with a divination, if he ever so prowled.
There were divinations he was unprepared for, and he
had at all events averted enquiry by the time Mrs. Muldoon
had left them, passing on to other parts.

There was happily enough to say, on so consecrated a
spot, that could be said freely and fairly; so that a whole
train of declarations was precipitated by his friend's having herself broken out, after a yearning look round: "But
I hope you don't mean they want you to pull *this* to
pieces!" His answer came, promptly, with his reawakened
wrath: it was of course exactly what they wanted, and
what they were "at" him for, daily, with the iteration of
people who couldn't for their life understand a man's
liability to decent feelings. He had found the place, just
as it stood and beyond what he could express, an interest
and a joy. There were values other than the beastly rent-
values, and in short, in short—! But it was thus Miss
Staverton took him up. "In short you're to make so good
a thing of your sky-scraper that, living in luxury on *those*
ill-gotten gains, you can afford for a while to be sentimental
here!" Her smile had for him, with the words, the particular mild irony with which he found half her talk

suffused; an irony without bitterness and that came, exactly, from her having so much imagination—not, like the cheap sarcasms with which one heard most people, about the world of "society," bid for the reputation of cleverness, from nobody's really having any. It was agreeable to him at this very moment to be sure that when he had answered, after a brief demur, "Well yes: so precisely, you may put it!" her imagination would still do him justice. He explained that even if never a dollar were to come to him from the other house he would nevertheless cherish this one; and he dwelt, further, while they lingered and wandered, on the fact of the stupefaction he was already exciting, the positive mystification he felt himself create.

He spoke of the value of all he read into it, into the mere sight of the walls, mere shapes of the rooms, mere sound of the floors, mere feel, in his hand, of the old silver-plated knobs of the several mahogany doors, which suggested the pressure of the palms of the dead; the seventy years of the past in fine that these things represented, the annals of nearly three generations, counting his grandfather's, the one that had ended there, and the impalpable ashes of his long-extinct youth, afloat in the very air like microscopic motes. She listened to everything; she was a woman who answered intimately but who utterly didn't chatter. She scattered abroad therefore no cloud of words; she could assent, she could agree, above all she could encourage, without doing that. Only at the last she went a little further than he had done himself. "And then how do you know? You may still, after all, want to live here." It rather indeed pulled him up, for it wasn't what he had been thinking, at least in her sense of the words. "You mean I may decide to stay on for the sake of it?"

"Well, *with* such a home—!" But, quite beautifully, she had too much tact to dot so monstrous an *i*, and it was precisely an illustration of the way she didn't rattle. How could anyone—of any wit—insist on anyone else's "wanting" to live in New York?

"Oh," he said, "I *might* have lived here (since I had my opportunity early in life); I might have put in here all these years. Then everything would have been different enough —and, I dare say, 'funny' enough. But that's another matter. And then the beauty of it—I mean of my perversity, of my refusal to agree to a 'deal'—is just in the total absence of a reason. Don't you see that if I had a reason about the matter at all it would *have* to be the other way, and would then be inevitably a reason of dollars? There are no reasons here *but* of dollars. Let us therefore have none whatever—not the ghost of one."

They were back in the hall then for departure, but from where they stood the vista was large, through an open door, into the great square main saloon, with its almost antique felicity of brave spaces between windows. Her eyes came back from that reach and met his own a moment. "Are you very sure the 'ghost' of one doesn't, much rather, serve—?"

He had a positive sense of turning pale. But it was as near as they were then to come. For he made answer, he believed, between a glare and a grin: "Oh ghosts—of course the place must swarm with them! I should be ashamed of it if it didn't. Poor Mrs. Muldoon's right, and it's why I haven't asked her to do more than look in."

Miss Staverton's gaze again lost itself, and things she didn't utter, it was clear, came and went in her mind. She might even for the minute, off there in the fine room, have imagined some element dimly gathering. Simplified like the death-mask of a handsome face, it perhaps produced for her just then an effect akin to the stir of an expression in the "set" commemorative plaster. Yet whatever her impression may have been she produced instead a vague platitude. "Well, if it were only furnished and lived in—!"

She appeared to imply that in case of its being still furnished he might have been a little less opposed to the idea of a return. But she passed straight into the vestibule, as if to leave her words behind her, and the next moment he had opened the house-door and was standing with her on the steps. He closed the door and, while he repocketed his key, looking up and down, they took in the comparatively harsh actuality of the Avenue, which reminded him of the assault of the outer light of the Desert on the traveller emerging from an Egyptian tomb. But he risked before they stepped into the street his gathered answer to her speech. "For me it *is* lived in. For me it *is* furnished." At which it was easy for her to sigh "Ah yes—!" all vaguely and discreetly; since his parents and his favourite sister, to say nothing of other kin, in numbers, had run their course and met their end there. That represented, within the walls, ineffaceable life.

It was a few days after this that, during an hour passed with her again, he had expressed his impatience of the too flattering curiosity—among the people he met—about his appreciation of New York. He had arrived at none at all that was socially producible, and as for that matter of his "thinking" (thinking the better or the worse of anything there) he was wholly taken up with one subject of thought. It was mere vain egoism, and it was moreover, if she liked, a morbid obsession. He found all things come back to the question of what he personally might have been, how he might have led his life and "turned out," if he had not so, at the outset, given it up. And confessing for the first time to the intensity within him of this absurd speculation—which but proved also, no doubt, the habit of too selfishly thinking—he affirmed the impotence there of any other source of interest, any other native appeal. "What would it have made of me, what would it have made of me? I keep for ever wondering, all idiotically; as if I could possibly know! I see what it has made of dozens of others, those I meet, and it positively aches within me, to the point of exasperation, that it would have made something of me as well. Only I can't make out *what,* and the worry of it, the small rage of curiosity never to be satisfied, brings back what I remember to have felt, once or twice, after judging best, for reasons, to burn some important letter unopened. I've been sorry, I've hated it— I've never known what was in the letter. You may of course say it's a trifle—!"

"I don't say it's a trifle," Miss Staverton gravely interrupted.

She was seated by her fire, and before her, on his feet and restless, he turned to and fro between this intensity of his idea and a fitful and unseeing inspection, through his single eye-glass, of the dear little old objects on her chimneypiece. Her interruption made him for an instant look at her harder. "I shouldn't care if you did!" he laughed, however; "and it's only a figure, at any rate, for the way I now feel. *Not* to have followed my perverse young course—and almost in the teeth of my father's curse, as I may say; not to have kept it up, so, 'over there,' from that day to this, without a doubt or a pang; not, above all, to have liked it, to have loved it, so much, loved it, no doubt, with such an abysmal conceit of my own preference: some variation from *that,* I say, must have produced some different effect for my life and for my 'form.' I should have stuck here—if it had been possible; and I was too young, at twenty-three, to judge, *pour deux sous,* whether it *were* possible. If I had waited I might have seen it was, and then I might have been, by staying here, something nearer to one of these types who have been hammered so hard and made so keen by their conditions. It isn't that I admire them so much—the question of any charm in them, or of any charm, beyond that of the rank money-passion, exerted by their conditions *for* them, has nothing to do with the matter: it's only a question of what fantastic, yet perfectly possible, development of my own nature I mayn't have missed. It comes over me that I had then a strange *alter ego* deep down somewhere within me, as the full-blown flower is in the small tight bud, and that I just took the course, I just transferred him to the climate, that blighted him for once and for ever."

"And you wonder about the flower," Miss Staverton said. "So do I, if you want to know; and so I've been wondering these several weeks. I believe in the flower," she continued, "I feel it would have been quite splendid, quite huge and monstrous."

"Monstrous above all!" her visitor echoed; "and I imagine, by the same stroke, quite hideous and offensive."

"You don't believe that," she returned; "if you did you wouldn't wonder. You'd know, and that would be enough for you. What you feel—and what I feel *for* you—is that you'd have had power."

"You'd have liked me that way?" he asked.

She barely hung fire. "How should I not have liked you?"

"I see. You'd have liked me, have preferred me, a billionaire!"

"How should I not have liked you?" she simply again asked.

He stood before her still—her question kept him motionless. He took it in, so much there was of it; and indeed his not otherwise meeting it testified to that. "I know at least what I am," he simply went on; "the other side

of the medal's clear enough. I've not been edifying—I
believe I'm thought in a hundred quarters to have been
barely decent. I've followed strange paths and worshipped
strange gods; it must have come to you again and again—
in fact you've admitted to me as much—that I was leading,
at any time these thirty years, a selfish frivolous scandalous
life. And you see what it has made of me."

She just waited, smiling at him. "You see what it has
made of *me*."

"Oh you're a person whom nothing can have altered.
You were born to be what you are, anywhere, anyway:
you've the perfection nothing else could have blighted.
And don't you see how, without my exile, I shouldn't have
been waiting till now—?" But he pulled up for the strange
pang.

"The great thing to see," she presently said, "seems to
me to be that it has spoiled nothing. It hasn't spoiled your
being here at last. It hasn't spoiled this. It hasn't spoiled
your speaking—" She also however faltered.

He wondered at everything her controlled emotion
might mean. "Do you believe then—too dreadfully!—that
I *am* as good as I might ever have been?"

"Oh no! Far from it!" With which she got up from her
chair and was near to him. "But I don't care," she smiled.

"You mean I'm good enough?"

She considered a little. "Will you believe it if I say so?
I mean will you let that settle your question for you?" And
then as if making out in his face that he drew back from
this, that he had some idea which, however absurd, he
couldn't yet bargain away: "Oh you don't care either—but
very differently: you don't care for anything but yourself."

Spencer Brydon recognised it—it was in fact what he
had absolutely professed. Yet he importantly qualified.
"*He* isn't myself. He's the just so totally other person. But
I do want to see him," he added. "And I can. And I
shall."

Their eyes met for a minute while he guessed from something in hers that she divined his strange sense. But neither
of them otherwise expressed it, and her apparent understanding, with no protesting shock, no easy derision,
touched him more deeply than anything yet, constituting
for his stifled perversity, on the spot, an element that was

like breathable air. What she said however was unexpected.
"Well, *I've* seen him."

"You—?"

"I've seen him in a dream."

"Oh a 'dream'—!" It let him down.

"But twice over," she continued. "I saw him as I see you now."

"You've dreamed the same dream—?"

"Twice over," she repeated. "The very same."

This did somehow a little speak to him, as it also gratified him. "You dream about me at that rate?"

"Ah about *him!*" she smiled.

His eyes again sounded her. "Then you know all about him." And as she said nothing more: "What's the wretch like?"

She hesitated, and it was as if he were pressing her so hard that, resisting for reasons of her own, she had to turn away. "I'll tell you some other time!"

II

It was after this that there was most of a virtue for him, most of a cultivated charm, most of a preposterous secret thrill, in the particular form of surrender to his obsession and of address to what he more and more believed to be his privilege. It was what in these weeks he was living for—since he really felt life to begin but after Mrs. Muldoon had retired from the scene and, visiting the ample house from attic to cellar, making sure he was alone, he knew himself in safe possession and, as he tacitly expressed it, let himself go. He sometimes came twice in the twenty-four hours; the moments he liked best were those of gathering dusk, of the short autumn twilight; this was the time of which, again and again, he found himself hoping most. Then he could, as seemed to him, most intimately wander and wait, linger and listen, feel his fine attention, never in his life before so fine, on the pulse of the great vague place: he preferred the lampless hour and only wished he might have prolonged each day the deep crepuscular spell. Later—rarely much before midnight, but then for a considerable vigil—he watched with his glimmering light; moving slowly, holding it high, playing it far, rejoicing above all, as much as he might, in open vistas, reaches of communication between rooms and by passages; the long straight chance or show, as he would have called it, for the revelation he pretended to invite. It was practice he found he could perfectly "work" without exciting remark; no one was in the least the wiser for it; even Alice Staverton, who was moreover a well of discretion, didn't quite fully imagine.

He let himself in and let himself out with the assurance of calm proprietorship; and accident so far favoured him that, if a fat Avenue "officer" had happened on occasion to see him entering at eleven-thirty, he had never yet, to the best of his belief, been noticed as emerging at two. He walked there on the crisp November nights, arrived regularly at the evening's end; it was as easy to do this after dining out as to take his way to a club or to his hotel. When he left his club, if he hadn't been dining out, it was ostensibly to go to his hotel; and when he left his hotel, if he had spent a part of the evening there, it was ostensibly to go to his club. Everything was easy in fine; everything conspired and promoted: there was truly even in the strain of his experience something that glossed over, something that salved and simplified, all the rest of consciousness. He circulated, talked, renewed, loosely and pleasantly, old relations—met indeed, so far as he could, new expectations and seemed to make out on the whole that in spite of the career, of such different contacts, which he had spoken of to Miss Staverton as ministering so little, for those who might have watched it, to edification, he was positively rather liked than not. He was a dim secondary social success—and all with people who had truly not an idea of him. It was all mere surface sound, this murmur of their welcome, this popping of their corks—just as his gestures of response were the extravagant shadows, emphatic in proportion as they meant little, of some game of *ombres chinoises*. He projected himself all day, in thought, straight over the bristling line of hard unconscious heads and into the other, the real, the waiting life; the life that, as soon as he had heard behind him the click of his great house-door, began for him, on the jolly corner, as beguilingly as the slow opening bars of some rich music follows the tap of the conductor's wand.

He always caught the first effect of the steel point of his stick on the old marble of the hall pavement, large black-and-white squares that he remembered as the admiration of his childhood and that had then made in him, as he now saw, for the growth of an early conception of style. This effect was the dim reverberating tinkle as of some far-off bell hung who should say where?—in the depths of the house, of the past, of that mystical other world that might have flourished for him had he not, for weal or woe, abandoned it. On this impression he did ever the same thing; he put his stick noiselessly away in a corner —feeling the place once more in the likeness of some great glass bowl, all precious concave crystal, set delicately humming by the play of a moist finger round its edge. The concave crystal held, as it were, this mystical other world, and the indescribably fine murmur of its rim was the sigh there, the scarce audible pathetic wail to his strained ear, of all the old baffled forsworn possibilities. What he did therefore by this appeal of his hushed presence was to wake them into such measure of ghostly life as they might still enjoy. They were shy, all but unappeasably shy, but they weren't really sinister; at least they weren't as he had hitherto felt them—before they had taken the Form he so yearned to make them take, the Form he at moments saw himself in the light of fairly hunting on tiptoe, the points of his evening-shoes, from room to room and from storey to storey.

That was the essence of his vision—which was all rank folly, if one would, while he was out of the house and otherwise occupied, but which took on the last verisimilitude as soon as he was placed and posted. He knew what he meant and what he wanted; it was as clear as the figure on a cheque presented in demand for cash. His *alter ego* "walked"—that was the note of his image of him, while his image of his motive for his own odd pastime was the desire to waylay him and meet him. He roamed, slowly, warily, but all restlessly, he himself did—Mrs. Muldoon had been right, absolutely, with her figure of their "craping"; and the presence he watched for would roam restlessly too. But it would be as cautious and as shifty; the conviction of its probable, in fact its already quite sensible, quite audible evasion of pursuit grew for him from night to night, laying on him finally a rigour to which nothing in his life had been comparable. It had been the theory of many superficially-judging persons, he knew, that he was wasting that life in a surrender to sensations, but he had tasted of no pleasure so fine as his actual tension, had been introduced to no sport that demanded at once the patience and the nerve of this stalking of a creature more subtle, yet at bay perhaps more formidable, than any beast of the forest. The terms, the comparisons, the very practices of the chase positively came again into play; there were even moments when passages of his occasional experience as a sportsman stirred memories, from his younger time, of moor and mountain and desert, revived for him— and to the increase of his keenness—by the tremendous force of analogy. He found himself at moments—once he had placed his single light on some mantel-shelf or in some recess—stepping back into shelter or shade, effacing himself behind a door or in an embrasure, as he had sought of old the vantage of rock and tree; he found himself holding his breath and living in the joy of the instant, the supreme suspense created by big game alone.

He wasn't afraid (though putting himself the question as he believed gentlemen on Bengal tiger-shoots or in close quarters with the great bear of the Rockies had been known to confess to having put it); and this indeed—since here at least he might be frank!—because of the impression, so intimate and so strange, that he himself produced as yet a dread, produced certainly a strain, beyond the liveliest he was likely to feel. They fell for him into categories, they fairly became familiar, the signs, for his own perception, of the alarm his presence and his vigilance created; though leaving him always to remark, portentously, on his probably having formed a relation, his probably enjoying a consciousness, unique in the experience of man. People enough, first and last, had been in terror of apparitions, but who had ever before so turned the tables and become himself, in the apparitional world, an incalculable terror? He might have found this sublime had he quite dared to think of it; but he didn't too much insist, truly, on that side of his privilege. With habit and repetition he gained to an extraordinary degree the power to penetrate the dusk of distances and the darkness of corners, to resolve back into their innocence the treacheries of uncertain light, the evil-looking forms taken in the gloom by mere shadows, by accidents of the air, by shifting effects of perspective; putting down his dim luminary he could still wander on without it, pass into other rooms, and, only knowing it was there behind him in case of need, see his way about, visually project for his purpose a comparative clearness. It made him feel, this acquired faculty, like some monstrous stealthy cat; he wondered if he would have glared at these moments with large shining yellow eyes, and what it mightn't verily be, for the poor hard-pressed *alter ego,* to be confronted with such a type.

He liked however the open shutters; he opened everywhere those Mrs. Muldoon had closed, closing them as carefully afterwards, so that she shouldn't notice: he liked —oh this he did like, and above all in the upper rooms!— the sense of the hard silver of the autumn stars through the window-panes, and scarcely less the flare of the street-lamps below, the white electric lustre which it would have taken curtains to keep out. This was human, actual, social; this was of the world he had lived in, and he was more at his ease certainly for the countenance, coldly general and impersonal, that all the while and in spite of his detachment it seemed to give him. He had support of course mostly in the rooms at the wide front and the prolonged side; it failed him considerably in the central shades and the parts at the back. But if he sometimes, on his rounds, was glad of his optical reach, so none the less often the rear of the house affected him as the very jungle of his prey. The place was there more subdivided; a large "extension" in particular, where small rooms for servants had been multiplied, abounded in nooks and corners, in closets and passages, in the ramifications especially of an ample back staircase over which he leaned, many a time, to look far down—not deterred from his gravity even while aware that he might, for a spectator, have figured some solemn simpleton playing at hide-and-seek. Outside in fact he might himself make that ironic *rapprochement;* but within the walls, and in spite of the clear windows, his consistency was proof against the cynical light of New York.

It had belonged to that idea of the exasperated consciousness of his victim to become a real test for him; since he had quite put it to himself from the first that, oh distinctly! he could "cultivate" his whole perception. He had felt it as above all open to cultivation—which indeed was but another name for his manner of spending his time. He was bringing it on, bringing it to perfection, by practice; in consequence of which it had grown so fine that he was now aware of impressions, attestations of his general postulate, that couldn't have broken upon him at once. This was the case more specifically with a phenomenon at last quite frequent for him in the upper rooms, the recognition—absolutely unmistakeable, and by a turn dating from a particular hour, his resumption of his campaign after a diplomatic drop, a calculated absence of three nights—of his being definitely followed, tracked at a distance carefully taken and to the express end that he should the less confidently, less arrogantly, appear to himself merely to pursue. It worried, it finally quite broke him up, for it proved, of all the conceivable impressions, the one least suited to his book. He was kept in sight while remaining himself—as regards the essence of his position —sightless, and his only recourse then was in abrupt turns, rapid recoveries of ground. He wheeled about, retracing his steps, as if he might so catch in his face at least the stirred air of some other quick revolution. It was indeed true that his fully dislocalised thought of these manœuvres recalled to him Pantaloon, at the Christmas farce, buffeted and tricked from behind by ubiquitous Harlequin; but it left intact the influence of the conditions themselves each time he was re-exposed to them, so that in fact this association, had he suffered it to become constant, would on a certain side have but ministered to his intenser gravity. He had made, as I have said, to create on the premises the baseless sense of a reprieve, his three absences; and the result of the third was to confirm the after-effect of the second.

On his return, that night—the night succeeding his last intermission—he stood in the hall and looked up the staircase with a certainty more intimate than any he had yet known. "He's *there,* at the top, and waiting—not, as in general, falling back for disappearance. He's holding his ground, and it's the first time—which is a proof, isn't it? that something has happened for him." So Brydon argued with his hand on the banister and his foot on the lowest stair; in which position he felt as never before the air chilled by his logic. He himself turned cold in it, for he seemed of a sudden to know what now was involved. "Harder pressed?—yes, he takes it in, with its thus making clear to him that I've come, as they say, 'to stay.' He finally doesn't like and can't bear it, in the sense, I mean,

that his wrath, his menaced interest, now balances with his
dread. I've hunted him till he has 'turned': that, up
there, is what has happened—he's the fanged or the
antlered animal brought at last to bay." There came to
him, as I say—but determined by an influence beyond
my notation!—the acuteness of this certainty; under which
however the next moment he had broken into a sweat that
he would as little have consented to attribute to fear as
he would have dared immediately to act upon it for
enterprise. It marked none the less a prodigious thrill, a
thrill that represented sudden dismay, no doubt, but also
represented, and with the self-same throb, the strangest,
the most joyous, possibly the next minute almost the
proudest, duplication of consciousness.

"He has been dodging, retreating, hiding, but now,
worked up to anger, he'll fight!"—this intense impression
made a single mouthful, as it were, of terror and applause.
But what was wondrous was that the applause, for the
felt fact, was so eager, since, if it was his other self he
was running to earth, this ineffable identity was thus in the
last resort not unworthy of him. It bristled there—somewhere near at hand, however unseen still—as the hunted
thing, even as the trodden worm of the adage *must* at last
bristle; and Brydon at this instant tasted probably of a
sensation more complex than had ever before found itself
consistent with sanity. It was as if it would have shamed
him that a character so associated with his own should
triumphantly succeed in just skulking, should to the end
not risk the open, so that the drop of this danger was, on
the spot, a great lift of the whole situation. Yet with
another rare shift of the same subtlety he was already
trying to measure by how much more he himself might
now be in peril of fear; so rejoicing that he could, in
another form, actively inspire that fear, and simultaneously quaking for the form in which he might passively
know it.

The apprehension of knowing it must after a little have
grown in him, and the strangest moment of his adventure
perhaps, the most memorable or really most interesting,
afterwards, of his crisis, was the lapse of certain instants of
concentrated conscious *combat,* the sense of a need to hold
on to something, even after the manner of a man slipping
and slipping on some awful incline; the vivid impulse, above

all, to move, to act, to charge, somehow and upon something—to show himself, in a word, that he wasn't afraid. The state of "holding-on" was thus the state to which he was momentarily reduced; if there had been anything, in the great vacancy, to seize, he would presently have been aware of having clutched it as he might under a shock at home have clutched the nearest chair-back. He had been surprised at any rate—of this he *was* aware—into something unprecedented since his original appropriation of the place; he had closed his eyes, held them tight, for a long minute, as with that instinct of dismay and that terror of vision. When he opened them the room, the other contiguous rooms, extraordinarily, seemed lighter—so light, almost, that at first he took the change for day. He stood firm, however that might be, just where he had paused; his resistance had helped him—it was as if there were some thing he had tided over. He knew after a little what this was—it had been in the imminent danger of flight. He had stiffened his will against going; without this he would have made for the stairs, and it seemed to him that, still with his eyes closed, he would have descended them, would have known how, straight and swiftly, to the bottom.

Well, as he had held out, here he was—still at the top, among the more intricate upper rooms and with the gauntlet of the others, of all the rest of the house, still to run when it should be his time to go. He would go at his time—only at his time: didn't he go every night very much at the same hour? He took out his watch—there was light for that: it was scarcely a quarter past one, and he had never withdrawn so soon. He reached his lodgings for the most part at two—with his walk of a quarter of an hour. He would wait for the last quarter—he wouldn't stir till then; and he kept his watch there with his eyes on it, reflecting while he held it that this deliberate wait, a wait with an effort, which he recognised, would serve perfectly for the attestation he desired to make. It would prove his courage—unless indeed the latter might most be proved by his budging at last from his place. What he mainly felt now was that, since he hadn't originally scuttled, he had his dignities—which had never in his life seemed so many— all to preserve and to carry aloft. This was before him in truth as a physical image, an image almost worthy of an age of greater romance. That remark indeed glimmered for him only to glow the next instant with a finer light; since what age of romance, after all, could have matched either the state of his mind or, "objectively," as they said, the wonder of his situation? The only difference would have been that, brandishing his dignities over his head as in a parchment scroll, he might then—that is, in the heroic time—have proceeded downstairs with a drawn sword in his other grasp.

At present, really, the light he had set down on the mantel of the next room would have to figure his sword; which utensil, in the course of a minute, he had taken the requisite number of steps to possess himself of. The door between the rooms was open, and from the second another door opened to a third. These rooms, as he remembered, gave all three upon a common corridor as well, but there was a fourth, beyond them, without issue save through the preceding. To have moved, to have heard his step again, was appreciably a help; though even in recognising this he lingered once more a little by the chimney-piece on which his light had rested. When he next moved, just hesitating where to turn, he found himself considering a circumstance that, after his first and comparatively vague apprehension of it, produced in him the start that often attends some pang of recollection, the violent shock of having ceased happily to forget. He had come into sight of the door in which the brief chain of communication ended and which he now surveyed from the nearer threshold, the one not directly facing it. Placed at some distance to the left of this point, it would have admitted him to the last room of the four, the room without other approach or egress, had it not, to his intimate conviction, been closed *since* his former visitation, the matter probably of a quarter of an hour before. He stared with all his eyes at the wonder of the fact, arrested again where he stood and again holding his breath while he sounded its sense. Surely it had been *subsequently* closed—that is, it had been on his previous passage indubitably open!

He took it full in the face that something had happened between—that he couldn't not have noticed before (by which he meant on his original tour of all the rooms that evening) that such a barrier had exceptionally presented itself. He had indeed since that moment undergone an agitation so extraordinary that it might have muddled for

him any earlier view; and he tried to convince himself that
he might perhaps then have gone into the room and,
inadvertently, automatically, on coming out, have drawn
the door after him. The difficulty was that this exactly was
what he never did; it was against his whole policy, as he
might have said, the essence of which was to keep vistas
clear. He had them from the first, as he was well aware,
quite on the brain: the strange apparition, at the far end
of one of them, of his baffled "prey" (which had become
by so sharp an irony so little the term now to apply!) was
the form of success his imagination had most cherished,
projecting into it always a refinement of beauty. He had
known fifty times the start of perception that had afterwards dropped; had fifty times gasped to himself "There!"
under some fond brief hallucination. The house, as the
case stood, admirably lent itself; he might wonder at the
taste, the native architecture of the particular time, which
could rejoice so in the multiplication of doors—the opposite extreme to the modern, the actual almost complete
proscription of them; but it had fairly contributed to
provoke this obsession of the presence encountered tele-
scopically, as he might say, focussed and studied in di-
minishing perspective and as by a rest for the elbow.

It was with these considerations that his present attention was charged—they perfectly availed to make what he
saw portentous. He *couldn't,* by any lapse, have blocked
that aperture; and if he hadn't, if it was unthinkable, why,
what else was clear but that there had been another agent?
Another agent?—he had been catching, as he felt, a moment back, the very breath of him; but when had he been
so close as in this simple, this logical, this completely
personal act? It was so logical, that is, that one might have
taken it for personal; yet for what did Brydon take it,
he asked himself, while, softly panting, he felt his eyes
almost leave their sockets. Ah this time at last they *were,*
the two, the opposed projections of him, in presence; and
this time, as much as one would, the question of danger
loomed. With it rose, as not before, the question of courage
—for what he knew the blank face of the door to say to
him was "Show us how much you have!" It stared, it
glared back at him with that challenge; it put to him the
two alternatives: should he just push it open or not? Oh
to have this consciousness was to *think*—and to think,

Brydon knew, as he stood there, was, with the lapsing moments, not to have acted! Not to have acted—that was the misery and the pang—was even still not to act; was in fact *all* to feel the thing in another, in a new and terrible way. How long did he pause and how long did he debate? There was presently nothing to measure it; for his vibration had already changed—as just by the effect of its intensity. Shut up there, at bay, defiant, and with the prodigy of the thing palpably proveably *done,* thus giving notice like some stark signboard—under that accession of accent the situation itself had turned; and Brydon at last remarkably made up his mind on what it had turned to.

It had turned altogether to a different admonition; to a supreme hint, for him, of the value of Discretion! This slowly dawned, no doubt—for it could take its time; so perfectly, on his threshold, had he been stayed, so little as yet had he either advanced or retreated. It was the strangest of all things that now when, by his taking ten steps and applying his hand to a latch, or even his shoulder and his knee, if necessary, to a panel, all the hunger of his prime need might have been met, his high curiosity crowned, his unrest assuaged—it was amazing, but it was also exquisite and rare, that insistence should have, at a touch, quite dropped from him. Discretion—he jumped at that; and yet not, verily, at such a pitch, because it saved his nerves or his skin, but because, much more valuably, it saved the situation. When I say he "jumped" at it I feel the consonance of this term with the fact that—at the end indeed of I know not how long—he did move again, he crossed straight to the door. He wouldn't touch it—it seemed now that he might *if* he would: he would only just wait there a little, to show, to prove, that he wouldn't. He had thus another station, close to the thin partition by which revelation was denied him; but with his eyes bent and his hands held off in a mere intensity of stillness. He listened as if there had been something to hear, but this attitude, while it lasted, was his own communication. "If you won't then —good: I spare you and I give up. You affect me as by the appeal positively for pity: you convince me that for reasons rigid and sublime—what do I know?—we both of us should have suffered. I respect them then, and, though moved and privileged as, I believe, it has never been given to man, I retire, I renounce—never, on my honour, to try again. So rest for ever—and let *me!*"

That, for Brydon was the deep sense of this last demonstration—solemn, measured, directed, as he felt it to be.
He brought it to a close, he turned away; and now verily
he knew how deeply he had been stirred. He retraced his
steps, taking up his candle, burnt, he observed, well-nigh
to the socket, and marking again, lighten it as he would,
the distinctness of his footfall; after which, in a moment,
he knew himself at the other side of the house. He did
here what he had not yet done at these hours—he opened
half a casement, one of those in the front, and let in the
air of the night; a thing he would have taken at any time
previous for a sharp rupture of his spell. His spell was
broken now, and it didn't matter—broken by his concession and his surrender, which made it idle henceforth
that he should ever come back. The empty street—its
other life so marked even by the great lamplit vacancy—
was within call, within touch; he stayed there as to be in it
again, high above it though he was still perched; he
watched as for some comforting common fact, some
vulgar human note, the passage of a scavenger or a thief,
some night-bird however base. He would have blessed that
sign of life; he would have welcomed positively the slow
approach of his friend the policeman, whom he had hitherto
only sought to avoid, and was not sure that if the patrol
had come into sight he mightn't have felt the impulse to
get into relation with it, to hail it, on some pretext, from
his fourth floor.

The pretext that wouldn't have been too silly or too
compromising, the explanation that would have saved his
dignity and kept his name, in such a case, out of the papers,
was not definite to him: he was so occupied with the
thought of recording his Discretion—as an effect of the
vow he had just uttered to his intimate adversary—that the
importance of this loomed large and something had over-
taken all ironically his sense of proportion. If there had
been a ladder applied to the front of the house, even one of
the vertiginous perpendiculars employed by painters and
roofers and sometimes left standing overnight, he would
have managed somehow, astride of the window-sill, to
compass by outstretched leg and arm that mode of descent.
If there had been some such uncanny thing as he had found
in his room at hotels, a workable fire-escape in the form
of notched cable or a canvas shoot, he would have availed
himself of it as a proof—well, of his present delicacy. He

nursed that sentiment, as the question stood, a little in vain, and even—at the end of he scarce knew once more, how long—found it, as by the action on his mind of the failure of response of the outer world, sinking back to vague anguish. It seemed to him he had waited an age for some stir of the great grim hush; the life of the town was itself under a spell—so unnaturally, up and down the whole prospect of known and rather ugly objects, the blankness and the silence lasted. Had they ever, he asked himself, the hard-faced houses, which had begun to look livid in the dim dawn, had they ever spoken so little to any need of his spirit? Great builded voids, great crowded stillnesses put on, often, in the heart of cities, for the small hours, a sort of sinister mask, and it was of this large collective negation that Brydon presently became conscious—all the more that the break of day was, almost incredibly, now at hand, proving to him what a night he had made of it.

He looked again at his watch, saw what had become of his time-values (he had taken hours for minutes—not, as in other tense situations, minutes for hours) and the strange air of the streets was but the weak, the sullen flush of a dawn in which everything was still locked up. His choked appeal from his own open window had been the sole note of life, and he could but break off at last as for a worse despair. Yet while so deeply demoralised he was capable again of an impulse denoting—at least by his present measure—extraordinary resolution; of retracing his steps to the spot where he had turned cold with the extinction of his last pulse of doubt as to there being in the place another presence than his own. This required an effort strong enough to sicken him; but he had his reason, which over-mastered for the moment everything else. There was the whole of the rest of the house to traverse, and how should he screw himself to that if the door he had seen closed were at present open? He could hold to the idea that the closing had practically been for him an act of mercy, a chance offered him to descend, depart, get off the ground and never again profane it. This conception held together, it worked; but what it meant for him depended now clearly on the amount of forbearance his recent action, or rather his recent inaction, had engendered. The image of the "presence," whatever it was, waiting there for him to go— this image had not yet been so concrete for his nerves as when he stopped short of the point at which certainty would have come to him. For, with all his resolution, or more exactly with all his dread, he did stop short—he hung back from really seeing. The risk was too great and his fear too definite: it took at this moment an awful specific form.

He knew—yes, as he had never known anything—that, *should* he see the door open, it would all too abjectly be the end of him. It would mean that the agent of his shame —for his shame was the deep abjection—was once more at large and in general possession; and what glared him thus in the face was the act that this would determine for him. It would send him straight about to the window he had left open, and by that window, be long ladder and dangling rope as absent as they would, he saw himself uncontrollably insanely fatally take his way to the street. The hideous chance of this he at least could avert; but he could only avert it by recoiling in time from assurance. He had the whole house to deal with, this fact was still there; only he now knew that uncertainty alone could start him. He stole back from where he had checked himself —merely to do so was suddenly like safety—and, making blindly for the greater staircase, left gaping rooms and sounding passages behind. Here was the top of the stairs, with a fine large dim descent and three spacious landings to mark off. His instinct was all for mildness, but his feet were harsh on the floors, and, strangely, when he had in a couple of minutes become aware of this, it counted somehow for help. He couldn't have spoken, the tone of his voice would have scared him, and the common conceit or resource of "whistling in the dark" (whether literally or figuratively) have appeared basely vulgar; yet he liked none the less to hear himself go, and when he had reached his first landing—taking it all with no rush, but quite steadily—that stage of success drew from him a gasp of relief.

The house, withal, seemed immense, the scale of space again inordinate; the open rooms to no one of which his eyes deflected, gloomed in their shuttered state like mouths of caverns; only the high skylight that formed the crown of the deep well created for him a medium in which he could advance, but which might have been, for queerness of colour, some watery under-world. He tried to think of something noble, as that his property was really grand, a splendid possession; but this nobleness took the form too of the clear delight with which he was finally to sacrifice it. They might come in now, the builders, the destroyers —they might come as soon as they would. At the end of two flights he had dropped to another zone, and from the middle of the third, with only one more left, he recognised the influence of the lower windows, of half-drawn blinds, of the occasional gleam of street-lamps, of the glazed spaces of the vestibule. This was the bottom of the sea, which showed an illumination of its own and which he even saw paved—when at a given moment he drew up to sink a long look over the banisters—with the marble squares of his childhood. By that time indubitably he felt, as he might have said in a commoner cause, better; it had allowed him to stop and draw breath, and the ease increased with the sight of the old black-and-white slabs. But what he most felt was that now surely, with the element of impunity pulling him as by hard firm hands, the case was settled for what he might have seen above had he dared that last look. The closed door, blessedly remote now, was still closed—and he had only in short to reach that of the house.

He came down further, he crossed the passage forming the access to the last flight; and if here again he stopped an instant it was almost for the sharpness of the thrill of assured escape. It made him shut his eyes—which opened again to the straight slope of the remainder of the stairs. Here was impunity still, but impunity almost excessive; inasmuch as the side-lights and the high fan-tracery of the entrance were glimmering straight into the hall; an appearance produced, he the next instant saw, by the fact that the vestibule gaped wide, that the hinged halves of the inner door had been thrown far back. Out of that again the *question* sprang at him, making his eyes, as he felt, half-start from his head, as they had done, at the top of the house, before the sign of the other door. If he had left that one open, hadn't he left this one closed, and wasn't he now in *most* immediate presence of some inconceivable occult activity? It was as sharp, the question, as a knife in his side, but the answer hung fire still and seemed to lose itself in the vague darkness to which the thin admitted dawn, glimmering archwise over the whole outer door, made a semicircular margin, a cold silvery nimbus that seemed to play a little as he looked—to shift and expand and contract.

It was as if there had been something within it, pro-

tected by indistinctness and corresponding in extent with
the opaque surface behind, the painted panels of the last
barrier to his escape, of which the key was in his pocket.
The indistinctness mocked him even while he stared,
affected him as somehow shrouding or challenging certitude, so that after faltering an instant on his step he let
himself go with the sense that here *was* at last something
to meet, to touch, to take, to know—something all unnatural and dreadful, but to advance upon which was the
condition for him either of liberation or of supreme defeat. The penumbra, dense and dark, was the virtual
screen of a figure which stood in it as still as some image
erect in a niche or as some black-vizored sentinel guarding
a treasure. Brydon was to know afterwards, was to recall
and make out, the particular thing he had believed during
the rest of his descent. He saw, in its great grey glimmering margin, the central vagueness diminish, and he felt
it to be taking the very form toward which, for so many
days, the passion of his curiosity had yearned. It gloomed,
it loomed, it was something, it was somebody, the prodigy
of a personal presence.

Rigid and conscious, spectral yet human, a man of his
own substance and stature waited there to measure himself
with his power to dismay. This only could it be—this only
till he recognised, with his advance, that what made the
face dim was the pair of raised hands that covered it and
in which, so far from being offered in defiance, it was
buried as for dark deprecation. So Brydon, before him,
took him in; with every fact of him now, in the higher
light, hard and acute—his planted stillness, his vivid truth,
his grizzled bent head and white masking hands, his queer
actuality of evening-dress, of dangling double eye-glass, of
gleaming silk lappet and white linen, of pearl button and
gold watch-guard and polished shoe. No portrait by a
great modern master could have presented him with more
intensity, thrust him out of his frame with more art, as if
there had been "treatment," of the consummate sort, in his
every shade and salience. The revulsion, for our friend,
had become, before he knew it, immense—this drop, in
the act of apprehension, to the sense of his adversary's
inscrutable manœuvre. That meaning at least, while he
gaped, it offered him; for he could but gape at his other
self in this other anguish, gape as a proof that *he,* standing
there for the achieved, the enjoyed, the triumphant life,

couldn't be faced in his triumph. Wasn't the proof in the splendid covering hands, strong and completely spread?— so spread and so intentional that, in spite of a special verity that surpassed every other, the fact that one of these hands had lost two fingers, which were reduced to stumps, as if accidentally shot away, the face was effectually guarded and saved.

"Saved," though, *would* it be?—Brydon breathed his wonder till the very impunity of his attitude and the very insistence of his eyes produced, as he felt, a sudden stir which showed the next instant as a deeper portent, while the head raised itself, the betrayal of a braver purpose. The hands, as he looked, began to move, to open; then, as if deciding in a flash, dropped from the face and left it uncovered and presented. Horror, with the sight, had leaped into Brydon's throat, gasping there in a sound he couldn't utter; for the bared identity was too hideous as *his,* and his glare was the passion of his protest. The face, *that* face, Spencer Brydon's?—he searched it still, but looking away from it in dismay and denial, falling straight from his height and sublimity. It was unknown, inconceivable, awful, disconnected from any possibility—! He had been "sold," he inwardly moaned, stalking such game as this: the presence before him was a presence, the horror within him a horror, but the waste of his nights had been only grotesque and the success of his adventure an irony. Such an identity fitted his at *no* point, made its alternative monstrous. A thousand times yes, as it came upon him nearer now—the face was the face of a stranger. It came upon him nearer now, quite as one of those expanding fantastic images projected by the magic lantern of childhood; for the stranger, whoever he might be, evil, odious, blatant, vulgar, had advanced as for aggression, and he knew himself give ground. Then harder pressed still, sick with the force of his shock, and falling back as under the hot breath and the roused passion of a life larger than his own, a rage of personality before which his own collapsed, he felt the whole vision turn to darkness and his very feet give way. His head went round; he was going; he had gone.

III

What had next brought him back, clearly—though after how long?—was Mrs. Muldoon's voice, coming to him from quite near, from so near that he seemed presently to see her as kneeling on the ground before him while he lay looking up at her; himself not wholly on the ground, but half-raised and upheld—conscious, yes, of tenderness of support and, more particularly, of a head pillowed in extraordinary softness and faintly refreshing fragrance. He considered, he wondered, his wit but half at his service; then another face intervened, bending more directly over him, and he finally knew that Alice Staverton had made her lap an ample and perfect cushion to him, and that she had to this end seated herself on the lowest degree of the staircase, the rest of his long person remaining stretched on his old black-and-white slabs. They were cold, these marble squares of his youth; but *he* somehow was not, in this rich return of consciousness—the most wonderful hour, little by little, that he had ever known, leaving him, as it did, so gratefully, so abysmally passive, and yet as with a treasure of intelligence waiting all round him for quiet appropriation; dissolved, he might call it, in the air of the place and producing the golden glow of a late autumn afternoon. He had come back, yes—come back from further away than any man but himself had ever travelled; but it was strange how with this sense what he had come back *to* seemed really the great thing, and as if his prodigious journey had been all for the sake of it. Slowly but surely his consciousness grew, his vision of his state thus completing itself: he had been miraculously *carried* back—lifted and carefully borne as from where he had been picked up, the uttermost end of an interminable grey passage. Even with this he was suffered to rest, and what had now brought him to knowledge was the break in the long mild motion.

It had brought him to knowledge, to knowledge—yes, this was the beauty of his state; which came to resemble more and more that of a man who has gone to sleep on some news of a great inheritance, and then, after dreaming it away, after profaning it with matters strange to it, has waked up again to serenity of certitude and has only to lie and watch it grow. This was the drift of his patience—that he had only to let it shine on him. He must moreover, with intermissions, still have been lifted and borne; since why and how else should he have known himself, later on, with the afternoon glow intenser, no longer at the foot of his stairs—situated as these now seemed at that dark other end of his tunnel—but on a deep window-bench of his high saloon, over which had been spread, couch-fashion, a mantle of soft stuff lined with grey fur that was familiar to his eyes and that one of his hands kept fondly feeling as for its pledge of truth. Mrs. Muldoon's face had gone, but the other, the second he had recognised, hung over him in a way that showed how he was still propped and pillowed. He took it all in, and the more he took it the more it seemed to suffice: he was as much at peace as if he had had food and drink. It was the two women who had found him, on Mrs. Muldoon's having plied, at her usual hour, her latch-key—and on her having above all arrived while Miss Staverton still lingered near the house. She had been turning away, all anxiety, from worrying the vain bell-handle—her calculation having been of the hour of the good woman's visit; but the latter, blessedly, had come up while she was still there, and they had entered together. He had then lain, beyond the vestibule, very much as he was lying now—quite, that is, as he appeared to have fallen, but all so wondrously without bruise or gash; only in a depth of stupor. What he most took in, however, at present, with the steadier clearance, was that Alice Staverton had for a long unspeakable moment not doubted he was dead.

"It must have been that I *was*." He made it out as she held him. "Yes—I can only have died. You brought me literally to life. Only," he wondered, his eyes rising to her, "only, in the name of all the benedictions, how?"

It took her but an instant to bend her face and kiss him, and something in the manner of it, and in the way her hands clasped and locked his head while he felt the cool charity and virtue of her lips, something in all this beatitude somehow answered everything. "And now I keep you," she said.

"Oh keep me, keep me!" he pleaded while her face still hung over him: in response to which it dropped again and stayed close, clingingly close. It was the seal of their situation—of which he tasted the impress for a long blissful moment in silence. But he came back. "Yet how did you know—?"

"I was uneasy. You were to have come, you remember —and you had sent no word."

"Yes, I remember—I was to have gone to you at one

today." It caught on to their "old" life and relation—which were so near and so far. "I was still out there in my strange darkness—where was it, what was it? I must have stayed there so long." He could but wonder at the depth and the duration of his swoon.

"Since last night?" she asked with a shade of fear for her possible indiscretion.

"Since this morning—it must have been: the cold dim dawn of today. Where have I been," he vaguely wailed, "where have I been?" He felt her hold him close, and it was as if this helped him now to make in all security his mild moan. "What a long dark day!"

All in her tenderness she had waited a moment. "In the cold dim dawn?" she quavered.

But he had already gone on piecing together the parts of the whole prodigy. "As I didn't turn up you came straight—?"

She barely cast about. "I went first to your hotel—where they told me of your absence. You had dined out last evening and hadn't been back since. But they appeared to know you had been at your club."

"So you had the idea of *this*—?"

"Of what?" she asked in a moment.

"Well—of what has happened."

"I believed at least you'd have been here. I've known, all along," she said, "that you've been coming."

" 'Known' it—?"

"Well, I've believed it. I said nothing to you after that talk we had a month ago—but I felt sure. I knew you *would*," she declared.

"That I'd persist, you mean?"

"That you'd see him."

"Ah but I didn't!" cried Brydon with his long wail. "There's somebody—an awful beast; whom I brought, too horribly, to bay. But it's not me."

At this she bent over him again, and her eyes were in his eyes. "No—it's not you." And it was as if, while her face hovered, he might have made out in it, hadn't it been so near, some particular meaning blurred by a smile. "No, thank heaven," she repeated—"it's not you! Of course it wasn't to have been."

"Ah but it *was*," he gently insisted. And he stared before him now as he had been staring for so many weeks. "I was to have known myself."

"You couldn't!" she returned consolingly. And then reverting, and as if to account further for what she had herself done, "But it wasn't only *that,* that you hadn't been at home," she went on. "I waited till the hour at which we had found Mrs. Muldoon that day of my going with you; and she arrived, as I've told you, while, failing to bring anyone to the door, I lingered in my despair on the steps. After a little, if she hadn't come, by such a mercy, I should have found means to hunt her up. But it wasn't," said Alice Staverton, as if once more with her fine intention— "it wasn't only that."

His eyes, as he lay, turned back to her. "What more then?"

She met it, the wonder she had stirred. "In the cold dim dawn, you say? Well, in the cold dim dawn of this morning I too saw you."

"Saw *me*—?"

"Saw *him,*" said Alice Staverton. "It must have been at the same moment."

He lay an instant taking it in—as if he wished to be quite reasonable. "At the same moment?"

"Yes—in my dream again, the same one I've named to you. He came back to me. Then I knew it for a sign. He had come to you."

At this Brydon raised himself; he had to see her better. She helped him when she understood his movement, and he sat up, steadying himself beside her there on the window-bench and with his right hand grasping her left. "*He* didn't come to me."

"You came to yourself," she beautifully smiled.

"Ah I've come to myself now—thanks to you, dearest. But this brute, with his awful face—this brute's a black stranger. He's none of *me,* even as I *might* have been," Brydon sturdily declared.

But she kept the clearness that was like the breath of infallibility. "Isn't the whole point that you'd have been different?"

He almost scowled for it. "As different as *that*—?"

Her look again was more beautiful to him than the things of this world. "Haven't you exactly wanted to know *how* different? So this morning," she said, "you appeared to me."

"Like *him?*"

"A black stranger!"

"Then how did you know it was I?"

"Because, as I told you weeks ago, my mind, my imagination, had worked so over what you might, what you mightn't have been—to show you, you see, how I've thought of you. In the midst of that you came to me—that my wonder might be answered. So I knew," she went on; "and believed that, since the question held you too so fast, as you told me that day, you too would see for yourself. And when this morning I again saw I knew it would be because you had—and also then, from the first moment, because you somehow wanted me. *He* seemed to tell me of that. So why," she strangely smiled, "shouldn't I like him?"

It brought Spencer Brydon to his feet. "You 'like' that horror—?"

"I *could* have liked him. And to me," she said, "he was no horror. I had accepted him."

" 'Accepted'—?" Brydon oddly sounded.

"Before, for the interest of his difference—yes. And as *I* didn't disown him, as *I* knew him—which you at last, confronted with him in his difference, so cruelly didn't, my dear—well, he must have been, you see, less dreadful to me. And it may have pleased him that I pitied him."

She was beside him on her feet, but still holding his hand—still with her arm supporting him. But though it all brought for him thus a dim light, "You 'pitied' him?" he grudgingly, resentfully asked.

"He has been unhappy; he has been ravaged," she said.

"And haven't I been unhappy? Am not I—you've only to look at me!—ravaged?"

"Ah I don't say I like him *better*," she granted after a thought. "But he's grim, he's worn—and things have happened to him. He doesn't make shift, for sight, with your charming monocle."

"No"—it struck Brydon: "I couldn't have sported mine 'downtown.' They'd have guyed me there."

"His great convex pince-nez—I saw it, I recognised the kind—is for his poor ruined sight. And his poor right hand—!"

"Ah!" Brydon winced—whether for his proved identity or for his lost fingers. Then, "He has a million a year," he lucidly added. "But he hasn't you."

"And he isn't—no, he isn't—*you!*" she murmured as he drew her to his breast.

1909

AMBROSE BIERCE

(1842–c1914)

A minor writer whose work still awaits a critically definitive statement, "Bitter" Bierce belongs with Poe, Stephen Crane, and Faulkner in his materials, humor, and attitudes. In his disenchantment he shares a large thematic community with most American writers, but this early Bohemian, free lance, and rebel probably is closer to the "sick" writers of the 1960's than to the respectably accepted first order of American authorship.

The youngest of nine children, Ambrose Bierce was born in Meigs County, Ohio, and moved with his family to Indiana when he was still a child. Brought up in a poverty that probably helped early to shape the bitterness that came to characterize him, he fled from his rural slum into the Kentucky Military Institute and thence into the ranks of the Grand Army of the Republic. His own serious injury at the battle of Kennesaw Mountain (which, however, did not deter him from completing his service through the end of the war) only deepened the sadness, savagery, contempt, and awe with which he viewed the human condition. In the army, so it seems, he had found the home that best satisfied his needs and suited his vision of reality. When the war was over, Bierce remained with the army and went West on a government map-making expedition. Finally, however, he resigned in order to avoid reduction in rank and traveled on to San Francisco. There he met Bret Harte and, as Harte had done, worked in the Mint and began to write for various newspapers.

A marriage contracted in San Francisco was an unhappy

adventure which served to confirm Bierce's dark view of human expectations. Abandoning his family in 1871 (the subsequent death of his two sons—one in gunplay, the other of alcohol—poisoned his perspective beyond remedy), he went to London to find the public that Mark Twain and Bret Harte enjoyed; he wrote for British periodicals, brought out two volumes of his selected San Francisco writings, and published his English writings under the pseudonym of Dod Grile. But the public he expected was not forthcoming, and in 1876 he went back to San Francisco to write for the *Wasp* and the *Argonaut*. Five years later he became a member of the Hearst organization, occupying various staff jobs (on the San Francisco *Examiner*, New York *American*, and *Cosmopolitan Magazine* and covering the Washington beat, where he helped to expose the railroad lobby) until 1909, when he retired from journalism as a career. Meanwhile his books continued to appear. In 1891 was published *Tales of Soldiers and Civilians* (later called *In the Midst of Life*); this was followed by *The Monk and the Hangman's Daughter* (Bierce's version of C. A. Danziger's translation from the German) and *Black Beetles in Amber*, a volume of his satiric, witty, and unsuccessful verse, in 1892 and *Can Such Things Be?* in 1893. The *Tales of Soldiers and Civilians* is probably his best work. Bierce was more adept at the short story than at any other form, and this collection of stories centers on his special materials: war, death, horror, with a tinge of the supernatural. They display a possibly important connection between Bierce and major serious national literature in their concentration on the impact of experience (usually war) on the innocent, beguiled, or romantic perception.

In all his writings, Bierce tried to maintain a strict distinction between journalism and literature. As a purist he insisted upon a proper use of the language (*Write It Right*, 1909), somewhat surprising in a writer whose subjects and attitudes deliberately departed from propriety and convention. In 1913 the seventy-year-old Bierce crossed the border into Mexico, disappeared, and became in his disappearance the subject for one of the favorite mysteries and legends of American literary biography.

In addition to the titles mentioned above, Bierce's works include *The Fiend's Delight* (1872); *Nuggets and Dust* (1872); *Cobwebs from an Empty Skull* (1873); *The Dance of Death* (1877); *Fantastic Fables* (1899); *Shapes of Clay* (1903); *The Cynic's Word Book* (1906; later called *The Devil's Dictionary*); and *The Shadow on the Dial* (1909).

Editions and accounts of the man and his work are to be found in W. Neale, ed. (with A. Bierce), *The Collected Works of Ambrose Bierce,* 12 vols. (1909–1912); V. Starrett, *Ambrose Bierce* (1920); B. C. Pope, ed., *The Letters of Ambrose Bierce* (1921); S. Lovman, ed., *Twenty-one Letters of Ambrose Bierce* (1922); A. de Castro, *Portrait of Ambrose Bierce* (1929); C. H. Grattan, *Bitter Bierce* (1929); C. McWilliams, *Ambrose Bierce* (1929); W. Neale, *The Life of Ambrose Bierce* (1929); C. D. Hall, *Bierce and the Poe Hoax* (1934); J. Gaer, *Ambrose Bierce* (1935); F. Walker, *San Francisco's Literary Frontier* (1939); J. Noel, *Footloose in Arcadia* (1940); F. Walker, *Ambrose Bierce* (1941); P. Fatout, *Ambrose Bierce, the Devil's Lexicographer* (1951); P. Fatout, *Ambrose Bierce and the Black Hills* (1956); L. A. Berkove, "Ambrose Bierce's Concern with Mind and Man," *Dissertation Abstracts* (1963); R. A. Wiggins, *Ambrose Bierce* (1964); S. C. Woodruff, *The Short Stories of Ambrose Bierce, A Study in Polarity* (1964).

An Occurrence at Owl Creek Bridge

I

A man stood upon a railroad bridge in northern Alabama, looking down into the swift water twenty feet below. The man's hands were behind his back, the wrists bound with a cord. A rope closely encircled his neck. It was attached to a stout crosstimber above his head and the slack fell to the level of his knees. Some loose boards laid upon the sleepers supporting the metals of the railway supplied a footing for him and his executioners—two private soldiers of the Federal army, directed by a sergeant who in civil life may have been a deputy sheriff. At a short remove upon the same temporary platform was an officer in the uniform of his rank, armed. He was a captain. A sentinel at each end of the bridge stood with his rifle in the position known as "support," that is to say, vertical in front of the left shoulder, the hammer resting on the forearm thrown straight across the chest—a formal and unnatural position, enforcing an erect carriage of the body. It did not appear to be the duty of these two men to know what was occurring at the centre of the bridge; they merely blockaded the two ends of the foot planking that traversed it.

Beyond one of the sentinels nobody was in sight; the railroad ran straight away into a forest for a hundred yards, then, curving, was lost to view. Doubtless there was an outpost farther along. The other bank of the stream was open ground—a gentle aclivity topped with a stockade of vertical tree trunks, loop-holed for rifles, with a single embrasure through which protruded the muzzle of a brass cannon commanding the bridge. Midway of the slope between bridge and fort were the spectators—a single company of infantry in line, at "parade rest," the butts of the rifles on the ground, the barrels inclining slightly backward against the right shoulder, the hands crossed upon the stock. A lieutenant stood at the right of the line, the point of his sword upon the ground, his left hand resting upon his right. Excepting the group of four at the center of the bridge, not a man moved. The company faced the bridge, staring stonily, motionless. The sentinels, facing the banks of the stream, might have been statues to adorn the bridge. The captain stood with folded arms, silent, observing the work of his subordinates, but making no sign. Death is a dignitary who when he comes announced is to be received with formal manifestations of respect, even by those most familiar with him. In the code of military etiquette silence and fixity are forms of deference.

The man who was engaged in being hanged was apparently about thirty-five years of age. He was a civilian, if one might judge from his habit, which was that of a planter. His features were good—a straight nose, firm mouth, broad forehead, from which his long, dark hair was combed straight back, falling behind his ears to the collar of his well-fitting frock-coat. He wore a mustache and pointed beard, but no whiskers; his eyes were large and dark gray, and had a kindly expression which one would hardly have expected in one whose neck was in the hemp. Evidently this was no vulgar assassin. The liberal military code makes provision for hanging many kinds of persons, and gentlemen are not excluded.

The preparations being complete, the two private soldiers stepped aside and each drew away the plank upon which he had been standing. The sergeant turned to the captain, saluted and placed himself immediately behind that officer, who in turn moved apart one pace. These movements left the condemned man and the sergeant standing on the two ends of the same plank, which spanned three of the cross-ties of the bridge. The end upon which the civilian stood almost, but not quite, reached a fourth. This plank had been held in place by the weight of the captain; it was now held by that of the sergeant. At a signal from the former the latter would step aside, the plank would tilt and the condemned man go down between two ties. The arrangement commended itself to his judgment as simple and effective. His face had not been covered nor his eyes bandaged. He looked a moment at his "unsteadfast footing," then let his gaze wander to the swirling water of the stream racing madly beneath his feet. A piece of dancing driftwood caught his attention and his eyes followed it down the current. How slowly it appeared to move! What a sluggish stream!

He closed his eyes in order to fix his last thoughts upon his wife and children. The water, touched to gold by the early sun, the brooding mists under the banks at some distance down the stream, the fort, the soldiers, the piece of drift—all had distracted him. And now he became conscious of a new disturbance. Striking through the thought of his dear ones was a sound which he could neither ignore nor understand, a sharp, distinct, metallic percussion like the stroke of a blacksmith's hammer upon the anvil; it had the same ringing quality. He wondered what it was, and whether immeasurably distant or near by—it seemed both. Its recurrence was regular, but as slow as the tolling of a death knell. He awaited each stroke with impatience and—he knew not why—apprehension. The intervals of silence grew progressively longer; the delays became maddening. With their greater infrequency the sounds increased in strength and sharpness. They hurt his ear like the thrust of a knife; he feared he would shriek. What he heard was the ticking of his watch.

He unclosed his eyes and saw again the water below him. "If I could free my hands," he thought, "I might throw off the noose and spring into the stream. By diving I could evade the bullets and, swimming vigorously, reach the bank, take to the woods and get away home. My home, thank God, is as yet outside their lines; my wife and little ones are still beyond the invader's farthest advance."

As these thoughts, which have here to be set down in words, were flashed into the doomed man's brain rather than evolved from it, the captain nodded to the sergeant. The sergeant stepped aside.

II

Peyton Farquhar was a well-to-do planter, of an old and highly respected Alabama family. Being a slave owner and, like other slave owners, a politician he was naturally an original secessionist and ardently devoted to the Southern cause. Circumstances of an imperious nature, which it is unnecessary to relate here, had prevented him from taking service with the gallant army that had fought the disastrous campaigns ending with the fall of Corinth, and he chafed under the inglorious restraint, longing for the release of his energies, the larger life of the soldier, the opportunity for distinction. That opportunity, he felt, would come, as it comes to all in war time. Meanwhile he did what he could. No service was too humble for him to perform in aid of the South, no adventure too perilous for him to undertake if consistent with the character of a civilian who was at heart a soldier, and who in good faith and without too much qualification assented to at least a part of the frankly villainous dictum that all is fair in love and war.

One evening while Farquhar and his wife were sitting on a rustic bench near the entrance to his grounds, a gray-clad soldier rode up to the gate and asked for a drink of water. Mrs. Farquhar was only too happy to serve him with her own white hands. While she was fetching the water her husband approached the dusty horseman and inquired eagerly for news from the front.

"The Yanks are repairing the railroads," said the man, "and are getting ready for another advance. They have reached the Owl Creek bridge, put it in order and built a stockade on the north bank. The commandant has issued an order, which is posted everywhere, declaring that any civilian caught interfering with the railroad, its bridges, tunnels or trains will be summarily hanged. I saw the order."

"How far is it to the Owl Creek bridge?" Farquhar asked.

"About thirty miles."

"Is there no force on this side the creek?"

"Only a picket post half a mile out, on the railroad, and a single sentinel at this end of the bridge."

"Suppose a man—a civilian and student of hanging—should delude the picket post and perhaps get the better of the sentinel," said Farquhar, smiling, "what could he accomplish?"

The soldier reflected. "I was there a month ago," he replied. "I observed that the flood of last winter had lodged a great quantity of driftwood against the wooden pier at this end of the bridge. It is now dry and would burn like tow."

The lady had now brought the water, which the soldier drank. He thanked her ceremoniously, bowed to her husband and rode away. An hour later, after nightfall, he repassed the plantation, going northward in the direction from which he had come. He was a Federal scout.

III

As Peyton Farquhar fell straight downward through the bridge he lost consciousness and was as one already dead. From this state he was awakened—ages later, it seemed to him—by the pain of a sharp pressure upon his throat, followed by a sense of suffocation. Keen, poignant agonies seemed to shoot from his neck downward through every fibre of his body and limbs. These pains appeared to flash along well-defined lines of ramification and to beat with an inconceivably rapid periodicity. They seemed like streams of pulsating fire heating him to an intolerable temperature. As to his head, he was conscious of nothing but a feeling of fulness—of congestion. These sensations were unaccompanied by thought. The intellectual part of his nature was already effaced; he had power only to feel, and feeling was torment. He was conscious of motion. Encompassed in a luminous cloud, of which he was now merely the fiery heart, without material substance, he swung through unthinkable arcs of oscillation, like a vast pendulum.

Then all at once, with terrible suddenness, the light about him shot upward with the noise of a loud plash; a frightful roaring was in his ears, and all was cold and dark. The power of thought was restored; he knew that the rope had broken and he had fallen into the stream. There was no additional strangulation; the noose about his neck was already suffocating him and kept the water from his lungs. To die of hanging at the bottom of a river!—the idea seemed to him ludicrous. He opened his eyes in the darkness and saw above him a gleam of light, but how distant, how inaccessible! He was still sinking, for the light became fainter and fainter until it was a mere glimmer. Then it began to grow and brighten, and he knew that he was rising toward the surface—knew it with reluctance, for he was now very comfortable. "To be hanged and drowned," he thought, "that is not so bad; but I do not wish to be shot. No; I will not be shot; that is not fair."

He was not conscious of an effort, but a sharp pain in his wrist apprised him that he was trying to free his hands. He gave the struggle his attention, as an idler might observe the feat of a juggler, without interest in the outcome. What splendid effort! What magnificent, what superhuman strength! Ah, that was a fine endeavor! Bravo! The cord fell away; his arms parted and floated upward, the hands dimly seen on each side in the growing light. He watched them with a new interest as first one and then the other pounced upon the noose at his neck. They tore it away and thrust it fiercely aside, its undulations resembling those of a water-snake. "Put it back, put it back!" He thought he shouted these words to his hands, for the undoing of the noose had been succeeded by the direst pang that he had yet experienced. His neck ached horribly; his brain was on fire; his heart, which had been fluttering faintly, gave a great leap, trying to force itself out at his mouth. His whole body was racked and wrenched with an insupportable anguish! But his disobedient hands gave no heed to the command. They beat the water vigorously with quick, downward strokes, forcing him to the surface. He felt his head emerge; his eyes were blinded by the sunlight; his chest expanded convulsively, and with a supreme and crowning agony his lungs engulfed a great draught of air, which instantly he expelled in a shriek!

He was now in full possession of his physical senses. They were, indeed, preternaturally keen and alert. Something in the awful disturbance of his organic system had so exalted and refined them that they made record of things never before perceived. He felt the ripples upon his face and heard their separate sounds as they struck. He looked at the forest on the bank of the stream, saw the individual trees, the leaves and the veining of each leaf—saw the very insects upon them: the locusts, the brilliant-bodied flies, the gray spiders stretching their webs from twig to twig. He noted the prismatic colors in all the dewdrops upon a million blades of grass. The humming of the gnats that danced above the eddies of the stream, the beating of the dragon-flies' wings, the strokes of the water-spiders' legs, like oars which had lifted their boat—all these made audible music. A fish slid along beneath his eyes and he heard the rush of its body parting the water.

He had come to the surface facing down the stream; in a moment the visible world seemed to wheel slowly round, himself the pivotal point, and he saw the bridge, the fort, the soldiers upon the bridge, the captain, the sergeant, the two privates, his executioners. They were in silhouette against the blue sky. They shouted and gesticulated, point-ing at him. The captain had drawn his pistol, but did not fire; the others were unarmed. Their movements were gro-tesque and horrible, their forms gigantic.

Suddenly he heard a sharp report and something struck the water smartly within a few inches of his head, spatter-ing his face with spray. He heard a second report, and saw one of the sentinels with his rifle at his shoulder, a light cloud of blue smoke rising from the muzzle. The man in the water saw the eye of the man on the bridge gazing into his own through the sights of the rifle. He observed that it was a gray eye and remembered having read that gray eyes were keenest, and that all famous marksmen had them. Nevertheless, this one had missed.

A counter-swirl had caught Farquhar and turned him half round; he was again looking into the forest on the bank opposite the fort. The sound of a clear, high voice in a monotonous singsong now rang out behind him and came across the water with a distinctness that pierced and subdued all other sounds, even the beating of the ripples in his ears. Although no soldier, he had frequented camps enough to know the dread significance of that deliberate, drawling, aspirated chant; the lieutenant on shore was tak-ing a part in the morning's work. How coldly and pitilessly —with what an even, calm intonation, presaging and en-forcing tranquillity in the men—with what accurately meas-ured intervals fell those cruel words:

"Attention, company! . . . Shoulder arms! . . . Ready! . . . Aim! . . . Fire!"

Farquhar dived—dived as deeply as he could. The water roared in his ears like the voice of Niagara, yet he heard the dulled thunder of the volley and, rising again toward the surface, met shining bits of metal, singularly flattened, oscil-

lating slowly downward. Some of them touched him on the
face and hands, then fell away, continuing their descent.
One lodged between his collar and neck; it was uncomfortably warm and he snatched it out.

As he rose to the surface, gasping for breath, he saw
that he had been a long time under water; he was perceptibly farther down stream—nearer to safety. The soldiers had almost finished reloading; the metal ramrods
flashed all at once in the sunshine as they were drawn from
the barrels, turned in the air, and thrust into their sockets.
The two sentinels fired again, independently and ineffectu-
ally.

The hunted man saw all this over his shoulder; he was
now swimming vigorously with the current. His brain was
as energetic as his arms and legs; he thought with the rapidity of lightning.

"The officer," he reasoned, "will not make that martinet's
error a second time. It is as easy to dodge a volley as a
single shot. He has probably already given the command
to fire at will. God help me, I cannot dodge them all!"

An appalling plash within two yards of him was followed
by a loud, rushing sound, *diminuendo,* which seemed to
travel back through the air to the fort and died in an ex-
plosion which stirred the very river to its deeps! A rising
sheet of water curved over him, fell down upon him,
blinded him, strangled him! The cannon had taken a hand
in the game. As he shook his head free from the commotion of the smitten water he heard the deflected shot humming through the air ahead, and in an instant it was crack-
ing and smashing the branches in the forest beyond.

"They will not do that again," he thought, "the next time
they will use a charge of grape. I must keep my eye upon
the gun; the smoke will apprise me—the report arrives too
late; it lags behind the missile. That is a good gun."

Suddenly he felt himself whirled round and round—
spinning like a top. The water, the banks, the forests, the
now distant bridge, fort and men—all were commingled
and blurred. Objects were represented by their colors only;
circular horizontal streaks of color—that was all he saw. He
had been caught in a vortex and was being whirled on
with a velocity of advance and gyration that made him
giddy and sick. In a few moments he was flung upon the
gravel at the foot of the left bank of the stream—the

southern bank—and behind a projecting point which concealed him from his enemies. The sudden arrest of his motion, the abrasion of one of his hands on the gravel, restored him, and he wept with delight. He dug his fingers into the sand, threw it over himself in handfuls and audibly blessed it. It looked like diamonds, rubies, emeralds; he could think of nothing beautiful which it did not resemble. The trees upon the bank were giant garden plants; he noted a definite order in their arrangement, inhaled the fragrance of their blooms. A strange, roseate light shone through the spaces among their trunks and the wind made in their branches the music of æolian harps. He had no wish to perfect his escape—was content to remain in that enchanting spot until retaken.

A whiz and rattle of grapeshot among the branches high above his head roused him from his dream. The baffled cannoneer had fired him a random farewell. He sprang to his feet, rushed up the sloping bank, and plunged into the forest.

All that day he traveled, laying his course by the rounding sun. The forest seemed interminable; nowhere did he discover a break in it, not even a woodman's road. He had not known that he lived in so wild a region. There was something uncanny in the revelation.

By nightfall he was fatigued, footsore, famishing. The thought of his wife and children urged him on. At last he found a road which led him in what he knew to be the right direction. It was as wide and straight as a city street, yet it seemed untraveled. No fields bordered it, no dwelling anywhere. Not so much as the barking of a dog suggested human habitation. The black bodies of the trees formed a straight wall on both sides, terminating on the horizon in a point, like a diagram in a lesson in perspective. Overhead, as he looked up through this rift in the wood, shone great golden stars looking unfamiliar and grouped in strange constellations. He was sure they were arranged in some order which had a secret and malign significance. The wood on either side was full of singular noises, among which—once, twice, and again—he distinctly heard whispers in an unknown tongue.

His neck was in pain and lifting his hand to it he found it horribly swollen. He knew that it had a circle of black where the rope had bruised it. His eyes felt congested; he could no longer close them. His tongue was swollen with thirst; he relieved its fever by thrusting it forward from between his teeth into the cold air. How softly the turf had carpeted the untraveled avenue—he could no longer feel the roadway beneath his feet!

Doubtless, despite his suffering, he had fallen asleep while walking, for now he sees another scene—perhaps he has merely recovered from a delirium. He stands at the gate of his own home. All is as he left it, and all bright and beautiful in the morning sunshine. He must have traveled the entire night. As he pushes open the gate and passes up the wide white walk, he sees a flutter of female garments; his wife, looking fresh and cool and sweet, steps down from the veranda to meet him. At the bottom of the steps she stands waiting, with a smile of ineffable joy, an attitude of matchless grace and dignity. Ah, how beautiful she is! He springs forward with extended arms. As he is about to clasp her he feels a stunning blow upon the back of the neck; a blinding white light blazes all about him with a sound like the shock of a cannon—then all is darkness and silence!

Peyton Farquhar was dead; his body, with a broken neck, swung gently from side to side beneath the timbers of the Owl Creek bridge.

1891

FROM

Fantastic Fables

Two Sons

A Man had Two Sons. The elder was virtuous and dutiful, the younger wicked and crafty. When the father was about to die, he called them before him and said: "I have only two things of value—my herd of camels and my blessing. How shall I allot them?"

"Give to me," said the Younger Son, "thy blessing, for it may reform me. The camels I should be sure to sell and squander the money."

The Elder Son, disguising his joy, said that he would try to be content with the camels and a pious mind.

It was so arranged and the Man died. Then the wicked Younger Son went before the Cadi and said: "Behold, my brother has defrauded me of my lawful heritage. He is so bad that our father, as is well known, denied him his blessing; is it likely that he gave him the camels?"

So the Elder Son was compelled to give up the herd and was soundly bastinadoed for his rapacity.

The Eligible Son-in-Law

A Truly Clever Person who conducted a savings bank and lent money to his sisters and his cousins and his aunts was approached by a Tatterdemalion who applied for a loan of one hundred thousand dollars.

"What security have you to offer?" asked the Truly Clever Person.

"The best in the world," the applicant replied, confidentially; "I am about to become your son-in-law."

"That would indeed be gilt-edged," said the Banker, gravely; "but what claim have you to the hand of my daughter?"

"One that cannot be lightly denied," said the Tatterdemalion. "I am about to become worth one hundred thousand dollars."

Unable to detect a weak point in this scheme of mutual advantage, the Financier gave the Promoter in Disguise an order for the money and wrote a note to his wife directing her to count out the girl.

Moral Principle and Material Interest

A Moral Principle met a Material Interest on a bridge wide enough for but one.

"Down, you base thing!" thundered the Moral Principle, "and let me pass over you!"

The Material Interest merely looked in the other's eyes without saying anything.

"Ah," said the Moral Principle, hesitatingly, "let us draw lots to see which one of us shall retire till the other has crossed."

The Material Interest maintained an unbroken silence and an unwavering stare.

"In order to avoid a conflict," the Moral Principle resumed, somewhat uneasily, "I shall myself lie down and let you walk over me."

Then the Material Interest found his tongue. "I don't think you are very good walking," he said. "I am a little particular about what I have underfoot. Suppose you get off into the water."

It occurred that way.

1899

FROM

The Cynic's Word Book

Definitions

ABSURDITY, *n.* A statement or belief manifestly inconsistent with one's own opinion.

AIR, *n.* A nutritious substance supplied by a bountiful Providence for the fattening of the poor.

COMFORT, *n.* A state of mind produced by contemplation of a neighbor's uneasiness.

CYNIC, *n.* A blackguard whose faulty vision sees things as they are, not as they ought to be. Hence the custom among the Scythians of plucking out a cynic's eyes to improve his vision.

DUTY, *n.* That which sternly impels us in the direction of profit, along the line of desire.

> Sir Lavender Portwine, in favor at court,
> Was wroth at his master, who'd kissed Lady Port.
> His anger provoked him to take the king's head,
> But duty prevailed, and he took the king's bread,
>   Instead.
>
>   G. J.

FUTURE, *n.* That period of time in which our affairs prosper, our friends are true, and our happiness is assured.

HISTORIAN, *n.* A broad-gauge gossip.

I is the first letter of the alphabet, the first word of the language, the first thought of the mind, the first object of affection. In grammar it is a pronoun of the first person and singular number. Its plural is said to be *We,* but how there can be more than one myself is doubtless clearer to the grammarians than it is to the author of this incomparable dictionary. Conception of two myselves is difficult, but fine. The frank yet graceful use of "I" distinguishes a good writer from a bad; the latter carries it with the manner of a thief trying to cloak his loot.

IMPUNITY, *n.* Wealth.

KLEPTOMANIAC, *n.* A rich thief.

OCEAN, *n.* A body of water occupying about two-thirds of a world made for man—who has no gills.

PLATITUDE, *n.* The fundamental element and special glory of popular literature. A thought that snores in words that smoke. The wisdom of a million fools in the diction of a dullard. A fossil sentiment in artificial rock. A moral without the fable. All that is mortal of a departed truth. A demitasse of milk-and-morality. The Pope's-nose of a featherless peacock. A jelly-fish withering on the shore of the sea of thought. The cackle surviving the egg. A desiccated epigram.

POSITIVE, *adj.* Mistaken at the top of one's voice.

PRAY, *v.* To ask that the laws of the universe be annulled in behalf of a single petitioner confessedly unworthy.

RADICALISM, *n.* The conservatism of to-morrow injected into the affairs of to-day.

REASON, *v.i.* To weigh probabilities in the scales of desire.

REFLECTION, *n.* An action of the mind whereby we obtain a clearer view of our relation to the things of yesterday and are able to avoid the perils that we shall not again encounter.

RESTITUTION, *n.* The founding or endowing of universities and public libraries by gift or bequest.

1906

JACK LONDON
(1876–1916)

London's career comes straight from a story book, much of which was published as his own semiautobiographical novel, *Martin Eden* (1909). As improbable as his life appears when viewed from the perspective of social conformity, it is curiously American in its constant note of expectation, aspiration, and disillusionment, as well as in its violence and range of experience. London is far beneath the level of Walt Whitman and Mark Twain, but the unifying appeal that makes European audiences see them all as representative national writers is that peculiarly American note.

His father was an astrologer, his mother was a medium, both were itinerants, and London was an illegitimate child. He grew up in the primitive poverty of back alleys, bowling alleys, and saloon alleys. By the time he was eighteen he had been a factory hand, an oyster pirate in San Francisco Bay, had sailed on a sealer to Japan, had "ridden the rods" cross-country, had identified himself with deprived and jobless workers, had been jailed in Buffalo for vagrancy, and had become a Socialist. His thought developed out of the ferment of socialism and Darwinian beliefs (he became a Spencerian evolutionist) at the brawling end of the nineteenth century. The idea of the survival of the superior organism, together with his ego's enormous demand for identification with the American promise of success, created in London a powerful drive for learning and literacy as a way to victory over his circumstances.

He quit the University of California in his freshman year—it was almost the only schooling he ever had—and rushed to the Klondike in 1897 with the other gold hunters. He returned to Oakland, California, the next year and began to write out the materials he had gathered in the north. Given the ideas of the times—the gospel of wealth, and a sense of great dislocation, change, and rags-to-power possibility—the American public was eager to read of the triumphant anarch and to see itself in the rugged individual who, as superman, conquered all. This theme London supplied in the stories he sent to the *Overland Monthly* and the *Atlantic*, stories developed in a crisp style with sensational settings and circumstances. In 1899, after many failures, he began to "hit" the market, and from 1900 to 1916 he achieved enormous success, publishing fifty volumes of novels, short stories, essays, and social criticism. His first collection of stories was *The Son of the Wolf* (1900); this set the patterns of violence, physical necessity, and supermanliness that he was to push to ridiculous extremes in his romantic celebration of the triumphant individual. *The Call of the Wild* (1903), like *The Sea Wolf* (1904) and *White Fang* (1906) among many others, continued his preoccupation with brutality, power, untrammeled self-aggrandizement, and atavism.

Yet, paradoxically, his sense of social injustice—*The Iron Heel* (1908) is one of the most terrifying visions of totalitarianism ever written—aligned him with the dream of the cooperative, socialist society in which no individual is subjugated by any other. London expressed his socialism in *The People of the Abyss* (1903), *War of the Classes* (1905), and *The Human Drift* (1917), but he was never able to reconcile adequately the tensions between individualism and Nietzsche on the one hand, and equality and Marx on the other. As voracious in reading as he was in experiencing life, he was not a thinker able to unite the polar energies of his allegiances. Some of his work is marred by unsatisfactory resolutions of the problems he raises; some of it is harmed by its sensationalism; and much of it is hurt by his frank haste to cash in on his popularity. Yet in a few works, such as *Martin Eden* and *The Call of the Wild*, London remains an important, if secondary, writer, not only for presenting the attitudes of the times and the issues of naturalism, but also for the quality of the work itself.

With his yacht, in which he cruised the South Seas, and his ranch in California, London achieved the class status with which he had early identified the liberation and triumph of the individual. But, as with F. Scott Fitzgerald a few years later, the close view turned the achievement to ashes in his mouth. After alcoholism, unhappy marriages, inconclusive alliances, and painful illnesses, London's life probably ended, like Martin Eden's, in suicide.

In addition to the titles mentioned above, some of London's works are *The Kempton-Wace Letters* (with Anna Strunsky, 1903); *Tales of the Fish Patrol* (1905); *Burning Daylight* (1910); *When God Laughs and Other Stories* (1911); *Adventure* (1911); *The Cruise of the Snark* (1911); *A Son of the Sun* (1912); *Smoke Bellew* (1912); *The Abysmal Brute* (1913); *John Barleycorn* (1913); *The Valley of the Moon* (1913); *The Strength of the Strong* (1914); *The Mutiny of the Elsinore* (1914); and *The Star Rover* (1915).

Editions and accounts of the man and his work are to be found in M. E. Johnson, *Through the South Seas with Jack London* (1913); C. London, *The Log of the Snark* (1915), *The Works of Jack London*, 12 vols. (1917); H. L. Mencken, *Prejudices, First Series* (1919); C. London, *The Book of Jack London*, 2 vols. (1921); *Complete Works of Jack London*, 21 vols. (1926); G. L. Bamford, *The Mystery of Jack London* (1931); J. Gaer, *Jack London* (1934); I. Stone, *Sailor on Horseback* (1938); Joan London, *Jack London and His Times* (1939); J. Noel, *Footloose in Arcadia* (1940); T. K. Whipple, *Study Out the Land* (1943); P. S. Foner, ed., *Jack London: American Rebel* (1947); R. Franchere, *Jack London: The Pursuit of a Dream* (1962); A. S. Shivers, "Romanticism in Jack London," *Dissertation Abstracts* (1962); Jack London and R. L. Fish, *The Assassination Bureau, Ltd.* (1963); A. Calder-Marshall, ed., *The Bodley Head Jack London* (1963–1967); F. Feied, *No Pie in the Sky* (1964); R. O'Connor, *Jack London* (1964); K. Hendricks and I. Shepard, eds., *Letters from Jack London* (1965); the Jack London issue of *American Book Collector*, XVII (Nov., 1966); C. C. Walcutt, *Jack London* (1966); and F. Walker, *Jack London and the Klondike* (1966).

The White Silence

"Carmen won't last more than a couple of days." Mason spat out a chunk of ice and surveyed the poor animal ruefully, then put her foot in his mouth and proceeded to bite out the ice which clustered cruelly between the toes.

"I never saw a dog with a highfalutin' name that ever was worth a rap," he said, as he concluded his task and shoved her aside. "They just fade away and die under the responsibility. Did ye ever see one go wrong with a sensible name like Cassiar, Siwash, or Husky? No, sir! Take a look at Shookum here; he's—"

Snap! The lean brute flashed up, the white teeth just missing Mason's throat.

"Ye will, will ye?" A shrewd clout behind the ear with

the butt of the dogwhip stretched the animal in the snow, quivering softly, a yellow slaver dripping from its fangs.

"As I was saying, just look at Shookum, here—he's got the spirit. Bet ye he eats Carmen before the week's out."

"I'll ˙bank another proposition against that," replied Malemute Kid, reversing the frozen bread placed before the fire to thaw. "We'll eat Shookum before the trip is over. What d' ye say, Ruth?"

The Indian woman settled the coffee with a piece of ice, glanced from Malemute Kid to her husband, then at the dogs, but vouchsafed no reply. It was such a palpable truism that none was necessary. Two hundred miles of unbroken trail in prospect, with a scant six days' grub for themselves and none for the dogs, could admit no other alternative. The two men and the woman grouped about the fire and began their meagre meal. The dogs lay in their harnesses, for it was a midday halt, and watched each mouthful enviously.

"No more lunches after to-day," said Malemute Kid. "And we've got to keep a close eye on the dogs,—they're getting vicious. They'd just as soon pull a fellow down as not, if they get a chance."

"And I was president of an Epworth once, and taught in the Sunday-school." Having irrelevantly delivered himself of this, Mason fell into a dreamy contemplation of his steaming moccasins, but was aroused by Ruth filling his cup. "Thank God, we've got slathers of tea! I've seen it growing, down in Tennessee. What wouldn't I give for a hot corn-pone just now! Never mind, Ruth; you won't starve much longer, nor wear moccasins either."

The woman threw off her gloom at this, and in her eyes welled up a great love for her white lord,—the first white man she had ever seen,—the first man she had known to treat a woman as something better than a mere animal or beast of burden.

"Yes, Ruth," continued her husband, having recourse to the macaronic jargon in which it was alone possible for them to understand each other, "wait till we clean up and pull for the Outside. We'll take the White Man's canoe and go to the Salt Water. Yes, bad water, rough water,— great mountains dance up and down all the time. And so big, so far, so far away,—you travel ten sleep, twenty sleep, forty sleep" (he graphically enumerated the days on his fingers), "all the time water, bad water. Then you come to great village, plenty people, just the same mosquitoes next summer. Wigwams oh, so high,—ten, twenty pines. Hi-yu skookum!"

He paused impotently, cast an appealing glance at Malemute Kid, then laboriously placed the twenty pines, end on end, by sign language. Malemute Kid smiled with cheery cynicism; but Ruth's eyes were wide with wonder, and with pleasure; for she half believed he was joking, and such condescension pleased her poor woman's heart.

"And then you step into a—a box, and pouf! up you go." He tossed his empty cup in the air by way of illustration, and as he deftly caught it, cried: "And biff! down you come. Oh, great medicine-men! You go Fort Yukon, I go Arctic City,—twenty-five sleep,—big string, all the time, —I catch him string,—I say, 'Hello, Ruth! How are ye?' —and you say, 'Is that my good husband?'—and I say 'Yes,'—and you say, 'No can bake good bread, no more soda,'—then I say, 'Look in cache, under flour; good-by.' You look and catch plenty soda. All the time you Fort Yukon, me Arctic City. Hi-yu medicine-man!"

Ruth smiled so ingenuously at the fairy story that both men burst into laughter. A row among the dogs cut short the wonders of the Outside, and by the time the snarling combatants were separated, she had lashed the sleds and all was ready for the trail.

"Mush! Baldy! Hi! Mush on!" Mason worked his whip smartly, and as the dogs whined low in the traces, broke out the sled with the gee-pole. Ruth followed with the second team, leaving Malemute Kid, who had helped her start, to bring up the rear. Strong man, brute that he was, capable of felling an ox at a blow, he could not bear to beat the poor animals, but humored them as a dog-driver rarely does,—nay, almost wept with them in their misery.

"Come, mush on there, you poor sore-footed brutes!" he murmured, after several ineffectual attempts to start the load. But his patience was at last rewarded, and though whimpering with pain, they hastened to join their fellows.

No more conversation; the toil of the trail will not permit such extravagance. And of all deadening labors, that of the Northland trail is the worst. Happy is the man who can weather a day's travel at the price of silence, and that on a beaten track.

And of all heart-breaking labors, that of breaking trail is the worst. At every step the great webbed shoe sinks till the snow is level with the knee. Then up, straight up, the deviation of a fraction of an inch being a certain precursor of disaster, the snowshoe must be lifted till the surface is cleared; then forward, down, and the other foot is raised perpendicularly for the matter of half a yard. He who tries this for the first time, if haply he avoids bringing his shoes in dangerous propinquity and measures not his length on the treacherous footing, will give up exhausted at the end of a hundred yards; he who can keep out of the way of the dogs for a whole day may well crawl into his sleeping-bag with a clear conscience and a pride which passeth all understanding; and he who travels twenty sleeps on the Long Trail is a man whom the gods may envy.

The afternoon wore on, and with the awe, born of the White Silence, the voiceless travellers bent to their work. Nature has many tricks wherewith she convinces man of his finity,—the ceaseless flow of the tides, the fury of the storm, the shock of the earthquake, the long roll of heaven's artillery,—but the most tremendous, the most stupefying of all, is the passive phase of the White Silence. All movement ceases, the sky clears, the heavens are as brass; the slightest whisper seems sacrilege, and man becomes timid, affrighted at the sound of his own voice. Sole speck of life journeying across the ghostly wastes of a dead world, he trembles at his audacity, realizes that his is a maggot's life, nothing more. Strange thoughts arise unsummoned, and the mystery of all things strives for utterance. And the fear of death, of God, of the universe, comes over him,—the hope of the Resurrection and the Life, the yearning for immortality, the vain striving of the imprisoned essence,—it is then, if ever, man walks alone with God.

So wore the day away. The river took a great bend, and Mason headed his team for the cut-off across the narrow neck of land. But the dogs balked at the high bank. Again and again, though Ruth and Malemute Kid were shoving on the sled, they slipped back. Then came the concerted effort. The miserable creatures, weak from hunger, exerted their last strength. Up—up—the sled poised on the top of the bank; but the leader swung the string of dogs behind him to the right, fouling Mason's snowshoes. The result was grievous. Mason was whipped off his feet; one of the dogs fell in the traces; and the sled toppled back, dragging everything to the bottom again.

Slash! the whip fell among the dogs savagely, especially upon the one which had fallen.

"Don't, Mason," entreated Malemute Kid; "the poor devil's on its last legs. Wait and we'll put my team on."

Mason deliberately withheld the whip till the last word had fallen, then out flashed the long lash, completely curling about the offending creature's body. Carmen—for it was Carmen—cowered in the snow, cried piteously, then rolled over on her side.

It was a tragic moment, a pitful incident of the trail,— a dying dog, two comrades in anger. Ruth glanced solicitously from man to man. But Malemute Kid restrained himself, though there was a world of reproach in his eyes, and bending over the dog, cut the traces. No word was spoken. The teams were double-spanned and the difficulty overcome; the sleds were under way again, the dying dog dragging herself along in the rear. As long as an animal can travel, it is not shot, and this last chance is accorded it,—the crawling into camp, if it can, in the hope of a moose being killed.

Already penitent for his angry action, but too stubborn to make amends, Mason toiled on at the head of the cavalcade, little dreaming that danger hovered in the air. The timber clustered thick in the sheltered bottom, and through this they threaded their way. Fifty feet or more from the trail towered a lofty pine. For generations it had stood there, and for generations destiny had had this one end in view,—perhaps the same had been decreed of Mason.

He stooped to fasten the loosened thong of his moccasin. The sleds came to a halt and the dogs lay down in the snow without a whimper. The stillness was weird; not a breath rustled the frost-encrusted forest; the cold and silence of outer space had chilled the heart and smote the trembling lips of nature. A sigh pulsed through the air,—they did not seem to actually hear it, but rather felt it, like the premonition of movement in a motionless void. Then the great tree, burdened with its weight of years and snow, played its last part in the tragedy of life. He heard the warning crash and attempted to spring up, but, almost erect, caught the blow squarely on the shoulder.

The sudden danger, the quick death,—how often had Malemute Kid faced it! The pine-needles were still quivering as he gave his commands and sprang into action. Nor did the Indian girl faint or raise her voice in idle wailing, as might many of her white sisters. At his order, she threw her weight on the end of a quickly extemporized handspike, easing the pressure and listening to her husband's groans, while Malemute Kid attacked the tree with his axe. The steel rang merrily as it bit into the frozen trunk, each stroke being accompanied by a forced, audible respiration, the "Huh!" "Huh!" of the woodsman.

At last the Kid laid the pitiable thing that was once a man in the snow. But worse than his comrade's pain was the dumb anguish in the woman's face, the blended look of hopeful, hopeless query. Little was said; those of the Northland are early taught the futility of words and the inestimable value of deeds. With the temperature at sixty-five below zero, a man cannot lie many minutes in the snow and live. So the sled-lashings were cut, and the sufferer, rolled in furs, laid on a couch of boughs. Before him roared a fire, built of the very wood which wrought the mishap. Behind and partially over him was stretched the primitive fly,—a piece of canvas, which caught the radiating heat and threw it back and down upon him,— a trick which men may know who study physics at the fount.

And men who have shared their bed with death know when the call is sounded. Mason was terribly crushed. The most cursory examination revealed it. His right arm, leg, and back were broken; his limbs were paralyzed from the hips; and the likelihood of internal injuries was large. An occasional moan was his only sign of life.

No hope; nothing to be done. The pitiless night crept slowly by,—Ruth's portion, the despairing stoicism of her race, and Malemute Kid adding new lines to his face of bronze. In fact, Mason suffered least of all, for he spent his time in Eastern Tennessee, in the Great Smoky Mountains, living over the scenes of his childhood. And most pathetic was the melody of his long-forgotten Southern vernacular, as he raved of swimming-holes and coon-hunts and watermelon raids. It was as Greek to Ruth, but the Kid understood and felt,—felt as only one can feel who has been shut out for years from all that civilization means.

Morning brought consciousness to the stricken man, and Malemute Kid bent closer to catch his whispers.

"You remember when we foregathered on the Tanana, four years come next ice-run? I didn't care so much for her then. It was more like she was pretty, and there was a smack of excitement about it, I think. But d'ye know, I've come to think a heap of her. She's been a good wife to me, always at my shoulder in the pinch, And when it comes to trading, you know there isn't her equal. D' ye recollect the time she shot the Moosehorn Rapids to pull you and me off that rock, the bullets whipping the water like hailstones?—and the time of the famine at Nukluk-yeto?—or when she raced the ice-run to bring the news? Yes, she's been a good wife to me, better 'n that other one. Didn't know I'd been there? Never told you, eh? Well, I tried it once, down in the States. That's why I'm here. Been raised together, too. I came away to give her a chance for divorce. She got it.

"But that's got nothing to do with Ruth. I had thought of cleaning up and pulling for the Outside next year,— her and I,—but it's too late. Don't send her back to her people, Kid. It's beastly hard for a woman to go back. Think of it!—nearly four years on our bacon and beans and flour and dried fruit, and then to go back to her fish and cariboo. It's not good for her to have tried our ways, to come to know they're better n' her people's, and then return to them. Take care of her, Kid,—why don't you, —but no, you always fought shy of them,—and you never told me why you came to this country. Be kind to her, and send her back to the States as soon as you can. But fix it so as she can come back,—liable to get homesick, you know.

"And the youngster—it's drawn us closer, Kid. I only hope it is a boy. Think of it!—flesh of my flesh, Kid. He mustn't stop in this country. And if it's a girl, why she can't. Sell my furs; they'll fetch at least five thousand, and I've got as much more with the company. And handle my interest with yours. I think that bench claim will show up. See that he gets a good schooling; and Kid, above all, don't let him come back. This country was not made for white men.

"I'm a gone man, Kid. Three or four sleeps at the best. You've got to go on. You must go on! Remember, it's my wife, it's my boy,—O God! I hope it's a boy! You can't stay by me,—and I charge you, a dying man, to pull on."

"Give me three days," pleaded Malemute Kid. "You may change for the better; something may turn up."

"No."

"Just three days."

"You must pull on."

"Two days."

"It's my wife and my boy, Kid. You would not ask it."

"One day."

"No, no! I charge—"

"Only one day. We can shave it through on the grub, and I might knock over a moose."

"No,—all right; one day, but not a minute more. And Kid, don't—don't leave me to face it alone. Just a shot, one pull on the trigger. You understand. Think of it! Think of it! Flesh of my flesh, and I'll never live to see him!

"Send Ruth here. I want to say good-by and tell her that she must think of the boy and not wait till I'm dead. She might refuse to go with you if I didn't. Good-by, old man; good-by.

"Kid! I say—a—sink a hole above the pup, next to the slide. I panned out forty cents on my shovel there.

"And Kid!" he stooped lower to catch the last faint words, the dying man's surrender of his pride. "I'm sorry —for—you know—Carmen."

Leaving the girl crying softly over her man, Malemute Kid slipped into his *parka* and snowshoes, tucked his rifle under his arm, and crept away into the forest. He was no tyro in the stern sorrows of the Northland, but never had he faced so stiff a problem as this. In the abstract, it was a plain, mathematical proposition,—three possible lives as against one doomed one. But now he hesitated. For five years, shoulder to shoulder, on the rivers and trails, in the camps and mines, facing death by field and flood and famine, had they knitted the bonds of their comradeship. So close was the tie, that he had often been conscious of a vague jealousy of Ruth from the first time she had come between. And now it must be severed by his own hand.

Though he prayed for a moose, just one moose, all

game seemed to have deserted the land, and nightfall found the exhausted man crawling into camp, light-handed, heavy-hearted. An uproar from the dogs and shrill cries from Ruth hastened him.

Bursting into the camp, he saw the girl in the midst of the snarling pack, laying about her with an axe. The dogs had broken the iron rule of their masters and were rushing the grub. He joined the issue with his rifle reversed, and the hoary game of natural selection was played out with all the ruthlessness of its primeval environment. Rifle and axe went up and down, hit or missed with monotonous regularity; lithe bodies flashed, with wild eyes and dripping fangs; and man and beast fought for supremacy to the bitterest conclusion. Then the beaten brutes crept to the edge of the firelight, licking their wounds, voicing their misery to the stars.

The whole stock of dried salmon had been devoured, and perhaps five pounds of flour remained to tide them over two hundred miles of wilderness. Ruth returned to her husband, while Malemute Kid cut up the warm body of one of the dogs, the skull of which had been crushed by the axe. Every portion was carefully put away, save the hide and offal, which were cast to his fellows of the moment before.

Morning brought fresh trouble. The animals were turning on each other. Carmen, who still clung to her slender thread of life, was downed by the pack. The lash fell among them unheeded. They cringed and cried under the blows, but refused to scatter till the last wretched bit had disappeared,—bones, hide, hair, everything.

Malemute Kid went about his work, listening to Mason, who was back in Tennessee, delivering tangled discourses and wild exhortations to his brethren of other days.

Taking advantage of neighboring pines, he worked rapidly, and Ruth watched him make a cache similar to those sometimes used by hunters to preserve their meat from the wolverines and dogs. One after the other, he bent the tops of two small pines toward each other and nearly to the ground, making them fast with thongs of moosehide. Then he beat the dogs into submission and harnessed them to two of the sleds, loading the same with everything but the furs which enveloped Mason. These he wrapped and lashed tightly about him, fastening either end of the robes to the bent pines. A single stroke of his hunting-knife would release them and send the body high in the air.

Ruth had received her husband's last wishes and made no struggle. Poor girl, she had learned the lesson of obedience well. From a child, she had bowed, and seen all women bow, to the lords of creation, and it did not seem in the nature of things for woman to resist. The Kid permitted her one outburst of grief, as she kissed her husband,—her own people had no such custom,—then led her to the foremost sled and helped her into her snowshoes. Blindly, instinctively, she took the gee-pole and whip, and "mushed" the dogs out on the trail. Then he returned to Mason, who had fallen into a coma; and long after she was out of sight, crouched by the fire, waiting, hoping, praying for his comrade to die.

It is not pleasant to be alone with painful thoughts in the White Silence. The silence of gloom is merciful, shrouding one as with protection and breathing a thousand intangible sympathies; but the bright White Silence, clear and cold, under steely skies, is pitiless.

An hour passed,—two hours,—but the man would not die. At high noon, the sun, without raising its rim above the southern horizon, threw a suggestion of fire athwart the heavens, then quickly drew it back. Malemute Kid roused and dragged himself to his comrade's side. He cast one glance about him. The White Silence seemed to sneer, and a great fear came upon him. There was a sharp report; Mason swung into his aerial sepulchre; and Malemute Kid lashed the dogs into a wild gallop as he fled across the snow.

1900

HAMLIN GARLAND

(1860–1940)

Garland was reared in circumstances that forced him to a first-hand recognition of the distance between the national image of the western lands as promise and fulfillment on the one hand and a much grimmer actuality on the other. His father stubbornly clung to the idea of the fortune yet to be made on the border farm and, faithful to the promissory note of America, emigrated from Maine to West Salem, Wisconsin, where Garland was born. The fortune never materialized, and the family moved to northeastern Iowa, where Garland lived for twelve years, attending the Cedar Valley Seminary. Still seeking, the family moved to Ordway, South Dakota; but instead of fortune, the Garlands met with toil, dullness, and the hostility of nature. Wanting to teach and to escape his environment, Hamlin sold his Dakota claim at a small profit and became one of the "back-trailers from the middle border" in fleeing to Boston. His movement from west to east was significant: although the national mind insisted that the land of the "folk" and of democratic realization lay westward, and that the east was effete, artificial and aristocratic, many nevertheless sought the very kind of life that the American was supposed to spurn. The split in perception, the double goals in Garland, are not merely personal but are typical of many American men of letters.

In Boston he lived alone and struggled to find a new life. He educated himself in the Boston public library and studied and taught in the Boston School of Oratory, all the while trying to write. He read in evolutionary thought popularized by Spencer, in Henry George's single-tax economics, and in the contemporary arguments raging about the issues of realism and impressionism in fiction. In 1887 he returned to the Midwest for a visit and saw with new perspective the treeless prairies, the unremittingly brutalizing toil, and the frontier's murderous effect on his parents. Enraged, he returned East and began to contribute stories to B. O. Flower's influential *Arena*. Encouraged by Joseph Kirkland, Flower, and William Dean Howells, he attempted to create "veritism" in fiction—a realism that would not stop short with accepted subjects and attitudes, but would also include the less pretty experiences that had led to his disenchantment. In 1891 he published *Main-Travelled Roads;* in the heat of his experience, he had written all the stories in this volume between 1887 and 1889. *Other Main-Travelled Roads* (1910) was, in turn, a collection made up out of *Prairie Folks* (1893) and *Wayside Courtships* (1897); these, too, consisted of stories written in the short, fruitful period. With the exception of *A Son of the Middle Border* (1917), none of his later books comes up to the strength and quality of his first collection. His impulse for reform was clearly seen in political novels and novels of protest such as the four he published in 1892—*Jason Edwards, A Little Norsk, A Member of the Third House,* and *A Spoil of Office.*

In 1894 he collected his literary rebellions and visions in *Crumbling Idols,* and published his grim *Rose of Dutcher's Coolly* in the following year. But after *Wayside Courtships* his fiction became more and more sentimental and romantic as he began to lose touch with the early anger of his writing and as success began to mellow experience in the rosy eye of retrospect. By the end of the century he was, as he himself said, "a club joiner and carpenter." Although he deplored the increasing debilitation of American public taste, he contributed to it with his books of supernaturalism, sensationalism, and celebration of a romanticized rugged-individual pioneer that was the obverse side of the coin of his early anger. Indeed, he was basically more romanticizer than rebel. He explained, in his discussion of "veritism," that the writer's propagandistic function is to show ugliness only in order to sigh for the beauty that is not but will be. As his own life became softer, that idealized and idealizing beauty seemed to settle sentimentally over his present and his past.

He absolved himself from the guilt he felt at abandoning the "good fight" by purchasing the old homestead for his mother, though he himself preferred Boston, Chicago, New York, and, from 1930 on, Los Angeles. Although most of his work has been relegated to a secondary position in American letters, the early work and the "middle border" series will remain Garland's valid claim to at least a small portion of American literary recognition. The latter includes *A Son of the Middle Border*, the semiautobiographical account of his own youth; *A Daughter of the Middle Border* (1921), the account of his wife's family and of the Garland career to World War I; *Trailmakers of the Middle Border* (1926), the account of the beginnings, the westward pioneering; and *Back-Trailers from the Middle Border* (1928), the account of Garland's final return to the East from which the fathers had come.

In addition to the titles mentioned above, some of Garland's works are *Boy Life on the Prairie* (1899); *The Captain of the Gray Horse Troop* (1902); *Hesper* (1903); *Cavanagh, Forest Ranger* (1910); *Roadside Meetings* (1930); *Companions on the Trail* (1931); *My Friendly Contemporaries* (1932); and *Forty Years of Psychic Research* (1936). There is no collected edition of Garland's works.

Accounts of the man and his work are to be found in C. Van Doren, *Contemporary American Novelists* (1922); F. L. Pattee, *The Development of the American Short Story* (1923); V. L. Parrington, *Main Currents in American Thought*, III (1930); A. H. Quinn, *American Fiction* (1936); F. B. Millett, *Contemporary American Authors* (1940); C. Van Doren, *The American Novel, 1789–1939* (1940); W. F. Taylor, *The Economic Novel in American Fiction* (1950); C. Walcutt, *American Literary Naturalism* (1956); J. Holloway, *Hamlin Garland* (1960); D. Piser, *Hamlin Garland's Early Work and Career* (1960); L. A. Arvidson, *Centennial Tributes and a Checklist of the Hamlin Garland Papers* (1962); R. E. Labrie, "American Naturalism," *Dissertation Abstracts* (1965).

Under the Lion's Paw

It was the last of autumn and first day of winter coming together. All day long the plowmen on their prairie farms had moved to and fro in their wide level fields through the falling snow, which melted as it fell, wetting them to the skin—all day, notwithstanding the frequent squalls of snow, the dripping, desolate clouds, and the muck of the furrows, black and tenacious as tar.

Under their dripping harness the horses swung to and fro silently, with that marvelous uncomplaining patience which marks the horse. All day the wild geese, honking wildly, as they sprawled sidewise down the wind, seemed to be fleeing from an enemy behind, and with neck out-thrust and wings extended, sailed down the wind, soon lost to sight.

Yet the plowman behind his plow, though the snow lay on his ragged great-coat, and the cold clinging mud rose on his heavy boots, fettering him like gyves, whistled in the very beard of the gale. As day passed, the snow, ceasing to melt, lay along the plowed land, and lodged in the depth of the stubble, till on each slow round the last furrow stood out black and shining as jet between the plowed land and the gray stubble.

When night began to fall, and the geese, flying low, be-gan to alight invisibly in the near corn-field, Stephen Council was still at work "finishing a land." He rode on his sulky plow when going with the wind, but walked when facing it. Sitting bent and cold but cheery under his slouch hat, he talked encouragingly to his four-in-hand.

"Come round there, boys!—Round agin! We got t' finish this land. Come in there, Dan! *Stiddy*, Kate,—stiddy! None o' y'r tantrums, Kittie. It's purty tuff, but got a be did. *Tchk! tchk!* Step along, Pete! Don't let Kate git y'r single-tree on the wheel. *Once* more!"

They seemed to know what he meant, and that this was the last round, for they worked with greater vigor than before.

"Once more, boys, an' then, sez I, oats an' a nice warm stall, an' sleep f'r all."

By the time the last furrow was turned on the land it was too dark to see the house, and the snow was changing to rain again. The tired and hungry man could see the light from the kitchen shining through the leafless hedge, and he lifted a great shout, "Supper f'r a half a dozen!"

It was nearly eight o'clock by the time he had finished his chores and started for supper. He was picking his way carefully through the mud, when the tall form of a man loomed up before him with a premonitory cough.

"Waddy ye want?" was the rather startled question of the farmer.

"Well, ye see," began the stranger, in a deprecating tone. "we'd like t' git in f'r the night. We've tried every house f'r the last two miles, but they hadn't any room f'r us. My wife's jest about sick, 'n' the children are cold and hungry——"

"Oh, y' want 'o stay all night, eh?"

"Yes, sir; it 'ud be a great accom——"

"Wall, I don't make it a practice t' turn anybuddy way hungry, not on sech nights as this. Drive right in. We ain't got much, but sech as it is——"

But the stranger had disappeared. And soon his steaming, weary team, with drooping heads and swinging singletrees, moved past the well to the block beside the path. Council stood at the side of the "schooner" and helped the children out—two little half-sleeping children—and then a small woman with a babe in her arms.

"There ye go!" he shouted jovially, to the children. "*Now* we're all right! Run right along to the house there, an' tell Mam' Council you wants sumpthin' t' eat. Right this way, Mis'—keep right off t' the right there. I'll go an' git a lantern. Come," he said to the dazed and silent group at his side.

"Mother," he shouted, as he neared the fragrant and warmly lighted kitchen, "here are some wayfarers an' folks who need sumpthin' t' eat an' a place t' snooze." He ended by pushing them all in.

Mrs. Council, a large, jolly, rather coarse-looking woman, took the children in her arms. "Come right in, you little rabbits. 'Most asleep, hey? Now here's a drink o' milk f'r each o' ye. I'll have s'm tea in a minute. Take off y'r things and set up t' the fire."

While she set the children to drinking milk, Council got out his lantern and went out to the barn to help the stranger about his team, where his loud, hearty voice could be heard as it came and went between the haymow and the stalls.

The woman came to light as a small, timid, and discouraged-looking woman, but still pretty, in a thin and sorrowful way.

"Land sakes! An' you've traveled all the way from Clear Lake t'-day in this mud! Waal! waal! No wonder you're all tired out. Don't wait f'r the men, Mis'——" She hesitated, waiting for the name.

"Haskins."

"Mis' Haskins, set right up to the table an' take a good swig o' tea whilst I make y' s'm toast. It's green tea, an' it's good. I tell Council as I git older I don't seem to enjoy Young Hyson n'r Gunpowder. I want the reel green tea, jest as it comes off'n the vines. Seems t'have more heart in it, some way. Don't s'pose it has. Council says it's all in m' eye." Going on in this easy way, she soon had the children filled with bread and milk and the woman thoroughly at home, eating some toast and sweet-melon pickles, and sipping the tea.

"See the little rats!" she laughed at the children. "They're full as they can stick now, and they want to go to bed. Now, don't git up, Mis' Haskins; set right where you are an' let me look after 'em. I know all about young ones, though I'm all alone now. Jane went an' married last fall. But, as I tell Council, it's lucky we keep our health. Set right there, Mis' Haskins; I won't have you stir a finger."

It was an unmeasured pleasure to sit there in the warm, homely kitchen, the jovial chatter of the housewife driving out and holding at bay the growl of the impotent, cheated wind.

The little woman's eyes filled with tears which fell down upon the sleeping baby in her arms. The world was not so desolate and cold and hopeless, after all.

"Now I hope Council won't stop out there and talk politics all night. He's the greatest man to talk politics an' read the *Tribune*—How old is it?"

She broke off and peered down at the face of the babe.

"Two months 'n' five days," said the mother, with a mother's exactness.

"Ye don't say! I want 'o know! The dear little pudzy-wudzy!" she went on, stirring it up in the neighborhood of the ribs with her fat forefinger. "Pooty tough on 'oo to go galivant'n' 'cross lots this way——"

"Yes, that's so; a man can't lift a mountain," said Council, entering the door. "Mother, this is Mr. Haskins, from Kansas. He's been eat up 'n' drove out by grasshoppers."

"Glad t' see yeh!—Pa, empty that wash-basin 'n' give him a chance t' wash."

Haskins was a tall man, with a thin, gloomy face. His hair was a reddish brown, like his coat, and seemed equally faded by the wind and sun, and his sallow face, though hard and set, was pathetic somehow. You would have felt that he had suffered much by the line of his mouth showing under his thin, yellow mustache.

"Hain't Ike got home yet, Sairy?"

"Hain't seem 'im."

"W-a-a-l, set right up, Mr. Haskins; wade right into what we've got; 'tain't much, but we manage to live on it—she gits fat on it," laughed Council, pointing his thumb at his wife.

After supper, while the women put the children to bed, Haskins and Council talked on, seated near the huge cook-ing-stove, the steam rising from their wet clothing. In the Western fashion Council told as much of his own life as he drew from his guest. He asked but few questions, but by and by the story of Haskins' struggles and defeat came out. The story was a terrible one, but he told it quietly, seated with his elbows on his knees, gazing most of the time at the hearth.

"I didn't like the looks of the country, anyhow," Haskins said, partly rising and glancing at his wife. "I was ust t' northern Ingyannie, where we have lots o' timber 'n' lots o' rain, 'n' I didn't like the looks o' that dry prairie. What galled me the worst was goin' s' far away acrosst so much fine land layin' all through here vacant."

"And the 'hoppers eat ye four years, hand runnin', did they?"

"Eat! They wiped us out. They chawed everything that was green. They jest set around waitin' f'r us to die t' eat us, too. My God! I ust t' dream of 'em sittin' 'round on the bedpost, six feet long, workin' their jaws. They eet the fork-handles. They got worse 'n' worse till they jest rolled on one another, piled up like snow in winter. Well, it ain't no use. If I was t' talk all winter I couldn't tell nawthin'. But all the while I couldn't help thinkin' of all that land back here that nobuddy was usin' that I ought 'o had 'stead o' bein' out there in that cussed country."

"Waal, why didn't ye stop an' settle here?" asked Ike, who had come in and was eating his supper.

"Fer the simple reason that you fellers wantid ten 'r fifteen dollars an acre fer the bare land, and I hadn't no money fer that kind o' thing."

"Yes, I do my own work," Mrs. Council was heard to say in the pause that followed. "I'm a-gettin' purty heavy t' be on m' laigs all day, but we can't afford t' hire, so I keep rackin' around somehow, like a foundered horse. S' lame— I tell Council he can't tell how lame I am, f'r I'm jest as lame in one laig as t' other." And the good soul laughed at the joke on herself as she took a handful of flour and dusted the biscuit-board to keep the dough from sticking.

"Well, I hain't *never* been very strong," said Mrs. Haskins. "Our folks was Canadians an' small-boned, and then since my last child I hain't got up again fairly. I don't like t' complain. Tim has about all he can bear now—but they was days this week when I jes wanted to lay right down an' die."

"Waal, now, I'll tell ye," said Council, from his side of the stove, silencing everybody with his good-natured roar, "I'd go down and *see* Butler, *anyway*, if I was you. I guess he'd let you have his place purty cheap; the farm's all run down. He's ben anxious t' let t' somebuddy next year. It 'ud be a good chance fer you. Anyhow, you go to bed and sleep like a babe. I've got some plowin' t' do, anyhow, an' we'll see if somethin' can't be done about your case. Ike, you go out an' see if the horses is all right, an' I'll show the folks t' bed."

When the tired husband and wife were lying under the generous quilts of the spare bed, Haskins listened a moment to the wind in the eaves, and then said, with a slow and solemn tone, "There are people in this world who are good enough t' be angels, an' only haff t' die to *be* angels."

II

Jim Butler was one of those men called in the West "land poor." Early in the history of Rock River he had come into the town and started in the grocery business in a small way, occupying a small building in a mean part of the town. At this period of his life he earned all he got, and was up early and late sorting beans, working over butter, and carting his goods to and from the station. But a change came over him at the end of the second year, when he sold a lot of land for four times what he paid for it. From that time forward he believed in land speculation as the surest way of getting rich. Every cent he could save or spare from his trade he put into land at forced sale, or mortgages on land, which were "just as good as the wheat," he was accustomed to say.

Farm after farm fell into his hands, until he was recognized as one of the leading land-owners of the county. His mortgages were scattered all over Cedar County, and as they slowly but surely fell in he sought usually to retain the former owner as tenant.

He was not ready to foreclose; indeed, he had the name of being one of the "easiest" men in the town. He let the debtor off again and again, extending the time whenever possible.

"I don't want y'r land," he said. "All I'm after is the int'rest on my money—that's all. Now, if y' want 'o stay on the farm, why, I'll give y' a good chance. I can't have the land layin' vacant." And in many cases the owner remained as tenant.

In the meantime he had sold his store; he couldn't spend time in it; he was mainly occupied now with sitting around town on rainy days smoking and "gassin' with the boys," or in riding to and from his farms. In fishing-time he fished a good deal. Doc Grimes, Ben Ashley, and Cal Cheatham were his cronies on these fishing excursions or hunting trips in the time of chickens or partridges. In winter they went to Northern Wisconsin to shoot deer.

In spite of all these signs of easy life Butler persisted in saying he "hadn't enough money to pay taxes on his land," and was careful to convey the impression that he was poor in spite of his twenty farms. At one time he was said to be worth fifty thousand dollars, but land had been a little slow of sale of late, so that he was not worth so much.

A fine farm, known as the Higley place, had fallen into his hands in the usual way the previous year, and he had not been able to find a tenant for it. Poor Higley, after working himself nearly to death on it in the attempt to lift the mortgage, had gone off to Dakota, leaving the farm and his curse to Butler. This was the farm which Council advised Haskins to apply for; and the next day Council hitched up his team and drove down town to see Butler.

"You jest let *me* do the talkin'," he said. "We'll find him wearin' out his pants on some salt barrel somew'ers; and if he thought you *wanted* a place he'd sock it to you hot and heavy. You jest keep quiet; I'll fix 'im."

Butler was seated in Ben Ashley's store telling fish yarns when Council sauntered in casually.

"Hello, But; lyin' agin, hey!"

"Hello, Steve! how goes it?"

"Oh, so-so. Too dang much rain these days. I thought it was goin' t' freeze up f'r good last night. Tight squeak if I get m' plowin' done. How's farmin' with *you* these days?"

"Bad. Plowin' ain't half done."

"It 'ud be a religious idee f'r you t' go out an' take a hand y'rself."

"I don't haff to," said Butler, with a wink.

"Got anybody on the Higley place?"

"No. Know anybody?"

"Waal, no; not eggsackly. I've got a relation back t' Michigan who's ben hot an' cold on the idee o' comin' West f'r some time. *Might* come if he could get a good layout. What do you talk on the farm?"

"Well, I d'know. I'll rent it on shares or I'll rent it money rent."

"Wall, how much money, say?"

"Well, say ten per cent, on the price—two-fifty."

"Wall, that ain't bad. Wait on 'im till 'e thrashes?"

Haskins listened eagerly to his important question, but Council was coolly eating a dried apple which he had speared out of a barrel with his knife. Butler studied him carefully.

"Well, knocks me out of twenty-five dollars interest."

"My relation'll need all he's got t' git his crops in," said Council, in the safe, indifferent way.

"Well, all right; *say* wait," concluded Butler.

"All right; this is the man. Haskins, this is Mr. Butler—no relation to Ben—the hardest-working man in Cedar County."

On the way home Haskins said: "I ain't much better off. I'd like that farm; it's a good farm, but it's all run down, an' so 'm I. I could make a good farm of it if I had half a show. But I can't stock it n'r seed it."

"Wall, now, don't you worry," roared Council in his ear. "We'll pull y' through somehow till next harvest. He's agreed t' hire it plowed, an' you can earn a hundred dollars plowin' an' y' c'n git the seed o' me, an' pay me back when y' can."

Haskins was silent with emotion, but at last he said, "I ain't got nothin' t' live on."

"Now, don't you worry 'bout that. You jest make your headquarters at ol' Steve Council's. Mother'll take a pile o' comfort in havin' y'r wife an' children 'round. Y' see, Jane's married off lately, an' Ike's away a good 'eal, so we'll be darn glad t' have y' stop with us this winter. Nex' spring we'll see if y' can't git a start agin." And he chirruped to the team, which sprang forward with the rumbling, clattering wagon.

"Say, looky here, Council, you can't do this. I never saw—" shouted Haskins in his neighbor's ear.

Council moved about uneasily in his seat and stopped his stammering gratitude by saying: "Hold on now: don't make such a fuss over a little thing. When I see a man down, an' things all on top of'm, I jest like t' kick 'em off an' help 'm up. That's the kind of religion I got, an' it's about the *only* kind."

They rode the rest of the way home in silence. And when the red light of the lamp shone out into the darkness of the cold and windy night, and he thought of this refuge for his children and wife, Haskins could have put his arm around the neck of his burly companion and squeezed him like a lover. But he contented himself with saying, "Steve Council, you'll git y'r pay f'r this some day."

"Don't want any pay. My religion ain't run on such business principles."

The wind was growing colder, and the ground was covered with a white frost, as they turned into the gate of the Council farm, and the children came rushing out, shouting, "Papa's come!" They hardly looked like the same children who had sat at the table the night before. Their torpidity, under the influence of sunshine and Mother Council, had given way to a sort of spasmodic cheerfulness, as insects in winter revive when laid on the hearth.

III

Haskins worked like a fiend, and his wife, like the heroic woman that she was, bore also uncomplainingly the most terrible burdens. They rose early and toiled without intermission till the darkness fell on the plain, then tumbled into bed, every bone and muscle aching with fatigue, to rise with the sun next morning to the same round of the same ferocity of labor.

The eldest boy drove a team all through the spring, plowing and seeding, milked the cows, and did chores innumerable, in most ways taking the place of a man.

An infinitely pathetic but common figure, this boy on the American farm, where there is no law against child labor.

To see him in his coarse clothing, his huge boots, and his ragged cap, as he staggered with a pail of water from the well, or trudged in the cold and cheerless dawn out into the frosty field behind his team, gave the city-bred visitor a sharp pang of sympathetic pain. Yet Haskins loved his boy, and would have saved him from this if he could, but he could not.

By June the first year the result of such Herculean toil began to show on the farm. The yard was cleaned up and sown to grass, the garden plowed and planted, and the house mended.

Council had given them four of his cows.

"Take 'em an' run 'em on shares. I don't want 'o milk s' many. Ike's away s' much now, Sat'd'ys an' Sund'ys, I can't stand the bother anyhow."

Other men, seeing the confidence of Council in the new-comer, had sold him tools on time; and as he was really an able farmer, he soon had round him many evidences of his care and thrift. At the advice of Council he had taken the farm for three years, with the privilege of re-renting or buying at the end of the term.

"It's a good bargain, an' y' want 'o nail it," said Council. "If you have any kind ov a crop, you c'n pay y'r debts, an' keep seed an' bread."

The new hope which now sprang up in the heart of Haskins and his wife grew great almost as a pain by the time the wide field of wheat began to wave and swirl in the winds of July. Day after day he would snatch a few moments after supper to go and look at it.

"Have ye seen the wheat t'-day, Nettie?" he asked one night as he rose from supper.

"No, Tim, I ain't had time."

"Well, take time now. Le's go look at it."

She threw an old hat on her head—Tommy's hat—and looking almost pretty in her thin, sad way, went out with her husband to the hedge.

"Ain't it grand, Nettie? Just look at it."

It was grand. Level, russet here and there, heavy-headed, wide as a lake, and full of multitudinous whispers and gleams of wealth, it stretched away before the gazers like the fabled field of the cloth of gold.

"Oh, I think—I *hope* we'll have a good crop, Tim; and oh, how good the people have been to us!"

"Yes; I don't know where we'd be t'-day if it hadn't ben f'r Council and his wife."

"They're the best people in the world," said the little woman, with a great sob of gratitude.

"We'll be in the field on Monday, sure," said Haskins, gripping the rail on the fence as if already at the work of the harvest.

The harvest came, bounteous, glorious, but the winds came and blew it into tangles, and the rain matted it here and there close to the ground, increasing the work of gathering it threefold.

Oh, how they toiled in those glorious days! Clothing dripping with sweat, arms aching, filled with briers, fingers raw and bleeding, backs broken with the weight of heavy bundles, Haskins and his man toiled on. Tommy drove the harvester, while his father and a hired man bound on the machine. In this way they cut ten acres every day, and almost every night after supper, when the hand went to bed, Haskins returned to the field shocking the bound grain in the light of the moon. Many a night he worked till his anxious wife came out at ten o'clock to call him in to rest and lunch.

At the same time she cooked for the men, took care of the children, washed and ironed, milked the cows at night, made the butter, and sometimes fed the horses and watered them while her husband kept at the shocking.

No slave in the Roman galleys could have toiled so frightfully and lived, for this man thought himself a free man, and that he was working for his wife and babes.

When he sank into his bed with a deep groan of relief, too tired to change his grimy, dripping clothing, he felt that he was getting nearer and nearer to a home of his own, and pushing the wolf of want a little farther from his door.

There is no despair so deep as the despair of a homeless man or woman. To roam the roads of the country or the streets of the city, to feel there is no rood of ground on which the feet can rest, to halt weary and hungry outside lighted windows and hear laughter and song within,—these are the hungers and rebellions that drive men to crime and women to shame.

It was the memory of this homelessness, and the fear of its coming again, that spurred Timothy Haskins and Nettie, his wife, to such ferocious labor during that first year.

IV

" 'M, yes; 'm, yes; first rate," said Butler, as his eye took in the neat garden, the pigpen, and the well-filled barnyard. "You're gitt'n' quite a stock around yeh. Done well, eh?"

Haskins was showing Butler around the place. He had not seen it for a year, having spent the year in Washington and Boston with Ashley, his brother-in-law, who had been elected to Congress.

"Yes, I've laid out a good deal of money durin' the last three years. I've paid out three hundred dollars f'r fencin'."

"Um—h'm! I see, I see," said Butler while Haskins went on:

"The kitchen there costs two hundred; the barn ain't cost much in money, but I've put a lot o' time on it. I've dug a new well, and I——"

"Yes, yes, I see. You've done well. Stock worth a thousand dollars," said Butler, picking his teeth with a straw.

"About that," said Haskins, modestly. "We begin to feel 's if we was gitt'n a home f'r ourselves; but we've worked hard. I tell you we begin to feel it, Mr. Butler, and we're goin' t' begin to ease up purty soon. We've been kind o' plannin' a trip back t' *her* folks after the fall plowin's done."

"*Eggs*-actly!" said Butler, who was evidently thinking of something else. "I suppose you've kind o' calc'lated on stayin' here three years more?"

"Well, yes. Fact is, I think I c'n buy the farm this fall, if you'll give me a reasonable show."

"Um—m! What do you call a reasonable show?"

"Well, say a quarter down and three years' time."

Butler looked at the huge stacks of wheat, which filled the yard, over which the chickens were fluttering and crawling, catching grasshoppers, and out of which the crickets were singing innumerably. He smiled in a peculiar way as he said, "Oh, I won't be hard on yeh. But what did you expect to pay f'r the place?"

"Why, about what you offered it for before, two thousand, five hundred, or *possibly* three thousand dollars," he added quickly as he saw the owner shake his head.

"This farm is worth five thousand and five hundred dollars," said Butler, in a careless and decided voice.

"What!" almost shrieked the astounded Haskins. "What's

this? Five thousand? Why that's double what you offered it for three years ago."

"Of course, and it's worth it. It was all run down then; now it's in good shape. You've laid out fifteen hundred dollars in improvements, according to your own story."

"But *you* had nothin' t' do about that. It's my work an' my money."

"You bet it was; but it's my land."

"But what's to pay me for all my——"

"Ain't you had the use of 'em?" replied Butler, smiling calmly into his face.

Haskins was like a man struck on the head with a sand-bag; he couldn't think; he stammered as he tried to say: "But—I never'd git the use— You'd rob me! More'n that: you agreed—you promised that I could buy or rent at the end of three years at——"

"That's all right. But I didn't say I'd let you carry off the improvements, nor that I'd go on renting the farm at two-fifty. The land is doubled in value, it don't matter how; it don't enter into the question; an' now you can pay me five hundred dollars a year rent, or take it on your own terms at fifty-five hundred, or—git out."

He was turning away when Haskins, the sweat pouring from his face, fronted him, saying again:

"But *you've* done nothing to make it so. You hain't added a cent. I put it all there myself, expectin' to buy. I worked an' sweat to improve it. I was workin' for myself an' babes——"

"Well, why didn't you buy when I offered to sell? What y' kickin' about?"

"I'm kickin' about payin' you twice f'r my own things,— my own fences, my own kitchen, my own garden."

Butler laughed. "You're too green t'eat, young feller. *Your* improvements! The law will sing another tune."

"But I trusted your word."

"Never trust anybody, my friend. Besides, I didn't prom-ise not to do this thing. Why, man, don't look at me like that. Don't take me for a thief. It's the law. The reg'lar thing. Everybody does it."

"I don't care if they do. It's stealin' jest the same. You take three thousand dollars of my money—the work o' my hands and my wife's." He broke down at this point. He was not a strong man mentally. He could face hardship, ceaseless toil, but he could not face the cold and sneering face of Butler.

"But I don't take it," said Butler, coolly. "All you've got to do is to go on jest as you've been a-doin', or give me a thousand dollars down, and a mortgage at ten per cent on the rest."

Haskins sat down blindly on a bundle of oats near by, and with staring eyes and drooping head went over the situation. He was under the lion's paw. He felt a horrible numbness in his heart and limbs. He was hid in a mist, and there was no path out.

Butler walked about, looking at the huge stacks of grain, and pulling now and again a few handfuls out, shelling the heads in his hands and blowing the chaff away. He hummed a little tune as he did so. He had an accommodating air of waiting.

Haskins was in the midst of the terrible toil of the last year. He was walking again in the rain and the mud behind his plow; he felt the dust and dirt of the threshing. The ferocious husking-time, with its cutting wind and biting, clinging snows, lay hard upon him. Then he thought of his wife, how she had cheerfully cooked and baked, without holiday and without rest.

"Well, what do you think of it?" inquired the cool, mocking, insinuating voice of Butler.

"I think you're a thief and a liar!" shouted Haskins, leaping up. "A blackhearted houn'!" Butler's smile maddened him; with a sudden leap he caught a fork in his hands, and whirled it in the air. "You'll never rob another man, damn ye!" he grated through his teeth, a look of pitiless ferocity in his accusing eyes.

Butler shrank and quivered, expecting the blow; stood, held hypnotized by the eyes of the man he had a moment before despised—a man transformed into an avenging demon. But in the deadly hush between the lift of the weapon and its fall there came a gush of faint, childish laughter and then across the range of his vision, far away and dim, he saw the sunbright head of his baby girl, as with the pretty, tottering run of a two-year-old, she moved across the grass of the dooryard. His hands relaxed; the fork fell to the ground; his head lowered.

"Make out y'r deed an' mor'gage, an' git off'n my land, an' don't ye never cross my line again; if y' do, I'll kill ye."

Butler backed away from the man in wild haste, and climbing into his buggy with trembling limbs drove off down the road, leaving Haskins seated dumbly on the sunny piles of sheaves, his head sunk into his hands.

1889

FROM

Crumbling Idols

V: Local Color in Art

Local color in fiction is demonstrably the life of fiction. It is the native element, the differentiating element. It corresponds to the endless and vital charm of individual peculiarity. It is the differences which interest us; the similarities do not please, do not forever stimulate and feed as do the differences. Literature would die of dry rot if it chronicled the similarities only, or even largely.

Historically, the local color of a poet or dramatist is of the greatest value. The charm of Horace is the side light he throws on the manners and customs of his time. The vital in Homer lies, after all, in his local color, not in his abstractions. Because the sagas of the North delineate more exactly how men and women lived and wrought in those days, therefore they have always appealed to me with infinitely greater power than Homer.

Similarly, it is the local color of Chaucer that interests us to-day. We yawn over his tales of chivalry which were in the manner of his contemporaries, but the Miller and the Priest interest us. Wherever the man of the past in literature showed us what he really lived and loved, he moves us. We understand him, and we really feel an interest in him.

Historically, local color has gained in beauty and suggestiveness and humanity from Chaucer down to the present day. Each age has embodied more and more of its actual life and social conformation until the differentiating qualities of modern art make the best paintings of Norway as distinct in local color as its fiction is vital and indigenous.

Every great moving literature to-day is full of local color. It is this element which puts the Norwegian and Russian almost at the very summit of modern novel writing, and it is the comparative lack of this distinctive flavor which makes the English and French take a lower place in truth and sincerity.

Everywhere all over the modern European world, men are writing novels and dramas as naturally as the grass or corn or flax grows. The Provençal, the Hun, the Catalonian, the Norwegian, is getting a hearing. This literature is not the literature of scholars; it is the literature of lovers and doers; of men who love the modern and who have not been educated to despise common things.

These men are speaking a new word. They are not hunting themes, they are struggling to express.

Conventional criticism does not hamper or confine them. They are rooted in the soil. They stand among the cornfields and they dig in the peat-bogs. They concern themselves with modern and very present words and themes, and they have brought a new word which is to divide in half the domain of beauty.

They have made art the re-creation of the beautiful *and the significant*. Mere beauty no longer suffices. Beauty is the world-old aristocrat who has taken for mate this mighty young plebeian Significance. Their child is to be the most human and humane literature ever seen.

It has taken the United States longer to achieve independence of English critics than it took to free itself from old-world political and economic rule. Its political freedom was won, not by its gentlemen and scholars, but by its yeomanry; and in the same way our national literature will come in its fulness when the common American rises spontaneously to the expression of his concept of life.

The fatal blight upon most American art has been, and is to-day, its imitative quality, which has kept it characterless and factitious,—a forced rose-culture rather than the free flowering of native plants.

Our writers despised or feared the home market. They rested their immortality upon the "universal theme," which was a theme of no interest to the public and of small interest to themselves.

During the first century and a half, our literature had very little national color. It was quite like the utterance of corresponding classes in England. But at length Bryant and Cooper felt the influence of our mighty forests and prairies. Whittier uttered something of New England boy-life, and Thoreau prodded about among newly discovered wonders, and the American literature got its first start.

Under the influence of Cooper came the stories of wild life from Texas, from Ohio, and from Illinois. The wild, rough settlements could not produce smooth and cultured poems or stories; they only furnished forth rough-and-ready anecdotes, but in these stories there were hints of something fine and strong and native.

As the settlements increased in size, as the pressure of the forest and the wild beast grew less, expression rose to a higher plane; men softened in speech and manner. All preparations were being made for a local literature raised to the level of art.

The Pacific slope was first in the line. By the exceptional interest which the world took in the life of the gold fields, and by the forward urge which seems always to surprise the pessimist and the scholiast, two young men were plunged into that wild life, led across the plains set in the shadow of Mount Shasta, and local literature received its first great marked, decided impetus.

To-day we have in America, at last, a group of writers who have no suspicion of imitation laid upon them. Whatever faults they may be supposed to have, they are at any rate, themselves. American critics can depend upon a characteristic American literature of fiction and the drama from these people.

The corn has flowered, and the cotton-boll has broken into speech.

Local color—what is it? It means that the writer spontaneously reflects the life which goes on around him. It is natural and unstrained art.

It is, in a sense, unnatural and artificial to find an American writing novels of Russia or Spain or the Holy Land. He cannot hope to do it so well as the native. The best he can look for is that poor word of praise, "He does it very well, considering he is an alien."

If a young writer complain that there are no themes at home, that he is forced to go abroad for perspective and romance, I answer there is something wrong in his education or his perceptive faculty. Often he is more anxious to win a money success than to be patiently one of art's unhurried devotees.

I can sympathize with him, however, for criticism has not helped him to be true. Criticism of the formal kind and spontaneous expression are always at war, like the old man and the youth. They may politely conceal it, but they are mutually destructive.

Old men naturally love the past; the books they read are the master-pieces; the great men are all dying off, they say; the young man should treat lofty and universal themes, as they used to do. These localisms are petty. These truths are disturbing. Youth annoys them. Spontaneousness is formlessness, and the criticism that does not call for the abstract and the ideal and the beautiful is leading to destruction, these critics say.

And yet there is a criticism which helps, which tends to keep a writer at his best; but such criticism recognizes the dynamic force of a literature, and tries to spy out tendencies. This criticism to-day sees that local color means national character, and is aiding the young writer to treat his themes in the best art.

I assert it is the most natural thing in the world for a man to love his native land and his native, intimate surroundings. Born into a web of circumstances, enmeshed in common life, the youthful artist begins to think. All the associations of that childhood and the love-life of youth combine to make that web of common affairs, threads of silver and beads of gold; the near-at-hand things are the dearest and sweetest after all.

As the reader will see, I am using local color to mean something more than a forced study of the picturesque scenery of a State.

Local color in a novel means that it has such quality of texture and back-ground that it could not have been written in any other place or by any one else than a native.

It means a statement of life as indigenous as the plant-growth. It means that the picturesque shall not be seen by the author,—that every tree and bird and mountain shall be dear and companionable and necessary, not picturesque; the tourist cannot write the local novel.

From this it follows that local color must not be put in for the sake of local color. It must go in, it *will* go in, because the writer naturally carries it with him half unconsciously, or conscious only of its significance, its interest to him.

He must not stop to think whether it will interest the reader or not. He must be loyal to himself, and put it in because he loves it. If he is an artist, he will make his reader feel it through his own emotion.

What we should stand for is not universality of theme, but beauty and strength of treatment, leaving the writer to choose his theme because he loves it.

Here is the work of the critic. Recognizing that the theme is beyond his control, let him aid the young writer to delineate simply and with unwavering strokes. Even here the critic can do little, if he is possessed of the idea that the young writer of to-day should model upon Addison or Macaulay or Swift.

There are new criterions to-day in writing as in painting, and individual expression is the aim. The critic can do much to aid a young writer to *not* copy an old master or any other master. Good criticism can aid him to be vivid and simple and unhackneyed in his technique, the subject is his own affair.

I agree with him who says, Local art must be raised to the highest levels in its expression; but in aiding this perfection of technique we must be careful not to cut into the artist's spontaneity. To apply ancient dogmas of criticism to our life and literature would be benumbing to artist and fatal to his art.

VI: The Local Novel

The local novel seems to be the heir-apparent to the kingdom of poesy. It is already the most promising of all literary attempts to-day; certainly it is the most sincere. It seems but beginning its work. It is "hopelessly contemporaneous"; that is its strength. It is (at its best) unaffected, natural, emotional. It is sure to become all-powerful. It will redeem American literature, as it has already redeemed the South from its conventional and highly wrought romanticism.

By reason of growing truth and sincerity the fiction of the South has risen from the dead. It is now in the spring season of shooting wilding plants and timorous blades of sown grains. Its future is assured. Its soil is fertilized with the blood of true men. Its women are the repositories of great, vital, sincere, emotional experiences which will inevitably appear in their children, and at last in art, and especially in fiction. The Southern people are in the midst of a battle more momentous than the Rebellion, because it is the result of the Rebellion; that is, the battle of intrenched privilege against the swiftly-spreading democratic idea of equality before the law and in the face of nature.

They have a terribly, mightily dramatic race-problem on their hands. The South is the meeting-place of winds. It is the seat of swift and almost incalculable change; and this change, this battle, this strife of invisible powers, is about to enter their fiction.

The Negro has already entered it. He has brought a musical speech to his masters, and to the new fiction. He has brought a strange and pleading song into music. The finest writers of the New South already find him a never-failing source of interest. He is not, of course, the only subject of Southern fiction, nor even the principal figure; but he is a necessary part, and a most absorbingly interesting part.

The future of fiction in the South will also depict the unreconstructed rebel unreservedly, and the race-problem without hate or contempt or anger; for the highest art will be the most catholic in its sympathy. It will delineate vast contending forces, and it will be a great literature.

The Negro will enter the fiction of the South, first, as subject; second, as artist in his own right. His first attempts will be imitative, but he will yet utter himself, as surely as he lives. He will contribute a poetry and a novel as peculiarly his own as the songs he sings. He may appear, also, in a strange half-song, half-chant, and possibly in a drama peculiar to himself; but in some form of fiction he will surely utter the sombre and darkly-florid genius for emotional utterance which characterizes him.

In the North the novel will continue local for some time to come. It will delineate the intimate life and speech of every section of our enormous and widely scattered republic. It will catch and fix in charcoal the changing, assimilating races, delineating the pathos and humor and the infinite drama of their swift adjustment to new conditions. California, New Mexico, Idaho, Utah, Oregon, each wonderful locality in our Nation of Nations will yet find its native utterance. The superficial work of the tourist and outsider will not do. The real novelist of these sections is walking behind the plow or trudging to school in these splendid potential environments.

This local movement will include the cities as well, and St. Louis, Chicago, San Francisco, will be delineated by artists born of each city, whose work will be so true that it could not have been written by any one from the outside. The real utterance of a city or a locality can only come when a writer is born out of its intimate heart. To such an one, nothing will be "strange" or "picturesque"; all will be familiar, and full of significance or beauty. The novel of the slums must be written by one who has played there as a child, and taken part in all its amusements; not out of curiosity, but out of pleasure seeking. It cannot be done from above nor from the outside. It must be done out of a full heart and without seeking for effect.

The artist should not look abroad to see how others are succeeding. Success does not always measure merit. It took nearly a third of a century for Whitman and Monet to be recognized. The great artist never conforms. He does not trail after some other man's success. He works out his individual perception of things.

The contrast of city and country, everywhere growing sharper, will find its reflection in this local novel of the immediate future,—the same tragedies and comedies, with the essential difference called local color, and taking place all over the land, wherever cities arise like fungi, unhealthy, yet absorbing as subjects of fictional art.

As I have elsewhere pointed out, the drama will join the novel in this study of local conditions. It will be derived from fiction, and in many cases the dramatist and novelist will be the same person. In all cases the sincerity of the author's love for his scenes and characters will find expression in tender care for truth, and there will be made to pass before our eyes wonderfully suggestive pictures of other lives and landscapes. The drama will grow in dignity and importance along these lines.

Both drama and novel will be colloquial. This does not mean that they will be exclusively in the dialects, but the actual speech of the people of each locality will unquestionably be studied more closely than ever before. Dialect is the life of a language, precisely as the common people of the nation form the sustaining power of its social life and art.

And so in the novel, in the short story, and in the drama —by the work of a multitude of loving artists, not by the work of an over-topping personality—will the intimate social, individual life of the nation be depicted. Before this localism shall pass away, such a study will have been made of this land and people as has never been made by any other age or social group,—a literature from the plain people, reflecting their unrestrained outlook on life, subtle in speech and color, humane beyond precedent, humorous, varied, simple in means, lucid as water, searching as sunlight.

To one who believes each age to be its own best interpreter, the idea of "decay of fiction" never comes. That which the absolutist takes for decay is merely change. The conservative fears change; the radical welcomes it. The conservative tries to argue that fundamentals cannot change; that they are the same yesterday, to-day, and to-morrow. If that were true, then a sorrowful outlook on the future would be natural. Such permanency would be death. Life means change.

As a matter of fact, the minute differentiations of literature which the conservative calls its non-essentials, are really its essentials. Vitality and growth are in these "non-essentials." It is the difference in characters, not their similarity, which is forever interesting. It is the subtle coloring individuality gives which vitalizes landscape art, and so it is the subtle differences in the interpretation of life which each age gives that vitalizes its literature and makes it its own.

The individuality of the artist is the saving grace of art; and landscape painting will not be fantastic so long as men study nature. It will never be mere reproduction so long as the artist represents it as he sees it. The fact will correct the fantasy. The artist will color the fact.

The business of the present is not to express fundamentals, but to sincerely present its own minute and characteristic interpretation of life. This point cannot be too often insisted upon. Unless a writer add something to the literature of his race, has he justification? Is there glory in imitation? Is the painter greatest who copies old masters, or is it more praiseworthy to embody an original conception? These are very important questions for the young artist.

To perceive the hopelessness of absolutism in literature,

you have but to stop a moment to think. Admit that there are perfect models to which must be referred all subsequent writing, and we are committed to a barren round of hopeless imitations. The young writer is disheartened or drawn off into imitations, and ruined for any real expression. This way of looking at literature produced our Barlows and Coltons and Hillhouses, with their "colossi of cotton-batting," and it produces blank-verse dramas to-day.

But the relativists in art are full of hope. They see that life is the model,—or, rather, that each man stands accountable to himself first, and to the perceived fact of life second. Life is always changing, and literature changes with it. It never decays; it changes. Poetry—that is to say *impassioned personal outlook on life*—is in no more danger of extinction to-day than in the days of Edmund Spenser. The American novel will continue to grow in truth to American life without regard to the form and spirit of the novel or drama of the past. Consciously or unconsciously, the point of view of the modern writer is that of the veritist, or truth stater.

Once out of the period of tutelage, it is natural for youth to overleap barriers. He naturally discards the wig and cloak of his grandfathers. He comes at last to reject, perhaps a little too brusquely, the models which conservatism regards with awe. He respects them as history, but he has life, abounding, fresh, contiguous life; life that stings and smothers and overwhelms and exalts, like the salt, green, snow-tipped ocean surf; life, with its terrors and triumphs, right here and now; its infinite drama, its allurement, its battle, and its victories. Life is the model, truth is the master, the heart of the man himself his motive power. The pleasure of re-creating in the image of nature is the artist's unfailing reward.

To him who sees that difference, not similarity, is the vitalizing quality, there is no sorrow at change. The future will take care of itself. In the space of that word "difference" lies all the infinite range of future art. Some elements are comparatively unchanging. The snow will fall, spring will come, men and women love, the stars will rise and set, and grass return again and again in vast rhythms of green, but society will not be the same.

The physical conformation of our nation will change. It will lose its wildness, its austerity. Its unpeopled plains will pass away, and gardens will bloom where the hot sand now drifts. Cities will rise where now the elk and the mountain lions are. Swifter means of transportation will bring the lives of different sections into closer relationship. It will tend to equalize intellectual opportunities. The physical and mental life of men and women will be changed, the relation of man to man, and man to woman, will change in detail, and the fiction of the future will express these changes.

To the veritist, therefore, the present is the vital theme. The past is dead, and the future can be trusted to look after itself. The young men and maidens of that time will find the stars of their present brighter than the stars of '92, the people around them more absorbing than books, and their own outlook on life more reasonable than that of dead men. Their writing and painting, in proportion to its vitality and importance, will reflect this, their natural attitude, toward life and history.

1894

STEPHEN CRANE

(1871–1900)

Writing to his brother in 1897 from England, where he had taken refuge from an American press which had exaggeratedly attributed to him a morally bizarre character like Poe's and Byron's, Stephen Crane announced: "Your little brother . . . knows that he is going on steadily to make his simple little place and he can't be stopped, he can't even be retarded. He is coming." Less than three years later death stopped him; but not before he had made for himself what is assuredly more than just a "little place" in American literary history.

Crane was the last of fourteen children born to a Methodist minister, Jonathan Townley Crane, and the daughter of a Methodist minister, Mary Peck Crane. (Although in his mature life Crane turned his back on the religion of his forebears to acccept a naturalistic view of the universe, his Methodist heritage manifests itself in the subject matter of a substantial portion of his poetry and in his penchant for religious metaphor and allusion in his prose.) In 1879 the Crane family finally settled in Port Jervis, New York, after living in various New Jersey cities—the composite locale of Stephen Crane's *Whilomville Stories* (1900). In 1882, two years after the father's death, Stephen (aged eleven) was acting as a reporter of vacation news items for his brother Townley's news-service agency in the resort town of Asbury Park, New Jersey. Crane's university days (1890–1891) were limited to two semesters—one at Lafayette College (where he was given a zero in theme writing), and one at Syracuse University (where he garnered an A in English Literature). But something of importance was going forward during this uninspired academic year: he wrote

at least the first draft of *Maggie: A Girl of the Streets*—
America's first wholly deterministic novel. Unable to find a
publisher for this account of a tenement girl's descent to
prostitution and suicide ("the most truthful . . . study of
the slums," Hamlin Garland called it), Crane borrowed money
and in 1893 brought it out himself in yellow paper wrappers
under the pseudonymn of "Johnston Smith." Financially the
book was stillborn, but it did serve to bring the young writer
to the attention of Garland (who wrote a sympathetic review)
and William Dean Howells. Howells not only encouraged the
despondent Crane, but also introduced him to the poetry of
Emily Dickinson (the most important influence on Crane's first
book of poems, *The Black Riders and Other Lines*, 1895,) and
later found a publisher for *The Red Badge of Courage* (1895).
In 1896, after the huge success of *The Red Badge of Courage*
(fourteen printings), a regular New York publisher reissued
Maggie with Crane's revisions and his name on the title page.
This slim novel, whose overarching intention, according to
Crane, was "to show that environment is a tremendous thing
in the world and frequently shapes lives regardless," is clearly
the inaugurator in fiction of an American literary tradition that
moves through writers such as Theodore Dreiser and James T.
Farrell.

It is not a little ironic that Crane subscribed to the notion
that an artist had actually to touch a segment of life before
he could recreate it imaginatively, for *The Red Badge of Courage*, America's first great war novel, was written before Crane
had "smelled even the powder of a sham battle." Books,
pictures, and veterans' accounts of Civil War fighting, rather
than any fighting itself, were the sources for his psychological
study of a boy soldier's struggle with the enormous horrors,
both within and without, which war unleashes. Nevertheless,
Crane sought personal experience as material for his art during
much of the last decade of his life. As a not too successful
reporter in New York, he had explored the bars and brothels
and flophouses of the Bowery. After the success of *The Red
Badge of Courage*, he toured the Far West and Mexico as a
correspondent for the Bacheller Syndicate (a job which gave
him the materials for "The Blue Hotel" and "The Bride Comes
to Yellow Sky"). Next he covered the activities of the filibus-
ters who were gunrunning from Florida to Cuba against Spain;
in the course of this activity he suffered the shipwreck and
consequent fifty-four hours' exposure at sea in a lifeboat
that became, after being passed through the alembic of his

imagination, one of his finest short stories, "The Open Boat."
In 1897 he covered the Greco-Turkish War for two newspapers; the following year it was the Spanish-American War.
By the time he settled down to a quiet but financially bankrupt
literary life at Brede Place in Sussex, England, in 1899—
playing host to such notable novelists as Henry James, Joseph
Conrad, H. G. Wells, and Ford Madox Ford—his frail body
had run down: he died of tuberculosis (and debts) in June
of the following year. Although he did not reach his twenty-
ninth birthday, his collected work fills twelve volumes, and
much of it is significant enough to have led several critics to
assert that modern American fiction began with Stephen Crane.

In addition to the titles mentioned above, Crane's works
include *The Little Regiment* (1896); *George's Mother* (1896);
The Third Violet (1897); *The Open Boat and Other Tales of
Adventure* (1898); *Active Service* (1899); *War is Kind* (1899);
The Monster and Other Stories (1899); *Wounds in the Rain*
(1900); *Great Battles of the World* (1901); *Last Words* (1902);
The O'Ruddy, with Robert Barr (1903).
Accounts of the man and his work can be found in H. G.
Wells, "Stephen Crane from an English Standpoint," *North
American Review*, CLXXI (1900); H. Garland, "Stephen Crane
as I Knew Him," *Yale Review*, n.s. III (1914); H. Monroe,
"Stephen Crane," *Poetry*, XIV (1919); T. Beer, *Stephen Crane:
A Study in American Letters* (1923); C. Van Doren, "Stephen
Crane," *American Mercury*, I (1924); W. Follett, ed., *The
Work of Stephen Crane*, 12 vols. (1925–27); W. Follett, ed.,
The Collected Poems of Stephen Crane (1930); M. Josephson,
"The Voyage of Stephen Crane," *Portrait of the Artist as
American* (1930); F. M. Ford, "Stephen Crane," *Portraits from
Life* (1937); H. Webster, "Wilbur F. Hinman's *Corporal Si
Klegg* and Stephen Crane's *The Red Badge of Courage*," *Amer-
ican Literature*, XI (1939); R. Nye, "Stephen Crane as Social
Critic," *Modern Quarterly*, XI (1940); A. Williams and V. Star-
rett, *Stephen Crane: A Bibliography* (1948); C. Gordon,
"Stephen Crane," *Accent*, IX (1949); M. Schoberlin, ed., *The
Sullivan County Sketches of Stephen Crane* (1949); L. Åhne-
brink, *The Beginnings of Naturalism in American Fiction*
(1950); J. Berryman, *Stephen Crane* (1950); R. Stallman, ed.,
Stephen Crane: An Omnibus (1952); R. Stallman, "Stephen
Crane," *Critiques and Essays on Modern Fiction* (1952); J.
Stevenson, "The Literary Reputation of Stephen Crane," *South
Atlantic Quarterly*, LI (1952); J. E. Hart, "*The Red Badge of
Courage* as Myth and Symbol," *University of Kansas City
Review*, XIX (1953); R. Adams, "Naturalistic Fiction: 'The
Open Boat,' " *Tulane Studies in English*, IV (1954); E. Cady
and L. Wells, eds., *Love Letters to Nellie Crouse* . . . (1954);
R. Stallman, "Stephen Crane's Revision of *Maggie: A Girl of*

IX (1956); C. Walcutt, *American Literary Naturalism, A Divided Stream* (1956); J. T. Cox, "Stephen Crane as Symbolic Naturalist: An Analysis of 'The Blue Hotel,' " *Modern Fiction Studies,* III (1957); D. Hoffman, ed. *The Red Badge of Courage & Other Stories* (1957); D. Hoffman, *The Poetry of Stephen Crane* (1957); E. Cady, ed., *My Stephen Crane* (by Corwin K. Linson, 1958); S. Greenfield, "The Unmistakable Stephen Crane," *PMLA,* LXXIII (1958); B. Weisberger, "The Red Badge of Courage," *Twelve Original Essays on Great American Novels* (1958); R. Lettis, R. McDonnell, and W. Morris, eds., *Stephen Crane's The Red Badge of Courage: Text and Criticism* (1959); *Modern Fiction Studies,* V (Autumn, 1959): a Stephen Crane issue; W. Stein, "Stephen Crane's *Homo Absurdus,"* *Bucknell Review,* VIII (1959); J. X. Brennan, "The Imagery and Art of *George's Mother," CLA Journal,* IV (1960); R. Stallman and L. Gilkes, eds., *Stephen Crane: Letters* (1960); L. Gilkes, *Cora Crane* (1960); V. S. Pritchett ed. *The Red Badge of Courage & Other Stories* (1960); R. W. Stallman, "Maggie in Review," *The Houses that James Built* (1961); A. J. Liebling, "The Dollars Damned Him," *The New Yorker,* XXXVII (August 5, 1961); S. Bradley, R. C. Beatty, E. H. Long, eds., *The Red Badge of Courage* (text, sources, criticism, 1962); E. H. Cady, *Stephen Crane* (1962); R. A. Toerne, "The Establishment of Stephen Crane," *Dissertation Abstracts* (1962); O. W. Fryckstedt, ed., *Stephen Crane: Uncollected Writings* (1963); T. A. Gullason, ed., *Complete Short Stories and Sketches* (1963); R. W. Stallman and E. R. Hagemann, eds., *The War Dispatches of Stephen Crane* (1964); E. Solomon, *Stephen Crane in England* (1964); M. LaFrance, "The Role of Illusion in the Works of Stephen Crane," *Dissertation Abstracts* (1965); R. E. Peck, "Method and Meaning in the Poetry of Stephen Crane," *Dissertation Abstracts* (1965); E. Solomon, *Stephen Crane: From Parody to Realism* (1966); R. Stallman and E. Hagemann, eds., *The New York City Sketches of Stephen Crane* (1966); and D. B. Gibson, *The Fiction of Stephen Crane* (1968). The definitive biography is *Stephen Crane* by R. W. Stallman (1968).

Maggie: A Girl of the Streets

I

A very little boy stood upon a heap of gravel for the honour of Rum Alley. He was throwing stones at howling urchins from Devil's Row, who were circling madly about the heap and pelting him. His infantile countenance was livid with the fury of battle. His small body was writhing in the delivery of oaths.

"Run, Jimmie, run! Dey'll git yehs!" screamed a retreating Rum Alley child.

"Naw," responded Jimmie with a valiant roar, "dese mugs can't make me run."

Howls of renewed wrath went up from Devil's Row throats. Tattered gamins on the right made a furious assault on the gravel-heap. On their small convulsed faces shone the grins of true assassins. As they charged, they threw stones and cursed in shrill chorus.

The little champion of Rum Alley stumbled precipitately down the other side. His coat had been torn to shreds in a scuffle, and his hat was gone. He had bruises on twenty parts of his body, and blood was dripping from a cut in his head. His wan features looked like those of a tiny insane demon. On the ground, children from Devil's Row closed in on their antagonist. He crooked his left arm defensively about his head and fought with madness. The little boys ran to and fro, dodging, hurling stones, and swearing in barbaric trebles.

From a window of an apartment-house that uprose from amid squat ignorant stables there leaned a curious woman. Some labourers, unloading a scow at a dock at the river, paused for a moment and regarded the fight. The engineer of a passive tugboat hung lazily over a railing and watched. Over on the island a worm of yellow convicts came from the shadow of a grey ominous building and crawled slowly along the river's bank.

A stone had smashed in Jimmie's mouth. Blood was bubbling over his chin and down upon his ragged shirt. Tears made furrows on his dirt-stained cheeks. His thin legs had begun to tremble and turn weak, causing his small body to reel. His roaring curses of the first part of the fight had changed to a blasphemous chatter. In the yells of the whirling mob of Devil's Row children there were notes of joy like songs of triumphant savagery. The little boys seemed to leer gloatingly at the blood upon the other child's face.

Down the avenue came boastfully sauntering a lad of sixteen years, although the chronic sneer of an ideal manhood already sat upon his lips. His hat was tipped over his eye with an air of challenge. Between his teeth a cigar-stump was tilted at the angle of defiance. He walked with a certain swing of the shoulders which appalled the timid. He glanced over into the vacant lot in which the little raving boys from Devil's Row seethed about the shrieking and tearful child from Rum Alley.

"Gee!" he murmured with interest, "a scrap. Gee!" He strode over to the cursing circle, swinging his shoulders in a manner which denoted that he held victory in his fists. He approached at the back of one of the most deeply engaged of the Devil's Row children. "Ah, what d' hell," he said, and smote the deeply engaged one on the back of the head.

The little boy fell to the ground and gave a tremendous howl. He scrambled to his feet, and perceiving, evidently, the size of his assailant, ran quickly off, shouting alarms. The entire Devil's Row party followed him. They came to a stand a short distance away and yelled taunting oaths at the boy with the chronic sneer.

The latter, momentarily, paid no attention to them. "What's wrong wi'che, Jimmie?" he asked of the small champion.

Jimmie wiped his blood-wet features with his sleeve. "Well, it was dis way, Pete, see? I was goin' teh lick dat Riley kid, an' dey all pitched on me."

Some Rum Alley children now came forward. The party stood for a moment exchanging vainglorious remarks with Devil's Row. A few stones were thrown at long distances, and words of challenge passed between small warriors. Then the Rum Alley contingent turned slowly in the direction of their home street. They began to give, each to each, distorted versions of the fight. Causes of retreat in particular cases were magnified. Blows dealt in the fight were enlarged to catapultian power, and stones thrown were alleged to have hurtled with infinite accuracy. Valour grew strong again, and the little boys began to brag with great spirit. "Ah, we blokies kin lick d' hull damn Row," said a child, swaggering.

Little Jimmie was trying to stanch the flow of blood from his cut lips. Scowling, he turned upon the speaker. "Ah, where was yehs when I was doin' all deh fightin'?" he demanded. "Youse kids makes me tired."

"Ah, go ahn!" replied the other argumentatively.

Jimmie replied with heavy contempt. "Ah, youse can't fight, Blue Billie! I kin lick yeh wid one han'."

"Ah, go ahn!" replied Billie again.

"Ah!" said Jimmie threateningly.

"Ah!" said the other in the same tone.

They struck at each other, clinched, and rolled over on the cobble-stones.

"Smash 'im, Jimmie, kick d' face off 'im!" yelled Pete, the lad with the chronic sneer, in tones of delight.

The small combatants pounded and kicked, scratched and tore. They began to weep, and their curses struggled in their throats with sobs. The other little boys clasped their hands and wriggled their legs in excitement. They formed a bobbing circle about the pair.

A tiny spectator was suddenly agitated. "Cheese it, Jimmie, cheese it! Here comes yer fader," he yelled.

The circle of little boys instantly parted. They drew away and waited in ecstatic awe for that which was about to happen. The two little boys, fighting in the modes of four thousand years ago, did not hear the warning.

Up the avenue there plodded slowly a man with sullen eyes. He was carrying a dinner-pail and smoking an apple-wood pipe. As he neared the spot where the little boys strove, he regarded them listlessly. But suddenly he roared an oath and advanced upon the rolling fighters. "Here, you Jim, git up, now, while I belt yer life out, yeh disorderly brat." He began to kick into the chaotic mass on the ground. The boy Billie felt a heavy boot strike his head. He made a furious effort and disentangled himself from Jimmie. He tottered away.

Jimmie arose painfully from the ground and, confronting his father, began to curse him. His parent kicked him. "Come home, now," he cried, "an' stop yer jawin', er I'll lam the everlasting head off yehs."

They departed. The man paced placidly along with the apple-wood emblem of serenity between his teeth. The boy followed a dozen feet in the rear. He swore luridly, for he felt that it was degradation for one who aimed to be some vague kind of soldier, or a man of blood with a sort of sublime license, to be taken home by a father.

II

Eventually they entered a dark region where, from a careening building, a dozen gruesome doorways gave up loads of babies to the street and the gutter. A wind of early autumn raised yellow dust from cobbles and swirled it against a hundred windows. Long streamers of garments fluttered from fire-escapes. In all unhandy places there were buckets, brooms, rags, and bottles. In the street infants played or fought with other infants or sat stupidly in the way of vehicles. Formidable women, with uncombed hair and disordered dress, gossiped while leaning on railings, or screamed in frantic quarrels. Withered persons, in curious postures of submission to something, sat smoking pipes in obscure corners. A thousand odours of cooking food came forth to the street. The building quivered and creaked from the weight of humanity stamping about in its bowels.

A small ragged girl dragged a red, bawling infant along the crowded ways. He was hanging back, baby-like, bracing his wrinkled, bare legs. The little girl cried out: "Ah, Tommie, come ahn. Dere's Jimmie and fader. Don't be a-pullin' me back." She jerked the baby's arm impatiently. He fell on his face, roaring. With a second jerk she pulled him to his feet, and they went on. With the obstinacy of his order, he protested against being dragged in a chosen direction. He made heroic endeavours to keep on his legs, denounced his sister, and consumed a bit of orange-peeling which he chewed between the times of his infantile orations.

As the sullen-eyed man, followed by the blood-covered boy, drew near, the little girl burst into reproachful cries. "Ah, Jimmie, youse bin fightin' agin."

The urchin swelled disdainfully. "Ah, what d' hell, Mag. See?"

The little girl upbraided him. "Youse allus fightin', Jimmie, an' yeh knows it puts mudder out when yehs come home half dead, an it's like we'll all get a poundin'." She began to weep. The babe threw back his head and roared at his prospects.

"Ah," cried Jimmie, "shut up er I'll smack yer mout'. See?" As his sister continued her lamentations, he suddenly struck her. The little girl reeled, and, recovering herself, burst into tears and quaveringly cursed him. As she slowly retreated, her brother advanced, dealing her cuffs.

The father heard, and turned about. "Stop that, Jim, d'yeh hear? Leave yer sister alone on the street. It's like I can never beat any sense into yer wooden head."

The urchin raised his voice in defiance to his parent, and continued his attacks. The babe bawled tremendously, protesting with great violence. During his sister's hasty manoeuvres he was dragged by the arm.

Finally the procession plunged into one of the gruesome doorways. They crawled up dark stairways and along cold, gloomy halls. At last the father pushed open a door, and they entered a lighted room in which a large woman was rampant.

She stopped in a career from a seething stove to a pan-covered table. As the father and children filed in she peered at them. "Eh, what? Been fightin' agin!" She threw herself upon Jimmie. The urchin tried to dart behind the others, and in the scuffle the babe, Tommie, was knocked down. He protested with his usual vehemence because they had bruised his tender shins against a table leg.

The mother's massive shoulders heaved with anger. Grasping the urchin by the neck and shoulder she shook him until he rattled. She dragged him to an unholy sink, and, soaking a rag in water, began to scrub his lacerated face with it. Jimmie screamed in pain, and tried to twist his shoulders out of the clasp of the huge arms.

The babe sat on the floor watching the scene, his face in contortions like that of a woman at a tragedy. The father, with a newly ladened pipe in his mouth, sat in a backless chair near the stove. Jimmie's cries annoyed him. He turned about and bellowed at his wife. "Let the kid alone for a minute, will yeh, Mary? Yer allus poundin' 'im. When I come nights I can't get no rest 'cause yer allus poundin' a kid. Let up, d'yeh hear? Don't be allus poundin' a kid." The woman's operations on the urchin instantly increased in violence. At last she tossed him to a corner, where he limply lay weeping.

The wife put her immense hands on her hips, and with a chieftain-like stride approached her husband. "Ho!" she said, with a great grunt of contempt. "An' what in the devil are you stickin' your nose for?" The babe crawled under the table, and, turning, peered out cautiously. The ragged girl retreated, and the urchin in the corner drew his legs carefully beneath him.

The man puffed his pipe calmly, and put his great muddied boots on the back part of the stove. "Go t' hell," he said tranquilly.

The woman screamed, and shook her fists before her husband's eyes. The rough yellow of her face and neck flared suddenly crimson. She began to howl.

He puffed imperturbably at his pipe for a time, but

finally arose and went to look out the window into the darkening chaos of back yards. "You've been drinkin', Mary," he said. "You'd better let up on the bot', ol' woman, or you'll git done."

"You're a liar. I ain't had a drop," she roared in reply. They had a lurid altercation.

The babe was staring out from under the table, his small face working in his excitement. The ragged girl went stealthily over to the corner where the urchin lay. "Are yehs hurted much, Jimmie?" she whispered timidly.

"Not a little bit. See?" growled the little boy.

"Will I wash d' blood?"

"Naw!"

"Will I——"

"When I catch dat Riley kid I'll break 'is face! Dat's right! See?" He turned his face to the wall as if resolved grimly to bide his time.

In the quarrel between husband and wife the woman was victor. The man seized his hat and rushed from the room, apparently determined upon a vengeful drunk. She followed to the door and thundered at him as he made his way downstairs.

She returned and stirred up the room until her children were bobbing about like bubbles. "Git outa d' way," she bawled persistently, waving feet with their dishevelled shoes near the heads of her children. She shrouded herself, puffing and snorting, in a cloud of steam at the stove, and eventually extracted a frying-pan full of potatoes that hissed. She flourished it. "Come t' yer suppers, now," she cried with sudden exasperation. "Hurry up, now, er I'll help yeh!"

The children scrambled hastily. With prodigious clatter they arranged themselves at table. The babe sat with his feet dangling high from a precarious infant's chair and gorged his small stomach. Jimmie forced, with feverish rapidity, the grease-enveloped pieces between his wounded lips. Maggie, with side glances of fear of interruption, ate like a small pursued tigress.

The mother sat blinking at them. She delivered reproaches, swallowed potatoes, and drank from a yellow-brown bottle. After a time her mood changed, and she wept as she carried little Tommie into another room and laid him to sleep, with his fists doubled, in an old quilt of

faded red-and-green grandeur. Then she came and moaned
by the stove. She rocked to and fro upon a chair, shedding
tears and crooning miserably to the two children about
their "poor mother" and "yer fader, damn 'is soul."

The little girl plodded between the table and the chair
with a dishpan on it. She tottered on her small legs beneath
burdens of dishes. Jimmie sat nursing his various wounds.
He cast furtive glances at his mother. His practised eye
perceived her gradually emerge from a mist of muddled
sentiment until her brain burned in drunken heat. He sat
breathless.

Maggie broke a plate.

The mother started to her feet as if propelled. "Good
Gawd!" she howled. Her glittering eyes fastened on her
child with sudden hatred. The fervent red of her face
turned almost to purple. The little boy ran to the hall,
shrieking like a monk in an earthquake. He floundered
about in darkness until he found the stairs. He stumbled,
panic-stricken, to the next floor.

An old woman opened a door. A light behind her threw
a flare on the urchin's face. "Eh, child, what is it dis time?
Is yer fader beatin' yer mudder, or yer mudder beatin' yer
fader?"

III

Jimmie and the old woman listened long in the hall.
Above the muffled roar of conversation, the dismal wailings of babies at night, the thumping of feet in unseen
corridors and rooms, and the sound of varied hoarse
shoutings in the street and the rattling of wheels over
cobbles, they heard the screams of the child and the roars
of the mother die away to a feeble moaning and a subdued
bass muttering.

The old woman was a gnarled and leathery personage
who could don at will an expression of great virtue. She
possessed a small music-box capable of one tune, and a collection of "God bless yeh's" pitched in assorted keys of
fervency. Each day she took a position upon the stones of
Fifth Avenue, where she crooked her legs under her and
crouched, immovable and hideous, like an idol. She received daily a small sum in pennies. It was contributed,
for the most part, by persons who did not make their homes
in that vicinity. Once, when a lady had dropped her purse

on the sidewalk, the gnarled woman had grabbed it and smuggled it with great dexterity beneath her cloak. When she was arrested she had cursed the lady into a partial swoon, and with her aged limbs, twisted from rheumatism, had kicked the breath out of a huge policeman whose conduct upon that occasion she referred to when she said, "The police, damn 'em!"

"Eh, Jimmie, it's a shame," she said. "Go, now, like a dear, an' buy me a can, an' if yer mudder raises 'ell all night yehs can sleep here." Jimmie took a tendered tin pail and seven pennies and departed. He passed into the side door of a saloon and went to the bar. Straining up on his toes he raised the pail and pennies as high as his arms would let him. He saw two hands thrust down to take them. Directly the same hands let down the filled.pail, and he left.

In front of the gruesome doorway he met a lurching figure. It was his father, swaying about on uncertain legs. "Give me deh can. See?" said the man.

"Ah, come off! I got dis can fer dat ol' woman, an' it 'ud be dirt teh swipe it. See?" cried Jimmie.

The father wrenched the pail from the urchin. He grasped it in both hands and lifted it to his mouth. He glued his lips to the under edge and tilted his head. His throat swelled until it seemed to grow near his chin. There was a tremendous gulping movement and the beer was gone. The man caught his breath and laughed. He hit his son on the head with the empty pail.

As it rolled clanging into the street, Jimmie began to scream, and kicked repeatedly at his father's shins. "Look at deh dirt what yeh done me," he yelled. "Deh ol' woman 'll be t'rowin' fits." He retreated to the middle of the street, but the old man did not pursue. He staggered toward the door. "I'll paste yeh when I ketch yeh!" he shouted, and disappeared.

During the evening he had been standing against a bar drinking whiskies, and declaring to all comers confidentially: "My home reg'lar livin' hell! Why do I come an' drin' whisk' here thish way? 'Cause home reg'lar livin' hell!"

Jimmie waited a long time in the street and then crept warily up through the building. He passed with great caution the door of the gnarled woman, and finally stopped outside his home and listened. He could hear his mother moving heavily about among the furniture of the room. She was chanting in a mournful voice, occasionally interjecting bursts of volcanic wrath at the father, who, Jimmie judged, had sunk down on the floor or in a corner.

"Why deh blazes don'cher try teh keep Jim from fightin'? I'll break yer jaw!" she suddenly bellowed.

The man mumbled with drunken indifference. "Ah, w'at's bitin' yeh? W'a' 's odds? W'a' makes kick?"

"Because he tears 'is clothes, yeh fool!" cried the woman in supreme wrath.

The husband seemed to become aroused. "Go chase yerself!" he thundered fiercely in reply. There was a crash against the door, and something broke into clattering fragments. Jimmie partially suppressed a yell and darted down the stairway. Below he paused and listened. He heard howls and curses, groans and shrieks—a confused chorus as if a battle were raging. With it all there was the crash of splintering furniture. The eyes of the urchin glared in his fear that one of them would discover him.

Curious faces appeared in doorways, and whispered comments passed to and fro. "Ol' Johnson's playin' horse agin."

Jimmie stood until the noises ceased and the other inhabitants of the tenement had all yawned and shut their doors. Then he crawled upstairs with the caution of an invader of a panther's den. Sounds of laboured breathing came through the broken door-panels. He pushed the door open and entered, quaking.

A glow from the fire threw red hues over the bare floor, the cracked and soiled plastering, and the overturned and broken furniture. In the middle of the floor lay his mother asleep. In one corner of the room his father's limp body hung across the seat of a chair.

The urchin stole forward. He began to shiver in dread of awakening his parents. His mother's great chest was heaving painfully. Jimmie paused and looked down at her. Her face was inflamed and swollen from drinking. Her yellow brows shaded eyelids that had grown blue. Her tangled hair tossed in waves over her forehead. Her mouth was set in the same lines of vindictive hatred that it had, perhaps, borne during the fight. Her bare red arms were thrown out above her head in an attitude of exhaustion, something, mayhap, like that of a sated villain.

The urchin bent over his mother. He was fearful lest she should open her eyes, and the dread within him was so strong that he could not forbear to stare, but hung as if fascinated over the woman's grim face. Suddenly her eyes opened. The urchin found himself looking straight into an expression which, it would seem, had the power to change his blood to salt. He howled piercingly and fell backward.

The woman floundered for a moment, tossed her arms about her head as if in combat, and again began to snore. Jimmie crawled back into the shadows and waited. A noise in the next room had followed his cry at the discovery that his mother was awake. He grovelled in the gloom, his eyes riveted upon the intervening door. He heard it creak, and then the sound of a small voice came to him. "Jimmie! Jimmie! Are yehs dere?" it whispered. The urchin started. The thin white face of his sister looked at him from the doorway of the other room. She crept to him across the floor.

The father had not moved, but lay in the same deathlike sleep. The mother writhed in an uneasy slumber, her chest wheezing as if she were in the agonies of strangulation. Out at the window a florid moon was peering over dark roofs, and in the distance the waters of a river glimmered pallidly.

The small frame of the ragged girl was quivering. Her features were haggard from weeping, and her eyes gleamed with fear. She grasped the urchin's arm in her little trembling hands and they huddled in a corner. The eyes of both were drawn, by some force, to stare at the woman's face, for they thought she need only to awake and all the fiends would come from below. They crouched until the ghost mists of dawn appeared at the window, drawing close to the panes, and looking in at the prostrate, heaving body of the mother.

IV

The babe, Tommie, died. He went away in an insignificant coffin, his small waxen hand clutching a flower that the girl, Maggie, had stolen from an Italian.

She and Jimmie lived.

The inexperienced fibers of the boy's eyes were hardened at an early age. He became a young man of leather.

He lived some red years without labouring. During that time his sneer became chronic. He studied human nature in the gutter, and found it no worse than he thought he had reason to believe it. He never conceived a respect for the world, because he had begun with no idols that it had smashed.

He clad his soul in armour by means of happening hilariously in at a mission church where a man composed his sermons of "you's." Once a philosopher asked this man why he did not say "we" instead of "you." The man replied, "What?" While they got warm at the stove he told his hearers just where he calculated they stood with the Lord. Many of the sinners were impatient over the pictured depths of their degradation. They were waiting for soup-tickets. A reader of the words of wind-demons might have been able to see the portions of a dialogue pass to and fro between the exhorter and his hearers. "You are damned," said the preacher. And the reader of sounds might have seen the reply go forth from the ragged people: "Where's our soup?" Jimmie and a companion sat in a rear seat, and commented upon the things that didn't concern them, with all the freedom of English tourists. When they grew thirsty and went out, their minds confused the speaker with Christ.

Momentarily, Jimmie was sullen with thoughts of a hopeless altitude where grew fruit. His companion said that if he should ever go to heaven he would ask for a million dollars and a bottle of beer. Jimmie's occupation for a long time was to stand at street corners and watch the world go by, dreaming blood-red dreams at the passing of pretty women. He menaced mankind at the intersections of streets. At the corners he was in life and of life. The world was going on and he was there to perceive it.

He maintained a belligerent attitude toward all well-dressed men. To him fine raiment was allied to weakness, and all good coats covered faint hearts. He and his orders were kings, to a certain extent, over the men of untarnished clothes, because these latter dreaded, perhaps, to be either killed or laughed at. Above all things he despised obvious Christians and ciphers with the chrysanthemums of aristocracy in their buttonholes. He considered himself above both of these classes. He was afraid of nothing.

When he had a dollar in his pocket his satisfaction with

existence was the greatest thing in the world. So, eventually, he felt obliged to work. His father died, and his mother's years were divided up into periods of thirty days.

He became a truck-driver. There was given to him the charge of a painstaking pair of horses and a large rattling truck. He invaded the turmoil and tumble of the downtown streets, and learned to breathe maledictory defiance at the police, who occasionally used to climb up, drag him from his perch; and punch him. In the lower part of the city he daily involved himself in hideous tangles. If he and his team chanced to be in the rear he preserved a demeanour of serenity, crossing his legs and bursting forth into yells when foot passengers took dangerous dives beneath the noses of his champing horses. He smoked his pipe calmly, for he knew that his pay was marching on. If his charge was in the front, and if it became the key-truck of chaos, he entered terrifically into the quarrel that was raging to and fro among the drivers on their high seats, and sometimes roared oaths and violently got himself arrested.

After a time his sneer grew so that it turned its glare upon all things. He became so sharp that he believed in nothing. To him the police were always actuated by malignant impulses, and the rest of the world was composed, for the most part, of despicable creatures who were all trying to take advantage of him, and with whom, in defence, he was obliged to quarrel on all possible occasions. He himself occupied a downtrodden position, which had a private but distinct element of grandeur in its isolation.

The greatest cases of aggravated idiocy were, to his mind, rampant upon the front platforms of all the street-cars. At first his tongue strove with these beings, but he eventually became superior. In him grew a majestic contempt for those strings of street-cars that followed him like intent bugs. He fell into the habit, when starting on a long journey, of fixing his eye on a high and distant object, commanding his horses to start, and then going into a trance of oblivion. Multitudes of drivers might howl in his rear, and passengers might load him with opprobrium, but he would not awaken until some blue policeman turned red and began frenziedly to seize bridles and beat the soft noses of the responsible horses.

When he paused to contemplate the attitude of the police toward himself and his fellows, he believed that

they were the only men in the city who had no rights.
When driving about, he felt that he was held liable by
the police for anything that might occur in the streets, and
that he was the common prey of all energetic officials. In
revenge, he resolved never to move out of the way of anything, until formidable circumstances or a much larger
man than himself forced him to it.

Foot passengers were mere pestering flies with an insane disregard for their legs and his convenience. He could
not comprehend their desire to cross the streets. Their
madness smote him with eternal amazement. He was continually storming at them from his throne. He sat aloft
and denounced their frantic leaps, plunges, dives, and
straddles. When they would thrust at, or parry, the noses
of his champing horses, making them swing their heads
and move their feet, and thus disturbing a stolid, dreamy
repose, he swore at the men as fools, for he himself could
perceive that Providence had caused it to be clearly written that he and his team had the inalienable right to stand
in the proper path of the sun-chariot and, if they so
minded, to obstruct its mission or take a wheel off. And if
the god driver had had a desire to step down, put up his
flame-coloured fists, and manfully dispute the right of way,
he would have probably been immediately opposed by a
scowling mortal with two sets of hard knuckles.

It is possible, perhaps, that this young man would have
derided, in an axle-wide alley, the approach of a flying
ferry-boat. Yet he achieved a respect for a fire-engine. As
one charged toward his truck, he would drive fearfully
upon a sidewalk, threatening untold people with annihila-
tion. When an engine struck a mass of blocked trucks,
splitting it into fragments as a blow annihilates a cake of
ice, Jimmie's team could usually be observed high and
safe, with whole wheels, on the sidewalk. The fearful
coming of the engine could break up the most intricate
muddle of heavy vehicles at which the police had been
storming for half an hour. A fire-engine was enshrined in
his heart as an appalling thing that he loved with a distant,
dog-like devotion. It had been known to overturn a streetcar. Those leaping horses, striking sparks from the cobbles
in their forward lunge, were creatures to be ineffably admired. The clang of the gong pierced his breast like a
noise of remembered war.

When Jimmie was a little boy he began to be arrested. Before he reached a great age, he had a fair record. He developed too great a tendency to climb down from his truck and fight with other drivers. He had been in quite a number of miscellaneous fights, and in some general barroom rows that had become known to the police. Once he had been arrested for assaulting a Chinaman. Two women in different parts of the city, and entirely unknown to each other, caused him considerable annoyance by breaking forth, simultaneously, at fateful intervals, into wailings about marriage and support and infants.

Nevertheless, he had, on a certain star-lit evening, said wonderingly and quite reverently, "Deh moon looks like hell, don't it?"

V

The girl, Maggie, blossomed in a mud-puddle. She grew to be a most rare and wonderful production of a tenement district, a pretty girl. None of the dirt of Rum Alley seemed to be in her veins. The philosophers, upstairs, downstairs, and on the same floor, puzzled over it. When a child, playing and fighting with gamins in the street, dirt disgusted her. Attired in tatters and grime, she went unseen.

There came a time, however, when the young men of the vicinity said, "Dat Johnson goil is a putty good looker." About this period her brother remarked to her: "Mag, I'll tell yeh dis! See? Yeh've eeder got t' go on d' toif er go t' work!" Whereupon she went to work, having the feminine aversion to the alternative. By a chance, she got a position in an establishment where they made collars and cuffs. She received a stool and a machine in a room where sat twenty girls of various shades of yellow discontent. She perched on the stool and treadled at her machine all day, turning out collars with a name which might have been noted for its irrelevancy to anything connected with collars. At night she returned home to her mother.

Jimmie grew large enough to take the vague position of head of the family. As incumbent of that office, he stumbled upstairs late at night, as his father had done before him. He reeled about the room, swearing at his relations, or went to sleep on the floor.

The mother had gradually risen to such a degree of fame that she could bandy words with her acquaintances

among the police justices. Court officials called her by
her first name. When she appeared they pursued a course
which had been theirs for months. They invariably grinned,
and cried out, "Hello, Mary, you here again?" Her grey
head wagged in many courts. She always besieged the bench
with voluble excuses, explanations, apologies, and prayers.
Her flaming face and rolling eyes were a familiar sight on
the island. She measured time by means of sprees, and was
swollen and dishevelled.

One day the young man Pete, who as a lad had smitten
the Devil's Row urchin in the back of the head and put to
flight the antagonists of his friend Jimmie, strutted upon
the scene. He met Jimmie one day on the street, promised
to take him to a boxing match in Williamsburg, and called
for him in the evening.

Maggie observed Pete.

He sat on a table in the Johnson home, and dangled his
checked legs with an enticing nonchalance. His hair was
curled down over his forehead in an oiled bang. His pugged
nose seemed to revolt from contact with a bristling moustache of short, wire-like hairs. His blue double-breasted
coat, edged with black braid, was buttoned close to a red
puff tie, and his patent leather shoes looked like weapons.
His mannerisms stamped him as a man who had a correct
sense of his personal superiority. There were valour and
contempt for circumstances in the glance of his eye. He
waved his hands like a man of the world who dismisses
religion and philosophy, and says "Rats!" He had certainly
seen everything, and with each curl of his lip he declared
that it amounted to nothing. Maggie thought he must be a
very "elegant" bartender.

He was telling tales to Jimmie. Maggie watched him furtively, with half-closed eyes lit with a vague interest.

"Hully gee! Dey makes me tired," he said. "Mos' e'ry
day some farmer comes in an' tries t' run d' shop. See? But
d' gits t'rowed right out. I jolt dem right out in d' street
before dey knows where dey is. See?"

"Sure," said Jimmie.

"Dere was a mug come in d' place d' odder day wid an
idear he was goin' t' own d' place. Hully gee! he was goin'
t' own d' place. I see he had a still on, an' I didn' wanna
giv 'im no stuff, so I says, 'Git outa here an' don' make no
trouble,' I says like dat. See? 'Git outa here an' don' make
no trouble;' like dat. 'Git outa here,' I says. See?"

Jimmie nodded understandingly. Over his features played an eager desire to state the amount of his valour in a similar crisis, but the narrator proceeded.

"Well, deh blokie he says: 'T' blazes wid it! I ain' lookin' for no scrap,' he says—see?—'but,' he says, 'I'm 'spectable cit'zen an' I wanna drink, an' quick, too.' See? 'Aw, go ahn!' I says, like dat. 'Aw, go ahn,' I says. See? 'Don' make no trouble,' I says, like dat. 'Don' make no trouble.' See? Den d' mug, he squared off an' said he was fine as silk wid his dukes—see?—an' he wan'ed a drink—quick. Dat's what he said. See?"

"Sure," repeated Jimmie.

Pete continued. "Say, I jes' jumped d' bar, an' d' way I plunked dat blokie was outa sight. See? Dat's right! In d' jaw! See? Hully gee! he t'rowed a spittoon t'rough d' front windee. Say, I t'ought I'd drop dead. But d' boss, he comes in after, an' he says: 'Pete, yehs done jes' right! Yeh've gotta keep order, an' it's all right.' See? 'It's all right,' he says. Dat's what he said."

The two held a technical discussion.

"Dat bloke was a dandy," said Pete, in conclusion, "but he hadn' oughta made no trouble. Dat's what I says t' dem: 'Don' come in here an' make no trouble,' I says, like dat. 'Don' make no trouble.' See?"

As Jimmie and his friend exchanged tales descriptive of their prowess, Maggie leaned back in the shadow. Her eyes dwelt wonderingly and rather wistfully upon Pete's face. The broken furniture, grimy walls, and general disorder and dirt of her home of a sudden appeared before her and began to take a potential aspect. Pete's aristocratic person looked as if it might soil. She looked keenly at him, occasionally wondering if he was feeling contempt. But Pete seemed to be enveloped in reminiscence.

"Hully gee!" said he, "dose mugs can't feaze me. Dey knows I kin wipe up d' street wid any t'ree of dem."

When he said, "Ah, what d' hell!" his voice was burdened with disdain for the inevitable and contempt for anything that fate might compel him to endure.

Maggie perceived that here was the ideal man. Her dim thoughts were often searching for faraway lands where the little hills sing together in the morning. Under the trees of her dream-gardens there had always walked a lover.

VI

Pete took note of Maggie. "Say, Mag, I'm stuck on yer shape. It's outa sight," he said parenthetically, with an affable grin.

As he became aware that she was listening closely, he grew still more eloquent in his descriptions of various happenings in his career. It appeared that he was invincible in fights. "Why," he said, referring to a man with whom he had had a misunderstanding, "dat mug scrapped like a dago. Dat's right. He was dead easy. See? He t'ought he was a scrapper. But he foun' out diff'ent. Hully gee!"

He walked to and fro in the small room, which seemed then to grow even smaller and unfit to hold his dignity, the attribute of a supreme warrior. That swing of the shoulders which had frozen the timid when he was but a lad had increased with his growth and education in the ratio of ten to one. It, combined with the sneer upon his mouth, told mankind that there was nothing in space which could appall him. Maggie marvelled at him and surrounded him with greatness. She vaguely tried to calculate the altitude of the pinnacle from which he must have looked down upon her.

"I met a chump deh odder day way up in deh city," he said. "I was goin' teh see a frien' of mine. When I was a-crossin' deh street deh chump runned plump inteh me, an' den he turns aroun' an' says, 'Yer insolen' ruffin!' he says, like dat. 'Oh, gee!' I says, 'oh, gee! git off d' eart'!' I says, like dat. See? 'Git off d' eart'!' like dat. Den deh blokie he got wild. He says I was a contempt'ble scoun'el, er somethin' like dat, an' he says I was doom' teh ever-lastin' pe'dition, er somethin' like dat. 'Gee!' I says, 'gee! Yer joshin' me,' I says. 'Yer joshin' me.' An' den I slugged 'im. See?"

With Jimmie in his company, Pete departed in a sort of blaze of glory from the Johnson home. Maggie, leaning from the window, watched him as he walked down the street. Here was a formidable man who disdained the strength of a world full of fists. Here was one who had contempt for brassclothed power; one whose knuckles could ring defiantly against the granite of law. He was a knight.

The two men went from under the glimmering street lamp and passed into shadows. Turning, Maggie contemplated the dark, dust-stained walls and the scant and crude furniture of her home. A clock in a splintered and battered oblong box of varnished wood she suddenly regarded as an abomination. She noted that it ticked raspingly. The almost vanished flowers in the carpet pattern, she conceived to be newly hideous. Some faint attempts which she had made with blue ribbon to freshen the appearance of a dingy curtain she now saw to be piteous.

She wondered what Pete dined on.

She reflected upon the collar-and-cuff factory. It began to appear to her mind as a dreary place of endless grinding. Pete's elegant occupation brought him, no doubt, into contact with people who had money and manners. It was probable that he had a large acquaintance with pretty girls. He must have great sums of money to spend.

To her the earth was composed of hardships and insults. She felt instant admiration for a man who openly defied it. She thought that if the grim angel of death should clutch his heart, Pete would shrug his shoulders and say, "Oh, ev'ryt'ing goes."

She anticipated that he would come again shortly. She spent some of her week's pay in the purchase of flowered cretonne for a lambrequin. She made it with infinite care, and hung it to the slightly careening mantel over the stove in the kitchen. She studied it with painful anxiety from different points in the room. She wanted it to look well on Sunday night when, perhaps, Jimmie's friend would come. On Sunday night, however, Pete did not appear. Afterward the girl looked at it with a sense of humiliation. She was now convinced that Pete was superior to admiration for lambrequins.

A few evenings later Pete entered with fascinating innovations in his apparel. As she had seen him twice and he wore a different suit each time, Maggie had a dim impression that his wardrobe was prodigious.

"Say, Mag," he said, "put on yer bes' duds Friday night an' I'll take yehs t' d' show. See?" He spent a few moments in flourishing his clothes, and then vanished without having glanced at the lambrequin.

Over the eternal collars and cuffs in the factory Maggie spent the most of three days in making imaginary sketches of Pete and his daily environment. She imagined some half-dozen women in love with him, and thought he must lean dangerously toward an indefinite one whom she pictured as endowed with great charms of person, but with an altogether contemptible disposition. She thought he must live in a blare of pleasure. He had friends and people who were afraid of him. She saw the golden glitter of the place where Pete was to take her. It would be an entertainment of many hues and many melodies, where she was afraid she might appear small and mouse-coloured

Her mother drank whisky all Friday morning. With lurid face and tossing hair she cursed and destroyed furniture all Friday afternoon. When Maggie came home at half-past six her mother lay asleep amid the wreck of chairs and a table. Fragments of various household utensils were scattered about the floor. She had vented some phase of drunken fury upon the lambrequin. It lay in a bedraggled heap in the corner.

"Hah!" she snorted, sitting up suddenly, "where yeh been? Why don' yeh come home earlier? Been loafin' 'round d' streets. Yer gettin' t' be a reg'lar devil."

When Pete arrived, Maggie, in a worn black dress, was waiting for him in the midst of a floor strewn with wreckage. The curtain at the window had been pulled by a heavy hand and hung by one tack, dangling to and fro in the draught through the cracks at the sash. The knots of blue ribbons appeared like violated flowers. The fire in the stove had gone out. The displaced lids and open doors showed heaps of sullen grey ashes. The remnants of a meal, ghastly, lay in a corner. Maggie's mother, stretched on the floor, blasphemed, and gave her daughter a bad name.

VII

An orchestra of yellow silk women and bald-headed men, on an elevated stage near the center of a great green-hued ball, played a popular waltz. The place was crowded with people grouped about little tables. A battalion of waiters slid among the throng, carrying trays of beer-glasses, and making change from the inexhaustible vaults of their trousers pockets. Little boys, in the costumes of French chefs, paraded up and down the irregular aisles vending fancy cakes. There was a low rumble of conversation and a subdued clinking of glasses. Clouds of tobacco smoke rolled and wavered high in air above the dull gilt of the chandeliers.

The vast crowd had an air throughout of having just quitted labour. Men with calloused hands, and attired in garments that showed the wear of an endless drudging for a living, smoked their pipes contentedly and spent five, ten, or perhaps fifteen cents for beer. There was a mere sprinkling of men who smoked cigars purchased elsewhere. The great body of the crowd was composed of people who showed that all day they strove with their hands. Quiet Germans, with maybe their wives and two or three children, sat listening to the music, with the expressions of happy cows. An occasional party of sailors from a war-ship, their faces pictures of sturdy health, spent the earlier hours of the evening at the small round tables. Very infre-quent tipsy men, swollen with the value of their opinions, engaged their companions in earnest and confidential conversation. In the balcony, and here and there below, shone the impassive faces of women. The nationalities of the Bowery beamed upon the stage from all directions.

Pete walked aggressively up a side aisle and took seats with Maggie at a table beneath the balcony. "Two beehs!" Leaning back, he regarded with eyes of superiority the scene before them. This attitude affected Maggie strongly. A man who could regard such a sight with indifference must be accustomed to very great things. It was obvious that Pete had visited this place many times before, and was very familiar with it. A knowledge of this fact made Maggie feel little and new.

He was extremely gracious and attentive. He displayed the consideration of a cultured gentleman who knew what was due. "Say, what's eatin' yeh? Bring d' lady a big glass! What use is dat pony?"

"Don't be fresh, now," said the waiter, with some warmth, as he departed.

"Ah, get off d' eart'!" said Pete, after the other's retreat-ing form.

Maggie perceived that Pete brought forth all his ele-gance and all his knowledge of high-class customs for her benefit. Her heart warmed as she reflected upon his con-descension.

The orchestra of yellow silk women and bald-headed

men gave vent to a few bars of anticipatory music, and a girl, in a pink dress with short skirts, galloped upon the stage. She smiled upon the throng as if in acknowledgment of a warm welcome, and began to walk to and fro, making profuse gesticulations, and singing, in brazen soprano tones, a song the words of which were inaudible. When she broke into the swift rattling measures of a chorus some half-tipsy men near the stage joined in the rollicking refrain, and glasses were pounded rhythmically upon the tables. People leaned forward to watch her and to try to catch the words of the song. When she vanished there were long rollings of applause. Obedient to more anticipatory bars, she reappeared among the half-suppressed cheering of the tipsy men. The orchestra plunged into dance music, and the laces of the dancer fluttered and flew in the glare of gas-jets. She divulged the fact that she was attired in some half-dozen skirts. It was patent that any one of them would have proved adequate for the purpose for which skirts are intended. An occasional man bent forward, intent upon the pink stockings. Maggie wondered at the splendour of the costume and lost herself in calculations of the cost of the silks and laces.

The dancer's smile of enthusiasm was turned for ten minutes upon the faces of her audience. In the finale she fell into some of those grotesque attitudes which were at the time popular among the dancers in the theaters uptown, giving to the Bowery public the diversions of the aristocratic theater-going public at reduced rates.

"Say, Pete," said Maggie, leaning forward, "dis is great."

"Sure!" said Pete, with proper complacence.

A ventriloquist followed the dancer. He held two fantastic dolls on his knees. He made them sing mournful ditties and say funny things about geography and Ireland.

"Do dose little men talk?" asked Maggie.

"Naw," said Pete, "it's some big jolly. See?"

Two girls, set down on the bills as sisters, came forth and sang a duet which is heard occasionally at concerts given under church auspices. They supplemented it with a dance, which, of course, can never be seen at concerts given under church auspices.

After they had retired, a woman of debatable age sang a Negro melody. The chorus necessitated some grotesque waddlings supposed to be an imitation of a plantation darky, under the influence, probably, of music and the moon. The audience was just enthusiastic enough over it to make her return and sing a sorrowful lay, whose lines told of a mother's love, and a sweetheart who waited, and a young man who was lost at sea under harrowing circumstances. From the faces of a score or so in the crowd the self-contained look faded. Many heads were bent forward with eagerness and sympathy. As the last distressing sentiment of the piece was brought forth, it was greeted by the kind of applause which rings as sincere.

As a final effort, the singer rendered some verses which described a vision of Britain annihilated by America, and Ireland bursting her bonds. A carefully prepared climax was reached in the last line of the last verse, when the singer threw out her arms and cried, "The star-spangled banner." Instantly a great cheer swelled from the throats of this assemblage of the masses, most of them of foreign birth. There was a heavy rumble of booted feet thumping the floor. Eyes gleamed with sudden fire, and calloused hands waved frantically in the air.

After a few moments' rest, the orchestra played noisily, and a small fat man burst out upon the stage. He began to roar a song and to stamp back and forth before the footlights, wildly waving a silk hat and throwing leers broadcast. He made his face into fantastic grimaces until he looked like a devil on a Japanese kite. The crowd laughed gleefully. His short, fat legs were never still a moment. He shouted and roared and bobbed his shock of red wig until the audience broke out in excited applause.

Pete did not pay much attention to the progress of events upon the stage. He was drinking beer and watching Maggie. Her cheeks were blushing with excitement and her eyes were glistening. She drew deep breaths of pleasure. No thoughts of the atmosphere of the collar-and-cuff factory came to her.

With the final crash of the orchestra they jostled their way to the sidewalk in the crowd. Pete took Maggie's arm and pushed a way for her, offering to fight with a man or two. They reached Maggie's home at a late hour and stood for a moment in front of the gruesome doorway.

"Say, Mag," said Pete, "give us a kiss for takin' yeh t' d' show, will yer?"

Maggie laughed, as if startled, and drew away from him. "Naw, Pete," she said, "dat wasn't in it."

"Ah, why wasn't it?" urged Pete.

The girl retreated nervously.

"Ah, go ahn!" repeated he.

Maggie darted into the hall and up the stairs. She turned and smiled at him, then disappeared.

Pete walked slowly down the street. He had something of an astonished expression upon his features. He paused under a lamp-post and breathed a low breath of surprise. "Gee!" he said, "I wonner if I've been played fer a duffer."

VIII

As thoughts of Pete came to Maggie's mind, she began to have an intense dislike for all of her dresses. "What ails yeh? What makes ye be allus fixin' and fussin'?" her mother would frequently roar at her. She began to note with more interest the well-dressed women she met on the avenues. She envied elegance and soft palms. She craved those adornments of person which she saw every day on the street, conceiving them to be allies of vast importance to women. Studying faces, she thought many of the women and girls she chanced to meet smiled with serenity as though forever cherished and watched over by those they loved.

The air in the collar-and-cuff establishment strangled her. She knew she was gradually and surely shrivelling in the hot, stuffy room. The begrimed windows rattled incessantly from the passing of elevated trains. The place was filled with a whirl of noises and odours. She became lost in thought as she looked at some of the grizzled women in the room, mere mechanical contrivances sewing seams and grinding out, with heads bent over their work, tales of imagined or real girlhood happiness, or of past drunks, or the baby at home, and unpaid wages. She wondered how long her youth would endure. She began to see the bloom upon her cheeks as something of value. She imagined herself, in an exasperating future, as a scrawny woman with an eternal grievance. She thought Pete to be a very fastidious person concerning the appearance of women.

She felt that she should love to see somebody entangle their fingers in the oily beard of the fat foreigner who owned the establishment. He was a detestable creature. He wore white socks with low shoes. He sat all day delivering orations in the depths of a cushioned chair. His pocket-book deprived them of the power of retort. "What do you sink I pie fife dolla a week for? Play? No, py tamn!"

Maggie was anxious for a friend to whom she could talk about Pete. She would have liked to discuss his admirable mannerisms with a reliable mutual friend. At home, she found her mother often drunk and always raving. It seemed that the world had treated this woman very badly, and she took a deep revenge upon such portions of it as came within her reach. She broke furniture as if she were at last getting her rights. She swelled with virtuous indignation as she carried the lighter articles of household use, one by one, under the shadows of the three gilt balls, where Hebrews chained them with chains of interest.

Jimmie came when he was obliged to by circumstances over which he had no control. His well-trained legs brought him staggering home and put him to bed some nights when he would rather have gone elsewhere.

Swaggering Pete loomed like a golden sun to Maggie. He took her to a dime museum, where rows of meek freaks astonished her. She contemplated their deformities with awe, and thought them a sort of chosen tribe. Pete, racking his brains for amusement, discovered the Central Park Menagerie and the Museum of Arts. Sunday afternoons would sometimes find them at these places. Pete did not appear to be particularly interested in what he saw. He stood around looking heavy, while Maggie giggled in glee.

Once at the menagerie he went into a trance of admiration before the spectacle of a very small monkey threatening to thrash a cageful because one of them had pulled his tail and he had not wheeled about quickly enough to discover who did it. Ever after Pete knew that monkey by sight, and winked at him, trying to induce him to fight with other and larger monkeys.

At the museum, Maggie said, "Dis is outa sight!"

"Aw, rats!" said Pete; "wait till next summer an' I'll take yehs to a picnic."

While the girl wandered in the vaulted rooms, Pete oc-

cupied himself in returning, stony stare for stony stare, the
appalling scrutiny of the watch-dogs of the treasures. Occasionally he would remark in loud tones, "Dat jay has
got glass eyes," and sentences of the sort. When he tired of
this amusement he would go to the mummies and moralize
over them.

Usually he submitted with silent dignity to all that he
had to go through, but at times he was goaded into comment. "Aw!" he demanded once. "Look at all dese little
jugs! Hundred jugs in a row! Ten rows in a case, an' 'bout
a t'ousand cases! What d' blazes use is dem?"

In the evenings of week days he often took her to see
plays in which the dazzling heroine was rescued from the
palatial home of her treacherous guardian by the hero with
the beautiful sentiments. The latter spent most of his time
out at soak in pale-green snow-storms, busy with a nickel-
plated revolver rescuing aged strangers from villains. Maggie lost herself in sympathy with the wanderers swooning
in snow-storms beneath happy-hued church windows, while
a choir within sang "Joy to the World." To Maggie and
the rest of the audience this was transcendental realism.
Joy always within, and they, like the actor, inevitably without. Viewing it, they hugged themselves in ecstatic pity of
their imagined or real condition. The girl thought the arro-
gance and granite-heartedness of the magnate of the play
were very accurately drawn. She echoed the maledictions
that the occupants of the gallery showered on this individual when his lines compelled him to expose his extreme
selfishness.

Shady persons in the audience revolted from the pictured villainy of the drama. With untiring zeal they hissed
vice and applauded virtue. Unmistakably bad men
evinced an apparently sincere admiration for virtue. The
loud gallery was overwhelmingly with the unfortunate and
the oppressed. They encouraged the struggling hero with
cries, and jeered the villain, hooting and calling attention
to his whiskers. When anybody died in the pale-green
snow-storms, the gallery mourned. They sought out the
painted misery and hugged it as akin.

In the hero's erratic march from poverty in the first act
to wealth and triumph in the final one, in which he for-
gives all the enemies that he has left, he was assisted by the
gallery, which applauded his generous and noble senti-

ments and confounded the speeches of his opponents by making irrelevant but very sharp remarks. Those actors who were cursed with the parts of villains were confronted at every turn by the gallery. If one of them rendered lines containing the most subtle distinctions between right and wrong, the gallery was immediately aware that the actor meant wickedness, and denounced him accordingly. The last act was a triumph for the hero, poor and of the masses, the representative of the audience, over the villain and the rich man, his pockets stuffed with bonds, his heart packed with tyrannical purposes, imperturbable amid suffering.

Maggie always departed with raised spirits from these melodramas. She rejoiced at the way in which the poor and virtuous eventually overcame the wealthy and wicked. The theater made her think. She wondered if the culture and refinement she had seen imitated, perhaps grotesquely, by the heroine on the stage, could be acquired by a girl who lived in a tenement house and worked in a shirt factory.

IX

A group of urchins were intent upon the side door of a saloon. Expectancy gleamed from their eyes. They were twisting their fingers in excitement. "Here she comes!" yelled one of them suddenly. The group of urchins burst instantly asunder and its individual fragments were spread in a wide, respectable half-circle about the point of interest. The saloon door opened with a crash, and the figure of a woman appeared upon the threshold. Her grey hair fell in knotted masses about her shoulders. Her face was crimsoned and wet with perspiration. Her eyes had a rolling glare. "Not a cent more of me money will yehs ever get—not a red! I spent me money here fer t'ree years, an' now yehs tells me yeh'll sell me no more stuff! Go fall on yerself, Johnnie Murckre! 'Disturbance'? Disturbance be blowed! Go fall on yerself, Johnnie—"

The door received a kick of exasperation from within, and the woman lurched heavily out on the sidewalk. The gamins in the half-circle became violently agitated. They began to dance about and hoot and yell and jeer. A wide dirty grin spread over each face.

The woman made a furious dash at a particularly outrageous cluster of little boys. They laughed delightedly, and scampered off a short distance, calling out to her over their shoulders. She stood tottering on the kerb-stone and thundered at them. "Yeh devil's kids!" she howled, shaking her fists. The little boys whooped in glee. As she started up the street they fell in behind and marched uproariously. Occasionally she wheeled about and made charges on them. They ran nimbly out of reach and taunted her.

In the frame of a gruesome doorway she stood for a moment cursing them. Her hair straggled, giving her red features a look of insanity. Her great fists quivered as she shook them madly in the air. The urchins made terrific noises until she turned and disappeared. Then they filed off quietly in the way they had come.

The woman floundered about in the lower hall of the tenement house, and finally stumbled up the stairs. On an upper hall a door was opened and a collection of heads peered curiously out, watching her. With a wrathful snort the woman confronted the door, but it was slammed hastily in her face and the key was turned.

She stood for a few minutes, delivering a frenzied challenge at the panels. "Come out in deh hall, Mary Murphy, if yehs want a scrap! Come ahn! yeh over-grown terrier, come ahn!" She began to kick the door. She shrilly defied the universe to appear and do battle. Her cursing trebles brought heads from all doors save the one she threatened. Her eyes glared in every direction. The air was full of her tossing fists. "Come ahn! deh hull gang of yehs, come ahn!" she roared at the spectators. An oath or two, cat-calls, jeers, and bits of facetious advice were given in reply. Missiles clattered about her feet.

"What's wrong wi'che?" said a voice in the gathered gloom, and Jimmie came forward. He carried a tin dinner-pail in his hand and under his arm a truckman's brown apron done in a bundle. "What's wrong?" he demanded.

"Come out! all of yehs, come out," his mother was howling. "Come ahn an' I'll stamp yer faces t'rough d' floor."

"Shet yer face, an' come home, yeh old fool!" roared Jimmie at her. She strode up to him and twirled her fingers in his face. Her eyes were darting flames of unreasoning rage, and her frame trembled with eagerness for a fight.

"An' who are youse? I ain't givin' a snap of me fingers

fer youse!" she bawled at him. She turned her huge back in tremendous disdain and climbed the stairs to the next floor.

Jimmie followed, and at the top of the flight he seized his mother's arm and started to drag her toward the door of their room. "Come home!" he gritted between his teeth.

"Take yer hands off me! Take yer hands off me!" shrieked his mother. She raised her arm and whirled her great fist at her son's face. Jimmie dodged his head, and the blow struck him in the back of the neck. "Come home!" he gritted again. He threw out his left hand and writhed his fingers about her middle arm. The mother and the son began to sway and struggle like gladiators.

"Whoop!" said the Rum Alley tenement house. The hall filled with interested spectators. "Hi, ol' lady, dat was a dandy!" "T'ree t' one on d' red!" "Ah, quit yer scrappin'!"

The door of the Johnson home opened and Maggie looked out. Jimmie made a supreme cursing effort and hurled his mother into the room. He quickly followed and closed the door. The Rum Alley tenement swore disappointedly and retired.

The mother slowly gathered herself up from the floor. Her eyes glittered menacingly upon her children.

"Here now," said Jimmie, "we've had enough of dis. Sit down, an' don' make no trouble."

He grasped her arm and, twisting it, forced her into a creaking chair.

"Keep yer hands off me!" roared his mother again.

"Say, yeh ol' bat! Quit dat!" yelled Jimmie, madly. Maggie shrieked and ran into the other room. To her there came the sound of a storm of crashes and curses. There was a great final thump and Jimmie's voice cried: "Dere, now! Stay still." Maggie opened the door now, and went warily out. "Oh, Jimmie!"

He was leaning against the wall and swearing. Blood stood upon bruises on his knotty forearms where they had scraped against the floor or the walls in the scuffle. The mother lay screeching on the floor, the tears running down her furrowed face.

Maggie, standing in the middle of the room, gazed about her. The usual upheaval of the tables and chairs had taken place. Crockery was strewn broadcast in fragments. The stove had been disturbed on its legs, and now leaned idiotically to one side. A pail had been upset and water spread in all directions.

The door opened and Pete appeared. He shrugged his shoulders. "Oh, gee!" he observed. He walked over to Maggie and whispered in her ear: "Ah, what d' hell, Mag? Come ahn and we'll have a outa-sight time."

The mother in the corner upreared her head and shook her tangled locks. "Aw, yer bote no good, needer of yehs," she said, glowering at her daughter in the gloom. Her eyes seemed to burn balefully. "Yeh've gone t' d' devil, Mag Johnson, yehs knows yehs have gone t' d' devil. Yer a disgrace t' yer people. An' now, git out an' go ahn wid dat doe-faced jude of yours. Go wid him, curse yeh, an' a good riddance. Go, an' see how yeh likes it."

Maggie gazed long at her mother.

"Go now, an' see how yeh likes it. Git out. I won't have sech as youse in me house! Git out, d' yeh hear! Damn yeh, git out!"

The girl began to tremble.

At this instant Pete came forward. "Oh, what d' hell, Mag, see?" whispered he softly in her ear. "Dis all blows over. See? D' ol' woman 'ill be all right in d' mornin'. Come ahn out wid me! We'll have a outa-sight time."

The woman on the floor cursed. Jimmie was intent upon his bruised forearms. The girl cast a glance about the room filled with a chaotic mass of debris, and at the writhing body of her mother.

"Git th' devil outa here."

Maggie went.

X

Jimmie had an idea it wasn't common courtesy for a friend to come to one's home and ruin one's sister. But he was not sure how much Pete knew about the rules of politeness.

The following night he returned home from work at a rather late hour in the evening. In passing through the halls he came upon the gnarled and leathery old woman who possessed the music-box. She was grinning in the dim light that drifted through dust-stained panes. She beckoned to him with a smudged forefinger.

"Ah, Jimmie, what do yehs t'ink I tumbled to, las' night! It was deh funnies' t'ing I ever saw," she cried, coming close to him and leering. She was trembling with eagerness to tell her tale. "I was by me door las' night when yer sister and her jude feller came in late, oh, very late. An' she, the dear, she was a-cryin' as if her heart would break, she was. It was deh funnies' t'ing I ever saw. An' right out here by me door she asked him did he love her, did he. An' she was a-cryin' as if her heart would break, poor t'ing. An' him, I could see be deh way what he said it dat she had been askin' orften; he says, 'Oh, gee, yes,' he says, says he. 'Oh, gee, yes.' "

Storm-clouds swept over Jimmie's face, but he turned from the leathery old woman and plodded on upstairs.

" 'Oh, gee, yes,' " she called after him. She laughed a laugh that was like a prophetic croak.

There was no one in at home. The rooms showed that attempts had been made at tidying them. Parts of the wreckage of the day before had been repaired by an unskilled hand. A chair or two and the table stood uncertainly upon legs. The floor had been newly swept. The blue ribbons had been restored to the curtains, and the lambrequin, with its immense sheaves of yellow wheat and red roses of equal size, had been returned, in a worn and sorry state, to its place at the mantel. Maggie's jacket and hat were gone from the nail behind the door.

Jimmie walked to the window and began to look through the blurred glass. It occurred to him to wonder vaguely, for an instant, if some of the women of his acquaintance had brothers.

Suddenly, however, he began to swear. "But he was me frien'! I brought 'im here! Dat's d' devil of it!" He fumed about the room, his anger gradually rising to the furious pitch. "I'll kill deh jay! Dat's what I'll do! I'll kill deh jay!"

He clutched his hat and sprang toward the door. But it opened, and his mother's great form blocked the passage. "What's d' matter wid yeh?" exclaimed she, coming into the room.

Jimmie gave vent to a sardonic curse and then laughed heavily. "Well, Maggie's gone teh d' devil! Dat's what! See?"

"Eh?" said his mother.

"Maggie's gone teh d' devil! Are yehs deaf?" roared Jimmie, impatiently.

"Aw, git out!" murmured the mother, astounded.

Jimmie grunted, and then began to stare out the window. His mother sat down in a chair, but a moment later sprang erect and delivered a maddened whirl of oaths. Her son turned to look at her as she reeled and swayed in the middle of the room, her fierce face convulsed with passion, her blotched arms raised high in imprecation.

"May she be cursed for ever!" she shrieked. "May she eat nothin' but stones and deh dirt in deh street. May she sleep in deh gutter an' never see deh sun shine again. D' bloomin'——"

"Here now," said her son. "Go fall on yerself, an' quit dat."

The mother raised lamenting eyes to the ceiling. "She's d' devil's own chil', Jimmie," she whispered. "Ah, who would t'ink such a bad girl could grow up in our fambly, Jimmie, me son. Many d' hour I've spent in talk wid dat girl an' tol' her if she ever went on d' streets I'd see her damned. An' after all her bringin'-up an' what I tol' her and talked wid her, she goes teh d' bad, like a duck teh water."

The tears rolled down her furrowed face. Her hands trembled. "An' den when dat Sadie MacMallister next door to us was sent teh d' devil by dat feller what worked in d' soap factory, didn't I tell our Mag dat if she——"

"Ah, dat's anudder story," interrupted the brother. "Of course, dat Sadie was nice an' all dat—but—see?—it ain't dessame as if—well, Maggie was diff'ent—see?—she was diff'ent." He was trying to formulate a theory that he had always unconsciously held, that all sisters excepting his own could, advisedly, be ruined.

He suddenly broke out again. "I'll go t'ump d' mug what done her d' harm. I'll kill 'im! He t'inks he kin scrap, but when he gits me a-chasin' 'im he'll fin' out where he's wrong, d' big stiff! I'll wipe up d' street wid 'im." In a fury he plunged out the doorway.

As he vanished the mother raised her head and lifted both hands, entreating. "May she be cursed for ever!" she cried.

In the darkness of the hallway Jimmie discerned a knot of women talking volubly. When he strode by they paid no attention to him. "She allus was a bold thing," he heard one of them cry in an eager voice. "Dere wasn't a feller come teh deh house but she'd try teh mash 'im. My Annie says deh shameless t'ing tried teh ketch her feller, her own feller, what we useter know his fader."

"I could' a' tol' yehs dis two years ago," said a woman, in a key of triumph. "Yes, sir, it was over two years ago dat I says teh my ol' man, I says, 'Dat Johnson girl ain't straight,' I says. 'Oh, rats!' he says. 'Oh, hell!' 'Dat's all right,' I says, 'but I know what I knows,' I says, 'an' it'll come out later. You wait an' see,' I says, 'you see.' "

"Anybody what had eyes could see dat dere was somethin' wrong wid dat girl. I didn't like her actions."

On the street Jimmie met a friend. "What's wrong?" asked the latter.

Jimmie explained. "An' I'll t'ump 'im till he can't stand."

"Oh, go ahn!" said the friend. "What's deh use! Yeh'll git pulled in! Everybody 'ill be on to it! An' ten plunks! Gee!"

Jimmie was determined. "He t'inks he kin scrap, but he'll fin' out diff'ent."

"Gee!" remonstrated the friend, "what's d' use?"

XI

On a corner a glass-fronted building shed a yellow glare upon the pavements. The open mouth of a saloon called seductively to passengers to enter and annihilate sorrow or create rage.

The interior of the place was papered in olive and bronze tints of imitation leather. A shining bar of counterfeit massiveness extended down the side of the room. Behind it a great mahogany-imitation sideboard reached the ceiling. Upon its shelves rested pyramids of shimmering glasses that were never disturbed. Mirrors set in the face of the sideboard multiplied them. Lemons, oranges, and paper napkins, arranged with mathematical precision, sat among the glasses. Many-hued decanters of liquor perched at regular intervals on the lower shelves. A nickel-plated cash-register occupied a place in the exact center of the general effect. The elementary senses of it all seemed to be opulence and geometrical accuracy.

Across from the bar a smaller counter held a collection of plates upon which swarmed frayed fragments of crackers, slices of boiled ham, dishevelled bits of cheese, and pickles swimming in vinegar. An odour of grasping, begrimed hands and munching mouths pervaded all.

Pete, in a white jacket, was behind the bar bending expectantly toward a quiet stranger. "A beeh," said the man. Peter drew a foam-topped glassful, and set it dripping upon the bar.

At this moment the light bamboo doors at the entrance swung open and crashed against the wall. Jimmie and a companion entered. They swaggered unsteadily but belligerently toward the bar, and looked at Pete with bleared and blinking eyes.

"Gin," said Jimmie.

"Gin," said the companion.

Pete slid a bottle and two glasses along the bar. He bent his head sideways as he assiduously polished away with a napkin at the gleaming wood. He wore a look of watchfulness.

Jimmie and his companion kept their eyes upon the bartender and conversed loudly in tones of contempt.

"He's a dandy masher, ain't he?" laughed Jimmie.

"Well, ain't he!" said the companion, sneering. "He's great, he is. Git on to deh mug on deh blokie. Dat's enough to make a feller turn handsprings in 'is sleep."

The quiet stranger moved himself and his glass a trifle farther away and maintained an attitude of obliviousness.

"Gee! ain't he hot stuff?"

"Git on to his shape!"

"Hey!" cried Jimmie, in tones of command. Pete came along slowly, with a sullen dropping of the under lip.

"Well," he growled, "what's eatin' yehs?"

"Gin," said Jimmie.

"Gin," said the companion.

As Pete confronted them with the bottle and the glasses they laughed in his face. Jimmie's companion, evidently overcome with merriment, pointed a grimy forefinger in Pete's direction. "Say, Jimmie," demanded he, "what's dat behind d' bar?"

"Looks like some chump," replied Jimmie. They laughed loudly.

Pete put down a bottle with a bang and turned a formidable face toward them. He disclosed his teeth, and his shoulders heaved restlessly. "You fellers can't guy me," he said. "Drink yer stuff an' git out an' don' make no trouble."

Instantly the laughter faded from the faces of the two

men, and expressions of offended dignity immediately came. "Aw, who has said anyt'ing t' you?" cried they in the same breath.

The quiet stranger looked at the door calculatingly.

"Ah, come off," said Pete to the two men. "Don't pick me up fer no jay. Drink yer rum an' git out an' don' make no trouble."

"Aw, go ahn!" airily cried Jimmie.

"Aw, go ahn!" airily repeated his companion.

"We goes when we git ready! See?" continued Jimmie.

"Well," said Pete in a threatening voice, "don' make no trouble."

Jimmie suddenly leaned forward with his head on one side. He snarled like a wild animal. "Well, what if we does? See?" said he.

Hot blood flushed into Pete's face, and he shot a lurid glance at Jimmie. "Well, den we'll see who's d' bes' man, you or me," he said.

The quiet stranger moved modestly toward the door.

Jimmie began to swell with valour. "Don' pick me up fer no tenderfoot. When yeh tackles me yeh tackles one of d' bes' men in d' city. See? I'm a scrapper, I am. Ain't dat right, Billie?"

"Sure, Mike," responded his companion in tones of conviction.

"Aw!" said Pete, easily. "Go fall on yerself."

The two men again began to laugh.

"What is dat talking?" cried the companion.

"Don' ast me," replied Jimmie with exaggerated contempt.

Pete made a furious gesture. "Git outa here now, an' don' make no trouble. See? Youse fellers er lookin' fer a scrap, an' it's like yeh'll fin' one if yeh keeps on shootin' off yer mout's. I know yehs! See? I kin lick better men dan yehs ever saw in yer lifes. Dat's right! See? Don' pick me up fer no stiff, er yeh might be jolted out in d' street before yeh knows where yeh is. When I comes from behind dis bar, I t'rows yehs bote inteh d' street. See?"

"Ah, go ahn!" cried the two men in chorus.

The glare of a panther came into Pete's eyes. "Dat's what I said! Unnerstan'?"

He came through a passage at the end of the bar and swelled down upon the two men. They stepped promptly forward and crowded close to him. They bristled like three roosters. They moved their heads pugnaciously and kept their shoulders braced. The nervous muscles about each mouth twitched with a forced smile of mockery.

"Well, what yer goin' t' do?" gritted Jimmie.

Pete stepped warily back, waving his hands before him to keep the men from coming too near.

"Well, what yer goin' t' do?" repeated Jimmie's ally. They kept close to him, taunting and leering. They strove to make him attempt the initial blow.

"Keep back now! Don' crowd me," said Pete ominously.

Again they chorused in contempt. "Aw, go ahn!"

In a small, tossing group, the three men edged for positions like frigates contemplating battle.

"Well, why don' yeh try t' t'row us out?" cried Jimmie and his ally with copious sneers.

The bravery of bulldogs sat upon the faces of the men. Their clenched fists moved like eager weapons. The allied two jostled the bartender's elbows, glaring at him with feverish eyes and forcing him toward the wall.

Suddenly Pete swore furiously. The flash of action gleamed from his eyes. He threw back his arm and aimed a tremendous, lightning-like blow at Jimmie's face. His foot swung a step forward and the weight of his body was behind his fist. Jimmie ducked his head, Bowery-like, with the quickness of a cat. The fierce answering blows of Jimmie and his ally crushed on Pete's bowed head.

The quiet stranger vanished.

The arms of the combatants whirled in the air like flails. The faces of the men, at first flushed to flame-coloured anger, now began to fade to the pallor of warriors in the blood and heat of a battle. Their lips curled back and stretched tightly over the gums in ghoul-like grins. Through their white, gripped teeth struggled hoarse whisperings of oaths. Their eyes glittered with murderous fire.

Each head was huddled between its owner's shoulders, and arms were swinging with marvellous rapidity. Feet scraped to and fro with a loud scratching sound upon the sanded floor. Blows left crimson blotches upon the pale skin. The curses of the first quarter-minute of the fight died away. The breaths of the fighters came wheezing from their lips and the three chests were straining and heaving. Pete at intervals gave vent to low, laboured hisses that sounded like a desire to kill. Jimmie's ally gibbered at times like a wounded maniac. Jimmie was silent, fighting with the face of a sacrificial priest. The rage of fear shone in all their eyes, and their blood-coloured fists whirled.

At a critical moment a blow from Pete's hand struck the ally, and he crashed to the floor. He wriggled instantly to his feet and, grasping the quiet stranger's beer-glass from the bar, hurled it at Pete's head.

High on the wall it burst like a bomb, shivering fragments flying in all directions. Then missiles came to every man's hand. The place had heretofore appeared free of things to throw, but suddenly glasses and bottles went singing through the air. They were thrown point-blank at bobbing heads. The pyramids of shimmering glasses, that had never been disturbed, changed to cascades as heavy bottles were flung into them. Mirrors splintered to nothing.

The three frothing creatures on the floor buried themselves in a frenzy for blood. There followed in the wake of missiles and fists some unknown prayers, perhaps for death.

The quiet stranger had sprawled very pyrotechnically out on the sidewalk. A laugh ran up and down the avenue for the half of a block. "Dey've t'rowed a bloke inteh deh street."

People heard the sound of breaking glass and shuffling feet within the saloon and came running. A small group, bending down to look under the bamboo doors, and watching the fall of glass and three pairs of violent legs, changed in a moment to a crowd. A policeman came charging down the sidewalk and bounced through the doors into the saloon. The crowd bent and surged in absorbing anxiety to see.

Jimmie caught the first sight of the oncoming interruption. On his feet he had the same regard for a policeman that, when on his truck, he had for a fire-engine. He howled and ran for the side door.

The officer made a terrific advance, club in hand. One comprehensive sweep of the long night-stick threw the ally to the floor and forced Pete to a corner. With his disengaged hand he made a furious effort at Jimmie's coat-tails. Then he regained his balance and paused. "Well, well, you are a pair of pictures. What have ye been up to?"

Jimmie, with his face drenched in blood, escaped up a side street, pursued a short distance by some of the more law-loving or excited individuals of the crowd.

Later, from a safe dark corner, he saw the policeman, the ally, and the bartender emerge from the saloon. Pete locked the doors and then followed up the avenue in the rear of the crowd-encompassed policeman and his charge.

At first Jimmie, with his heart throbbing at battle heat, started to go desperately to the rescue of his friend, but he halted. "Ah, what's d' use?" he demanded of himself.

XII

In a hall of irregular shape sat Pete and Maggie drinking beer. A submissive orchestra, dictated to by a spectacled man with frowsy hair and in soiled evening dress, industriously followed the bobs of his head and the waves of his baton. A ballad-singer, in a gown of flaming scarlet, sang in the inevitable voice of brass. When she vanished, men seated at the tables near the front applauded loudly, pounding the polished wood with their beer-glasses. She returned attired in less gown and sang again. She received another enthusiastic encore. She reappeared in still less gown and danced. The deafening rumble of glasses and clapping of hands that followed her exit indicated an overwhelming desire to have her come on for the fourth time, but the curiosity of the audience was not gratified.

Maggie was pale. From her eyes had been plucked all look of self-reliance. She leaned with a dependent air toward her companion. She was timid, as if fearing his anger or displeasure. She seemed to beseech tenderness of him.

Pete's air of distinguished valour had grown upon him until it threatened to reach stupendous dimensions. He was infinitely gracious to the girl. It was apparent to her that his condescension was a marvel. He could appear to strut even while sitting still, and he showed that he was a lion of lordly characteristics by the air with which he spat.

With Maggie gazing at him wonderingly, he took pride in commanding the waiters, who were, however, indifferent or deaf. "Hi, you, git a russle on yehs! What yehs lookin' at? Two more beehs, d' yeh hear?" He leaned back and critically regarded the person of a girl with a straw-coloured wig who was flinging her heels about upon the stage in somewhat awkward imitation of a well-known *danseuse*.

At times Maggie told Pete long confidential tales of her former home life, dwelling upon the escapades of the other members of the family and the difficulties she had had to combat in order to obtain a degree of comfort. He responded in the accents of philanthropy. He pressed her arm with an air of reassuring proprietorship.

"Dey was cursed jays," he said, denouncing the mother and brother.

The sound of the music which, through the efforts of the frowsy-headed leader, drifted to her ears in the smoke-filled atmosphere, made the girl dream. She thought of her former Rum Alley environment and turned to regard Pete's strong protecting fists. She thought of a collar-and-cuff manufactory and the eternal moan of the proprietor: "What een hale do you sink I pie fife dolla a week for? Play? No, py tamn!" She contemplated Pete's man-subduing eyes and noted that wealth and prosperity were indicated by his clothes. She imagined a future rose-tinted because of its distance from all that she had experienced before.

As to the present she perceived only vague reasons to be miserable. Her life was Pete's, and she considered him worthy of the charge. She would be disturbed by no particular apprehensions so long as Pete adored her as he now said he did. She did not feel like a bad woman. To her knowledge she had never seen any better.

At times men at other tables regarded the girl furtively. Pete, aware of it, nodded at her and grinned. He felt proud. "Mag, yer a bloomin' good looker," he remarked, studying her face through the haze. The men made Maggie fear, but she blushed at Pete's words as it became apparent to her that she was the apple of his eye.

Grey-headed men, wonderfully pathetic in their dissipation, stared at her through clouds. Smooth-cheeked boys, some of them with faces of stone and mouths of sin, not nearly so pathetic as the grey heads, tried to find the girl's eyes in the smoke-wreaths. Maggie considered she was not what they thought her. She confined her glances to Pete and the stage.

The orchestra played Negro melodies, and a versatile drummer pounded, whacked, clattered, and scratched on a dozen machines to make noise.

Those glances of the men, shot at Maggie from under half-closed lids, made her tremble. She thought them all to be worse men than Pete. "Come, let's go," she said.

As they went out Maggie perceived two women seated at a table with some men. They were painted, and their cheeks had lost their roundness. As she passed them the girl, with a shrinking movement, drew back her skirts.

XIII

Jimmie did not return home for a number of days after the fight with Pete in the saloon. When he did, he approached with extreme caution.

He found his mother raving. Maggie had not returned home. The parent continually wondered how her daughter could come to such a pass. She had never considered Maggie as a pearl dropped unstained into Rum Alley from Heaven, but she could not conceive how it was possible for her daughter to fall so low as to bring disgrace upon her family. She was terrific in denunciation of the girl's wickedness.

The fact that the neighbours talked of it maddened her. When women came in, and in the course of their conversation casually asked, "Where's Maggie dese days?" the mother shook her fuzzy head at them and appalled them with curses. Cunning hints inviting confidence she rebuffed with violence.

"An' wid all d' bringin'-up she had, how could she?" moaningly she asked of her son. "Wid all d' talkin' wid her I did an' d' t'ings I tol' her to remember. When a girl is bringed up d' way I bringed up Maggie, how kin she go teh d' devil?"

Jimmie was transfixed by these questions. He could not conceive how, under the circumstances, his mother's daughter and his sister could have been so wicked.

His mother took a drink from a bottle that sat on the table. She continued her lament. "She had a bad heart, dat girl did, Jimmie. She was wicked t' d' heart an' we never knowed it."

Jimmie nodded, admitting the fact.

"We lived in d' same house wid her an' I brought her up, an' we never knowed how bad she was."

Jimmie nodded again.

"Wid a home like dis an' a mudder like me, she went teh d' bad," cried the mother, raising her eyes.

One day Jimmie came home, sat down in a chair, and began to wriggle about with a new and strange nervousness. At last he spoke shamefacedly. "Well, look-a-here, dis t'ing queers us! See? We're queered! An' maybe it 'ud be better if I—well, I t'ink I kin look 'er up an'—maybe it 'ud be better if I fetched her home an'——"

The mother started from her chair and broke forth into a storm of passionate anger. "What! Let 'er come an' sleep under deh same roof wid her mudder agin? Oh, yes, I will, won't I! Sure! Shame on yehs, Jimmie Johnson, fer sayin' such a t'ing teh yer own mudder! Little did I t'ink when yehs was a babby playin' about me feet dat ye'd grow up teh say sech a t'ing teh yer mudder—yer own mudder. I never t'ought——"

Sobs choked her and interrupted her reproaches.

"Dere ain't nottin' teh make sech trouble about," said Jimmie. "I on'y says it 'ud be better if we keep dis t'ing dark, see? It queers us! See?"

His mother laughed a laugh that seemed to ring through the city and be echoed and re-echoed by countless other laughs. "Oh, yes, I will, won't I? Sure!"

"Well, yeh must take me fer a damn fool," said Jimmie, indignant at his mother for mocking him. "I didn't say we'd make 'er inteh a little tin angel, ner nottin', but deh way it is now she can queer us! Don'che see?"

"Ay, she'll git tired of deh life atter a while, an' den she'll wanna be a-comin' home, won' she, deh beast! I'll let 'er in den, won't I?"

"Well, I didn't mean none of dis prod'gal bus'ness anyway," explained Jimmie.

"It wa'n't no prod'gal daughter, yeh fool," said the mother. "It was prod'gal son, anyhow."

"I know dat," said Jimmie.

For a time they sat in silence. The mother's eyes gloated on the scene which her imagination called before her. Her lips were set in a vindictive smile. "Ay, she'll cry, won' she, an' carry on, an' tell how Pete, or some odder feller, beats 'er, an' she'll say she's sorry an' all dat, an' she ain't happy, she ain't, an' she wants to come home agin, she does." With grim humour the mother imitated the possible wailing notes of the daughter's voice. "Den I'll take 'er in, won't I? She kin cry 'er two eyes out on deh stones of deh street before I'll dirty d' place wid her. She abused an' ill-treated her own mudder—her own mudder what loved her, an' she'll never git anodder chance."

Jimmie thought he had a great idea of women's frailty, but he could not understand why any of his kin should be victims. "Curse her!" he said fervidly. Again he wondered vaguely if some of the women of his acquaintance had brothers. Nevertheless, his mind did not for an instant confuse himself with those brothers nor his sister with theirs.

After the mother had, with great difficulty, suppressed the neighbours, she went among them and proclaimed her grief. "May Heaven forgive dat girl," was her continual cry. To attentive ears she recited the whole length and breadth of her woes. "I bringed 'er up deh way a daughter oughta be bringed up, an' dis is how she served me! She went teh deh devil deh first chance she got! May Heaven forgive her."

When arrested for drunkenness she used the story of her daughter's downfall with telling effect upon the police justices. Finally one of them said to her, peering down over his spectacles: "Mary, the records of this and other courts show that you are the mother of forty-two daughters who have been ruined. The case is unparalleled in the annals of this court, and this court thinks—"

The mother went through life shedding large tears of sorrow. Her red face was a picture of agony.

Of course Jimmie publicly damned his sister that he might appear on a higher social plane. But, arguing with himself, stumbling about in ways that he knew not, he, once, almost came to a conclusion that his sister would have been more firmly good had she better known how. However, he felt that he could not hold such a view. He threw it hastily aside.

XIV

In a hilarious hall there were twenty-eight tables and twenty-eight women and a crowd of smoking men. Valiant noise was made on a stage at the end of the hall by an or-

chestra composed of men who looked as if they had just
happened in. Soiled waiters ran to and fro, swooping down
like hawks on the unwary in the throng; clattering along
the aisles with trays covered with glasses; stumbling over
women's skirts and charging two prices for everything but
beer, all with a swiftness that blurred the view of the coco-
nut palms and dusty monstrosities painted upon the walls
of the room. A "bouncer," with an immense load of business upon his hands, plunged about in the crowd, dragging
bashful strangers to prominent chairs, ordering waiters
here and there, and quarrelling furiously with men who
wanted to sing with the orchestra.

The usual smoke-cloud was present, but so dense that
heads and arms seemed entangled in it. The rumble of
conversation was replaced by a roar. Plenteous oaths
heaved through the air. The room rang with the shrill voices
of women bubbling over with drink-laughter. The chief element in the music of the orchestra was speed. The musicians played in intent fury. A woman was singing and
smiling upon the stage, but no one took notice of her. The
rate at which the piano, cornet, and violins were going
seemed to impart wildness to the half-drunken crowd.
Beer-glasses were emptied at a gulp and conversation became a rapid chatter. The smoke eddied and swirled like
a shadowy river hurrying toward some unseen falls. Pete
and Maggie entered the hall and took chairs at a table near
the door. The woman who was seated there made an
attempt to occupy Pete's attention, and, failing, went away.

Three weeks had passed since the girl had left home. The
air of spaniel-like dependence had been magnified and
showed its direct effect in the peculiar off-handedness and
ease of Pete's ways toward her. She followed Pete's eyes
with hers, anticipating with smiles gracious looks from him.

A woman of brilliance and audacity, accompanied by a
mere boy, came into the place and took a seat near them.
At once Pete sprang to his feet, his face beaming with
glad surprise. "Hully gee, dere's Nellie!" he cried. He went
over to the table and held out an eager hand to the
woman.

"Why, hello, Pete, me boy, how are you?" said she,
giving him her fingers.

Maggie took instant note of the woman. She perceived
that her black dress fitted her to perfection. Her linen collar
and cuffs were spotless. Tan gloves were stretched over

her well-shaped hands. A hat of a prevailing fashion perched jauntily upon her dark hair. She wore no jewellery and was painted with no apparent paint. She looked clear-eyed through the stares of the men.

"Sit down, and call your lady friend over," she said to Pete. At his beckoning Maggie came and sat between Pete and the mere boy.

"I t'ought yeh was gone away fer good," began Pete, at once. "When did yeh git back? How did dat Buff'lo business turn out?"

The woman shrugged her shoulders. "Well, he didn't have as many stamps as he tried to make out, so I shook him, that's all."

"Well, I'm glad teh see ychs back in deh city," said Pete, with gallantry. He and the woman entered into a long conversation, exchanging reminiscences of days together. Maggie sat still, unable to formulate an intelligent sentence as her addition to the conversation, and painfully aware of it.

She saw Pete's eyes sparkle as he gazed upon the handsome stranger. He listened smilingly to all she said. The woman was familiar with all his affairs, asked him about mutual friends, and knew the amount of his salary. She paid no attention to Maggie, looking toward her once or twice and apparently seeing the wall beyond.

The mere boy was sulky. In the beginning he had welcomed the additions with acclamations. "Let's all have a drink! What'll you take, Nell? And you, Miss What's-your-name. Have a drink, Mr.—you, I mean." He had shown a sprightly desire to do the talking for the company and tell all about his family. In a loud voice he declaimed on various topics. He assumed a patronizing air toward Pete. As Maggie was silent, he paid no attention to her. He made a great show of lavishing wealth upon the woman of brilliance and audacity.

"Do keep still, Freddie! You talk like a clock," said the woman to him. She turned away and devoted her attention to Pete. "We'll have many a good time together again, eh?"

"Sure, Mike," said Pete, enthusiastic at once.

"Say," whispered she, leaning forward, "let's go over to Billie's and have a time."

"Well, it's dis way! See?" said Pete. "I got dis lady frien' here."

"Oh, g'way with her," argued the woman.

Pete appeared disturbed.

"All right," said she, nodding her head at him. "All right for you! We'll see the next time you ask me to go anywheres with you."

Pete squirmed. "Say," he said, beseechingly, "come wid me a minute an' I'll tell yer why."

The woman waved her hand. "Oh, that's all right, you needn't explain, you know. You wouldn't come merely because you wouldn't come, that's all." To Pete's visible distress she turned to the mere boy, bringing him speedily out of a terrific rage. He had been debating whether it would be the part of a man to pick a quarrel with Pete, or would he be justified in striking him savagely with his beer-glass without warning. But he recovered himself when the woman turned to renew her smilings. He beamed upon her with an expression that was somewhat tipsy and inexpressibly tender.

"Say, shake that Bowery jay," requested he, in a loud whisper.

"Freddie, you are so funny," she replied.

Pete reached forward and touched the woman on the arm. "Come out a minute while I tells yeh why I can't go wid yer. Yer doin' me dirt, Nell! I never t'ought ye'd do me dirt, Nell. Come on, will yer?" He spoke in tones of injury.

"Why, I don't see why I should be interested in your explanations," said the woman, with a coldness that seemed to reduce Pete to a pulp.

His eyes pleaded with her. "Come out a minute while I tells yeh. On d' level, now."

The woman nodded slightly at Maggie and the mere boy, saying, " 'Scuse me."

The mere boy interrupted his loving smile and turned a shrivelling glare upon Pete. His boyish countenance flushed and he spoke in a whine to the woman: "Oh, I say, Nellie, this ain't a square deal, you know. You aren't goin' to leave me and go off with that duffer, are you? I should think—"

"Why, you dear boy, of course I'm not," cried the woman, affectionately. She bent over and whispered in his ear. He smiled again and settled in his chair as if resolved to wait patiently.

As the woman walked down between the rows of tables, Pete was at her shoulder talking earnestly, apparently in explanation. The woman waved her hands with studied airs of indifference. The doors swung behind them leaving Maggie and the mere boy seated at the table.

Maggie was dazed. She could dimly perceive that something stupendous had happened. She wondered why Pete saw fit to remonstrate with the woman, pleading forgiveness with his eyes. She thought she noted an air of submission about her leonine Pete. She was astounded.

The mere boy occupied himself with cocktails and a cigar. He was tranquilly silent for half an hour. Then he bestirred himself and spoke. "Well," he said, sighing, "I knew this was the way it would be. They got cold feet." There was another stillness. The mere boy seemed to be musing. "She was pulling m' leg. That's the whole amount of it," he said, suddenly. "It's a bloomin' shame the way that girl does. Why, I've spent over two dollars in drinks tonight. And she goes off with that plug-ugly, who looks as if he had been hit in the face with a coin die. I call it rocky treatment for a fellah like me. Here, waiter, bring me a cocktail, and make it strong."

Maggie made no reply. She was watching the doors.

"It's a mean piece of business," complained the mere boy. He explained to her how amazing it was that anybody should treat him in such a manner. "But I'll get square with her, you bet. She won't get far ahead of yours truly, you know," he added, winking. "I'll tell her plainly that it was bloomin' mean business. And she won't come it over me with any of her 'now-Freddie-dear's.' She thinks my name is Freddie, you know, but of course it ain't. I always tell these people some name like that, because if they got on to your right name they might use it sometime. Understand? Oh, they don't fool me much."

Maggie was paying no attention, being intent upon the doors. The mere boy relapsed into a period of gloom, during which he exterminated a number of cocktails with a determined air, as if replying defiantly to fate. He occasionally broke forth into sentences composed of invectives joined together in a long chain.

The girl was still staring at the doors. After a time the mere boy began to see cobwebs just in front of his nose. He spurred himself into being agreeable and insisted upon her having a Charlotte Russe and a glass of beer.

"They's gone," he remarked, "they's gone." He looked

at her through the smoke-wreaths. "Shay, lil' girl, we mightish well make bes' of it. You ain't such bad-lookin' girl, y' know. Not half bad. Can't come up to Nell, though. No, can't do it! Well, I should shay not! Nell fine-lookin' girl! F-i-n-ine. You look bad longsider her, but by y'self ain't so bad. Have to do, anyhow. Nell gone. O'ny you left. Not half bad, though."

Maggie stood up. "I'm going home," she said.

The mere boy started. "Eh? What? Home!" he cried, struck with amazement. "I beg pardon, did hear say home?"

"I'm going home," she repeated.

"Great heavens! what hav' a struck?" demanded the mere boy of himself, stupefied. In a semi-comatose state he conducted her on board an uptown car, ostentatiously paid her fare, leered kindly at her through the rear window, and fell off the steps.

XV

A forlorn woman went along a lighted avenue. The street was filled with people desperately bound on missions. An endless crowd darted at the elevated station stairs, and the horse-cars were thronged with owners of bundles.

The pace of the forlorn woman was slow. She was apparently searching for some one. She loitered near the doors of saloons and watched men emerge from them. She furtively scanned the faces in the rushing stream of pedestrians. Hurrying men, bent on catching some boat or train, jostled her elbows, failing to notice her, their thoughts fixed on distant dinners.

The forlorn woman had a peculiar face. Her smile was no smile. But when in repose her features had a shadowy look that was like a sardonic grin, as if some one had sketched with cruel forefinger indelible lines about her mouth.

Jimmie came strolling up the avenue. The woman encountered him with an aggrieved air. "Oh, Jimmie, I've been lookin' all over for yehs—" she began.

Jimmie made an impatient gesture and quickened his pace. "Ah, don't bodder me!" he said, with the savageness of a man whose life is pestered.

The woman followed him along the sidewalk in somewhat the manner of a suppliant. "But, Jimmie," she said, "yehs told me yehs—"

Jimmie turned upon her fiercely as if resolved to make

a last stand for comfort and peace. "Say, Hattie, don' foller me from one end of deh city teh deh odder. Let up, will yehs! Give me a minute's res', can't yehs? Yehs makes me tired, allus taggin' me. See? Ain' yehs got no sense? Do yehs want people teh get on to me? Go chase yerself."

The woman stepped closer and laid her fingers on his arm. "But, look a' here—"

Jimmie snarled. "Oh, go teh blazes!" He darted into the front door of a convenient saloon and a moment later came out into the shadows that surrounded the side door. On the brilliantly lighted avenue he perceived the forlorn woman dodging about like a scout. Jimmie laughed with an air of relief and went away.

When he returned home he found his mother clamouring. Maggie had returned. She stood shivering beneath the torrent of her mother's wrath.

"Well, I'm damned!" said Jimmie in greeting.

His mother, tottering about the room, pointed a quivering forefinger. "Look ut her, Jimmie, look ut her. Dere's yer sister, boy. Dere's yer sister. Look ut her! Look ut her!" She screamed at Maggie with scoffing laughter.

The girl stood in the middle of the room. She edged about as if unable to find a place on the floor to put her feet.

"Ha ha, ha!" bellowed the mother. "Dere she stands! Ain't she purty? Look ut her! Ain' she sweet, deh beast? Look ut her! Ha, ha! look ut her!" She lurched forward and put her red and seamed hands upon her daughter's face. She bent down and peered keenly up into the eyes of the girl. "Oh, she's jes' dessame as she ever was, ain' she? She's her mudder's putty darlin' yit, ain' she? Look ut her, Jimmie. Come here and look ut her."

The loud, tremendous railing of the mother brought the denizens of the Rum Alley tenement to their doors. Women came in the hallways. Children scurried to and fro.

"What's up? Dat Johnson party on anudder tear?"

"Naw! Young Mag's come home!"

"Git out!"

Through the open doors curious eyes stared in at Maggie. Children ventured into the room and ogled her as if they formed the front row at a theater. Women, without, bent toward each other and whispered, nodding their heads with airs of profound philosophy.

A baby, overcome with curiosity concerning this object

at which all were looking, sidled forward and touched her dress, cautiously, as if investigating a red-hot stove. Its mother's voice rang out like a warning trumpet. She rushed forward and grabbed her child, casting a terrible look of indignation at the girl.

Maggie's mother paced to and fro, addressing the doorful of eyes, expounding like a glib showman. Her voice rang through the building. "Dere she stands," she cried, wheeling suddenly and pointing with dramatic finger. "Dere she stands! Look ut her! Ain' she a dandy? An' she was so good as to come home teh her mudder, she was! Ain' she a beaut'? Ain' she a dandy?"

The jeering cries ended in another burst of shrill laughter.

The girl seemed to awaken. "Jimmie—"

He drew hastily back from her. "Well, now, yer a t'ing, ain' yeh?" he said, his lips curling in scorn. Radiant virtue sat upon his brow, and his repelling hands expressed horror of contamination.

Maggie turned and went.

The crowd at the door fell back precipitately. A baby falling down in front of the door wrenched a scream like that of a wounded animal from its mother. Another woman sprang forward and picked it up with a chivalrous air, as if rescuing a human being from an oncoming express train.

As the girl passed down through the hall, she went before open doors framing more eyes strangely microscopic, and sending broad beams of inquisitive light into the darkness of her path. On the second floor she met the gnarled old woman who possessed the music-box.

"So," she cried, " 'ere yehs are back again, are yehs? An' dey've kicked yehs out? Well, come in an' stay wid me t'-night. I ain' got no moral standin'."

From above came an unceasing babble of tongues, over all of which rang the mother's derisive laughter.

XVI

Pete did not consider that he had ruined Maggie. If he had thought that her soul could never smile again, he would have believed the mother and brother, who were pyrotechnic over the affair, to be responsible for it. Besides, in his world, souls did not insist upon being able to smile. "What d' hell?"

He felt a trifle entangled. It distressed him. Revelations and scenes might bring upon him the wrath of the owner of the saloon, who insisted upon respectability of an advanced type. "What do dey wanna raise such a smoke about it fer?" demanded he of himself, disgusted with the attitude of the family. He saw no necessity that people should lose their equilibrium merely because their sister or their daughter had stayed away from home. Searching about in his mind for possible reasons for their conduct, he came upon the conclusion that Maggie's motives were correct, but that the two others wished to snare him. He felt pursued.

The woman whom he had met in the hilarious hall showed a disposition to ridicule him. "A little pale thing with no spirit," she said. "Did you note the expression of her eyes? There was something in them about pumpkin pie and virtue. That is a peculiar way the left corner of her mouth has of twitching, isn't it? Dear, dear, Pete, what are you coming to?"

Pete asserted at once that he never was very much interested in the girl. The woman interrupted him, laughing. "Oh, it's not of the slightest consequence to me, my dear young man. You needn't draw maps for my benefit. Why should I be concerned about it?" But Pete continued with his explanations. If he was laughed at for his tastes in women, he felt obliged to say that they were only temporary or indifferent ones.

The morning after Maggie had departed from home Pete stood behind the bar. He was immaculate in white jacket and apron, and his hair was plastered over his brow with infinite correctness. No customers were in the place. Pete was twisting his napkined fist slowly in a beer-glass, softly whistling to himself, and occasionally holding the object of his attention between his eyes and a few weak beams of sunlight that found their way over the thick screens and into the shaded rooms.

With lingering thoughts of the woman of brilliance and audacity, the bartender raised his head and stared through the varying cracks between the swaying bamboo doors. Suddenly the whistling pucker faded from his lips. He saw Maggie walking slowly past. He gave a great start, fearing for the previously mentioned eminent respectability of the place.

He threw a swift, nervous glance about him, all at once feeling guilty. No one was in the room. He went hastily over to the side door. Opening it and looking out, he perceived Maggie standing, as if undecided, at the corner. She was searching the place with her eyes. As she turned her face toward him, Pete beckoned to her hurriedly, intent upon returning with speed to a position behind the bar, and to the atmosphere of respectability upon which the proprietor insisted.

Maggie came to him, the anxious look disappearing from her face and a smile wreathing her lips. "Oh, Pete—" she began brightly.

The bartender made a violent gesture of impatience. "Oh, say," cried he vehemently. "What d' yeh wanna hang aroun' here fer? Do yer wanna git me inteh trouble?" he demanded with an air of injury.

Astonishment swept over the girl's features. "Why, Pete! yehs tol' me—"

Pete's glance expressed profound irritation. His countenance reddened with the anger of a man whose respectability is being threatened. "Say, yehs makes me tired! See? What d' yeh wanna tag aroun' atter me fer? Yeh'll do me dirt wid d' ol' man an' dey'll be trouble! If he sees a woman roun' here he'll go crazy an' I'll lose me job! See? Ain' yehs got no sense? Don' be allus bodderin' me. See? Yer brudder came in here an' made trouble an' d' ol' man hadda put up fer it! An' now I'm done! See? I'm done."

The girl's eyes stared into his face. "Pete, don' yeh remem—"

"Oh, go ahn!" interrupted Pete, anticipating.

The girl seemed to have a struggle with herself. She was apparently bewildered and could not find speech. Finally she asked in a low voice, "But where kin I go?"

The question exasperated Pete beyond the powers of endurance. It was a direct attempt to give him some responsibility in a matter that did not concern him. In his indignation he volunteered information. "Oh, go to hell!" cried he. He slammed the door furiously and returned, with an air of relief, to his respectability.

Maggie went away. She wandered aimlessly for several blocks. She stopped once and asked aloud a question of herself: "Who?" A man who was passing near her shoulder humorously took the questioning word as intended for him. "Eh! What? Who? Nobody! I didn't say anything," he laughingly said, and continued his way.

Soon the girl discovered that if she walked with such apparent aimlessness, some men looked at her with calculating eyes. She quickened her step, frightened. As a protection, she adopted a demeanour of intentness as if going somewhere.

After a time she left rattling avenues and passed between rows of houses with sternness and stolidity stamped upon their features. She hung her head, for she felt their eyes grimly upon her.

Suddenly she came upon a stout gentleman in a silk hat and a chaste black coat, whose decorous row of buttons reached from his chin to his knees. The girl had heard of the grace of God and she decided to approach this man. His beaming, chubby face was a picture of benevolence and kind-heartedness. His eyes shone good will.

But as the girl timidly accosted him he made a convulsive movement and saved his respectability by a vigorous side-step. He did not risk it to save a soul. For how was he to know that there was a soul before him that needed saving?

XVII

Upon a wet evening, several months later, two interminable rows of cars, pulled by slipping horses, jangled along a prominent side street. A dozen cabs, with coatenshrouded drivers, clattered to and fro. Electric lights, whirring softly, shed a blurred radiance. A flower-dealer, his feet tapping impatiently, his nose and his wares glistening with raindrops, stood behind an array of roses and chrysanthemums. Two or three theaters emptied a crowd upon the stormswept sidewalks. Men pulled their hats over their eyebrows and raised their collars to their ears. Women shrugged impatient shoulders in their warm cloaks and stopped to arrange their skirts for a walk through the storm. People who had been constrained to comparative silence for two hours burst into a roar of conversation, their hearts still kindling from the glowings of the stage.

The sidewalks became tossing seas of umbrellas. Men stepped forth to hail cabs or cars, raising their fingers in varied forms of polite· request or imperative demand. An endless procession wended toward elevated stations. An atmosphere of pleasure and prosperity seemed to hang over the throng, born, perhaps, of good clothes and of two hours in a place of forgetfulness.

In the mingled light and gloom of an adjacent park, a handful of wet wanderers, in attitudes of chronic dejection, were scattered among the benches.

A girl of the painted cohorts of the city went along the street. She threw changing glances at men who passed her, giving smiling invitations to those of rural or untaught pattern and usually seeming sedately unconscious of the men with a metropolitan seal upon their faces. Crossing glittering avenues, she went into the throng emerging from the places of forgetfulness. She hurried forward through the crowd as if intent upon reaching a distant home, bending forward in her handsome cloak, daintily lifting her skirts, and picking for her well-shod feet the dryer spots upon the sidewalks.

The restless doors of saloons, clashing to and fro, disclosed animated rows of men before bars and hurrying barkeepers. A concert-hall gave to the street faint sounds of swift, machine-like music, as if a group of phantom musicians were hastening.

A tall young man, smoking a cigarette with a sublime air, strolled near the girl. He had on evening dress, a moustache, a chrysanthemum, and a look of *ennui,* all of which he kept carefully under his eye. Seeing the girl walk on as if such a young man as he was not in existence, he looked back transfixed with interest. He stared glassily for a moment, but gave a slight convulsive start when he discerned that she was neither new, Parisian, nor theatrical. He wheeled about hastily and turned his stare into the air, like a sailor with a searchlight.

A stout gentleman, with pompous and philanthropic whiskers, went stolidly by, the broad of his back sneering at the girl. A belated man in business clothes, and in haste to catch a car, bounced against her shoulder. "Hi, there, Mary, I beg your pardon! Brace up, old girl." He grasped her arm to steady her, and then was away running down the middle of the street.

The girl walked on out of the realm of restaurants and saloons. She passed more glittering avenues and went into darker blocks than those where the crowd travelled.

A young man in light overcoat and derby hat received a

glance shot keenly from the eyes of the girl. He stopped and looked at her, thrusting his hands into his pockets and making a mocking smile curl his lips. "Come, now, old lady," he said, "you don't mean to tell me that you sized me up for a farmer?"

A labouring man marched along with bundles under his arms. To her remarks replied, "It's a fine evenin', ain't it?"

She smiled squarely into the face of a boy who was hurrying by with his hands buried in his overcoat pockets, his blond locks bobbing on his youthful temples, and a cheery smile of unconcern upon his lips. He turned his head and smiled back at her, waving his hands. "Not this eve—some other eve."

A drunken man, reeling in her pathway, began to roar at her. "I ain' go' no money!" he shouted, in a dismal voice. He lurched on up the street, wailing to himself: "I ain' go' no money. Ba' luck. Ain' go' no more money."

The girl went into gloomy districts near the river, where the tall black factories shut in the street and only occasional broad beams of light fell across the sidewalks from saloons. In front of one of these places, whence came the sound of a violin vigorously scraped, the patter of feet on boards, and the ring of loud laughter, there stood a man with blotched features.

Farther on in the darkness she met a ragged being with shifting, bloodshot eyes and grimy hands.

She went into the blackness of the final block. The shutters of the tall buildings were closed like grim lips. The structure seemed to have eyes that looked over them, beyond them, at other things. Afar off the lights of the avenues glittered as if from an impossible distance. Streetcar bells jingled with a sound of merriment.

At the feet of the tall buildings appeared the deathly black hue of the river. Some hidden factory sent up a yellow glare that lit for a moment the waters lapping oilily against timbers. The varied sounds of life, made joyous by distance and seeming unapproachableness, came faintly and died away to a silence.

XVIII

In a partitioned-off section of a saloon sat a man with a half-dozen women, gleefully laughing, hovering about him.

The man had arrived at that stage of drunkenness where affection is felt for the universe. "I'm good f'ler, girls," he said, convincingly. "I'm good f'ler. An'body trea's me right, I allus trea's zem right! See?"

The women nodded their heads approvingly. "To be sure," they cried in hearty chorus. "You're the kind of a man we like, Pete. You're outa sight! What yeh goin' to buy this time, dear?"

"An't'ing yehs wants!" said the man in an abandonment of good will. His countenance shone with the true spirit of benevolence. He was in the proper mood of missionaries. He would have fraternized with obscure Hottentots. And above all he was overwhelmed in tenderness for his friends, who were all illustrious. "An't'ing yehs wants!" repeated he, waving his hands with beneficent recklessness. "I'm good f'ler, girls, an' if an'body trea's me right I— Here," called he through an open door to a waiter, "bring girls drinks. What 'ill yehs have, girls? An't'ing yehs want."

The waiter glanced in with the disgusted look of the man who serves intoxicants for the man who takes too much of them. He nodded his head shortly at the order from each individual, and went.

"W' 're havin' great time," said the man. "I like you girls! Yer right sort! See?" He spoke at length and with feeling concerning the excellences of his assembled friends. "Don' try pull man's leg, but have a good time! Dass right! Dass way teh do! Now, if I s'ought yehs tryin' work me fer drinks, wouldn' buy notting! But yer right sort! Yehs know how ter treat a f'ler, an' I stays by yehs till spen' las' cent! Dass right!" I'm good f'ler an' I knows when an'body trea's me right!"

Between the times of the arrival and departure of the waiter, the man discoursed to the women on the tender regard he felt for all living things. He laid stress upon the purity of his motives in all dealings with men in the world, and spoke of the fervour of his friendship for those who were amiable. Tears welled slowly from his eyes. His voice quavered when he spoke to his companions.

Once when the waiter was about to depart with an empty tray, the man drew a coin from his pocket and held it forth. "Here," said he, quite magnificently, "here's quar'."

The waiter kept his hands on his tray. "I don't want yer money," he said.

The other put forth the coin with tearful insistence. "Here's quar'!" cried he, "take 't! Yer goo' f'ler an' I wan' yehs take 't!"

"Come, come, now," said the waiter, with the sullen air of a man who is forced into giving advice. "Put yer mon in yer pocket! Yer loaded an' yehs on'y makes a fool of yerself."

As the waiter passed out of the door the man turned pathetically to the women. "He don' know I'm goo' f'ler," cried he, dismally.

"Never you mind, Pete, dear," said the woman of brilliance and audacity, laying her hand with great affection upon his arm. "Never you mind, old boy! We'll stay by you, dear!"

"Dass ri'!" cried the man, his face lighting up at the soothing tones of the woman's voice. "Dass ri'; I'm goo' f'ler, an' w'en any one trea's me ri', I trea's zem ri'! Shee?"

"Sure!" cried the women. "And we're not goin' back on you, old man."

The man turned appealing eyes to the woman. He felt that if he could be convicted of a contemptible action he would die. "Shay, Nell, I allus trea's yehs shquare, didn' I? I allus been goo' f'ler wi' yehs, ain't I, Nell?"

"Sure you have, Pete," assented the woman. She delivered an oration to her companions. "Yessir, that's a fact. Pete's a square fellah, he is. He never goes back on a friend. He's the right kind an' we stay by him, don't we, girls?"

"Sure!" they exclaimed. Looking lovingly at him they raised their glasses and drank his health.

"Girlsh," said the man, beseechingly, "I allus trea's yehs ri', didn' I? I'm goo' f'ler, ain' I, girlsh?"

"Sure!" again they chorused.

"Well," said he finally, "le's have nozzer drink, zen."

"That's right," hailed a woman, "that's right. Yer no bloomin' jay! Yer spends yer money like a man. Dat's right."

The man pounded the table with his quivering fists. "Yessir," he cried, with deep earnestness, as if some one disputed him. "I'm goo' f'ler, an' w'en any one trea's me ri', I allus trea's—le's have nozzer drink." He began to beat the wood with his glass. "Shay!" howled he, growing suddenly impatient. As the waiter did not then come, the man swelled with wrath. "Shay!" howled he again. The waiter appeared at the door. "Bringsh drinksh," said the man.

The waiter disappeared with the orders.

"Zat f'ler fool!" cried the man. "He insul' me! I'm ge'man! Can' stan' be insul'! I'm goin' lick 'im when comes!"

"No, no!" cried the women, crowding about and trying to subdue him. "He's all right! He didn't mean anything! Let it go! He's a good fellah!"

"Di'n' he insul' me?" asked the man earnestly.

"No," said they. "Of course he didn't! He's all right!"

"Sure he didn' insul' me?" demanded the man, with deep anxiety in his voice.

"No, no! We know him! He's a good fellah. He didn't mean anything."

"Well, zen," said the man resolutely, "I'm go 'pol'gize!"

When the waiter came, the man struggled to the middle of the floor. "Girlsh shed you insul' me! I shay—lie! I 'pol'gize!"

"All right," said the waiter.

The man sat down. He felt a sleepy but strong desire to straighten things out and have a perfect understanding with everybody. "Nell, I allus trea's yeh shquare, di'n' I? Yeh likes me, don' yehs, Nell? I'm goo' f'ler?"

"Sure!" said the woman.

"Yeh knows I'm stuck on yehs, don' yehs, Nell?"

"Sure!" she repeated carelessly.

Overwhelmed by a spasm of drunken adoration, he drew two or three bills from his pocket and, with the trembling fingers of an offering priest, laid them on the table before the woman. "Yehs knows yehs kin have all I got, 'cause I'm stuck on yehs, Nell, I—I'm stuck on yehs, Nell—buy drinksh—we're havin' grea' time—w'en any one trea's me ri'—I—Nell—we're havin' heluva—time."

Presently he went to sleep with his swollen face fallen forward on his chest.

The women drank and laughed, not heeding the slumbering man in the corner. Finally he lurched forward and fell groaning to the floor.

The women screamed in disgust and drew back their skirts. "Come ahn!" cried one, starting up angrily, "let's get out of here."

The woman of brilliance and audacity stayed behind,

taking up the bills and stuffing them into a deep, irregularly shaped pocket. A guttural snore from the recumbent man caused her to turn and look down at him. She laughed. "What a fool!" she said, and went.

The smoke from the lamps settled heavily down in the little compartment, obscuring the way out. The smell of oil, stifling in its intensity, pervaded the air. The wine from an overturned glass dripped softly down upon the blotches on the man's neck.

XIX

In a room a woman sat at a table eating like a fat monk in a picture.

A soiled, unshaven man pushed open the door and entered.

"Well," said he, "Mag's dead."

"What?" said the woman, her mouth filled with bread.

"Mag's dead," repeated the man.

"Deh blazes she is!" said the woman. She continued her meal. When she finished her coffee she began to weep.

"I kin remember when her two feet was no bigger dan yer t'umb an' she weared worsted boots," moaned she.

"Well, whata dat?" said the man.

"I kin remember when she weared worsted boots," she cried.

The neighbours began to gather in the hall, staring in at the weeping woman as if watching the contortions of a dying dog. A dozen women entered and lamented with her. Under their busy hands the room took on that appealing appearance of neatness and order with which death is greeted.

Suddenly the door opened and a woman in a black gown rushed in with outstretched arms. "Ah, poor Mary!" she cried, and tenderly embraced the moaning one.

"Ah, what ter'ble affliction is dis!" continued she. Her vocabulary was derived from mission churches. "Me poor Mary, how I feel fer yehs! Ah, what a ter'ble affliction is a disobed'ent chile."

Her good, motherly face was wet with tears. She trembled in eagerness to express her sympathy. The mourner sat with bowed head, rocking her body heavily to and fro, and crying out in a high, strained voice that sounded like a dirge on some forlorn pipe.

"I kin remember when she weared worsted boots an' her two feets was no bigger dan yer t'umb an' she weared worsted boots, Miss Smith," she cried, raising her streaming eyes.

"Ah, me poor Mary!" sobbed the woman in black. With low, coddling cries, she sank on her knees by the mourner's chair, and put her arms about her. The other women began to groan in different keys.

"Yer poor misguided chil' is gone now, Mary, an' let us hope it's fer deh bes'. Yeh'll fergive her now, Mary, won't yehs, dear, all her disobed'ence? All her t'ankless behaviour to her mudder an' all her badness? She's gone where her ter'ble sins will be judged."

The woman in black raised her face and paused. The inevitable sunlight came streaming in at the window and shed a ghastly cheerfulness upon the faded hues of the room. Two or three of the spectators were sniffing, and one was weeping loudly. The mourner arose and staggered into the other room. In a moment she emerged with a pair of faded baby shoes held in the hollow of her hand. "I kin remember when she used to wear dem!" cried she. The women burst anew into cries as if they had all been stabbed. The mourner turned to the soiled and unshaven man. "Jimmie, boy, go git yer sister! Go git yer sister an' we'll put deh boots on her feets!"

"Dey won't fit her now, yeh fool," said the man.

"Go git yer sister, Jimmie!" shrieked the woman confronting him fiercely.

The man swore sullenly. He went over to a corner and slowly began to put on his coat. He took his hat and went out, with a dragging, reluctant step.

The woman in black came forward and again besought the mourner. "Yeh'll fergive her, Mary! Yeh'll fergive yer bad, bad chil'! Her life was a curse an' her days were black, an' yeh'll fergive yer bad girl? She's gone where her sins will be judged."

"She's gone where her sins will be judged!" cried the other women, like a choir at a funeral.

"Deh Lord gives and deh Lord takes away," said the woman in black, raising her eyes to the sunbeams.

"Deh Lord gives and deh Lord takes away," responded the others.

"Yeh'll fergive her, Mary?" pleaded the woman in black.

The mourner essayed to speak, but her voice gave way. She shook her great shoulders frantically, in an agony of grief. The tears seemed to scald her face. Finally her voice came and arose in a scream of pain. "Oh, yes, I'll fergive her! I'll fergive her!"

1893

The Open Boat

I

None of them knew the color of the sky. Their eyes glanced level, and were fastened upon the waves that swept toward them. These waves were of the hue of slate, save for the tops, which were of foaming white, and all of the men knew the colors of the sea. The horizon narrowed and widened, and dipped and rose, and at all times its edge was jagged with waves that seemed thrust up in points like rocks. Many a man ought to have a bath-tub larger than the boat which here rode upon the sea. These waves were most wrongfully and barbarously abrupt and tall, and each froth-top was a problem in small-boat navigation.

The cook squatted in the bottom and looked with both eyes at the six inches of gunwale which separated him from the ocean. His sleeves were rolled over his fat fore-arms, and the two flaps of his unbottoned vest dangled as he bent to bail out the boat. Often he said: "Gawd! That was a narrow clip." As he remarked it he invariably gazed eastward over the broken sea.

The oiler, steering with one of the two oars in the boat, sometimes raised himself suddenly to keep clear of water that swirled in over the stern. It was a thin little oar and it seemed often ready to snap.

The correspondent, pulling at the other oar, watched the waves and wondered why he was there.

The injured captain, lying in the bow, was at this time buried in that profound dejection and indifference which comes, temporarily at least, to even the bravest and most enduring when, willy nilly, the firm fails, the army loses, the ship goes down. The mind of the master of a vessel is rooted deep in the timbers of her, though he commanded for a day or a decade, and this captain had on him the stern impression of a scene in the grays of dawn of seven turned faces, and later a stump of a top-mast with a white ball on it that slashed to and fro at the waves, went low and lower, and down. Thereafter there was something strange in his voice. Although steady, it was deep with mourning, and of a quality beyond oration or tears.

"Keep 'er a little more south, Billie," said he.

" 'A little more south,' sir," said the oiler in the stern.

A seat in this boat was not unlike a seat upon a bucking broncho, and by the same token, a broncho is not much smaller. The craft pranced and reared, and plunged like an animal. As each wave came, and she rose for it, she seemed like a horse making at a fence outrageously high. The manner of her scramble over these walls of water is a mystic thing, and, moreover, at the top of them were ordinarily these problems in white water, the foam racing down from the summit of each wave, requiring a new leap, and a leap from the air. Then, after scornfully bumping a crest, she would slide, and race, and splash down a long incline, and arrive bobbing and nodding in front of the next menace.

A singular disadvantage of the sea lies in the fact that after successfully surmounting one wave you discover that there is another behind it just as important and just as nervously anxious to do something effective in the way of swamping boats. In a ten-foot dingey one can get an idea of the resources of the sea in the line of waves that is not probable to the average experience which is never at sea in a dingey. As each slatey wall of water approached, it shut all else from the view of the men in the boat, and it was not difficult to imagine that this particular wave was the final outburst of the ocean, the last effort of the grim water. There was a terrible grace in the move of the waves, and they came in silence, save for the snarling of the crests.

In the wan light, the faces of the men must have been gray. Their eyes must have glinted in strange ways as they gazed steadily astern. Viewed from a balcony, the whole thing would doubtless have been weirdly picturesque. But the men in the boat had not time to see it, and if they had had leisure there were other things to occupy their minds. The sun swung steadily up the sky, and they knew it was broad day because the color of the sea changed from slate to emerald-green, streaked with amber lights, and the foam was like tumbling snow. The process of the breaking day was unknown to them. They were aware only of this effect upon the color of the waves that rolled toward them.

In disjointed sentences the cook and the correspondent argued as to the difference between a life-saving station and a house of refuge. The cook had said: "There's a house of refuge just north of the Mosquito Inlet Light, and as soon as they see us, they'll come off in their boat and pick us up."

"As soon as who see us?" said the correspondent.

"The crew," said the cook.

"Houses of refuge don't have crews," said the correspondent. "As I understand them, they are only places where clothes and grub are stored for the benefit of shipwrecked people. They don't carry crews."

"Oh, yes, they do," said the cook.

"No, they don't," said the correspondent.

"Well, we're not there yet, anyhow," said the oiler, in the stern.

"Well," said the cook, "perhaps it's not a house of refuge that I'm thinking of as being near Mosquito Inlet Light. Perhaps it's a life-saving station."

"We're not there yet," said the oiler, in the stern.

II

As the boat bounced from the top of each wave, the wind tore through the hair of the hatless men, and as the craft plopped her stern down again the spray splashed past them. The crest of each of these waves was a hill, from the top of which the men surveyed, for a moment, a broad tumultuous expanse, shining and wind-riven. It was probably splendid. It was probably glorious, this play of the free sea, wild with lights of emerald and white and amber.

"Bully good thing it's an on-shore wind," said the cook. "If not, where would we be? Wouldn't have a show."

"That's right," said the correspondent.

The busy oiler nodded his assent.

Then the captain, in the bow, chuckled in a way that expressed humor, contempt, tragedy, all in one.

"Do you think we've got much of a show now, boys?" said he.

Whereupon the three were silent, save for a trifle of hemming and hawing. To express any particular optimism at this time they felt to be childish and stupid, but they all doubtless possessed this sense of the situation in their minds. A young man thinks doggedly at such times. On the other hand, the ethics of their condition was decidedly against any open suggestion of hopelessness. So they were silent.

"Oh, well," said the captain, soothing his children, "we'll get ashore all right."

But there was that in his tone which made them think, so the oiler quoth: "Yes! If this wind holds!"

The cook was bailing: "Yes! If we don't catch hell in the surf."

Canton flannel gulls flew near and far. Sometimes they sat down on the sea, near patches of brown seaweed that rolled on the waves with a movement like carpets on a line in a gale. The birds sat comfortably in groups, and they were envied by some in the dingey, for the wrath of the sea was no more to them than it was to a covey of prairie chickens a thousand miles inland. Often they came very close and stared at the men with black bead-like eyes. At these times they were uncanny and sinister in their unblinking scrutiny, and the men hooted angrily at them, telling them to be gone.

One came, and evidently decided to alight on the top of the captain's head. The bird flew parallel to the boat and did not circle, but made short sidelong jumps in the air in chicken-fashion. His black eyes were wistfully fixed upon the captain's head. "Ugly brute," said the oiler to the bird. "You look as if you were made with a jack-knife." The cook and the correspondent swore darkly at the creature. The captain naturally wished to knock it away with the end of the heavy painter; but he did not dare do it, because anything resembling an emphatic gesture would have capsized this freighted boat, and so with his open hand, the captain gently and carefully waved the gull away. After it had been discouraged from the pursuit the captain breathed easier on account of his hair, and others breathed easier because the bird struck their minds at this time as being somehow gruesome and ominous.

In the meantime the oiler and the correspondent rowed. And also they rowed.

They sat together in the same seat, and each rowed an oar. Then the oiler took both oars; then the correspondent took both oars; then the oiler; then the correspondent. They rowed and they rowed. The very ticklish part of the business was when the time came for the reclining one in the stern to take his turn at the oars. By the very last star of truth, it is easier to steal eggs from under a hen than it was to change seats in the dingey. First the man in the stern slid his hand along the thwart and moved with care, as if he were of Sèvres. Then the man in the rowing seat slid his hand along the other thwart. It was all done with the most extraordinary care. As the two sidled past each other, the whole party kept watchful eyes on the coming wave, and the captain cried: "Look out now! Steady there!"

The brown mats of seaweed that appeared from time to time were like islands, bits of earth. They were traveling, apparently, neither one way nor the other. They were, to all intents, stationary. They informed the men in the boat that it was making progress slowly toward the land.

The captain, rearing cautiously in the bow, after the dingey soared on a great swell, said that he had seen the lighthouse at Mosquito Inlet. Presently the cook remarked that he had seen it. The correspondent was at the oars then, and for some reason he too wished to look at the lighthouse, but his back was toward the far shore and the waves were important, and for some time he could not seize an opportunity to turn his head. But at last there came a wave more gentle than the others, and when at the crest of it he swiftly scoured the western horizon.

"See it?" said the captain.

"No," said the correspondent slowly, "I didn't see anything."

"Look again," said the captain. He pointed. "It's exactly in that direction."

At the top of another wave, the correspondent did as he was bid, and this time his eyes chanced on a small still thing on the edge of the swaying horizon. It was precisely like the point of a pin. It took an anxious eye to find a lighthouse so tiny.

"Think we'll make it, captain?"

"If this wind holds and the boat don't swamp, we can't do much else," said the captain.

The little boat, lifted by each towering sea, and splashed viciously by the crests, made progress that in the absence of seaweed was not apparent to those in her. She seemed just a wee thing wallowing, miraculously top-up, at the mercy of five oceans. Occasionally, a great spread of water, like white flames, swarmed into her.

"Bail her, cook," said the captain serenely.

"All right, captain," said the cheerful cook.

III

It would be difficult to describe the subtle brotherhood of men that was here established on the seas. No one said that it was so. No one mentioned it. But it dwelt in the boat, and each man felt it warm him. They were a captain, an oiler, a cook, and a correspondent, and they were friends, friends in a more curiously iron-bound degree than may be common. The hurt captain, lying against the water-jar in the bow, spoke always in a low voice and calmly, but he could never command a more ready and swiftly obedient crew than the motley three of the dingey. It was more than a mere recognition of what was best for the common safety. There was surely in it a quality that was personal and heartfelt. And after this devotion to the commander of the boat there was this comradeship that the correspondent, for instance, who had been taught to be cynical of men, knew even at the time was the best experience of his life. But no one said that it was so. No one mentioned it.

"I wish we had a sail," remarked the captain. "We might try my overcoat on the end of an oar and give you two boys a chance to rest."

So the cook and the correspondent held the mast and spread wide the overcoat. The oiler steered, and the little boat made good way with her new rig. Sometimes the oiler had to scull sharply to keep a sea from breaking into the boat, but otherwise sailing was a success.

Meanwhile the lighthouse had been growing slowly larger. It had now almost assumed color, and appeared like a little gray shadow on the sky. The man at the oars could not be prevented from turning his head rather often to try for a glimpse of this little gray shadow.

At last, from the top of each wave the men in the tossing boat could see land. Even as the lighthouse was an upright shadow on the sky, this land seemed but a long black shadow on the sea. It certainly was thinner than paper. "We must be about opposite New Smyrna," said the cook, who had coasted this shore often in schooners. "Captain, by the way, I believe they abandoned that life-saving station there about a year ago."

"Did they?" said the captain.

The wind slowly died away. The cook and the correspondent were not now obliged to slave in order to hold high the oar. But the waves continued their old impetuous swooping at the dingey, and the little craft, no longer under way, struggled woundily over them. The oiler or the correspondent took the oars again.

Shipwrecks are *à propos* of nothing. If men could only train for them and have them occur when the men had reached pink condition, there would be less drowning at sea.

Of the four in the dingey none had slept any time worth mentioning for two days and two nights previous to embarking in the dingey, and in the excitement of clambering about the deck of a foundering ship they had also forgotten to eat heartily.

For these reasons, and for others, neither the oiler nor the correspondent was fond of rowing at this time. The correspondent wondered ingenuously how in the name of all that was sane could there be people who thought it amusing to row a boat. It was not an amusement; it was a diabolical punishment, and even a genius of mental aberrations could never conclude that it was anything but a horror to the muscles and a crime against the back. He mentioned to the boat in general how the amusement of rowing struck him, and the weary-faced oiler smiled in full sympathy. Previously to the foundering, by the way, the oiler had worked double-watch in the engine-room of the ship.

"Take her easy, now, boys," said the captain. "Don't spend yourselves. If we have to run a surf you'll need all your strength, because we'll sure have to swim for it. Take your time."

Slowly the land arose from the sea. From a black line it became a line of black and a line of white, trees and sand. Finally, the captain said that he could make out a house on the shore.

"That's the house of refuge, sure," said the cook. "They'll see us before long, and come out after us."

The distant lighthouse reared high. "The keeper ought to be able to make us out now, if he's looking through a glass," said the captain. "He'll notify the life-saving people."

"None of those other boats could have got ashore to give word of the wreck," said the oiler, in a low voice. "Else the life-boat would be out hunting us."

Slowly and beautifully the land loomed out of the sea.

The wind came again. It had veered from the north-east to the south-east.

Finally, a new sound struck the ears of the men in the boat. It was the low thunder of the surf on the shore. "We'll never be able to make the lighthouse now," said the captain. "Swing her head a little more north, Billie," said he.

" 'A little more north,' sir," said the oiler.

Whereupon the little boat turned her nose once more down the wind, and all but the oarsman watched the shore grow. Under the influence of this expansion doubt and direful apprehension was leaving the minds of the men. The management of the boat was still most absorbing, but it could not prevent a quiet cheerfulness. In an hour, perhaps, they would be ashore.

Their backbones had become thoroughly used to balancing in the boat, and they now rode this wild colt of a dingey like circus men. The correspondent thought that he had been drenched to the skin, but happening to feel in the top pocket of his coat, he found therein eight cigars. Four of them were soaked with sea-water; four were perfectly scatheless. After a search, somebody produced three dry matches, and thereupon the four waifs rode impudently in their little boat, and with an assurance of an impending rescue shining in their eyes, puffed at the big cigars and judged well and ill of all men. Everybody took a drink of water.

IV

"Cook," remarked the captain, "there don't seem to be any signs of life about your house of refuge."

"No," replied the cook. "Funny they don't see us!"

A broad stretch of lowly coast lay before the eyes of the men. It was of dunes topped with dark vegetation. The roar of the surf was plain, and sometimes they could see the white lip of a wave as it spun up the beach. A tiny house was blocked out black upon the sky. Southward, the slim lighthouse lifted its little gray length.

Tide, wind, and waves were swinging the dingey northward. "Funny they don't see us," said the men.

The surf's roar was dulled, but its tone was, nevertheless, thunderous and mighty. As the boat swam over the great rollers, the men sat listening to this roar. "We'll swamp sure," said everybody.

It is fair to say here that there was not a life-saving station within twenty miles in either direction, but the men did not know this fact, and in consequence they made dark and opprobrious remarks concerning the eyesight of the nation's life-savers. Four scowling men sat in the dingey and surpassed records in the invention of epithets.

"Funny they don't see us."

The lightheartedness of a former time had completely faded. To their sharpened minds it was easy to conjure pictures of all kinds of incompetency and blindness and, indeed, cowardice. There was the shore of the populous land, and it was bitter and bitter to them that from it came no sign.

"Well," said the captain, ultimately, "I suppose we'll have to make a try for ourselves. If we stay out here too long, we'll none of us have strength left to swim after the boat swamps."

And so the oiler, who was at the oars, turned the boat straight for the shore. There was a sudden tightening of muscle. There was some thinking.

"If we don't all get ashore——" said the captain. "If we don't all get ashore, I suppose you fellows know where to send news of my finish?"

They then briefly exchanged some addresses and admonitions. As for the reflections of the men, there was a great deal of rage in them. Perchance they might be formulated thus: "If I am going to be drowned—if I am going to be drowned—if I am going to be drowned, why, in the name of the seven mad gods who rule the sea, was I allowed to come thus far and contemplate sand and trees? Was I brought here merely to have my nose dragged away as I was about to nibble the sacred cheese of life? It is preposterous. If this old ninny-woman, Fate, cannot do better than this, she should be deprived of the management of men's fortunes. She is an old hen who knows not her intention. If she has decided to drown me, why did she not do it in the beginning and save me all this trouble? The whole affair is absurd. . . . But no, she cannot mean to drown me. She dare not drown me. She cannot drown me. Not after all this work." Afterward the man might have had an impulse to shake his fist at the clouds: "Just you drown me, now, and then hear what I call you!"

The billows that came at this time were more formidable. They seemed always just about to break and roll over the little boat in a turmoil of foam. There was a preparatory and long growl in the speech of them. No mind unused to the sea would have concluded that the dingey could ascend these sheer heights in time. The shore was still afar.

The oiler was a wily surfman. "Boys," he said swiftly, "she won't live three minutes more, and we're too far out to swim. Shall I take her to sea again, captain?"

"Yes! Go ahead!" said the captain.

This oiler, by a series of quick miracles, and fast and steady oarsmanship, turned the boat in the middle of the surf and took her safely to sea again.

There was a considerable silence as the boat bumped over the furrowed sea to deeper water. Then somebody in gloom spoke. "Well, anyhow, they must have seen us from the shore by now."

The gulls went in slanting flight up the wind toward the gray desolate east. A squall, marked by dingy clouds, and clouds brick-red, like smoke from a burning building, appeared from the south-east.

"What do you think of those life-saving people? Ain't they peaches?"

"Funny they haven't seen us."

"Maybe they think we're out here for sport! Maybe they think we're fishin'. Maybe they think we're damned fools."

It was a long afternoon. A changed tide tried to force them southward, but the wind and wave said northward. Far ahead, where coast-line, sea, and sky formed their mighty angle, there were little dots which seemed to indicate a city on the shore.

"St. Augustine?"

The captain shook his head. "Too near Mosquito Inlet."

And the oiler rowed, and then the correspondent rowed. Then the oiler rowed. It was a weary business. The human back can become the seat of more aches and pains than are registered in books for the composite anatomy of a regiment. It is a limited area, but it can become the theater of innumerable muscular conflicts, tangles, wrenches, knots, and other comforts.

"Did you ever like to row, Billie?" asked the correspondent.

"No," said the oiler. "Hang it!"

When one exchanged the rowing-seat for a place in the bottom of the boat, he suffered a bodily depression that

caused him to be careless of everything save an obligation
to wiggle one finger. There was cold sea-water swashing
to and fro in the boat, and he lay in it. His head, pillowed
on a thwart, was within an inch of the swirl of a wave
crest, and sometimes a particularly obstreperous sea came
in-board and drenched him once more. But these matters
did not annoy him. It is almost certain that if the boat
had capsized he would have tumbled comfortably out upon
the ocean as if he felt sure that it was a great soft mattress.

"Look! There's a man on the shore!"

"Where?"

"There! See 'im? See 'im?"

"Yes, sure! He's walking along."

"Now he's stopped. Look! He's facing us!"

"He's waving at us!"

"So he is! By thunder!"

"Ah, now we're all right! Now we're all right! There'll
be a boat out here for us in half-an-hour."

"He's going on. He's running. He's going up to that
house there."

The remote beach seemed lower than the sea, and it
required a searching glance to discern the little black figure.
The captain saw a floating stick and they rowed to it. A
bath-towel was by some weird chance in the boat, and,
tying this on the stock, the captain waved it. The oarsman
did not dare turn his head, so he was obliged to ask questions.

"What's he doing now?"

"He's standing still again. He's looking, I think . . .
There he goes again. Toward the house . . . Now he's
stopped again."

"Is he waving at us?"

"No, not now! he was, though."

"Look! There comes another man!"

"He's running."

"Look at him go, would you."

"Why, he's on a bicycle. Now he's met the other man.
They're both waving at us. Look!"

"There comes something up the beach."

"What the devil is that thing?"

"Why, it looks like a boat."

"Why, certainly it's a boat."

"No, it's on wheels."

"Yes, so it is. Well, that must be the life-boat. They drag them along shore on a wagon."

"That's the life-boat, sure."

"No, by————, it's—it's an omnibus."

"I tell you it's a life-boat."

"It is not! It's an omnibus. I can see it plain. See? One of these big hotel omnibuses."

"By thunder, you're right. It's an omnibus, sure as fate. What do you suppose they are doing with an omnibus? Maybe they are going around collecting the life-crew, hey?"

"That's it, likely. Look! There's a fellow waving a little black flag. He's standing on the steps of the omnibus. There comes those other two fellows. Now they're all talking together. Look at the fellow with the flag. Maybe he ain't waving it."

"That ain't a flag, is it? That's his coat. Why, certainly, that's his coat."

"So it is. It's his coat. He's taken it off and is waving it around his head. But would you look at him swing it."

"Oh, say, there isn't any life-saving station there. That's just a winter resort hotel omnibus that has brought over some of the boarders to see us drown."

"What's that idiot with the coat mean? What's he signaling, anyhow?"

"It looks as if he were trying to tell us to go north. There must be a life-saving station up there."

"No! He thinks we're fishing. Just giving us a merry hand. See? Ah, there, Willie!"

"Well, I wish I could make something out of those signals. What do you suppose he means?"

"He don't mean anything. He's just playing."

"Well, if he'd just signal us to try the surf again, or to go to sea and wait, or go north, or go south, or go to hell —there would be some reason in it. But look at him. He just stands there and keeps his coat revolving like a wheel. The ass!"

"There come more people."

"Now there's quite a mob. Look! Isn't that a boat?"

"Where? Oh, I see where you mean. No, that's no boat."

"That fellow is still waving his coat."

"He must think we like to see him do that. Why don't he quit it? It don't mean anything."

"I don't know. I think he is trying to make us go north. It must be that there's a life-saving station there somewhere."

"Say, he ain't tired yet. Look at 'im wave."

"Wonder how long he can keep that up. He's been revolving his coat ever since he caught sight of us. He's an idiot. Why aren't they getting men to bring a boat out? A fishing boat—one of those big yawls—could come out here all right. Why don't he do something?"

"Oh, it's all right, now."

"They'll have a boat out here for us in less than no time, now that they've seen us."

A faint yellow tone came into the sky over the low land. The shadows on the sea slowly deepened. The wind bore coldness with it, and the men began to shiver.

"Holy smoke!" said one, allowing his voice to express his impious mood, "if we keep on monkeying out here! If we've got to flounder out here all night!"

"Oh, we'll never have to stay here all night! Don't you worry. They've seen us now, and it won't be long before they'll come chasing out after us."

The shore grew dusky. The man waving a coat blended gradually into this gloom, and it swallowed in the same manner the omnibus and the group of people. The spray, when it dashed uproariously over the side, made the voyagers shrink and swear like men who were being branded.

"I'd like to catch the chump who waved the coat. I feel like soaking him one, just for luck."

"Why? What did he do?"

"Oh, nothing, but then he seemed so damned cheerful."

In the meantime the oiler rowed, and then the correspondent rowed, and then the oiler rowed. Gray-faced and bowed forward, they mechanically, turn by turn, plied the leaden oars. The form of the lighthouse had vanished from the southern horizon, but finally a pale star appeared, just lifting from the sea. The streaked saffron in the west passed before the all-merging darkness, and the sea to the east was black. The land had vanished, and was expressed only by the low and drear thunder of the surf.

"If I am going to be drowned—if I am going to be drowned—if I am going to be drowned, why, in the name of the seven mad gods who rule the sea, was I allowed to come this far and contemplate sand and trees? Was I brought here merely to have my nose dragged away as I was about to nibble the sacred cheese of life?"

The patient captain, drooped over the water-jar, was sometimes obliged to speak to the oarsman.

"Keep her head up! Keep her head up!"

" 'Keep her head up,' sir." The voices were weary and low.

This was surely a quiet evening. All save the oarsman lay heavily and listlessly in the boat's bottom. As for him, his eyes were just capable of noting the tall black waves that swept forward in a most sinister silence, save for an occasional subdued growl of a crest.

The cook's head was on a thwart, and he looked without interest at the water under his nose. He was deep in other scenes. Finally he spoke. "Billie," he murmured, dreamfully, "what kind of pie do you like best?"

V

"Pie," said the oiler and the correspondent, agitatedly. "Don't talk about those things, blast you!"

"Well," said the cook, "I was just thinking about ham sandwiches, and——"

A night on the sea in an open boat is a long night. As darkness settled finally, the shine of the light, lifting from the sea in the south, changed to full gold. On the northern horizon a new light appeared, a small bluish gleam on the edge of the waters. These two lights were the furniture of the world. Otherwise there was nothing but waves.

Two men huddled in the stern, and distances were so magnificent in the dingey that the rower was enabled to keep his feet partly warmed by thrusting them under his companions. Their legs indeed extended far under the rowing-seat until they touched the feet of the captain forward. Sometimes, despite the efforts of the tired oarsmen, a wave came piling into the boat, an icy wave of the night, and the chilling water soaked them anew. They would twist their bodies for a moment and groan, and sleep the dead sleep once more, while the water in the boat gurgled about them as the craft rocked.

The plan of the oiler and the correspondent was for one to row until he lost the ability, and then arouse the other from his sea-water couch in the bottom of the boat.

The oiler plied the oars until his head dropped forward, and the overpowering sleep blinded him. And he rowed yet afterward. Then he touched a man in the bottom of the boat, and called his name. "Will you spell me for a little while?" he said, meekly.

"Sure, Billie," said the correspondent, awakening and dragging himself to a sitting position. They exchanged places carefully, and the oiler, cuddling down in the sea-water at the cook's side, seemed to go to sleep instantly.

The particular violence of the sea had ceased. The waves came without snarling. The obligation of the man at the oars was to keep the boat headed so that the tilt of the rollers would not capsize her, and to preserve her from filling when the crests rushed past. The black waves were silent and hard to be seen in the darkness. Often one was almost upon the boat before the oarsman was aware.

In a low voice the correspondent addressed the captain. He was not sure that the captain was awake, although this iron man seemed to be always awake. "Captain, shall I keep her making for that light north, sir?"

The same steady voice answered him. "Yes. Keep it about two points off the port bow."

The cook had tied a life-belt around himself in order to get even the warmth which this clumsy cork contrivance could donate, and he seemed almost stove-like when a rower, whose teeth invariably chattered wildly as soon as he ceased his labor, dropped down to sleep.

The correspondent, as he rowed, looked down at the two men sleeping under-foot. The cook's arm was around the oiler's shoulders, and, with their fragmentary clothing and haggard faces, they were the babes of the sea, a grotesque rendering of the old babes in the wood.

Later he must have grown stupid at his work, for suddenly there was a growling of water, and a crest came with a roar and a swash into the boat, and it was a wonder that it did not set the cook afloat in his lifebelt. The cook continued to sleep, but the oiler sat up, blinking his eyes and shaking with the new cold.

"Oh, I'm awful sorry, Billie," said the correspondent contritely.

"That's all right, old boy," said the oiler, and lay down again and was asleep.

Presently it seemed that even the captain dozed, and the

correspondent thought that he was the one man afloat on all the oceans. The wind had a voice as it came over the waves, and it was sadder than the end.

There was a long, loud swishing astern of the boat, and a gleaming trail of phosphorescence, like blue flame, was furrowed on the black waters. It might have been made by a monstrous knife.

Then there came a stillness, while the correspondent breathed with the open mouth and looked at the sea.

Suddenly there was another swish and another long flash of bluish light, and this time it was alongside the boat, and might almost have been reached with an oar. The correspondent saw an enormous fin speed like a shadow through the water, hurling the crystalline spray and leaving the long glowing trail.

The correspondent looked over his shoulder at the captain. His face was hidden, and he seemed to be asleep. He looked at the babes of the sea. They certainly were asleep. So being bereft of sympathy, he leaned a little way to one side and swore softly into the sea.

But the thing did not then leave the vicinity of the boat. Ahead or astern, on one side or the other, at intervals long or short, fled the long sparkling streak, and there was to be heard the whirroo of the dark fin. The speed and power of the thing was greatly to be admired. It cut the water like a gigantic and keen projectile.

The presence of this biding thing did not affect the man with the same horror that it would if he had been a picnicker. He simply looked at the sea dully and swore in an undertone.

Nevertheless, it is true that he did not wish to be alone. He wished one of his companions to awaken by chance and keep him company with it. But the captain hung motionless over the water-jar and the oiler and the cook in the bottom of the boat were plunged in slumber.

VI

"If I am going to be drowned—if I am going to be drowned—if I am going to be drowned, why, in the name of the seven mad gods who rule the sea, was I allowed to come thus far and contemplate sand and trees?"

During this dismal night, it may be remarked that a man would conclude that it was really the intention of the seven mad gods to drown him, despite the abominable injustice of it. For it was certainly an abominable injustice to drown a man who had worked so hard, so hard. The man felt it would be a crime most unnatural. Other people had drowned at sea since galleys swarmed with painted sails, but still——

When it occurs to a man that Nature does not regard him as important, and that she feels she would not maim the universe by disposing of him, he at first wishes to throw bricks at the temple, and he hates deeply the fact that there are no bricks and no temples. Any visible expression of Nature would surely be pelleted with jeers.

Then, if there be no tangible thing to hoot, he feels, perhaps, the desire to confront a personification and indulge in pleas, bowed to one knee, and with hands supplicant, saying: "Yes, but I love myself."

A high cold star on a winter's night is the word he feels that she says to him. Thereafter he knows the pathos of his situation.

The men in the dingey had not discussed these matters, but each had, no doubt, reflected upon them in silence and according to his mind. There was seldom any expression upon their faces save the general one of complete weariness. Speech was devoted to the business of the boat.

To chime the notes of his emotion, a verse mysteriously entered the correspondent's head. He had even forgotten that he had forgotten this verse, but it suddenly was in his mind.

"A soldier of the Legion lay dying in Algiers,
There was lack of woman's nursing, there was dearth of
woman's tears;
But a comrade stood beside him, and he took that com-
rade's hand,
And he said: 'I never more shall see my own, my native
land.' "

In his childhood, the correspondent had been made acquainted with the fact that a soldier of the Legion lay dying in Algiers, but he had never regarded the fact as important. Myriads of his school-fellows had informed him of the soldier's plight, but the dinning had naturally ended by making him perfectly indifferent. He had never considered it his affair that a soldier of the Legion lay dying in Algiers, nor had it appeared to him as a matter for sorrow. It was less to him than the breaking of a pencil's point.

Now, however, it quaintly came to him as a human, living thing. It was no longer merely a picture of a few throes in the breast of a poet, meanwhile drinking tea and warming his feet at the grate; it was an actuality—stern, mournful, and fine.

The correspondent plainly saw the soldier. He lay on the sand with his feet out straight and still. While his pale left hand was upon his chest in an attempt to thwart the going of his life, the blood came between his fingers. In the far Algerian distance, a city of low square forms was set against a sky that was faint with the last sunset hues. The correspondent, plying the oars and dreaming of the slow and slower movements of the lips of the soldier, was moved by a profound and perfectly impersonal comprehension. He was sorry for the soldier of the Legion who lay dying in Algiers.

The thing which had followed the boat and waited, had evidently grown bored at the delay. There was no longer to be heard the slash of the cut-water, and there was no longer the flame of the long trail. The light in the north still glimmered, but it was apparently no nearer to the boat. Sometimes the boom of the surf rang in the correspondent's ears, and he turned the craft seaward then and rowed harder. Southward, some one had evidently built a watch-fire on the beach. It was too low and too far to be seen, but it made a shimmering, roseate reflection upon the bluff back of it, and this could be discerned from the boat. The wind came stronger, and sometimes a wave suddenly raged out like a mountain-cat, and there was to be seen the sheen and sparkle of a broken crest.

The captain, in the bow, moved on his water-jar and sat erect. "Pretty long night," he observed to the correspondent. He looked at the shore. "Those life-saving people take their time."

"Did you see that shark playing around?"

"Yes, I saw him. He was a big fellow, all right."

"Wish I had known you were awake."

Later the correspondent spoke into the bottom of the boat.

"Billie!" There was a slow and gradual disentanglement. "Billie, will you spell me?"

"Sure," said the oiler.

As soon as the correspondent touched the cold comfortable sea-water in the bottom of the boat, and had huddled close to the cook's lifebelt he was deep in sleep, despite the fact that his teeth played all the popular airs. This sleep was so good to him that it was but a moment before he heard a voice call his name in a tone that demonstrated the last stages of exhaustion. "Will you spell me?"

"Sure, Billie."

The light in the north had mysteriously vanished, but the correspondent took his course from the wide-awake captain.

Later in the night they took the boat farther out to sea, and the captain directed the cook to take one oar at the stern and keep the boat facing the seas. He was to call out if he should hear the thunder of the surf. This plan enabled the oiler and the correspondent to get respite together. "We'll give those boys a chance to get into shape again," said the captain. They curled down and, after a few preliminary chatterings and trembles, slept once more the dead sleep. Neither knew they had bequeathed to the cook the company of another shark, or perhaps the same shark.

As the boat caroused on the waves, spray occasionally bumped over the side and gave them a fresh soaking, but this had no power to break their repose. The ominous slash of the wind and the water affected them as it would have affected mummies.

"Boys," said the cook, with the notes of every reluctance in his voice, "she's drifted in pretty close. I guess one of you had better take her to sea again." The correspondent, aroused, heard the crash of the toppled crests.

As he was rowing, the captain gave him some whisky-and-water, and this steadied the chills out of him. "If I ever get ashore and anybody shows me even a photograph of an oar——"

At last there was a short conversation.

"Billie . . . Billie, will you spell me?"

"Sure," said the oiler.

VII

When the correspondent again opened his eyes, the sea and the sky were each of the gray hue of the dawning. Later, carmine and gold was painted upon the waters. The morning appeared finally, in its splendor, with a sky of pure blue, and the sunlight flamed on the tips of the waves.

On the distant dunes were set many little black cottages, and a tall white windmill reared above them. No man, nor dog, nor bicycle appeared on the beach. The cottages might have formed a deserted village.

The voyagers scanned the shore. A conference was held in the boat. "Well," said the captain, "if no help is coming we might better try a run through the surf right away. If we stay out here much longer we will be too weak to do anything for ourselves at all." The others silently acquiesced in this reasoning. The boat was headed for the beach. The correspondent wondered if none ever ascended the tall windtower, and if then they never looked seaward. This tower was a giant, standing with its back to the plight of the ants. It represented in a degree, to the correspondent, the serenity of Nature amid the struggles of the individual—Nature in the wind, and Nature in the vision of men. She did not seem cruel to him then, nor beneficent, nor treacherous, nor wise. But she was indifferent, flatly indifferent. It is, perhaps, plausible that a man in this situation, impressed with the unconcern of the universe, should see the innumerable flaws of his life, and have them taste wickedly in his mind and wish for another chance. A distinction between right and wrong seems absurdly clear to him, then, in this new ignorance of the grave-edge, and he understands that if he were given another opportunity he would mend his conduct and his words, and be better and brighter during an introduction or at a tea.

"Now, boys," said the captain, "she is going to swamp, sure. All we can do is to work her in as far as possible, and then, when she swamps, pile out and scramble for the beach. Keep cool now, and don't jump until she swamps sure."

The oiler took the oars. Over his shoulder he scanned the surf "Captain," he said, "I think I'd better bring her about, and keep her head-on to the seas and back her in."

"All right, Billie," said the captain. "Back her in." The oiler swung the boat then and, seated in the stern, the cook and the correspondent were obliged to look over their shoulders to contemplate the lonely and indifferent shore.

The monstrous in-shore rollers heaved the boat high until the men were again enabled to see the white sheets of water scudding up the slanted beach. "We won't get in very close," said the captain. Each time a man could wrest his attention from the rollers, he turned his glance toward the shore, and in the expression of the eyes during this contemplation there was a singular quality. The correspondent, observing the others, knew that they were not afraid, but the full meaning of their glances was shrouded.

As for himself, he was too tired to grapple fundamentally with the fact. He tried to coerce his mind into thinking of it, but the mind was dominated at this time by the muscles, and the muscles said they did not care. It merely occurred to him that if he should drown it would be a shame.

There were no hurried words, no pallor, no plain agitation. The men simply looked at the shore. "Now, remember to get well clear of the boat when you jump," said the captain.

Seaward the crest of a roller suddenly fell with a thunderous crash, and the long white comber came roaring down upon the boat.

"Steady now," said the captain. The men were silent. They turned their eyes from the shore to the comber and waited. The boat slid up the incline, leaped at the furious top, bounced over it, and swung down the long back of the wave. Some water had been shipped and the cook bailed it out.

But the next crest crashed also. The tumbling, boiling flood of white water caught the boat and whirled it almost perpendicular. Water swarmed in from all sides. The correspondent had his hands on the gunwale at this time, and when the water entered at that place he swiftly withdrew his fingers, as if he objected to wetting them.

The little boat, drunken with this weight of water, reeled and snuggled deeper into the sea.

"Bail her out, cook! Bail her out!" said the captain.

"All right, captain," said the cook.

"Now, boys, the next one will do for us, sure," said the oiler. "Mind to jump clear of the boat."

The third wave moved forward, huge, furious, implacable. It fairly swallowed the dingey, and almost simultaneously the men tumbled into the sea. A piece of lifebelt had lain in the bottom of the boat, and as the correspondent went overboard he held this to his chest with his left hand.

The January water was icy, and he reflected immediately that it was colder than he had expected to find it on the coast of Florida. This appeared to his dazed mind as a fact important enough to be noted at the time. The coldness of the water was sad; it was tragic. This fact was somehow so mixed and confused with his opinion of his own situation that it seemed almost a proper reason for tears. The water was cold.

When he came to the surface he was conscious of little but the noisy water. Afterward he saw his companions in the sea. The oiler was ahead in the race. He was swimming strongly and rapidly. Off to the correspondent's left, the cook's great white and corked back bulged out of the water, and in the rear the captain was hanging with his one good hand to the keel of the overturned dingey.

There is a certain immovable quality to a shore, and the correspondent wondered at it amid the confusion of the sea.

It seemed also very attractive, but the correspondent knew that it was a long journey, and he paddled leisurely. The piece of life preserver lay under him, and sometimes he whirled down the incline of a wave as if he were on a hand-sled.

But finally he arrived at a place in the sea where travel was beset with difficulty. He did not pause swimming to inquire what manner of current had caught him, but there his progress ceased. The shore was set before him like a bit of scenery on a stage, and he looked at it and understood with his eyes each detail of it.

As the cook passed, much farther to the left, the captain was calling to him, "Turn over on your back, cook! Turn over on your back and use the oar."

"All right, sir." The cook turned on his back, and, paddling with an oar, went ahead as if he were a canoe.

Presently the boat also passed to the left of the correspondent with the captain clinging with one hand to the keel. He would have appeared like a man raising himself to look over a board fence, if it were not for the extraordinary gymnastics of the boat. The correspondent marvelled that the captain could still hold to it.

They passed on, nearer to shore—the oiler, the cook, the captain—and following them went the water-jar, bouncing gaily over the seas.

The correspondent remained in the grip of this strange

new enemy—a current. The shore, with its white slope of sand and its green bluff, topped with little silent cottages, was spread like a picture before him. It was very near to him then, but he was impressed as one who in a gallery looks at a scene from Brittany or Holland.

He thought: "I am going to drown? Can it be possible? Can it be possible? Can it be possible?" Perhaps an individual must consider his own death to be the final phenomenon of nature.

But later a wave perhaps whirled him out of this small, deadly current, for he found suddenly that he could again make progress toward the shore. Later still, he was aware that the captain, clinging with one hand to the keel of the dingey, had his face turned away from the shore and toward him, and was calling his name. "Come to the boat! Come to the boat!"

In his struggle to reach the captain and the boat, he reflected that when one gets properly wearied, drowning must really be a comfortable arrangement, a cessation of hostilities accompanied by a large degree of relief, and he was glad of it, for the main thing in his mind for some months had been horror of the temporary agony. He did not wish to be hurt.

Presently he saw a man running along the shore. He was undressing with most remarkable speed. Coat, trousers, shirt, everything flew magically off him.

"Come to the boat," called the captain.

"All right, captain." As the correspondent paddled, he saw the captain let himself down to bottom and leave the boat. Then the correspondent performed his one little marvel of the voyage. A large wave caught him and flung him with ease and supreme speed completely over the boat and far beyond it. It struck him even then as an event in gymnastics, and a true miracle of the sea. An overturned boat in the surf is not a plaything to a swimming man.

The correspondent arrived in water that reached only to his waist, but his condition did not enable him to stand for more than a moment. Each wave knocked him into a heap, and the undertow pulled at him.

Then he saw the man who had been running and undressing, and undressing and running, come bounding into the water. He dragged ashore the cook, and then waded towards the captain, but the captain waved him away, and sent him to the correspondent. He was naked, naked as a tree in winter, but a halo was about his head, and he shone like a saint. He gave a strong pull, and a long drag, and a bully heave at the correspondent's hand. The correspondent, schooled in the minor formulae, said: "Thanks, old man." But suddenly the man cried: "What's that?" He pointed a swift finger. The correspondent said: "Go."

In the shallows, face downward, lay the oiler. His forehead touched sand that was periodically, between each wave, clear of the sea.

The correspondent did not know all that transpired afterward. When he achieved safe ground he fell, striking the sand with each particular part of his body. It was as if he dropped from a roof, but the thud was grateful to him.

It seems that instantly the beach was populated with men with blankets, clothes, and flasks, and women with coffee-pots and all the remedies sacred to their minds. The welcome of the land to the men from the sea was warm and generous, but a still and dripping shape was carried slowly up the beach, and the land's welcome for it could only be the different and sinister hospitality of the grave.

When it came night, the white waves paced to and fro in the moonlight, and the wind brought the sound of the great sea's voice to the men on shore, and they felt that they could then be interpreters.

1898

The Blue Hotel

I

The Palace Hotel at Fort Romper was painted a light blue, a shade that is on the legs of a kind of heron, causing the bird to declare its position against any background. The Palace Hotel, then, was always screaming and howling in a way that made the dazzling winter landscape of Nebraska seem only a gray swampish hush. It stood alone on the prairie, and when the snow was falling the town two hundred yards away was not visible. But when the traveler alighted at the railway station he was obliged to pass the Palace Hotel before he could come upon the company of low clapboard houses which composed Fort Romper, and it was not to be thought that any traveler could pass the Palace Hotel without looking at it. Pat Scully, the proprietor, had proved himself a master of strategy when he chose his paints. It is true that on clear days, when the great transcontinental expresses, long lines of swaying Pullmans, swept through Fort Romper, passengers were overcome at the sight, and the cult that knows the brown-reds and the subdivisions of the dark greens of the East expressed shame, pity, horror, in a laugh. But to the citizens of this prairie town and to the people who would naturally stop there, Pat Scully had performed a feat. With this opulence and splendor, these creeds, classes, egotisms, that streamed through Romper on the rails day after day, they had no color in common.

As if the displayed delights of such a blue hotel were not sufficiently enticing, it was Scully's habit to go every morning and evening to meet the leisurely trains that stopped at Romper and work his seductions upon any man that he might see wavering, gripsack in hand.

One morning, when a snow-crusted engine dragged its long string of freight cars and its one passenger coach to the station, Scully performed the marvel of catching three men. One was a shaky and quick-eyed Swede, with a great shining cheap valise; one was a tall bronzed cowboy, who was on his way to a ranch near the Dakota line; one was a little silent man from the East, who didn't look it, and didn't announce it. Scully practically made them prisoners. He was so nimble and merry and kindly that each probably felt it would be the height of brutality to try to escape. They trudged off over the creaking board sidewalks in the wake of the eager little Irishman. He wore a heavy fur cap squeezed tightly down on his head. It caused his two red ears to stick out stiffy, as if they were made of tin.

At last, Scully, elaborately, with boisterous hospitality, conducted them through the portals of the blue hotel. The room which they entered was small. It seemed to be merely a proper temple for an enormous stove, which, in the center, was humming with godlike violence. At various points on its surface the iron had become luminous and glowed yellow from the heat. Beside the stove Scully's son Johnnie was playing High-Five with an old farmer who had whiskers both gray and sandy. They were quarreling. Frequently the old farmer turned his face toward a box of sawdust—colored brown from tobacco juice—

that was behind the stove, and spat with an air of great impatience and irritation. With a loud flourish of words Scully destroyed the game of cards, and bustled his son upstairs with part of the baggage of the new guests. He himself conducted them to three basins of the coldest water in the world. The cowboy and the Easterner burnished themselves fiery red with this water, until it seemed to be some kind of metal-polish. The Swede, however, merely dipped his fingers gingerly and with trepidation. It was notable that throughout this series of small ceremonies the three travelers were made to feel that Scully was very benevolent. He was conferring great favors upon them. He handed the towel from one to another with an air of philanthropic impulse.

Afterward they went to the first room, and, sitting about the stove, listened to Scully's officious clamor at his daughters, who were preparing the midday meal. They reflected in the silence of experienced men who tread carefully amid new people. Nevertheless, the old farmer, stationary, invincible in his chair near the warmest part of the stove, turned his face from the sawdust-box frequently and addressed a glowing common-place to the strangers. Usually he was answered in short but adequate sentences by either the cowboy or the Easterner. The Swede said nothing. He seemed to be occupied in making furtive estimates of each man in the room. One might have thought that he had the sense of silly suspicion which comes to guilt. He resembled a badly frightened man.

Later, at dinner, he spoke a little, addressing his conversation entirely to Scully. He volunteered that he had come from New York, where for ten years he had worked as a tailor. These facts seemed to strike Scully as fascinating, and afterward he volunteered that he had lived at Romper for fourteen years. The Swede asked about the crops and the price of labor. He seemed barely to listen to Scully's extended replies. His eyes continued to rove from man to man.

Finally, with a laugh and a wink, he said that some of these Western communities were very dangerous; and after this statement he straightened his legs under the table, tilted his head, and laughed again, loudly. It was plain that the demonstration had no meaning to the others. They looked at him wondering and in silence.

II

As the men trooped heavily back into the front room, the two little windows presented views of a turmoiling sea of snow. The huge arms of the wind were making attempts—mighty, circular, futile—to embrace the flakes as they sped. A gate-post like a still man with a blanched face stood aghast amid this profligate fury. In a hearty voice Scully announced the presence of a blizzard. The guests of the blue hotel, lighting their pipes, assented with grunts of lazy masculine contentment. No island of the sea could be exempt in the degree of this little room with its humming stove. Johnnie, son of Scully, in a tone which defined his opinion of his ability as a card-player, challenged the old farmer of both gray and sandy whiskers to a game of High-Five. The farmer agreed with a contemptuous and bitter scoff. They sat close to the stove, and squared their knees under a wide board. The cowboy and the Easterner watched the game with interest. The Swede remained near the window, aloof, but with a countenance that showed signs of an inexplicable excitement.

The play of Johnnie and the gray-beard was suddenly ended by another quarrel. The old man arose while casting a look of heated scorn at his adversary. He slowly buttoned his coat, and then stalked with fabulous dignity from the room. In the discreet silence of all other men the Swede laughed. His laughter rang somehow childish. Men by this time had begun to look at him askance, as if they wished to inquire what ailed him.

A new game was formed jocosely. The cowboy volunteered to become the partner of Johnnie, and they all then turned to ask the Swede to throw in his lot with the little Easterner. He asked some questions about the game, and, learning that it wore many names, and that he had played it when it was under an alias, he accepted the invitation. He strode toward the men nervously, as if he expected to be assaulted. Finally, seated, he gazed from face to face and laughed shrilly. This laugh was so strange that the Easterner looked up quickly, the cowboy sat intent and with his mouth open, and Johnnie paused, holding the cards with still fingers.

Afterward there was a short silence. Then Johnnie said, "Well, let's get at it. Come on now!" They pulled their chairs forward until their knees were bunched under the board. They began to play, and their interest in the game caused the others to forget the manner of the Swede.

The cowboy was a board-whacker. Each time that he held superior cards he whanged them, one by one, with exceeding force, down upon the improvised table, and took the tricks with a glowing air of prowess and pride that sent thrills of indignation into the hearts of his opponents. A game with a board-whacker in it is sure to become intense. The countenances of the Easterner and the Swede were miserable whenever the cowboy thundered down his aces and kings, while Johnnie, his eyes gleaming with joy, chuckled and chuckled.

Because of the absorbing play none considered the strange ways of the Swede. They paid strict heed to the game. Finally, during a lull caused by a new deal, the Swede suddenly addressed Johnnie: "I suppose there have been a good many men killed in this room." The jaws of the others dropped and they looked at him.

"What in hell are you talking about?" said Johnnie.

The Swede laughed again his blatant laugh, full of a kind of false courage and defiance. "Oh, you know what I mean all right," he answered.

"I'm a liar if I do!" Johnnie protested. The card was halted, and the men stared at the Swede. Johnnie evidently felt that as the son of the proprietor he should make a direct inquiry. "Now, what might you be drivin' at, mister?" he asked. The Swede winked at him. It was a wink full of cunning. His fingers shook on the edge of the board. "Oh, maybe you think I have been to nowheres. Maybe you think I'm a tenderfoot?"

"I don't know nothin' about you," answered Johnnie, "and I don't give a damn where you've been. All I' got to say is that I don't know what you're driving at. There hain't never been nobody killed in this room."

The cowboy, who had been steadily gazing at the Swede, then spoke: "What's wrong with you, mister?"

Apparently it seemed to the Swede that he was formidably menaced. He shivered and turned white near the corners of his mouth. He sent an appealing glance in the direction of the little Easterner. During these moments he did not forget to wear his air of advanced pot-valor.

"They say they don't know what I mean," he remarked mockingly to the Easterner.

The latter answered after prolonged and cautious reflection. "I don't understand you," he said, impassively.

The Swede made a movement then which announced that he thought he had encountered treachery from the only quarter where he had expected sympathy, if not help. "Oh, I see you are all against me, I see——"

The cowboy was in a state of deep stupefaction. "Say," he cried, as he tumbled the deck violently down upon the board, "say, what are you gittin' at, hey?"

The Swede sprang up with the celerity of a man escaping from a snake on the floor. "I don't want to fight!" he shouted. "I don't want to fight!"

The cowboy stretched his long legs indolently and deliberately. His hands were in his pockets. He spat into the sawdust-box. "Well, who the hell thought you did?" he inquired.

The Swede backed rapidly toward a corner of the room. His hands were out protectingly in front of his chest, but he was making an obvious struggle to control his fright. "Gentleman," he quavered, "I suppose I am going to be killed before I can leave this house! I suppose I am going to be killed before I can leave this house!" In his eyes was the dying-swan look. Through the windows could be seen the snow turning blue in the shadow of dusk. The wind tore at the house, and some loose thing beat regularly against the clapboards like a spirit tapping.

A door opened, and Scully himself entered. He paused in surprise as he noted the tragic attitude of the Swede. Then he said, "What's the matter here?"

The Swede answered him swiftly and eagerly: "These men are going to kill me."

"Kill you!" ejaculated Scully. "Kill you! What are you talkin'?"

The Swede made the gesture of a martyr.

Scully wheeled sternly upon his son. "What is this, Johnnie?"

The lad had grown sullen. "Damned if I know," he answered. "I can't make no sense to it." He began to shuffle the cards, fluttering them together with an angry snap. "He says a good many men have been killed in

this room, or something like that. And he says he's goin'
to be killed here too. I don't know what ails him. He's
crazy, I shouldn't wonder.".

Scully then looked for explanation to the cowboy, but
the cowboy simply shrugged his shoulders.

"Kill you?" said Scully again to the Swede. "Kill you?
Man, you're off your nut."

"Oh, I know," burst out the Swede. "I know what will
happen. Yes, I'm crazy—yes. Yes, of course, I'm crazy—
yes. But I know one thing——" There was a sort of sweat
of misery and terror upon his face. "I know I won't get
out of here alive."

The cowboy drew a deep breath, as if his mind was
passing into the last stages of dissolution. "Well, I'm dog-
goned," he whispered to himself.

Scully wheeled suddenly and faced his son. "You've
been troublin' this man!"

Johnnie's voice was loud with its burden of grievance.
"Why, good Gawd, I ain't done nothin' to 'im."

The Swede broke in. "Gentlemen, do not disturb yourselves. I will leave this house. I will go away, because"—
he accused them dramatically with his glance—"because
I do not want to be killed."

Scully was furious with his son. "Will you tell me what
is the matter, you young divil? What's the matter, anyhow? Speak out!"

"Blame it!" cried Johnnie in despair, "don't I tell you
I don't know? He—he says we want to kill him, and that's
all I know. I can't tell what ails him."

The Swede continued to repeat: "Never mind, Mr.
Scully; never mind. I will leave this house. I will go away,
because I do not wish to be killed. Yes, of course, I am
crazy—yes. But I know one thing! I will go away. I will
leave this house. Never mind, Mr. Scully; never mind. I
will go away."

"You will not go 'way," said Scully. "You will not go
'way until I hear the reason of this business. If anybody
has troubled you I will take care of him. This is my house.
You are under my roof, and I will not allow any peaceable
man to be troubled here." He cast a terrible eye upon
Johnnie, the cowboy, and the Easterner.

"Never mind, Mr. Scully; never mind. I will go away.
I do not wish to be killed." The Swede moved toward the

door which opened upon the stairs. It was evidently his intention to go at once for his baggage.

"No, no," shouted Scully peremptorily; but the white-faced man slid by him and disappeared. "Now," said Scully severely, "what does this mane?"

Johnnie and the cowboy cried together: "Why, we didn't do nothin' to 'im!"

Scully's eyes were cold. "No," he said, "you didn't?"

Johnnie swore a deep oath. "Why, this is the wildest loon I ever see. We didn't do nothin' at all. We were jest sittin' here playin' cards, and he——"

The father suddenly spoke to the Easterner, "Mr. Blanc," he said, "what has these boys been doin'?"

The Easterner reflected again. "I didn't see anything wrong at all," he said at last, slowly.

Scully began to howl. "But what does it mane?" He started ferociously at his son. "I have a mind to lather you for this, me boy."

Johnnie was frantic. "Well, what have I done?" he bawled at his father.

III

"I think you are tongue-tied," said Scully finally to his son, the cowboy, and the Easterner; and at the end of this scornful sentence he left the room.

Upstairs the Swede was swiftly fastening the straps of his great valise. Once his back happened to be half turned toward the door, and, hearing a noise there, he wheeled and sprang up, uttering a loud cry. Scully's wrinkled visage showed grimly in the light of the small lamp he carried. This yellow effulgence, streaming upward, colored only his prominent features, and left his eyes, for instance, in mysterious shadow. He resembled a murderer.

"Man! man!" he exclaimed, "have you gone daffy?"

"Oh, no! Oh, no!" rejoined the other. "There are people in this world who know pretty nearly as much as you do —understand?"

For a moment they stood gazing at each other. Upon the Swede's deathly pale cheeks were two spots brightly crimson and sharply edged, as if they had been carefully painted. Scully placed the light on the table and sat himself on the edge of the bed. He spoke ruminatively. "By cracky, I never heard of such a thing in my life. It's a complete muddle. I can t, for the soul of me, think how you ever got this idea into your head." Presently he lifted his eyes and asked: "And did you sure think they were going to kill you?"

The Swede scanned the old man as if he wished to see into his mind. "I did," he said at last. He obviously suspected that this answer might precipitate an outbreak. As he pulled on a strap his whole arm shook, the elbow wavering like a bit of paper.

Scully banged his hand impressively on the footboard of the bed. "Why, man, we're goin' to have a line of ilictric street-cars in this town next spring."

" 'A line of electric street-cars,' " repeated the Swede, stupidly.

"And," said Scully, "there's a new railroad goin' to be built down from Broken Arm to here. Not to mintion the four churches and the smashin' big brick school house. Then there's the big factory, too. Why, in two years Romper'll be a metro-pol-is."

Having finished the preparation of his baggage, the Swede straightened himself. "Mr. Scully," he said, with sudden hardihood, "how much do I owe you?"

"You don't owe me anythin'," said the old man, angrily.

"Yes, I do," retorted the Swede. He took seventy-five cents from his pocket and tendered it to Scully; but the latter snapped his fingers in disdainful refusal. However, it happened that they both stood gazing in a strange fashion at three silver pieces on the Swede's open palm.

"I'll not take your money," said Scully at last. "Not after what's been goin' on here." Then a plan seemed to strike him. "Here," he cried, picking up his lamp and moving toward the door. "Here! Come with me a minute."

"No," said the Swede, in overwhelming alarm.

"Yes," urged the old man. "Come on! I want you to come and see a picter—just across the hall—in my room."

The Swede must have concluded that his hour was come. His jaw dropped and his teeth showed like a dead man's. He ultimately followed Scully across the corridor, but he had the step of one hung in chains.

Scully flashed the light high on the wall of his own chamber. There was revealed a ridiculous photograph of a little girl. She was leaning against a balustrade of gorgeous decoration, and the formidable bang to her hair was prominent. The figure was as graceful as an upright sled-stake, and, withal, it was the hue of lead. "There," said Scully, tenderly, "that's the picter of my little girl that died. Her name was Carrie. She had the purtiest hair you ever saw! I was that fond of her, she——"

Turning then, he saw that the Swede was not contemplating the picture at all, but, instead, was keeping keen watch on the gloom in the rear.

"Look, man!" cried Scully, heartily. "That's the picter of my little gal that died. Her name was Carrie. And then here's the picter of my oldest boy, Michael. He's a lawyer in Lincoln, an' doin' well. I gave that boy a grand eddication, and I'm glad for it now. He's a fine boy. Look at 'im now. Ain't he bold as blazes, him there in Lincoln, an honored an' respicted gintleman! An honored and respicted gintleman," concluded Scully with a flourish. And, so saying, he smote the Swede jovially on the back.

The Swede faintly smiled.

"Now," said the old man, "there's only one more thing." He dropped suddenly to the floor and thrust his head beneath the bed. The Swede could hear his muffled voice. "I'd keep it under my piller if it wasn't for that boy Johnnie. Then there's the old woman—— Where is it now? I never put it twice in the same place. Ah, now come out with you!"

Presently he backed clumsily from under the bed, dragging with him an old coat rolled into a bundle. "I've fetched him," he muttered. Kneeling on the floor, he unrolled the coat and extracted from its heart a large yellow-brown whisky-bottle.

His first maneuver was to hold the bottle up to the light. Reassured, apparently that nobody has been tampering with it, he thrust it with a generous movement toward the Swede.

The weak-kneed Swede was about to eagerly clutch this element of strength, but he suddenly jerked his hand away and cast a look of horror upon Scully.

"Drink," said the old man affectionately. He had risen to his feet, and now stood facing the Swede.

There was a silence. Then again Scully said: "Drink!"

The Swede laughed wildly. He grabbed the bottle, put it to his mouth; and as his lips curled absurdly around the opening and his throat worked, he kept his glance, burning with hatred, upon the old man's face.

IV

After the departure of Scully the three men, with the cardboard still upon their knees, preserved for a long time an astounded silence. Then Johnnie said: "That's the dod-dangedest Swede I ever see."

"He ain't no Swede," said the cowboy, scornfully.

"Well, what is he then?" cried Johnnie. "What is he then?"

"It's my opinion," replied the cowboy deliberately, "he's some kind of a Dutchman." It was a venerable custom of the country to entitle as Swedes all light-haired men who spoke with a heavy tongue. In consequence the idea of the cowboy was not without its daring. "Yes, sir," he repeated. "It's my opinion this feller is some kind of a Dutchman."

"Well, he says he's a Swede, anyhow," muttered Johnnie, sulkily. He turned to the Easterner: "What do you think, Mr. Blanc?"

"Oh, I don't know," replied the Easterner.

"Well, what do you think makes him act that way?" asked the cowboy.

"Why, he's frightened." The Easterner knocked his pipe against a rim of the stove. "He's clear frightened out of his boots."

"What at?" cried Johnnie and the cowboy together.

The Easterner reflected over his answer.

"What at?" cried the others again.

"Oh, I don't know, but it seems to me this man has been reading dime novels, and he thinks he's right out in the middle of it—the shootin' and stabbin' and all."

"But," said the cowboy, deeply scandalized, "this ain't Wyoming, ner none of them places. This is Nebrasker."

"Yes," added Johnnie, "an' why don't he wait till he gits *out West?*"

The traveled Easterner laughed. "It isn't different there even—not in these days. But he thinks he's right in the middle of hell."

Johnnie and the cowboy mused long.

"It's awful funny," remarked Johnnie at last.

"Yes," said the cowboy. "This is a queer game. I hope we don't git snowed in, because then we'd have to stand this here man bein' around with us all the time. That wouldn't be no good."

"I wish pop would throw him out," said Johnnie.

Presently they heard a loud stamping on the stairs, accompanied by ringing jokes in the voice of old Scully, and laughter, evidently from the Swede. The men around the stove stared vacantly at each other. "Gosh!" said the cowboy. The door flew open, and old Scully, flushed and anecdotal, came into the room. He was jabbering at the Swede, who followed him, laughing bravely. It was the entry of two roisterers from a banquet hall.

"Come now," said Scully sharply to the three seated men, "move up and give us a chance at the stove." The cowboy and the Easterner obediently sidled their chairs to make room for the new-comers. Johnnie, however, simply arranged himself in a more indolent attitude, and then remained motionless.

"Come! Git over, there," said Scully.

"Plenty of room on the other side of the stove," said Johnnie.

"Do you think we want to sit in the draught?" roared the father.

But the Swede here interposed with a grandeur of confidence. "No, no. Let the boy sit where he likes," he cried in a bullying voice to the father.

"All right! All right!" said Scully, deferentially. The cowboy and the Easterner exchanged glances of wonder.

The five chairs were formed in a crescent about one side of the stove. The Swede began to talk; he talked arrogantly, profanely, angrily. Johnnie, the cowboy, and the Easterner maintained a morose silence, while old Scully appeared to be receptive and eager, breaking in constantly with sympathetic ejaculations.

Finally the Swede announced that he was thirsty. He moved in his chair, and said that he would go for a drink of water.

"I'll git it for you," cried Scully at once.

"No," said the Swede, contemptuously. "I'll get it for myself." He arose and stalked with the air of an owner off into the executive parts of the hotel.

As soon as the Swede was out of hearing, Scully sprang to his feet and whispered intensely to the others: "Upstairs he thought I was tryin' to poison 'im."

"Say," said Johnnie, "this makes me sick. Why don't you throw 'im out in the snow?"

"Why, he's all right now," declared Scully. "It was only

that he was from the East, and he thought this was a tough place. That's all. He's all right now."

The cowboy looked with admiration upon the Easterner. "You were straight," he said. "You were on to that there Dutchman."

"Well," said Johnnie to his father, "he may be all right now, but I don't see it. Other time he was scared, but now he's too fresh."

Scully's speech was always a combination of Irish brogue and idiom, Western twang and idiom, and scraps of curiously formal diction taken from the story-books and newspapers. He now hurled a strange mass of language at the head of his son. "What do I keep? What do I keep? What do I keep?" he demanded, in a voice of thunder. He slapped his knee impressively, to indicate that he himself was going to make reply, and that all should heed. "I keep a hotel," he shouted. "A hotel, do you mind? A guest under my roof has sacred privileges. He is to be intimidated by none. Not one word shall he hear that would prijudice him in favor of goin' away. I'll not have it. There's no place in this here town where they can say they iver took in a guest of mine because he was afraid to stay here." He wheeled suddenly upon the cowboy and the Easterner. "Am I right?"

"Yes, Mr. Scully," said the cowboy, "I think you're right."

"Yes, Mr. Scully," said the Easterner, "I think you're right."

V

At six-o'clock supper, the Swede fizzed like a firewheel. He sometimes seemed on the point of bursting into riotous song, and in all his madness he was encouraged by old Scully. The Easterner was encased in reserve; the cowboy sat in wide-mouthed amazement, forgetting to eat, while Johnnie wrathily demolished great plates of food. The daughters of the house, when they were obliged to replenish the biscuits, approached as warily as Indians, and, having succeeded in their purpose, fled with ill-concealed trepidation. The Swede domineered the whole feast, and he gave it the appearance of a crucl bacchanal. He seemed to have grown suddenly taller; he gazed, brutally disdainful, into every face. His voice rang through the room. Once when he jabbed out harpoon-fashion with his fork to pinion a

biscuit, the weapon nearly impaled the hand of the Easterner, which had been stretched quietly out for the same
biscuit.

After supper, as the men filed toward the other room, the
Swede smote Scully ruthlessly on the shoulder. "Well, old
boy, that was a good, square meal." Johnnie looked hopefully at his father; he knew that shoulder was tender from
an old fall; and, indeed, it appeared for a moment as if
Scully was going to flame out over the matter, but in the
end he smiled a sickly smile and remained silent. The others
understood from his manner that he was admitting his responsibility for the Swede's new viewpoint.

Johnnie, however, addressed his parent in an aside.
"Why don't you license somebody to kick you downstairs?"
Scully scowled darkly by way of reply.

When they were gathered about the stove, the Swede insisted on another game of High-Five. Scully gently deprecated the plan at first, but the Swede turned a wolfish glare
upon him. The old man subsided, and the Swede can-
vassed the others. In his tone there was always a great
threat. The cowboy and the Easterner both remarked indifferently that they would play. Scully said that he would
presently have to go to meet the 6.58 train, and so the
Swede turned menacingly upon Johnnie. For a moment
their glances crossed like blades, and then Johnnie smiled
and said. "Yes, I'll play."

They formed a square, with the little board on their
knees. The Easterner and the Swede were again partners.
As the play went on, it was noticeable that the cowboy
was not boardwhacking as usual. Meanwhile, Scully, near
the lamp, had put on his spectacles and, with an appearance
curiously like an old priest, was reading a newspaper. In
time he went out to meet the 6.58 train, and, despite his
precautions, a gust of polar wind whirled into the room as
he opened the door. Besides scattering the cards, it chilled
the players to the marrow. The Swede cursed frightfully.
When Scully returned, his entrance disturbed a cozy and
friendly scene. The Swede again cursed. But presently they
were once more intent, their heads bent forward and their
hands moving swiftly. The Swede had adopted the fashion
of board-whacking.

Scully took up his paper and for a long time remained
immersed in matters which were extraordinarily remote
from him. The lamp burned badly, and once he stopped to

adjust the wick. The newspaper, as he turned from page to page, rustled with a slow and comfortable sound. Then suddenly he heard three terrible words: "You are cheatin'!"

Such scenes often prove that there can be little of dramatic import in environment. Any room can present a tragic front; any room can be comic. This little den was now hideous as a torture-chamber. The new faces of the men themselves had changed it upon the instant. The Swede held a huge fist in front of Johnnie's face, while the latter looked steadily over it into the blazing orbs of his accuser. The Easterner had grown pallid; the cowboy's jaw had dropped in that expression of bovine amazement which was one of his important mannerisms. After the three words, the first sound in the room was made by Scully's paper as it floated forgotten to his feet. His spectacles had also fallen from his nose, but by a clutch he had saved them in air. His hand, grasping the spectacles, now remained poised awkwardly and near his shoulder. He stared at the card-players.

Probably the silence was while a second elapsed. Then, if the floor had been suddenly twitched out from under the men they could not have moved quicker. The five had projected themselves headlong toward a common point. It happened that Johnnie, in rising to hurl himself upon the Swede, had stumbled slightly because of his curiously instinctive care for the cards and the board. The loss of the moment allowed time for the arrival of Scully, and also allowed the cowboy time to give the Swede a great push which sent him staggering back. The men found tongue together, and hoarse shouts of rage, appeal, or fear burst from every throat. The cowboy pushed and jostled feverishly at the Swede, and the Easterner and Scully clung wildly to Johnnie; but through the smoky air, above the swaying bodies of the peace-compellers, the eyes of the two warriors ever sought each other in glances of challenge that were at once hot and steely.

Of course the board had been overturned, and now the whole company of cards was scattered over the floor, where the boots of the men trampled the fat and painted kings and queens as they gazed with their silly eyes at the war that was waging above them.

Scully's voice was dominating the yells. "Stop now! Stop, I say! Stop, now——"

Johnnie, as he struggled to burst through the rank formed by Scully and the Eastener, was crying, "Well, he says I cheated! He says I cheated! I won't allow no man to say I cheated! If he says I cheated, he's a—— ——!"

The cowboy was telling the Swede, "Quit, now! Quit, d'ye hear——"

The screams of the Swede never ceased: "He did cheat! I saw him! I saw him——"

As for the Easterner, he was importuning in a voice that was not heeded: "Wait a moment, can't you? Oh, wait a moment. What's the good of a fight over a game of cards? Wait a moment——"

In this tumult no complete sentences were clear. "Cheat" —"Quit"—"He says"—these fragments pierced the uproar and rang out sharply. It was remarkable that, whereas Scully undoubtedly made the most noise, he was the least heard of any of the riotous band.

Then suddenly there was a great cessation. It was as if each man had paused for breath; and although the room was still lighted with the anger of men, it could be seen that there was no danger of immediate conflict, and at once Johnnie, shouldering his way forward, almost succeeded in confronting the Swede. "What did you say I cheated for? What did you say I cheated for? I don't cheat, and I won't let no man say I do!"

The Swede said, "I saw you! I saw you!"

"Well," cried Johnnie, "I'll fight any man what says I cheat!"

"No, you won't," said the cowboy. "Not here."

"Ah, be still, can't you?" said Scully, coming between them.

The quiet was sufficient to allow the Easterner's voice to be heard. He was repeating, "Oh, wait a moment, can't you? What's the good of a fight over a game of cards? Wait a moment!"

Johnnie, his red face appearing above his father's shoulders, hailed the Swede again. "Did you say I cheated?"

The Swede showed his teeth. "Yes."

"Then," said Johnnie, "we must fight."

"Yes, fight," roared the Swede. He was like a demoniac. "Yes, fight! I'll show you what kind of a man I am! I'll show you who you want to fight! Maybe you think I can't fight! Maybe you think I can't! I'll show you, you skin, you cardsharp! Yes, you cheated! You cheated! You cheated!"

"Well, let's go at it, then, mister," said Johnnie, coolly.

The cowboy's brow was beaded with sweat from his efforts in intercepting all sorts of raids. He turned in despair to Scully. "What are you goin' to do now?"

A change had come over the Celtic visage of the old man. He now seemed all eagerness; his eyes glowed.

"We'll let them fight," he answered, stalwartly. "I can't put up with it any longer. I've stood this damned Swede till I'm sick. We'll let them fight."

VI

The men prepared to go out of doors. The Easterner was so nervous that he had great difficulty in getting his arms into the sleeves of his new leather coat. As the cowboy drew his fur cap down over his ears his hands trembled. In fact, Johnnie and old Scully were the only ones who displayed no agitation. These preliminaries were conducted without words.

Scully thew open the door. "Well, come on," he said. Instantly a terrific wind caused the flame of the lamp to struggle at its wick, while a puff of black smoke sprang from the chimney-top. The stove was in mid-current of the blast, and its voice swelled to equal the roar of the storm. Some of the scarred and bedabbled cards were caught up from the floor and dashed helplessly against the farther wall. The men lowered their heads and plunged into the tempest as into a sea.

No snow was falling, but great whirls and clouds of flakes, swept up from the ground by the frantic winds, were streaming southward with the speed of bullets. The covered land was blue with the sheen of an unearthly satin, and there was no other hue save where, at the low, black railway station—which seemed incredibly distant—one light gleamed like a tiny jewel. As the men floundered into a thigh-deep drift, it was known that the Swede was bawling out something. Scully went to him, put a hand on his shoulder, and projected an ear. "What's that you say?" he shouted.

"1 say," bawled the Swede again, "I won't stand much show against this gang. I know you'll all pitch on me."

Scully smote him reproachfully on the arm.

"Tut, man!" he yelled. The wind tore the words from Scully's lips and scattered them far alee.

"You are all a gang of——" boomed the Swede, but the storm also seized the remainder of this sentence.

Immediately turning their backs upon the wind, the men had swung around a corner to the sheltered side of the hotel. It was the function of the little house to preserve here, amid this great devastation of snow, an irregular V-shape of heavily encrusted grass, which crackled beneath the feet. One could imagine the great drifts piled against the windward side. When the party reached the comparative peace of this spot, it was found that the Swede was still bellowing.

"Oh, I know what kind of a thing this is! I know you'll all pitch on me. I can't lick you all!"

Scully turned upon him panther-fashion. "You'll not have to whip all of us. You'll have to whip my son Johnnie. An' the man what troubles you durin' that time will have me to dale with."

The arrangements were swiftly made. The two men faced each other, obedient to the harsh commands of Scully, whose face, in the subtly luminous gloom, could be seen set in the austere impersonal lines that are pictured on the countenances of the Roman veterans. The Easterner's teeth were chattering, and he was hopping up and down like a mechanical toy. The cowboy stood rock-like.

The contestants had not stripped off any clothing. Each was in his ordinary attire. Their fists were up, and they eyed each other in a calm that had the elements of leonine cruelty in it.

During this pause, the Easterner's mind, like a film, took lasting impressions of three men—the iron-nerved master of the ceremony; the Swede, pale, motionless, terrible; and Johnnie, serene yet ferocious, brutish yet heroic. The entire prelude had in it a tragedy greater than the tragedy of action, and this aspect was accentuated by the long, mellow cry of the blizzard, as it sped the tumbling and wailing flakes into the black abyss of the south.

"Now!" said Scully.

The two combatants leaped forward and crashed together like bullocks. There was heard the cushioned sound of blows, and of a curse squeezing out from between the tight teeth of one.

As for the spectators, the Easterner's pent-up breath ex-

ploded from him with a pop of relief, absolute relief from
the tension of the preliminaries. The cowboy bounded into
the air with a yowl. Scully was immovable as from supreme
amazement and fear at the fury of the fight which he himself had permitted and arranged.

For a time the encounter in the darkness was such a
perplexity of flying arms that it presented no more detail
than would a swiftly revolving wheel. Occasionally a face,
as if illumined by a flash of light, would shine out, ghastly
and marked with pink spots. A moment later, the men
might have been known as shadows, if it were not for the
involuntary utterance of oaths that came from them in
whispers.

Suddenly a holocaust of warlike desire caught the cowboy, and he bolted forward with the speed of a broncho.
"Go it, Johnnie! go it! Kill him! Kill him!"

Scully confronted him. "Kape back," he said; and by his
glance the cowboy could tell that this man was Johnnie's
father.

To the Easterner there was a monotony of unchangeable
fighting that was an abomination. This confused mingling
was eternal to his sense, which was concentrated in a
longing for the end, the priceless end. Once the fighters
lurched near him, and as he scrambled hastily backward
he heard them breathe like men on the rack.

"Kill him, Johnnie! Kill him! Kill him! Kill him!" The
cowboy's face was contorted like one of those agony masks
in museums.

"Keep still," said Scully, icily.

Then there was a sudden loud grunt, incomplete, cut
short, and Johnnie's body swung away from the Swede and
fell with sickening heaviness to the grass. The cowboy was
barely in time to prevent the mad Swede from flinging
himself upon his prone adversary. "No, you don't," said
the cowboy, interposing an arm. "Wait a second."

Scully was at his son's side. "Johnnie! Johnnie, me boy!"
His voice had a quality of melancholy tenderness. "Johnnie!
Can you go on with it?" He looked anxiously down into
the bloody, pulpy face of his son.

There was a moment of silence, and then Johnnie answered in his ordinary voice, "Yes, I—it—yes."

Assisted by his father he struggled to his feet. "Wait a
bit now till you git your wind," said the old man.

A few paces away the cowboy was lecturing the Swede. "No, you don't! Wait a second!"

The Easterner was plucking at Scully's sleeve. "Oh, this is enough," he pleaded. "This is enough! Let it go as it stands. This is enough!"

"Bill," said Scully, "git out of the road." The cowboy stepped aside. "Now." The combatants were actuated by a new caution as they advanced toward collision. They glared at each other, and then the Swede aimed a lightning blow that carried with it his entire weight. Johnnie was evidently half stupid from weakness, but he miraculously dodged, and his fist sent the over-balanced Swede sprawling.

The cowboy, Scully, and the Easterner burst into a cheer that was like a chorus of triumphant soldiery, but before its conclusion the Swede had scuffed agilely to his feet and come in berserk abandon at his foe. There was another perplexity of flying arms, and Johnnie's body again swung away and fell, even as a bundle might fall from a roof. The Swede instantly staggered to a little wind-waved tree and leaned upon it, breathing like an engine, while his savage and flame-lit eyes roamed from face to face as the men bent over Johnnie. There was a splendor of isolation in his situation at this time which the Easterner felt once when, lifting his eyes from the man on the ground, he beheld that mysterious and lonely figure, waiting.

"Are you any good yet, Johnnie?" asked Scully in a broken voice.

The son gasped and opened his eyes languidly. After a moment he answered, "No—I ain't—any good—any—more." Then, from shame and bodily ill, he began to weep, the tears furrowing down through the bloodstain on his face. "He was too—too—too heavy for me."

Scully straightened and addressed the waiting figure. "Stranger," he said, evenly, "it's all up with our side." Then his voice changed into that vibrant huskiness which is commonly the tone of the most simple and deadly announcements. "Johnnie is whipped."

Without replying, the victor moved off on the route to the front door of the hotel.

The cowboy was formulating new and unspellable blasphemies. The Easterner was startled to find that they were out in a wind that seemed to come direct from the shadowed arctic floes. He heard again the wail of the snow as it was flung to its grave in the south. He knew now that all this time the cold had been sinking into him deeper and deeper, and he wondered that he had not perished. He felt indifferent to the condition of the vanquished man.

"Johnnie, can you walk?" asked Scully.

"Did I hurt—hurt him any?" asked the son.

"Can you walk, boy? Can you walk?"

Johnnie's voice was suddenly strong. There was a robust impatience in it. "I asked you whether I hurt him any!"

"Yes, yes, Johnnie," answered the cowboy, consolingly; "he's hurt a good deal."

They raised him from the ground, and as soon as he was on his feet he went tottering off, rebuffing all attempts at assistance. When the party rounded the corner they were fairly blinded by the pelting of the snow. It burned their faces like fire. The cowboy carried Johnnie through the drift to the door. As they entered, some cards again rose from the floor and beat against the wall.

The Easterner rushed to the stove. He was so profoundly chilled that he almost dared to embrace the glowing iron. The Swede was not in the room. Johnnie sank into a chair and, folding his arms on his knees, buried his face in them. Scully, warming one foot and then the other at a rim of the stove, muttered to himself with Celtic mournfulness. The cowboy had removed his fur cap, and with a dazed and rueful air he was running one hand through his tousled locks. From overhead they could hear the creaking of boards, as the Swede tramped here and there in his room.

The sad quiet was broken by the sudden flinging open of a door that led toward the kitchen. It was instantly followed by an inrush of women. They precipitated themselves upon Johnnie amid a chorus of lamentation. Before they carried their prey off to the kitchen, there to be bathed and harangued with that mixture of sympathy and abuse which is a feat of their sex, the mother straightened herself and fixed old Scully with an eye of stern reproach. "Shame be upon you, Patrick Scully!" she cried. "Your own son, too. Shame be upon you!"

"Shame be upon you, Patrick Scully!" The girls, rallying to this slogan, sniffed disdainfully in the direction of those trembling accomplices, the cowboy and the Easterner. Presently they bore Johnnie away, and left the three men to dismal reflection.

VII

"I'd like to fight this here Dutchman myself," said the cowboy, breaking a long silence.

Scully wagged his head sadly. "No, that wouldn't do. It wouldn't be right. It wouldn't be right."

"Well, why wouldn't it?" argued the cowboy. "I don't see no harm in it."

"No," answered Scully, with mournful heroism. "It wouldn't be right. It was Johnnie's fight, and now we musn't whip the man just because he whipped Johnnie."

"Yes, that's true enough," said the cowboy; "but—he better not get fresh with me, because I couldn't stand no more of it."

"You'll not say a word to him," commanded Scully, and even then they heard the tread of the Swede on the stairs. His entrance was made theatric. He swept the door back with a bang and swaggered to the middle of the room. No one looked at him. "Well," he cried, insolently, at Scully, "I s'pose you'll tell me now how much I owe you?"

The old man remained stolid. "You don't owe me nothin'."

"Huh!" said the Swede, "huh! Don't owe 'im nothin'."

The cowboy addressed the Swede. "Stranger, I don't see how you come to be so gay around here."

Old Scully was instantly alert. "Stop!" he shouted, holding his hand forth, fingers upward. "Bill, you shut up!"

The cowboy spat carelessly into the sawdust-box. "I didn't say a word, did I?" he asked.

"Mr. Scully," called the Swede, "how much do I owe you?" It was seen that he was attired for departure, and that he had his valise in his hand.

"You don't owe me nothin'," repeated Scully in the same imperturbable way.

"Huh!" said the Swede. "I guess you're right. I guess if it was any way at all, you'd owe me somethin'. That's what I guess," He turned to the cowboy. " 'Kill him! Kill him! Kill him!' " he mimicked, and then guffawed victoriously. " 'Kill him!' " He was convulsed with ironical humor.

But he might have been jeering the dead. The three men were immovable and silent, staring with glassy eyes at the stove.

The Swede opened the door and passed into the storm,

giving one derisive glance backward at the still group.

As soon as the door was closed, Scully and the cowboy leaped to their feet and began to curse. They trampled to and fro, waving their arms and smashing into the air with their fists. "Oh, but that was a hard minute!" wailed Scully. "That was a hard minute! Him there leerin' and scoffin'! One bang at his nose was worth forty dollars to me that minute! How did you stand it, Bill!"

"How did I stand it?" cried the cowboy in a quivering voice. "How did I stand it? Oh!"

The old man burst into sudden brogue. "I'd loike to take that Swade," he wailed, "and hould 'im down on a shtone flure and bate 'im to a jeelly wid a shtick!"

The cowboy groaned in sympathy. "I'd like to git him by the neck and ha-ammer him"—he brought his hand down on a chair with a noise like a pistol-shot—"hammer that there Dutchman until he couldn't tell himself from a dead coyote!"

"I'd bate 'im until he——"

"I'd show *him* some things——"

And then together they raised a yearning, fanatic cry—"Oh-o-oh! if we only could—"

"Yes!"

"Yes!"

"And then I'd——"

"O-o-oh!"

VIII

The Swede, tightly gripping his valise, tacked across the face of the storm as if he carried sails. He was following a line of little naked, gasping trees which, he knew, must mark the way of the road. His face, fresh from the pounding of Johnnie's fists, felt more pleasure than pain in the wind and the driving snow. A number of square shapes loomed upon him finally, and he knew them as the houses of the main body of the town. He found a street and made travel along it, leaning heavily upon the wind whenever, at a corner, a terrific blast caught him.

He might have been in a deserted village. We picture the world as thick with conquering and elate humanity, but here, with the bugles of the tempest pealing, it was hard to imagine a peopled earth. One viewed the existence of man then as a marvel, and conceded a glamour of wonder to these lice which were caused to cling to a whirling, fire-smitten, ice-locked, disease-striken, space-lost bulb. The conceit of man was explained by this storm to be the very engine of life. One was a coxcomb not to die in it. However, the Swede found a saloon.

In front of it an indomitable red light was burning, and the snowflakes were made blood-color as they flew through the circumscribed territory of the lamp's shining. The Swede pushed open the door of the saloon and entered. A sanded expanse was before him, and at the end of it four men sat about a table drinking. Down one side of the room extended a radiant bar, and its guardian was leaning upon his elbows listening to the talk of the men at the table. The Swede dropped his valise upon the floor and, smiling fraternally upon the barkeeper, said, "Gimme some whisky, will you?" The man placed a bottle, a whisky-glass, and a glass of ice-thick water upon the bar. The Swede poured himself an abnormal portion of whisky and drank it in three gulps. "Pretty bad night," remarked the bartender, indifferently. He was making the pretension of blindness which is usually a distinction of his class; but it could have been seen that he was furtively studying the half-erased bloodstains on the face of the Swede. "Bad night," he said again.

"Oh, it's good enough for me," replied the Swede, hardily, as he poured himself some more whisky. The barkeeper took his coin and maneuvered it through its reception by the highly nickeled cash-machine. A bell rang; a card labeled "20 cts." had appeared.

"No," continued the Swede, "this isn't too bad weather. It's good enough for me."

"So?" murmured the barkeeper, languidly.

The copious drams made the Swede's eyes swim, and he breathed a trifle heavier. "Yes, I like this weather. I like it. It suits me." It was apparently his design to impart a deep significance to these words.

"So?" murmured the bartender again. He turned to gaze dreamily at the scroll-like birds and bird-like scrolls which had been drawn with soap upon the mirrors in back of the bar.

"Well, I guess I'll take another drink," said the Swede, presently. "Have something?"

"No, thanks; I'm not drinkin'," answered the bartender. Afterward he asked, "How did you hurt your face?"

The Swede immediately began to boast loudly. "Why, in a fight. I thumped the soul out of a man down here at Scully's hotel."

The interest of the four men at the table was at last aroused.

"Who was it?" said one.

"Johnnie Scully," blustered the Swede. "Son of the man what runs it. He will be pretty near dead for some weeks, I can tell you. I made a nice thing of him, I did. He couldn't get up. They carried him in the house. Have a drink?"

Instantly the men in some subtle way encased themselves in reserve. "No, thanks," said one. The group was of curious formation. Two were prominent local business men; one was the district attorney; and one was a professional gambler of the kind known as "square." But a scrutiny of the group would not have enabled an observer to pick the gambler from the men of more reputable pursuits. He was, in fact, a man so delicate in manner, when among people of fair class, and so judicious in his choice of victims, that in the strictly masculine part of the town's life he had come to be explicitly trusted and admired. People called him a thoroughbred. The fear and contempt with which his craft was regarded were undoubtedly the reason why his quiet dignity shone conspicuous above the quiet dignity of men who might be merely hatters, billiard-markers, or grocery clerks. Beyond an occasional unwary traveler who came by rail, this gambler was supposed to prey solely upon reckless and senile farmers, who, when flush with good crops, drove into town in all the pride and confidence of an absolutely invulnerable stupidity. Hearing at times in circuitous fashion of the despoilment of such a farmer, the important men of Romper invariably laughed in contempt of the victim, and if they thought of the wolf at all, it was with a kind of pride at the knowledge that he would never dare think of attacking their wisdom and courage. Besides, it was popular that this gambler had a real wife and two real children in a neat cottage in a suburb, where he led an exemplary home life; and when anyone even suggested a discrepancy in his character, the crowd immediately voci-

ferated descriptions of this virtuous family circle. Then
men who led exemplary home lives, and men who did not
lead exemplary home lives, all subsided in a bunch, remarking that there was nothing more to be said.

However, when a restriction was placed upon him—as,
for instance, when a strong clique of members of the new
Pollywog Club refused to permit him, even as a spectator,
to appear in the rooms of the organization—the candor and
gentleness with which he accepted the judgment disarmed
many of his foes and made his friends more desperately
partisan. He invariably distinguished between himself and
a respectable Romper man so quickly and frankly that his
manner actually appeared to be a continual broadcast
compliment.

And one must not forget to declare the fundamental fact
of his entire position in Romper. It is irrefutable that in all
affairs outside his business, in all matters that occur eternally and commonly between man and man, this thieving
card-player was so generous, so just, so moral, that, in a
contest, he could have put to flight the consciences of nine
tenths of the citizens of Romper.

And so it happened that he was seated in this saloon
with the two prominent local merchants and the district attorney.

The Swede continued to drink raw whisky, meanwhile
babbling at the barkeeper and trying to induce him to indulge in potations. "Come on. Have a drink. Come on.
What—no? Well, have a little one, then. By gawd, I've
whipped a man tonight, and I want to celebrate. I whipped
him good, too. Gentlemen," the Swede cried to the men at
the table, "have a drink?"

"Ssh!" said the barkeeper.

The group at the table, although furtively attentive, had
been pretending to be deep in talk, but now a man lifted
his eyes toward the Swede and said, shortly, "Thanks. We
don't want any more."

At this reply the Swede ruffled out his chest like a rooster.
"Well," he exploded, "it seems I can't get anybody to
drink with me in this town. Seems so, don't it? Well!"

"Ssh!" said the barkeeper.

"Say," snarled the Swede, "don't you try to shut me up.
I won't have it. I'm a gentleman, and I want people to

drink with me. And I want 'em to drink with me now. *Now*—do you understand?" He rapped the bar with his knuckles.

Years of experience had calloused the bartender. He merely grew sulky. "I hear you," he answered.

"Well," cried the Swede, "listen hard then. See those men over there? Well, they're going to drink with me, and don't you forget it. Now you watch."

"Hi," yelled the barkeeper, "this won't do!"

"Why won't it?" demanded the Swede. He stalked over to the table, and by chance laid his hand upon the shoulder of the gambler. "How about this?" he asked wrathfully. "I asked you to drink with me."

The gambler simply twisted his head and spoke over his shoulder. "My friend, I don't know you."

"Oh, hell!" answered the Swede, "come and have a drink."

"Now, my boy," advised the gambler kindly, "take your hand off my shoulder and go 'way and mind your own business." He was a little, slim man, and it seemed strange to hear him use this tone of heroic patronage to the burly Swede. The other men at the table said nothing.

"What! You won't drink with me, you little dude? I'll make you, then! I'll make you!" The Swede had grasped the gambler frenziedly at the throat, and was dragging him from his chair. The other men sprang up. The barkeeper dashed around the corner of his bar. There was a great tumult, and then was seen a long blade in the hand of the gambler. It shot forward, and a human body, this citadel of virtue, wisdom, power, was pierced as easily as if it had been a melon. The Swede fell with a cry of supreme astonishment.

The prominent merchants and the district attorney must have at once tumbled out of the place backward. The bartender found himself hanging limply to the arm of a chair and gazing into the eyes of a murderer.

"Henry," said the latter, as he wiped his knife on one of the towels that hung beneath the bar rail, "you tell 'em where to find me. I'll be home, waiting for 'em." Then he vanished. A moment afterward the barkeeper was in the street dinning through the storm for help and, moreover, companionship.

The corpse of the Swede, alone in the saloon, had its eyes

fixed upon a dreadful legend that dwelt atop of the cash-machine: "This registers the amount of your purchase."

IX

Months later, the cowboy was frying pork over the stove of a little ranch near the Dakota line, when there was a quick thud of hoofs outside, and presently the Easterner entered with the letters and the papers.

"Well," said the Easterner at once, "the chap that killed the Swede has got three years. Wasn't much, was it?"

"He has? Three years?" The cowboy poised his pan of pork, while he ruminated upon the news. "Three years. That ain't much."

"No. It was a light sentence," replied the Easterner as he unbuckled his spurs. "Seems there was a good deal of sympathy for him in Romper."

"If the bartender had been any good," observed the cow-boy, thoughtfully, "he would have gone in and cracked that there Dutchman on the head with a bottle in the beginnin' of it and stopped all this here murderin'."

"Yes, a thousand things might have happened," said the Easterner, tartly.

The cowboy returned his pan of pork to the fire, but his philosophy continued. "It's funny, ain't it? If he hadn't said Johnnie was cheatin' he'd be alive this minute. He was an awful fool. Game played for fun, too. Not for money. I believe he was crazy."

"I feel sorry for that gambler," said the Easterner.

"Oh, so do I," said the cowboy. "He don't deserve none of it for killin' who he did."

"The Swede might not have been killed if everything had been square."

"Might not have been killed?" exclaimed the cowboy. "Everythin' square? Why, when he said that Johnnie was cheatin' and acted like such a jackass? And then in the saloon he fairly walked up to git hurt?" With these arguments the cowboy browbeat the Easterner and reduced him to rage.

"You're a fool!" cried the Easterner, viciously. "You're a bigger jackass than the Swede by a million majority. Now let me tell you one thing. Let me tell you something. Listen! Johnnie *was* cheating!"

" 'Johnnie,' " said the cowboy, blankly. There was a

minute of silence, and then he said, robustly, "Why, no. The game was only for fun."

"Fun or not," said the Easterner, "Johnnie was cheating. I saw him. I know it. I saw him. And I refused to stand up and be a man. I let the Swede fight it out alone. And you —you were simply puffing around the place and wanting to fight. And then old Scully himself! We are all in it! This poor gambler isn't even a noun. He is kind of an adverb. Every sin is the result of a collaboration. We, five of us, have collaborated in the murder of this Swede. Usually there are from a dozen to forty women really involved in every murder, but in this case it seems to be only five men—you, I, Johnnie, old Scully; and that fool of an unfortunate gambler came merely as a culmination, the apex of a human movement, and gets all the punishment."

The cowboy, injured and rebellious, cried out blindly into this fog of mysterious theory: "Well, I didn't do anythin', did I?"

1898

God Fashioned the Ship of the World Carefully

God fashioned the ship of the world carefully.
With the infinite skill of an All-Master
Made He the hull and the sails,
Held He the rudder
Ready for adjustment.
Erect stood He, scanning His work proudly.
Then—at fateful time—a wrong called,
And God turned, heeding.
Lo, the ship, at this opportunity, slipped slyly,
Making cunning noiseless travel down the ways.   10
So that, for ever rudderless, it went upon the seas
Going ridiculous voyages,
Making quaint progress,
Turning as with serious purpose
Before stupid winds.
And there were many in the sky
Who laughed at this thing.

1895

Should the Wide World Roll Away

Should the wide world roll away,
Leaving black terror,
Limitless night,
Nor God, nor man, nor place to stand
Would be to me essential,
If thou and thy white arms were there,
And the fall to doom a long way.

1895

A Youth in Apparel that Glittered

A youth in apparel that glittered
Went to walk in a grim forest.
There he met an assassin
Attired all in garb of old days;
He, scowling through the thickets,
And dagger poised quivering,
Rushed upon the youth.
"Sir," said this latter,
"I am enchanted, believe me,
To die, thus,   10
In this mediæval fashion,
According to the best legends;
Ah, what joy!"
Then took he the wound, smiling,
And died, content.

1895

A Man Went before a Strange God

A man went before a strange God—
The God of many men, sadly wise.
And the Deity thundered loudly,
Fat with rage, and puffing,
"Kneel, mortal, and cringe

And grovel and do homage
To My Particularly Sublime Majesty."
The man fled.

Then the man went to another God—
The God of his inner thoughts.   10
And this one looked at him
With soft eyes
Lit with infinite comprehension,
And said, "My poor child!"

                                                    1895

War Is Kind

Do not weep, maiden, for war is kind.
Because your lover threw wild hands toward the sky
And the affrighted steed ran on alone,
Do not weep.
War is kind.

Hoarse, booming drums of the regiment,
Little souls who thirst for fight,
These men were born to drill and die.
The unexplained glory flies above them,
Great is the battle-god, great, and his kingdom—   10
A field where a thousand corpses lie.

Do not weep, babe, for war is kind.
Because your father tumbled in the yellow trenches,
Raged at his breast, gulped and died,
Do not weep.
War is kind.

Swift blazing flag of the regiment,
Eagle with crest of red and gold,
These men were born to drill and die.
Point for them the virtue of slaughter,   20
Make plain to them the excellence of killing
And a field where a thousand corpses lie.

Mother whose heart hung humble as a button
On the bright splendid shroud of your son,
Do not weep.
War is kind.

1899

A Little Ink More or Less!

A little ink more or less!
It surely can't matter?
Even the sky and the opulent sea,
The plains and the hills, aloof,
Hear the uproar of all these books.
But it is only a little ink more or less.

What?
You define me God with these trinkets.
Can my misery meal on an ordered walking
Of surpliced numskulls?   10
And a fanfare of lights?
Or even upon the measured pulpitings
Of the familiar false and true?
Is this God?
Where, then, is hell?
Show me some bastard mushroom
Sprung from a pollution of blood.
It is better.

Where is God?

1899

A Newspaper Is a Collection of Half-Injustices

A newspaper is a collection of half-injustices
Which, bawled by boys from mile to mile,
Spreads its curious opinion
To a million merciful and sneering men,
While families cuddle the joys of the fireside
When spurred by tale of dire lone agony.
A newspaper is a court
Where everyone is kindly and unfairly tried

By a squalor of honest men.
A newspaper is a market   10
Where wisdom sells its freedom
And melons are crowned by the crowd.
A newspaper is a game
Where his error scores the player victory
While another's skill wins death.
A newspaper is a symbol;
It is feckless life's chronicle,
A collection of loud tales
Concentrating eternal stupidities,
That in remote ages lived unhaltered,
Roaming through a fenceless world.

1899

A Slant of Sun on Dull Brown Walls

A slant of sun on dull brown walls,
A forgotten sky of bashful blue.

Toward God a mighty hymn,
A song of collisions and cries,
Rumbling wheels, hoof-beats, bells,
Welcomes, farewells, love-calls, final moans,
Voices of joy, idiocy, warning, despair,
The unknown appeals of brutes,
The chanting of flowers,
The screams of cut trees,   10
The senseless babble of hens and wise men—
A cluttered incoherency that says at the stars:
"O God, save us!"

1899

A Man Said to the Universe

A man said to the universe:
"Sir, I exist!"
"However," replied the universe,
"The fact has not created in me
A sense of obligation."

1899

The Trees in the Garden Rained Flowers

The trees in the garden rained flowers.
Children ran there joyously.
They gathered the flowers
Each to himself.
Now there were some
Who gathered great heaps—
Having opportunity and skill—
Until, behold, only chance blossoms
Remained for the feeble.
Then a little spindling tutor   10
Ran importantly to the father, crying:
"Pray, come hither!
"See this unjust thing in your garden!"
But when the father had surveyed
He admonished the tutor:
"Not so, small sage!
"This thing is just.
"For, look you,
"Are not they who possess the flowers
"Stronger, bolder, shrewder   20
"Than they who have none?
"Why should the strong—
"The beautiful strong—
"Why should they not have the flowers?"
Upon reflection, the tutor bowed to the ground.
"My lord," he said,
"The stars are displaced
"By this towering wisdom."

1899

FRANK NORRIS

(1870–1902)

Norris's life was short but full; his writings second-rank but important. The son of a successful businessman and an actress, Norris was fourteen when his family moved to San Francisco from Chicago. Three years later he was in Paris as an art student—devoting himself, however, more to literature than to painting. In 1890, at his father's insistence, he returned home to become a student at the University of California, which he attended for four years without earning his degree. In 1894 he enrolled at Harvard as a special student in English; there, under the expert tutelage of Professor Lewis E. Gates (a literary critic of some note), he completed *McTeague* (1899), a relentless novel in the naturalistic manner of Zola—a manner which Norris, confusingly, termed "romantic" because of its willingness to expose and explore sordid deviations from "the normal life." He pleaded for "romantic" fiction as a release from the probability in characterization and incident demanded by Howells. With Stephen Crane's *Maggie* (published in 1893, but not influential until several years later), *McTeague,* a study of an unlicensed dentist whose disintegration was brought about by the interaction of hostile circumstances and bad heredity, was one of the first steps beyond the kind of realism that Norris characterized as being as "respectable as a church and proper as a deacon." *Vandover and the Brute,* another daring (but inferior) piece of naturalism, was written about the same time as *McTeague,* but it was not published until 1914, and then from an uncorrected draft of the novel.

University days behind him, Norris, ever energetic, took

himself off to South Africa during the Boer War to write a series of sketches; he was captured by the Boers, suffered an attack of fever, and was ordered to leave the country. Back home, he joined the staff of a San Francisco magazine, the *Wave*, to which he made frequent contributions. In 1898, *McClure's Magazine* sent him to Cuba to cover the Spanish American War; there he met Stephen Crane, who was also reporting the war, but the two did not become friends. The last few years of his life were spent in writing and, for a brief time, editorial reading for Doubleday, Page, the publishing company. In this latter activity, his work was not without significance: Norris got the company to publish Dreiser's *Sister Carrie*, despite great opposition. But Norris's potential service to the cultural community as editor and writer was cut short in his thirty-second year. He died of post-operative complications resulting from an appendectomy.

Although Norris was not himself a great novelist, he had a grandiose concept of the role of the novelist in society. Of the three great "molders of public opinion and public morals"— the press, the pulpit, and the novel—Norris felt the last to be potentially the most powerful. His championing of "the novel with a purpose" was the logical result. Suddenly in 1899 he conceived an idea ("big as all outdoors," he called it) consonant with his vision—"the big American novel is going to come out of the West," he wrote a friend. This is the origin of his projected "Epic of the Wheat," a trilogy which was to tell the story of the production, distribution, and consumption of American wheat. *The Octopus* (1901) portrays the struggle of the California wheat growers against more powerful interests; *The Pit* (1903) concerns the greedy struggles on the old Chicago Board of Trade; *The Wolf* (unwritten) was to have dealt with the relation of American wheat to starving countries. With all their faults, *The Octopus* and *The Pit* loom as large in the history of the American economic novel as does *Mc-Teague* in the history of American literary naturalism, and this is no small accomplishment.

In addition to the titles mentioned above, Norris's works include *Moran of the Lady Letty* (1898); *Blix* (1899); *A Man's Woman* (1900); *The Responsibilities of the Novelist* (1903); *A Deal in Wheat and Other Stories* (1903); *The Joyous Miracle* (1906); and *The Third Circle* (1909).

Editions and accounts of the man and his work are to be found in W. D. Howells, "Frank Norris," *North American Review*, CLXXV (1902); J. Underwood, *Literature and Insurgency*

(1914); C. Dobie, "Frank Norris, Or Up from Culture," American Mercury, XIII (1928); O. Lewis, ed., Frank Norris of "The Wave": Stories and Sketches from the San Francisco Weekly, 1893–1897 (1931); The Complete Works of Frank Norris (1928); F. Walker, Frank Norris: A Biography (1932); H. Reninger, "Norris Explains The Octopus: A Correlation of His Theory and Practice," American Literature, XII (1940); E. Marchand, Frank Norris: A Study (1942); W. Taylor, The Economic Novel in America (1942); G. Meyer, "A New Interpretation of The Octopus," College English, IV (1943); L. Åhnebrink, The Influence of Emile Zola on Frank Norris (1947); L. Åhnebrink, The Beginnings of Naturalism in American Fiction (1950); C. Walcutt, American Literary Naturalism, A Divided Stream (1956); F. Walker, ed., The Letters of Frank Norris (1956); R. Chase, The American Novel and Its Tradition (1957); K. Lohf and E. Sheehy, Frank Norris: A Bibliography (1959); W. French, Frank Norris (1962); R. J. Ray, "Symbolism in the Novels of Frank Norris," Dissertation Abstracts (1962); G. A. Schloss, "Frank Norris, Form and Development," Dissertation Abstracts (1963); R. A. Davison, "Frank Norris' Aesthetic Theory and Artistic Practice," Dissertation Abstracts (1964); D. Pizer, ed., The Literary Criticism of Frank Norris (1964); D. Pizer, The Novels of Frank Norris (1966).

A Plea for Romantic Fiction

Let us at the start make a distinction. Observe that one speaks of romanticism and not of sentimentalism. One claims that the latter is as distinct from the former as is that other form of art which is called Realism. Romance has been often put upon and overburdened by being forced to bear the onus of abuse that by right should fall to sentiment; but the two should be kept very distinct; for a very high and illustrious place will be claimed for romance, while sentiment will be handed down the scullery stairs.

Many people to-day are composing mere sentimentalism, and calling it and causing it to be called romance; so with those who are too busy to think much upon these subjects, but who none the less love honest literature, Romance, too, has fallen into disrepute. Consider now the cut-and-thrust stories. They are all labeled Romances, and it is very easy to get the impression that Romance must be an affair of cloaks and daggers, or moonlight and golden hair. But this is not so at all. The true Romance is a more serious business than this. It is not merely a conjurer's trick-box full of flimsy quackeries, tinsel and claptraps, meant only to amuse, and relying upon deception to do even that. Is it not something better than this? Can we not see in it an instrument, keen, finely tempered, flawless—an instrument with which we may go straight through the clothes and tissues and wrappings of flesh down deep into the red, living heart of things?

Is all this too subtle, too merely speculative and intrinsic, too *precieuse* and nice and "literary"? Devoutly one hopes the contrary. So much is made of so-called Romanticism in present-day fiction that the subject seems worthy of discussion, and a protest against the misuse of a really noble and honest formula of literature appears to be timely—misuse, that is, in the sense of a limited use. Let us suppose for the moment that a romance can be made out of a cut-and-thrust business. Good Heavens, are there no other things that are romantic, even in this—falsely, falsely called —humdrum world of today? Why should it be that so soon as the novelist addresses himself—seriously—to the consideration of contemporary life he must abandon Romance and take up the harsh, loveless, colorless, blunt tool called Realism?

Now, let us understand at once what is meant by Romance and what by Realism. Romance, I take it, is the kind of fiction that takes cognizance of variations from the type of normal life. Realism is the kind of fiction that confines itself to the type of normal life. According to this definition, then, Romance may even treat of the sordid, the unlovely—as for instance, the novels of M. Zola. (Zola has been dubbed a Realist, but he is, on the contrary, the very head of the Romanticists.) Also, Realism, used as it sometimes is as a term of reproach, need not be in the remotest sense or degree offensive, but on the other hand respectable as a church and proper as a deacon—as, for instance, the novels of Mr. Howells.

The reason why one claims so much for Romance, and quarrels so pointedly with Realism, is that Realism stultifies itself. It notes only the surface of things. For it, Beauty is not even skin deep, but only a geometrical plane, without dimensions and depth, a mere outside. Realism is very excellent so far as it goes, but it goes no further than the Realist himself can actually see, or actually hear. Realism is minute; it is the drama of a broken teacup, the tragedy of a walk down the block, the excitement of an afternoon call, the adventure of an invitation to dinner. It is the visit to my neighbor's house, a formal visit, from which I may draw no conclusions. I see my neighbor and his friends—very, oh, such very! probable people—and that is all. Realism bows upon the doormat and goes away and says to me, as we link arms on the sidewalk: "That is life." And I say it is not. It is not, as you would very well see if you took Romance with you to call upon your neighbor.

Lately you have been taking Romance a weary journey across the water—ages and the flood of years—and haling her into the fuzzy, musty, worm-eaten, moth-riddled, rust-corroded "Grandes Salles" of the Middle Ages and the Renaissance, and she has found the drama of a bygone age for you there. But would you take her across the street to your neighbor's front parlor (with the bisque fisher-boy on the mantel and the photograph of Niagara Falls on glass hanging in the front window); would you introduce her there? Not you. Would you take a walk with her on Fifth Avenue, or Beacon Street, or Michigan Avenue? No, indeed. Would you choose her for a companion of a morning spent in Wall Street, or an afternoon in the Waldorf-Astoria? You just guess you would not.

She would be out of place, you say—inappropriate. She might be awkward in my neighbor's front parlor, and knock over the little bisque fisher-boy. Well, she might. If she did, you might find underneath the base of the statuette, hidden away, tucked away—what? God knows. But something that would be a complete revelation of my neighbor's secretest life.

So you think Romance would stop in the front parlor and discuss medicated flannels and mineral waters with the ladies? Not for more than five minutes. She would be off upstairs with you, prying, peeping, peering into the closets of the bedroom, into the nursery, into the sitting-room; yes, and into that little iron box screwed to the lower shelf of the closet in the library; and into those compartments and pigeon-holes of the *secretaire* in the study. She would find a heartache (maybe) between the pillows of the mistress's bed, and a memory carefully secreted in the master's deed-box. She would come upon a great hope amid the books and papers of the study-table of the young man's room, and—perhaps—who knows—an affair, or great Heavens, an intrigue, in the scented ribbons and gloves and hairpins of the young lady's bureau. And she would pick here a little and there a little, making up a bag of hopes and fears and a package of joys and sorrows—great ones, mind you—and then come down to the front door, and, stepping out into the street, hand you the bags and package and say to you—"That is Life!"

Romance does very well in the castles of the Middle Ages and the Renaissance chateaux, and she has the *entree* there and is very well received. That is all well and good. But let us protest against limiting her to such places and such times. You will find her, I grant you, in the chatelaine's chamber and the dungeon of the man-at-arms; but, if you choose to look for her, you will find her equally at home in the brownstone house on the corner and in the office-building downtown. And this very day, in this very hour, she is sitting among the rags and wretchedness, the dirt and despair of the tenements of the East Side of New York.

"What?" I hear you say, "look for Romance—the lady of the silken robes and golden crown, our beautiful, chaste maiden of soft voice and gentle eyes—look for her among the vicious ruffians, male and female, of Allen Street and Mulberry Bend?" I tell you she is there, and to your shame be it said you will not know her in those surroundings. You, the aristocrats, who demand the fine linen and the purple in your fiction; you, the sensitive, the delicate, who will associate with your Romance only so long as she wears a silken gown. You will not follow her to the slums, for you believe that Romance should only amuse and entertain you, singing you sweet songs and touching the harp of silver strings with rosy-tipped fingers. If haply she should call to you from the squalor of a dive, or the awful degradation of a disorderly house, crying: "Look! listen! This, too, is life. These, too, are my children! Look at them, know them and, knowing, help!" Should she call thus you would stop your ears; you would avert your eyes and you would answer, "Come from there, Romance. Your place is not there!" And you would make of her a harlequin, a tumbler, a sword-dancer, when, as a matter of fact, she should be by right divine a teacher sent from God.

She will not often wear the robe of silk, the gold crown, the jeweled shoon; will not always sweep the silver harp. An iron note is hers if so she choose, and coarse garments, and stained hands; and, meeting her thus, it is for you to know her as she passes—know her for the same young queen of the blue mantle and lilies. She can teach you if you will be humble to learn—teach you by showing. God help you if at last you take from Romance her mission of teaching; if you do not believe that she has a purpose—a nobler purpose and a mightier than mere amusement, mere entertainment. Let Realism do the entertaining with its meticulous presentation of teacups, rag carpets, wall-paper and haircloth sofas, stopping with these, going no deeper than it sees, choosing the ordinary, the untroubled, the commonplace.

But to Romance belongs wide world for range, and the unplumbed depths of the human heart, and the mystery of sex, and the problems of life, and the black, unsearched penetralia of the soul of man. You, the indolent, must not always be amused. What matter the silken clothes, what matter the prince's houses? Romance, too, is a teacher, and if—throwing aside the purple—she wears the camel's hair and feeds upon the locusts, it is to cry aloud unto the people, "Prepare ye the way of the Lord; make straight his path."

1902

A Deal in Wheat

I The Bear—Wheat at Sixty-two

As Sam Lewiston backed the horse into the shafts of his buckboard and began hitching the tugs to the whiffletree, his wife came out from the kitchen door of the house and drew near, and stood for some time at the horse's head, her arms folded and her apron rolled around them. For a long moment neither spoke. They had talked over the situation so long and so comprehensively the night before that there seemed to be nothing more to say.

The time was late in the summer, the place a ranch in southwestern Kansas, and Lewiston and his wife were two of a vast population of farmers, wheat growers, who at that moment were passing through a crisis—a crisis that at any moment might culminate in tragedy. Wheat was down to sixty-six.

At length Emma Lewiston spoke.

"Well," she hazarded, looking vaguely out across the ranch toward the horizon, leagues distant; "well, Sam, there's always that offer of brother Joe's. We can quit—and go to Chicago—if the worst comes."

"And give up!" exclaimed Lewiston, running the lines through the torets. "Leave the ranch! Give up! After all these years!"

His wife made no reply for the moment. Lewiston climbed into the buckboard and gathered up the lines. "Well, here goes for the last try, Emmie," he said. "Good-by, girl. Maybe things will look better in town to-day."

"Maybe," she said gravely. She kissed her husband good-by and stood for some time looking after the buckboard traveling toward the town in a moving pillar of dust.

"I don't know," she murmured at length; "I don't know just how we're going to make out."

When he reached town, Lewiston tied the horse to the iron railing in front of the Odd Fellows' Hall, the ground floor of which was occupied by the post-office, and went across the street and up the stairway of a building of brick and granite—quite the most pretentious structure of the town—and knocked at a door upon the first landing. The door was furnished with a pane of frosted glass, on which, in gold letters, was inscribed "Bridges & Co., Grain Dealers."

Bridges himself, a middle-aged man who wore a velvet skullcap and who was smoking a Pittsburg stogie, met the farmer at the counter and the two exchanged perfunctory greetings.

"Well," said Lewiston, tentatively, after a while.

"Well, Lewiston," said the other, "I can't take that wheat of yours at any better than sixty-two."

"Sixty-*two*."

"It's the Chicago price that does it, Lewiston. Truslow is bearing the stuff for all he's worth. It's Truslow and the bear clique that stick the knife into us. The price broke again this morning. We've just got a wire."

"Good heavens," murmured Lewiston, looking vaguely from side to side. "That—that ruins me. I *can't* carry my grain any longer—what with storage charges and—and—Bridges, I don't see just how I'm going to make out. Sixty-two cents a bushel! Why, man, what with this and with that it's cost me nearly a dollar a bushel to raise that wheat, and now Truslow—"

He turned away abruptly with a quick gesture of infinite discouragement.

He went down the stairs, and making his way to where his buckboard was hitched, got in, and, with eyes vacant, the reins slipping and sliding in his limp, half-open hands, drove slowly back to the ranch. His wife had seen him coming, and met him as he drew up before the barn.

"Well?" she demanded.

"Emmie," he said as he got out of the buckboard, laying his arm across her shoulder, "Emmie, I guess we'll take up with Joe's offer. We'll go to Chicago. We're cleaned out!"

II   The Bull—Wheat at a Dollar-ten

. . .—*and said Party of the Second Part further covenants and agrees to merchandise such wheat in foreign ports, it being understood and agreed between the Party of the First Part and the Party of the Second Part that the wheat hereinbefore mentioned is released and sold to the Party of the Second Part for export purposes only, and not for consumption or distribution within the boundaries of the United States of America or of Canada.*

"Now, Mr. Gates, if you will sign for Mr. Truslow, I guess that'll be all," remarked Hornung when he had finished reading.

Hornung affixed his signature to the two documents and passed them over to Gates, who signed for his principal client, Truslow—or, as he had been called ever since he had gone into the fight against Hornung's corner—the Great Bear. Hornung's secretary was called in and witnessed the signatures, and Gates thrust the contract into his Gladstone bag and stood up, smoothing his hat.

"You will deliver the warehouse receipts for the grain," began Gates.

"I'll send a messenger to Truslow's office before noon," interrupted Hornung. "You can pay by certified check through the Illinois Trust people."

When the other had taken himself off, Hornung sat

for some moments gazing abstractedly toward his office windows, thinking over the whole matter. He had just agreed to release to Truslow, at the rate of one dollar and ten cents per bushel, one hundred thousand out of the two million and odd bushels of wheat that he, Hornung, controlled, or actually owned. And for the moment he was wondering if, after all, he had done wisely in not goring the Great Bear to actual financial death. He had made him pay one hundred thousand dollars. Truslow was good for this amount. Would it not have been better to have put a prohibitive figure on the grain and forced the Bear into bankruptcy? True, Hornung would then be without his enemy's money, but Truslow would have been eliminated from the situation, and that—so Hornung told himself—was always a consummation most devoutly, strenuously and diligently to be striven for. Truslow once dead was dead, but the Bear was never more dangerous than when desperate.

"But so long as he can't get *wheat*," muttered Hornung at the end of his reflections, "he can't hurt me. And he can't get it. That I *know*."

For Hornung controlled the situation. So far back as the February of that year an "unknown bull" had been making his presence felt on the floor of the Board of Trade. By the middle of March the commercial reports of the daily press had begun to speak of "the powerful bull clique"; a few weeks later that legendary condition of affairs implied and epitomized in the magic words "Dollar Wheat" had been attained, and by the first of April, when the price had been boosted to one dollar and ten cents a bushel, Hornung had disclosed his hand, and in place of mere rumors, the definite and authoritative news that May wheat had been cornered in the Chicago Pit went flashing around the world from Liverpool to Odessa and from Duluth to Buenos Aires.

It was—as the veteran operators were persuaded—Truslow himself who had made Hornung's corner possible. The Great Bear had for once overreached himself, and believing himself all-powerful, had hammered the price just the fatal fraction too far down. Wheat had gone to sixty-two —for the time, and under the circumstances, an abnormal price. When the reaction came it was tremendous. Hornung saw his chance, seized it, and in a few months had turned the tables, had cornered the product, and virtually driven the bear clique out of the pit.

On the same day that the delivery of the hundred thousand bushels was made to Truslow, Hornung met his broker at his lunch club.

"Well," said the latter, "I see you let go that line of stuff to Truslow."

Hornung nodded; but the broker added:

"Remember, I was against it from the very beginning. I know we've cleared up over a hundred thou'. I would have fifty times preferred to have lost twice that and *smashed Truslow dead*. Bet you what you like he makes us pay for it somehow."

"Huh!" grunted his principal. "How about insurance and warehouse charges, and carrying expenses on that lot? Guess we'd have had to pay those, too, if we'd held on."

But the other put up his chin, unwilling to be persuaded. "I won't sleep easy," he declared, "till Truslow is busted."

III The Pit

Just as Going mounted the steps on the edge of the pit the great gong struck, a roar of a hundred voices developed with the swiftness of successive explosions, the rush of a hundred men surging downward to the center of the pit filled the air with the stamp and grind of feet, a hundred hands in eager strenuous gestures tossed upward from out the brown of the crowd, the official reporter in his cage on the margin of the pit leaned far forward with straining ear to catch the opening bid, and another day of battle was begun.

Since the sale of the hundred thousand bushels of wheat to Truslow the "Hornung crowd" had steadily shouldered the price higher until on this particular morning it stood at one dollar and a half. That was Hornung's price. No one else had any grain to sell.

But not ten minutes after the opening Going was surprised out of all countenance to hear shouted from the other side of the pit these words:

"Sell May at one-fifty."

Going was for the moment touching elbows with Kimbark on one side and with Merriam on the other, all three belonging to the "Hornung crowd." Their answering challenge of *"Sold"* was as the voice of one man. They did not pause to reflect upon the strangeness of the circumstance. (That was for afterward.) Their response to the offer was as unconscious as reflex action and almost as rapid, and before the pit was well aware of what had happened the transaction of one thousand bushels was down upon Going's trading-card and fifteen hundred dollars had changed hands. But here was a marvel—the whole available supply of wheat cornered, Hornung master of the situation, invincible, unassailable; yet behold a man willing to sell, a Bear bold enough to raise his head.

"That was Kennedy, wasn't it, who made that offer?" asked Kimbark, as Going noted down the trade—"Kennedy, that new man?"

"Yes; who do you suppose he's selling for; who's willing to go short at this stage of the game?"

"Maybe he ain't short."

"Short! Great heavens, man; where'd he get the stuff?"

"Blamed if I know. We can account for every handful of May. Steady! Oh, there he goes again."

"Sell a thousand May at one-fifty," vociferated the bear-broker, throwing out his hand, one finger raised to indicate the number of "contracts" offered. This time it was evident that he was attacking the Hornung crowd deliberately, for, ignoring the jam of traders that swept toward him, he looked across the pit to where Going and Kimbark were shouting *"Sold! Sold!"* and nodded his head.

A second time Going made memoranda of the trade, and either the Hornung holdings were increased by two thousand bushels of May wheat or the Hornung bank account swelled by at least three thousand dollars of some unknown short's money.

Of late—so sure was the bull crowd of its position—no one even thought of glancing at the inspection sheet on the bulletin board. But now one of Going's messengers hurried up to him with the announcement that this sheet showed receipts at Chicago for that morning of twenty-five thousand bushels, and not credited to Hornung. Some one had got hold of a line of wheat overlooked by the "clique" and was dumping it upon them.

"Wire the chief," said Going over his shoulder to Merriam. This one struggled out of the crowd, and on a telegraph blank scribbled:

"Strong bear movement—New man—Kennedy—Selling in lots of five contracts—Chicago receipts twenty-five thousand."

The message was despatched, and in a few moments the answer came back, laconic, of military terseness.

"Support the market."

And Going obeyed, Merriam and Kimbark following, the new broker fairly throwing the wheat at them in thousand-bushel lots.

"Sell May at 'fifty; sell May; sell May." A moment's indecision, an instant's hesitation, the first faint suggestion of weakness, and the market would have broken under them. But for the better part of four hours they stood their ground, taking all that was offered, in constant communication with the Chief, and from time to time stimulated and steadied by his brief, unvarying command:

"Support the market."

At the close of the session they had bought in the twenty-five thousand bushels of May. Hornung's position was as stable as a rock, and the price closed even with the opening figure—one dollar and a half.

But the morning's work was the talk of all La Salle Street. Who was back of that raid? What was the meaning of this unexpected selling? For weeks the Pit trading had been merely nominal. Truslow, the Great Bear, from whom the most serious attack might have been expected, had gone to his country seat at Geneva Lake, in Wisconsin, declaring himself to be out of the market entirely. He went bass fishing every day.

IV The Belt Line

On a certain day toward the middle of the month, at a time when the mysterious Bear had unloaded some eighty thousand bushels upon Hornung, a conference was held in the library of Hornung's home. His broker attended it, and also a clean-faced, bright-eyed individual whose name of Cyrus Ryder might have been found upon the payroll of a rather well-known detective agency. For upward of half an hour after the conference began the detective spoke, the other two listening attentively, gravely.

"Then, last of all," concluded Ryder, "I made out I was a hobo, and began stealing rides on the Belt Line Railroad. Know the road? It just circles Chicago. Truslow owns it. Yes? Well, then I began to catch on. I noticed that cars of certain numbers—thirty-one naught thirty-four, thirty-two one ninety—well, the numbers don't matter, but anyhow, these cars were always switched on to the sidings by Mr. Truslow's main elevator D soon as they came in. The wheat was shunted in, and they were pulled out again. Well, I spotted one car and stole a ride on her. Say, look here, *that car went right around the city on the Belt, and came back to D again, and the same wheat in her all the time.* The grain was reinspected—it was raw, I tell you—and the warehouse receipts made out just as though the stuff had come in from Kansas or Iowa."

"The same wheat all the time!" interrupted Hornung.

"The same wheat—your wheat, that you sold to Truslow."

"Great snakes!" ejaculated Hornung's broker. "Truslow never took it abroad at all."

"Took it abroad! Say, he's just been running it around Chicago, like the supers in 'Shenandoah,' round an' round, so you'd think it was a new lot, an' selling it back to you again."

"No wonder we couldn't account for so much wheat."

"Bought it from us at one-ten, and made us buy it back —our own wheat—at one-fifty."

Hornung and his broker looked at each other in silence for a moment. Then all at once Hornung struck the arm of his chair with his fist and exploded in a roar of laughter. The broker stared for one bewildered moment, then followed his example.

"Sold! Sold!" shouted Hornung almost gleefully. "Upon my soul it's as good as a Gilbert and Sullivan show. And we—Oh, Lord! Billy, shake on it, and hats off to my distinguished friend, Truslow. He'll be President some day. Hey! What? Prosecute him? Not I."

"He's done us out of a neat hatful of dollars for all that," observed the broker, suddenly grave.

"Billy, it's worth the price."

"We've got to make it up somehow."

"Well, tell you what. We were going to boost the price to one seventy-five next week, and make that our settlement figure."

"Can't do it now. Can't afford it."

"No. Here; we'll let out a big link; we'll put wheat at two dollars, and let it go at that."

"Two it is, then," said the broker.

V   The Bread Line

The street was very dark and absolutely deserted. It was a district on the "South Side," not far from the Chicago River, given up largely to wholesale stores, and after nightfall was empty of all life. The echoes slept but lightly hereabouts, and the slightest footfall, the faintest noise, woke them upon the instant and sent them clamoring up and down the length of the pavement between the iron-shuttered fronts. The only light visible came from the side door of a certain "Vienna" bakery, where at one o'clock in the morning loaves of bread were given away to any who should ask. Every evening about nine o'clock the outcasts began to gather about the side door. The stragglers came in rapidly, and the line—the "bread line," as it was called—began to form. By midnight it was usually some hundred yards in length, stretching almost the entire length of the block.

Toward ten in the evening, his coat collar turned up against the fine drizzle that pervaded the air, his hands in his pockets, his elbows gripping his sides, Sam Lewiston came up and silently took his place at the end of the line.

Unable to conduct his farm upon a paying basis at the time when Truslow, the "Great Bear," had sent the price of grain to sixty-two cents a bushel, Lewiston had turned over his entire property to his creditors, and, leaving Kansas for good, had abandoned farming, and had left his wife at her sister's boarding-house in Topeka with the understanding that she was to join him in Chicago so soon as he had found a steady job. Then he had come to Chicago and had turned workman. His brother Joe conducted a small hat factory on Archer Avenue, and for a time he found there a meagre employment. But difficulties had occurred, times were bad, the hat factory was involved in

debts, the repealing of a certain import duty on manu-
factured felt overcrowded the home market with cheap
Belgian and French products, and in the end his brother
had resigned and gone to Milwaukee.

Thrown out of work, Lewiston drifted aimlessly about
Chicago, from pillar to post, working a little, earning here
a dollar, there a dime, but always sinking, till at last the
ooze of the lowest bottom dragged at his feet and the
rush of the great ebb went over him and engulfed him
and shut him from the light, and a park bench became his
home and the "bread line" his chief makeshift of sub-
sistence.

He stood now in the infolding drizzle, sodden, stupefied
with fatigue. Before and behind stretched the line. There
was no talking. There was no sound. The street was empty.
It was so still that the passing of a cable-car in the adjoining thoroughfare grated like prolonged rolling explosions,
beginning and ending at immeasurable distances. The
drizzle descended incessantly. After a long time midnight
struck.

There was something ominous and gravely impressive in
this interminable line of dark figures, close-pressed, soundless; a crowd, yet absolutely still; a close-packed, silent
file, waiting, waiting in the vast deserted night-ridden street;
waiting without a word, without a movement, there under
the night and under the slow-moving mists of rain.

Few in the crowd were professional beggars. Most of
them were workmen, long since out of work, forced into
idleness by long-continued "hard times," by ill luck, by
sickness. To them the "bread line" was a godsend. At
least they could not starve. Between jobs here in the end
was something to hold them up—a small platform, as
it were, above the sweep of black water, where for a
moment they might pause and take breath before the
plunge.

The period of waiting on this night of rain seemed endless to those silent, hungry men; but at length there was
a stir. The line moved. The side door opened. Ah, at last!
They were going to hand out the bread.

But instead of the usual white-aproned undercook with
his crowded hampers there now appeared in the doorway
a new man—a young fellow who looked like a bookkeeper's assistant. He bore in his hand a placard, which

he tacked to the outside of the door. Then he disappeared within the bakery, locking the door after him.

A shudder of poignant despair, an unformed, inarticulate sense of calamity, seemed to run from end to end of the line. What had happened? Those in the rear, unable to read the placard, surged forward, a sense of bitter disappointment clutching at their hearts.

The line broke up, disintegrated into a shapeless throng —a throng that crowded forward and collected in front of the shut door whereon the placard was affixed. Lewiston, with the others, pushed forward. On the placard he read these words:

"Owing to the fact that the price of grain has been increased to two dollars a bushel, there will be no distribution of bread from this bakery until further notice."

Lewiston turned away, dumb, bewildered. Till morning he walked the streets, going on without purpose, without direction. But now at last his luck had turned. Overnight the wheel of his fortunes had creaked and swung upon its axis, and before noon he had found a job in the street-cleaning brigade. In the course of time he rose to be first shift-boss, then deputy inspector, then inspector, promoted to the dignity of driving a red wagon with rubber tires and drawing a salary instead of mere wages. The wife was sent for and a new start made.

But Lewiston never forgot. Dimly he began to see the significance of things. Caught once in the cogs and wheels of a great and terrible engine, he had seen—none better —its workings. Of all the men who had vainly stood in the "bread line" on that rainy night in early summer, he, perhaps, had been the only one who had struggled up to the surface again. How many others had gone down in the great ebb? Grim question; he dared not think how many.

He had seen the two ends of a great wheat operation— a battle between Bear and Bull. The stories (subsequently published in the city's press) of Truslow's counter move in selling Hornung his own wheat, supplied the unseen section. The farmer—he who raised the wheat—was ruined upon one hand; the working-man—he who consumed it —was ruined upon the other. But between the two, the great operators, who never saw the wheat they traded in, bought and sold the world's food, gambled in the nourishment of entire nations, practiced their tricks, chicanery and oblique shifty "deals," were reconciled in their differences, and went on through their appointed way, jovial, contented, enthroned, and unassailable.

1903

WILLIAM VAUGHN MOODY

(1869–1910)

Born in the same year as his friend Edwin Arlington Robinson, Moody died just as American poetry was entering a new and revolutionary phase. Had he lived as long as his friend (who outlived him by twenty-five years), he might well have made a substantial contribution to the "new poetry," for there is no reason to believe that his genuine lyric talent would not have responded significantly to the twentieth-century's poetic ways of approaching experience. As it is, he is chiefly remembered as a transitional poet (the best of them, it should be added) whose traditional forms, rhetorical opulence, and moral idealism look back to the classics of English poetry from the Victorian era to the Renaissance, but whose mythic use of symbolism, employment of ugly realistic detail, and direct confrontation of contemporary social and political problems point, even if somewhat tentatively, to an age yet to come.

The son of a riverboat captain who lost his fortune in the Civil War, Moody was a precocious young man with an almost instinctive affinity for the life of learning and sensibility. ("To be a poet is a much better thing than to write poetry," he once remarked.) Eventually he made his way from the small Indiana town in which he was born to Riverside Academy in New York and finally, in 1889, to Harvard. Although he had to work his way through the university, with the academic brilliance he was to display all his life he finished the course in three years and spent his fourth year touring Europe as the tutor for a wealthy man's son. In 1895, the year after receiving his master's degree from Harvard, he joined the English faculty of the newly founded University of Chicago, where he remained as an instructor and assistant professor until 1903. Like some of our present-day professor-poets, Moody was a brilliant teacher but found the academic routine irritatingly restrictive. He was also a fine scholar, publishing studies of several English authors and editing the poetry of Milton and Homer. His *Poems* appeared in 1901. But when *A History of English Literature* (1902), which he wrote in collaboration with his friend and colleague, Robert Morss Lovett, proved a financial success, he bade a not-too-sad farewell to faculty life. His marriage to Harriet Brainerd, delayed four years for various reasons, took place in 1909, one year before his death in Colorado.

A word must be said about Moody's plays, which are interesting enough to have led one scholar to suggest that had Moody lived longer he might have been second only to Eugene O'Neill as a writer of dramas in which the romantic and the realistic are symbolically blended. *The Masque of Judgment* (1900), *The Fire Bringer* (1904), and *The Death of Eve* (which he never lived to complete) form a poetic trilogy that deals with the conflicts between man and God and their ultimate reconciliation in the creation of woman. None of these works has been produced. *The Great Divide* (1909)—a prose drama which, when it was first put on the stage under the title *A Sabine Woman* in 1906, had a successful two-year run—pivots on a theme that lies at the heart of much of American literature: the contrast of an inhibiting Puritan tradition with the freer moral stance of the frontier West. *The Faith Healer* (1909) is a much less satisfactory product, being marred by an excessively exalted moral idealism.

Editions and accounts of the man and his work include J. Manly, ed., *The Poems and Plays of William Vaughn Moody*, 2 vols. (1912); D. Mason, ed., *Some Letters of William Vaughn Moody* (1913); C. Lewis, "William Vaughn Moody," *Yale Review*, n.s. II (1913); C. Walker, "The Poetry of William Vaughn Moody," *Texas Review*, I (1915); H. Jones, "William Vaughn Moody: An American Milton," *Double Dealer*, IV (1922); N. Adkins, "The Poetic Philosophy of William Vaughn Moody," *Texas Review*, IX (1924); B. Weireck, *From Whitman to Sandburg in American Poetry* (1924); A. Kreymborg, *Our Singing Strength* (1929); R. Lovett, ed., *Selected Poems* (1931); D. Henry, *William Vaughn Moody* (1934); P. MacKaye, ed., *Letters to Harriet* (1935); F. and A. Glasheen, "Moody's 'An Ode in Time of Hesitation,'" *College English*, V (1943); T. Riggs, Jr., "Prometheus 1900," *American Literature*, XXII (1951); R. Cary, "Robinson on Moody," *Colby Library Quarterly*, Ser. VI (1962); M. Halpern, *William Vaughn Moody* (1964).

An Ode in Time of Hesitation

I

Before the solemn bronze Saint-Gaudens made
To thrill the heedless passer's heart with awe,
And set here in the city's talk and trade
To the good memory of Robert Shaw,
This bright March morn I stand,
And hear the distant spring come up the land;
Knowing that what I hear is not unheard
Of this boy soldier and his Negro band,
For all their gaze is fixed so stern ahead,
For all the fatal rhythm of their tread.   10
The land they died to save from death and shame
Trembles and waits, hearing the spring's great name,
And by her pangs these resolute ghosts are stirred.

II

Through street and mall the tides of people go
Heedless; the trees upon the Common show
No hint of green; but to my listening heart
The still earth doth impart
Assurance of her jubilant emprise,
And it is clear to my long-searching eyes
That love at last has might upon the skies.   20
The ice is runneled on the little pond;
A telltale patter drips from off the trees;
The air is touched with southland spiceries,
As if but yesterday it tossed the frond
Of pendant mosses where the live-oaks grow
Beyond Virginia and the Carolines,
Or had its will among the fruits and vines
Of aromatic isles asleep beyond
Florida and the Gulf of Mexico.

III

Soon shall the Cape Ann children shout in glee,   30
Spying the arbutus, spring's dear recluse;
Hill lads at dawn shall hearken the wild goose
Go honking northward over Tennessee;
West from Oswego to Sault Sainte-Marie,

And on to where the Pictured Rocks are hung,
And yonder where, gigantic, wilful, young,
Chicago sitteth at the northwest gates,
With restless violent hands and casual tongue
Moulding her mighty fates,
The Lakes shall robe them in ethereal sheen;   40
And like a larger sea, the vital green
Of springing wheat shall vastly be outflung
Over Dakota and the prairie states.
By desert people immemorial
On Arizonan mesas shall be done
Dim rites unto the thunder and the sun;
Nor shall the primal gods lack sacrifice
More splendid, when the white Sierras call
Unto the Rockies straightway to arise
And dance before the unveiled ark of the year,   50
Sounding their windy cedars as for shawms,
Unrolling rivers clear
For flutter of broad phylacteries;
While Shasta signals to Alaskan seas
That watch old sluggish glaciers downward creep
To fling their icebergs thundering from the steep,
And Mariposa through the purple calms
Gazes at far Hawaii crowned with palms
Where East and West are met,—
A rich seal on the ocean's bosom set   60
To say that East and West are twain,
With different loss and gain:
The Lord hath sundered them; let them be sundered yet.

                           IV
Alas! what sounds are these that come
Sullenly over the Pacific seas,—
Sounds of ignoble battle, striking dumb
The season's half-awakened ecstasies?
Must I be humble, then,
Now when my heart hath need of pride?
Wild love falls on me from these sculptured men;   70
By loving much the land for which they died
I would be justified.
My spirit was away on pinions wide
To soothe in praise of her its passionate mood
And ease it of its ache of gratitude.

Too sorely heavy is the debt they lay
On me and the companions of my day.
I would remember now
My country's goodliness, make sweet her name.
Alas! what shade art thou   80
Of sorrow or of blame
Liftest the lyric leafage from her brow,
And pointest a slow finger at her shame?

V

Lies! lies! It cannot be! The wars we wage
Are noble, and our battles still are won
By justice for us, ere we lift the gage.
We have not sold our loftiest heritage.
The proud republic hath not stooped to cheat
And scramble in the market-place of war:
Her forehead weareth yet its solemn star.   90
Here is her witness: this, her perfect son,
This delicate and proud New England soul
Who leads despised men, with just-unshackled feet
Up the large ways where death and glory meet,
To show all peoples that our shame is done,
That once more we are clean and spirit-whole.

VI

Crouched in the sea-fog on the moaning sand
All night he lay, speaking some simple word
From hour to hour to the slow minds that heard,
Holding each poor life gently in his hand   100
And breathing on the base rejected clay
Till each dark face shone mystical and grand
Against the breaking day;
And lo, the shard the potter cast away
Was grown a fiery chalice crystal-fine,
Fulfilled of the divine
Great wine of battle wrath by God's ring-finger stirred.
Then upward, where the shadowy bastion loomed
Huge on the mountain in the west sea light,
Whence now, and now, infernal flowerage bloomed,   110
Bloomed, burst, and scattered down its deadly seed,
They swept, and died like freemen on the height,
Like freemen, and like men of noble breed;
And when the battle fell away at night

By hasty and contemptuous hands were thrust
Obscurely in a common grave with him
The fair-haired keeper of their love and trust.
Now limb doth mingle with dissolved limb
In nature's busy old democracy
To flush the mountain laurel when she blows   120
Sweet by the southern sea,
And heart with crumbled heart climbs in the rose:—
The untaught hearts with the high heart that knew
This mountain fortress for no earthly hold
Of temporal quarrel, but the bastion old
Of spiritual wrong,
Built by an unjust nation sheer and strong,
Expugnable but by a nation's rue
And bowing down before that equal shrine
By all men held divine,   130
Whereof his band and he were the most holy sign.

VII

O bitter, bitter shade!
Wilt thou not put the scorn
And instant tragic question from thine eye?
Do thy dark brows yet crave
That swift and angry stave—
Unmeet for this desirous morn—
That I have striven, striven to evade?
Gazing on him, must I not deem they err
Whose careless lips in street and shop aver   140
As common tidings, deeds to make his cheek
Flush from the bronze, and his dead throat to speak?
Surely some elder singer would arise,
Whose harp hath leave to threaten and to mourn
Above this people when they go astray.
Is Whitman, the strong spirit, overworn?
Has Whittier put his yearning wrath away?
I will not and I dare not yet believe!
Though furtively the sunlight seems to grieve,
And the spring-laden breeze   150
Out of the gladdening west is sinister
With sounds of nameless battle overseas;
Though when we turn and question in suspense
If these things be indeed after these ways,
And what things are to follow after these,

Our fluent men of place and consequence
Fumble and fill their mouths with hollow phrase,
Or for the end-all of deep arguments
Intone their dull commercial liturgies—
I dare not yet believe! My ears are shut!   160
I will not hear the thin satiric praise
And muffled laughter of our enemies,
Bidding us never sheathe our valiant sword
Till we have changed our birthright for a gourd
Of wild pulse stolen from a barbarian's hut:
Showing how wise it is to cast away
The symbols of our spiritual sway,
That so our hands with better ease
May wield the driver's whip and grasp the jailer's keys.

VIII

Was it for this our fathers kept the law?   170
This crown shall crown their struggle and their ruth?
Are we the eagle nation Milton saw
Mewing its mighty youth,
Soon to possess the mountain winds of truth,
And be a swift familiar of the sun
Where aye before God's face his trumpets run?
Or have we but the talons and the maw,
And for the abject likeness of our heart
Shall some less lordly bird be set apart?—
Some gross-billed wader where the swamps are fat?   180
Some gorger in the sun? Some prowler with the bat?

IX

Ah, no!
We have not fallen so.
We are our fathers' sons: let those who lead us know!
'Twas only yesterday sick Cuba's cry
Came up the tropic wind, "Now help us, for we die!"
Then Alabama heard,
And rising, pale, to Maine and Idaho
Shouted a burning word.
Proud state with proud impassioned state conferred,   190
And at the lifting of a hand sprang forth,
East, west, and south, and north,
Beautiful armies. Oh, by the sweet blood and young
Shed on the awful hill slope at San Juan,

By the unforgotten names of eager boys
Who might have tasted girl's love and been stung
With the old mystic joys
And starry griefs, now the spring nights come on,
But that the heart of youth is generous,—
We charge you, ye who lead us,   200
Breathe on their chivalry no hint of stain!
Turn not their new-world victories to gain!
One least leaf plucked for chaffer from the bays
Of their dear praise,
One jot of their pure conquest put to hire,
The implacable republic will require;
With clamor, in the glare and gaze of noon,
Or subtly, coming as a thief at night,
But surely, very surely, slow or soon,
That insult deep we deeply will require.   210
Tempt not our weakness, our cupidity!
For save we let the island men go free,
Those baffled and dislaureled ghosts
Will curse us from the lamentable coasts
Where walk the frustrate dead.
The cup of trembling shall be drained quite,
Eaten the sour bread of astonishment,
With ashes of the hearth shall be made white
Our hair, and wailing shall be in the tent;
Then on your guiltier head   220
Shall our intolerable self-disdain
Wreak suddenly its anger and its pain;
For manifest in that disastrous light
We shall discern the right
And do it, tardily,—O ye who lead,
Take heed!
Blindness we may forgive, but baseness we will smite.

                                                                  1900

Gloucester Moors

A mile behind is Gloucester town
Where the fishing fleets put in,
A mile ahead the land dips down
And the woods and farms begin.
Here, where the moors stretch free

In the high blue afternoon,
Are the marching sun and talking sea,
And the racing winds that wheel and flee
On the flying heels of June.

Jill-o'er-the-ground is purple blue,   10
Blue is the quaker-maid,
The wild geranium holds its dew
Long in the boulder's shade.
Wax-red hangs the cup
From the huckleberry boughs,
In barberry bells the grey moths sup
Or where the choke-cherry lifts high up
Sweet bowls for their carouse.

Over the shelf of the sandy cove
Beach-peas blossom late.   20
By copse and cliff the swallows rove
Each calling to his mate.
Seaward the sea-gulls go,
And the land-birds all are here;
That green-gold flash was a vireo,
And yonder flame where the marsh-flags grow
Was a scarlet tanager.

This earth is not the steadfast place
We landsmen build upon;
From deep to deep she varies pace,   30
And while she comes is gone.
Beneath my feet I feel
Her smooth bulk heave and dip;
With velvet plunge and soft upreel
She swings and steadies to her keel
Like a gallant, gallant ship.

These summer clouds she sets for sail,
The sun is her masthead light,
She tows the moon like a pinnace frail
Where her phosphor wake churns bright.   40
Now hid, now looming clear,
On the face of the dangerous blue
The star fleets tack and wheel and veer,

But on, but on does the old earth steer
As if her port she knew.

God, dear God! Does she know her port,
Though she goes so far about?
Or blind astray, does she make her sport
To brazen and chance it out?
I watched when her captains passed: 50
She were better captainless.
Men in the cabin, before the mast,
But some were reckless and some aghast,
And some sat gorged at mess.

By her battened hatch I leaned and caught
Sounds from the noisome hold,—
Cursing and sighing of souls distraught
And cries too sad to be told.
Then I strove to go down and see;
But they said, "Thou art not of us!" 60
I turned to those on the deck with me
And cried, "Give help!" But they said, "Let be:
Our ship sails faster thus."

Jill-o'er-the-ground is purple blue,
Blue is the quaker-maid,
The alder-clump where the brook comes through
Breeds cresses in its shade.
To be out of the moiling street
With its swelter and its sin!
Who has given to me this sweet, 70
And given my brother dust to eat?
And when will his wage come in?

Scattering wide or blown in ranks,
Yellow and white and brown,
Boats and boats from the fishing banks
Come home to Gloucester town.
There is cash to purse and spend,
There are wives to be embraced,
Hearts to borrow and hearts to lend,
And hearts to take and keep to the end,— 80
O little sails, make haste!

But thou, vast outbound ship of souls,
What harbor town for thee?
What shapes, when thy arriving tolls,
Shall crowd the banks to see?
Shall all the happy shipmates then
Stand singing brotherly?
Or shall a haggard ruthless few
Warp her over and bring her to,
While the many broken souls of men   90
Fester down in the slaver's pen,
And nothing to say or do?

                                                     1900

The Menagerie

Thank God my brain is not inclined to cut
Such capers every day! I'm just about
Mellow, but then—There goes the tent-flap shut.
Rain's in the wind. I thought so: every snout
Was twitching when the keeper turned me out.
That screaming parrot makes my blood run cold
Gabriel's trump! the big bull elephant
Squeals "Rain!" to the parched herd. The monkeys scold,
And jabber that it's rain water they want.
(It makes me sick to see a monkey pant.)   10

I'll foot it home, to try and make believe
I'm sober. After this I stick to beer,
And drop the circus when the sane folks leave.
A man's a fool to look at things too near:
They look back, and begin to cut up queer.

Beasts do, at any rate; especially
Wild devils caged. They have the coolest way
Of being something else than what you see:
You pass a sleek young zebra nosing hay,
A nylghau looking bored and distingué,—   20

And think you've seen a donkey and a bird.
Not on your life! Just glance back, if you dare

The zebra chews, the nylghau hasn't stirred;
But something's happened, Heaven knows what or where,
To freeze your scalp and pompadour your hair.

I'm not precisely an æolian lute
Hung in the wandering winds of sentiment,
But drown me if the ugliest, meanest brute
Grunting and fretting in that sultry tent
Didn't just floor me with embarrassment!   30

'Twas like a thunder-clap from out the clear,—
One minute they were circus beasts, some grand,
Some ugly, some amusing, and some queer:
Rival attractions to the hobo band,
The flying jenny, and the peanut stand.

Next minute they were old hearth-mates of mine!
Lost people, eyeing me with such a stare!
Patient, satiric, devilish, divine;
A gaze of hopeless envy, squalid care,
Hatred, and thwarted love, and dim despair.   40

Within my blood my ancient kindred spoke,—
Grotesque and monstrous voices, heard afar
Down ocean caves when behemoth awoke,
Or through fern forests roared the plesiosaur
Locked with the giant-bat in ghastly war.

And suddenly, as in a flash of light,
I saw great Nature working out her plan;
Through all her shapes from mastodon to mite
Forever groping, testing, passing on
To find at last the shape and soul of Man.   50

Till in the fullness of accomplished time,
Comes brother Forepaugh, upon business bent,
Tracks her through frozen and through torrid clime,
And shows us, neatly labeled in a tent,
The stages of her huge experiment;

Blabbing aloud her shy and reticent hours;
Dragging to light her blinking, slothful moods;

Publishing fretful seasons when her powers
Worked wild and sullen in her solitudes,
Or when her mordant laughter shook the woods.   60

Here, round about me, were her vagrant births;
Sick dreams she had, fierce projects she essayed;
Her qualms, her fiery prides, her crazy mirths;
The troublings of her spirit as she strayed,
Cringed, gloated, mocked, was lordly, was afraid,

On that long road she went to seek mankind;
Here were the darkling coverts that she beat
To find the Hider she was sent to find;
Here the distracted footprints of her feet
Whereby her soul's Desire she came to greet.   70

But why should they, her botch-work, turn about
And stare disdain at me, her finished job?
Why was the place one vast suspended shout
Of laughter? Why did all the daylight throb
With soundless guffaw and dumb-stricken sob?

Helpless I stood among those awful cages;
The beasts were walking loose, and I was bagged!
I, I, last product of the toiling ages,
Goal of heroic feet that never lagged,—
A little man in trousers, slightly jagged.   80

Deliver me from such another jury!
The Judgment-day will be a picnic to 't.
Their satire was more dreadful than their fury,
And worst of all was just a kind of brute
Disgust, and giving up, and sinking mute.

Survival of the fittest, adaptation,
And all their other evolution terms,
Seem to omit one small consideration,
To wit, that tumblebugs and angelworms
Have souls: there's soul in everything that squirms.   90

And souls are restless, plagued, impatient things,
All dream and unaccountable desire;
Crawling, but pestered with the thought of wings;

Spreading through every inch of earth's old mire
Mystical hanker after something higher.

Wishes *are* horses, as I understand.
I guess a wistful polyp that has strokes
Of feeling faint to gallivant on land
Will come to be a scandal to his folks;
Legs he will sprout, in spite of threats and jokes.   100

And at the core of every life that crawls
Or runs or flies or swims or vegetates—
Churning the mammoth's heart-blood, in the galls
Of shark and tiger planting gorgeous hates,
Lighting the love of eagles for their mates;

Yes, in the dim brain of the jellied fish
That is and is not living—moved and stirred
From the beginning a mysterious wish,
A vision, a command, a fatal Word:
The name of Man was uttered, and they heard.   110

Upward along the æons of old war
They sought him: wing and shank-bone, claw and bill
Were fashioned and rejected; wide and far
They roamed the twilight jungles of their will;
But still they sought him, and desired him still.

Man they desired, but mind you, Perfect Man,
The radiant and the loving, yet to be!
I hardly wonder, when they came to scan
The upshot of their strenuosity,
They gazed with mixed emotions upon *me*.   120

Well, my advice to you is, Face the creatures,
Or spot them sideways with your weather eye,
Just to keep tab on their expansive features;
It isn't pleasant when you're stepping high
To catch a giraffe smiling on the sly.

If nature made you graceful, don't get gay
Back-to before the hippopotamus;
If meek and godly, find some place to play

Besides right where three mad hyenas fuss:
You may hear language that we won't discuss.   130

If you're a sweet thing in a flower-bed hat,
Or her best fellow with your tie tucked in,
Don't squander love's bright springtime girding at
An old chimpanzee with an Irish chin:
There may be hidden meaning in his grin.

                                                                                    1901

On a Soldier Fallen in the Philippines

Streets of the roaring town,
Hush for him, hush, be still!
He comes, who was stricken down
Doing the word of our will.
Hush! Let him have his state,
Give him his soldier's crown.
The grists of trade can wait
Their grinding at the mill,
But he cannot wait for his honor, now the trumpet has
been blown;
Wreathe pride now for his granite brow, lay love on his
breast of stone.

Toll! Let the great bells toll
Till the clashing air is dim.
Did we wrong this parted soul?
We will make up it to him.
Toll! Let him never guess
What work we set him to.
Laurel, laurel, yes;
He did what we bade him do.
Praise, and never a whispered hint but the fight he fought
was good;
Never a word that the blood on his sword was his country's
own heart's-blood.

A flag for the soldier's bier
Who dies that his land may live;
O, banners, banners here,
That he doubt not nor misgive!

That he heed not from the tomb
The evil days draw near
When the nation, robed in gloom,
With its faithless past shall strive.
Let him never dream that his bullet's scream went wide
of its island mark,
Home to the heart of his darling land where she stumbled
and sinned in the dark.

1901

TRUMBULL STICKNEY

(1874–1904)

Joseph Trumbull Stickney reached maturity in the tragic generation of the "Harvard poets" and, like them, is highly representative of the *fin de siècle*. At Harvard he met William Vaughn Moody, and obtained his B.A. in 1895, a year after his older friend earned his master's degree. Unlike Moody, however, Stickney did not come from a family of ruined fortunes. His father, Austin, was the head of the Latin Department at Trinity College, and Trumbull, born in Geneva, Switzerland, was brought up in Europe under the private tutelage of his father.

Having lived abroad most of his life, Stickney continued his international education by going from Harvard to the Sorbonne, where he spent seven years studying Greek and Sanskrit, and where, in 1903, he was the first American to receive the degree of Docteur ès Lettres. In 1902 he published *Dramatic Verses*, the one volume of his poetry that was to appear in his lifetime. The next year, when his degree was granted, he was appointed to teach Greek at Harvard. He planned to combine his teaching with translations from Aeschylus and the production of a second volume of poetry. He worked hard on the poems during that first year at Harvard, which was the last year of his life: in 1904, aged thirty, he died of brain cancer. Although his brief life and small output consigned him to obscurity for many years and will perhaps always relegate him to minor status, he is nevertheless one of our truly gifted poets, whose sense of craftsmanship we can now see as foreshadowing the influences that were brought to bear on American poetry by Pound and Eliot.

The Poems of Trumbull Stickney (1905) was posthumously edited by William Vaughn Moody, George Cabot Lodge, and J. E. Lodge. Accounts of Stickney are to be found in W. V. Moody, "The Poems of Trumbull Stickney," *North American Review*, 183 (1906); R. P. Blackmur, "Stickney's Poetry," *Poetry*, 42 (1933); T. Riggs, Jr., "Trumbull Stickney (1874–1904)"—an unpublished dissertation at Princeton (1955); J. W. Myers, "A Complete Stickney Bibliography," *Twentieth Century Literature* (1964); A. R. Whittle, "Time in the Poetry of Trumbull Stickney," *Sewanee Review*, LXXIV (1966).

Mnemosyne

It's autumn in the country I remember.

How warm a wind blew here about the ways!
And shadows on the hillside lay to slumber
During the long sun-sweetened summer-days.

It's cold abroad the country I remember.

The swallows veering skimmed the golden grain
At midday with a wing aslant and limber;
And yellow cattle browsed upon the plain.

It's empty down the country I remember.

I had a sister lovely in my sight:
Her hair was dark, her eyes were very sombre;
We sang together in the woods at night.

It's lonely in the country I remember.

The babble of our children fills my ears,
And on our hearth I stare the perished ember
To flames that show all starry thro' my tears.

It's dark about the country I remember.

There are the mountains where I lived. The path
Is slushed with cattle-tracks and fallen timber,

The stumps are twisted by the tempests' wrath.   20
But that I knew these places are my own,
I'd ask how come such wretchedness to cumber
The earth, and I to people it alone.

It rains across the country I remember.

1905

Be Still. The Hanging Gardens Were a Dream

Be still. The Hanging Gardens were a dream
That over Persian roses flew to kiss
The curlèd lashes of Semiramis.
Troy never was, nor green Skamander stream.
Provence and Troubadour are merest lies,
The glorious hair of Venice was a beam
Made within Titian's eye. The sunsets seem,
The world is very old and nothing is.
Be still. Thou foolish thing, thou canst not wake,
Nor thy tears wedge thy soldered lids apart,   10
But patter in the darkness of thy heart.
Thy brain is plagued. Thou art a frightened owl
Blind with the light of life thou'ldst not forsake,
And error loves and nourishes thy soul.

1905

In Ampezzo

Only once more and not again—the larches
Shake to the wind their echo. "Not again,"—
We see, below the sky that over-arches
Heavy and blue, the plain

Between Tofana lying and Cristallo
In meadowy earths above the ringing stream:
Whence interchangeably desire may follow,
Hesitant as in dream,

At sunset, south, by lilac promontories
Under green skies to Italy, or forth   10
By calms of morning beyond Lavinores
Tyrolward and to north:

As now, this last of latter days, when over
The brownish field by peasants are undone
Some widths of grass, some plots of mountain clover
Under the autumn sun,

With honey-warm perfume that risen lingers
In mazes of low heat, or takes the air,
Passing delicious as a woman's fingers
Passing amid the hair;   20

When scythes are swishing and the mower's muscle
Spans a repeated crescent to and fro,
Or in dry stalks of corn the sickles rustle,
Tangle, detach and go,

Far thro' the wide blue day and greening meadow
Whose blots of amber beaded are with sheaves,
Whereover pallidly a cloud-shadow
Deadens the earth and leaves:

Whilst high around and near, their heads of iron
Sunken in sky whose azure overlights   30
Ravine and edges, stand the gray and maron
Desolate Dolomites,—

And older than decay from the small summit
Unfolds a stream of pebbly wreckage down
Under the suns of midday, like some comet
Struck into gravel stone.

Faintly across this gold and amethystine
September, images of summer fade;
And gentle dreams now freshen on the pristine
Viols, awhile unplayed,   40

Of many a place where lovingly we wander,
More dearly held that quickly we forsake,—
A pine by sullen coasts, an oleander
Reddening on the lake.

And there, each year with more familiar motion,
From many a bird and windy forestries,
Or along shaking fringes of the ocean
Vapors of music rise.

From many easts the morning gives her splendor;
The shadows fill with colors we forget;
Remembered tints at evening grow tender,
Tarnished with violet.

Let us away! soon sheets of winter metal
On this discolored mountain-land will close,
While elsewhere Spring-time weaves a crimson petal,
Builds and perfumes a rose.

Away! for here the mountain sinks in gravel.
Let us forget the unhappy site with change,
And go, if only happiness be travel
After the new and strange:—   60

Unless 'twere better to be very single,
To follow some diviner monotone,
And in all beauties, where ourselves commingle,
Love but a love, but one,

Across this shadowy minute of our living,
What time our hearts so magically sing,
To mitigate our fever, simply giving
All in a little thing?

Just as here, past yon dumb and melancholy
Sameness of ruin, while the mountains ail,   70
Summer and sunset-colored autumn slowly
Dissipate down the vale;

And all these lines along the sky that measure,
Sorapis and the rocks of Mezzodi
Crumble by foamy miles into the azure
Mediterranean sea:

Whereas to-day at sunrise, under brambles,
A league above the moss and dying pines
I picked this little—in my hand that trembles—
Parcel of columbines.   80

1905

At Sainte-Marguerite

The gray tide flows and flounders in the rocks
Along the crannies up the swollen sand.
Far out the reefs lie naked—dunes and blocks
Low in the watery wind. A shaft of land
Going to sea thins out the western strand.

It rains, and all along and always gulls
Career sea-screaming in and weather-glossed.
It blows here, pushing round the cliff; in lulls
Within the humid stone a motion lost
Ekes out the flurried heart-beat of the coast.   10

It blows and rains a pale and whirling mist
This summer morning. I that hither came—
Was it to pluck this savage from the schist.
This crazy yellowish bloom without a name,
With leathern blade and tortured wiry frame?

Why here alone, away, the forehead pricked
With dripping salt and fingers damp with brine,
Before the offal and the derelict
And where the hungry sea-wolves howl and whine
Like human hours? now that the columbine   20

Stands somewhere shaded near the fields that fall
Great starry sheaves of the delighted year,
And globing rosy on the garden wall
The peach and apricot and soon the pear
Drip in the teasing hand their sugared tear.

Inland a little way the summer lies.
Inland a little and but yesterday
I saw the weary teams, I heard the cries
Of sicklemen across the fallen hay,
And buried in the sunburned stacks I lay   30

Tasting the straws and tossing, laughing soft
Into the sky's great eyes of gold and blue
And nodding to the breezy leaves aloft

Over the harvest's mellow residue.
But sudden then—then strangely dark it grew.

How good it is, before the dreary flow
Of cloud and water, here to lie alone
And in this desolation to let go
Down the ravine one with another, down
Across the surf to linger or to drown   40

The loves that none can give and none receive,
The fearful asking and the small retort,
The life to dream of and the dream to live!
Very much more is nothing than a part,
Nothing at all and darkness in the heart.

I would my manhood now were like the sea.—
Thou at high-tide, when compassing the land
Thou find'st the issue short, questioningly
A moment poised, thy floods then down the strand
Sink without rancor, sink without command,   50

Sink of themselves in peace without despair,
And turn as still the calm horizon turns,
Till they repose little by little nowhere
And the long light unfathomable burns
Clear from the zenith stars to the sea-ferns.

Thou art thy Priest, thy Victim and thy God.
Thy life is bulwarked with a thread of foam,
And of the sky, the mountains and the sod
Thou askest nothing, evermore at home
In thy own self's perennial masterdom.   60

1905

WILLIAM JAMES

(1842–1910)

Born in New York City, William James and his novelist brother, Henry, were afforded an unconventional, international, and brilliant education by their wealthy Swedenborgian father, Henry, Sr. William resided in Germany and in France, studied painting, returned to America to study biology at Harvard, interrupted his medical schooling for an expedition with Louis Agassiz, and received his M. D. degree from Harvard in 1869. He remained at Harvard to teach physiology, conducting the first laboratory course in that subject ever offered at the school; but his temperament and the desire to explore the wider significance of human experience gradually steered him out of medicine and into philosophy. In his thinking he attempted to merge the empiricism of science with his father's intuitionalism. His persistently radical, rational, and pragmatic attitude, a result of his journey to philosophy from physiology by way of psychology, is clearly evident in works such as *The Principles of Psychology* (1890). For the last three decades of his life he lectured extensively and traveled widely to present his ideas; he published many books, reviews, and articles, met his classes, and rounded out the picture of the busy academician with membership and leadership in the American Psychological Association, the Society for Psychical Research, and the American Philosophical Association.

In 1897 he published *The Will to Believe*, in which he defended beliefs beyond empirical validation, yet providing empirical arguments for his defense. In 1902 he published *The Varieties of Religious Experience*, which explored the empirical and conditional bases of faith and used them, in psychological, social, and practical terms, for a defense of the mystical response. The development of James's ideas reaches its logical conclusion in *Pragmatism* (1907), an inevitable American philosophy that reflects the insistence of a frontier culture on empiricism, utilitarianism, and faith in man's control of his existence. In 1907, after thirty-five years of inspired teaching, he delightedly retired from the profession, to be, as he put it, "my own man after thirty-five years of being owned by others." James has been one of the most influential of all American philosophers; he continued the efforts of Emerson to evolve a viable philosophy of experience, the need for which has been one of the chief motive forces in our serious literature.

In addition to the works mentioned above, some of James's books are *Human Immortality* (1898); *Talks to Teachers on Psychology* (1899); *A Pluralistic Universe* (1909); and *The Meaning of Truth* (1909).

Collections and accounts of the man and his work are to be found in H. James, ed., *Memories and Studies* (1911); J. Royce, *William James and Other Essays on the Philosophy of Life* (1911); H. Knox, *The Philosophy of William James* (1914); H. James, ed., *The Letters of William James*, 2 vols. (1920); R. B. Perry, *Annotated Bibliography of the Writings of William James* (1920); H. M. Kallen, ed., *The Philosophy of William James* (1925); R. B. Perry, *The Thought and Character of William James*, 2 vols. (1935); R. B. Perry, *In the Spirit of William James* (1938); J. S. Bixler, J. Dewey, et al., *In Commemoration of William James, 1842–1942* (1942); J. S. Bixler, J. Dewey, et al., *William James: The Man and the Thinker* (1942); F. O. Matthiessen, *The James Family* (1947); L. Morris, *William James: The Message of a Modern Mind* (1950); B. P. Brennan, *The Ethics of William James* (1962); T. R. Martland, *The Metaphysics of William James and John Dewey* (1963); E. C. Moore, *William James* (1965); R. C. LeClair, ed., *The Letters of William James and Théodore Flournoy* (1966); and G. W. Allen, *William James* (1967).

F R O M

Pragmatism

From Chapter II: What Pragmatism Means

Some years ago, being with a camping party in the mountains, I returned from a solitary ramble to find every one engaged in a ferocious metaphysical dispute. The *corpus* of the dispute was a squirrel—a live squirrel supposed to be clinging to one side of a tree-trunk; while over against the tree's opposite side a human being was imagined to stand. This human witness tries to get sight of the squirrel by moving rapidly round the tree, but no matter how fast he goes, the squirrel moves as fast in the opposite direction, and always keeps the tree between himself and the man, so that never a glimpse of him is caught. The resultant metaphysical problem now is this: *Does the man go round the squirrel or not?* He goes round the tree, sure enough, and the squirrel is on the tree; but does he go round the squirrel? In the unlimited leisure of the wilderness, discussion had been worn threadbare. Every one had taken sides, and was obstinate; and the numbers on both sides were even. Each side, when I appeared therefore appealed to me to make it a majority. Mindful of the scholastic adage that whenever you meet a contradiction you must make a distinction, I immediately sought and found one, as follows: "Which party is right," I said, "depends on what you *practically mean* by 'going round' the squirrel. If you mean passing from the north of him to the east, then to the south, then to the west, and then to the north of him again, obviously the man does go round him, for he occupies these successive positions. But if on the contrary you mean being first in front of him, then on the right of him, then behind him, then on his left, and finally in front again, it is quite as obvious that the man fails to go round him, for by the compensating movements the squirrel makes, he keeps his belly turned towards the man all the time, and his back turned away. Make the distinction, and there is no occasion for any farther dispute. You are both right and both wrong according as you conceive the verb 'to go round' in one practical fashion or the other."

Although one or two of the hotter disputants called my speech a shuffling evasion, saying they wanted no quibbling or scholastic hairsplitting, but meant just plain honest English 'round,' the majority seemed to think that the distinction had assuaged the dispute.

I tell this trivial anecdote because it is a peculiarly simple example of what I wish now to speak of as *the pragmatic method*. The pragmatic method is primarily a method of settling metaphysical disputes that otherwise might be interminable. Is the world one or many?—fated or free?—material or spiritual?—here are notions either of which may or may not hold good of the world; and disputes over such notions are unending. The pragmatic method in such cases is to try to interpret each notion by tracing its respective practical consequences. What difference would it practically make to any one if this notion rather than that notion were true? If no practical difference whatever can be traced, then the alternatives mean practically the same thing, and all dispute is idle. Whenever a dispute is serious, we ought to be able to show some practical difference that must follow from one side or the other's being right.

A glance at the history of the idea will show you still better what pragmatism means. The term is derived from the same Greek word πράγμα, meaning action, from which our words 'practice' and 'practical' come. It was first introduced into philosophy by Mr. Charles Peirce in 1878. In an article entitled "How to Make Our Ideas Clear," in the *Popular Science Monthly* for January of that year Mr. Peirce, after pointing out that our beliefs are really rules for action, said that, to develop a thought's meaning, we need only determine what conduct it is fitted to produce: that conduct is for us its sole significance. And the tangible fact at the root of all our thought-distinctions, however subtle, is that there is no one of them so fine as to consist in anything but a possible difference of practice. To attain perfect clearness in our thoughts of an object, then, we need only consider what conceivable effects of a practical kind the object may involve—what sensations we are to expect from it, and what reactions we must prepare. Our conceptions of these effects, whether immediate or remote, is then for us the whole of our conception of the object, so far as that conception has positive significance at all.

This is the principle of Peirce, the principle of pragmatism. It lay entirely unnoticed by any one for twenty years, until I, in an address before Professor Howison's philosophical union at the University of California, brought it forward again and made a special application of it to religion. By that date (1898) the times seemed ripe for its reception. The word 'pragmatism' spread, and at present it fairly spots the pages of the philosophic journals. On all hands we find the 'pragmatic movement' spoken of, sometimes with respect, sometimes with contumely, seldom with clear understanding. It is evident that the term applies itself conveniently to a number of tendencies that hitherto have lacked a collective name, and that it has 'come to stay.'

To take in the importance of Peirce's principle, one must get accustomed to applying it to concrete cases. I found a few years ago that Ostwald, the illustrious Leipzig chemist, had been making perfectly distinct use of the principle of pragmatism in his lectures on the philosophy of science, though he had not called it by that name.

"All realities influence our practice," he wrote me, "and that influence is their meaning for us. I am accustomed to put questions to my classes in this way: In what respects would the world be different if this alternative or that were true? If I can find nothing that would become different, then the alternative has no sense."

That is, the rival views mean practically the same thing, and meaning, other than practical, there is for us none. Ostwald in a published lecture gives this example of what he means. Chemists have long wrangled over the inner constitution of certain bodies called 'tautomerous.' Their properties seemed equally consistent with the notion that an instable hydrogen atom oscillates inside of them, or that they are instable mixtures of two bodies. Controversy raged, but never was decided. "It would never have begun," says Ostwald, "if the combatants had asked themselves what particular experimental fact could have been made different by one or the other view being correct. For it would then have appeared that no difference of fact could possibly ensue; and the quarrel was as unreal as if, theorizing in primitive times about the raising of dough by yeast, one party should have invoked a 'brownie,' while another insisted on an 'elf' as the true cause of the phenomenon."

It is astonishing to see how many philosophical disputes collapse into insignificance the moment you subject them to this simple test of tracing a concrete consequence. There can *be* no difference anywhere that doesn't *make* a difference elsewhere—no difference in abstract truth that doesn't express itself in a difference in concrete fact and in conduct consequent upon that fact, imposed on somebody, somehow, somewhere, and somewhen. The whole function of philosophy ought to be to find out what definite difference it will make to you and me at definite instants of our life, if this world-formula or that world-formula be the true one.

There is absolutely nothing new in the pragmatic method. Socrates was an adept at it. Aristotle used it methodically. Locke, Berkeley, and Hume made momentous contributions to truth by its means. Shadworth Hodgson keeps insisting that realities are only what they are 'known as.' But these forerunners of pragmatism used it in fragments: they were preluders only. Not until in our time has it generalized itself, become conscious of a universal mission, pretended to a conquering destiny. I believe in that destiny, and I hope I may end by inspiring you with my belief.

Pragmatism represents a perfectly familiar attitude in philosophy, the empiricist attitude, but it represents it, as it seems to me, both in a more radical and in a less objectionable form than it has ever yet assumed. A pragmatist turns his back resolutely and once for all upon a lot of inveterate habits dear to professional philosophers. He turns away from abstraction and insufficiency, from verbal solutions, from bad *a priori* reasons, from fixed principles, closed systems, and pretended absolutes and origins. He turns towards concreteness and adequacy, towards facts, towards action and towards power. That means the empiricist temper regnant and the rationalist temper sincerely given up. It means the open air and possibilities of nature, as against dogma, artificiality, and the pretence of finality in truth.

At the same time it does not stand for any special results. It is a method only. But the general triumph of that method would mean an enormous change in what I called in my last lecture the 'temperament' of philosophy. Teachers of the ultra-rationalistic type would be frozen out, much as the courtier type is frozen out in republics, as the ultramontane type of priest is frozen out in protestant lands. Science and metaphysics would come much nearer together, would in fact work absolutely hand in hand.

Metaphysics has usually followed a very primitive kind of quest. You know how men have always hankered after unlawful magic, and you know what a great part in magic *words* have always played. If you have his name, or the formula of incantation that binds him, you can control the spirit, genie, afrite, or whatever the power may be. Solomon knew the names of all the spirits, and having their names, he held them subject to his will. So the universe has always appeared to the natural mind as a kind of enigma, of which the key must be sought in the shape of some illuminating or power-bringing word or name. That word names the universe's *principle,* and to possess it is after a fashion to possess the universe itself. 'God,' 'Matter,' 'Reason,' 'the Absolute,' 'Energy,' are so many solving names. You can rest when you have them. You are at the end of your metaphysical quest.

But if you follow the pragmatic method, you cannot look on any such word as closing your quest. You must bring out of each word its practical cash-value, set it at work within the stream of your experience. It appears less as a solution, then, than as a program for more work, and more particularly as an indication of the ways in which existing realities may be *changed.*

Theories thus become instruments, not answers to enigmas, in which we can rest. We don't lie back upon them, we move forward, and, on occasion, make nature over again by their aid. Pragmatism unstiffens all our theories, limbers them up and sets each one at work. Being nothing essentially new, it harmonizes with many ancient philosophic tendencies. It agrees with nominalism for instance, in always appealing to particulars; with utilarianism in emphasizing practical aspects; with positivism in its disdain for verbal solutions, useless questions and metaphysical abstractions.

All these, you see, are *anti-intellectualist* tendencies. Against rationalism as a pretension and a method pragmatism is fully armed and militant. But, at the outset, at least, it stands for no particular results. It has no dogmas, and no doctrines save its method. As the young Italian pragmatist Papini has well said, it lies in the midst of our theories, like a corridor in a hotel. Innumerable chambers open out of it. In one you may find a man writing an atheistic volume; in the next some one on his knees praying for faith and strength; in a third a chemist investigating a body's properties. In a fourth a system of idealistic metaphysics is being excogitated; in a fifth the impossibility of metaphysics is being shown. But they all own the corridor, and all must pass through it if they want a practicable way of getting into or out of their respective rooms.

No particular results then, so far, but only an attitude of orientation, is what the pragmatic method means. The *attitude of looking away from first things, principles, 'cate-*

gories,' supposed necessities; and of looking towards last things, fruits, consequences, facts.

So much for the pragmatic method! You may say that I have been praising it rather than explaining it to you, but I shall presently explain it abundantly enough by showing how it works on some familiar problems. Meanwhile the word pragmatism has come to be used in a still wider sense, as meaning also a certain *theory of truth.* I mean to give a whole lecture to the statement of that theory, after first paving the way, so I can be very brief now. But brevity is hard to follow, so I ask for your redoubled attention for a quarter of an hour. If much remains obscure, I hope to make it clearer in the later lectures.

One of the most successfully cultivated branches of philosophy in our time is what is called inductive logic, the study of the conditions under which our sciences have evolved. Writers on this subject have begun to show a singular unanimity as to what the laws of nature and elements of fact mean, when formulated by mathematicians, physicists and chemists. When the first mathematical, logical, and natural uniformities, the first *laws,* were discovered, men were so carried away by the clearness, beauty and simplification that resulted, that they believed themselves to have deciphered authentically the eternal thoughts of the Almighty. His mind also thundered and reverberated in syllogisms. He also thought in conic sections, squares and roots and ratios, and geometrized like Euclid. He made Kepler's laws for the planets to follow; he made velocity increase proportionally to the time in falling bodies; he made the law of the sines for light to obey when refracted; he established the classes, orders, families and genera of plants and animals, and fixed the distances between them. He thought the archetypes of all things, and devised their variations; and when we rediscover any one of these his wondrous institutions, we seize his mind in its very literal intention.

But as the sciences have developed farther, the notion has gained ground that most, perhaps all, of our laws are only approximations. The laws themselves, moreover, have grown so numerous that there is no counting them; and so many rival formulations are proposed in all the branches of science that investigators have become accustomed to the notion that no theory is absolutely a transcript of reality, but that any one of them may from some point of view be useful. Their great use is to summarize old facts and to lead to new ones. They are only a man-made language, a conceptual short-hand, as some one calls them, in which we write our reports of nature; and languages, as is well known, tolerate much choice of expression and many dialects.

Thus human arbitrariness has driven divine necessity from scientific logic. If I mention the names of Sigwart, Mach, Ostwald, Pearson, Milhaud, Poincaré, Duhem, Ruyssen, those of you who are students will easily identify the tendency I speak of, and will think of additional names.

Riding now on the front of this wave of scientific logic Messrs. Schiller and Dewey appear with their pragmatistic account of what truth everywhere signifies. Everywhere, these teachers say, 'truth' in our ideas and beliefs means the same thing that it means in science. It means, they say, nothing but this, *that ideas (which themselves are but parts of our experience) become true just in so far as they help us to get into satisfactory relation with other parts of our experience,* to summarize them and get about them by conceptual short-cuts instead of following the interminable succession of particular phenomena. Any idea upon which we can ride, so to speak; any idea that will carry us prosperously from any one part of our experience to any other part, linking things satisfactorily, working securely, simplifying, saving labor; is true for just so much, true in so far forth, true *instrumentally.* This is the 'instrumental' view of truth taught so successfully at Chicago, the view that truth in our ideas means their power to 'work,' promulgated so brilliantly at Oxford.

Messrs. Dewey, Schiller and their allies, in reaching this general conception of all truth, have only followed the example of geologists, biologists and philologists. In the establishment of these other sciences, the successful stroke was always to take some simple process actually observable in operation—as denudation by weather, say, or variation from parental type, or change of dialect by incorporation of new words and pronunciations—and then to generalize it, making it apply to all times, and produce great results by summating its effects through the ages.

The observable process which Schiller and Dewey particularly singled out for generalization is the familiar one by which any individual settles into *new opinions.* The process here is always the same. The individual has a stock of old opinions already, but he meets a new experience that puts them to a strain. Somebody contradicts them; or in a reflective moment he discovers that they contradict each other; or he hears of facts with which they are incompatible; or desires arise in him which they cease to satisfy. The result is an inward trouble to which his mind till then had been a stranger, and from which he seeks to escape by modifying his previous mass of opinions. He saves as much of it as he can, for in this matter of belief we are all extreme conservatives. So he tries to change first this opinion, and then that (for they resist change very variously), until at last some new idea comes up which he can graft upon the ancient stock with a minimum of disturbance of the latter, some idea that mediates between the stock and the new experience and runs them into one another most felicitously and expediently.

This new idea is then adopted as the true one. It preserves the older stock of truths with a minimum of modification, stretching them just enough to make them admit the novelty, but conceiving that in ways as familiar as the case leaves possible. An *outrée* explanation, violating all our preconceptions, would never pass for a true account of a novelty. We should scratch round industriously till we found something less excentric. The most violent revolutions in an individual's beliefs leave most of his old order standing. Time and space, cause and effect, nature and history, and one's own biography remain untouched. New truth is always a go-between, a smoother-over of transitions. It marries old opinion to new fact so as ever to show a minimum of jolt, a maximum of continuity. We hold a theory true just in proportion to its success in solving this 'problem of maxima and minima.' But success in solving this problem is eminently a matter of approximation. We say this theory solves it on the whole more satisfactorily than that theory; but that means more satisfactorily to ourselves, and individuals will emphasize their points of satisfaction differently. To a certain degree, therefore, everything here is plastic.

The point I now urge you to observe particularly is the part played by the older truths. Failure to take account of it is the source of much of the unjust criticism levelled against pragmatism. Their influence is absolutely controlling. Loyalty to them is the first principle—in most cases it is the only principle; for by far the most usual way of handling phenomena so novel that they would make for a serious rearrangement of our preconception is to ignore them altogether, or to abuse those who bear witness for them.

You doubtless wish examples of this process of truth's growth, and the only trouble is their superabundance. The simplest case of new truth is of course the mere numerical addition of new kinds of facts, or of new single facts of old kinds, to our experience—an addition that involves no alteration in the old beliefs. Day follows day, and its contents are simply added. The new contents themselves are not true, they simply *come* and *are*. Truth is *what we say about* them, and when we say that they have come, truth is satisfied by the plain additive formula.

But often the day's contents oblige a rearrangement. If I should now utter piercing shrieks and act like a maniac on this platform, it would make many of you revise your ideas as to the probable worth of my philosophy. 'Radium' came the other day as part of the day's content, and seemed for a moment to contradict our ideas of the whole order of nature, that order having come to be identified with what is called the conservation of energy. The mere sight of radium paying heat away indefinitely out of its own pocket seemed to violate that conservation. What to think? If the radiations from it were nothing but an escape of unsuspected 'potential' energy, pre-existent inside of the atoms, the principle of conservation would be saved. The discovery of 'helium' as the radiation's outcome, opened a way to this belief. So Ramsay's view is generally held to be true, because, although it extends our old ideas of energy, it causes a minimum of alteration in their nature.

I need not multiply instances. A new opinion counts as 'true' just in proportion as it gratifies the individual's desire to assimilate the novel in his experience to his beliefs in stock. It must both lean on old truth and grasp new fact; and its success (as I said a moment ago) in doing this, is a matter for the individual's appreciation. When old truth grows, then, by new truth's addition, it is for subjective reasons. We are in the process and obey the reasons. That new idea is truest which performs most felicitously its function of satisfying our double urgency. It makes itself true, gets itself classed as true, by the way it works; grafting itself then upon the ancient body of truth, which thus grows much as a tree grows by the activity of a new layer of cambium.

Now Dewey and Schiller proceed to generalize this observation and to apply it to the most ancient parts of truth. They also once were plastic. They also were called true for human reasons. They also mediated between still earlier truths and what in those days were novel observations. Purely objective truth, truth in whose establishment the function of giving human satisfaction in marrying previous parts of experience with newer parts played no rôle whatever, is nowhere to be found. The reason why we call things true is the reason why they *are* true, for 'to be true' *means* only to perform this marriage-function.

The trail of the human serpent is thus over everything. Truth independent; truth that we *find* merely; truth no longer malleable to human need; truth incorrigible, in a word; such truth exists indeed superabundantly—or is supposed to exist by rationalistically minded thinkers; but then it means only the dead heart of the living tree, and its being there means only that truth also has its paleontology, and its 'prescription,' and may grow stiff with years of veteran service and petrified in men's regard by sheer antiquity. But how plastic even the oldest truths nevertheless really are has been vividly shown in our day by the transformation of logical and mathematical ideas, a transformation which seems even to be invading physics. The ancient formulas are reinterpreted as special expressions of much wider principles, principles that our ancestors never got a glimpse of in their present shape and formulation.

Mr. Schiller still gives to all this view of truth the name of 'Humanism,' but, for this doctrine too, the name of pragmatism seems fairly to be in the ascendant, so I will treat it under the name of pragmatism in these lectures.

Such then would be the scope of pragmatism—first, a method; and second, a genetic theory of what is meant by truth. And these two things must be our future topics.

What I have said of the theory of truth will, I am sure, have appeared obscure and unsatisfactory to most of you by reason of its brevity. I shall make amends for that hereafter. In a lecture on 'common sense' I shall try to show what I mean by truths grown petrified by antiquity. In another lecture I shall expatiate on the idea that our thoughts become true in proportion as they successfully exert their go-between function. In a third I shall show how hard it is to discriminate subjective from objective factors in Truth's development. You may not follow me wholly in these lectures; and if you do, you may not wholly agree with me. But you will, I know, regard me at least as serious, and treat my effort with respectful consideration.

You will probably be surprised to learn, then, that Messrs. Schiller's and Dewey's theories have suffered a hailstorm of contempt and ridicule. All rationalism has risen against them. In influential quarters Mr. Schiller, in particular, has been treated like an impudent schoolboy who deserves a spanking. I should not mention this, but for the fact that it throws so much sidelight upon that rationalistic temper to which I have opposed the temper of pragmatism. Pragmatism is uncomfortable away from facts. Rationalism is comfortable only in the presence of abstractions. This pragmatist talk about truths in the plural, about their utility and satisfactoriness, about the success with which they 'work,' etc., suggests to the typical intellectualist mind a sort of coarse lame second-rate makeshift article of truth. Such truths are not real truth. Such tests are merely subjective. As against this, objective truth must be something non-utilitarian, haughty, refined, remote, august, exalted. It must be an absolute correspondence of our thoughts with an equally absolute reality. It must be what we *ought* to think unconditionally. The conditioned ways in which we *do* think are so much irrelevance and matter for psychology. Down with psychology, up with logic, in all this question!

See the exquisite contrast of the types of mind! The pragmatist clings to facts and concreteness, observes truth at its work in particular cases, and generalizes. Truth, for him, becomes a class-name for all sorts of definite working-values in experience. For the rationalist it remains a pure abstraction, to the bare name of which we must defer. When the pragmatist undertakes to show in detail just *why* we must defer, the rationalist is unable to recognize the concretes from which his own abstraction is taken. He accuses us of *denying* truth; whereas we have only sought to trace exactly why people follow it. Your typical ultra-abstractionist fairly shudders at concreteness: other things equal, he positively prefers the pale and spectral. If the two universes were offered, he would always choose the skinny outline rather than the rich thicket of reality. It is so much purer, clearer, nobler.

I hope that as these lectures go on, the concreteness and closeness to facts of the pragmatism which they advocate may be what approves itself to you as its most satisfactory peculiarity. It only follows here the example of the sister-sciences, interpreting the unobserved by the observed. It brings old and new harmoniously together. It converts the absolutely empty notion of a static relation of 'correspondence' (what that may mean we must ask later) between our minds and reality, into that of a rich and active commerce (that any one may follow in detail and understand) between particular thoughts of ours, and the great universe of other experiences in which they play their parts and have their uses.

But enough of this at present? The justification of what I say must be postponed. I wish now to add a word in further explanation of the claim I made at our last meeting, that pragmatism may be a happy harmonizer of empiricist ways of thinking with the more religious demands of human beings.

Men who are strongly of the fact-loving temperament, you may remember me to have said, are liable to be kept at a distance by the small sympathy with facts which that philosophy from the present-day fashion of idealism offers them. It is far too intellectualistic. Old-fashioned theism was bad enough, with its notion of God as an exalted monarch, made up of a lot of unintelligible or preposterous 'attributes'; but, so long as it held strongly by the argument from design, it kept some touch with concrete realities. Since, however, darwinism has once for all displaced design from the minds of the 'scientific,' theism has lost that foothold; and some kind of an immanent or pantheistic deity working *in* things rather than above them is, if any, the kind recommended to our contemporary imagination. Aspirants to a philosophic religion turn, as a rule, more hopefully nowadays towards idealistic pantheism than towards the older dualistic theism, in spite of the fact that the latter still counts able defenders.

But, as I said in my first lecture, the brand of pantheism

offered is hard for them to assimilate if they are lovers of facts, or empirically minded. It is the absolutistic brand, spurning the dust and reared upon pure logic. It keeps no connexion whatever with concreteness. Affirming the Absolute Mind, which is its substitute for God, to be the rational presupposition of all particulars of fact, whatever they may be, it remains supremely indifferent to what the particular facts in our world actually are. Be they what they may, the Absolute will father them. Like the sick lion in Esop's fable, all footprints lead into his den, but *nulla vestigia retrorsum* [no footprints back]. You cannot redescend into the world of particulars by the Absolute's aid, or deduce any necessary consequences of detail important for your life from your idea of his nature. He gives you indeed the assurance that all is well with *Him,* and for his eternal way of thinking; but thereupon he leaves you to be finitely saved by your own temporal devices.

Far be it from me to deny the majesty of this conception, or its capacity to yield religious comfort to a most respectable class of minds. But from the human point of view, no one can pretend that it doesn't suffer from the faults of remoteness and abstractness. It is eminently a product of what I have ventured to call the rationalistic temper. It disdains empiricism's needs. It substitutes a pallid outline for the real world's richness. It is dapper, it is noble in the bad sense, in the sense in which to be noble is to be inapt for humble service. In this real world of sweat and dirt, it seems to me that when a view of things is 'noble,' that ought to count as a presumption against its truth, and as a philosophic disqualification. The prince of darkness may be a gentleman, as we are told he is, but whatever the God of earth and heaven is, he can surely be no gentleman. His menial services are needed in the dust of our human trials, even more than his dignity is needed in the empyrean.

Now pragmatism, devoted though she be to facts, has no such materialistic bias as ordinary empiricism labors under. Moreover, she has no objection whatever to the realizing of abstractions, so long as you get about among particulars with their aid and they actually carry you somewhere. Interested in no conclusions but those which our minds and our experiences work out together, she has no *a priori* prejudices against theology. *If theological ideas prove to*

*have a value for concrete life, they will be true, for prag-
matism, in the sense of being good for so much. For how
much more they are true, will depend entirely on their relations to the other truths that also have to be acknowledged.*

What I said just now about the Absolute, of transcendental idealism, is a case in point. First, I called it majestic and
said it yielded religious comfort to a class of minds, and
then I accused it of remoteness and sterility. But so far as
it affords such comfort, it surely is not sterile; it has that
amount of value; it performs a concrete function. As a
good pragmatist, I myself ought to call the Absolute true
'in so far forth,' then; and I unhesitatingly now do so.

But what does *true in so far forth* mean in this case? To
answer, we need only apply the pragmatic method. What
do believers in the Absolute mean by saying that their belief affords them comfort? They mean that since, in the Absolute finite evil is 'overruled' already, we may, therefore,
whenever we wish, treat the temporal as if it were potentially the eternal, be sure that we can trust its outcome, and,
without sin, dismiss our fear and drop the worry of our
finite responsibility. In short, they mean that we have a
right ever and anon to take a moral holiday, to let the
world wag in its own way, feeling that its issues are in better hands than ours and are none of our business.

The universe is a system of which the individual members may relax their anxieties occasionally, in which the
don't-care mood is also right for men, and moral holidays
in order,—that, if I mistake not, is part, at least, of what
the Absolute is 'known-as,' that is the great difference in
our particular experiences which his being true makes, for
us, that is his cash-value when he is pragmatically interpreted. Farther than that the ordinary lay-reader in philosophy who thinks favorably of absolute idealism does not
venture to sharpen his conceptions. He can use the Absolute
for so much, and so much is very precious. He is pained
at hearing you speak incredulously of the Absolute, therefore, and disregards your criticisms because they deal with
aspects of the conception that he fails to follow.

If the Absolute means this, and means no more than
this, who can possibly deny the truth of it? To deny it
would be to insist that men should never relax, and that
holidays are never in order.

I am well aware how odd it must seem to some of you to

hear me say that an idea is 'true' so long as to believe it
is profitable to our lives. That it is *good,* for as much as it
profits, you will gladly admit. If what we do by its aid is
good, you will allow the idea itself to be good in so far
forth, for we are the better for possessing it. But is it not
a strange misuse of the word 'truth,' you will say, to call
ideas also 'true' for this reason?

To answer this difficulty fully is impossible at this stage
of my account. You touch here upon the very central point
of Messrs. Schiller's, Dewey's and my own . doctrine of
truth, which I can not discuss with detail until my sixth
lecture. Let me now say only this, that truth is *one species
of good,* and not, as is usually supposed, a category distinct
from good, and co-ordinate with it. *The true is the name of
whatever proves itself to be good in the way of belief, and
good, too, for definite, assignable reasons.* Surely you must
admit this, that if there were *no* good for life in true ideas,
or if the knowledge of them were positively disadvanta-
geous and false ideas the only useful ones, then the current
notion that truth is divine and precious, and its pursuit a
duty, could never have grown up or become a dogma. In
a world like that, our duty would be to *shun* truth, rather.
But in this world, just as certain foods are not only agreeable to our taste, but good for our teeth, our stomach, and
our tissues; so certain ideas are not only agreeable to think
about, or agreeable as supporting other ideas that we are
fond of, but they are also helpful in life's practical struggles.
If there be any life that it is really better we should lead,
and if there be any idea which, if believed in, would help
us to lead that life, then it would be really *better for us* to
believe in that idea, *unless, indeed, belief in it incidentally
clashed with other greater vital benefits.*

'What would be better for us to believe'! This sounds very
like a definition of truth. It comes very near to saying
'what we *ought* to believe': and in *that* definition none of
you would find any oddity. Ought we ever not to believe
what it is *better for us* to believe? And can we then keep
the notion of what is better for us, and what is true for us,
permanently apart?

Pragmatism says no, and I fully agree with her. Probably you also agree, so far as the abstract statement goes,
but with a suspicion that if we practically did believe everything that made for good in our own personal lives, we

should be found indulging all kinds of fancies about this world's affairs, and all kinds of sentimental superstitions about a world hereafter. Your suspicion here is undoubtedly well founded, and it is evident that something happens when you pass from the abstract to the concrete that complicates the situation.

I said just now that what is better for us to believe is true *unless the belief incidentally clashes with some other vital benefit*. Now in real life what vital benefits is any particular belief of ours most liable to clash with? What indeed except the vital benefits yielded by *other beliefs* when these prove incompatible with the first ones? In other words, the greatest enemy of any one of our truths may be the rest of our truths. Truths have once for all this desperate instinct of self-preservation and of desire to extinguish whatever contradicts them. My belief in the Absolute, based on the good it does me, must run the gauntlet of all my other beliefs. Grant that it may be true in giving me a moral holiday. Nevertheless, as I conceive it,—and let me speak now confidentially, as it were, and merely in my own private person,—it clashes with other truths of mine whose benefits I hate to give up on its account. It happens to be associated with a kind of logic of which I am the enemy, I find that it entangles me in metaphysical paradoxes that are inacceptable, etc., etc. But as I have enough trouble in life already without adding the trouble of carrying these intellectual inconsistencies, I personally just give up the Absolute. I just *take* my moral holidays; or else as a professional philosopher, I try to justify them by some other principle.

If I could restrict my notion of the Absolute to its bare holiday-giving value, it wouldn't clash with my other truths. But we can not easily thus restrict our hypotheses. They carry supernumerary features, and these it is that clash so. My disbelief in the Absolute means then disbelief in those other supernumerary features, for I fully believe in the legitimacy of taking moral holidays.

You see by this what I meant when I called pragmatism a mediator and reconciler and said, borrowing the word from Papini, that she 'unstiffens' our theories. She has in fact no prejudices whatever, no obstructive dogmas, no rigid canons of what shall count as proof. She is completely genial. She will entertain any hypothesis, she will consider any evidence. It follows that in the religious field she is at a great advantage both over positivistic empiricism, with its anti-theological bias, and over religious rationalism, with its exclusive interest in the remote, the noble, the simple, and the abstract in the way of conception.

In short, she widens the field of search for God. Rationalism sticks to logic and the empyrean. Empiricism sticks to the external senses. Pragmatism is willing to take anything, to follow either logic or the senses and to count the humblest and most personal experiences. She will count mystical experiences if they have practical consequences. She will take a God who lives in the very dirt of private fact—if that should seem a likely place to find him.

Her only test of probable truth is what works best in the way of leading us, what fits every part of life best and combines with the collectivity of experience's *demands,* nothing being omitted. If theological ideas should do this, if the notion of God, in particular, should prove to do it, how could pragmatism possibly deny God's existence? She could see no meaning in treating as 'not true' a notion that was pragmatically so successful. What other kind of truth could there be, for her, than all this agreement with concrete reality?

In my last lecture I shall return again to the relations of pragmatism with religion. But you see already how democratic she is. Her manners are as various and flexible, her resources as rich and endless, and her conclusions as friendly as those of mother nature.

1907

HENRY ADAMS

(1838–1918)

Perhaps no one ever came into this world with more in his favor than Boston-born Henry Adams. His mother was a Brooks, one of the wealthiest families in the nation; his father was Charles Francis Adams, later minister to England; his grandfather was President John Quincy Adams; his great-grandfather was President John Adams; and the family also included many scholars and diplomats. Moreover, he was blessed with a brilliant mind and a sound education. He was graduated from Harvard in 1858, studied in Europe, acted as his father's secretary in England during the Civil War, worked at journalism after the War, edited the influential *North American Review* from 1870 to 1876, taught medieval history at Harvard until 1877 (when he resigned to take up residence in Washington, D. C.), and was a celebrated interpreter of United States history.

Although he wrote two novels—*Democracy* (1880) and *Esther* (1884)—he is remembered in American literary history as an essayist, a biographer, and a thinker rather than as a novelist. His books on Gallatin and his nine-volume *History of the United States during the Administrations of Jefferson and Madison* (1889–1891) made his reputation as a historian. But it was with *Mont-Saint-Michel and Chartres* (1904) that he began to develop his theory of history as a science of force. He saw medieval man, nourished by the power of his belief in the Virgin, as a man who "held the highest idea of himself as a unit in a unified universe." Adams saw history since the Middle Ages as the discovery that the universe is multiplistic, chaotic, and anarchic, and that order exists only in man's wishful projections. Troubled by his inability to achieve an identity for himself as an intellectual in an increasingly commercial culture, Adams attempted to find in his own career a clue to the atomization of society in modern times.

In this attempt, he viewed his own life as a continuing education, representative of dispersions that destroyed the old medieval certitudes and answers to the problems of living. In 1907 he privately printed the third-person autobiography that chronicled his life-as-education. This was *The Education of Henry Adams*, which did not become publicly available until his death in 1918. The book became one of the leading voices of the times, centering as it does on modern man's growing sense of isolation and uncertainty. In the *Education* he continued his scientific theories of history, adapting them from laws of physics in an endeavor to furnish history with the same kind of predictability enjoyed by the physical sciences. One does not wish Adams success as a prognosticator beyond that which he has already met—he predicted that as sheer power increasingly becomes the characteristic of modern society, the twentieth century would be one of barbarically violent revolutions and repeated wars, that Russia and China would combine to overthrow the West, and that man would develop a bomb with which he would blow apart the planet.

In addition to the works mentioned above, some of Adams's books are *Documents Relating to New England Federalism, 1800–1815* (1879); The Life of Albert Gallatin (1879); *The Writings of Albert Gallatin* (1879); *John Randolph* (1882); *Memoirs of Marau Taaroa* (1893); and *The Degradation of the Democratic Dogma* (1919), edited with an introduction by his brother Brooks Adams.

Collections and accounts of the man and his work are to be found in W. C. Ford, ed., *A Cycle of Adams Letters, 1861–1865,* 2 vols. (1920); T. K. Whipple, *Spokesmen* (1928); W. C. Ford, ed., *Letters of Henry Adams, 1858–1891* (1930); J. T. Adams, *Henry Adams* (1933); W. Thoron, ed., *The Letters of Mrs. Henry Adams* (1936); W. C. Ford, ed., *Letters of Henry Adams, 1892–1918* (1938); H. D. Cater, ed., *Henry Adams and His Friends* (1947); E. Samuels, *Young Henry Adams* (1948); N. Arvin, ed., *The Selected Letters of Henry Adams* (1951); M. I. Baym, *The French Education of Henry Adams* (1951); R. E. Hume, *Runaway Star* (1951); W. H. Jordy, *Henry Adams: Scientific Historian* (1952); J. Blanck, *Bibliography of American Literature,* I (1955); E. Stevenson, *Henry Adams* (1955); J. C. Levenson, *The Mind and Art of Henry Adams* (1958); E. Samuels, *Henry Adams: The Middle Years,*

1877–1891 (1958); E. Stevenson, ed., *A Henry Adams Reader* (1958); H. Munford, "Henry Adams and the Tendency of History," *New England Quarterly*, XXXII (1959); G. Hochfield, *Henry Adams: An Introduction and Interpretation* (1962); and E. Samuels, *Henry Adams, The Major Phase* (1964).

FROM

The Education of Henry Adams

Chapter XXV

The Dynamo and the Virgin

Until the Great Exposition of 1900 closed its doors in November, Adams haunted it, aching to absorb knowledge, and helpless to find it. He would have liked to know how much of it could have been grasped by the best-informed man in the world. While he was thus meditating chaos, Langley came by, and showed it to him. At Langley's behest, the Exhibition dropped its superfluous rags and stripped itself to the skin, for Langley knew what to study, and why, and how; while Adams might as well have stood outside in the night, staring at the Milky Way. Yet Langley said nothing new, and taught nothing that one might not have learned from Lord Bacon, three hundred years before; but though one should have known the "Advancement of Science" as well as one knew the "Comedy of Errors," the literary knowledge counted for nothing until some teacher should show how to apply it. Bacon took a vast deal of trouble in teaching King James I and his subjects, American or other, towards the year 1620, that true science was the development or economy of forces; yet an elderly American in 1900 knew neither the formula nor the forces; or even so much as to say to himself that his historical business in the Exposition concerned only the economies or developments of force since 1893, when he began the study at Chicago.

Nothing in education is so astonishing as the amount of ignorance it accumulates in the form of inert facts. Adams had looked at most of the accumulations of art in the storehouses called Art Museums; yet he did not know how to look at the art exhibits of 1900. He had studied Karl Marx and his doctrines of history with profound attention, yet he could not apply them at Paris. Langley, with the ease of a great master of experiment, threw out of the field every exhibit that did not reveal a new application of force, and naturally threw out, to begin with, almost the whole art exhibit. Equally, he ignored almost the whole industrial exhibit. He led his pupil directly to the forces. His chief interest was in new motors to make his airship feasible, and he taught Adams the astonishing complexities of the new Daimler motor, and of the automobile, which, since 1893, had become a nightmare at a hundred kilometres an hour, almost as destructive as the electric tram which was only ten years older; and threatening to become as terrible as the locomotive steam-engine itself, which was almost exactly Adams's own age.

Then he showed his scholar the great hall of dynamos, and explained how little he knew about electricity or force of any kind, even of his own special sun, which spouted heat in inconceivable volume, but which, as far as he knew, might spout less or more, at any time, for all the certainty he felt in it. To him, the dynamo itself was but an ingenious channel for conveying somewhere the heat latent in a few tons of poor coal hidden in a dirty engine-house carefully kept out of sight; but to Adams the dynamo became a symbol of infinity. As he grew accustomed to the great gallery of machines, he began to feel the forty-foot dynamos as a moral force, much as the early Christians felt the Cross. The planet itself seemed less impressive, in its old-fashioned, deliberate, annual or daily revolution, than this huge wheel, revolving within arm's-length at some vertiginous speed, and barely murmuring—scarcely humming an audible warning to stand a hair's-breadth further for respect of power—while it would not wake the baby lying close against its frame. Before the end, one began to pray for it; inherited instinct taught the natural expression of man before silent and infinite force. Among the thousand symbols of ultimate energy, the dynamo was not so human as some, but it was the most expressive.

Yet the dynamo, next to the steam-engine, was the most familiar of exhibits. For Adams's objects its value lay chiefly in its occult mechanism. Between the dynamo in the gallery of machines and the engine-house outside, the break of continuity amounted to abysmal fracture for a historian's objects. No more relation could he discover between the steam and the electric current than between the Cross and the cathedral. The forces were interchangeable if not reversible, but he could see only an absolute *fiat* in electricity as in faith. Langley could not help him. Indeed, Langley seemed to be worried by the same trouble, for he constantly repeated that the new forces were anarchical, and specially that he was not responsible for the new rays, that were little short of parricidal in their wicked spirit towards science. His own rays, with which he had doubled the solar spectrum, were altogether harmless and beneficent; but Radium denied its God—or, what was to Langley the same thing, denied the truths of his Science. The force was wholly new.

A historian who asked only to learn enough to be as futile as Langley or Kelvin, made rapid progress under this teaching, and mixed himself up in the tangle of ideas until he achieved a sort of Paradise of ignorance vastly consoling to his fatigued senses. He wrapped himself in vibrations and rays which were new, and he would have hugged Marconi and Branly had he met them, as he hugged the dynamo; while he lost his arithmetic in trying to figure out the equation between the discoveries and economies of force. The economies, like the discoveries, were absolute, supersensual, occult; incapable of expression in horsepower. What mathematical equivalent could he suggest as the value of a Branly coherer? Frozen air, or the electric furnace, had some scale of measurement, no doubt, if somebody could invent a thermometer adequate to the purpose; but X-rays had played no part whatever in man's consciousness, and the atom itself had figured only as a fiction of thought. In these seven years man had translated himself into a new universe which had no common scale of measurement with the old. He had entered a supersensual world, in which he could measure nothing except by chance collisions of movements imperceptible to his senses, perhaps even imperceptible to his instruments, but perceptible to each other, and so to some known ray at the end of the scale. Langley seemed prepared for anything, even for an indeterminable number of universes interfused—physics stark mad in metaphysics.

Historians undertake to arrange sequences,—called stories, or histories—assuming in silence a relation of cause and effect. These assumptions, hidden in the depths of dusty libraries, have been astounding, but commonly unconscious and childlike; so much so, that if any captious critic were to drag them to light, historians would probably reply, with one voice, that they had never supposed themselves required to know what they were talking about. Adams, for one, had toiled in vain to find out what he meant. He had even published a dozen volumes of American history for no other purpose than to satisfy himself whether, by the severest process of stating, with the least possible comment, such facts as seemed sure, in such order as seemed rigorously consequent, he could fix for a familiar moment a necessary sequence of human movement. The result had satisfied him as little as at Harvard College. Where he saw sequence, other men saw something quite different, and no one saw the same unit of measure. He cared little about his experiments and less about his statesmen, who seemed to him quite as ignorant as himself and as a rule, no more honest; but he insisted on a relation of sequence, and if he could not reach it by one method, he would try as many methods as science knew. Satisfied that the sequence of men led to nothing and that the sequence of their society could lead no further, while the mere sequence of time was artificial, and the sequence of thought was chaos, he turned at last to the sequence of force; and thus it happened that, after ten years' pursuit, he found himself lying in the Gallery of Machines at the Great Exposition of 1900, his historical neck broken by the sudden irruption of forces totally new.

Since no one else showed much concern, an elderly person without other cares had no need to betray alarm. The year 1900 was not the first to upset schoolmasters. Copernicus and Galileo had broken many professorial necks about 1600; Columbus had stood the world on its head towards 1500; but the nearest approach to the revolution of 1900 was that of 310, when Constantine set up the Cross. The rays that Langley disowned, as well as those which he fathered, were occult, supersensual, irrational; they were what, in terms of medieval science, were called immediate modes of the divine substance.

The historian was thus reduced to his last resources. Clearly if he was bound to reduce all these forces to a common value, this common value could have no measure but that of their attraction on his own mind. He must treat them as they had been felt; as convertible, reversible, interchangeable attractions on thought. He made up his mind to venture it; he would risk translating rays into faith. Such a reversible process would vastly amuse a chemist, but the chemist could not deny that he, or some of his fellow physicists, could feel the force of both. When Adams was a boy in Boston, the best chemist in the place had probably never heard of Venus except by way of scandal, or of the Virgin except as idolatry; neither had he heard of dynamos or automobiles or radium; yet his mind was ready to feel the force of all, though the rays were unborn and the women were dead.

Here opened another totally new education, which promised to be by far the most hazardous of all. The knife-edge along which he must crawl, like Sir Lancelot in the twelfth century, divided two kingdoms of force which had nothing in common but attraction. They were as different as a magnet is from gravitation, supposing one knew what a magnet was, or gravitation, or love. The force of the Virgin was still felt at Lourdes, and seemed to be as potent as X-rays but in America neither Venus nor Virgin ever had value as a force—at most as sentiment. No American had ever truly been afraid of either.

This problem in dynamics gravely perplexed an American historian. The Woman had once been supreme; in France she still seemed potent, not merely as a sentiment, but as a force. Why was she unknown in America? For evidently America was ashamed of her, and she was ashamed of herself, otherwise they would not have strewn fig-leaves so profusely all over her. When she was a true force, she was ignorant of fig-leaves, but the monthly-magazine-made American female had not a feature that would have been recognized by Adam. The trait was notorious, and often humorous, but any one brought up among Puritans knew that sex was a sin. In any previous age, sex was strength. Neither art nor beauty was needed. Every one, even among Puritans, knew that neither Diana of the Ephesians nor any of the Oriental goddesses was worshipped for her beauty. She was goddess because of her force; she was the animated dynamo; she was reproduction—the greatest and most mysterious of all energies; all she needed was to be fecund. Singularly enough, not one of Adams's many schools of education had ever drawn his

attention to the opening lines of Lucretius, though they
were perhaps the finest in all Latin literature, where the
poet invoked Venus exactly as Dante invoked the Virgin:—

"Quae quoniam rerum naturam *sola* gubernas."
[Since thou art, above all, sole mistress of the nature of things]

The Venus of Epicurean philosophy survived in the Virgin
of the Schools:—

> "Donna, sei tanto grande, e tanto vali,
> Che qual vuol grazia, e a te non ricorse,
> Sua disianza vuol volar senz' ali."
> [Lady, thou art so great in all things,
> That he who wishes grace and seeks thee not
> His desires fly upwards without wings.]

All this was to American thought as though it had never
existed. The true American knew something of the facts,
but nothing of the feelings; he read the letter, but he never
felt the law. Before this historical chasm, a mind like that
of Adams felt itself helpless; he turned from the Virgin to
the Dynamo as though he were a Branly coherer. On one
side, at the Louvre and at Chartres, as he knew by the
record of work actually done and still before his eyes, was
the highest energy ever known to man, the creator of four-
fifths of his noblest art, exercising vastly more attraction
over the human mind than all the steam-engines and dynamos ever dreamed of; and yet this energy was unknown
to the American mind. An American Virgin would never
dare command; an American Venus would never dare
exist.

The question, which to any plain American of the nineteenth century seemed as remote as it did to Adams, drew
him almost violently to study, once it was posed; and on
this point Langleys were as useless as though they were
Herbert Spencers or dynamos. The idea survived only as
art. There one turned as naturally as though the artist were
himself a woman. Adams began to ponder, asking himself
whether he knew of any American artist who had ever insisted on the power of sex, as every classic had always done;
but he could think only of Walt Whitman; Bret Harte, as
far as the magazines would let him venture; and one or two
painters, for the flesh-tones. All the rest had used sex for
sentiment, never for force; to them, Eve was a tender

flower, and Herodias an unfeminine horror. American art, like the American language and American education, was as far as possible sexless. Society regarded this victory over sex as its greatest triumph, and the historian readily admitted it, since the moral issue, for the moment, did not concern one who was studying the relations of unmoral force. He cared nothing for the sex of the dynamo until he could measure its energy.

Vaguely seeking a clue, he wandered through the art exhibit, and, in his stroll, stopped almost every day before St. Gaudens's General Sherman, which had been given the central post of honor. St. Gaudens himself was in Paris, putting on the work his usual interminable last touches, and listening to the usual contradictory suggestions of brother sculptors. Of all the American artists who gave to American art whatever life it breathed in the seventies, St. Gaudens was perhaps the most sympathetic, but certainly the most inarticulate. General Grant or Don Cameron had scarcely less instinct of rhetoric than he. All the others—the Hunts, Richardson, John La Farge, Stanford White—were exuberant; only St. Gaudens could never discuss or dilate on an emotion, or suggest artistic arguments for giving to his work the forms that he felt. He never laid down the law, or affected the despot, or became brutalized like Whistler by the brutalities of his world. He required no incense; he was no egoist; his simplicity of thought was excessive; he could not imitate, or give any form but his own to the creations of his hand. No one felt more strongly than he the strength of other men, but the idea that they could affect him never stirred an image in his mind.

This summer his health was poor and his spirits were low. For such a temper, Adams was not the best companion, since his own gaiety was not *folle;* but he risked going now and then to the studio on Mont Parnasse to draw him out for a stroll in the Bois de Boulogne, or dinner as pleased his moods, and in return St. Gaudens sometimes let Adams go about in his company.

Once St. Gaudens took him down to Amiens, with a party of Frenchmen, to see the cathedral. Not until they found themselves actually studying the sculpture of the western portal, did it dawn on Adams's mind that, for his purposes, St. Gaudens on that spot had more interest to him than the cathedral itself. Great men before great monuments express great truths, provided they are not taken too solemnly. Adams never tired of quoting the supreme phrase of his idol Gibbon, before the Gothic cathedrals: "I darted a contemptuous look on the stately monuments of superstition." Even in the footnotes of his history, Gibbon had never inserted a bit of humor more human than this, and one would have paid largely for a photograph of the fat little historian, on the background of Notre Dame of Amiens, trying to persuade his readers—perhaps himself— that he was darting a contemptuous look on the stately monument, for which he felt in fact the respect which every man of his vast study and active mind always feels before objects worthy of it; but besides the humor, one felt also the relation. Gibbon ignored the Virgin, because in 1789 religious monuments were out of fashion. In 1900 his remark sounded fresh and simple as the green fields to ears that had heard a hundred years of other remarks, mostly no more fresh and certainly less simple. Without malice, one might find it more instructive than a whole lecture of Ruskin. One sees what one brings, and at that moment Gibbon brought the French Revolution. Ruskin brought reaction against the Revolution. St. Gaudens had passed beyond all. He liked the stately monuments much more than he liked Gibbon or Ruskin; he loved their dignity; their unity; their scale; their lines; their lights and shadows; their decorative sculpture; but he was even less conscious than they of the force that created it all—the Virgin, the Woman—by whose genius "the stately monuments of superstition" were built, through which she was expressed. He would have seen more meaning in Isis with the cow's horns, at Edfoo, who expressed the same thought. The art remained, but the energy was lost even upon the artist.

Yet in mind and person St. Gaudens was a survival of the 1500; he bore the stamp of the Renaissance, and should have carried an image of the Virgin round his neck, or stuck in his hat, like Louis XI. In mere time he was a lost soul that had strayed by chance into the twentieth century, and forgotten where it came from. He writhed and cursed at his ignorance, much as Adams did at his own, but in the opposite sense. St. Gaudens was a child of Benvenuto Cellini, smothered in an American cradle. Adams was a quintessence of Boston, devoured by curiosity to think like Ben-venuto. St. Gaudens's art was starved from birth, and Adams's instinct was blighted from babyhood. Each had but half of a nature, and when they came together before the Virgin of Amiens they ought both to have felt in her the force that made them one; but it was not so. To Adams she became more than ever a channel of force; to St. Gaudens she remained as before a channel of taste.

For a symbol of power, St. Gaudens instinctively pre-ferred the horse, as was plain in his horse and Victory of the Sherman monument. Doubtless Sherman also felt it so. The attitude was so American that, for at least forty years, Adams had never realized that any other could be in sound taste. How many years had he taken to admit a notion of what Michael Angelo and Rubens were driving at? He could not say; but he knew that only since 1895 had he begun to feel the Virgin or Venus as force, and not every-where even so. At Chartres—perhaps at Lourdes—possibly at Cnidos if one could still find there the divinely naked Aphrodite of Praxiteles—but otherwise one must look for force to the goddesses of Indian mythology. The idea died out long ago in the German and English stock. St. Gaudens at Amiens was hardly less sensitive to the force of the female energy than Matthew Arnold at the Grande Char-treuse. Neither of them felt goddesses as power—only as reflected emotion, human expression, beauty, purity, taste, scarcely even as sympathy. They felt a railway train as power; yet they, and all other artists, constantly complained that the power embodied in a railway train could never be embodied in art. All the steam in the world could not, like the Virgin, build Chartres.

Yet in mechanics, whatever the mechanicians might think, both energies acted as interchangeable forces on man, and by action on man all known force may be meas-ured. Indeed, few men of science measured force in any other way. After once admitting that a straight line was the shortest distance between two points, no serious mathemati-cian cared to deny anything that suited his convenience, and rejected no symbol, unproved or unproveable, that helped him to accomplish work. The symbol was force, as a compass-needle or a triangle was force, as the mechanist might prove by losing it, and nothing could be gained by ignoring their value. Symbol or energy, the Virgin had acted as the greatest force the Western world ever felt, and had drawn man's activities to herself more strongly than any other power, natural or supernatural, had ever done; the historian's business was to follow the track of the energy; to find where it came from and where it went to; its complex source and shifting channels; its values, equivalents, conversions. It could scarcely be more complex than radium; it could hardly be deflected, diverted, polarized, absorbed more perplexingly than other radiant matter. Adams knew nothing about any of them, but as a mathematical problem of influence on human progress, though all were occult, all reacted on his mind, and he rather inclined to think the Virgin easiest to handle.

The pursuit turned out to be long and tortuous, leading at last into the vast forests of scholastic science. From Zeno to Descartes, hand in hand with Thomas Aquinas, Montaigne, and Pascal, one stumbled as stupidly as though one were still a German student of 1860. Only with the instinct of despair could one force one's self into this old thicket of ignorance after having been repulsed at a score of entrances more promising and more popular. Thus far, no path had led anywhere, unless perhaps to an exceedingly modest living. Forty-five years of study had proved to be quite futile for the pursuit of power; one controlled no more force in 1900 than in 1850, although the amount of force controlled by society had enormously increased. The secret of education still hid itself somewhere behind ignorance, and one fumbled over it as feebly as ever. In such labyrinths, the staff is a force almost more necessary than the legs; the pen becomes a sort of blind-man's dog, to keep him from falling into the gutters. The pen works for itself, and acts like a hand, modelling the plastic material over and over again to the form that suits it best. The form is never arbitrary, but is a sort of growth like crystallization, as any artist knows too well; for often the pencil or pen runs into side-paths and shapelessness, loses its relations, stops or is bogged. Then it has to return on its trail, and recover, if it can, its line of force. The result of a year's work depends more on what is struck out than on what is left in; on the sequence of the main lines of thought, than on their play or variety. Compelled once more to lean heavily on this support, Adams covered more thousands of pages with figures as formal as though they were algebra, laboriously striking out, altering, burning, experimenting, until the year had expired, the Exposition had long been closed, and winter drawing to its end before he sailed from Cherbourg, on January 19, 1901 for home.

1907

EDITH WHARTON

(1862–1937)

Born into a social world that provided her with some of the same materials as those of Henry James, Edith Wharton explored her circumstances with a satiric intelligence and a delicate deftness that did not preclude a grimly realistic vision. She was born in New York to a substantial and distinguished family that provided her with private governesses, private education, and frequent trips abroad. In 1885 she married a Boston banker, Edward Wharton. The couple wintered in their New York town house and summered in fashionable Newport and Lenox in the Berkshires. Their annual trips to Europe led to their permanent move to Paris in 1906. On either side of the Atlantic, Mrs. Wharton belonged to the *haut monde,* moving easily and bilingually in American, English, and French aristocracy. It was perhaps inevitable that, at home in society in the New and Old Worlds, she should write novels which are moral explorations of manners and social codes.

Although she did not use her twin perspectives for a contrast of the American and European character as James did, she was, like him, concerned with the limitations of a vanishing aristocracy whose values and customs no longer expressed essential human feelings and whose modes of living became the restrictive enemy of human needs. Perhaps the American quality of her writing lies precisely in this universal theme, for many of her short stories, and more particularly her novels, indicate an awareness of the deterioration of a social image that once had a meaning based in national reality, but that no longer possessed either substance or the homogeneity of living tradition.

Her first volume of short stories, *The Greater Inclination*

(1899), was followed shortly by a long historical novel, The Valley of Decision (1902). Serious recognition of her exquisite craftsmanship and sharp observations came to her with The Descent of Man and Other Stories (1904) and The House of Mirth (1905), generally regarded as her best novel of manners. Throughout her life she continued to produce distinguished fiction: Ethan Frome appeared in 1911, The Custom of the Country in 1913, Xingu and Other Stories in 1916, and The Age of Innocence in 1920.

Her short stories have a greater variety of circumstances than her novels, ranging from the medieval to the supernatural to the sociological. She pointed out that her stories centered on situations that, in the brevity of the form, provided for the swift drama of plot. Her novels, on the other hand, unwound from characters, whose development demanded the slower, more detailed, and larger form. Always, she insisted, the novelist had to preselect only those circumstances which would reveal character, so that the end of the novel would be implicit in the events of the beginning. She deplored the naturalists and identified herself as a realist, emphasizing that the events of a novel must grow from the probability of choice a character would make once the purpose and identity of that character were defined in the author's mind.

Mrs. Wharton's critical theories are most explicitly given in The Writing of Fiction (1925) and in "The Great American Novel" (Yale Review, XVI [1927]), "Visibility in Fiction" (Yale Review, XVII [1929]), "The Writing of Ethan Frome" (Colophon, III [1932]), and "Confessions of a Novelist" (Atlantic Monthly, CLI [1933]). In four novelettes, published as Old New York in 1924, she attempted to reconstruct the New York society of the nineteenth century: False Dawn concentrated on the 1840's, The Old Maid on the 1850's, The Spark on the 1860's, and New Year's Day on the 1870's. Although some of the settings are placed before her own lifetime, the tetralogy is representative of Mrs. Wharton's theme and method and constitutes her last important fictional exploration of society. Many aspects of her own life are furnished in her autobiography, A Backward Glance, published in 1934.

Among her other books are Sanctuary (1903); The Fruit of the Tree (1907); The Hermit and the Wild Woman and Other Stories (1908); Tales of Men and Ghosts (1910); Summer (1917); The Glimpses of the Moon (1922); Here and Beyond (1926); Twilight Sleep (1927); Hudson River Bracketed (1929);

The Gods Arrive (1932); *Human Nature* (1933); *Ghosts* (1937); and *The Buccaneers* (1938).

There is no collected edition of Edith Wharton's works. Accounts of the woman and her writings are to be found in C. Waldstein, "Social Ideals," *North American Review*, CLXXXII (1906); H. D. Sedgwick, *The New American Type* (1908); H. James, *Notes on Novelists* (1914); K. F. Gerould, *Edith Wharton* (1922); R. M. Lovett, *Edith Wharton* (1925); L. M. Melish, *A Bibliography of the Collected Writings of Edith Wharton* (1927); L. R. Davis, *A Bibliography of the Writings of Edith Wharton* (1933); E. K. Brown, *Edith Wharton* (1935); Q. D. Leavis, "Henry James's Heiress: The Importance of Edith Wharton," *Scrutiny*, VII (1938); E. Wilson, "Justice to Edith Wharton," *New Republic*, XCV (1938); M. E. Monroe, *The Novel and Society* (1941); P. Lubbock, *Portrait of Edith Wharton* (1947); A. H. Quinn, ed., *An Edith Wharton Treasury* (1950); B. Nevius, *Edith Wharton* (1953); M. Bell, "Edith Wharton and Henry James: The Literary Relation," *PMLA*, LXXIV (1959); M. Lyde, *Edith Wharton* (1959); I. Howe, ed., *Edith Wharton: A Collection of Critical Essays* (1962); P. R. Plante, "The Critical Reception of Edith Wharton's Fiction in America with an Annotated . . . Bibliography of Wharton Criticism from 1900 to 1961," *Dissertation Abstracts* (1962); J. W. Tuttleton, "Edith Wharton and the Novel of Manners," *Dissertation Abstracts* (1964); M. Bell, *Edith Wharton and Henry James* (1965); G. Kellogg, *The Two Lives of Edith Wharton* (1965); and O. Coolidge, *Edith Wharton, 1862–1937* (1966).

The Other Two

I

Waythorn, on the drawing-room hearth, waited for his wife to come down to dinner.

It was their first night under his own roof, and he was surprised at his thrill of boyish agitation. He was not so old, to be sure—his glass gave him little more than the five-and-thirty years to which his wife confessed—but he had fancied himself already in the temperate zone; yet here he was listening for her step with a tender sense of all it symbolized, with some old trail of verse about the garlanded nuptial door-posts floating through his enjoyment of the pleasant room and the good dinner just beyond it.

They had been hastily recalled from their honeymoon by the illness of Lily Haskett, the child of Mrs. Waythorn's first marriage. The little girl, at Waythorn's desire, had been transferred to his house on the day of her mother's wedding, and the doctor, on their arrival, broke the news that she was ill with typhoid, but declared that all the symptoms were favorable. Lily could show twelve years of unblemished health, and the case promised to be a light one. The nurse spoke as reassuringly, and after a moment of alarm Mrs. Waythorn had adjusted herself to the situation. She was very fond of Lily—her affection for the child had perhaps been her decisive charm in Waythorn's eyes—but she had the perfectly balanced nerves which her little girl had inherited, and no woman ever wasted less tissue in unproductive worry. Waythorn was therefore quite prepared to see her come in presently, a little late because of a last look at Lily, but as serene and well-appointed as if her good-night kiss had been laid on the brow of health. Her composure was restful to him; it acted as ballast to his somewhat unstable sensibilities. As he pictured her bending over the child's bed he thought how soothing her presence must be in illness: her very step would prognosticate recovery.

His own life had been a gray one, from temperament rather than circumstance, and he had been drawn to her by the unperturbed gaiety which kept her fresh and elastic at an age when most women's activities are growing either slack or febrile. He knew what was said about her; for, popular as she was, there had always been a faint undercurrent of detraction. When she had appeared in New York, nine or ten years earlier, as the pretty Mrs. Haskett whom Gus Varick had unearthed somewhere—was it in Pittsburgh or Utica?—society, while promptly accepting her, had reserved the right to cast a doubt on its own indiscrimination. Enquiry, however, established her undoubted connection with a socially reigning family, and explained her recent divorce as the natural result of a runaway match at seventeen; and as nothing was known of Mr. Haskett it was easy to believe the worst of him.

Alice Haskett's remarriage with Gus Varick was a passport to the set whose recognition she coveted, and for a few years the Varicks were the most popular couple in town. Unfortunately the alliance was brief and stormy, and this time the husband had his champions. Still, even Varick's stanchest supporters admitted that he was not meant for matrimony, and Mrs. Varick's grievances were of a nature to bear the inspection of the New York courts.

A New York divorce is in itself a diploma of virtue, and in the semi-widowhood of this second separation Mrs. Varick took on an air of sanctity, and was allowed to confide her wrongs to some of the most scrupulous ears in town. But when it was known that she was to marry Waythorn there was a momentary reaction. Her best friends would have preferred to see her remain in the rôle of the injured wife, which was as becoming to her as crape to a rosy complexion. True, a decent time had elapsed, and it was not even suggested that Waythorn had supplanted his predecessor. People shook their heads over him, however, and one grudging friend, to whom he affirmed that he took the step with his eyes open, replied oracularly: "Yes—and with your ears shut."

Waythorn could afford to smile at these innuendoes. In the Wall Street phrase, he had "discounted" them. He knew that society has not yet adapted itself to the consequences of divorce, and that till the adaptation takes place every woman who uses the freedom the law accords her must be her own social justification. Waythorn had an amused confidence in his wife's ability to justify herself. His expectations were fulfilled, and before the wedding took place Alice Varick's group had rallied openly to her support. She took it all imperturbably: she had a way of surmounting obstacles without seeming to be aware of them, and Waythorn looked back with wonder at the trivialities over which he had worn his nerves thin. He had the sense of having found refuge in a richer, warmer nature than his own, and his satisfaction, at the moment, was humorously summed up in the thought that his wife, when she had done all she could for Lily, would not be ashamed to come down and enjoy a good dinner.

The anticipation of such enjoyment was not, however, the sentiment expressed by Mrs. Waythorn's charming face when she presently joined him. Though she had put on her most engaging teagown she had neglected to assume the smile that went with it, and Waythorn thought he had never seen her look so nearly worried.

"What is it?" he asked. "Is anything wrong with Lily?"

"No; I've just been in and she's still sleeping." Mrs. Waythorn hesitated. "But something tiresome has happened."

He had taken her two hands, and now perceived that he was crushing a paper between them.

"This letter?"

"Yes—Mr. Haskett has written—I mean his lawyer has written."

Waythorn felt himself flush uncomfortably. He dropped his wife's hands.

"What about?"

"About seeing Lily. You know the courts—"

"Yes, yes," he interrupted nervously.

Nothing was known about Haskett in New York. He was vaguely supposed to have remained in the outer darkness from which his wife had been rescued, and Waythorn was one of the few who were aware that he had given up his business in Utica and followed her to New York in order to be near his little girl. In the days of his wooing, Waythorn had often met Lily on the doorstep, rosy and smiling, on her way "to see papa."

"I am so sorry," Mrs. Waythorn murmured.

He roused himself. "What does he want?"

"He wants to see her. You know she goes to him once a week."

"Well—he doesn't expect her to go to him now, does he?"

"No—he has heard of her illness; but he expects to come here."

"Here?"

Mrs. Waythorn reddened under his gaze. They looked away from each other.

"I'm afraid he has the right. . . . You'll see. . . ." She made a proffer of the letter.

Waythorn moved away with a gesture of refusal. He stood staring about the softly lighted room, which a moment before had seemed so full of bridal intimacy.

"I'm so sorry," she repeated. "If Lily could have been moved—"

"That's out of the question," he returned impatiently.

"I suppose so."

Her lip was beginning to tremble, and he felt himself a brute.

"He must come, of course," he said. "When is—his day?"

"I'm afraid—to-morrow."

"Very well. Send a note in the morning."

The butler entered to announce dinner.

Waythorn turned to his wife. "Come—you must be tired.

It's beastly, but try to forget about it," he said, drawing her hand through his arm.

"You're so good, dear. I'll try," she whispered back.

Her face cleared at once, and as she looked at him across the flowers, between the rosy candle-shades, he saw her lips waver back into a smile.

"How pretty everything is!" she sighed luxuriously.

He turned to the butler. "The champagne at once, please. Mrs. Waythorn is tired."

In a moment or two their eyes met above the sparkling glasses. Her own were quite clear and untroubled: he saw that she had obeyed his injunction and forgotten.

II

Waythorn, the next morning, went down town earlier than usual. Haskett was not likely to come till the afternoon, but the instinct of flight drove him forth. He meant to stay away all day—he had thoughts of dining at his club. As his door closed behind him he reflected that before he opened it again it would have admitted another man who had as much right to enter it as himself, and the thought filled him with a physical repugnance.

He caught the "elevated" at the employees' hour, and found himself crushed between two layers of pendulous humanity. At Eighth Street the man facing him wriggled out, and another took his place. Waythorn glanced up and saw that it was Gus Varick. The men were so close together that it was impossible to ignore the smile of recognition on Varick's handsome overblown face. And after all—why not? They had always been on good terms, and Varick had been divorced before Waythorn's attentions to his wife began. The two exchanged a word on the perennial grievance of the congested trains, and when a seat at their side was miraculously left empty the instinct of self-preservation made Waythorn slip into it after Varick.

The latter drew the stout man's breath of relief. "Lord— I was beginning to feel like a pressed flower." He leaned back, looking unconcernedly at Waythorn. "Sorry to hear that Sellers is knocked out again."

"Sellers?" echoed Waythorn, starting at his partner's name.

Varick looked surprised. "You didn't know he was laid up with the gout?"

"No, I've been away—I only got back last night." Waythorn felt himself reddening in anticipation of the other's smile.

"Ah—yes; to be sure. And Seller's attack came on two days ago. I'm afraid he's pretty bad. Very awkward for me, as it happens, because he was just putting through a rather important thing for me."

"Ah?" Waythorn wondered vaguely since when Varick had been dealing in "important things." Hitherto he had dabbled only in the shallow pools of speculation, with which Waythorn's office did not usually concern itself.

It occurred to him that Varick might be talking at random, to relieve the strain of their propinquity. That strain was becoming momentarily more apparent to Waythorn, and when, at Cortlandt Street, he caught sight of an acquaintance and had a sudden vision of the picture he and Varick must present to an initiated eye, he jumped up with a muttered excuse.

"I hope you'll find Sellers better," said Varick civilly, and he stammered back: "If I can be of any use to you—" and let the departing crowd sweep him to the platform.

At his office he heard that Sellers was in fact ill with the gout, and would probably not be able to leave the house for some weeks.

"I'm sorry it should have happened so, Mr. Waythorn," the senior clerk said with affable significance. "Mr. Sellers was very much upset at the idea of giving you such a lot of extra work just now."

"Oh, that's no matter," said Waythorn hastily. He secretly welcomed the pressure of additional business, and was glad to think that, when the day's work was over, he would have to call at his partner's on the way home.

He was late for luncheon, and turned in at the nearest restaurant instead of going to his club. The place was full, and the waiter hurried him to the back of the room to capture the only vacant table. In the cloud of cigar-smoke Waythorn did not at once distinguish his neighbors; but presently, looking about him, he saw Varick seated a few feet off. This time, luckily, they were too far apart for conversation, and Varick, who faced another way, had probably not even seen him; but there was an irony in their renewed nearness.

Varick was said to be fond of good living, and as Waythorn sat despatching his hurried luncheon he looked across half enviously at the other's leisurely degustation of his meal. When Waythorn first saw him he had been helping himself with critical deliberation to a bit of Camembert at the ideal point of liquefaction, and now, the cheese removed, he was just pouring his *café double* from its little two-storied earthen pot. He poured slowly, his ruddy profile bent above the task, and one beringed white hand steadying the lid of the coffee-pot; then he stretched his other hand to the decanter of cognac at his elbow, filled a liqueur-glass, took a tentative sip, and poured the brandy into his coffee-cup.

Waythorn watched him in a kind of fascination. What was he thinking of—only of the flavor of the coffee and the liqueur? Had the morning's meeting left no more trace in his thoughts than on his face? Had his wife so completely passed out of his life that even this odd encounter with her present husband, within a week after her remarriage, was no more than an incident in his day? And as Waythorn mused, another idea struck him: had Haskett ever met Varick as Varick and he had just met? The recollection of Haskett perturbed him, and he rose and left the restaurant, taking a circuitous way out to escape the placid irony of Varick's nod.

It was after seven when Waythorn reached home. He thought the footman who opened the door looked at him oddly.

"How is Miss Lily?" he asked in haste.

"Doing very well, sir. A gentleman—"

"Tell Barlow to put off dinner for half an hour," Waythorn cut him off, hurrying upstairs.

He went straight to his room and dressed without seeing his wife. When he reached the drawing-room she was there, fresh and radiant. Lily's day had been good; the doctor was not coming back that evening.

At dinner Waythorn told her of Sellers' illness and of the resulting complications. She listened sympathetically, adjuring him not to let himself be overworked, and asking vague feminine questions about the routine of the office. Then she gave him the chronicle of Lily's day; quoted the nurse and doctor, and told him who had called to inquire. He had never seen her more serene and unruffled. It struck him, with a curious pang, that she was very happy in being with him, so happy that she found a childish pleasure in rehearsing the trivial incidents of her day.

After dinner they went to the library, and the servant put the coffee and liqueurs on a low table before her and left the room. She looked singularly soft and girlish in her rosy pale dress, against the dark leather of one of his bachelor armchairs. A day earlier the contrast would have charmed him.

He turned away now, choosing a cigar with affected deliberation.

"Did Haskett come?" he asked, with his back to her.

"Oh, yes—he came."

"You didn't see him, of course?"

She hesitated a moment. "I let the nurse see him."

That was all. There was nothing more to ask. He swung round toward her, applying a match to his cigar. Well, the thing was over for a week, at any rate. He would try not to think of it. She looked up at him, a trifle rosier than usual, with a smile in her eyes.

"Ready for your coffee, dear?"

He leaned against the mantelpiece, watching her as she lifted the coffee-pot. The lamplight struck a gleam from her bracelets and tipped her soft hair with brightness. How light and slender she was, and how each gesture flowed into the next! She seemed a creature all compact of harmonies. As the thought of Haskett receded, Waythorn felt himself yielding again to the joy of possessorship. They were his, those white hands with their flitting motions, his the light haze of hair, the lips and eyes. . . .

She set down the coffee-pot, and reaching for the decanter of cognac, measured off a liqueur-glass and poured it into his cup.

Waythorn uttered a sudden exclamation.

"What is the matter?" she said, startled.

"Nothing; only—I don't take cognac in my coffee."

"Oh, how stupid of me," she cried.

Their eyes met, and she blushed a sudden agonized red.

III

Ten days later, Mr. Sellers, still house-bound, asked Waythorn to call on his way down town.

The senior partner, with his swaddled foot propped up

by the fire, greeted his associate with an air of embarrassment.

"I'm sorry, my dear fellow; I've got to ask you to do an awkward thing for me."

Waythorn waited, and the other went on, after a pause apparently given to the arrangement of his phrases: "The fact is, when I was knocked out I had just gone into a rather complicated piece of business for—Gus Varick."

"Well?" said Waythorn, with an attempt to put him at his ease.

"Well—it's this way: Varick came to me the day before my attack. He had evidently had an inside tip from somebody, and had made about a hundred thousand. He came to me for advice, and I suggested his going in with Vanderlyn."

"Oh, the deuce!" Waythorn exclaimed. He saw in a flash what had happened. The investment was an alluring one, but required negotiation. He listened quietly while Sellers put the case before him, and, the statement ended, he said: "You think I ought to see Varick?"

"I'm afraid I can't as yet. The doctor is obdurate. And this thing can't wait. I hate to ask you, but no one else in the office knows the ins and outs of it."

Waythorn stood silent. He did not care a farthing for the success of Varick's venture, but the honor of the office was to be considered, and he could hardly refuse to oblige his partner.

"Very well," he said, "I'll do it."

That afternoon, apprised by telephone, Varick called at the office. Waythorn, waiting in his private room, wondered what the others thought of it. The newspapers, at the time of Mrs. Waythorn's marriage, had acquainted their readers with every detail of her previous matrimonial ventures, and Waythorn could fancy the clerks smiling behind Varick's back as he was ushered in.

Varick bore himself admirably. He was easy without being undignified, and Waythorn was conscious of cutting a much less impressive figure. Varick had no experience of business, and the talk prolonged itself for nearly an hour while Waythorn set forth with scrupulous precision the details of the proposed transaction.

"I'm awfully obliged to you," Varick said as he rose.

"The fact is I'm not used to having much money to look after, and I don't want to make an ass of myself—" He smiled, and Waythorn could not help noticing that there was something pleasant about his smile. "It feels uncommonly queer to have enough cash to pay one's bills. I'd have sold my soul for it a few years ago!"

Waythorn winced at the allusion. He had heard it rumored that a lack of funds had been one of the determining causes of the Varick separation, but it did not occur to him that Varick's words were intentional. It seemed more likely that the desire to keep clear of embarrassing topics had fatally drawn him into one. Waythorn did not wish to be outdone in civility.

"We'll do the best we can for you," he said. "I think this is a good thing you're in."

"Oh, I'm sure it's immense. It's awfully good of you—" Varick broke off, embarrassed. "I suppose the thing's settled now—but if—"

"If anything happens before Sellers is about, I'll see you again," said Waythorn quietly. He was glad, in the end, to appear the more self-possessed of the two.

The course of Lily's illness ran smooth, and as the days passed Waythorn grew used to the idea of Haskett's weekly visit. The first time the day came round, he stayed out late, and questioned his wife as to the visit on his return. She replied at once that Haskett had merely seen the nurse downstairs, as the doctor did not wish any one in the child's sick-room till after the crisis.

The following week Waythorn was again conscious of the recurrence of the day, but had forgotten it by the time he came home to dinner. The crisis of the disease came a few days later, with a rapid decline of fever, and the little girl was pronounced out of danger. In the rejoicing which ensued the thought of Haskett passed out of Waythorn's mind, and one afternoon, letting himself into the house with a latch-key, he went straight to his library without noticing a shabby hat and umbrella in the hall.

In the library he found a small effaced-looking man with a thinnish gray beard sitting on the edge of a chair. The stranger might have been a piano-tuner, or one of those mysteriously efficient persons who are summoned in emergencies to adjust some detail of the domestic machinery. He blinked at Waythorn through a pair of gold-rimmed spectacles and said mildly: "Mr. Waythorn, I presume? I am Lily's father."

Waythorn flushed. "Oh—" he stammered uncomfortably. He broke off, disliking to appear rude. Inwardly he was trying to adjust the actual Haskett to the image of him projected by his wife's reminiscences. Waythorn had been allowed to infer that Alice's first husband was a brute.

"I am sorry to intrude," said Haskett, with his over-the-counter politeness.

"Don't mention it," returned Waythorn, collecting himself. "I suppose the nurse has been told?"

"I presume so. I can wait," said Haskett. He had a resigned way of speaking, as though life had worn down his natural powers of resistance.

Waythorn stood on the threshold, nervously pulling off his gloves.

"I'm sorry you've been detained. I will send for the nurse," he said; and as he opened the door he added with an effort: "I'm glad we can give you a good report of Lily." He winced as the *we* slipped out, but Haskett seemed not to notice it.

"Thank you, Mr. Waythorn. It's been an anxious time for me."

"Ah, well, that's past. Soon she'll be able to go to you." Waythorn nodded and passed out.

In his own room he flung himself down with a groan. He hated the womanish sensibility which made him suffer so acutely from the grotesque chances of life. He had known when he married that his wife's former husbands were both living, and that amid the multiplied contacts of modern existence there were a thousand chances to one that he would run against one or the other, yet he found himself as much disturbed by his brief encounter with Haskett as though the law had not obligingly removed all difficulties in the way of their meeting.

Waythorn sprang up and began to pace the room nervously. He had not suffered half as much from his two meetings with Varick. It was Haskett's presence in his own house that made the situation so intolerable. He stood still, hearing steps in the passage.

"This way, please," he heard the nurse say. Haskett

was being taken upstairs, then: not a corner of the house but was open to him. Waythorn dropped into another chair, staring vaguely ahead of him. On his dressing-table stood a photograph of Alice, taken when he had first known her. She was Alice Varick then—how fine and exquisite he had thought her! Those were Varick's pearls about her neck. At Waythorn's instance they had been returned before her marriage. Had Haskett ever given her any trinkets—and what had become of them, Waythorn wondered? He realized suddenly that he knew very little of Haskett's past or present situation; but from the man's appearance and manner of speech he could reconstruct with curious precision the surroundings of Alice's first marriage. And it startled him to think that she had, in the background of her life, a phase of existence so different from anything with which he had connected her. Varick, whatever his faults, was a gentleman, in the conventional, traditional sense of the term: the sense which at that moment seemed, oddly enough, to have most meaning to Waythorn. He and Varick had the same social habits, spoke the same language, understood the same allusions. But this other man . . . it was grotesquely uppermost in Waythorn's mind that Haskett had worn a made-up tie attached with an elastic. Why should that ridiculous detail symbolize the whole man? Waythorn was exasperated by his own paltriness, but the fact of the tie expanded, forced itself on him, became as it were the key to Alice's past. He could see her, as Mrs. Haskett, sitting in a "front parlor" furnished in plush, with a pianola, and a copy of *Ben Hur* on the center-table. He could see her going to the theater with Haskett—or perhaps even to a "Church Sociable"— she in a "picture hat" and Haskett in a black frock-coat, a little creased, with the made-up tie on an elastic. On the way home they would stop and look at the illuminated shop-windows, lingering over the photographs of New York actresses. On Sunday afternoons Haskett would take her for a walk, pushing Lily ahead of them in a white enameled perambulator, and Waythorn had a vision of the people they would stop and talk to. He could fancy how pretty Alice must have looked, in a dress adroitly constructed from the hints of a New York fashion-paper, and how she must have looked down on the other women chafing at her life, and secretly feeling that she belonged in a bigger place.

For the moment his foremost thought was one of wonder at the way in which she had shed the phase of existence which her marriage with Haskett implied. It was as if her whole aspect, every gesture, every inflection, every allusion, were a studied negation of that period of her life. If she had denied being married to Haskett she could hardly have stood more convicted of duplicity than in this obliteration of the self which had been his wife.

Waythorn started up, checking himself in the analysis of her motives. What right had he to create a fantastic effigy of her and then pass judgment on it? She had spoken vaguely of her first marriage as unhappy, had hinted, with becoming reticence, that Haskett had wrought havoc among her young illusions. . . . It was a pity for Waythorn's peace of mind that Haskett's very inoffensiveness shed a new light on the nature of those illusions. A man would rather think that his wife has been brutalized by her first husband than that the process has been reversed.

IV

"Mr. Waythorn, I don't like that French governess of Lily's."

Haskett, subdued and apologetic, stood before Waythorn in the library, revolving his shabby hat in his hand.

Waythorn, surprised in his armchair over the evening paper, stared back perplexedly at his visitor.

"You'll excuse my asking to see you," Haskett continued. "But this is my last visit, and I thought if I could have a word with you it would be a better way than writing to Mrs. Waythorn's lawyer."

Waythorn rose uneasily. He did not like the French governess either; but that was irrelevant.

"I am not so sure of that," he returned stiffly; "but since you wish it I will give your message to—my wife." He always hesitated over the possessive pronoun in addressing Haskett.

The latter sighed. "I don't know as that will help much. She didn't like it when I spoke to her."

Waythorn turned red. "When did you see her?" he asked.

"Not since the first day I came to see Lily—right after

she was taken sick. I remarked to her then that I didn't like the governess."

Waythorn made no answer. He remembered distinctly that, after that first visit, he had asked his wife if she had seen Haskett. She had lied to him then, but she had respected his wishes since; and the incident cast a curious light on her character. He was sure she would not have seen Haskett that first day if she had divined that Waythorn would object, and the fact that she did not divine it was almost as disagreeable to the latter as the discovery that she had lied to him.

"I don't like the woman," Haskett was repeating with mild persistency. "She ain't straight, Mr. Waythorn—she'll teach the child to be underhand. I've noticed a change in Lily—she's too anxious to please—and she don't always tell the truth. She used to be the straightest child, Mr. Waythorn—" He broke off, his voice a little thick. "Not but what I want her to have a stylish education," he ended.

Waythorn was touched. "I'm sorry, Mr. Haskett; but frankly, I don't quite see what I can do."

Haskett hesitated. Then he laid his hat on the table, and advanced to the hearth-rug, on which Waythorn was standing. There was nothing aggressive in his manner, but he had the solemnity of a timid man resolved on a decisive measure.

"There's just one thing you can do, Mr. Waythorn," he said. "You can remind Mrs. Waythorn that, by the decree of the courts, I am entitled to have a voice in Lily's bringing up." He paused, and went on more deprecatingly: "I'm not the kind to talk about enforcing my rights, Mr. Waythorn. I don't know as I think a man is entitled to rights he hasn't known how to hold on to; but this business of the child is different. I've never let go there—and I never mean to."

The scene left Waythorn deeply shaken. Shamefacedly, in indirect ways, he had been finding out about Haskett; and all that he had learned was favorable. The little man, in order to be near his daughter, had sold out his share in a profitable business in Utica, and accepted a modest clerkship in a New York manufacturing house. He boarded in a shabby street and had few acquaintances. His passion for

Lily filled his life. Waythorn felt that this exploration of Haskett was like groping about with a dark-lantern in his wife's past; but he saw now that there were recesses his lantern had not explored. He had never enquired into the exact circumstances of his wife's first matrimonial rupture. On the surface all had been fair. It was she who had obtained the divorce, and the court had given her the child. But Waythorn knew how many ambiguities such a verdict might cover. The mere fact that Haskett retained a right over his daughter implied an unsuspected compromise. Waythorn was an idealist. He always refused to recognize unpleasant contingencies till he found himself confronted with them, and then he saw them followed by a special train of consequences. His next days were thus haunted, and he determined to try to lay the ghosts by conjuring them up in his wife's presence.

When he repeated Haskett's request a flame of anger passed over her face; but she subdued it instantly and spoke with a slight quiver of outraged motherhood.

"It is very ungentlemanly of him," she said.

The word grated on Waythorn. "That is neither here nor there. It's a bare question of rights."

She murmured: "It's not as if he could ever be a help to Lily—"

Waythorn flushed. This was even less to his taste. "The question is," he repeated, "what authority has he over her?"

She looked downward, twisting herself a little in her seat. "I am willing to see him—I thought you objected," she faltered.

In a flash he understood that she knew the extent of Haskett's claims. Perhaps it was not the first time she had resisted them.

"My objecting has nothing to do with it," he said coldly; "if Haskett has a right to be consulted you must consult him."

She burst into tears, and he saw that she expected him to regard her as a victim.

Haskett did not abuse his rights. Waythorn had felt miserably sure that he would not. But the governess was dismissed, and from time to time the little man demanded an interview with Alice. After the first outburst she accepted the situation with her usual adaptability. Haskett had once reminded Waythorn of the piano-tuner, and Mrs. Waythorn, after a month or two, appeared to class him with that domestic familiar. Waythorn could not but respect the father's tenacity. At first he had tried to cultivate the suspicion that Haskett might be "up to" something, that he had an object in securing a foothold in the house. But in his heart Waythorn was sure of Haskett's single-mindedness; he even guessed in the latter a mild contempt for such advantages as his relation with the Waythorns might offer. Haskett's sincerity of purpose made him invulnerable, and his successor had to accept him as a lien on the property.

Mr. Sellers was sent to Europe to recover from his gout, and Varick's affairs hung on Waythorn's hands. The negotiations were prolonged and complicated; they necessitated frequent conferences between the two men, and the interests of the firm forbade Waythorn's suggesting that his client should transfer his business to another office.

Varick appeared well in the transaction. In moments of relaxation his coarse streak appeared, and Waythorn dreaded his geniality; but in the office he was concise and clear-headed, with a flattering deference to Waythorn's judgment. Their business relations being so affably established, it would have been absurd for the two men to ignore each other in society. The first time they met in a drawing-room, Varick took up their intercourse in the same easy key, and his hostess's grateful glance obliged Waythorn to respond to it. After that they ran across each other frequently, and one evening at a ball Waythorn, wandering through the remoter rooms, came upon Varick seated beside his wife. She colored a little, and faltered in what she was saying; but Varick nodded to Waythorn without rising, and the latter strolled on.

In the carriage, on the way home, he broke out nervously: "I didn't know you spoke to Varick."

Her voice trembled a little. "It's the first time—he happened to be standing near me; I didn't know what to do. It's so awkward, meeting everywhere—and he said you had been very kind about some business."

"That's different," said Waythorn.

She paused a moment. "I'll do just as you wish," she

returned pliantly. "I thought it would be less awkward to speak to him when we meet."

Her pliancy was beginning to sicken him. Had she really no will of her own—no theory about her relation to these men? She had accepted Haskett—did she mean to accept Varick? It was "less awkward," as she had said, and her instinct was to evade difficulties or to circumvent them. With sudden vividness Waythorn saw how the instinct had developed. She was "as easy as an old shoe"—a shoe that too many feet had worn. Her elasticity was the result of tension in too many different directions. Alice Haskett—Alice Varick—Alice Waythorn—she had been each in turn, and had left hanging to each name a little of her privacy, a little of her personality, a little of the inmost self where the unknown god abides.

"Yes—it's better to speak to Varick," said Waythorn wearily.

V

The winter wore on, and society took advantage of the Waythorns' acceptance of Varick. Harassed hostesses were grateful to them for bridging over a social difficulty, and Mrs. Waythorn was held up as a miracle of good taste. Some experimental spirits could not resist the diversion of throwing Varick and his former wife together, and there were those who thought he found a zest in the propinquity. But Mrs. Waythorn's conduct remained irreproachable. She neither avoided Varick nor sought him out. Even Waythorn could not but admit that she had discovered the solution of the newest social problem.

He had married her without giving much thought to that problem. He had fancied that a woman can shed her past like a man. But now he saw that Alice was bound to hers both by the circumstances which forced her into continued relation with it, and by the traces it had left on her nature. With grim irony Waythorn compared himself to a member of a syndicate. He held so many shares in his wife's personality and his predecessors were his partners in the business. If there had been any element of passion in the transaction he would have felt less deteriorated by it. The fact that Alice took her change of husbands like a change of weather reduced the situation to mediocrity. He could have forgiven her for blunders, for excesses; for resisting Haskett, for yielding to Varick; for anything but her acquiescence and her tact. She reminded him of a juggler tossing knives; but the knives were blunt and she knew they would never cut her.

And then, gradually, habit formed a protecting surface for his sensibilities. If he paid for each day's comfort with the small change of his illusions, he grew daily to value the comfort more and set less store upon the coin. He had drifted into a dulling propinquity with Haskett and Varick and he took refuge in the cheap revenge of satirizing the situation. He even began to reckon up the advantages which accrued from it, to ask himself if it were not better to own a third of a wife who knew how to make a man happy than a whole one who had lacked opportunity to acquire the art. For it *was* an art, and made up, like all others, of concessions, eliminations and embellishments; of lights judiciously thrown and shadows skilfully softened. His wife knew exactly how to manage the lights, and he knew exactly to what training she owed her skill. He even tried to trace the source of his obligations, to discriminate between the influences which had combined to produce his domestic happiness: he perceived that Haskett's commonness had made Alice worship good breeding, while Varick's liberal construction of the marriage bond had taught her to value the conjugal virtues; so that he was directly indebted to his predecessors for the devotion which made his life easy if not inspiring.

From this phase he passed into that of complete acceptance. He ceased to satirize himself because time dulled the irony of the situation and the joke lost its humor with its sting. Even the sight of Haskett's hat on the hall table had ceased to touch the springs of epigram. The hat was often seen there now, for it had been decided that it was better for Lily's father to visit her than for the little girl to go to his boarding-house. Waythorn, having acquiesced in this arrangement, had been surprised to find how little difference it made. Haskett was never obtrusive, and the few visitors who met him on the stairs were unaware of his identity. Waythorn did not know how often he saw Alice, but with himself Haskett was seldom in contact.

One afternoon, however, he learned on entering that Lily's father was waiting to see him. In the library he found

Haskett occupying a chair in his usual provisional way. Waythorn always felt grateful to him for not leaning back.

"I hope you'll excuse me, Mr. Waythorn," he said rising. "I wanted to see Mrs. Waythorn about Lily, and your man asked me to wait here till she came in."

"Of course," said Waythorn, remembering that a sudden leak had that morning given over the drawing-room to the plumbers.

He opened his cigar-case and held it out to his visitor, and Haskett's acceptance seemed to mark a fresh stage in their intercourse. The spring evening was chilly, and Waythorn invited his guest to draw up his chair to the fire. He meant to find an excuse to leave Haskett in a moment; but he was tired and cold, and after all the little man no longer jarred on him.

The two were enclosed in the intimacy of their blended cigar-smoke when the door opened and Varick walked into the room. Waythorn rose abruptly. It was the first time that Varick had come to the house, and the surprise of seeing him, combined with the singular inopportuneness of his arrival, gave a new edge to Waythorn's blunted sensibilities. He stared at his visitor without speaking.

Varick seemed too preoccupied to notice his host's embarrassment.

"My dear fellow," he exclaimed in his most expansive tone, "I must apologize for tumbling in on you in this way, but I was too late to catch you down town, and so I thought—"

He stopped short, catching sight of Haskett, and his sanguine colour deepened to a flush which spread vividly under his scant blond hair. But in a moment he recovered himself and nodded slightly. Haskett returned the bow in silence, and Waythorn was still groping for speech when the footman came in carrying a tea-table.

The intrusion offered a welcome vent to Waythorn's nerves, "What the deuce are you bringing this here for?" he said sharply.

"I beg your pardon, sir, but the plumbers are still in the drawing-room, and Mrs. Waythorn said she would have tea in the library." The footman's perfectly respectful tone implied a reflection on Waythorn's reasonableness.

"Oh, very well," said the latter resignedly, and the footman proceeded to open the folding tea-table and set out its complicated appointments. While this interminable process continued the three men stood motionless, watching it with a fascinated stare, till Waythorn, to break the silence, said to Varick: "Won't you have a cigar?"

He held out the case he had just tendered to Haskett, and Varick helped himself with a smile. Waythorn looked about for a match, and finding none, proffered a light from his own cigar. Haskett, in the background, held his ground mildly, examining his cigar-tip now and then, and stepping forward at the right moment to knock its ashes into the fire.

The footman at last withdrew, and Varick immediately began: "If I could just say half a word to you about this business—"

"Certainly," stammered Waythorn; "in the dining-room—"

But as he placed his hand on the door it opened from without, and his wife appeared on the threshold.

She came in fresh and smiling, in her street dress and hat, shedding a fragrance from the boa which she loosened in advancing.

"Shall we have tea in here, dear?" she began; and then she caught sight of Varick. Her smile deepened, veiling a slight tremor of surprise.

"Why, how do you do?" she said with a distinct note of pleasure.

As she shook hands with Varick she saw Haskett standing behind him. Her smile faded for a moment, but she recalled it quickly, with a scarcely perceptible sideglance at Waythorn.

"How do you do, Mr. Haskett?" she said, and shook hands with him a shade less cordially.

The three men stood awkwardly before her, till Varick, always the most self-possessed, dashed into an explanatory phrase.

"We—I had to see Waythorn a moment on business," he stammered, brick-red from chin to nape.

Haskett stepped forward with his air of mild obstinacy. "I am sorry to intrude; but you appointed five o'clock—" he directed his resigned glance to the time-piece on the mantel.

She swept aside their embarrassment with a charming gesture of hospitality.

"I'm so sorry—I'm always late; but the afternoon was so lovely." She stood drawing off her gloves, propitiatory and graceful, diffusing about her a sense of ease and familiarity in which the situation lost its grotesqueness. "But before talking business," she added brightly, "I'm sure every one wants a cup of tea."

She dropped into her low chair by the tea-table, and the two visitors, as if drawn by her smile, advanced to receive the cups she held out.

She glanced about for Waythorn, and he took the third cup with a laugh.

1904

INDEX OF AUTHORS, TITLES, AND FIRST LINES OF POEMS

CONTENTS OF OTHER VOLUMES
IN THIS SERIES

Colonial and Federal · To 1800

☆ ☆

The American Romantics · 1800–1860

The Twentieth Century